Ever a Princess

Awakened one night by her father's most trusted servant, Princess Giana is given her father's ring—signifying her as ruler of Saxe-Wallerstein-Karolya. Her parents have been slain by her treacherous cousin in a coup to seize the throne. But with the princess still alive, no one can claim the crown. With only a handful of loyal servants left to attend and protect her, Giana flees to an abandoned hunting lodge in Scotland to hide.

Adam McKendrick is a successful hotel owner from Nevada—and the unfortunate subject of a series of embarrassing dime novels. A stroke of luck at poker wins him a Scottish hunting lodge giving him the excuse he needs to leave the States and his infamous reputation for a while. To his surprise, he finds the lodge has a domestic staff, headed by a very clumsy, yet quite beautiful maid named Giana. . .

Turn the page for acclaim for Rebecca Hagan Lee . . .

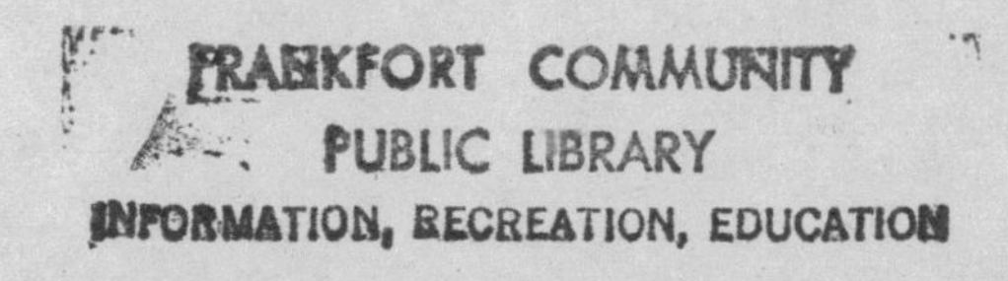

A Hint of Heather

"Rebecca Hagan Lee captures the allure of Scotland through the eyes of her memorable characters. Her gift for describing a time and place enables her to enchant readers."

—*Romantic Times*

"*A Hint of Heather* gets stronger and more exciting as the pages turn. The sensuality . . . is steamy, the wit and humor bring smiles, the romance has you sighing, and the ending has you cheering."

—*Under the Covers*

"A seductive Scottish historical . . . *A Hint of Heather* is going to be a big hit."

—*The Romance Reader*

"For those who love Scottish romances . . . *A Hint of Heather* is likely to please. [It] features the sort of well-defined characters that enrich the world of the romance novel. A real treat."

—*All About Romance*

"An entertaining Scottish romance . . . filled with action and intrigue."

—*Painted Rock Reviews*

Gossamer

"*Gossamer* is a tender treasure of a book."

—Teresa Medeiros

"Warmth, love, tenderness and humanity fill the pages to overflowing in another beautifully rendered romance. Following an original plotline, tackling important themes and creating memorable characters ensure Ms. Lee a place among the finest writers." —*Romantic Times*

"Beautifully written and very touching . . . if you're looking for something a little different from the norm, this is the one to read." —*Old Book Barn Gazette*

"Outstanding and unforgettable." —*Bell, Book & Candle*

"A moving and emotional love story." —*All About Romance*

"*Gossamer* is an incredible diamond." —*Affaire de Coeur*

Titles by Rebecca Hagan Lee

EVER A PRINCESS
ONCE A MISTRESS
A HINT OF HEATHER
WHISPER ALWAYS
GOSSAMER
SOMETHING BORROWED

Ever a Princess

Rebecca Hagan Lee

J

JOVE BOOKS, NEW YORK

EVER A PRINCESS

A Jove Book / published by arrangement with
the author

PRINTING HISTORY
Jove edition / February 2002

Cover art by Leslie Peck.

For information address: The Berkley Publishing Group,
a division of Penguin Putnam Inc.,
375 Hudson Street, New York, New York 10014.

Visit our website at
www.penguinputnam.com

ISBN: 0-515-13250-0

A JOVE BOOK®
Jove Books are published by The Berkley Publishing Group,
a division of Penguin Putnam Inc.,
375 Hudson Street, New York, New York 10014.

PRINTED IN THE UNITED STATES OF AMERICA

10 9 8 7 6 5 4 3 2 1

For Maria Isabel Fernandez Marrero.
Here's your story, Mari.
Enjoy!

Codicil to the Last Will and Testament of

George Ramsey, fifteenth Marquess of Templeston

My fondest wish is that I shall die a very old man beloved of my family and surrounded by children and grandchildren, but because one cannot always choose the time of one's Departure from the Living, I charge my legitimate son and heir, Andrew Ramsey, twenty-eighth Earl of Ramsey, Viscount Birmingham and Baron Selby, on this the 3rd day of August in the Year of Our Lord 1818, with the support and responsibility for my beloved mistresses and any living children born of their bodies in the nine months immediately following my death.

As discretion is the mark of a true gentleman, I shall not give name to the extraordinary ladies who have provided me with abiding care and comfort since the death of my beloved wife, but shall charge my legitimate son and heir with the duty of awarding to any lady who should present to him, his legitimate heir, or representative, a gold-and-diamond locket engraved with my seal, containing my likeness, stamped by my jeweler, and matching in every way the locket enclosed with this document, an annual sum not to exceed twenty thousand pounds to ensure the bed and board of the lady and any living children born of her body in the nine months immediately following my Departure from the Living.

The ladies who present such a locket have received it as a promise from me that they shall not suffer ill for having offered me abiding care and comfort. Any offspring who presents such a locket shall have done so at their mother's bequest and shall be recognized as children of the fifteenth Marquess of Templeston and shall be entitled to his or her mother's portion of my estate for themselves and their legitimate heirs in perpetuity according to my wishes as set forth in this, my Last Will and Testament.

George Ramsey,

Fifteenth Marquess of Templeston

Prologue

The first duty of a Princess of the Blood Royal is to serve the House of Saxe-Wallerstein-Karolya.

—First Maxim of Protocol and Court Etiquette of Princesses of the Blood Royal of the House of Saxe-Wallerstein-Karolya, as decreed by His Serene Highness, Prince Karol I, 1432.

April 18, 1874
PALACE AT LAKEN
BALTIC PRINCIPALITY OF
SAXE-WALLERSTEIN-KAROLYA

"*You must wake up, Your Highness!*"

Her Royal Highness Georgiana Victoria Elizabeth May heard the whisper, recognized the voice, and placed her hand against the soft fur at her side to quiet the low, menacing growl coming from the throat of Wagner, the huge wolfhound sharing her bed. She opened her eyes and found Lord Maximillian Gudrun, her father's private secretary, standing in the dim glow of the lamplight beside her bed.

"Thank the All Highest," he whispered reverently. "I've reached you in time."

Alarmed by the old man's reaction, Princess Giana pushed herself into a sitting position, leaning against the mound of feather pillows propped against the headboard of the old-fashioned half-canopied tester.

"What is it, Max? What are you doing here? You're supposed to be in Christianberg with Father and Mother."

A sheen of tears sparkled in Lord Gudrun's eyes and ran unchecked down the weathered planes of his face. The old man clutched at his side, then dropped to his knees by the side of the bed and bowed his head. "Something terrible has happened at the palace, Your Highness."

A frisson of foreboding prickled the fine hairs at the back of Giana's neck, and her voice echoed her terror. "Max?"

Lord Gudrun reached across the fine snowy-white linen and thick eiderdown comforters to clasp Giana's right hand. His hand left a dark smear of blood on the covers, and Giana drew in a sharp horrified breath as he slipped a heavy gold signet ring onto her right thumb.

"His Serene Highness Prince Christian Frederick Randolph George of Saxe-Wallerstein-Karolya bid me bring this to you, Your Highness."

"No." Giana began to tremble as she stared down at the gold ring Max had slipped on her thumb. The royal seal. The seal of state worn by every ruler of Saxe-Wallerstein-Karolya since the principality's beginnings in 1448—a gold seal now stained with blood. "My father . . . Max?" She glanced up at him. "He can't be . . ."

Lord Gudrun bit down on his lip to stop its quivering, and then gave a sharp affirmative nod. "I'm afraid so, Your Highness."

Although she understood the meaning of the transfer of the royal signet ring, and had always known that one day, this day would come, Giana couldn't bring herself to utter the words. To do so would be to confirm the thing her heart and her mind could not accept. Her beloved father was dead. She was now ruler of the principality.

A sudden rush of hot, salty tears stung her eyes as Giana pushed back the covers and scrambled to her feet. The wolfhound bounded to his feet beside her. "We must go to the palace at Christianberg at once. My mother will . . ." Her mother would know what to do. Her mother would put aside her own deep overflowing grief and help Giana get through the ordeal ahead; to do what must be done.

Lord Gudrun struggled to stand, then gripped Princess Giana's hand with his left one and squeezed it hard. "I'm sorry, Your Highness, but your mother . . ."

Giana wrenched her hand out of his and shook her head. "No, Max, please . . . Not my mother, too."

"I'm sorry, Your Highness."

"How?" she asked. Giana was willing to admit that a healthy, hearty man in his early fifties might meet an untimely death, but she could not concede that his wife might meet the same fate. Unless . . .

"Treachery, Your Highness. Your father and your mother were stabbed this evening by hired assassins."

Giana's breath left her body in a rush. "Why? Who?"

"Prince Victor has been inciting the young men of the ruling class, denouncing your father's support of a constitution and a Declaration of Rights for the Masses. Victor has been promising estate grants, titles, and funds to the foolish younger sons of aristocratic families to gain their support, and he has convinced these young traitors that your father's aim was to reward the poor with the landed estates of the rich."

"Victor?" Giana struggled to comprehend the meaning of Max's words. "My cousin assassinated my parents?"

"Yes, Your Highness," Max confirmed. "Your parents were murdered in their bedchamber after retiring from the state dinner celebrating the opening of Parliament. The palace has been overrun. Your father's loyal servants are being slaughtered, and Victor's men are searching for you."

"How did you escape?" She asked the question, though she dreaded hearing the answer.

"I was delivering the nightly dispatch box to your father's bedchamber. I heard Prince Christian cry out a warning as your mother entered the room. I entered your mother's chamber from the south door through the dressing room and hid the dispatch box under a bonnet in one of the princess's hatboxes, then I drew my dress sword and entered your father's bedchamber." Lord Gudrun took a breath. "Your father lay on the floor, bleeding from several wounds. Your mother lay dead beside him. One of the traitors was attempting to remove the seal from the prince's hand. He turned and discharged his pistol as I entered the room."

Giana suddenly realized Max was bleeding—that the blood from the seal hadn't belonged only to her father. "How badly are you injured?"

Max shrugged. "A minor wound, Your Highness. The ball glanced off my rib." He uncovered the wound in his side so Giana could assess the damage.

Giana's face whitened at the sight of the spreading red stain. Please, don't let me faint, she begged, please; let me do what must be done. Her stomach muscles clenched and her head began to spin, but she refused to give in to the weakness. Stiffening her resolve, Giana reached across the bed for the nearest pillow, stripped off the pillowcase, and pressed the white linen into Max's hand to help staunch the flow of blood. She found, to her amazement, that the task was what she needed to help dispel her light-headedness. "It may require stitching." She bit her bottom lip. "But for now, I think it best if we wrap it."

"Yes, Your Royal Highness."

Giana met Max's gaze. His eyes were dark and shadowed with pain as she withdrew her hand from the makeshift bandage at his side. Giana wiped her bloody hands on the sheets, then took a deep breath to steady herself. She reached for another pillow, removed its case, and bit a hole in the seam, tearing the fine linen into strips of bandage. She repeated the procedure with another pillowcase, then helped Max remove his waistcoat and jacket. He lifted the bandage as Giana unbuttoned his shirt, then placed it back over the wound as she wrapped the strips of linen around his chest. She talked as she worked, speaking in the clipped and precise regal tone that was as much of an imitation of her father as she could manage, hoping her questions would keep the old man's mind off his pain. "The traitor who shot you?"

"I ran him through, Your Highness."

Giana tightened the last strip of linen, knotted it into place, and stepped back to view the results. "And Papa? Did he suffer?" She knew the answer. She knew her father had suffered terribly, but she wanted Max's reassurance, so she had to ask.

"No, Princess," Max answered, softening his tone and reverting to the familiar form of address. "Nor your mother. She died instantly. Your father tried to save her and when he could not, he bid me to deliver his seal to you, to get you to safety, and to guard you with my life. Those were his final orders to me." Prince Christian had given him one other order before he died, but Max could not muster the strength to deliver it yet. *Tell Giana never to be afraid to follow her heart. Promise me, Max. Promise you will help her find a way.* His voice broke on a sob and his rounded shoulders shook from the force of his grief. "And I shall, Your Highness, I will not fail you again."

Max buttoned his shirt over the bandage and struggled into his brocade waistcoat and wool jacket. He stared at the princess. To him, she was still a girl—barefoot, dressed in a demure white lawn nightgown with her long blond hair plaited into a single braid. She was too young to be the ruler of a wealthy principality. Too young to bear the crushing burdens of the state. Her blue eyes were darkened with sorrow and red-rimmed from the sting of tears she refused to let flow. She stood tall and looked him in the eye, her gaze unflinching as she accepted responsibility for her country and for her people. She was a girl on the brink of womanhood, a princess and rightful heir to the throne, filled with strength and courage and compassion.

Her Serene Highness Princess Georgiana Victoria Elizabeth May of the house of Saxe-Wallerstein-Karolya.

Max knelt before her, kissed the ring that had belonged to her father, and swore to serve her as he had served her father and as his father and grandfathers had served the rulers of Saxe-Wallerstein-Karolya for four hundred years.

Giana reached down and buried her fingers in the soft brindle-colored fur just above her wolfhound's shoulders. She held on to Wagner, bracing herself against the tide of anguish that threatened to overtake her. She was the sovereign ruler of her country, and she was alone and terribly afraid. She wanted to throw herself into Max's arms and weep as she had done many times as a child, but she stayed the impulse. The ruler of Saxe-Wallerstein-Karolya could not succumb to emotions. She couldn't behave like a grief-stricken daughter. She had to behave like a princess—like the ruler of her country. She had to behave as her father would have behaved, so she accepted her due, nodding regally as she helped Max to his feet. "Wake the others," she ordered. "We must prepare for the journey to Christianberg."

"Your Highness, you cannot return to the capital," Max told her. "Your cousin will kill you if he finds you."

"Finds me?" Giana asked. "The fact that I'm on holiday here is common knowledge. My program is published each month. Victor knows I'm at Laken."

"No, Your Highness, he does not. Your schedule was altered before it was made public."

"By whom?" Giana demanded.

"Your father."

"But why?"

"Prince Christian knew of the unrest among the young aristocrats in the capital and suspected your cousin might be behind it. Prince Christian received word of your cousin's traitorous activities shortly after he refused to consider Victor's request for your hand in marriage."

"Victor offered for me?"

Max nodded. "Your father knew Victor was plotting to overthrow him. He refused his offer for your hand because he feared Victor would use you to gain the throne. But Victor was incensed by Prince Christian's refusal, so your father suggested this trip to Laken in order to get you out of the capital and away from possible danger."

Giana's eyes widened at the revelation. "Papa sent me away? On purpose?"

"Yes," Max confirmed. "He suspected Victor might try to use the opening of Parliament to incite rebellion."

"He sent me away. But he allowed Mother . . ." Giana couldn't finish the thought.

"You were the heir apparent," Max reminded her.

"But—"

"Prince Christian tried to send your mother away. He begged her to accompany you, but Princess May refused to leave him. She refused to allow him to face the traitors alone."

"Oh, Mama." Giana tried mightily to keep her sorrow in check, tried to keep the tears at bay, but one solitary droplet slipped through her lashes and rolled down her cheek. While her father had ruled the principality, her mother had been the glue that held everything together. Prince Christian was the hereditary leader of Saxe-Wallerstein-Karolya, the embodiment of goodness, justice, and might, but Princess May was the heart and soul of the country—the mother of its heir, the champion of the common people, keeper of centuries-old traditions, and social arbiter. Without her mother to guide her, Giana was lost. Overwhelmed. Terrified. Unequipped to rule. She didn't understand government; she didn't understand the nuances of negotiating treaties, or foreign trade rights. Giana had always known that the continued beating of her father's heart was all that kept her from assuming the throne, but somehow the knowledge hadn't seemed real. She had never seen herself ascending the throne, had always assumed her role as heir apparent was temporary—until a brother came along. She didn't know how to do her father's job. She wasn't prepared to be a ruler. She only knew how to be a princess. She glanced at Max. He had been her father's confidant and adviser for more than twenty years. Surely he would know what to do. Surely he would have all the answers.

"How many people do we have, Max?"

"Only myself, Your Highness, and those serving you here at Laken."

Giana frowned. The permanent staff at Laken was kept to a minimum. Those presently serving at Laken were Langstrom, the butler, and Isobel, his wife, who served as housekeeper, Josef, the stable master, and Brenna, Giana's personal maid. Everyone else lived in the village and came into work on a daily basis. "That gives us four," Giana said. "Six counting you and me. Seven with Wagner." She glanced down at her beloved wolfhound. "Seven against Victor's traitors."

"There are many landowners and men in the government and the army who will remain loyal to your father," Max assured her.

"Then we must return to Christianberg to rally them."

"You cannot, Your Highness. I swore a solemn oath to your father that I would see you to safety. The palace isn't safe and neither is the capital."

"But we can't let Victor win," Giana protested. "We can't stand idly by and allow Victor to ascend my father's throne. To get away with murder—with regicide."

"We must for now," Max assured her. "The tide of rebellion is running high. Victor will not risk losing his chance to gain the throne—however briefly. We cannot risk your life. We cannot risk the life of the rightful heir to the crown."

"The crown," Giana breathed slowly, reverently, as understanding dawned. "The crown. If Victor wishes to wear the crown of Saxe-Wallerstein-Karolya, he must abide by the Law of Succession. He must endure the wait. He cannot marry until the traditional period of mourning for the late ruler is over. And he cannot be crowned until he is married. Until that year is over, Victor can govern the principality, but he cannot be recognized as its rightful ruler."

Max managed a slight smile. "And because you are recognized as your father's successor, not Victor, the People's Parliament of Karolya will require him to marry a princess of Karolyan blood."

"There are no princesses of Karolyan blood left to marry. I am the only one." She looked at Max. "Unless he marries one of his sisters."

"An act none of the other European ruling families could or would condone." Max shook his head. "No, Your Highness, in order to be crowned His Serene Highness, Prince Victor IV of Saxe-Wallerstein-Karolya, your cousin must marry you."

"Or produce my body," Giana reminded him. "And my father's seal of state."

"Then we have no more time to waste. We have only one year."

"We must leave the country before Victor closes the borders. For the time being, we must bide our time, go to ground like the fox, and endure the wait."

Max studied his princess, marveling at the strength and sense of determination he heard in her voice. He knew, even if she did not, that until the year was up there was no safe haven left to them, knew Princess Giana's life was forfeit if her cousin found her, knew she would never agree to marry her parents' murderer, and he also knew that Victor would search the countryside for the princess and post spies in every remaining monarchy in Europe in an effort to find her. "Where shall we go?" he asked. "What is to be our destination?"

Giana's mouth thinned into a firm hard line. "I don't know. But it must be a place where no one would ever think to look for a princess."

Chapter 1

The Bountiful Baron never refuses a woman in need.

—THE FIRST INSTALLMENT OF THE TRUE ADVENTURES OF THE BOUNTIFUL BARON: WESTERN BENEFACTOR TO BLOND, BEAUTIFUL, AND BETRAYED WOMEN WRITTEN BY JOHN J. BOOKMAN, 1874.

June 18, 1874
USS *YANKEE BELLE*
FROM NEW YORK TO LONDON

"Call."

Adam McKendrick studied the cards in his hand for a moment longer before spreading them out on the table. "Full house. Gents and ladies."

Ignoring the groans and the round of good-natured teasing, Adam pulled a gold watch from the pocket of his waistcoat, flipped open the lid, and stared down at the face. Squinting through the blue haze of cigar smoke that hovered over the tables and seemed to swirl beneath the prisms of the crystal chandeliers, he made out the time. Three forty-seven A.M. In a couple of hours the first light of dawn would begin to break the horizon, but none of the men in the Gentlemen's Gaming Salon would see it.

The man across the table from him picked up the deck of cards. "You in or out?"

"Out." Adam grabbed his hat from the hat rack and raked his earnings into it. He left his hat sitting on the table while he stood up and stretched his arms over his head, easing the tension in his neck from the long hours at cards. His head ached from the smoke he'd inhaled and the whiskey he'd consumed, and his body was stiff and sore from sitting at a card table all evening. "It's late, gentlemen. I'm calling it a night."

"What about you?" The dealer nodded toward Murphy O'Brien, Adam's friend and traveling companion.

Murph glanced at Adam and winked. "I need to recoup my earnings. I'll play another hand or two before I turn in."

"Suit yourself." Adam shrugged into his jacket and picked up his hat. No one else at the table looked up as he crossed the room to the cashier's window.

Adam helped himself to an expensive cigar from the humidor while he waited for the cashier to exchange his poker chips for currency. He snipped the end off the cigar and struck a match to it while the clerk counted out his cash. Adam pulled a bill from the pile and handed it to the clerk, then recounted the bills, folded the money, and tucked it into his pocket.

Opening the door to the Gentlemen's Gaming Salon, he stepped into the passageway and made his way to the purser's office, where he deposited the bulk of his cash into the safe. Once he had his receipt in hand, Adam left the purser's office and climbed the steps to the deck. He circled the deck twice, then leaned against the rail of the ship to breathe in the cool air and study the stars as he smoked his cigar.

Half an hour later Adam left the deck and made his way back down the passageway to his stateroom.

A steward smiled broadly and greeted him as he unlocked the door. "Have a good evening, Mr. McKendrick."

"Thanks," Adam replied as he stepped through the door and into his room.

"Shall I light a lamp for you, sir?"

Adam shook his head. "That won't be necessary. I can manage." He closed the door behind him and fumbled for a match. The odor of sulfur filled his nostrils as he scraped the match against the striking plate. He lifted the lamp globe and touched the flame to the wick, then turned toward his bunk. "Aw, hell! Not again!"

A curvaceous blonde, naked except for the bedsheet, lay in the center of his bunk. "Hello, handsome," came the husky voice. "I've been waiting for you."

"Dammit!" Adam crossed the room in four angry strides. "This is the third time this week. How did you get in?"

"I bribed the steward."

Adam managed a half-laugh. "No wonder he was smiling. If this keeps up, he'll be a rich man."

The woman stretched luxuriously like a cat and allowed the sheet covering her breasts to slip lower, giving Adam an enticing view.

"Get your clothes and get out."

She pouted. "I thought you helped women in need."

"You don't need my help," he reasoned. "Or you wouldn't be bribing the steward."

"A woman doesn't have to be financially destitute to need help." She smiled a meaningful smile. "I require a different sort of assistance."

Adam looked her in the eye. "You've got the wrong man."

"But you're Adam McKendrick," she purred.

"Let me put this another way," he said firmly. "Madam, I'm not interested."

"Helena," she continued, undaunted. "Helena Compton."

"Mrs. Samuel Compton?"

"The same." She wet her lips with the tip of her tongue in a move too practiced to be an accident. "I could be very good to you, you know."

Compton. Adam raked his fingers through his hair. He'd just spent most of the night playing poker with Samuel Compton, a Chicago railroad tycoon, almost twice her age. "I don't want you to be good to me, Mrs. Compton," Adam told her. "I don't want you to be anything to me. And I don't want to come back to my room and find you in my bed again. Understand?"

"No." She pouted prettily.

"Too bad." He glanced around the stateroom. "I don't mind winning a man's money, but I draw the line at winning his money and bedding his wife. Now, where are your clothes?" he asked.

"I didn't wear any."

Adam raised an eyebrow at that. "How did you get from your room if you didn't have on any clothes?"

"I had an accomplice. She came with me, waited while I undressed, then took my clothes back with her."

"The woman who was here the other night?" Adam guessed.

"My cousin." She shrugged. "We figure one of us will get lucky sooner or later. And we don't mind sharing."

"I do." Adam rang for the steward, then leaned down and scooped Helena Compton into his arms, sheet and all.

"Won't you at least give me reason to hope?" She wrapped her arms around Adam's neck and pressed herself against him.

"Nope."

The steward knocked on the door almost immediately, and Adam invited him to enter. "You rang for me, sir?"

Adam carried Helena Compton across the room and deposited her in the steward's arms. "This lady has mistaken my room for hers," he said, removing a crisp fifty-dollar bill from his pocket. "Please see that she finds her way back to the correct one."

"But, sir, the lady assured me that you and she—"

"Please bring another sheet for my bunk." Adam folded the money and tucked it into the steward's breast pocket. "As you can see, the lady was mistaken. I know she can rely on your discretion in rectifying her error." He stared at the other man. "And I'm sure her husband would appreciate it if you'll see that this sort of mistake doesn't happen again." Adam backed the steward into the passage and closed the door in his face.

How the hell was he going to face Samuel Compton over the poker table again? And how in the hell was he going to explain if the older man learned of his wife's escapade and took exception? Adam stripped off his jacket and shirt, tossed them over the nearest chair, and sat down on the edge of the bunk. His unwanted notoriety was beginning to be a pain in the ass.

He blew out the breath he'd been holding and rubbed the throbbing spot on his temple. There were days when he'd give every penny he'd ever made to find a place where no one knew or cared who he was.

Today was shaping up to be one of them.

Chapter 2

The Bountiful Baron defends the weak and helps the poor.

—The Second Installment of the True Adventures of the Bountiful Baron: Western Benefactor to Blond, Beautiful, and Betrayed Women written by John J. Bookman, 1874.

Later that morning
USS *Yankee Belle*
From New York to London

Adam started as a dime novel sailed past his shoulder and landed on the table in the main dining room, rattling his cup and saucer. He looked up from the newspaper he'd just opened and frowned at his friend. "What the . . . ?"

"You're famous, my friend," O'Brien replied. "Your reputation has preceded you."

Adam sat at his usual table, nursing a scalding hot cup of strong black coffee and battling the effects of a wicked hangover while he watched a group of fellow travelers file into the room for breakfast. He folded his newspaper and laid it aside, then picked up the small book and glanced at the title. *The Second Installment of the True Adventures of the Bountiful Baron: Western Benefactor to Blond, Beautiful, and Betrayed Women.*

"What do you think of that?" Murphy asked.

Christ! There was another one! Adam opened the novel, scanned the first couple of pages, and let out a derisive snort. One good deed, he thought. If the truth were known, he'd probably never done an entirely unselfish deed in his life—including the one that was currently causing so much trouble. He'd been furious at his sister Kirstin's husband because the bastard had beaten her for attending a suffragette rally. Adam shoved his fingers through his hair. The truth was that he'd been angry enough at his brother-in-law to kill him, and he'd taken his frustration out on a cowboy he'd caught slapping a saloon girl around. Adam let out another snort. He'd done one good deed, protected one saloon girl from an abusive customer, and this was the result. He flipped through the pages. The pen and ink drawings in the first installment had depicted him as a gentleman defending a saloon girl from a ruffian; this installment appeared to have expanded upon the theme with drawings of women from all walks of life—rich and poor—escaping tyranny and neglect, turning to him for help.

Adam groaned. Instead of confining his good deed to the defense of one saloon girl, this installment depicted him as an avenging angel defending blond womanhood everywhere. Well, at least that explained Helena Compton's uninvited appearance in his bed. She'd seen the book and wanted to share a pillow with the Bountiful Baron. "I think that if I'd eaten breakfast, I'd be losing it about now."

Murphy laughed, then reached over and helped himself to the pot of coffee on the table.

"Need my cup and saucer?" Adam cocked an eyebrow at his friend.

"No, thanks." Murphy held up a thick mug. "I brought my own. I figured that since the *Bountiful Baron* would provide the coffee, the least I could do was bring my own cup." He commandeered the chair across from Adam and sat down.

"*Very* funny." Adam shoved the book back across the table and glared at Murphy. "Where'd you get this?"

"From one of the dudes at the poker table last night."

"Which one?"

"The one with the foreign accent and the fancy embroidered vest," Murphy replied.

Adam narrowed his gaze, wrinkling his forehead and drawing his brows together in a concentration.

"You won't remember him. He came into the salon with three companions—all foreigners—after you raked up your winnings and left."

"It was nearly four before I left the table," Adam told him. "I thought you were right behind me."

O'Brien chuckled. "I couldn't help myself. I had to stay awhile longer and pad my winnings. You'd left the table and I couldn't stand the thought of anyone else winning the cash those foreigners were flashing around." He smiled at Adam. "And when one of them started showing this"—Murphy picked up the dime novel and stared at the cover—"around the table and asking if any of us had ever heard of him, I became curious." He dropped the book on the table and turned back to Adam.

Adam rubbed his forehead in a futile effort to rub away his headache. "Did anyone answer?"

Murphy shook his head. "Fortunately, no one else at the table had seen a copy of the book and the foreigner referred to you as the baron instead of by name. But you're a passenger on this ship and your name is on the manifest. If they want to find you, it won't take them long."

"Jesus, Joseph, and Mary! How many of those are there?" He nodded toward the dime novel. "I've bought up as many copies of the first installment as I can find. Am I going to have to buy the publisher just to put an end to this? Why did"—Adam stared at the author's pseudonym—"John J. Bookman print my name? He doesn't use *his* real one." He muttered a curse beneath his breath. "It was bad enough when the first one came out. Now there are two of them." His reputation for lending a helping hand to women in need had spread like wildfire through the mining camps to Virginia City, Sacramento, and San Francisco before the publication of the first installment. Now a second installment had appeared. At least there was some truth to the first installment. The second one was pure fiction. "You're the Pinkerton. Do something useful. Find out where these things are coming from." He picked up the book and slapped it down on the table. "This is almost as bad as having a reputation as a gunslinger. I can't turn around without tripping over someone who's read all about me. . . ."

Murphy commiserated. "Yeah, beautiful blondes every time you turn around and all of them desperately seeking aid and succor. Damn the luck."

"Luck and beauty have nothing to do with it," Adam protested. "There will be women and girls of all shapes and sizes, from sixteen to sixty looking for help. My life is going to be living hell when I get back home."

Home for Adam McKendrick was Queen City in the Nevada Territory, a town built from the fortunes made on the silver ore of the Comstock Lode. Adam owned the largest hotel in town and the Queen City Opera House, a fancy name for a saloon and gambling house, but one the city council insisted would lure moneyed visitors to town. Adam doubted that the grand name he'd given his saloon had as much to do with the draw as the fact that new silver strikes occurred in Queen City on a regular basis and the fact that it was the last large town on the main stage line to Virginia City and San Francisco. But the city fathers were right about one thing—business was booming.

"If you get back." Murphy took a sip of his coffee.

"If? What do you mean, if?" Adam demanded.

Murphy shrugged. "You're going to the Scottish Highlands to check out the hunting lodge you inherited. You might decide to stay and be lord of the manor."

Adam snorted. "I didn't inherit the lodge. I won it in a poker game. And why would I decide to stay in Scotland and be lord of a manor when I've got several perfectly good businesses to run back home?"

"The Highlands are known for their wild and desolate beauty. And McKendrick is a Scottish name. You may develop a fondness for the auld sod."

"I don't give a damn how beautiful the Highlands are or what the name is. I'm an American. And any fondness I develop for the auld sod will come from the fact that there's money to be made there."

"Not to worry, then." Murphy laughed. "You won't be forming any undue attachment to Scottish soil. They may be beautiful, but there's nothing in the Highlands but poor people, shaggy cattle, heather, and sheep. If there was a way to turn that into money, surely someone would have found it by now."

"Maybe they weren't looking at it the right way." Adam reached over and cuffed Murphy on the shoulder. "The world is changing, my friend. Wealth isn't confined to the aristocracy anymore. Men are making fortunes in gold and silver mining, in railroads and steel mills. There's a whole new class of millionaires looking for new ways to spend money and new things to spend it on." He grinned. "I earned my first fortune breaking my back digging silver from the Comstock, and I can tell you that the money pouring into the hotel and the opera house is a hell of a lot easier to make. That's why I decided to see if the hunting lodge has potential."

"Potential for what?"

"For recreation. Manly recreation that relies heavily on hunting and fishing, drinking whisky, and playing cards, polo, and golf."

"Golf?" Murphy raised his eyebrows as if he'd never heard the word before. "I know hunting and fishing and playing cards and drinking whisky. And I've heard of polo. But what the hell is golf?"

Adam smiled. "A game Scotsmen like to play."

"Where did you hear about this game?"

"From an old Scotsman who worked the claim next to mine. He always talked about going back to Scotland and building a gentleman's club where men could play golf."

"Is it an indoor or an outdoor game?" O'Brien asked.

"Outdoor," Adam answered.

O'Brien threw back his head and laughed so hard that he had to wipe tears from the corner of his eyes. "It's so damned cold and windy in Scotland that a man would have to be a fool to pay good money to play any kind of game outdoors."

"McTavish swore his kinsmen loved it."

O'Brien continued to chuckle as he looked at Adam. "Are you sure that old Scotsman was right in the head?"

"Absolutely," Adam replied without hesitation.

"This I've got to see."

"That's why I asked you to come along," Adam told him.

O'Brien helped himself to another cup of coffee. "You didn't just ask me to come along. You're paying me to come along because you wanted someone other than your sister to talk to during the crossing."

Adam grimaced. "That's true. I love my sister, but she gets on my nerves." He did love his sister. There was no one in the world he loved more than his mother and his four older sisters, but there was no doubting the fact that they could try the patience of a cathedral full of saints. And Adam was no saint. Still, he'd grown up with them. He knew what to expect. Conversing with his other three sisters could be a trial, at times, because they were so opinionated and stubborn, but talking to Kirstin about anything of importance or of real interest was next to impossible. His mother and his other three sisters might be budding suffragettes, but they hadn't succeeded in converting Kirstin. She didn't understand what the fuss was all about. Kirstin was just as beautiful, but she wasn't as smart as his mother or his other sisters. Learning to read had been difficult for her and schoolwork, a chore. But their mother had always preached about using the talents God gave you, so Kirstin used hers—a beautiful face and body and stubborn persistence—to get what she wanted out of life.

Unfortunately, she had wanted an English lord for a husband. And she had gotten one.

Kirstin had never had any intention of preaching equality of the sexes to the ladies of London. She didn't care about equal rights. She cared about prestige—the kind of prestige that could only be achieved by being the wife of a peer. Kirstin didn't talk politics all the time, but her conversation began and ended with fashion and gossip. And that, Adam discovered, was a mixed blessing. Because there was a limit to the number of times a man—even an adoring and indulgent brother—could listen to her rapturous descriptions of bows and frills. And unless the lodge proved to have commercial potential, Adam didn't care a fig for the gossip of London society. Although he could successfully avoid constant association with Kirstin during the day, society demanded she have a suitable escort at night.

Adam heaved a sigh. Wrestling with a dozen forks and

spoons and knives and the dizzying array of plates and glasses included in the twelve-course dinners was such a chore, he and Murphy cut cards each night for the dubious honor of escorting her. So far, Adam had won the cut more than he'd lost and Murphy was suffering through the gossip and the fashion reviews. Still, Adam was honor bound to pay the man for his trouble and provide other amenities like cigars and fine liquor to make it up to him. Because the truth was that he liked Murphy O'Brien and he would have died of boredom on the crossing if Murph hadn't taken him up on the offer. Adam reached for his coffee cup, took a tentative sip and studied O'Brien over the rim. "Which reminds me, it's your turn to escort her into dinner tonight."

"If you hate the job so much, how did you allow yourself to get talked into taking her back to her husband?"

"You know what they say." Adam met O'Brien's gaze. "No good deed goes unpunished."

"How's that?"

"It all started with the party my oldest sister, Astrid, planned for my mother's sixtieth birthday. We all made the trip to Astrid's house—including Kirstin and her husband, the English lord . . ."

"Like mother, like daughter." O'Brien chuckled.

"Not quite." Adam pinned O'Brien with a look that told him he could do without the commentary. "The difference is that Kirstin wanted one. Even if the English lord was strapped for cash and looking to marry an heiress. Unfortunately, he's turning out to be the bad penny that turns up every so often asking for more. My father was just the opposite. He had plenty of money and he didn't stay around long after he married my mother because she encouraged him to go. She says she knew their marriage was a mistake from the start because they were so different. Personally, I've always thought he left before I was born because the thought that I might be a twin and a girl probably scared the bejesus out of him."

Adam laughed. He had to admit his family was unique. All four of his sisters were twins. The two older ones were twins and the two younger ones were twins and they all looked alike. Like his mother, his sisters were all blonde and blue-eyed. He was the odd man out. The youngest child. The only boy. The only one in the family with dark hair and the one whose father decided a return to London was preferable to remaining in an ill-advised marriage to a widow with four daughters. "Anyway, Kirstin and His Lordship made the trip to Denver to celebrate my mother's birthday."

"So it was a nice family gathering," Murphy commented.

"It was hell," Adam said. "My mother is as stubborn and independent as ever. She's still running the farm in Kansas and worrying about the weather and the price of corn and wheat and she's become a leader in the women's suffragette movement." He smiled at the mental image of his mother carrying a placard. "I've always been proud of her strength and independence and I'm certainly in favor of women's suffrage, but I sometimes wish my mother . . ." He'd been about to say that he wished his mother hadn't been quite so independent, wished that she hadn't chosen her first husband's legacy over her second husband's love, but Adam shrugged off the thought. His mother was who she was and he loved her. She wasn't the type to show affection. It wasn't in her nature to boast or to coddle. Her nature was to push, to work hard to succeed, and to see that her children succeeded. And she'd been successful. "My sister, Astrid, is helping her husband expand his medical practice into a hospital, despite the fact that she's pregnant with her seventh child. And Erika has hired three new teachers—all suffragettes—for her school. Her husband is an engineer with the railroad. He travels a lot and Erika spends her energy on the school." Adam shrugged. "Greta and her husband purchased the farm adjacent to Ma's, and Greta gave up her position at the newspaper in town, but she's publishing a weekly bulletin for female farmers. And now, Ma, Astrid, Erika, and Greta have formed a Women's Temperance League with other local suffragettes." He glanced over at Murphy. "The other three of my sisters' husbands don't seem to find their politics threatening, but *His Lordship* . . ." Adam shook his head and swore viciously. "His bloody Lordship has turned out to be a real bastard. The legitimate kind. He beat the hell out of Kirstin because she dared—she dared—accompany my mother and sisters to a temperance rally. Kirstin was sporting a black eye when I arrived. And all because *His Lordship* is afraid she might take her suffragette ways back to England—to the wives and daughters of his House of Lords friends. The irony is that Kirstin only went to the rally because all of the other women in town were going. She didn't care about temperance or the suffragette movement; she went because she didn't want to be left out. But His bloody Lordship beat the hell out of her anyway."

"Sheesh!" Murphy ran his fingers through his thick brown hair, shuddering at the thought of ugly bruises marring Kirstin Marshfeld's gorgeous flesh. "But I hate English lords. Bloody arrogant bastards, the lot of them." He looked over at Adam. "With one notable exception."

"Don't make an exception on my account," Adam told him. "I agree with you."

"But you're a . . ."

Adam shook his head. "My father is the younger son of an English lord. He was supposed to inherit money and property instead of a title, but he'd never claimed his inheritance. Ma said he didn't need it. She said he had the Midas touch and loads of charm to go with it. He could have made a go of anything he tried, but when she met him, he was living for adventure. He wanted to see the world and although my mother loved him, she refused to give up the farm she inherited from her first husband in order to explore the world. At any rate, they parted company. Eventually my father had the marriage annulled. Although I wasn't born one, technically I became a bastard when my father dissolved his marriage to my mother in order to marry someone else." He paused. "Ma didn't get anything out of the marriage except me. But that was her choice. After she wrote to tell him I'd been born, he sent passage money to England for all of us and an old gold locket he told her to give to me." Adam pulled out his watch chain to show O'Brien the locket he wore as a fob. "She kept the locket and returned the money. *This* was my inheritance. When the marriage was annulled I was no longer entitled to bear the McKendrick name, but Ma insisted I keep it. She says it's the name I was born with and neither the law nor the church has the right to take it away." He shoved the watch back into his pocket and continued his story. "Kirstin's husband is the real English lord. I tried to persuade her to leave him, but she wouldn't consider it." Adam traced the rim of his coffee cup with his index finger. "There was nothing I could do except promise His Lordship I'd kill him if he touched my sister in anger again. And I promised him I'd be watching from now on."

"Did he believe you?" O'Brien asked.

"He believed me enough to leave Kirstin to visit with Ma while he took the next train east and a boat back to England," Adam answered. "And so did the guy slapping one of the girls around in the Gold Nugget Saloon later that night."

"Hence the first installment of the true adventures of the Bountiful Baron . . ."

Adam nodded. "There must have been a journalist in the saloon. Someone who heard me offer the girl a job and a place to stay. She turned down the offer of a job, but she accepted a train ticket back home to her parents' farm in Indiana."

"The girl might have sold her story to the dime novel."

"Could be." Adam refilled his coffee cup, and then signaled to the waiter for a fresh pot. "Or Kirstin's decided on a novel way of earning pin money. However it came about, it's a pain in the ass."

"Speaking of which," O'Brien said. "Where is Her Ladyship?"

"Breakfasting in her stateroom," Adam replied. "She says it isn't done for a viscountess to be seen before one or two in the afternoon."

"What does she do in there all morning?" O'Brien asked. "She can't be primping. She's already gorgeous enough to stop clocks."

"I don't know and I don't care as long as I don't have to listen to one more description of the new gowns she's ordered for the Season." Adam waited until the waiter removed the empty coffeepot and replaced it with a fresh one. He refilled his cup and took a swallow. "Thank God we'll be docking in a few days. Her husband can listen to her for a while." He glanced at Murphy. "Don't get me wrong about this. I despise the man. I think Kirstin made a big mistake in marrying His

Lordship and is making another one in going back to him. But it's her life and her decision. I worry about her. But my hands are tied unless she changes her mind about being a viscountess." He thought for a moment. "If she does, I'll only be as far away as Scotland."

Murphy murmured an agreement. He'd spent enough time in Kirstin Marshfeld's company to know that she wasn't about to give up the prestige that went with an old and honorable title—even if that meant suffering beatings at the hands of her husband. And he knew Adam well enough to know that he felt duty bound to protect her—even if that meant protecting her from her own ambition. "Look at the bright side." He picked up the dime novel and waved it at Adam. "Nobody in Scotland will know about the Bountiful Baron."

Adam saluted O'Brien with his coffee cup. "I won't have to look at that thing every time I turn around."

"Or attempt to live up to his reputation." Murph grinned.

Adam matched Murph's grin with one of his own. "You can bet on that. I've had my fill of blond, blue-eyed darlings. If they have 'em in Scotland, I don't want to know about it."

"You're sure about that?" O'Brien teased.

"Completely," Adam pronounced. "You can have 'em all."

Chapter 3

A Princess of the Blood Royal must attend all loyal subjects of the House of Saxe-Wallerstein-Karolya.

—MAXIM 5: PROTOCOL AND COURT ETIQUETTE OF PRINCESSES OF THE BLOOD ROYAL OF THE HOUSE OF SAXE-WALLERSTEIN-KAROLYA, AS DECREED BY HIS SERENE HIGHNESS, PRINCE KAROL I, 1432.

"There is trouble, Your Royal Highness."

Giana sighed. "Max . . ." She had reminded him a thousand times that it did no good for them to travel incognito, pretending to be a family, or to remain in hiding if he insisted on speaking Karolyan and using her title every time he addressed her. She was supposed to be the daughter of a well-traveled cook and butler. Max was supposed to be her paternal uncle, and Josef and Brenna, her cousins. They had come to Scotland on holiday from their jobs in the household of a recently deceased Slovenian countess to visit Gordon, her mother's brother. English was to be spoken at all times, but Giana had learned to make allowances when she and Max were alone.

Max glanced over his shoulder to be certain no one overheard. The habits of a lifetime were difficult to break. "We're alone, Your—Giana."

She dropped the dress she had started mending into the basket sitting on the stone floor of the massive gathering room. It was too dark to sew. The daylight had faded with the gloaming and a soft mist had begun to fall and the fire in the huge hearth gave meager light. The gathering room had become her favorite room in the lodge. The stone walls, high ceilings, and exposed timbers of the gathering room reminded her of the summer palace at Laken. Giana squared her shoulders and prepared for the worst, as she calmly waited for Max to explain. He didn't have to announce bad news. She could tell by the expression on his face that the news he bore wasn't good. "Is there news of Victor?"

Max shook his head. "No, Your Highness."

"Then what?"

"We must find another hiding place," he told her. "The owner of this one is on his way here."

Giana frowned. After spending six weeks crisscrossing the back roads of Europe from Karolya to the Mediterranean and up through Spain and France, Giana and Max had finally felt safe enough to lead their little band of refuges to their current hiding place—an uninhabited hunting lodge hidden deep in the highlands of Scotland where Isobel's brother, Gordon, was gamekeeper and caretaker. The empty hunting lodge had been a godsend. Isobel had lived in Karolya for more than twenty years, and the fact that she and Langstrom lived and worked at Laken, away from the capital, made the likelihood of any of Victor's minions realizing that she had a brother in Scotland remote. "But Gordon said Lord Bascombe hadn't come to the lodge in years. He hates the place."

"Gordon was correct," Max told her. "Apparently, Lord Bascombe hated the lodge enough to sell it. There was a telegraph awaiting Gordon in the village saying the new owner is on his way to inspect the property. He instructed Gordon to make the lodge habitable."

"When?" Giana breathed.

"Any day now," Max said. "The telegraph operator waited for Gordon to come into the village to collect his mail and messages instead of riding out here to deliver them." He glanced at the princess. "I'm afraid that doesn't give us much time to find another place, Your Highness."

Giana worried her bottom lip with her teeth. "Do we know if the person who purchased the lodge is someone who might recognize us?"

"The origin of the name is Scottish," he said. "But according to the telegram, the gentleman is from America."

Giana smiled. "Then we need not worry about finding a new place to hide, Max."

"Why not?"

"We shall be safe and comfortable here until it's time to return to Karolya and reclaim the throne." She hoped she sounded more confident than she felt.

"How can you be so certain Highness?"

"It has become common knowledge, among royals, that Americans pay little attention to our goings-on."

"But, Princess, we cannot remain in a lodge the new owner expects to find uninhabited," he protested.

She thought for a moment. "We can if we're the staff."

Max groaned. He recognized the look of determination in her eye. "The staff? Highness, please . . . I beg you to reconsider."

"It's perfect, Max." Giana smiled. "We'll become the staff."

He bit back another groan, but he couldn't prevent his wince. Princess Giana's last attempt at domesticity had been an unmitigated disaster. She'd set herself and the palace kitchens in Christianberg on fire in a failed attempt to master the art of French cuisine. She hadn't been burned, but in her efforts to gain practical experience in homemaking skills, the princess had reduced the goose she'd been preparing to ash, and her skirts and the oven had suffered irreparable damage. The palace chef, always temperamental at best, had refused to continue the princess's cooking lessons and had forbidden Her Royal Highness from entering his domain. Even Isobel, who was the most forgiving of souls, forbade the princess to try her hand at meal preparation, saying they could not afford to sacrifice the lodge's only working cookstove.

Max tried again. "Your Highness, I beg you to remember your Sixteenth."

Giana's smile faded. According to Karolyan custom, young girls born to common families could not marry until they reached the age of six and ten. In order to prepare for that momentous rite of passage, they spent their fifteenth year learning the skills they would need to care for a husband and family. Although the custom excluded females born to the nobility, who were often betrothed before they reached the age of consent, Giana was the exception. As heir apparent to the throne, she was expected to set an example and encourage every girl born in the principality of Karolya to prepare for her Sixteenth by learning to cook and sew and clean. Prince Christian and Princess May had arranged for the palace chef to teach her to cook and for individual members of the staff to teach her ordinary housekeeping skills. "That was an accident, Max."

"Of course it was, Your Highness, but the fact remains that you have no practical experience in staffing a hunting lodge."

"I've greater practical experience, Max. *I* grew up in a palace."

"Growing up in a palace and working in a palace are two very different things."

She frowned at the secretary. "I am aware of that. But I've watched the staff. And I do have some experience aside from cooking. I learned to perform other vital tasks in preparation for my Sixteenth. I swept and mopped the floor and dusted furniture and helped beat the rugs, and I washed dishes and clothes."

She neglected to mention that those lessons had come to an end when she left her lawn nightgowns and delicate undergarments soaking in lye and forgot to rinse the floor of the entry to her father's reception hall after washing it. The lye soap had eaten holes in all of her underclothes, and the palace seamstresses had had to work around the clock to make new ones, and a German ambassador had slipped and fallen on the hard marble floor leading into the reception hall, sending two Papal emissaries skidding across the floor, where they'd landed at the feet of the Chancellor of the Exchequer. Papa had laughed about it later, saying the ambassador had rolled through the emissaries like a bowling ball through pins, but he'd declared her lessons in scrubbing floors and doing laundry at an end.

Her other lessons continued, and two days later she accidentally demolished several pieces of her mother's priceless Venetian crystal by plopping them into scalding hot dishwater.

A week after that she'd unpropped the lid of the grand piano, dropping it onto the fingers of the Russian counsel while practicing her dusting in the Music Room, and shattered one Ming Dynasty horse when she knocked it off its pedestal while beating the dust from a tapestry chair. The next day her father had instructed that her lessons be confined to sewing, then immediately revised that order to exclude sewing done by machine. From that day forward, her homemaking skills were directed toward the traditional ladylike arts of the nobility—menu planning, flower arranging, embroidery, and gardening. The palace topiaries had suffered slight damage, the goldfish had been fed more often than usual, and a few of the roses had been pruned too enthusiastically, but her name was read along with all the other girls in Christianberg who marked their Sixteenth with a bouquet of white flowers and a silver pin in the shape of a bouquet, inscribed with the year and the Karolyan motto: *love, duty, family.* The silver pin had been her mother's idea—a commemoration given to all the young women in the land upon the occasion of their sixteenth birthday.

Giana had worn hers ever since. She cherished her pin, placing as much value on it as she did the Karolyan Crown Jewels. With the exception of that silver pin and the locket her mother had given her on her twentieth birthday, everything she had—her wealth, her titles, her position in life—had all been awarded to her by virtue of her birth. But her silver pin had been earned. She had worked for it. She reached up and traced the familiar contours through the bodice of her gown. She didn't dare wear it where anyone might see it and inquire about it, so she wore it pinned to her chemise, just above the edge of her corset, close to where her locket hung around her neck, suspended from a fine gold chain. The Seal of State hung on a sturdier chain fastened about her waist where no one would ever see it. "I earned my pin."

"Yes, Your Highness, but . . ." Max stared into his princess's shining blue eyes. He couldn't, in good conscience, recommend a course of action that he feared might expose her identity and compromise her safety. But he couldn't refuse her, either.

"We can do this, Max."

"Princess, have you considered that by taking the work meant for the surrounding villagers, you may deprive them of wages and the livelihoods they need to survive?"

Giana hesitated. She hadn't considered that. And, in truth, she had no wish to deprive the crofters of badly needed wages. She had had no idea, when she arrived, that Scottish Highlanders were so impoverished or that her godmother, Queen Victoria, had failed to provide her beloved Highland people with a means of earning a sufficient living. Giana looked at her adviser. "We—I—" She was trying to learn to use the singular pronoun, but it was very hard to remember to be an "I" rather than the "we" she had always been. "I shan't accept wages."

"Oh, but you must, Your Highness," Max informed her. "To do otherwise would raise suspicions. These days no one works as a domestic except as a means of earning wages."

"Then we—I—shall donate my wages to charity. You and Gordon shall arrange for them to go to the needy so that I might become an anonymous benefactor."

"Very good, Your Highness." Max didn't have the heart to tell her that the meager wage she would earn as a domestic would do very little to alleviate the suffering of the poor.

"The staff, of course, shall keep whatever they earn. Isobel and Langstrom shall resume their roles as housekeeper and butler. Josef shall be in charge of the stable. Brenna and I shall be the maids, and you shall be the lodge steward."

Max cleared his throat. "I believe that is the position Gordon currently holds, Highness."

"Oh." She thought a moment. "Then you shall be the . . ." She frowned, searching her brain for the common equivalent for the title of Lord Chamberlain, the head of the royal household. "Overseer."

"I beg your pardon, Your Royal Highness, but *paid* employees do not require an overseer. I believe that, in English, the term is most commonly used to describe the taskmasters assigned to direct slaves and convicts."

Giana felt the heat rise in her cheeks. "We didn't mean to insult you, Max. We—I—only meant that you shall be whatever it is that Scottish commoners call the Lord Chamberlain," she pronounced. "You shan't be just the Master of the Household, you shall be the person responsible for the maintenance and staffing of the royal residence—wherever that may be—in exile and when we return to Karolya."

Her announcement brought tears to Max's eyes. For nearly four hundred years Gudrun men had been assigned to the Prince of Saxe-Wallerstein-Karolya's household, and not one of them had ever risen above the position of Private Secretary to His or Her Serene Highness. His princess had, in one sentence, promoted him to the highest office any member of his family had ever achieved. Or ever hoped to achieve because the Lord Chamberlain was the highest-ranking member in the royal household, answering only to the royal family.

He bowed his head. "I am deeply honored, Princess."

Giana managed a sad smile. "You deserve far better," she said. "The position of Lord Chamberlain isn't much of an honor at the moment. We've only a borrowed royal residence and a staff of six for you to supervise, but we hope to make it up to you when we return to the palace at Christianberg."

"You need not worry about making anything up to me, Your Highness," Max told her. "I'm honored to serve you in any capacity."

"And *I* am honored to have you." She stood up. "I shall require help," she said softly. "Although I earned my Sixteenth pin, I do not, as you reminded me, have quite enough practical experience to attend to all of the duties necessary to run a hunting lodge. Although I'm extremely proficient in mopping and dusting, my skills in cooking and laundry are not as proficient. You may secure additional staff from among the crofters to instruct and assist us."

Max winced again. "Of course, it shall be as you command, Princess. But may I suggest that Your Highness might put her skills to better use in a supervisory capacity?"

Giana shook her head. "I cannot occupy a higher position in the household than Langstrom and Isobel," she said. "They are supposed to be my parents. I fear that having a daughter supervise their activities might arouse suspicions as to our identity."

Max bowed. "You are correct, Princess."

"Then assemble the other guests and inform them of the owner's arrival." Giana reached out and placed her palm against Max's cheek.

"Guests, Princess?" He looked up and lifted an eyebrow in surprise.

"Guests for one more night," she explained. "For tomorrow we become staff." She gifted Max with mischievous smile. "I may be a Princess, but even *I* noticed that none of the staff normally occupied bedchambers on the same floor as the family." Giana didn't know about the accommodations of the other members of her little entourage, but she suspected that the rooms they occupied bore little resemblance to the room she had chosen for herself—the one with the large marble fireplace and a massive four-poster bed piled high with feather mattresses.

"There is still time for you to change your mind, Your Royal Highness, and avoid the attic." He winked at her. "The position of housekeeper includes a private room."

"I'm tempted," she replied honestly, "because I shall hate to give up that wonderful bed, but Isobel will be a better housekeeper than I."

"Isobel will have no need of the housekeeper's quarters. She's Langstrom's wife. She'll share his bedchamber."

"And I will share a bedchamber in the attic with Brenna."

Max shook his head. "If you feel you must, Your Highness."

"I must." She laughed. "But not until tomorrow."

Chapter 4

A Princess of the Blood Royal never disagrees with those of higher rank, or expresses a difference of opinion to those of lesser rank.

—MAXIM 201: PROTOCOL AND COURT ETIQUETTE OF PRINCESSES OF THE BLOOD ROYAL OF THE HOUSE OF SAXE-WALLERSTEIN-KAROLYA, AS DECREED BY HIS SERENE HIGHNESS, PRINCE KAROL I, 1432.

"Open up!" Adam banged his fists against the solid oak front door, and then began a rapid tattoo with the brass doorknocker. "Open up!"

By the time he reached the front door of Larchmont Lodge, the light mist that had greeted him in at the train station in Glasgow had become a torrential downpour with wind gusts that threatened to sweep him off the steps. Holding on to the doorknocker with one hand to brace himself against the gale-force winds, he fumbled in his coat pocket for the front door key. Bascombe hadn't had the key on him when he'd lost the deed to the place to Adam in a high-stakes poker game during his tour of Nevada and the American West. Adam hadn't wanted to accept the deed in the first place. He enjoyed winning his opponents' cash as long as he knew they could afford to lose it, but the thought of winning family property made him uncomfortable. His attempts to excuse Lord Bascombe's debt had been rebuffed. The man had insisted he accept the lodge as payment for his losses, and Adam had been compelled to do so. He'd filed the deed away in his safe and had all but forgotten about it until a key to the front door arrived by mail some three months later along with a note detailing the outbuildings and the furnishings and informing Adam that although the lodge was no longer fully staffed, a caretaker named Gordon Ross remained in residence to look after the place.

When he'd ridden onto the grounds, Adam had thought the lodge was empty. He'd sent a telegram to the caretaker from London instructing him to hire a staff and make the lodge ready for his arrival, but that didn't mean the man had done it or if he'd received the telegram telling him to do it. Murphy had tried to warn him when they left the train in Glasgow, suggesting they spend the night in a hotel in the city and send another telegram before continuing the journey into the Highlands, but Adam wouldn't hear of it. He'd been cooped up long enough—first on the ship, then in London, and finally on the train. He was ready to see the countryside, ready to see Larchmont Lodge and weigh its commercial appeal.

Because he didn't want to be shot for trespassing, Adam had planned to go to the Ross's cottage first to apprise the man of his arrival. He'd meant to ride around to where he knew the caretaker's cottage sat some distance from the main house at the back of the property, but a flicker of light through the window of the lodge caught his eye. It was late, and although no one hurried across the yard with an umbrella and a lantern to greet him, the light at the window and the smell of chimney smoke told him that lodge was inhabited. It seemed that Gordon Ross had gotten his telegram after all. The staff—if there was staff—had most likely retired for the night, but someone was inside the lodge, and he might as well join whoever it was—after all, he owned the place.

Adam let go of the brass knocker, reached up, and readjusted the brim of his hat and the collar of his mackintosh in an effort to redirect the steady stream of rain dripping down his neck. He shivered as a gust of wind blew across the lawn, but he managed to fit the front door key into the lock. He was wet, cold, and thoroughly road weary and had spent the last few miles of the journey looking forward to a roaring fire, a hot meal, and a bed. Adam knew that he might have to do without those comforts tonight, but not without a fight.

"I know you're in there." He lifted his hand to bang on the

door once again. "Open up!" Adam shouted one final warning, then turned the key in the lock and pushed open the door.

The door flew open, crashing against the interior wall with a thud that shook the frame. The key bounced out of the lock and skidded across the marble entry while a man and a woman dressed in nightclothes leapt back to avoid the torrent of cold rain. Adam stepped over the threshold, grabbed hold of the front door, and slammed it shut. He leaned his back against it, breathing heavily as he removed his hat and raked his fingers through his hair.

"I'm Adam McKendrick." Adam dropped his hat on the marble-topped table in the entry hall and offered his hand to the other man. "You must be Gordon Ross."

The older man retreated, shaking his head as he stepped away from Adam's outstretched hand.

Adam withdrew his hand and frowned. "Then, who?"

The woman stepped forward, responding with the answer to Adam's question before the man could form a response. "Staff," she replied in a thick Scottish burr. "I'm Isobel Langstrom and this is my husband, Albert. We're part of the staff."

"Staff . . . ," Adam breathed a sigh of relief. "Thank God." He removed his mackintosh, shaking the water from the folds as he glanced around for a place to hang it.

Albert took the coat from him.

"Thanks." Adam left the couple standing in the foyer and started up the staircase. He took the stairs two at a time. "I've been traveling all day. I'm wet, cold, and tired. I'd like a roaring fire and a soft bed as soon as possible. And please see that my horse is tended to right away." Pausing at the top of the landing, he asked, "Where's the master suite?"

"Last one on the left," Isobel replied automatically, "but, my lord . . . wait . . ." She started up the stairs behind him.

Adam waved her off. "No need to show me," he said. "I'll find it."

He heard the low noise and recognized it as a warning growl seconds before he opened the door of the master suite. "What the devil—" The air left Adam's lungs in a rush and a series of white-hot stars danced against a black background as the base of his skull thudded against the hard floor.

He couldn't see his attacker until he was flat on his back with a hundred plus pounds of a massive animal—an ugly shaggy-coated brute that appeared to be some sort of missing link—a cross between a dog and a Shetland pony—standing on his chest. The soft glow of the lamplight illuminated the brindle-colored fur on the dog's legs and the white fur of his underbelly. A flash of light sparkled off the dog's neck, and Adam realized he was staring at a black velvet collar trimmed with gold braid and studded with what appeared to be paste diamonds. He lifted his head to get a better look, and the dog growled another warning.

"Wagner! Cease!"

The beast was obedient, responding immediately to the command. Unfortunately, he responded instantly by lying down. Adam's head connected with the floor once more. He let out a groan and another whoosh of air as the dog's elbows pressed against his stomach.

"Wagner, you may have killed him!"

The animal whined at the rebuke, shifting his weight as he buried his nose in the hollow beneath Adam's left ear and his elbows deeper into Adam's ribs.

"Not quite." Adam gasped the words.

"Good," she breathed. "You are alive."

Blinking hard to clear the stars from his eyes, Adam looked up and beheld his savior standing in the center of the bed. He groaned again, this time in abject disappointment. His savior was blond and beautiful and female, and if the length of her legs was anything to go by, very nearly tall enough to look him in the eye. Her body, silhouetted through her long white nightgown by the light from the table lamp behind her, was slim and curved in all the right places. A thick rope of tightly braided hair hung past her hips and she bore the delicate, classical facial features that had graced the canvases of great painters for centuries. He couldn't see her feet, buried as they were in the mound of bedclothes, but he supposed they were as classically beautiful as the rest of her. "What the hell is this? Who the hell are you? And what are you doing in my bed?"

Her eyes widened in shock. "Wagner is one of the finest

wolfhounds ever bred, and I am Her Ser—" she began in a haughty tone that set Adam's teeth on edge.

"Our daughter!" The shout echoed through the room, covering whatever it was the girl was about to say.

Adam turned his head in time to see Isobel rush through the doorway. He looked from Isobel to the Amazon standing on the bed. The top of Isobel's head was several inches below his chin, and Albert was only an inch or so taller than his wife. "Your *daughter*?" Adam's tone of voice held a healthy measure of disbelief.

"Yes," Isobel and Albert nodded in unison. "Our daughter, Georgiana Langstrom." Isobel turned to the girl. "Georgiana, meet Mr. Adam McKendrick from America, the new owner of Larchmont Lodge."

"How do you do, Mr. McKendrick?" she asked.

He stared at her as she extended her hand with the grace of a prima ballerina and waited patiently for him to take it. Adam rolled his eyes. Beauty appeared to hold an entitlement all its own. His sister, Kirstin, would have responded in exactly the same manner. All the world was a stage—populated by blondes aspiring to be great tragediennes. Adam didn't know whether to laugh or to cry, to shake hands with her or crawl to his knees and pay homage. He settled for indignation. "How do I do? How do I do?" He sputtered. "I'm lying flat on my back in the middle of the floor with a hundred-pound dog on my chest. How do you think I do?"

"Rude." Georgiana narrowed her gaze at him. "And there's no need to be rude, Mr. McKendrick."

"Really?" He tried to shove the dog off him, but the beast refused to budge. "I can think of a dozen reasons—beginning with him." He glared at the wolfhound.

"Wagner! Off!" She pointed to the dog, then patted her thigh. "Come!"

Wagner obeyed, first by standing on Adam, then stepping over him in order to hurry to his mistress's side.

Adam pushed himself to his feet.

Wagner growled in warning once again and Adam growled back.

Georgiana clucked her tongue at him. " 'Manners maketh man,' " she quoted. "William of Wykeham."

" 'She speaks, yet she says nothing,' " he retorted. "William Shakespeare." Adam smiled. "And if we've concluded this war of quotations, I'll take the opportunity to remind you that you haven't answered my question."

"What question was that, Mr. McKendrick?" Georgiana pretended ignorance.

"What are you doing in my bed?"

"We didn't know when to expect you, sir," Isobel hastened to explain. "The attic quarters need cleaning and repair and the beds are short and narrow . . ." She sighed. "And, as you can see, our Giana is taller than most girls. So tall that her feet hang off the mattresses." She shrugged her shoulders. "But the master suite has a huge bed, and we saw no harm in allowing her to sleep in comfort until you arrived. If that has offended you, then I beg your pardon, sir."

"You must not blame my parents for wanting to provide the best for me," Giana told him.

"Why not?" Adam lifted an eyebrow in query.

Giana smiled her most angelic smile and fluttered her eyelashes at him. "To do otherwise would be against their nature."

The smile and the fluttering lashes almost worked, but Adam had been raised in a household of consummate actresses. Wheedling and coy feminine wiles no longer had the power to sway him. Especially when he sensed that employing them wasn't part of the Amazon's nature. He liked her better when she challenged him. "Is its size the only reason you happened to be in my bed?"

Giana blinked. "What other reason could there be?"

"I'm a very wealthy man," Adam said.

"How very nice for you," Giana politely replied.

Adam inhaled sharply, swallowed his breath, and began to cough.

Giana waited patiently for him to recover from his fit of coughing. She stared at him with an expectant look on her face.

"I'm also young and healthy."

"Then you are to be congratulated, Mr. McKendrick, for I

understand that Scotland can be a very harsh land. You are very fortunate to have youth and health on your side, for one cannot overestimate their importance. I feel quite certain that those qualities will go a long way in alleviating the hardships one encounters here."

Adam was fascinated by the words that came out of her mouth each time she spoke. Her words sounded like English, but he couldn't quite grasp the meaning. Nor did she appear to grasp the meaning of his. Maybe it was because he was American and she was . . . well . . . foreign . . . but the Amazon couldn't take a hint. "I'm also generally considered to be reasonably attractive," he informed her.

She cocked her head to one side and studied him. "I do not agree."

"You don't?"

"No, I do not." She sighed. "I do not wish to find fault with the opinions of the people who have commented on your appearance, but I would have to say that you are more than reasonably attractive—"

Adam grinned. "More?"

"Of course," she replied matter-of-factly. "I have only just made your acquaintance, and know nothing of your character, but I would judge your outward appearance to be *very* attractive."

"Is that so?" Adam gave her a slow, appraising glance.

"Yes, Mr. McKendrick, it is so." She frowned, unable to understand why he insisted on questioning her answers or why he appeared to have difficulty understanding her English. Although it was not her native tongue, Giana knew her command of the English language was exceptional because her mother had taught her to speak it, and her mother had been a cousin to Queen Victoria.

"You must have been aware that I'm a bachelor."

"No, Mr. McKendrick, I know nothing of the details of your private life." Giana frowned even more. "What have they to do with me?"

"Let's see," Adam drawled sarcastically, raising his hand and pretending to count on his fingers. "What *could* the details of my private life have to do with you?" He paused for effect.

"Especially since I'm young, healthy, wealthy, and reasonably—no, make that *very*—attractive, unmarried, and the owner of the bed you're currently occupying." He looked up at her. "I would have to be extremely unenlightened not to realize that, in most circles, I'm considered to be quite a catch."

"In most circles, perhaps," Giana informed him. "But not in mine."

Adam cocked an eyebrow once again. "Indeed?" He'd have to be an extremely unenlightened man not to realize that the daughter of his new housekeeper and butler had just declared her circle closed to him. Adam had deliberately baited her, but her answer still stung, and Adam didn't know whether to find the idea amusing or pathetic.

Isobel stepped forward. "Come, Giana, we'll leave the McKendrick to settle in here while we find you another bed."

"Wait." Adam glanced from mother to daughter. "Tell me what you've heard about the *Bountiful Baron*?"

Isobel was clearly puzzled by the demand. "I don't understand."

Adam turned to Giana. "What about you?"

Giana lifted her chin. "That baron is not among my acquaintances."

"Then you can stay where you are," he said. "For tonight. But tomorrow you and the dog find someplace else to sleep." Adam lifted his chin and gave her his most winning smile. "You're welcome to sleep indoors, but fancy collar or no, the dog sleeps outside."

Giana glared at him, her nostrils flaring in anger. "You cannot . . ." she sputtered.

He grinned. "Sorry, sweetheart, but I outrank you. You may be tall, but I'm taller and I own the place." Adam turned his back on Giana and headed for the bedroom door.

The other occupants of the room gasped.

"What?" Adam paused in the doorway and glanced over his shoulder at the Amazon standing in the center of his bed. Her mouth gaped open, and he noticed for the first time that the ribbons threaded through the neckline of her nightgown were black and untied.

Giana was stunned. She knew, even if he did not, that he was in the presence of royalty, and one simply did not turn one's back on royalty. Since she could not bring her royal status to his attention, she settled for chastising him for his rudeness. "Manners, Mr. McKendrick," she called out in a too-sweet singsong voice. "Shall we find you some? Along with your warm fire and comfortable bed? Because you seem to have forgotten yours again."

"Not at all." Adam put his thumb and forefinger up to his forehead, inclined his head, and pretended to tip his hat to her. "Pleasure meeting you, George."

Chapter 5

A Princess of the Blood Royal calmly addresses the concerns of her loyal subjects.

—Maxim 104: Protocol and Court Etiquette of Princesses of the Blood Royal of the House of Saxe-Wallerstein-Karolya, as decreed by His Serene Highness, Prince Karol I, 1432.

"George!" Isobel propped her fists on her hips and sniffed her disapproval to Giana and the rest of the staff as they huddled around the kitchen table discussing the night's events.

The new owner of Larchmont Lodge had been fed and comfortably settled into a room in the opposite wing of the lodge more than an hour ago. Isobel and Albert had returned from tending to McKendrick's needs and promptly awakened Max, who insisted on rousing the rest of the staff in order to hold a family meeting to determine the best way to avert a crisis and proceed with the plan.

Giana politely covered her yawn with her hand. As far as she was concerned, the best way to proceed with the plan was to proceed. She saw no reason to rob the others of a few hours' sleep by holding a midnight meeting. But Max had wanted to make certain everyone knew of McKendrick's arrival and understood their roles, and Max had always been cautious and a stickler when it came to planning. Giana swallowed another yawn. If holding an urgent meeting on the crisis eased his mind, then she was willing to comply. But the fact remained that the crisis, if one could call it that, had already been averted. McKendrick had willingly accepted their explanations, and as long as McKendrick believed they were staff, they were safe. And McKendrick had no reason not to believe them. Isobel and Albert had made certain that he'd been fed and made comfortable in his room, and Josef had seen to the care and feeding of his horse in the barn.

Still, the family had been surprised and upset by McKendrick's unexpected arrival, and the least she could do as their leader was to listen to their worries and do her best to reassure them.

"The McKendrick called you George, Your Highness," Isobel repeated.

"So he did." A half-smile played at the corner of Giana's lips. Her mother had called her Fleur when she was growing up because, she said, Giana was the most precious bloom in the principality. Her father's name for her hadn't been quite as elegant. To him, she had always been Monkey. Her father had said it was because she'd come out of the womb all arms and legs, red-wrinkled face, and grasping hands. He'd told her that she hadn't looked like a princess at all and had more closely resembled the monkeys in the Christianberg zoo.

Giana sighed. She hadn't been called anything except Giana or Your Royal Highness since the night her father was mur . . . her father died. How she missed hearing her father's voice. Missed hearing the sound of his footsteps echoing down the marble halls of the palace at Christianberg, the clink of his dress spurs and the rattle of his scabbard as he hurried from room to room, greeting guests and attending to business. Her Royal Highness Princess Monkey. Her father was the only person who had ever called her that. And she'd loved it because it made her feel special. Because she was the heir apparent to a crown, everyone else in the world addressed her by her given names or by the title she held. Only her parents dared to call her anything else. Until now . . .

"And he insulted you," Albert said.

Giana frowned. He might have seemed insulting to Isobel and Josef, but she preferred to think of his manner as challenging rather than insulting. Except on rare occasions when Max did it, there was no one to question her decisions or challenge her ideals or opinions the way her parents had done.

There wasn't anyone to tease her or chastise her for her royal hauteur or remind her that her position in life existed so that she might serve, rather than be served. "When?"

"He deliberately turned his back on you, Your Highness," Albert explained.

"Oh, that." She'd dismissed his action as thoughtless and unintentional. He hadn't known he was in the presence of royalty or that turning his back on royalty was the height of insult, so the sight of the three of them—Isobel, Albert, and herself—standing in stunned silence with their mouths agape must have seemed quite strange. Giana smiled at the memory. "I rather doubt that Mr. McKendrick's *practical experience*"—she used her father's favorite expression—"with royalty is as great as yours or Isobel's."

"Turning his back on you wasn't the only insult he paid you, Your Highness," Isobel continued her list of grievances against the American. "He stared at you in a most impolite manner."

"Did he?" Giana asked.

Isobel nodded. "He stared at you as if he thought you were something on display in a sweet shop window. How is it that you did not notice?"

Giana smiled her mysterious princess smile—the one that said she knew a great deal more than she was telling. "Let's see," she said, mimicking Adam's drawl, "could it be because most everyone we've—I've—ever met stares at me as if I'm something on display in a shop window? And the fact is that I have *been* on display like merchandise in a shop window since the day I was born. Over the years I have grown quite immune to impolite stares. How is it that you failed to notice that?" She teased, reaching over to pat Isobel's hand.

"You've only us to protect you." Isobel glanced around the table and nodded at each of her companions, all of them subjects who had remained loyal to their beloved princess and the memory of her late parents. "We must have Max speak to the McKendrick about his presumptuous and forward manner toward you," Isobel said.

"No," Giana said. "Max must not speak to the McKendrick." She looked at the older woman. "Would you have had Max or Albert speak to my father or any other gentleman about his manner of speaking to a member of the female staff?"

"Of course not," Isobel answered. "But Prince Christian was the sovereign ruler of Karolya."

"Adam McKendrick is the sovereign ruler of Larchmont Lodge and all the land surrounding it," Giana replied. "We have no where else to go. We cannot risk discovery."

Isobel grudgingly admitted Giana was right, but she didn't have to like it. "That is true, Your Highness, but you should not allow him such familiarity."

"I could do nothing to prevent his familiarity. You told him that my name was Georgiana and that I was your daughter." She softened her tone of voice. "He's an *American*, Isobel, and unaccustomed to royalty." She shrugged her shoulders in a gesture her mother would have declared most unbecoming a princess. "As long as he thinks I'm a servant in his employ, you cannot expect him to address me properly or hold his ignorance of my royal heritage against him."

"Maybe not," Isobel conceded, "but we can certainly hold his *familiar* manner against him, Your Highness."

"I have already taken the man to task for his lack of manners, Isobel," Giana reminded her.

"I understand, Your Royal Highness, but as you said, he is an American ignorant of our ways"—she turned to the other members of the staff—"but we are not. We are Karolyan citizens. We cannot put any job above our duty to our princess and our duty is to serve and protect our princess first and foremost." Isobel narrowed her gaze. "One of the ways we shall protect our princess is by keeping watchful eyes on the McKendrick."

Chapter 6

The men and women in the Bountiful Baron's employ sing his praises.

—The First Installment of the True Adventures of the Bountiful Baron: Western Benefactor to Blond, Beautiful, and Betrayed Women written by John J. Bookman, 1874.

"Good morning, sir."

Adam automatically grabbed at the bedclothes and yanked them from his waist to his chest. Good lord! His new housekeeper was as bad as his mother—barging into his room and waking him up without so much as a knock in warning. Keeping one hand on the covers to ensure his modesty remained intact, Adam raked his hand through his hair to smooth down the locks he knew, from experience, were standing on end.

Isobel struggled to keep from smiling. "I brought your breakfast, sir. And your clothes." She plopped the breakfast tray across his lap and pointed to the neatly pressed suit hanging on a brass hook on the open door of the mahogany wardrobe.

He frowned at her. "You're the last person I expected to see this morning, ma'am. Where is Albert? Why didn't he bring my clothes?"

"Albert is meeting with Max in the library. They're discussing the refurbishing of the servants' quarters and the hiring of additional staff from among those available in the village."

"Who is Max?"

"Private secretary to Her . . ." Isobel caught herself. "Your private secretary."

Adam shook his head. "I don't have a private secretary."

"Of course you do, sir," Isobel said. "Owners of hunting lodges always have private secretaries to attend to their correspondence and the correspondence of their guests."

"I attend to my own correspondence," Adam replied. "It's more private than employing a private secretary, and I prefer it that way."

His answer came as a surprise to Isobel. "But what of your guests, sir?"

Adam shrugged his shoulders. "If they wish to correspond with anyone, they'll have to write the letters themselves," he said. "I'm not going to do it."

"Of course not, sir," Isobel replied. "That would be an unthinkable breach of protocol—especially since it is Max's duty to attend to it for you."

"Max has no duty to attend to for me," Adam told her. "Because I don't have a private secretary."

Isobel turned and gestured toward the china pot sitting upon the breakfast tray. "How do you take your tea, sir?"

"I don't drink tea."

Isobel frowned. I can fetch you a cup of hot chocolate from the pot I made for Giana."

"Giana." Adam repeated aloud, rolling the name around on his tongue, liking the sound of it.

"Our daughter," Isobel reminded him. "You met her last night."

George. The Amazon. How could he forget? He smiled at the memory of the young woman standing in the center of the bed. He thought of her as an Amazon, not because she was masculine in any way, but because she was tall and beautiful and able to look a man in the eye. "I thought her name was . . ."

"Georgiana."

"George."

They spoke in unison and the housekeeper narrowed her gaze and frowned at him. "We call her Giana."

Adam lifted an eyebrow. "And you prepare a pot of hot chocolate for her each morning?"

"Of course, sir," Isobel replied. "Hot and frothy, just the way she likes it."

Adam snorted. "And deliver it on a tray to her bed."

She nodded. "Just as I delivered this one to you."

"Quite the little princess, isn't she?"

Isobel froze. "Sir?" The single query came out as a high-pitched squeak.

"I thought my mother spoiled my sisters, but you . . ." He shook his head. "You treat your daughter like a queen."

Isobel looked puzzled. "That is a mother's duty, is it not?"

"But your daughter . . ." He paused for a moment, as if he couldn't believe what he'd heard. "Georgiana gets the master suite, the largest bed, and chocolate hot and frothy just the way she likes it every morning."

"That's right, sir. Shall I fetch you a cup?" Isobel ventured.

Adam shook his head. "I prefer coffee."

"I'm sorry sir, but I didn't bring coffee. Only tea."

"Then I'll take tea," Adam replied, wincing as he did so.

"Very good, sir." She turned to the tray, filled a cup with steaming liquid from the china pot, and handed it to him.

He accepted the cup and saucer she handed to him but refused the milk and sugar she offered. "I take it straight." He swallowed a sip of the strong brew. It wasn't coffee, but it was hot and since it was all he could do to keep his teeth from chattering with cold, he drank it. "Thank you."

"You're welcome, sir."

"Not at all, sir," she replied. "I made an exception this morning because I thought you might appreciate having your clothes. But now that your man has arrived, I'm certain he will assume that duty."

"My man?" She had surprised him once again.

"Your valet, sir."

"I don't have a valet."

"Of course you do, sir. All gentlemen have valets to see to their wardrobes. Although I've never met an Irish one before." She thinned her lips in a disapproving line. "O'Brien, I believe he said. Murphy O'Brien. He arrived early this morning in a coach piled high with your luggage."

Adam laughed. "O'Brien isn't my valet," he replied. "He's

my friend." He poured himself another cup of tea, then lifted a piece of bacon from the rasher on the tray and scooped up a forkful of eggs.

Isobel sniffed. "You could ha' fooled me."

"Why do you say that?"

"Because the only men I've ever known who fussed that much over luggage were valets," she said.

Adam laughed again. "O'Brien has reason to be concerned about the luggage," he told her. "Because over half of it is his, and he spent a small fortune to procure it in time for the journey."

"Then he's a gentleman like yourself."

"I'm not sure either of us qualify for the title of gentleman," Adam said. "But he's my friend nonetheless. My closest friend." His voice held a warning note to remind Isobel that O'Brien was a friend and she was staff.

"Very good, sir." Isobel understood the warning. "I'll prepare a room for Mr. O'Brien." She bobbed a slight curtsy.

"Thank you."

"The staff will await you in the library, sir, when you've finished your breakfast and completed your morning ablutions."

Adam quirked an eyebrow in question.

"They expect to be presented, sir."

"Please ask the members of the staff to assemble in the library in half an hour," Adam instructed. "And ask Mr. O'Brien to join me here."

"Very good, sir."

Adam waited until the sound of the housekeeper's footsteps faded on the stairs before he lifted the breakfast tray off his lap and placed it on the table beside the bed. He flipped back the covers and climbed out of bed. Pulling the coverlet off the bed, Adam wrapped it around his waist, holding it with one fist as he padded barefoot across the cold floor to the privacy screen in the corner of the bedchamber.

He answered the call of nature, then made his way to where his suit hung on the door of the wardrobe. The top drawer of the wardrobe was opened, and his shirt and linen undergarments were dried and neatly folded inside it. His boots stood beside the wardrobe, and his leather saddlebags hung on a brass hook inside the wardrobe door.

Adam let the coverlet fall to the floor as he removed his trousers from their hook. He stepped into his underwear and trousers and pulled his shirt over his head. Still shivering with cold, he retrieved his boots and saddlebags, silently thanking the brave soul who had ventured out in the cold rain to tend to his horse and claim his belongings. Adam hopped from one foot to the other as he crossed over to the fire and set his boots on the hearth to warm. He stoked the peat fire, stirring the embers into a small flame before he made his way back across the room to the washstand. Christ! He was so cold his teeth were chattering. No wonder Bascombe sold the place. The rest of the world was enjoying a moderately warm summer, but a man could freeze to death in Larchmont Lodge in Scotland unless he kept a close proximity to the fire, and Adam had already learned that peat fires tended to smoke more than they heated.

Sucking in a breath, Adam broke the thin film of ice on the water in the china pitcher on the washstand. He poured the icy water into the bowl, gritted his teeth, removed his mug and brush and a bar of soap from his saddlebags, and prepared to shave. Adam managed a grim laugh. He thought he'd put this particular brand of discomfort behind him. When he'd struck it rich working his silver claim, he vowed he'd have hot water to shave in every morning for the rest of his life. But he hadn't counted on winning a hunting lodge in the wilds of Scotland. He washed his face in the cold water and grimaced at his reflection in the mirror. What good was a staff when no one thought to provide him with hot water for shaving? Unless that was one of the duties of a valet . . .

"Where are you, McKendrick?"

Adam recognized the sound of O'Brien's hearty chuckle before his friend opened the bedroom door. He dipped his shaving brush in the basin of water and rubbed it across the bar of shaving soap. Murphy announced his arrival by entering the room.

"Hold it!"

Adam froze.

"Yer handsome face will look like raw meat if you shave in water from that." He nodded toward the bowl. "Especially if it's been sitting overnight. Besides, the bossy little woman downstairs told me I should do my duty and bring this up to you." O'Brien held up a kettle, its handle wrapped to keep from burning him.

Adam reached for it.

"Careful, boyo, it's boiling," Murphy warned as he handed the kettle over.

"Thank God," Adam breathed. He poured hot water into the basin, tested the temperature, then added some more. "I was ready to sell my soul for hot water."

"Good." Murphy grinned. "You can pay me for it later."

Adam met O'Brien's grin with one of his own. Trust Murphy to take him up on his offer to pay. He turned his attention to the mirror and began to lather his face.

"Well, boyo, what do you think?" O'Brien asked. "I don't know about it's commercial appeal, but this is some setup you've got here." He gave a low whistle of admiration and lifted a scone from one of the plates on Adam's breakfast tray. Murphy slathered the scone with butter and marmalade, swallowed the biscuit in three bites, then crossed the room and stretched out on Adam's bed. He stacked his hands beneath his head and watched while Adam shaved. "Have you seen the place?" Murphy whistled again.

Adam frowned. "I arrived during a storm. I saw gale-force winds, freezing rain, the outside of the lodge, and the shadow of a barn."

"I don't know how to break the news to you, but you didn't win the deed to a hunting lodge," Murphy told him. "You won the deed to an estate that takes up half the bloody county." He scratched his forehead. "I should be so lucky."

"Why aren't you?" Adam deadpanned. "I thought the Irish were famous for their luck."

Murphy chuckled. "It never applied to the common Irish, only the wealthy landlords."

Adam finished shaving, wiped his face on a length of toweling, then pointed to a garment hanging in the wardrobe. "Hand me that waistcoat, will you?"

Murphy reached up and lifted the waistcoat off its hook and tossed it to Adam.

Adam caught the waistcoat in one hand and shrugged into it. "Thanks."

"Anything for you, Your Lordship," Murphy replied in an exaggerated British accent.

"I'm not Your Lordship."

"All right, then, Mr. McKendrick, what say we saddle up and spend the morning surveying your estate, evaluating its potential?" O'Brien rolled off the bed and onto his feet.

"Can't," Adam answered.

"Too sore to ride?" O'Brien speculated.

Adam shook his head. "I have to inspect the staff," he answered in a near perfect imitation of Murph's exaggerated English accent.

"Inspect the staff?" O'Brien nearly doubled over laughing.

"A place this size has to have staff," Adam reminded him. "And I've been informed that they're waiting for me to pass judgment."

"Well, lead on, boyo, I wouldn't miss this for the world."

"Of course you wouldn't," Adam agreed. "Because I believe you've just become a part of it."

"What?" O'Brien's mirth died a quick dead.

"The bossy little woman who sent you up here with the hot water is the housekeeper," Adam explained. "And she thinks you're my valet."

"Your *what?*"

"My gentleman's gentleman."

O'Brien cast a suspicious glance Adam's way. "And just how would she get an idea like that?"

Adam held up his hands. "Don't look at me. You're the one who gave her the idea."

"Impossible!" Murphy scoffed.

"And I quote, 'The only men I've ever known who fussed over luggage that much were valets.' "

"Criminy," Murphy swore. "That luggage cost me a bloody fortune!"

"I explained that," Adam said. "And I told her you were my friend and traveling companion, but apparently she chose to believe otherwise." He clucked his tongue. "It's amazing, really. I thought she'd take one look at you and know."

"Why should she?" O'Brien demanded. "What's wrong with the way I look?"

"Nothing," Adam teased. "Except your clothes, your hair, and your manner." O'Brien's clothes were the latest fashion and made of fine cloth, but he would never be considered stylish. He was too big, too brawny, and too ruggedly handsome to fit the image of a valet.

"What about them?"

"There's no way in hell you'll ever pass inspection."

Chapter 7

A Princess of the Blood Royal is obliged to attend all court presentations.

—Maxim 8: Protocol and Court Etiquette of Princesses of the Blood Royal of the House of Saxe-Wallerstein-Karolya, as decreed by His Serene Highness Prince Karol I, 1432.

And all other mundane and tedious presentations…

—Addendum to Maxim 8: Her Serene Highness, Princess May, 1850.

The staff of Parchmont Lodge weren't the only ones under scrutiny. Adam couldn't walk down the halls of the lodge without feeling the fine hairs on the back of his neck prickle in reaction. The walls lining the central corridor were hung with massive portraits of long-dead ancestors of the previous owners, and dozens of pairs of painted eyes seemed to follow his progress as he made his way from his bedchamber to the library.

And the sensation of being watched increased as he entered the comfortable oak and leather confines of the lodge's magnificent library and glanced around to find eight—nine, if he counted Murphy O'Brien's—pairs of actual eyes staring at him.

Albert Langstrom stepped forward, bowed to Adam, then turned to another slightly older gentleman with jet-black hair liberally streaked with silver and a ramrod-straight posture. He spoke in a language Adam didn't understand, which seemed odd for a Scottish staff. Odder still, since Adam thought he understood English—even English spoken with a Scot's burr. When he finished speaking, whatever he was speaking, Langstrom took his place in line beside his wife.

The older man turned to Adam. "My name is Maximillian . . . umm . . . Langstrom," he said. "I am Your Lordship's private secretary. You may call me Max. My brother"—he paused ever-so-slightly—"Albert begs your pardon for his failure to perform his duty as expected, but his English is limited. He asks that you allow me to stand in his stead and perform the required introductions." Max's English was heavily accented, but Adam had no trouble understanding it. "May I present to you the remaining staff of Larchmont Lodge?"

They stood in a line in the center of the room—obviously according to position and rank, rather than height.

"You're not Scottish?"

Max shook his head. "Gordon and Isobel are Scottish. They are brother and sister. The rest of us are from continental households, most recently from the late Countess of Brocavia's household."

"There are only eight of you?" Adam's tone of voice mirrored his surprise at finding the lodge so thinly staffed.

"Eight at present, my lord . . ."

Adam held up his hand. "I know you're accustomed to addressing Lord Bascombe as my lord, but I'm an American, not a lord."

"But, my lord—"

"McKendrick," Adam told him, extending his hand for a handshake. "Adam McKendrick."

Max glanced at Adam's outstretched hand. Adam clamped his teeth together as the older man accepted his hand in a brief handshake, then quickly released it and stepped away. Max's discomfit at being asked to shake his employer's hand was patently apparent.

"Jesus!" Adam swore beneath his breath. "You'd think I was contagious. Haven't they heard that 'all men are created equal'?"

"Easy, boyo," O'Brien whispered, placing a hand on

Adam's shoulder to steady him. "You're in the old world now."

Adam shot him a look of disbelief. "I realized that."

"Then you should realize that here America is a distant dream. It's not you. In America all men are created equal. Here, they occupy different stations in life," Murphy told him. "Act like a bloody lord and they'll respect ya. Act like an American and they'll look down on ya."

Adam focused his attention on Maximillian Langstrom. "Sir." He didn't raise his voice, but spoke in a firm tone loud enough for everyone to hear. "Not my lord. I prefer to be called sir."

"Yes, sir." The male members of the staff bowed their heads, and the female members of the staff bobbed a brief curtsy—with one notable exception.

George stood straight and tall with her shoulders back and her head held at a regal angle. Unusual in a girl so tall. His sisters had tended to hunch their shoulders and to slouch to keep from appearing taller than the boys they knew from school and church. That habit had been a continuous source of concern in the household. Adam remembered his mother commanding his sisters to stand straight and tall and to look a fellow right in the eye, forcing them to walk around the house with books on their heads to make certain they did so. Unfortunately, looking the fellows right in the eye was the problem, since like George, his sisters tended to tower over their would-be beaus.

But George appeared to have no qualms about standing straight and tall and looking a fellow right in the eye. Even when she wasn't supposed to. Adam bit the inside of his cheek to keep from smiling as a younger, smaller girl elbowed George in the ribs and motioned for her to curtsy.

Langstrom rushed to cover George's gaffe by clearing his throat and resuming the inspection. "Would you care to introduce your man, my . . . sir . . . and have him join us so that we might continue our inspection?"

He couldn't be serious. He couldn't really believe that O'Brien was a valet. Or could he? Adam glanced at Maximillian and realized that Langstrom was entirely serious. Apparently, Isobel hadn't believed him when he'd told her that O'Brien wasn't his valet because she hadn't seen fit to pass the word along to her husband or brother-in-law. "O'Brien is my friend. He's not my—"

"I'm honored that you consider me so, sir," O'Brien interrupted smoothly. Leaving his place beside Adam, O'Brien crossed the Turkish carpet and stepped into line with the rest of the staff. Turning to Langstrom, he replied in a thick Irish brogue, "My name is Murphy O'Brien and I'm proud to serve Mr. McKendrick not just as his valet, but as his gentleman's gentleman."

Adam lifted an eyebrow at Murph's bold claim, but he didn't dispute it.

A couple of inches shorter than Adam, O'Brien stood at least a head taller than everyone else in line except George, who stood at the end of the line, with the dog seated beside her. O'Brien gingerly took his place on the other side of the dog. He and George stood shoulder to shoulder with the wolfhound sandwiched between them. Adam watched as O'Brien cautiously patted the wolfhound on the head and winked at the girl peeking around George to get a better look at him.

Adam was doing his best to give the introduction ceremony the attention Max and the rest of the staff thought it deserved, but his stomach tightened at O'Brien's flirtatious manner and Adam gestured for the older man to precede him down the line. "Shall we continue?"

"Very well." With one quick nod of his head Maximillian Langstrom acknowledged O'Brien's introduction and dismissed it. There was, after all, a hierarchy and a schedule to maintain.

Max gave another of his characteristic bows. He cleared his throat and walked to Albert. "Sir, may I present to you Albert Langstrom, butler at Larchmont Lodge, last in service as head of household to the late countess of Brocavia."

"Albert." Adam acknowledged the butler.

"Sir." Albert inclined his head.

Max stepped down the line to the next person. "Sir, may I present to you Isobel Langstrom, housekeeper at Larchmont

Lodge, last in service as housekeeper to the late countess of Brocavia."

"Mrs. L.," Adam said.

"Sir." Isobel bobbed a curtsey as Max and Adam moved to the next person.

Max continued down the line introducing Isobel's brother the gamekeeper, Gordon Ross.

His official title was houndsman and gamekeeper, but Gordon Ross had been responsible for taking care of the lodge in the absence of its previous owner, Lord Bascombe. He was the man Adam had telegraphed requesting that the lodge be suitably staffed. It came as no surprise to Adam that, upon such short notice, the gamekeeper would turn to his family for help in staffing the house, but it came as something of a surprise to learn that an experienced household staff with such sterling qualifications and references had been available.

Unfortunately, there weren't enough former members of the countess of Brocavia's to go around. The grounds and stable staff consisted of two men: Gordon Ross and the master of the stables, Josef Langstrom, who was Max's son.

Adam turned to Gordon Ross. "I'd like a tour of the grounds and the stables as soon as possible. If the property proves suitable for my purposes, you'll need to hire more men to tend the grounds and the horses." He glanced at Josef. "There will be more work than the two of you to handle."

"Understood, sir."

Adam nodded in reply and moved to stand before the two remaining members of the household staff: Brenna and Georgiana Langstrom, Albert and Isobel's daughters, who worked as housemaids.

The younger petite Brenna looked nothing like her sister. She was short and small-boned with brown hair and eyes. She appeared shy and favored her mother more than her father.

Adam knew that sisters didn't necessarily have to look alike to be sisters, but coming from a family with four sisters who were pairs of identical twins made the other reality seem strange. In his family Adam was the different one. In George's family she was. It gave them an unexpected bond.

And Adam supposed the bond also extended to the dog, which

bore no resemblance to any breed of dog he had ever encountered. He stared at the animal sitting quietly beside George. Beauty and the beast.

"What about the beast?" He asked the question of Max, but Adam kept his gaze on George to see if she would speak for herself and for her pet.

The girl opened her mouth, but Max smoothly interrupted. "The beast, as you call him, sir, is an Irish wolfhound. The countess of Brocavia was a great lover of dogs. She gave this one to my niece, Giana, when he was orphaned at birth. Giana raised him, and as you can see, he's as devoted to her as she is to him."

"With the exception of the beast, the countess of Brocavia's loss appears to have been my gain," Adam commented.

"He isn't a beast. He's a dog. His name is Wagner." Unable to contain herself any longer, George ignored her uncle's warning look and challenged Adam's authority. "And he goes where I go."

"I trust you have no objections." Max's response wasn't a question but a statement.

Adam ignored Max and focused all of his attention on the girl. "That depends."

"Upon what?" she retorted.

"Upon whether the two of you intend to occupy my bed again tonight."

Chapter 8

A Princess of the Blood Royal never acknowledges, encourages, or engages in vulgar flirtations.

—Maxim 71: Protocol and Court Etiquette of Princesses of the Blood Royal of the House of Saxe-Wallerstein-Karolya, as decreed by His Serene Highness Prince Karol I, 1432.

Adam ignored the gasp that echoed through the massive library like the collected breath of a cathedral choir. He kept his attention focused solely on George. "I trust you found it to your liking."

"We found it very much to our liking." Giana tangled her fingers in Wagner's fur and lifted her chin a fraction higher than usual in order to meet McKendrick's gaze.

"Sir," Adam reminded her.

Giana frowned.

"We found it very much to our liking, *sir,*" he repeated, emphasizing his proper address.

"Sir." She uttered the word through clenched teeth.

Adam grinned at her. "There," he said, "that wasn't so hard, now was it?"

Giana glared back at him. "I do not understand your meaning."

"You're a clever girl," he answered. "You'll figure it out."

The tension between Adam and Giana crackled like lightning across the sky, and everyone in the room felt it.

Adam recognized the tension for what it was. He knew lust when he felt it, and he felt it whenever he was around George. His nerve endings sizzled with awareness, and his body responded to her presence in a way that wreaked havoc on his peace of mind. He was playing a dangerous game and knew that he was in danger of being burned. He'd never subjected any of his other female employees to the sort of forward and ungentlemanly behavior he'd displayed toward George. But he'd never found himself attracted to any of his other female employees. And all he could think to do was to make her family aware of his unwanted feelings and hope that they would help keep her safely out of harm's way. Out of *his* way.

Adam was honest enough with himself to admit that he didn't want to be attracted to her or approve of the way he was handling his unwanted emotion. But he was also honest enough to admit that he seemed to have no control over it or his behavior.

Nor did he understand how George's family could stand by and allow him to flirt with her or to engage her in unsavory wordplay. Anyone with half an eye could see that despite her ability to defend herself, George was an innocent who didn't understand the sexual undertones in his manner. But that was no excuse for his behavior or for her parents. Albert and Isobel had to understand what was happening. His meaning must be as apparent to them as it was to him. It couldn't lose that much in translation. So why didn't her father or brother or uncle put a stop to it? Why didn't they protect George by boxing his ears or punching him in the nose? Why weren't they looking out for her?

Giana shivered. Until she met Adam McKendrick, no one except her mother and father had ever spoken to her in an irreverent manner. She liked the change. She liked the tingle in her blood and the way her senses seemed to go on alert whenever he was near. She bit her bottom lip to keep from laughing aloud at the sheer joy of engaging him in a battle of wits. Giana liked the way he talked to her, liked the way he took it for granted that she was his intellectual equal and that he was hers. And she enjoyed knowing she was able to challenge him without fear of reprisal.

His words reminded her of her parents' witty, flirtatious teasing—teasing that almost always led to passionate embraces and time spent alone behind locked doors. Yes, she liked the

McKendrick's teasing. She liked it enough to encourage more of the same. She glanced up at him from beneath her lashes. "Are you going to allow us to occupy your bed once again?" she asked.

"*Your* presence in my bed is most welcome," Adam told her. "But I'd prefer the dog sleep elsewhere."

There was another collective gasp from the assembled staff. Adam prepared himself to face her father's or uncle's or cousin's wrath, but it was not forthcoming. Apart from the audible gasp, the Langstrom men did nothing to defend George's honor.

But then, Georgiana Langstrom was perfectly capable of defending her own honor.

"That is not possible," Giana answered. "For Wagner sleeps where I sleep."

Adam shrugged his shoulders. "I suppose I could make an exception for you."

"There is no need for you to make such a sacrifice, sir." Giana favored McKendrick with a smug smile. "For Wagner and I have already made our bed elsewhere."

Adam shook his head and clucked his tongue in mock sympathy. "I can't say that I'll miss Wagner, but not having you in my bed again is something I'll truly regret."

"I feel for you." She looked him in the eye. "Because, I fear, it will be a terrible waste for a gentleman like you to mourn what will never come to pass. *Sir*."

"You've been in my bed once," Adam reminded her, enjoying their verbal sparring much more than he cared to admit. "And you could easily be there again." He grinned at her. "Never is a very long time. You may be surprised by what the future holds for you."

She glanced at Max, then turned to Adam and shook her head. "I do not think so," she answered honestly. "My future was decided the day I was born."

The flash of sadness in her eyes startled him. "Fortunes change, George," he replied. "Lady Luck smiles on everyone once in a while." He shrugged his shoulders. "Even housemaids."

Giana reacted to the innuendo and the arrogance behind his

words. "It is possible," she retorted, holding his gaze for a long moment. "But not very likely, *sir.*"

Although he'd tried to mask it, Adam knew she'd seen his empathy mirrored in his eyes. He knew the expression on his face had given him away the moment George looked down at the floor and bobbed a respectful curtsey.

Adam gritted his teeth. Her respectful curtsey was harder for Adam to swallow than her saucy impertinence. George was tall, blond, and blue-eyed, and she bore more than a passing resemblance to his four sisters. The sad look in her eyes and that slight, almost imperceptible tremor in her voice shouldn't bother him. But it did.

Her unexpected subservience tore at his conscience and left a hollow feeling in the pit of his stomach.

Adam turned to the staff. "Everyone except Josef and my valet, Mr. O'Brien, is excused to return to their duties."

No one budged.

Adam tried again, waving the staff toward the library door. But the staff remained where they were, and Adam turned to Max Langstrom for help. "Thank you for introducing me to your family. And to you, Mr. Ross"—he looked at Gordon Ross—"for hiring them. Now, I'd like you to dismiss everyone except Josef and my valet."

"Have you any instructions for the rest of us?" Max asked.

"Brenna and George can return to their daily chores while you assist Albert and Isobel with the hiring of a cook, a kitchen staff, and a few more maids to help Brenna and George," Adam replied. "Mr. Ross can see to the recruitment of additional staff for the stables and grounds, and Josef can see to the saddling of horses so that Mr. O'Brien and I might ride out over the estate."

"But, sir, you cannot!" Max sputtered in protest.

Isobel said something in a language Adam didn't understand, and Albert began vigorously shaking his head.

"I can't ride out over my estate?"

"You cannot ride out with your valet," Max corrected.

"Why not?"

"Gentlemen do not ride out with their valets." Max leveled a firm look at O'Brien. "And valets do not accompany their employers on pleasure jaunts unless they are needed to attend to wardrobe or luggage."

O'Brien raised an eyebrow at that. While he was familiar with many of the ways of the aristocracy, he hadn't expected to be mistaken for a valet or taken to task by Adam's new private secretary. O'Brien exchanged amused glances with his friend. Such was the life of a Pinkerton agent. "Is that so?"

Max nodded. "Sir, it simply isn't done."

"Gentlemen don't ride out with their valets in Scotland," Adam told him. "But they do ride out with their friends. Murphy O'Brien is a friend first and a valet second."

"Your friend, sir?" Max gave voice to his confusion. "I've never met a gentleman who would call his valet or any servant a friend."

"You have now," Adam replied. "Tell me, Max, have you ever been to America?"

"No, sir."

Adam smiled. "Well, in America, gentlemen ride out with their valets or anyone else they call friends—no matter what their station in life. That's why I'm going to ride out and look over my estate with my friend, Murphy O'Brien." He gave Max a firm look that brooked no further protest and walked over to stand in front of the stable master. "Do you understand English?"

Josef didn't respond.

"How about French?" Adam repeated the question in French.

Josef smiled. "*Oui.*"

"*Bon,*" Adam answered, continuing to speak the universal language of aristocrats. "Please saddle my horse and Mr. O'Brien's horse, as we'll be riding out momentarily."

Adam waited for the stable master to leave the room, and when he didn't, Adam attempted to hurry him along. "*Au revoir,* Josef," he said. "Mr. O'Brien and I will join you in the stable shortly."

Josef backed toward the doorway, paused long enough to receive an almost imperceptible nod from George and from Max, then left the room.

Adam glanced at his private secretary and the Amazon. "Thank you for your assistance, Max, and for yours, Miss Langstrom. . . ." he acknowledged George's unspoken interference. "I'll call if I need you. *Au revoir*." He waved his arm and shooed the staff out the door.

Chapter 9

The Bountiful Baron always behaves in a gentlemanly fashion. He treats all women as if they are ladies.

—The Second Installment of the True Adventures of the Bountiful Baron: Western Benefactor to Blond, Beautiful, and Betrayed Women written by John J. Bookman, 1874.

"That was enlightening," Murphy commented wryly as he and McKendrick rode out of the stable yard.

Adam glanced over at Murphy to gauge his measure. "Was it?"

O'Brien chuckled. "I always knew the English—above- and belowstairs—considered the Irish to be beneath contempt." He winked at McKendrick. "But I didn't realize the European Continent followed suit until today."

"Don't take it personally," Adam advised. "You may be Irish, but at least you're from the Old Country. Those of us born in the New World rank lower than the Irish because we don't understand the aristocracy or its class system—above- or belowstairs."

Murphy agreed. "Americans are a threat. Not because you don't understand the aristocracy or class system, but because you hold the aristocracy and the class system in greater contempt than they hold you."

"There's no doubt about it." Adam loosened his grip on the reins and urged his horse into a faster gait. "We're rough and ready, unrefined and unrepentant. America is bursting at the seams with people escaping the class system in search of a better life—people who have no respect for centuries of cultural refinement and superiority."

"Some of whom should have had better taste than to become *nouveau riche,*" Murphy pronounced in his best upper-crust accent.

"You sound like my brother-in-law, the Legitimate Bastard," Adam said, reverting to the title he'd given Kirstin's husband, the Viscount Marshfeld.

O'Brien shuddered. "God forbid."

Adam laughed. "You know the main difference between the Bastard and me?"

"He enjoys slapping women around and you don't?" O'Brien quipped.

"That's part of it," Adam replied.

"You're rich and he's not?"

"You know as well as I do that in America, anyone can become *nouveau riche* if he's willing to work hard and get a little dirt under his fingernails. The men and women who struck it rich during the Rush of Forty-nine and the Comstock got lucky—sure—but they worked hard to make that luck possible." Adam grinned at his friend, then took off, cantering his horse up a hill.

"Like you," Murphy shouted.

"Like me," Adam answered. He topped the rise of the hill and waited for O'Brien to catch up. "The difference between me and the Bastard is that the Bastard can't understand why I got lucky and he didn't. He's supposed to be lucky. Because he has a much better pedigree than I have and a far superior place in society. *He* was given every advantage—an old family name with land and titles, a guaranteed place in society, and an expensive education. I had none of those things. My only advantage was being born in America to a mother who taught me the value of hard work and big dreams.

"But my brother-in-law, like his father and grandfather before him, was too bored, too sophisticated, and too lazy to work or to dream. He squandered what was left of his inheritance and wasted his advantages.

"I didn't. I made the most of my advantages. That's the

primary difference between the Legitimate Bastard and me."

O'Brien disagreed. "Character. That's the main difference between the two of you. You have it and he wants it."

"He wants my money." Adam snorted. "He doesn't give a fig about my character."

"I disagree," O'Brien said. "The Bastard wants to be you. Hell, Adam, a lot of men want to be you! John J. Bookman wants to be you! Most of the time even *I* want to be you!"

Adam laughed out loud.

"It's true!" O'Brien protested. "Who do you think is buying *The Second Installment of the True Adventures of the Bountiful Baron: Western Benefactor to Blond, Beautiful, and Betrayed Women?*"

"Too damn many blondes for my comfort," Adam joked. "And let me tell you, that they aren't all beautiful, betrayed, or natural blondes."

"Yeah, well, there are suckers like me, who ought to know better, buying 'em, too."

"What?" Adam turned to his friend, a look of pure astonishment on his face.

"That's right, boyo," O'Brien confirmed. "I gave the dude at the poker table a five-dollar chip for it."

"Good god, why?"

"Because I'd already read the first installment and I wanted to see what else Bookman had to say about you."

"That's a hell of a reason."

O'Brien gave him a sheepish grin. "The fact is that you inspired someone to write a book about you."

"A dime novel, Murph, not a book," Adam reminded him. "If I hadn't been at the wrong place at the wrong time, he'd have found someone else to inspire it."

"Yeah, well, I'm a Pinkerton agent and nobody's written a dime novel about me," Murphy grumbled.

"Thank your lucky stars," Adam breathed.

"I don't have lucky stars," Murphy said. "I wasn't willing to do what it takes to get them. You were. That's the point." He grinned at McKendrick. "That's what men admire about you. You have dreams. Dreams you work hard to make come true. Most of us simply take the easy path."

"You work hard," Adam said. "And you stand up for the things you believe in."

"That's right," Murphy agreed. "I stand up for what I believe in and I work hard. But I work hard for Allan Pinkerton, not Murphy O'Brien, because it's easier. And safer than risking everything." He paused to see what Adam would say. "No wonder the Bastard envies you. Think how hard it must be to be a poor aristocrat. Because it's hard enough to be poor without carrying the expectations that come with the pedigree."

Uncomfortable with the topic and unable to sit still any longer, Adam urged his horse forward. Murphy followed and the two of them rode over the estate, admiring the scenery without saying a word until Adam crested another hill and stared out at the moors below. "Christ! This place is beautiful. Too damn cold. But beautiful. And it's perfect for what I have in mind."

"Then it's a good thing that you're the lord of all you survey," O'Brien said.

"Yes, it is." Adam exhaled. He paused for a long moment. "That was enlightening."

"Was it?"

Adam chuckled. "I always knew the English—above- and belowstairs—considered the *nouveau riche* to be beneath contempt." He winked at O'Brien. "But I didn't realize the European Continent followed suit until today."

"Don't take it personally," O'Brien advised. "You may be *nouveau riche* and beneath contempt, but the girl likes you."

Adam lifted a brow and pretended ignorance. "The girl?"

"Yeah, the tall, blond Valkyrie," O'Brien answered.

"Valkyrie, eh?" Adam looked at O'Brien with new eyes. "I thought of her as an Amazon."

O'Brien shrugged. "I like opera. Her dog's name is Wagner. I made the connection."

Adam shook his head. "I can't quite see her as a Brunnhilde. My mother—even Erika or Astrid—yes. But George—no." He was thoughtful for a moment. "I see George not just as an Amazon warrior, but as Artemis."

"And how long have you known this Artemis?"

"I met her last night," Adam told him. "She and the dog were in my bed when I arrived."

"I gathered as much from your earlier exchange." O'Brien made a face. "The question is: Did she and the dog remain in your bed after you arrived?"

"Yes."

"Did you?"

"No," Adam answered.

O'Brien snorted. "Would you tell me if you had?"

Adam shot him a meaningful look. "Have I ever?"

"No."

"And I'm not going to start now. You should know that discretion is the mark of a true gentleman, and that means that a gentleman doesn't kiss and tell."

"Ah, but you're no gentleman." O'Brien's tone of voice took on a more serious note. "Or else she's no lady. . . ."

"She's definitely a lady."

"She's a housemaid, Adam."

"Who cares? Jesus! O'Brien!" Adam took off his hat and raked his fingers through his hair. "Didn't you hear a word I said to Maximillian Langstrom? Didn't I defend my friendship with you? Didn't I tell them that you are my friend? Do you really think I care that she's a housemaid or that you're my valet?"

"No," Murphy replied. "But then, I'm not your valet."

"The rest of the staff thinks you are."

"But you know I'm not."

"That's right," Adam said. "I know you're not my gentleman's gentleman. But the point is that it wouldn't matter to me if you were. You would still be my friend."

"So, why didn't you tell them who I really am?"

"I did," Adam protested. "I told them you were my friend. They chose not to believe me."

"You told them I'm your friend who works for the Pinkerton Detective Agency?"

"No, I told them you were my friend." Adam met Murphy's unwavering gaze.

"Why didn't you set them straight about what I do for a living instead of allowing them to believe that I'm your valet?"

"I tried. You're the one who volunteered to step into the role of my valet," Adam countered. "Why did you do that? You had as much of an opportunity to correct their misconception as I did."

Murphy shrugged his shoulders. "I don't know."

"Neither do I," Adam admitted. "Other than the fact that something simply doesn't feel—"

"—quite right." They answered in unison.

"Exactly," Murphy pronounced. "I can't put my finger on what's bothering me. But I know something is bothering me. I'm not entirely comfortable with this situation."

"Neither am I." Adam paused. "Did you notice the way everyone looked to Max or to George before they moved?"

"I noticed," O'Brien said. "I didn't know if you did."

"I kept telling myself that it was because they didn't understand me, but Max and Isobel and George and Gordon Ross all speak English, so that couldn't be the reason." Adam scratched his forehead. "So why didn't anyone try to help defend her from me?"

"Who?" O'Brien asked.

"You know who," Adam snapped. "The Valkyrie. The Amazon. George."

"You said you didn't sleep with her." Murphy O'Brien enjoyed ruffling Adam McKendrick's feathers, loved seeing him loose some of his control, so he relished his role as devil's advocate every chance he got.

"I didn't," Adam repeated.

Murphy narrowed his gaze. "You wouldn't speak to the Valkyrie the way I heard you speak to her this morning unless you didn't think she was a lady or an innocent or unless you intended to find out."

Adam was thoughtful. "I can't deny that," he said softly. "I spoke to her in a way no gentleman should ever speak to a lady—especially one who is still an innocent."

"How do you know she still innocent?"

Adam shot O'Brien a look that spoke volumes about the continued wisdom of playing devil's advocate or of asking patently stupid questions. "She's still innocent. I'd bet my life on it."

"So would I," O'Brien agreed.

"Then why didn't her father or brother or uncle punch me in the nose?" Adam stared at his friend. "You would have defended your sister's honor. God knows I've defended my sisters' honor often enough." Adam frowned. "So why didn't George's family defend her honor? There's no excuse for it."

"Unless they've something to fear," Murphy suggested.

"Such as?"

"Losing their positions."

"I'm more inclined to dismiss them for *not* defending her honor than I would be *for* defending it," Adam said.

"You know that and I know that," O'Brien replied. "But they don't know that because they don't know you. You heard them, Adam, their employer died. They're starting over in a new place. Maybe they were afraid of jeopardizing their positions here."

"I hope so," Adam fervently replied. "I hope it's as simple as that."

"Would you dismiss them?" Murphy asked. "Knowing they may have nowhere else to go?"

"Who me?" Adam put on his most innocent face. "I'm the Bountiful Baron, remember? Western Benefactor to Blond, Beautiful, and Betrayed Women everywhere."

"Ah, criminy," Murphy swore. "I knew it!"

"Knew what?"

"You're preparin' for a third installment."

Adam grinned. "Then let the adventures begin. . . ."

Chapter 10

The Bountiful Baron is a man of action and few words.

—THE SECOND INSTALLMENT OF THE TRUE ADVENTURES OF THE BOUNTIFUL BARON: WESTERN BENEFACTOR TO BLOND, BEAUTIFUL, AND BETRAYED WOMEN WRITTEN BY JOHN J. BOOKMAN, 1874.

Once Adam decided the lodge was ideally suited for the purpose he intended, plans for the building and the grounds got under way.

No one knew exactly what the McKendrick had in mind for the lodge, but everyone wanted to watch the progress and share in the process. The word went out that the McKendrick was a rich, eccentric American who paid top wages to workers willing to help renovate the lodge and construct a private golf links. McKendrick was looking for permanent staff, and that was all that was needed to entice the men and women in Kinlochen and the surrounding crofts and villages to travel to Larchmont to offer their services as craftsmen and day laborers and as housemaids, laundresses, cooks, and kitchen and scullery maids; as stewards and footmen, gardeners and gardeners' helpers, stable boys and caddies. Permanent staff lived in and was allowed one day off a week, paid holidays, and time off for sickness and emergencies. They were guaranteed perquisites at Easter and Christmas and the end of every year of service. A permanent position in a house like Larchmont Lodge was the best form of employment one could hope for in the Highlands, and dozens of applicants vied for every position.

Adam had never lived or worked in a house the size of

Larchmont Lodge. He didn't know everything he needed to know in order to run a huge household, but he owned and operated a hotel and saloon back home in Nevada, and he knew enough to hire the best people he could find and allow them to take pride in doing their jobs. At Larchmont Lodge the man charged with the task of finding the right people for the jobs was Gordon Ross. Gordon quickly learned that Adam McKendrick was a man who held his staff to high standards. In that regard, he was like every aristocrat and royal Gordon had ever come across, but unlike most royalty, the McKendrick expected and was willing to pay well for quality service.

And Adam believed in allowing a man the opportunity to pursue his dreams. No one employed at Larchmont Lodge had to remain in his current station simply because the men in his family had always held that position. If a gardener aspired to become a butler or a stable boy or stable master or valet, Adam McKendrick believed in allowing him the opportunity. He believed in providing the men and women who lived and worked on his domain with opportunities for advancement and the means to live a better life.

To that end, Adam asked Gordon to create as many jobs as possible, and to arrange to have a roster of additional help available at all times. The additional staff would earn quarter day wages for agreeing to work at the lodge when needed and would receive full day wages to supplement their regular income for substituting for permanent employees on off-days, holidays, sickness, or emergencies. This meant that the local farmers, craftsmen, shop owners, housewives, and crofters could continue to work for themselves, but would also have the opportunity to receive training in other positions and to earn additional wages by working at the lodge or on the grounds. Max, Isobel, and Albert were in charge of training all household workers, and Gordon and Josef were in charge of training all outside workers.

Except children. Adam specifically instructed Gordon not to hire children. Any young man or girl hoping to work at Larchmont Lodge or for the McKendrick had to have reached their sixteenth year. Children could be paid for helping with the daily chores like running errands or sweeping steps and walkways, for walking ponies, mucking stalls, and weeding borders and flower beds, and other traditional childhood tasks so long as they worked no more than a half day.

Gordon agreed, and although the grounds of the lodge echoed with the sounds of children, it was the sound of laughter and play. Once the staff and the day laborers were in force, the creation of the golf links began near one of the old stone gatehouses that was being renovated to include a bar and wine cellar overlooking the eighteenth green.

Adam sent to St. Andrew's, the oldest golf links in Scotland, for help in designing the one at Larchmont. He also sent for instructors and craftsmen to fashion the clubs and balls used in the game. Because he was paying top wages, men who loved the game of golf flocked to Larchmont looking for work. That influx of workers dictated that the next step in the renovation was the refurbishing of the staff quarters.

Adam's decision to begin with the women's wing of the servants' quarters was a result of a simple but earnest desire to remove George Langstrom's wolfhound from the second floor—and his close proximity to Adam's bed. Work began at the top. Laborers repaired the leaking roof and ceiling by installing new slate roofing tiles and a new plaster ceiling. Oilskin shades and thick wooden interior shutters were added to the windows to help keep out the cold night air and interior walls removed so that bats of thatch and straw could be stuffed between the wooden timbers and the stone exterior wall as additional insulation.

The dormitory-style quarters, though efficient and practical for children, allowed little privacy for adults, so Adam ordered the room partitioned off into private areas that each contained a bed with feather mattresses, a nightstand, a chair, a washstand and a mirror. One larger, separate, more spacious area contained a bed long and wide enough for a very tall woman and an Irish wolfhound to sleep on. Two water closets with twin sinks and bathtubs, hot and cold running water, and two toilets were added.

No one in the village of Kinlochen had ever seen a water

closet, and workers had to be brought in from Glasgow, along with the supplies, in order to construct them. But Adam felt it was worth the expense and the effort.

In his journeys to England escorting or visiting his sister, Kirstin, Adam had discovered that the water closets, if they existed at all, left a great deal to be desired. Those with running water worked intermittently, and the others weren't water closets at all, but earth closets or worse, chamber pots in wooden cabinets. Wealthy gentlemen expected better facilities, and the employees who provided service for wealthy gentlemen deserved better.

Unfortunately, the construction of the water closets and the bathing facilities was proving to be more of a challenge than Adam had anticipated. The employees and the locals who kept stopping by the construction site to gawk hampered the craftsmen and laborers from Glasgow.

The only employees who seemed immune to gawking were Gordon Ross and the Langstrom family. The women's wing was in chaos, but the rest of the house ran as smoothly as clockwork. It didn't run to suit him, but it ran smoothly.

It was hard to believe. Especially in light of the fact that the only members of the staff who followed his instructions were the laborers working on the renovations. He was the undisputed head of the household, but nothing in the household ran according to his directions.

In the three weeks he'd been at Larchmont Lodge, Adam discovered that breakfast was never served when he ordered it. Nor luncheon or dinner. None of his domestic instructions were followed as he issued them—all of them seemed to be circumvented by someone—either Isobel, or Albert or Max—but Adam had to admit that the household ran smoothly—with or without his instructions.

His sister Kirstin had told him once that England's great country houses were run for the convenience of the staff and not for the convenience of the owners. Adam had scoffed at the notion, but now he wasn't so sure. He didn't like it, but he didn't seem to be able to do very much about it. He couldn't even control the dog.

Adam entered his bedchamber to find the wolfhound lying

in the center of his bed. The dog lay snoring on his back with all four paws in the air. Careful not to wake the beast, Adam backed out of his bedroom and closed the door. "Miss Langstrom!"

A door down the hall opened. Shy, dark-haired Brenna stepped onto the threshold and covered a yawn with her hand.

"Not you." Adam pointed toward his bedroom door. "The other Miss Langstrom."

Brenna frowned at him.

Adam frowned back at her. "George. I want George. Your sister Georgiana . . . Where is she?"

Brenna pointed to the valet's room across the hall.

Adam crossed the hall and opened the door. "Miss Langstrom!"

The Langstrom in question sat before the coal grate, a pair of leather work gloves, a pail of ashes, and a container of lead black beside her. She turned at the sound of his voice and Adam noticed several things at once—she wore a black silk moire gown—a Worth from the look of it—covered by a plain white cotton pinafore. The black set her blond hair and her figure off to perfection, much better than the soot streaked on her right cheek and across her forehead.

"Yes?"

"We need to talk about your dog."

"Oh?" George wiped her hands on her skirt and jumped to her feet so fast she stepped on the hem of her dress, lost her balance, and fell against the mantel. A porcelain shepherdess toppled off her pedestal and crashed to the hearth.

Adam moved as quickly as possible, but he wasn't fast enough to save the delicate bone china. The shepherdess figurine splintered against the marble.

A look of sheer horror crossed George's face as she dropped to her knees and began collecting the pieces of the broken shepherdess. It wasn't the first object she'd broken in his presence. Yesterday she had dropped a tray of dishes she'd been carrying to the kitchen when she met him in the corridor, and three days before that she had broken one of the collection of clay pipes in his study, and the day before that she had lost her grip on a china cup and saucer when he walked into the dining room.

"I am too sorry," she apologized.

"It's all right." Adam bent to help her. He took several large pieces of the figurine she'd retrieved from the hearth out of her hand and placed them in the ash pail.

"But . . ." Embarrassed beyond belief at her unprincesslike clumsiness, Giana resumed her hurried attempt to gather all the bits of the broken shepherdess. She collected the largest pieces of china, then unthinkingly swept her palm across the hearth to corral the smaller pieces.

"No!" Adam grabbed hold of her wrist to stop her. The touch of his fingers on her hand sent a jolt of electricity through him, but he was so intent on preventing the mishap he knew was coming that he barely noticed. But he was too late.

Adam flinched almost as badly as Giana as a piece of one of the lambs that had adorned the base of the figurine sliced through the fleshy portion of her palm.

"Oh." She gasped in pain and surprise and instinctively closed her hand to halt the flow of bright crimson blood that ran from the cut down the side of her hand.

"Don't!" Adam eased his grip and gently caressed her wrist with the pads of his fingers, feeling the steady throb of her pulse against them, as he gently pried open her fist. "Please." He looked into her eyes. "Let me."

Giana opened her hand, relaxing her grip and allowing the McKendrick to inspect the wound.

There were blisters on her palm and a jagged wound. Adam ran his thumb over the cut, wincing as he felt the sliver of china from the shepherdess protruding from her hand. The wound was small, but fairly deep, and droplets of blood pooled around his thumb, staining the nail.

George sucked in a breath.

Gritting his teeth, Adam carefully removed the porcelain shard. It had to hurt, but she didn't complain.

Adam noticed the tears sparkling on her lashes and the incredibly fragile feel of her hand in his. He was immediately struck by the contrast of their skin tones—his dark, hers so pale and translucent that he could see the fine network of blue veins beneath her skin.

Reaching for the handkerchief in his breast pocket, Adam carefully dabbed at the bloody cut, before wrapping it around her palm to help stanch the crimson flow. The expression on her face tugged at his heart. It was filled with equal amounts of bewilderment and betrayal. She looked like a lost child who can't understand how she came to be that way. Adam impulsively pressed a kiss against her palm to make the hurt go away the way his mother and sisters had kissed away his childhood wounds.

Giana shivered at the rush of warmth flooding her body when Adam gently pressed his lips against her hand. A shock of awareness jolted her. She stared up at him. The flicker of deep emotion in his dark eyes pleased her. She held his gaze for what seemed like an eternity, reluctant to let it go. The look in his eyes sent a tingle of awareness down her spine. "I am too sorry about the little shepherdess."

"It doesn't matter," Adam told her.

"Oh, but it does," Giana insisted. She recognized the fact that the little shepherdess had been a priceless bit of sixteenth-century porcelain.

"I will pay for it and for all the other things I have damaged."

"There's no need." He shrugged his shoulders. "I'm as much to blame for the accident as you are. I startled you. If I hadn't burst in here shouting at you about the dog, you wouldn't have knocked the shepherdess off the mantel. Besides, it was only a bit of pottery."

"But it was Meissen porcelain . . ." Giana murmured.

That caught his attention. Adam lifted an eyebrow in query. "How did you know it was Meissen?"

Giana bit her bottom lip. "We . . . I . . . She . . . had a collection of Meissen shepherdesses."

"Who?" He asked.

"The countess of Brocadia." Giana glanced at him from beneath her lashes. "I dusted them."

"Brocavia," Adam corrected, caressing her wrist with his thumb.

"Pardon?"

Her pulse fluttered beneath his thumb. "The countess of Brocavia," he explained. "You said you dusted the countess of Brocadia's Meissen shepherdesses."

Giana lowered her gaze. "I meant the countess of Brocavia. My English is not—"

"Your English is fine," Adam told her. "It's your countess I question." He also questioned the countess's wisdom in allowing George to dust her collection of little shepherdesses. But that was supposing the countess actually existed and Adam wasn't so sure.

"I do not know what you mean," she said.

"I think you do."

Giana's eyes momentarily flashed fire as she pulled her hand from his grasp and scrambled to her feet. It was the second time the McKendrick had accused her of telling an untruth. And the fact that he was right only made it worse. Before her parents' death, Giana had never knowingly told a lie, but her parents' death had necessitated a huge deception and an intricate web of half-truths. But she wasn't a liar by nature, and Giana couldn't help but take exception to the fact that Adam McKendrick believed she was.

Adam didn't get to his feet right away. He stayed where he was, kneeling on the hearth, wishing he didn't have to force the issue, wishing he didn't have to acknowledge what he knew must be the truth. But wishing didn't change the truth or make the confrontation any easier. Adam let out a breath and pushed himself to his feet. He expected to tower over her and was pleasantly surprised, once again, when he was able to look her in the eye. "There was no countess of Brocavia."

Giana crossed her fingers behind her back and hid her uninjured hand in the folds of her skirt. "O-of course there was."

Adam studied her closely, then slowly shook his head. "Was there? If I were to look through a few of those European lineage books in the library, would I find any reference to the countess of Brocavia? If I send for letters of reference from the countess's family, will I get them or will they be forged by one of your family members?" The blood seemed to drain from her face. Adam reached out to steady her. "That's it, isn't it?" he asked.

Giana couldn't answer. She bit her bottom lip and sat perfectly still, barely breathing as she waited for his next move.

The fact that she didn't offer to defend herself or to offer an argument sent a quiver of alarm up his spine. Adam took a deep breath, then slowly exhaled. The wounded look in her eyes twisted his gut into knots. He didn't think he could feel any worse if he'd spent the morning robbing defenseless widows and orphans. Adam was suddenly deeply, inexplicably ashamed of himself. "I'm not going to check.

She didn't respond.

"I'm not going to investigate the countess, George. Do you understand? I don't care about references. You and your family have done a wonderful job here so far. I have no complaints."

Her eyes lit up and she managed a brief smile. "Truly?"

"Well . . ." He hesitated.

Too long. He hesitated too long. "It's me, isn't it?" Giana glanced down at the handkerchief wrapped around her hand. "Because I am so clumsy." She picked at the edge of the linen. The bleeding had ceased.

"You aren't clumsy."

"I am like the bull in the teapot," she confided.

Adam furrowed his brow, unable to comprehend her logic.

She returned his frown, unable to understand why he didn't understand her perfectly correct English. The way he frowned one would think that she was speaking Karolyan to him. She unwrapped his handkerchief and handed it to him. "I am as efficient and careful as the other members of the house . . . of my family . . ." She gave a most unprincesslike shrug. "But it seems that the more careful I am, the more I break things."

Like a bull in a china shop. It took a moment for him to grasp her meaning. Adam bit the inside of his cheek to keep from laughing at her mangled idiom. Adam handed the handkerchief back to her. "You keep it. You may need it again should the wound reopen."

Giana recognized the wisdom of that advice. "Very well."

She gave him her most regal nod. "But I will pay you for the shepherdess."

"Forget the shepherdess!" Adam burst out. "I don't care about the shepherdess! I care about finding that blasted beast of yours in my bed again!"

Chapter 11

A Princess of the Blood Royal of the House of Saxe-Wallerstein-Karolya is ever mindful of the whereabouts and behavior of her royal pets. She protects her royal pets from palace guests or staff that might wish to do them harm and protects her guests and staff from the pets that might do harm to them or cause them to do harm to themselves.

—Maxim 1112: Protocol and Court Etiquette of Princesses of the Blood Royal of the House of Saxe-Wallerstein-Karolya, as decreed by Her Serene Highness, Princess May, 1867.

"Wagner?" Her voice held a note of panic. She sat back on her heels and looked up at him.

"Yes, Wagner," Adam retorted. "Who else?"

Giana glanced around. "Where is he?"

"When last I saw him, he was snoring soundly."

"Was Brenna with him?"

Adam frowned. "Brenna? What does Brenna have to do with anything? She wasn't there. He was alone and stretched out in the center of my bed."

"When I began cleaning Mr. O'Brien's room, I left Wagner with Brenna. Where was she and why was he not with her?"

"Perhaps it's because your sister finds her bed more comfortable than mine," Adam commented, remembering Brenna's half-hearted attempts to cover her yawns and the sleep marks on her face. "Unlike the dog. Or maybe it's because she prefers a human sleeping companion to a canine one."

"Wagner sleeps only with me."

Adam snorted in amusement. "Apparently, he's more selective in his choice of bed partners than he is in his choice of beds."

"On the contrary," Giana told him. "He is equally selective in his choice of beds. It was my bed until you arrived. He returns to it because it retains my scent."

"Of orange blossoms and woman," Adam muttered beneath his breath. He couldn't argue with her logic. Although the linens had been laundered several times since she'd removed to another bedchamber, his bed still retained the scent of her perfume. He had thought the fragrance came from something the laundry staff added to the final rinse when they washed the sheets. He hadn't realized, until this moment, that the tantalizing perfume originated with George. But now he recognized the surprisingly erotic scent of orange blossoms and musk that emanated from her hair and her skin—a scent that was still faintly detectable despite the pungent metallic smell of fresh blood, coal ash, and lead blackening.

Adam had always appreciated the fresh, clean scent of orange blossoms, but never more than he did now. And the scent of her wasn't all he found appealing. He was fascinated by George's words and even more fascinated by her mouth, so much so that he found himself staring at it. Everything about her mouth intrigued him from the perfect shape of her upper and lower lips to the subtle pattern of textures imprinted there.

Giana had spent her entire life as an object of curious speculation. She was accustomed to having people stare at her and generally found it easy to overlook their rudeness, but Adam McKendrick's intense blue-eyed gaze disturbed her in a way she had never expected because it made her feel things she had never known existed. For the first time in her life she felt like a woman instead of a royal princess. But awareness of new feelings brought another kind of awareness—an awareness of Adam McKendrick as a man—a man who had an uncanny knack for making her forget who she was and the responsibilities she had been born to bear.

Forcing herself to look away, Giana turned and reached for the pair of leather gloves balanced on the rim of the ash pail. "Pardon me."

"No." Adam took the gloves from her and stuck them in his jacket pocket.

"Excuse me." Assuming her English was to blame for his failure to understand her, Giana politely repeated her request, then picked up the pail and tried to move past him, but the McKendrick refused to let her by.

"What do you think you're doing?" This time Adam reached for the ash pail.

"I have to collect Wagner," Giana answered. "And complete my work."

Adam set the pail out of her reach. "Your work day is finished."

"But there is more to do. . . ." she protested.

"That may be. But you're not going to be the one to do it. You've a nasty cut on your hand. Someone else can finish cleaning the grates." Adam was suddenly struck by the notion that while Giana had been cleaning and polishing the coal grates in the second-floor bedrooms, Brenna had been napping. "Someone like your sister."

Giana shook her head.

"Why not?" he demanded.

"Brenna's duties do not include work of this sort."

Adam lifted an eyebrow at that. "But yours do . . ."

"Yes, of course."

"Why?" He asked. "Why are you cleaning fireplaces while your sister sleeps? Other than watching the beast, which she has failed to do, what exactly are her duties?"

"Brenna is a lady's maid," Giana explained.

"Which means . . ."

"Her duty is to attend the lady of the house. To personally dress and undress her, arrange her hair, attend to needlework and repair personal items of clothing, and serve as companion."

"There is no lady in the house for Brenna to personally attend," Adam reminded her.

Giana had never behaved coyly in her life, but she supposed there was a first time for everything. She turned her mysterious princess smile on the McKendrick and glanced up at him from beneath the cover of her lashes. "There will be."

"Oh?" Adam gave her another speculative look. "How so?"

"When gentlemen begin extensive and costly repairs to their homes, it is generally supposed that they mean to settle down and begin their families. . . ." Giana pretended to knowledge of the ways of the world that princesses of the blood royal were supposed to inherit at birth. "Naturally, we supposed that once the renovations to the lodge are concluded, you would do likewise. . . ."

"You supposed that?" Adam hadn't grown up with four sisters without learning more than he had ever wanted to know about the way their minds worked. He recognized a blatant fishing expedition when he saw it, and he also recognized the fact that none of his four sisters would ever had tried such an obvious ploy to gather information. His sisters were experts at toying with a man's sensibilities. George was a rank novice. Adam decided to respond in kind, gifting her with a devilish grin and an equally devilish reply, "Surely, you're not naïve enough to think that renovating a building has anything to do with whether or not I intend to begin a family or that beginning a family necessarily includes marriage or having a lady in or of the house."

She opened her mouth to reply, but no words came out.

Unable to resist, Adam reached out and smoothed a smear of soot off her cheek with the pad of his thumb. "Who are you? And what have you done with George?"

Giana's felt the color leave her face as she straightened her backbone, stiffened her spine, and prepared to have her deception revealed. "I do not understand what you mean."

Adam exhaled. She had proved to be such a stimulating adversary in verbal sparring he'd forgotten that, for all her pretense to the contrary, she *was* a naïve young woman for whom English was obviously a second language. "I mean that coyness doesn't become you, George."

Giana moistened her lips with the tip of her tongue. "Nor you, sir."

"I've been called many things, George, but never coy." He smiled to show that there was no censure in his words. "When a woman answers the way you did, it's generally thought that she's deliberately being coy. When a man answers that way, it's generally *supposed* that he's being evasive."

"Are you?"

Adam's smile widened into a grin. "Now, there's the George I know and lo—" He broke off abruptly.

Jesus, Mary, and Joseph! Adam wiped his hand over his face. Where had that thought come from? He was in trouble. Big trouble. George was everything he had always said he didn't want in a woman. But his preferences no longer seemed to matter. God, she was a beauty. And worse than that, she was a beauty who sent his pulse racing. He was definitely in trouble. He recognized the warning signs, but he wasn't sure he could prevent the damage. He might be too late to prevent the damage. He might be too late to save himself.

Unless . . .

He'd never before been tempted by a woman like George. He'd always preferred more demure women. . . . He tended to be attracted to petite, dark-haired, dark-eyed beauties. Never blondes. Which made those damned dime novels so laughable. But he hadn't shared a bed with a woman since he'd left Nevada. There was always the chance that he might simply be attracted to the novelty of kissing a woman who could look him in the eye. . . .

Adam bent his head and leaned closer. There was always the chance that kissing her would prove to be nothing more than a pleasant distraction—an enjoyable way to pass the time while in Scotland. . . . And there was always the chance that he was a bigger damned liar than she was. He'd have to be a fool to find out. . . .

And he had never been a fool. Until now . . .

Adam made one last valiant attempt to save himself. He tried to back away, tried to give her room to retreat, but George showed no signs of retreating. Standing on tiptoe, she leaned toward him, lifted her chin, parted her lips, and closed her eyes. . . .

He stared down at her face, at her softly parted lips, and was lost. . . . Adam covered her mouth with his and licked at the seam of her lips. She gave a startled gasp at the intimacy of that gesture. He took advantage of the opportunity and slipped his tongue inside her mouth.

And discovered he was both a liar and a fool. George was sweet and innocent and incredibly tempting. Although he used his tongue to tease, tantalize, and seduce, it was quite apparent to Adam that the woman he held in his arms had never had anyone kiss her the way he was kissing her. And it was equally apparent to Adam that he never wanted anyone else to have the chance.

The idea scared him so much, Adam broke off the kiss. He stepped back and fought for control, but he knew he was fighting a losing battle when George looped her arms around his neck and pressed herself against him.

"God help me!" He murmured the heartfelt prayer moments before he bent and traced the delicate contours of her cheekbones with the pads of his thumbs. Leaning forward, Adam pressed a gentle kiss on her eyelids, then worked his way down her face, back to her lips. He kissed her again and again, paying particular attention to her plump bottom lip, savoring the texture, flicking his tongue over it, touching the roughness of the myriad tiny abrasions she made with her teeth each time she bit her bottom lip. He lavished her mouth with attention, sucking on her lower lip, teasing her, tempting her to open her mouth and allow him further access.

She yielded to temptation, and the touch of his mouth was a revelation, producing an avalanche of hidden emotions. Giana parted her lips, allowing him to deepen the kiss. He complied, moving his lips on hers, kissing her harder, then softer, then harder once more, testing her response, slipping his tongue past her teeth, exploring the sweet hot interior of her mouth with practiced finesse. As he leisurely stroked the inside of her mouth in a provocative imitation of the mating dance, George followed his lead. She moved her lips on his and kissed him back. Her abundant talent and enthusiasm inspired him as much as it surprised him, and Adam made love to her mouth, teaching her everything he knew about the fine art of kissing.

And George was an excellent pupil. She progressed rapidly, mirroring his actions and inventing a few of her own as she moved from novice to expert in the space of a few heartbeats.

The jolt of pure pleasure he felt as she used her newfound talent with her tongue and teeth and mouth to entice him shook him down to his toes, threatening to steal his breath away along with his suddenly tenuous control.

"Stop." Adam let go of her. He needed distance. He needed space. He needed to let go of her before he took her on the floor of O'Brien's bedroom.

"Why?" Now that she'd discovered kissing, Giana meant to continue practicing it for as long as possible. "I like it."

"I'm gratified to hear it," he answered curtly. "But your lesson is over." He clenched his fists to keep from touching her.

"I do not want the lesson to end," Giana informed him in the imperious tone she had long ago learned to use in order to get her way. Being a princess of the blood royal did have its uses, and one of them was being able to order people of lesser rank to obey one's commands.

Adam stared down into bright blue eyes. "You probably don't want to end up on the floor on your back with your skirts over your head, either, but that's what's going to happen if we don't stop kissing."

"Truly?" Giana had no idea why she'd be on the floor on her back with her skirts over her head, but the notion of such a thing happening to her intrigued her. "How extraordinary!"

"Yes," Adam agreed, "it's extraordinary. So extraordinary that millions of people do it every day."

"Do they?"

Adam shook his head in wonder. "Yes, they really do. Why do you think there are so many babies?"

He could tell from the expression on her face that he had finally succeeded in shocking her.

"Babies?" She stared up at him in awe. So that was how babies were born. She knew, of course, that babies were a natural result of marriage, just as she knew that her duty as a princess of the blood royal was to marry for the good of her country and provide her husband and country with an heir. After kissing Adam McKendrick, Giana could finally understand how children might come to be born out of wedlock. "I had no idea."

The expression on her face was so appealing that Adam fought an almost overwhelming urge to kiss her again. "You still have no idea," he told her. "And I intend to keep it that way. For both our sakes." He turned and started toward the door. "Stay out of my way, George. Stay out of my room and out of my bed and keep that beast of yours away as well."

Giana attempted to point out the fact that he had come in search of her and not the other way around. "But, sir . . ."

Sir. She had called him sir. After kissing him senseless and nearly causing him to lose control of his *extraordinary* control, she'd called him sir. He'd become a caricature of every lusty landowner who'd ever tumbled a serving wench in his employ. He wiped a hand over his forehead. Christ! He couldn't feel any worse if she'd kicked him in the groin. "Adam," he said softly. "When a man teaches a woman to kiss, the least she can do is call him by name."

"And the least a man can do, after teaching her, is to continue, *Adam.*" Giana didn't wait to hear his reply. She simply turned and walked out of the bedroom, leaving Adam McKendrick staring after her.

Chapter 12

The Bountiful Baron hates a mystery or a riddle and feels duty bound to solve it.

—The Second Installment of the True Adventures of the Bountiful Baron: Western Benefactor to Blond, Beautiful, and Betrayed Women written by John J. Bookman, 1874.

"*There's something strange going on here,* boyo." O'Brien swirled his whisky around the bottom of his glass before taking a hefty swallow.

"Oh?" Adam quirked an eyebrow at him and gave an ironic chuckle. "What makes you think so? The fact that every manservant in this household has taken the lord of the house to task for daring to drink whisky instead of brandy after dinner or for sharing the bottle with his valet?" He and Murphy had retreated to the library after dinner and remained there long after the other members of the household had retired for the night. Neither Albert's frowning disapproval or Max's pointed comments had dissuaded Adam from treating Murphy like the friend he was instead of the gentleman's gentleman he was pretending to be.

"All you're subjected to is a few frowns and a comment or two," O'Brien reminded him. "While I'll have to endure another in a series of lectures regarding my lack of training in the proper etiquette for a gentleman's gentleman."

"What?" Adam asked.

"Some lord of the manor you are," O'Brien teased. "Don't ya know that your private secretary feels he's duty bound to lecture me following breakfast in the upper servants' quarters each morning?" He spoke in an exaggerated Irish brogue. "Of course you don't." He answered his own question. "But it's time you opened your eyes, boyo, and paid attention to what's going on inside the walls of the lodge, instead of outside them."

"What does he lecture you about?"

"The usual topic is the relationship between a particular gentleman's gentleman and his employer and why said gentleman's gentleman should maintain a proper distance between his employer and himself and not attempt to overreach his station in life by believing he is his employer's equal." O'Brien drained the last of mouthful of whisky from his glass and set it down on the table beside his chair.

"Despite his employer's words and actions to the contrary."

O'Brien laughed. "Despite that."

Adam joined in the laughter. "I have complete faith in your ability to handle Maximillian Langstrom."

"That's good," O'Brien told him. "Because I'm beginning to lose faith in yours."

Adam stopped laughing.

"Face it, boyo, you've been spending too much time outdoors supervising the building of that golf track. . . ."

"Links," Adam corrected automatically. "It's called a golf links."

"Track. Links. No matter," O'Brien said. "Whatever it's called, you've spent so much time there that your instructions carry little weight with the indoor staff around here."

"My words and actions carry *no* weight with any of the staff around here," Adam corrected. "Except the day laborers from the village, the workers from Glasgow, and the men from St. Andrews . . ."

O'Brien shook his head. "The workers from Glasgow and St. Andrews maybe, but the villagers are taking their orders from Isobel and Gordon, who take them from Max, the reigning head of the household. You may own the place, boyo, but you've been usurped."

"I can't have been usurped." Adam gave a self-deprecating snort. "Because I've never been in control of the household staff." He poured himself another finger of whisky, offered some to O'Brien, then set the bottle aside when O'Brien refused. "I haven't even managed to gain control over that damned dog."

"Caught him on your bed again, eh?"

"On his back with all four paws in the air, snoring loud enough to wake the dead."

"Where was his owner?" O'Brien asked.

"On her hands and knees cleaning the ashes and soot from the fireplace in your room," Adam replied.

Murphy knew that one of the many duties of a housemaid was to clean and blacken the fireplace grates, but he could not reconcile the image of Georgiana Langstrom on her hands and knees scrubbing like a charwoman. "You're joking."

"I wish I were," Adam answered honestly. "But seeing George on her hands and knees cleaning the hearth in a Worth gown was no joke."

O'Brien wondered suddenly if he'd heard correctly or if Adam had simply consumed too much whisky. "Did you say Worth gown?"

Adam nodded. "A black silk moiré day dress with jet beading, a small bustle and short train."

"How do you know it was Worth?"

"I crossed the Atlantic with Kirstin, the Honorable Lady Marshfeld." Adam smiled. "So did you. And I happen to know that we were treated to the latest Parisian fashions including several by Monsieur Worth. I recognized the style."

"I've always said that you were a man of many talents," O'Brien retorted.

"Talented enough to know that the white pinafore George wore over her gown was not Worth. It was ordinary, run-of-the mill, standard housemaid attire."

"How many other households can lay claim to a housemaid who wears Worth gowns?" O'Brien couldn't control his smirk. He pushed himself to his feet and sketched an elaborate bow. "You are, indeed, the Bountiful Baron."

Adam shook his head. "I'm not *that* bountiful. I didn't supply the staff with Worth gowns."

"Then who did?" O'Brien set his whisky glass aside and exchanged glances with Adam.

"Certainly not the Langstroms," Adam answered. "If they could afford Worth originals, there would be no need for them to work as domestics."

"Maybe the gown was one of the countess of Brocavia's castoffs."

Adam paused for a moment, debating whether or not he should confide his suspicions about the countess of Brocavia, but thought better of it. Murphy O'Brien was the soul of discretion, but Adam had promised George he'd keep silent. "I don't think so," he said at last. "Brenna is the lady's maid, and as a lady's maid, she would be entitled to any of her mistress's cast-off garments."

"But Brenna's not wearing Worth originals," O'Brien finished Adam's train of thought.

"That could be because she hasn't done anything to merit them," Adam grumbled.

O'Brien shrugged. "You said it yourself. Brenna is a lady's maid. What is there for her to do?"

"She could be helping her sister with the dusting and cleaning," Adam told him.

"Not so, boyo."

"Why not?"

"Belowstairs doesn't work that way. Belowstairs has its own hierarchy. A lady's maid ranks higher than a housemaid. Ordinary dusting and cleaning is beneath her."

"I know what a lady's maid does and I understand her place within the household," Adam retorted. "George explained it. But it galls me to know that while George is on her hands and knees scrubbing hearths, Brenna does nothing to earn her keep except watch the dog." Adam snorted. "And she's a dismal failure at that."

O'Brien laughed. "The dog sleeps all the time. He must not be very interesting to watch, because Brenna is much better at watching her sister and her mother and me work."

"You?" Adam was surprised.

O'Brien winked. "Shy Brenna isn't as shy as we thought. She watches me as I go about my duties as your gentleman's gentleman."

"That is interesting," Adam mused.

"It may not be as interesting as you think," Murphy said.

"She may not be watching me, so much as hoping to keep an eye on you."

"Unless the Langstroms have Brenna watching you because they know you're not what you pretend to be."

O'Brien shrugged. "They have no doubt that I'm a vastly inexperienced valet," he said. "But I don't think they know I'm only masquerading as one—or that I'm a private detective. And there's no doubt that Brenna is watching us—but whether she's been instructed to or whether she is doing it on her own—or whether she's watching me or you—remains to be seen," O'Brien said.

"In your role as a valet you're a more likely prospect for a lady's maid than I am," Adam reminded him.

"That's true. But you're better looking and a better catch."

"I think she finds you attractive. . . ." Adam teased.

"She might," O'Brien agreed. "Or she might have decided to use me to get to you." He shrugged his shoulders once again. "I don't know. Unfortunately, my French is worse than her English, and I can't begin to guess what her other language is. I do know that Brenna isn't as lazy as you think," O'Brien added. "Or as unfeeling. She may not help Georgiana take care of the housework, but she helps in other ways."

"What other ways?"

"According to Max, Brenna practices her lady's maid skills by taking care of George—by drawing her sister's baths and attending to her clothes and hair."

Adam got up out of his chair and began to pace the length of the library. "You mean to tell me that I'm paying one member of the staff to take care of another?"

"I hear she needs it now that she's sliced her hand."

"She cut her hand"—Adam stopped his pacing and turned to face his friend—"on a shard of broken porcelain. She didn't slice it."

"Isobel and Albert and Max made such fuss over the wound while Isobel was cleaning it and dressing it with salve, you would have sworn that it was mortal." O'Brien gave a sharp whistle as he reached over Adam's abandoned chair and helped himself to another whisky. "I don't know what they found more shocking—the fact that Georgiana cut her hand or the fact that you refused to allow her to continue to work until it healed. Let me tell you, boyo, there was quite a family discussion when Georgiana appeared for the noonday meal, all pink-cheeked and rosy-lipped, presenting her cut and your soiled handkerchief to Isobel." O'Brien took a sip of whisky, then refilled Adam's empty glass and held it up to him as Adam resumed his pacing. They kept their voices low and I didn't catch more than a word or two of the conversation, but your name and the word *porcelain* came up more than once."

"Thanks." Adam snagged the glass of whisky as he walked past.

Murphy winked and pretended to tip his cap. "At your service, sir." He grinned as Adam swallowed a mouthful of liquor. "I gathered from those two bits of information and the wound on Georgiana's hand that there was more breakage. . . ."

Adam laughed. "I seem to have that effect on her."

"What was it this time?" O'Brien asked more out of curiosity than anything else.

"The little shepherdess that used to sit upon the mantel in your bedchamber."

Recalling the pretty little porcelain figurine, O'Brien frowned. "Was she valuable?"

"The ones in Kirstin's house are."

"Ouch."

"Yes, ouch," Adam agreed. "That brings the breakage total to a tray of dishes, a clay pipe, a cup and saucer, and a porcelain shepherdess."

"It's a good thing Georgiana doesn't work at your saloon," O'Brien joked, "or there would be a severe shortage of beer mugs by now."

"Yes, but the value of the breakage would be much lower."

"Did she offer to repay you?"

Adam nodded. "She's offered to repay me for all of it. But it's out of the question," he said. "Worth gown or not, she doesn't make enough to replace what she's broken. Besides, there's no need. And it doesn't matter. The loss of a few pieces of expensive china isn't going to break me."

"What about the girl?" O'Brien asked, turning his unflinching stare on Adam.

Adam sighed. "The china is of no consequence, but George may prove to be the death of me."

Chapter 13

A Princess of the Blood Royal of the House of Saxe-Wallerstein-Karolya understands and willingly accepts the personal sacrifices she must make in order to do her duty to her country.

—MAXIM 2: PROTOCOL AND COURT ETIQUETTE OF PRINCESSES OF THE BLOOD ROYAL OF THE HOUSE OF SAXE-WALLERSTEIN-KAROLYA, AS DECREED BY HIS SERENE HIGHNESS, PRINCE KAROL I, 1432.

He had kissed her. Adam McKendrick had pulled her into his arms and kissed her. She had felt the heat of his body penetrating the fabric of her white cotton pinafore and the silk of her black dress beneath it. But the heat of his body had been nothing compared to the heat of his mouth.

Giana remembered the taste of him, the rasp of his tongue against her teeth as it slipped between her lips into her mouth. She recalled the urgency of his kiss and the way she had echoed it, moving her lips under his, allowing him further access. Giana moved her own tongue, then experienced the jolt of pure pleasure as it found, and mated with, Adam's. She had looped her arms around his neck, and her hands had somehow found their way onto his broad shoulders. She remembered the feel of the superfine of his coat against her fingertips. She had traced little circles against the fabric before trailing her fingers up the column of his neck to caress his thick, silky black hair.

As she lay in her bed staring up at the ceiling, Giana knew that as long as she lived she would remember the thrill, the sweetness, the romance, the absolute terror of her first kiss. It would remain firmly embedded in her heart and on her soul until her dying day. She pressed her fingertips against her mouth. A man had kissed her, and her life would never be the same.

Wagner moaned in his sleep, and Giana wiggled her toes against his back as he slept at the foot of her bed. Adam McKendrick complained about finding Wagner on his bed every time he turned around, but she didn't understand why. She preferred the comfort and companionship of a warm body cuddled beside her—even a canine one—because it kept her from feeling so alone and being so lonely.

She had always been alone. Her mother and father had had each other, and in many ways they had never needed anyone else. When she outgrew the nursery and her nanny, Giana had been alone. She was a princess surrounded by people, yet isolated from them by her position and rank. But for a few precious moments while Adam McKendrick was sharing his life's breath with her, she had felt as if she were a part of him. She, who had always felt apart and different, had felt as if she finally belonged, not to the people of Karolya, but to him. In his arms Giana had found the safety and security that had eluded her since the night she had learned that her parents were gone.

She reached up and traced the outline of the gold locket that lay beneath her nightgown, nestled in the valley between her breasts. It had belonged to her mother. Princess May had taken it from around her own neck and presented it to her daughter on the anniversary of Giana's twentieth year of life. Inside the locket was a miniature of her maternal grandparents copied from their official wedding portrait and a miniature of an informal portrait of her father and mother and herself on the day of her christening. Giana had always loved the expression on her parents' faces as they gazed down at the child their love had created. She swiped at a tear with the back of her hand and managed a tiny smile.

Her father had often said that he'd taken one look at her mother and known that May was the woman God sent to share his life. They had fallen in love and married despite the objections of her father's ministers, clergy, and the high aristocracy.

His Serene Highness Prince Christian of Saxe-Wallerstein-Karolya had married for reasons of the heart instead of for reasons of state. And because he had married for love, he had married beneath his rank.

Giana sighed. Now she understood why her mother had never explained how wonderful kissing could be. It was a feeling that couldn't be put into words. It could only be experienced. It could only be felt. And her parents had felt it. They had known that incredible feeling of wonder and the sense of belonging to someone else and to each other.

But Giana was a princess of the Blood Royal and princesses of the Blood Royal were not permitted to belong to anyone except their subjects, nor were they permitted to kiss a man until they had been pronounced man and wife. As to enjoying the experience, Giana suspected that that depended a great deal on the man chosen to be their husbands. She shuddered. Now that she knew what it was like to kiss and be kissed by Adam McKendrick, she found it impossible to imagine kissing any of the royal suitors who had petitioned her father for her hand in marriage or allowing them to kiss her—and sharing a bed with any of them was out of the question—especially her cousin Victor.

Unfortunately, princesses of the Blood Royal of the House of Saxe-Wallerstein-Karolya historically had little or no say in the man chosen to be their husbands. But in this Giana had been exceptionally lucky. Her father had not only refused her cousin Victor's suit, but had kept it a secret from her. The fact that he had done so had been a blessing because the idea of marrying her first cousin was so abhorrent to her it made her skin crawl.

Giana rolled onto her side and hugged her pillow closer. When she was a little girl, her mother had kept her entertained for hours with stories of how she and Prince Christian had met and fallen in love. But as she grew older, her mother had grown more and more reluctant to regale her with those romantic tales. And now she understood why.

Her mother wouldn't discuss the particulars of the marriage bed with her because her mother's tutelage in the intimacies to be found in the marriage bed had come from a loving husband. They were precious and private, not meant to be shared with anyone—even a daughter. Especially when the daughter's introduction into the intimacies of the marriage bed would most likely come from a stranger—a husband chosen by her father and his cabinet ministers for state reasons.

Giana exhaled the breath she hadn't realized she was holding. Her parents' marriage was unique in Karolyan history. They had been allowed to marry for love—not out of sentimentality, but because her father, as sovereign, had had the power to make the match he wanted. But her father was a man.

She was a female, and while the "Female Provision" of the Karolyan Charter allowed Giana to assume the throne, it did not allow her the complete freedom to rule as she saw fit. Giana suddenly realized that the sadness she had seen in her mother's eyes when she had begged to hear the romantic stories of her parents' courtship and marriage was there because Princess May had known that her daughter might not be as fortunate.

Princess May hadn't been born a princess, she became one when she married Prince Christian. She hadn't even been born Karolyan. Lady Caroline Frances Alexandra May, only child of the elderly marquess of Barracksford and his young marchioness, Lady May—as she preferred to be called—came into the world as the sole heiress to a tidy fortune.

There had been whispers surrounding the birth of Barracksford's heir, but none of that meant anything to the marquess and marchioness. Let the gossips speculate and whisper about the fact that Lady May bore no resemblance to the marquess. She was born a Barracksford and nothing could change that. The marquess and marchioness held their heads high and ignored the gossip. Antoinette Barracksford had married the marquess without regret and she had been rewarded with a daughter who became the light of her life and who exceeded her grandest expectations by marrying Prince Christian of Saxe-Wallerstein-Karolya, becoming a princess, and presenting her adopted country with an heir.

An heir who was currently working as a chambermaid in a hunting lodge deep in the Scottish highlands and sharing a bed with an Irish wolfhound while she built girlish fantasies around a man with dark hair and sky-blue eyes who kissed like a dream.

A dark-haired, blue-eyed man who had not only kissed her lips, but had kissed away the pain of the cut on her palm. A man who overlooked her embarrassing spate of clumsiness and the destruction of his objets d'art and household china. Although he refused to accept payment for the damages, Giana intended to find a way to repay him. And she knew, without a doubt, that if she thought about it long enough, she would come up with a way.

A Princess of the Blood Royal of the House of Saxe-Wallerstein-Karolya had been kissed by a man who was not her husband. A miracle had occurred. Anything was possible.

Chapter 14

Princesses of the Blood Royal should always defer to their nearest male relative of the House of Saxe-Wallerstein-Karolya in all matters of state.

—MAXIM 6: PROTOCOL AND COURT ETIQUETTE OF PRINCESSES OF THE BLOOD ROYAL OF THE HOUSE OF SAXE-WALLERSTEIN-KAROLYA, AS DECREED BY HIS SERENE HIGHNESS, PRINCE KAROL I, 1432.

"How dare you stand before me and announce that you have failed to locate her!" The white dueling scar that bisected Prince Victor Lucien of Saxe-Wallerstein-Karolya's left cheek stood out in stark contrast to the vivid scarlet hue staining the rest of his face as he berated the captain of the guard standing stiffly at attention before him.

"I regret that I must do so, Your Highness, but after searching every city, town, village, and encampment in Karolya from Christianberg to the mountains beyond Laken, we have failed in our quest to locate Princess Giana or Lord Gudrun." Captain Peter Tolsen betrayed no emotion as he stood before the regent and reported that the anarchists holding their beloved princess had eluded His Highness's Royal Palace Guard for nearly three months.

"He must have sent her out of the country," Prince Victor said.

"He, Your Highness, or they?" the captain asked.

"He, you incompetent cur!" Prince Victor exploded.

"Lord Gudrun?"

"Not Lord Gudrun! My uncle, Prince Christian!" Prince Victor forced himself to rein in his temper. It wouldn't do to let the earnest young captain know that he was playing an unwitting part in a scheme to cover up the identity of Princess May's and Prince Christian's real murderer or to lay the blame for their deaths at Gudrun's feet. "Maximillian Gudrun is nothing more than a glorified scribe. He has neither the skill nor the courage to spirit the princess out of the country."

"According to the reports of those of your household guards who attempted to aid my men, Lord Gudrun had the skill and the courage to murder Prince Christian and Princess May and abduct Princess Giana."

"And you lacked the skill to keep him from escaping with our princess." Prince Victor snapped at the captain.

"He could not have abducted or escaped with the princess," Captain Tolsen announced. "Because Princess Giana wasn't in the palace on the night of the murders."

Victor whirled around to face the captain. "How do you know that?"

"Your personal guard reported that the anarchists killed the guardsman on duty outside the princess's apartments."

"Which of my personal guard reported this? And to whom?" Victor tried to sound mildly interested, but he was seething inside.

"I sent word from the hospital that I wanted to speak to the guard who found my guardsman's body. Captain Mareska presented himself and related the details of the incident," Tolsen answered.

Victor stared down at his right hand. The finger that should have been home to the royal seal of state was bare. He did not have the seal or the princess and the only witness to Prince Christian's murder was still alive. Victor clenched his hand into a fist. "Did Mareska report anything else? Anything that might help us find the princess?"

Captain Tolsen shook his head. "He told me that the rabble broke into her rooms, forcing the doors, only to find her apartments unoccupied."

Mareska had reported too much. Tomorrow he would be replaced. And weeks from now, his family would receive word that he had died in the line of duty protecting the Prince Regent. The Karolyan people would learn that the anarchists who had murdered Prince Christian and Princess May and abducted their princess had also attempted to assassinate the Prince Regent. The same would be true of Captain Tolsen when his usefulness ended. Victor focused his gaze on the captain. "My uncle must have suspected something. He must have gotten wind of the anarchists' plot and sent Princess Giana to safety somewhere outside the border. But where? Where would he send her? And why hasn't she come forward?"

"I do not know, sir," Tolsen admitted.

"Why not?" Prince Victor asked. "You're captain of His Highness's Royal Palace Guards. You must have escorted her somewhere. . . ."

Captain Tolsen shook his head. "The Royal Guard did not escort her. If she left the country, she did so by force or by traveling incognito."

"You had no orders from Prince Christian? Or Lord Gudrun?"

"No, Your Highness." The captain looked up and met the prince's unnerving gaze.

"How do you explain her absence?"

"I cannot explain it, Your Highness. The surviving members of His Highness's guard were told that our princess had been taken hostage by anarchists." Captain Tolsen frowned. After escorting Prince Christian and Princess May to their apartments, the members of the Royal Guard not standing guard outside the doors leading to Prince Christian's and Princess May's private chambers and Princess Giana's private chambers, had retired to their barracks for the night. Most of those guards had never awakened. The anarchists had set upon them while they slept. Captain Tolsen had been fortunate. He'd recovered from his stab wounds, but many of his friends and fellow guardsmen had not.

Prince Victor's contingent of guards had escaped the massacre. Their barracks were in the Tower at the opposite end of the palace close to Prince Victor's apartments. Victor's guards had raised the alarm after the Prince and Princess were murdered.

Victor narrowed his gaze at the captain of the guard. "And so she was," the prince regent agreed. "But we have it on the highest authority that the anarchists were in league with Lord Gudrun. We must assume that Lord Gudrun ordered the princess taken."

"Whose authority, sir?" Captain Tolsen forgot himself long enough to demand an answer. "I should like to speak to the person from whom you've received this information."

Prince Victor stared at Tolsen, daring him to continue. "The identity of the informant does not concern you, Captain Tolsen."

"You charged me with the investigation into Princess Giana's disappearance, sir. If you have information as to her whereabouts, it concerns me." The young captain stood his ground, refusing to allow the prince regent to intimidate him.

"I did not charge you with the duty of *investigating* my cousin's disappearance! I charged you with the duty of *locating* her and with rescuing her from her abductors," the prince told him. "The princess is gone! That much is quite apparent! How she disappeared is of little consequence now!" He pointed a finger at the captain of the guard. "You are charged with the task of finding her! And soon! Time is running out, Captain. For both of us!" Prince Victor drew his dress sword from its scabbard.

Captain Tolsen remained silent. He had failed in his mission to find and rescue the heir to the throne and in so doing had angered and frustrated the volatile prince regent. Up until this moment Captain Tolsen believed that the anarchists who had murdered Prince Christian and Princess May had abducted Princess Giana, but now, he wondered. . . .

As he stared at the Prince Regent, Captain Tolsen understood that if it pleased him to do so, Prince Victor could dispense with the niceties of military protocol and dispatch the current captain of the royal guard with one clean thrust of his sword and replace him with someone more loyal to the prince regent than he appeared to be.

Tolsen looked into the prince regent's eyes and saw death. He drew himself up to his full height and stood ramrod straight, waiting for the thrust that would end his life—and conceal his failure.

But he was granted a reprieve. A knock sounded on the

salon doors as the prince regent's equerry announced the arrival of his savior, "The special envoy from the Court of St. James has arrived, Your Highness."

Prince Victor growled his frustration, then wielded his sword against the household furnishings, severing the legs of a dainty French cabriole table, sending it crashing to the floor.

Captain Tolsen breathed a silent, heartfelt sigh of relief, but Prince Victor wasn't finished with him yet.

"Find her!" Victor ordered. "Find Princess Giana and find her fast, or I will find a captain of the guard who can!"

Captain Tolsen gave a crisp nod, clicked his heels together, and backed out of the salon, withdrawing from Prince Victor's presence before the prince regent could change his mind about allowing him to escape. He passed the British Special Envoy, Lord Everleigh, on the way into the room and wondered how the prince regent would explain the splintered gilt table.

Lord Everleigh greeted Prince Victor with a brief bow. He did not slight the prince regent intentionally, but neither did he show the deference usually reserved for ruling heads of state.

His action angered the prince regent, but Lord Everleigh ignored the prince's displeasure.

A handsome man, in his late fifties, the marquess of Everleigh had spent more than thirty years in the diplomatic corps as ambassador to the Habsburg court in Vienna and as special envoy to Russia, Crimea, and the Balkans. In his current role as special envoy to Saxe-Wallerstein-Karolya, Lord Everleigh was acting on personal instructions from the Queen's Most Trusted, Loyal, and Special Advisor, the sixteenth marquess of Templeston.

Lord Templeston had charged Lord Everleigh with the task of discovering what happened in Christianberg and if the prince and princess were murdered by anarchists or by someone hoping to usurp the throne. As godmother to Princess Giana, Queen Victoria felt it her duty to assist the Karolyan government in finding her. Although she knew Prince Victor was hoping for official recognition from the British government, the queen refused to grant it. If Princess Giana was still alive, she must have a country and a throne to return to. If Princess Giana had been abducted and murdered, the prince regent, according to the Karolyan State Charter, must present her body or the state seal in order to be proclaimed ruler.

"Our beloved queen sends her greetings and her deepest condolences on the deaths of Prince Christian and Princess May and the disappearance of Her Serene Highness Princess Giana," Lord Everleigh offered.

Prince Victor lowered his gaze and inclined his head. "Please relay our deepest thanks to Her Majesty."

"Of course, sir." Lord Everleigh studied the prince. "Her Majesty and Her Majesty's government is quite alarmed by the state of affairs in Karolya. . . ."

The prince regent took umbrage to the special envoy's statement. "I assure you, sir, so that you may assure your queen, that she has no cause for concern about the state of affairs in Karolya."

"I beg your pardon, Your Highness," Lord Everleigh replied, "but Her Majesty disagrees. Anarchists who seek to abolish all monarchies have apparently murdered the hereditary ruler of Karolya, and his wife. That is reason enough to concern our gracious queen. The fact that her goddaughter, Princess Giana, is missing only adds to her concern. You are second in line to the throne of Karolya, behind the heir apparent. You are regent because Princess Giana has yet to be found. The government is in complete disarray and you lack the support you require in the parliament." He paused. "Those facts give Our Gracious Majesty plenty of reason to be concerned and plenty of reason to express it."

Prince Victor attempted to conceal his anger and failed miserably. Lord Everleigh noted that the prince regent's dueling scar gave him away, serving as a barometer for his moods. "I am quite capable of governing the country in my cousin's absence."

"And the Karolyan Charter gives you that right," Lord Everleigh commented. "But as prince regent, you are acting in Princess Giana's stead and on her behalf until she is returned."

"We have been searching for the princess for weeks now—

to no avail—and we fear that something terrible has happened to her."

"Something terrible *has* happened to her," Lord Everleigh replied. "She has been kidnapped by the person or persons who murdered her parents and is being held against her will."

"Our cousin, Princess Giana, was kidnapped by anarchists in league with a traitor. We have evidence that suggests that Prince Christian's private secretary, Lord Maximillian Gudrun, conspired with the anarchists to arrange the deaths of Prince Christian and Princess May and the abduction of the heir."

"For what purpose?" Lord Everleigh asked. "Why would Lord Gudrun betray his country?"

"For Karolya's iron ore deposits," Prince Victor responded promptly. "His Highness, Prince Christian, refused to barter or sell the iron ore deposits that would greatly enrich Karolya's coffers."

The consummate diplomat, Lord Everleigh gave no hint as to his political leaning or partisanship. "It is our understanding that Karolya's coffers are already full. Prince Christian was a very wealthy man, and the country has one of the highest standards of living in Europe. There was no need for Prince Christian to sell the iron ore deposits or rape the landscape in order to add to the country's already overflowing treasury."

"That may be true," Victor agreed, "but the fact remains that we have uncovered evidence that Lord Gudrun engineered the deaths of the prince and princess and the abduction of the Princess Royal in order to gain control of Karolya and the iron ore deposits."

"Then it is fortunate for the people of Karolya that your life was spared, Your Highness." Lord Everleigh met the prince regent's unwavering gaze.

"It was, indeed, most fortunate," the prince regent agreed.

"A great deal more fortunate than the other members of your family." Lord Everleigh didn't blink as he asked the barbed question, "Why do you suppose that came to be, Your Highness?"

Prince Victor's complexion was a mottled mix of red and scarlet hues. "I beg your pardon?"

"Anarchists aren't ordinarily so discriminating," Lord Everleigh responded. "They usually kill as many royal personages as possible. And generally do not leave a member of the ruling house in a position to take over the country." He paused for effect. "Our Gracious Majesty, Queen Victoria, held the late Prince Christian and Princess May in the highest regard and felt very deep affection for them. She is eager to honor our country's alliance with Karolya and assist your government in its efforts to locate Princess Giana. . . ."

"That will not be necessary," Prince Victor replied. "We thank Her Majesty for the offer, but we are quite capable of negotiating with the anarchists for Princess Giana's safe return."

"Then you have located the anarchist leader?"

Victor faltered for a moment. "No, we have not."

"With whom will you negotiate?"

"The anarchists have made their demands known."

"Have they?" Lord Everleigh pursed his lips in thought. "We were not aware . . ."

"The anarchists made their demands known through the democratic newspaper," Prince Victor answered in a flash of brilliance.

"I see," Lord Everleigh said. "It was our understanding that the publication of Karolya's democratic newspaper had been suspended since the night of the murders so as not to further alarm the people about the disappearance of the heir apparent."

"The official newspaper has been suspended," Victor recovered. "But we have continued to issue bulletins informing our people of our efforts to locate our beloved princess. The anarchists contacted the editor to make their demands known. They've assured us that the princess is alive and well cared for. Of course, the editor immediately contacted the military police."

"Why the military police?"

"Because Karolya is under martial law until the negotiations are completed and the princess royal is returned."

"I see." Lord Everleigh nodded his head in understanding. "And what have these anarchists demanded?"

"That we not add a Declaration of Rights for the Masses to the Karolyan Charter and that ownership of Karolya's iron ore deposits be surrendered to them as representatives of the people."

Lord Everleigh paused. "That's odd. One would think that anarchists would support any legislation created to provide and protect the basic rights of the common people." He looked at Prince Victor. "So, they wish to exchange the princess for the iron ore."

"Yes."

"I do not envy you, Your Highness. That is a terrible decision for a ruler to have to make." The empathy in the special envoy's words sounded entirely genuine. "The loss of either one will have a profound effect on Karolya's future."

"Yes, but our cousin would be the greater loss." Prince Victor didn't flinch as he looked the older diplomat in the eye.

"One would imagine that if sold to the highest bidder, the iron ore deposits would be worth an enormous sum of money."

"Yes, one might imagine that." Victor glanced down at his right hand.

Lord Everleigh followed his gaze. "It is a great deal to lose."

"No more so than the Crown." Prince Victor gave Lord Everleigh a brilliant smile. "But that is not going to happen. I am most confident that our cousin, Princess Giana, will be found and that the people and the parliament will unite behind its new ruler. I hope that is what you shall report to Her Majesty."

"Most definitely, Your Highness," Everleigh agreed. "I shall be most happy to report that you have everything in Karolya under control and that your efforts to secure Princess Giana's release from her captors is currently under way."

"Will that satisfy Her Majesty?"

Lord Everleigh smiled. "I've no doubt that Lord Templeston and Her Majesty will be most satisfied to learn that they need not worry about Karolya's future. Your assurances, Your Highness, have left us with no doubt as to who is responsible for these heinous and cowardly acts against the Crown, and I am sure Her Majesty and her most trusted adviser will be as relieved as I am to know that you have proven yourself to be a completely formidable adversary—"

Victor took a step toward the special envoy.

"For the anarchists," Lord Everleigh continued. He shook his head. "Until today I would never have believed anyone so close to Prince Christian and Princess May could be capable of such treachery. Nor could I ever have imagined Maximillian Gudrun in the role of anarchist leader or thought to point a finger at him. But you, Your Highness, have managed to make me see things in their true light."

"Have we?"

"Yes, indeed. I seldom mistake a person's character." Lord Everleigh sketched another bow.

"We are very glad we were able to help." Victor grinned.

"I'm sure Her Majesty will be most grateful to know that you have been so forthcoming."

"Will you be sending your report soon, Lord Everleigh?"

"I shall have it ready for the next post," he answered.

Prince Victor nodded. "If there is nothing more—"

"There is one other thing," Lord Everleigh told him.

"Yes?"

"I must confess to a certain amount of curiosity as to what happened to that small gilt table. I thought I heard a crash upon my arrival. . . ." Lord Everleigh nodded to the remains of the French cabriole.

The prince regent attempted a boyish shrug. "You must have been mistaken. You see, the anarchists invaded this part of the palace and wreaked havoc the night our aunt and uncle were murdered. It remained closed and sealed until we chose to use it for this meeting. We did not realize it had not been properly cleared and cleaned."

The special envoy glanced around the room. Except for the gilt table that lay splintered on the marble floor, the room was clean, the surfaces of the furniture, dusted. If the anarchists had wreaked havoc upon the room, they had done it very neatly, for nothing else was disturbed. No china smashed or paintings slashed. No obvious signs of looting. "Thank you for indulging my curiosity, Your Highness."

"Good day, Lord Everleigh." Prince Victor dismissed him.

Lord Everleigh bowed to the prince regent, then respectfully backed out of the room.

Three quarters of an hour later the marquess of Everleigh sat down at the desk in his borrowed office in the British Embassy to write his report. He would follow up his written report with a face-to-face audience with the queen and the marquess, but first he had to relay the details of his audience with Karolya's acting ruler to the marquess of Templeston.

"Lord Everleigh? Am I disturbing you?"

Lord Everleigh looked up from his writing to find Lord Sissingham, the British ambassador in Karolya, standing in the doorway. "No. Please, come in, Sissingham."

"How did it go?" Sissingham asked.

Everleigh put down his pen and invited the ambassador to sit down and help himself to the tea tray. "I believe you have accurately judged the situation."

Sissingham raised an eyebrow. "Then you agree?"

"Most definitely," Lord Everleigh replied. "There are no anarchists."

"We were suspicious when we heard rumors that Prince Victor was inciting young men of the ruling class to denounce Prince Christian's support of a constitution and a Declaration of Rights for the Masses."

"Your suspicions appear to be correct," Lord Everleigh said, grimly. "Prince Victor has usurped his uncle's throne."

"Have we any idea what has become of Her Serene Highness Princess Giana?"

Everleigh shook his head. "Prince Victor is a desperate man. Desperate to hold on to the Crown—a Crown he has stolen first from his uncle and from his cousin, Princess Giana."

"Do you think he has her?" Sissingham asked.

Everleigh thought for a moment before he replied, "I don't think so. He wasn't wearing the royal seal."

Sissingham was impressed. "You noticed."

"Victor didn't appear nervous, but he kept glancing at his right hand. It struck me as odd until I recalled that Prince Christian shook hands with me at a meeting in Geneva once and the state seal cut into my hand. Prince Christian apologized by saying that he rarely shook hands because the seal tended to bruise him and maim the handshake recipient. He laughed and said he'd made an exception in Geneva because he didn't want to appear to be a stuffy old monarchist at a meeting on the modernization of Europe. He always wore the seal of state on his right hand. Victor's right hand was bare."

"Have you had an occasion to read a copy of the Karolyan Charter?" Sissingham asked.

"On the journey here from London."

"Then you're aware that Victor cannot be crowned unless he abides by the Law of Succession. He cannot marry until the traditional period of mourning for the late ruler is over and he cannot be crowned until he is married."

"The traditional period of mourning is one year," Everleigh said. "He can govern for seven more months before he's required him to marry a princess of Karolyan blood."

"The only available princesses of Karolyan blood are Victor's sisters and Princess Giana."

"In order to be crowned His Serene Highness, Prince Victor IV of Saxe-Wallerstein-Karolya, the prince regent will have to marry Princess Giana or submit proof of her death and produce the seal of state." Lord Everleigh ran his fingers through his hair. "He's desperate to find her."

"So are we," Sissingham said.

"Yes, but he wants the crown and the iron ore deposits. We only want to see that she is safely returned so that we can help her reclaim her country and her crown."

"How much damage can Victor do to the country in seven months?" Sissingham wondered.

"If he finds Princess Giana before we do, Victor could force her into marrying him."

"I don't think the princess would ever agree to marry her parents' killer," Sissingham said.

"Under normal circumstances, I don't think she would either. But these aren't normal circumstances. If she is being held captive somewhere, she may not know who is holding her or who is responsible for her parents' deaths," Everleigh expounded. "And if she's in voluntary hiding and Victor finds her, she may not have a choice. Marriage and the opportunity to regain your country are preferable to death."

Sissingham frowned. "And even if he chose not to marry her, Victor could coerce her into handing over the seal . . ."

"We are, of course, assuming that she is still alive and that the seal is in her possession," Everleigh interrupted. "And that she wants to regain her crown . . ." Deep in thought, Everleigh rested his elbow on the desk, propped his chin on his thumb and lightly tapped his lower lip with the tip of his index finger.

"We might try negotiating," Sissingham volunteered.

"With imaginary anarchists?"

"No, with Victor."

Everleigh looked askance at the ambassador.

"Hear me out," Sissingham said.

Everleigh nodded.

"Suppose the princess is in voluntary hiding and suppose the price of her freedom is her signature on the rights to the Karolyan timber and iron ore deposits, do you think there is any chance that she might come forward?"

"Would you with every newspaper in Europe and Britain, including *The Times*, carrying the latest news of Victor's search for the missing princess?" Everleigh asked.

The ambassador frowned. "What if we promised to protect her?"

"We can promise," Everleigh admitted, "but I don't know if we can ensure her complete safety if Victor sets assassins on her. And if we were successful in our negotiations, what is the likelihood of Prince Victor honoring such an agreement with her?"

"None." Sissingham admitted. "Her life would be forfeit."

"Agreed," Everleigh said. "The only way Victor can rule is if she's his wife or if she's a corpse." He glanced at Sissingham. "You are more familiar with the princess than I am. Do you think she is politically well-versed or intelligent enough to arrive at the same conclusion we've come to?"

Sissingham nodded. "Especially if Maximillian Gudrun is with her."

"Suppose she is alive and Lord Gudrun is with her. Where

would they go? Is there anyone in Europe—any relatives she can trust?"

The ambassador met the special envoy's gaze. "Princess May was an only child and all of her family, except distant cousins, are gone. The only close relatives Princess Giana has left are Prince Victor, his mother, three sisters and two younger brothers."

"She wouldn't turn to them. And even if she did, it's doubtful that any of them would hide Princess Giana from Victor." Lord Everleigh sighed. "What about her paternal aunt? Prince Christian's older sister?"

"Princess Pauline lives in Saint Therese's Convent outside Salzburg."

"Could Princess Giana seek asylum there?"

The ambassador shrugged. "I don't think so. Women seeking sanctuary at Saint Therese's are admitted only if they intend to remain there. Princess Giana has no immediate relatives to turn to except Victor's family and a few distant cousins who've married into the other royal families of Europe."

"Some of whom are negotiating to buy iron ore and timber and who may or may not be in league with Victor," Lord Everleigh said.

"That leaves her godmother. Our gracious queen."

"Who remains secluded at Windsor." Everleigh looked at the ambassador.

"If Victor is searching for her, he's sure to have men in London and around Windsor."

"What about Scotland? The queen will make her annual trek to Balmoral in August. Do you think Princess Giana is aware of the queen's schedule?"

"Of course she is," Sissingham said. "She and her parents have visited the queen at Balmoral." He met the special envoy's gaze. "But so has Victor."

"True," Lord Everleigh nodded. "But if I were Princess Giana and I were hiding from my enemies, I'd do my damnedest to obtain an audience with someone I knew I could trust and someone I knew could protect me and who better than my godmother, the queen of England?"

"And it would be a great deal easier to obtain an audience with the queen in Scotland than it would be at Windsor . . ." the ambassador agreed.

"I think we would be remiss if we didn't begin a discreet investigation of the towns and villages within a day's journey of Balmoral."

Several blocks away at the Christianberg Palace, Prince Victor Lucien sent for his equerry. "Find a goldsmith," he ordered.

"Sir?"

"Find a goldsmith," Prince Victor repeated his order. "And every tall blond female bearing a resemblance to our princess that you can find." He pointed to a miniature of Princess Giana that sat on what had once been Prince Christian's desk. "Take that with you for comparison."

"I do not understand," the equerry replied.

"What is there to understand?" Prince Victor demanded. "We've given an order we expect you to follow. We require a goldsmith." He stared as his equerry. "The British government is snapping at our heels. Time is running out. We need the Karolyan State Seal, and if we cannot locate the original, we must produce a well-crafted replacement. The same is true of the princess."

Chapter 15

The Bountiful Baron is a man who is keenly aware and always in control of his surroundings.

—The First Installment of the True Adventures of the Bountiful Baron: Western Benefactor to Blond, Beautiful, and Betrayed Women written by John J. Bookman, 1874.

"Wake up, boyo, or you'll be missing your breakfast." O'Brien burst into Adam's bedchamber carrying a tray with a pot of tea, a kettle of boiling water, and a cup and saucer on it in one hand and a pair of Adam's trousers and a white linen shirt over his arm. He set the tray on the table beside Adam's bed, then tossed his trousers and his shirt at him.

Adam shoved his shirt off his face and sat up. "What time is it?"

"Half past six." O'Brien poured Adam a cup of tea and handed it to him, then carried the kettle of water to the basin in the shaving stand and filled the bowl.

Adam accepted the tea. "Where's yours?" he grumbled, glaring up at his friend and drinking companion, who was perfectly groomed and showing no ill effects from the previous night's indulgence.

"I had mine earlier this morning."

"What are you doing up? I ordered breakfast served at half past eight."

"The staff eats before they begin their workday," O'Brien recited. "In a well-run household a proper gentleman's gentleman rises with the rest of the staff to prepare for his employer's awakening."

"Was that the topic of this morning's lecture?"

"Aye."

"And you stood for it?"

"I suffered through it," Murphy replied. "I am supposed to be a proper gentleman's gentleman, remember?"

Adam took a sip of tea, grimacing as the hot, sweet liquid burned its way down his throat to his stomach. He wasn't sure what had happened to the cook, because he specifically remembered asking the woman if she knew how to brew coffee. But if someone didn't teach her how to make a pot of coffee soon, he was going to have to give up drinking coffee and learn to drink the scalding and disgustingly sweet tea she sent up to him every morning—or find another cook. "Where do I have to go to get a cup of coffee?"

"Kinlochen."

"Why is that?"

"Because proper households serve tea."

"I don't care about being proper. I want a cup of coffee. I need a cup of coffee!" Adam growled. "And so do you. You couldn't have had more than three hours of sleep."

"Closer to two," O'Brien admitted. "But your proper household is running smoothly. The question is who does it run to suit? Because it does not run to suit Adam McKendrick."

"No, it does not," Adam replied. "And it's about time I did something about it."

O'Brien smiled.

Adam swung his legs over the side of the bed, but kept his grip on the covers, anchoring them across his lap. He was naked except for a pair of dark woolen socks.

"You're wearing socks."

"Of course, I'm wearing socks," Adam said. "It's as cold as an icehouse in here." He shot his friend a dirty look. "So get the hell out of here so I can cover the rest of me before I freeze to death."

"A proper gentleman's gentleman assists his employer with his dressing."

"I can dress myself," Adam reminded him. "I've been doing

it for quite a while now. I'm going to get breakfast. You go back to bed."

"And miss all the fun when you take on the household staff? Not on your life."

"At least have the decency to turn your back."

O'Brien obliged.

Adam stood up, stepped into his trousers, and pulled his linen shirt over his head. He walked over to his shaving stand and dropped a towel in the hot water. He took out his razor, removed it from its case, and stroked it against the razor strop. When he finished stropping his razor, he laid it aside, then wrung the hot water from the towel and placed the steaming linen over the lower portion of his face. "Ah . . ." He closed his eyes and allowed the heat from the cloth to clear his head, penetrate his pores, and soften his whisker stubble.

"Shall I attend to your shaving, sir?" O'Brien couldn't keep the note of laughter out of his voice when he asked the facetious question.

"It may surprise you to learn that I can dress and *shave* myself," Adam shot back. He removed the cloth and opened his eyes. "I've been doing that for quite some time now, too." He stared into the mirror as he dipped his shaving brush in the basin of hot water, then into his shaving mug where he worked the spicy sandalwood soap into a frothy lather. Adam coated his beard with the soap, then lifted his razor and began to carefully scrape away his whiskers.

"You're the one who accused me of being a valet." Murphy still loved baiting Adam over the whole valet misunderstanding. It was practically a daily ritual now. He went to the armoire and took out a collar and tie from one drawer and a waistcoat from another, then turned his attention to the selection of coats and jackets. O'Brien held up two coats—a dark green and a heather tweed.

"I didn't accuse you of being a valet," Adam corrected. "I told you Isobel thought you were my gentleman's gentleman." He glanced at the jackets O'Brien held.

"You could have set her straight," Murphy said.

"I did set her straight, but she chose not to believe me because you arrived with a wagonload of new and expensive luggage—something she said only a valet would do. You decided to masquerade as one." Adam finished shaving and donned his collar and tie.

"And I'm becoming quite good at it, don't you think?" He winked. "Solid or tweed?"

Adam shrugged into a brown waistcoat that contrasted very nicely with his buff trousers. "Tweed."

O'Brien took the jacket off its hanger and held it out for Adam to slip into, then tilted the cheval glass so Adam could inspect his appearance.

Adam raked his fingers through his hair and laughed at his reflection. "Well, what do you think? How do I look?"

O'Brien grinned. "You look like the lord who's about to retake his manor."

"Good morning, sir," Albert greeted Adam as soon as he entered the dining room.

"Good morning." Adam took a plate from the stack on the sideboard and filled it with an array of food warming in the silver chafing dishes, then walked over to the dining table and sat down.

Albert filled a cup with steaming hot tea and set it down beside Adam's plate.

Adam picked up the cup of tea and handed it back to Albert. "I don't drink tea."

The butler took the cup of tea, removed it to the sideboard, then returned to the dining table and silently placed a cup of hot chocolate beside Adam's plate.

Adam frowned at it. "I don't want chocolate." He looked up at Albert. "I drink coffee."

Albert shook his head. "No coffee."

"Why not?" Adam demanded. "I drink coffee. Hot, black coffee. Every morning. Not tea. Not chocolate. Coffee." He knew he was running the risk of sounding like a spoiled child, but it was time he began enforcing his authority in his home and now was as good a time as any to begin.

"No coffee," Albert repeated.

"Then find some," Adam ordered, raising his voice loud enough to be heard in the next room. "Can't a man get a cup of coffee in his own house?"

Max came running. "Good morning, sir."

Adam acknowledged him with a quick nod. Trust Max to come translate Adam's simple, but largely ignored, instructions for his brother.

"A mail packet arrived for you from London," Max continued. "I placed it on the desk in your study, and I took the liberty of giving the newspapers to Albert to iron for you." Max turned to Albert and questioned him in a language Adam didn't understand.

Albert nodded.

"He says he ironed them well so there's no need to worry about the ink smearing your hands or clothing. They are neatly stacked on your desk. I hope that meets with your satisfaction."

Adam smiled. "As a matter of fact, it's the first thing he's done that meets with my satisfaction."

"Sir?"

Adam waited while the clock on the mantel chimed seven times, then focused his attention on his private secretary. "It's seven o'clock in the morning."

"Yes, sir," Max answered with a puzzled look on his face.

"Max, why am I sitting down to a breakfast of scrambled eggs at seven o'clock in the morning?" Adam asked. "When I ordered it to be served at half past eight?"

"The household runs on a schedule, sir," Max replied stiffly.

"Yes, it does," Adam agreed. "But not at the expense of its owner. I'm eating scrambled eggs because I don't like kidneys, blood pudding, or ptarmigan, and the steak I ordered isn't on the menu. Nor is the coffee I drink."

"Sir?"

"This household will be run to suit me." Adam's voice held an unyielding note of steel resolve. "Me. Adam McKendrick. No one else. Is that clear?"

"It is very clear. But I fail to understand the reason for your displeasure, sir." Max faltered for a moment, then cast a speculative look at Adam. "With the exception of Her—Giana's—

unfortunate accidents with the china, the household has been run to suit you."

"Really?" Adam quickly finished eating his scrambled eggs, then laid his fork aside and pushed back his chair and stood up. "Let's go see."

"Sir?" Max was clearly taken aback.

"Let's take a look," Adam reiterated. "We'll start with the kitchen." He turned and led the way out of the dining room, down the corridor to the kitchen, where he stopped in the doorway and stared at the cook. He was male and, from the looks of it, French. "Where's Mrs. Dunham, the cook I recommended Mrs. Langstrom hire?"

"Mrs. Dunham was a local woman who cooked local fare," Max explained. "She did not cook in the French style."

"I know," Adam said. "She cooked good, plain, hearty fare. That is why I recommended that Mrs. Langstrom hire her."

"I'm sure she is a wonderful cook," Max said, "but the food she cooks is not the sort of food Her—to which we were accustomed. We were among the staff of the countess of Brocavia, which set an exquisite table. That is why Isobel—I mean Mrs. Langstrom—hired Monsieur Henri."

The temper Adam had been struggling to contain exploded. *"Henri!"*

"Oui?" The chef glanced up as he answered.

"Do you speak English?" he asked in French.

"Non."

Adam exhaled and slowly counted to ten, then asked if Henri could make coffee. *"Est-ce que vous pouvez faire le café?"*

"Oui," Henri replied in his native tongue. "but, there isn't any."

Adam ordered, "Find some, or find someplace else to cook, because from now on I expect a pot of hot coffee every morning. Understand?"

"Oui." The French chef nodded to show his understanding.

Adam turned to Max. "Find Mrs. Dunham and hire her back right away."

"Sir, how will I explain to Henri?"

"Explain that from now on, Henri and Mrs. Dunham will share the kitchen duties. For breakfast, I'll expect a variety of Scottish and French dishes. Mrs. Dunham will prepare luncheons and tea and Henri will be responsible for dinner and desserts. Larchmont Lodge will offer its owner, guests, and staff a choice of fare."

"Chef Henri will not be happy," Maximillian warned. "He prefers to be in control of his kitchens."

"And I prefer to be in control of my household," Adam replied. "If you can't manage to run it to my satisfaction, without countermanding my orders, I'll find a staff who will." With that, Adam turned and stalked out of the kitchen, his long legs eating up the distance as he left the kitchen and made his way to his library.

Maximillian followed close on his heels, managing to cross the threshold before Adam slammed the door in his face.

"Out!" Adam ordered.

"Sir?"

"That will be all, Max," Adam said.

"But, sir . . ."

Christ, but he was tired of having all of his instructions and decisions questioned and circumvented! "Please leave, Max." Adam struggled to rein his temper in. "I want a few minutes alone."

Max opened his mouth to protest, but Adam cut him off. "Perhaps I was remiss in not explaining my purpose in renovating Larchmont Lodge. But I plan to open it as a gentleman's club. A place of refuge for men of wealth and stature—businessmen, aristocrats, and world leaders—to come to—" Adam broke off as a slight noise caught his attention. It sounded as if someone had drawn a quick breath. He turned toward the sound and noticed a triangle of black silk on the carpet behind the leather sofa. There it was again, another almost imperceptible noise, only this time it sounded like a mouse crawling across the open pages of a book. Adam suspected it might be a very big mouse—one who stood nearly six feet tall in her stocking feet. He bit the inside of his cheek to keep from smiling.

The older man blanched. Max had heard it, too. "Do I understand, sir, that you intend to open the doors of Larchmont Lodge to the public?" Max asked.

Max sounded as if Adam had just announced that he intended to assassinate the queen. "I intend to open the doors of Larchmont Lodge to the well-paying public." Although the links required another six months or so of work to become established, Adam had decided to extend an invitation to preview the lodge to a few select guests during the week of the Cowes Regatta. "The best way to turn this pile of stone into a profitable enterprise is to convert it into a place where the rich and famous can rest and relax far away from the pressures of everyday life. I hope it will be a place men will come to hunt and fish, to ride and walk the moors, to golf or lounge around playing cards or reading. I've already issued private invitations for the week of the Cowes Regatta." He gave a little snort. "You needn't worry about riffraff, Max. They won't be able to afford to holiday here."

Adam waited until the private secretary regained some color in his face before he waved him back over the threshold. "Thank you, Max, that will be all." He closed the door to the library, barely missing the highly polished toes of Max's shoes.

Adam turned the key in the lock, then closed his eyes and leaned against the door, resting his forehead against its cool, wood grain surface. His body ached from hours spent overseeing the construction of the golf links and from hours of instruction in the game of golf. For what was the use of building a golf links to entice the richest and most powerful men in the world if he didn't know how to play the game with them? His head was pounding from too much drink, too little sleep, and no coffee. He pushed away from the door and eyed the long leather sofa.

Adam glanced at his desk where a packet of mail and a pile of neatly ironed newspapers lay stacked on the blotter just as Max had left them. He should attend to his correspondence, but he couldn't concentrate on the mail or the newspapers with an aching head. He had to admit the sofa was more enticing than the mail. A brief nap would do him a world of good. Besides, Adam reasoned, he hadn't planned to get up before half-past eight anyway. But there was the small problem of George. What to do about her? Adam covered a yawn with his hand, then slipped the key to the door inside his waistcoat pocket and stretched out on the sofa. She was the interloper. Let her wait. He just needed to close his eyes for a few moments. . . .

Chapter 16

A Princess of the Blood Royal of the House of Saxe-Wallerstein-Karolya respects the privacy and the property of her subjects.

—MAXIM 803: PROTOCOL AND COURT ETIQUETTE OF PRINCESSES OF THE BLOOD ROYAL OF THE HOUSE OF SAXE-WALLERSTEIN-KAROLYA, AS DECREED BY HIS SERENE HIGHNESS, PRINCE CHRISTIAN I, 1864.

Giana leaned against the back of the long leather sofa and reread the article printed in the bottom corner of the front page of the *Times of London*. Shocked by the deaths of Their Serene Highnesses, Prince Christian and Princess May of Saxe-Wallerstein-Karolya at the hands of anarchists, Britain's Queen Victoria had sent a special envoy to Christianberg, the capital of Karolya, to assist Prince Victor, the prince regent, in the investigation of the murders and in negotiating the return of Her Serene Highness Princess Georgiana, who had been taken hostage and was currently being held for ransom by the anarchists, whom it was believed were in league with the late prince's private secretary.

She had stumbled across the newspaper while cleaning the McKendrick's office, and although she had been taught to contain her curiosity and ignore the reams of official documents she saw lying scattered across the surface of her father's massive desk, Giana couldn't ignore a newspaper article about her family. Not when it affected her future and the futures of the men and women who had risked their lives in order to save her.

Giana swallowed her tears and bit back a sob. Victor had accused Max of being in league with anarchists who were supposed to have murdered her parents and kidnapped her! But the anarchists were a figment of Victor's imagination. Victor had murdered her parents and was trying to murder her, and now he had enlisted the help of her godmother's government in finding her.

Giana glanced at the date on the paper. It was more than a fortnight old, and although this edition had been lying on the top of the stack, she didn't know whether or not it was the most recent one. McKendrick had arrived before she had had time to look through the rest of the stack. She had grabbed the newspaper and hidden behind the sofa to read it. She hadn't intended to eavesdrop on his conversation with Max any more than she had intended to neglect her household duties by reading the newspaper instead of cleaning the library, but there had been no way to avoid overhearing the McKendrick's conversation with Max.

And the conversation she had overheard was as shocking as the newspaper article. She was so shocked by what she'd heard she hadn't been able to prevent a gasp of surprise—a gasp that had almost led to her discovery. Adam McKendrick intended to open Larchmont Lodge to the public—to the wealthy male public. Time was running out. The regatta was only a few weeks away. If she didn't think of some way of reaching Balmoral or of delaying the preview, there would be no place for her to hide.

Giana bit her bottom lip. Max had been horrified by the news and must be beside himself with anxiety for her safety. To think that the one safe place they had been able to find was about to become a haven for the very men she was trying to avoid! She needed to talk to Max, needed to consult with the rest of her entourage before they panicked. She needed to come up with a plan.

Unfortunately, she couldn't do anything until she made her way out of the library without waking McKendrick. McKendrick. Giana ground her teeth together and looked up at the ceiling. She hadn't expected McKendrick to remain in the library. She had expected him to follow Max out the door, but McKendrick had slammed the door almost in Max's face and decided to take a nap. A nap! Who would have thought that he'd decide to take a nap so soon after breakfast?

Folding the newspaper as quietly as possible, Giana lifted her skirts and tucked it in the waistband of her drawers. She didn't like the idea of borrowing McKendrick's newspaper, but she needed to show it to Max, needed to share her fears with the one person who had as much to lose as she did. Giana took a deep breath, screwed her courage to the sticking place, and crawled around the sofa.

The McKendrick—Adam—was sleeping soundly. His breathing, deep and even. Giana knew she should keep moving, but she couldn't help but stop and look at him. At Adam McKendrick. At the man who had given her her first kiss.

She liked the way he looked when he slept, liked the way his dark eyelashes fanned against his cheekbones and the way his nostrils flared ever-so-slightly as he breathed. And Giana especially liked the way his lips remained slightly parted. His lower lip was slightly plumper than his upper lip, but both were exquisitely shaped. Giana leaned closer—close enough to study the subtle pattern of lines on his lips. She remembered the taste and touch and feel of his lips on hers, his warm breath, and the way he had used his tongue to tempt and torment her. Had there ever been anything quite as enticing as the soft, rough feel of Adam McKendrick's tongue mating with hers?

Fighting an almost overwhelming urge to press her lips against his, Giana took one last look and began the long crawl across the library. She inched her way across the Aubusson carpet, past his desk and the last wall of bookcases to the door where she reached up and stealthily turned the brass doorknob.

But the door didn't open. It was locked. She felt for the key that had been in the lock when she entered the room. It was gone. Giana pushed herself to her knees and stared through the open keyhole. She was locked in the library with Adam McKendrick. There was no way for her to escape unless she located the missing key—and Giana wasn't at all sure she wanted to. But duty compelled her to look.

She tiptoed over to his desk and began looking for the key.

She searched his desk from top to bottom, carefully opening each drawer and rifling through the contents in a futile search for the key. She had never plundered through anyone else's private belongings, and the idea that she was invading *his* privacy made her feel slightly queasy. And the fact that she failed to locate the key to the library door only served to increase her queasiness.

If the key was not to be found in the McKendrick's desk, then it had to be on his person. Giana tiptoed back to the sofa and knelt beside it. She slipped her hand beneath his jacket and began a stealthy search of his pockets.

Adam moaned in his sleep and moved his head against the arm of the sofa. He smoothed his hand over the fabric of his waistcoat and his fingers met hers. He closed his hand over around her wrist. "Looking for something, Miss Langstrom?"

The sound of his voice startled her. Giana jumped back, upsetting a table and the lead crystal vase of hothouse flowers sitting on it.

"Oh!" She grabbed for the vase, but Adam was quicker. He reached behind his head and caught hold of the vase seconds before it hit the ground or spilled its contents over his head.

"Is it me?" Adam chuckled. "Or do you have something against fragile household objects?" He righted the vase, then caught hold of Giana's hand before she could do further damage.

"I-it is you," Giana replied. "I am not normally so clumsy. But I become clumsy around you."

Her honest answer surprised him. When she tried to withdraw her hand, Adam wouldn't let go. He let his gaze roam over her. His seat on the sofa gave him a unique view of the underside of her black silk and white cotton pinafore-covered breasts. They were magnificent. "Why do you think that is, Miss Langstrom?" he asked.

"I think it is because you kissed me."

Adam lifted an eyebrow at that. "You were breaking the china and the crockery before I kissed you."

Giana answered him with her most mysterious smile. "Why do you think that is, Mr. McKendrick?"

"I think it's because you were trying to get my attention," he teased. "Because you were hoping I'd kiss you."

She opened her mouth to deny his charge or protest it, but she was too honest to deny the truth. She swallowed hard, inhaling the scent of him. She loved the way he smelled and the way he tasted and she did want him to kiss her. She did want to taste him again.

Adam watched as she parted her lips until her mouth formed a perfect circle. A perfectly kissable circle. "Are you waiting for more of my kisses? Is that why you locked yourself in the library with me?"

"I did not lock the door, sir. You did," she pointed out. "I was seeking the key."

"What are you doing in here?"

He gave her hand a little tug. Giana lost her balance and fell forward, sprawling across his chest. "I appear to be locked in."

Adam turned his most devastating grin on her. "You *are* locked in," he told her. "The question is why."

Her china-blue eyes widened in surprise, and her pink, pouting lips were slightly opened and quiet, for a change.

"What's the matter?" he asked, placing his hands on her waist and pulled her closer to his face. "Cat got your tongue? No? Maybe that's because I have," he murmured sympathetically an instant before his mouth found hers.

Giana inhaled the spicy sandalwood scent of him, allowing it to engulf her as she felt the exotic touch of his tongue on hers. She felt the heat of his body penetrating through her pinafore and her dress, but it was nothing compared to the heat of his mouth. She tasted him, feeling the rasp of his tongue against her teeth as it slipped between her lips into her mouth. She felt the urgency of his mouth and she echoed it, moving her lips under his, allowing him further access. Giana experienced the jolt of pure pleasure as her tongue mated with his.

Adam caressed her back through the fabric of her dress. The fabric hampered him, frustrated him. He wanted to feel the softness of her flesh beneath the layers of clothing. He wanted to move his hands over her, count her ribs, and test the weight of those wonderful, pear-shaped breasts, but all he could really feel was fabric. Too much fabric, masking the curves pressed against him. He moved his hand down her back, over one firm buttock, to the back of her thigh. Fumbling with her skirts, he reached beneath them, then ran his fingers under the lace of her drawers, caressing the bare flesh of her knee while his mouth ate at hers. Over and over again.

The twin pinpoints pressing into his chest were hard and tight and driving him mad. Adam reversed their positions, shifting his weight until George lay on the sofa. He stopped kissing her mouth long enough to roll her onto her back, then began pressing warm, wet kisses against her line of her jaw, her neck, and beneath one ear.

Giana gasped when Adam's probing tongue explored the contours of her ear. She was hot, breathless, light-headed. She whimpered.

Adam took that as a sign of encouragement. He became bolder, slipping his hand farther up the lace-edged leg of her drawers and higher along her thigh.

Hearing a slight rustle and remembering the newspaper she had secreted in the waistband of her drawers, Giana pulled away. "What are you doing?" she murmured against his lips.

"I was touching you," Adam answered, caressing her thigh once more with his fingers before he withdrew his hand. "Because I want to undress you and spend the rest of the morning touching you all over."

"I have never been undressed by anyone except my"—she almost said lady's maid, but she recovered in time—"Brenna when she's practicing her lady's maid skills." Giana bit her bottom lip and shyly averted her gaze. "I did not realize that a man might choose to undress a woman or that she might allow him to do it."

"The privilege is usually reserved for a husband or a lover," Adam whispered. "And if a lady decides to allow it, the man chosen for the privilege is honored to make sure the lady enjoys it."

"Is that permissible?"

"It's not only permissible, it's desirable," Adam whispered.

Giana shivered as his warm breath caressed her ear. "For ladies as well?"

"As far as I'm concerned," he said. "When a woman grants me the privilege of undressing her, I like to touch all of her. Beginning with her eyes, her lips, her breasts, and continuing until I know all her secret places." He touched each part of her with his gaze as he explained his preferences. "Shall I demonstrate?"

Giana's eyes widened with each husky word, then darkened to a deeper blue as his meaning became clearer. "Adam!"

"George," he breathed, bending closer to kiss her mouth, hard.

She kissed him back, stopping only when she felt him deftly unhook the bodice of her pinafore and unbutton the top button of her dress.

"Yes?" he queried.

She was tempted. Tempted in a way that Princesses of the Blood Royal should never be tempted, but the newspaper stuck in the waistband of her drawers wasn't the only thing she was hiding. She couldn't allow Adam to unbutton her dress because she was wearing a fortune in family heirlooms concealed in the bodice of her dress, and that wasn't all. . . .

Giana was a walking, talking jewelry safe. There were gems sewn into the lining of her corset cover, the padding of her corset and the hems of most of her skirts. About the only thing not sewn into her clothing was the tiara she wore during official functions. It was concealed in the false bottom of her traveling case. There would be no way to conceal her identity if she allowed him to continue, for how would a chambermaid ever explain the presence of a king's, or in her case a princess's, ransom in precious stones.

"I cannot," she whispered.

"I should not," he admitted as his conscience returned with a vengeance. The girl lying with him on the leather sofa was an innocent in his employ. An apparently willing innocent, but an innocent nonetheless. And he knew better than to turn his attention to innocents. Especially innocents who looked like George.

He knew better. But that didn't seem to matter. He wanted her. And what was worse than wanting to make love to her was knowing that she was everything he had always avoided in a lover. Adam exhaled.

What was it about George that fascinated him so? He had never been attracted to tall, leggy, blondes before. They tended to remind him of his family. But he was attracted now. He wanted George. He couldn't seem to keep his gaze off her. He'd made a valiant effort, but he'd failed. She excited him. She challenged him. She fascinated him.

He wasn't breaking the china and the crockery, but she was having a similar effect on him. It was all he could do to keep his hands off her. He wanted to taste her, to feel her. And that made him very nervous.

The best thing he could do for the both of them would be to make her forget about him by turning his attention to someone else. Someone different. Someone safe. Someone like her sister, Brenna.

Adam shifted his weight off her and helped her sit up. Reaching into his waistcoat pocket, he removed the door key and handed it to her. "I believe this is what you were looking for."

Giana accepted it. "Thank you, sir." She stood up, walked over to the library door, and unlocked it.

"My pleasure," Adam said. "Thank you most kindly for a very entertaining morning, Miss Langstrom."

Giana opened the door, then glanced back over her shoulder to look at him. She was blushing. "You are most kindly welcome, sir."

Adam grinned back at her. "Am I?"

She met his gaze and gave him her most regal look. "More than you know." Giana glanced back one last time, then slipped through the doorway and disappeared.

Chapter 17

Princesses of the Blood Royal of the House of Saxe-Wallerstein-Karolya do not conspire with members of their households or indulge in petty schemes or squabbles.

—MAXIM 307: PROTOCOL AND COURT ETIQUETTE OF PRINCESSES OF THE BLOOD ROYAL OF THE HOUSE OF SAXE-WALLERSTEIN-KAROLYA, AS DECREED BY HIS SERENE HIGHNESS, PRINCE KAROL IV, 1611.

"This cannot be!" Max's hands shook as he read the article in the newspaper Giana had borrowed from Adam's office. He sat at the table in the housekeeper's room and covered his face with his hands. "This simply cannot be."

Giana studied his hands—the raised blue veins, the swollen joints, and the dark blotches on his skin—and suddenly realized how much Max had aged since her parents' deaths. He had spent more than thirty years of his adult life in Christianberg Palace and the strain of living a lie in a country far from home was beginning to show. Although their sojourn at Larchmont Lodge had been safe and uneventful, life in exile did not agree with him.

"I was certain that you had seen it and that you had kept silent in order to spare me." She and Max were meeting in Isobel and Albert's room because the housekeeper's room was larger than Max's and because it offered complete privacy from the rest of the staff. Although Isobel laid out a tea table for the staff, no one entered without permission.

Max was shocked. "I would never keep important information regarding matters of state from you, Your Highness."

"I apologize, Max, but I thought that you collected the mail."

"Yes, I did, Your Highness. I placed the mail packet on the McKendrick's desk and gave the bundle of newspapers to Albert to iron."

Giana nodded her understanding. Foreign languages were not Albert's forte and despite having lived with Isobel for nearly a quarter of a century, his grasp of English was rudimentary. The butler had performed one of his many daily chores, ironing the newsprint without realizing that one of the articles on it could have a profound affect on their futures.

"What about the other editions?" Max asked. "Do they contain similar articles?"

"I do not know," Giana replied. "McKendrick arrived before I had the opportunity to read the other editions."

"We must find out," Max said. "We must discover a way to get our hands on those newspapers."

"The newspapers are only a part of our worries," Giana reminded him. "You heard what A—McKendrick said. He intends to open the lodge to several very rich, very powerful, very important guests during the week of the Cowes Regatta. We haven't much time." She was more terrified by the possibility of having Victor or someone else she knew, visit the lodge than she was by the prospect of Adam discovering her true identity.

Giana sighed. Having Adam discover her true identity might be more of a relief than a hardship for her because she disliked lying to him. But the same might not be true for the rest of her staff and until she was certain she could trust him completely, Giana would not risk it.

"I think the time has come for us to send Gordon to London to seek an audience with the queen," Max said.

"The queen remains in seclusion at Windsor," Giana said. "And the courtiers around Queen Victoria will never grant a simple gamekeeper an audience," Giana said. "It's time *I* left our cozy little nest and sought an audience with the queen."

Max nodded. "You cannot go to Windsor alone. I will accompany you."

"You cannot go," Giana told him. "I will not allow it."

"But, Princess . . ." Max resorted to the less formal use of her title.

"You have been accused of murdering my parents and of kidnapping me. I will not risk having you arrested."

"That would not happen, Princess, as long as you are there to explain."

"What if I am not there to explain? What if something should happen to me to prevent me from explaining? Who would bear witness to the truth then? Who would tell the world of the murders of my parents or denounce Victor as the murderer? Who would prevent him from becoming Prince Regnant?" Giana shook her head. "I cannot fulfill my duty to my country and my people unless I am certain that you are safe and that you will bear witness for my parents if I cannot. And you will not be safe until I am able to speak to the queen."

Max opened his mouth to protest, but Giana held up a hand to silence him. "Please, Max. I could not bear to lose you. You're not just my private secretary, you're my Lord Chamberlain and you are the only witness to my father and my mother's murder. You are the only one who saw the assassins—the only one who can identify them as part of Victor's entourage. I trust you, Max, and I need you." She smiled at him. "I need to know that you are here with me."

"If the McKendrick invites his guests to the lodge before Regatta week begins, it may be too dangerous for us to remain. We may have to leave before the queen arrives in Scotland."

"Then we will leave," Giana assured him, "and if we leave, we will find a way to contact our ambassador in London."

"Princess, have you considered that we may not be able to trust our ambassador—that he may be in league with your cousin?"

"Of course, I've considered it." She frowned at Max. "I've also considered that while Queen Victoria may be perfectly willing to offer me protection and to support my claim to the throne, her government might not."

Max lifted an eyebrow in surprise.

"You still see me as a child, Max. And because you still see me as the little girl in pinafores and plaits, you forget that I cut my teeth on politics and government. I learned from the best. From the time I was old enough to sit at my father's knee. I am not a naïve little girl. I realize that some of my father's policies were unpopular. I know there were those in our country who were against creating a modern constitution and a Declaration of Rights for the Masses. I know they feared the loss of power. My father spoke to me about it. He explained that there were those in power in Karolya who wanted to harvest our timber and extract our rich iron ore deposits in order to add more gold to their coffers and that there were those in power in other countries who would be only too happy to assist in the harvesting of timber or the mining of iron ore or in the buying and selling of it. And while I don't know who all of the traitors in our country were, I can guess. I am not entirely sure where our ambassador's loyalties lie, but I cannot let that dissuade me from claiming my crown. I am the rightful heir to the crown of Saxe-Wallerstein-Karolya. My father died preserving my heritage and I don't intend to allow his murderer to steal what is rightfully mine or to exercise control over my subjects any longer than necessary. If that means I must put my faith in the fact that our ambassador is loyal to us and that Queen Victoria's government is as well, then I will do so. I am more than willing to risk my life for my country, but I prefer to do it once I know my godmother has arrived on Scottish soil." Giana felt safe at Larchmont Lodge, but she would be safer at Balmoral under the protection of the British government. Giana had known from the beginning that her stay at Larchmont Lodge would be temporary—simply a place to rest and regroup until she was able to present herself to the world and rescue her people and her country by proving her cousin, Victor, was the murderer and usurper she knew him to be.

But knowing her stay was temporary wouldn't make it any easier to leave. It wasn't home, but the lodge had served her well. It had become a place of refuge and sanctuary and even though she didn't want to admit it, even to herself, Giana knew in her heart of hearts that the primary reason she was reluctant to leave Larchmont Lodge had nothing to do with safety or security and everything to do with Adam McKendrick.

"What shall we do, Your Highness?"

Giana took a deep breath, then slowly expelled it. Max expected answers. He expected her to be the leader of her country, not just a figurehead, but the heart and soul and common sense of her country. "We must find a way to prevent the McKendrick from inviting guests during Cowes." She worried her bottom lip with her teeth. "And we must find a way to do it without alarming the McKendrick."

"Have you something in mind?"

"I suggest we do what we do best," she told him. "We simply do more of it."

Max frowned.

Giana grinned. "Instead of discouraging Albert from attempting to institute a proper dress code and rules of conduct for the workmen renovating the lodge, we encourage him to do so. I will begin by encouraging him to be the butler he would be if we had stayed at Laken." She turned to Max. "Your mission will be to take over as much of McKendrick's correspondence as you possibly can. Move into his office and do the same job for him that you would do for my father or for me if we were in Christianberg."

Max's smile began at one corner of his mouth and grew. "What of the rest of the staff?"

"We will simply instruct the members of our household to pretend they are back home and attend to their duties accordingly. We can issue specific instructions as we think of them." In a very unprincesslike gesture, Giana propped her elbows on the table and propped her chin on her hands. "Brenna presents a problem," she said at last, "because her traditional duties require that she take care of me. But I am sure that with a bit of thought, I will be able to discover Brenna's skills and her finest qualities." She snapped her fingers. "Since she cannot perform physical labor that does not include taking care of me, we will concentrate on allowing her to supervise the redecoration of the lodge."

Max winced. The McKendrick was sure to disapprove for like most lady's maids, Brenna's tastes tended toward flowers and frills—not at all what the McKendrick had in mind for Larchmont Lodge. "The McKendrick is already angry. You heard him threaten to dismiss us all if we didn't run the household according to his wishes."

Giana turned her most proper princess smile on Max. "That is another risk I am willing to take."

"When do we tell the others?" Max asked.

"Tonight at dinner in the housekeeper's room," Giana answered. "After the rest of the staff has gone home or retired."

"What about Mr. O'Brien?"

"I'll take care of Mr. O'Brien," she promised.

Giana was as good as her word. She knocked on Murphy O'Brien's bedchamber door a quarter of an hour before the rest of the upper staff were to meet in the housekeeper's room.

"Yes?" O'Brien opened the door to find Georgiana standing in the corridor holding a butler's table loaded with a variety of dishes under silver covers.

"I have brought your dinner, Mr. O'Brien," she announced, thrusting the table at him.

Afraid his dinner was about to hit the floor, Murphy grabbed the tray in self-defense. "I see that. Thanks."

"You are welcome." Giana gave him a brief nod and whirled around to leave.

"Wait a moment!" Murphy set his dinner tray on the floor inside his room.

Giana paused. "Yes, Mr. O'Brien?"

The expression on her face and her tone of voice told him that she hadn't expected him to question her. O'Brien felt the corner of his mouth curve upward in the beginning of a smile and he fought to conceal his amusement. "Are you delivering dinner trays to all of the other members of the staff or might I conclude that I'm the only one?"

"We thought it best if Henri prepared a tray for you, Mr. O'Brien," Giana explained.

"We, Miss Langstrom?" he asked.

"The family, Mr. O'Brien," she replied. "The housekeeper's room is reserved for members of our family tonight. We are dining together *enfamile*."

"Is there some special occasion of which I should be aware?" O'Brien asked.

Giana shook her head. "No, Mr. O'Brien."

"Just a quiet Langstrom family dinner?"

"That is correct."

"Fine." Murphy heaved a dramatic sigh in an effort to win her sympathy and gain more information. "I guess I'll have to make do with a tray. I can't change my name. O'Brien isn't Langstrom."

Giana felt a surge of guilt. O'Brien had the right to feel left out and hurt. He had the right to feel slighted. She understood how it felt to be the odd fellow out, but she didn't know O'Brien well enough to trust him—not with her life or the lives of the other members of the "family." "We regret that we must exclude you, Mr. O'Brien. We did not intend to injure your feelings or cause harm, but we have family matters to discuss and these things must remain private."

The note of distress in her voice was real and Murphy decided to let her off the hook. "I understand, Miss Langstrom," he said. "Enjoy your *family* dinner."

"And you, Mr. O'Brien."

"I'm sure the food will be excellent. But I am not a man who enjoys solitary meals," he said. "Now, if you or your lovely sister would care to join me . . ." He made the suggestion to see how she reacted.

"Thank you most kindly for the invitation," she replied. "I am sure that my lovely sister and I will be honored to join you for dinner tomorrow night in the housekeeper's room."

O'Brien laughed as Georgiana saw through his invitation and called his bluff.

Giana smiled at him, then turned and made her way down the stairs to the housekeeper's room.

Murphy was mesmerized by her smile. It was the kind of smile to which men dedicated sonnets. Murphy thought that he might easily fall in love with a smile like that, if she hadn't already caught the eye of his best friend. It didn't matter that Adam had freely relinquished his rights to all the blond, blue-eyed darlings in Scotland. O'Brien smiled. He might not want to be attracted to Valkyries and Amazons, but Adam Mc-Kendrick had grown up in a family of extraordinarily lovely women. He would never be happy with the plain, petite, timid women he chose to squire around. Once Adam realized he was hopelessly attracted to the tall, blond, blue-eyed and beautiful Miss Langstrom, he would want her back. The Bountiful Baron was nothing if not predictable.

Chapter 18

The Bountiful Baron defends the rights of women and will always rush to the side of a woman in need. It is not in his character to do otherwise.

—The Second Installment of the True Adventures of the Bountiful Baron: Western Benefactor to Blond, Beautiful, and Betrayed Women written by John J. Bookman, 1874.

O'Brien related the incident to Adam an hour or so later when they met in the library for their customary after-dinner whisky and cigars.

"George brought your dinner to your room?" Adam asked.

O'Brien nodded. "Yes. On a butler's table that she handed over to me without rattling a dish."

"You were witness to a miracle," Adam commented dryly.

O'Brien laughed. "It's a fairly commonplace miracle." He shot a pointed look at his friend. "But *I* don't affect her the way you do."

"*I* make her nervous."

"Of course you do," O'Brien said. "Because you look at her as if she's the rabbit and you're the fox."

Adam lifted an eyebrow at that.

"And she looks at you as if you're a rabbit and she's the fox."

"You've been paying attention."

"I'm a Pinkerton agent," O'Brien reminded him. "I'm supposed to pay attention."

"Yet you have no idea what the family meeting was about?" Adam poured a glass of whisky for each of them.

"I imagine it was about you," Murphy said. "But I can't

prove it. Despite my attempt to appeal to her sense of fair play."

Adam smirked. "You're losing your touch, *boyo*." He handed O'Brien a glass of whisky.

"Not quite," O'Brien retorted. "She felt sorry for me and she felt guilty about excluding me from the family gathering, but not enough to induce her to tell me what the meeting was about."

"You tried."

"Yeah, well, I tried to entice her into having dinner with me, too."

"What?"

It was Murphy's turn to smirk. "That got your attention."

"What are you talking about?"

"I'm talking about you, boyo, trying to ignore your attraction to the Valkyrie, when anyone with half an eye can see it's impossible. When's the last time you took any notice of the women I invite to dinner?"

Adam glared at his best friend. There would be hell to pay if O'Brien found out just how attracted to the Valkyrie he was. And if Murph got wind of the kisses he and George had exchanged behind the library's locked doors, he would never let him hear the end of it. "You needn't worry about it," Adam said. "I'm sure that any attraction I might be tempted to feel for the Valkyrie will die a quick death once we return to London."

"London?" Murphy choked on the mouthful of Scotch he'd just swallowed, coughing until his eyes watered.

"That got your attention." Adam reached over and pounded O'Brien on the back.

"Did you say we were going to London?" O'Brien asked in a high-pitched voice that sounded nothing like his normal baritone.

"That's what I said."

"Why?"

Adam pulled a white linen envelope from the pile of mail stacked on the corner of his desk and waved it in the air. "I received a letter from Kirstin today."

O'Brien frowned. "Is *His Bastard Lordship* up to his old tricks?"

"She doesn't say." Adam pulled the letter out of the envelope and handed it to O'Brien.

O'Brien read Kirstin's letter, then folded it and handed it back to Adam. "Any idea why she wants you to come to London?"

Adam shrugged his shoulders. "Nope. Unless she's missing us already," he joked.

"She saw us three weeks ago," Murphy said. "I wouldn't think she'd be missing us so soon." He winked at Adam. "But it's possible. I've always believed Lady Marshfeld harbors a *tendresse* for me."

Adam bit the inside of his cheek to keep from smiling as the whisky loosened O'Brien's tongue. He had always believed that O'Brien harbored a deep *tendresse* for Kirstin. Not that Kirstin would ever notice since O'Brien didn't come from a prominent family or possess either fortune or title. But O'Brien had always exhibited much more patience with Kirstin than she had ever exhibited toward him or toward anyone else. She was his sister and Adam loved her dearly. Although she was the elder by two years, Adam had always felt protective of her and Greta, her twin, and there was nothing he wouldn't do for her—including journeying to London simply because she asked him to. "You know Kirstin nearly as well as I do," Adam said. "What do you think?"

"I think I'd better call it a night." Murphy set his glass on the side table and pushed his chair back. "I've got some packing to do."

Down the hall, in the housekeeper's room, another meeting was taking place. Giana showed everyone the newspaper she'd found in McKendrick's library, passing it around the table, before she carefully folded it and laid it on the seat of one of the chairs. After everyone at the table had an opportunity to look at the article in the newspaper, Giana explained their other dilemma—that Adam McKendrick planned to open the lodge to the public—and not just any public, but the wealthy, aristocratic public. A public that could jeopardize their lives.

Giana outlined her ideas for delaying the opening of the lodge to guests until Queen Victoria arrived in Scotland for her Balmoral holiday. If they could delay the opening of the lodge long enough for the queen to reach Scotland, Giana might be able to request an audience with her godmother without risking her discovery by Victor's spies.

The trick would be to delay the opening without risking their positions. Adam McKendrick meant to make the lodge profitable, and he would not allow anyone to stop him. They ran the risk of losing their jobs if they angered the McKendrick. But losing their jobs was better than losing their lives. And the risk was worth the taking.

Giana took a deep breath, then faced her "adopted" family. Everyone had specific roles to fulfill, and each role was dependent upon the other in order that they might succeed. "We must rely on each other," Giana reminded them. "For we do not know who else to trust."

She looked at Albert. "We must be able to read McKendrick's newspapers. As butler, you are responsible for ironing them before you give them to McKendrick. But the newspapers carry stories about us and about Karolya. You must confiscate those papers."

Albert nodded in agreement.

"We cannot hazard the chance that McKendrick will read those newspapers. We must think of a way to get them before he sees the photograph of me and puts the pieces of the puzzle together. If he recognizes me, our masquerade is over." As if in answer to her prayers, Giana heard the soft sound of paper ripping. She looked down at her feet to find that Wagner had pulled the newspaper from the seat of the chair beside her and was systematically shredding it. Giana smiled. Although he was nearly three years old, Wagner still exhibited occasional bouts of puppy behavior. And one of his favorite vices was the destruction of newspapers and shoes. Her father had twice scolded her for allowing Wagner access to his office and his closets. On both occasions Wagner had chewed the toes of his boots and had created a whirlwind of destruction by ripping newspapers and a batch of state papers into hundreds of tiny pieces that littered the floor of his office. It seemed her pet wolfhound adored the taste of newsprint and of the mink oil used to polish and waterproof her father's boots.

Now Giana realized that Wagner's bad habits could aid in preventing Adam from reading his morning papers. From now on she would grant Wagner access to the newspapers.

But doing so was not without its risks. For it meant that from now on, she and Wagner would have to bear the full brunt of Adam's wrath at the dog. She sighed. Wagner spent his life protecting her. She would learn to protect him. And she would begin just as soon as this meeting concluded. There were more newspapers on the desk in the library, and she had to get her hands on all of them.

Giana turned to Max. "Do you all understand what we are asking you to do?"

Everyone nodded.

"Good," she pronounced. "We begin tomorrow."

The library smelled of expensive cigars, leather book bindings, the lemon beeswax she used on the furniture, and Adam McKendrick. She tiptoed over to his desk and carefully lifted the globe on the lamp and struck a match to the wick.

"Returning to the scene of the crime? Or for another lesson in kissing?"

The globe rattled against the base of the lamp.

"Easy," Adam cautioned. "If you break that, you're liable to set the whole place on fire." He got up from the leather sofa and walked over to Giana.

"How did you know it was me?" she asked.

Adam gently removed the lamp globe from her fingers and placed it back on the lamp. "Orange blossoms."

"Pardon?" She looked up at him from beneath the cover of her lashes.

"You smell of orange blossoms," Adam said softly. "You're the only one here who does."

"And you are the only one here who smells of sandalwood and cigars."

"You noticed." He sounded more pleased than surprised.

She glanced toward the leather sofa. "How could I not?"

Adam heard the unspoken meaning behind her question. He stepped forward and opened his arms.

She knew she should obey his earlier directive and stay away from him, knew she should stand her ground, but it was impossible to keep her distance. How could she obey his command to stay away from him when he paid it no heed? She took a step forward and found herself held firmly against his chest as he bent his head and kissed her for the second time in as many days.

And this time she had a better idea of what to expect and how to respond. She kissed him back, silently granting him permission to deepen the kiss. And Adam obeyed, tightening his embrace around her waist, pulling her closer until it was impossible to tell where he stopped and she began.

Giana sighed. His kiss was everything she remembered and more. It was soft and gentle and tender and sweet and enticing and hungry and hot and wet and deep and persuasive at once. It coaxed and demanded, asked and expected a like response, and she obliged. She parted her lips when he asked entrance into the warm recesses of her mouth. She shivered with delight at the first tentative, exploratory thrust of his tongue against hers. She met his tongue with her own, returning each stroke, practicing everything she had learned in her first lesson in kissing him and began a devastatingly thorough exploration of her own.

She grabbed a fistful of his shirt and held on, losing herself in Adam's kiss. She hadn't thought it was possible for a man's kiss to steal her heart and her soul, but she learned it was more than possible—it had happened. She wasn't just a princess anymore, but the princess in the fairy tale—sleeping for years—waiting for her handsome prince to come along and awaken her. Adam McKendrick kissed her as if she were the most desirable woman in the world and reawakened the dreams and desires Giana had put aside the night her parents were murdered.

Adam teased. He coaxed. He promised. He held her as if she belonged in his arms. And that was exactly where Giana wanted to be.

As he held her, Giana suddenly realized how great the sacrifice her position demanded of her. She was a princess of the House of Saxe-Wallerstein-Karolya. She could not marry for love if her country required that she marry for political or economic purposes. And while the Female Provision of the Karolyan Charter allowed her to marry a man of lesser rank, it did not allow her to marry a man without a hereditary title. Nor could a female heir apparent marry without the consent of her nearest male relative, and Victor would never consent to her marrying anyone other than himself. He would see her dead first. And since he had already murdered her parents, Giana had no reason to hope that Victor would miraculously decide to spare her or the man she chose to marry. Especially an American. And Adam McKendrick was an American.

She could not marry him. But she could love him. For as long as she remained at Larchmont Lodge and in Scotland, for as long as she remained on the earth, she could love him. Giana loosened her grip on his shirtfront and pressed her hand on his chest over his heart.

Adam immediately broke the kiss and stepped back. He looked down at her and sanity returned. Jesus, Joseph, and Mary! He was at it again! He was kissing a chambermaid. A long-legged, blue-eyed, blond chambermaid who worked for him. What was he thinking? What had happened to his code of honor? What had happened to his morals? What had happened to his sense of self-preservation?

"I thought I told you to stay away from me," he said hoarsely.

"You did," she whispered.

"Then what are you doing here?"

Giana didn't want to lie, so she told as much of the truth as possible. "I came for something to read."

Adam stared at her as if the words she'd uttered made no sense. "Something to read?"

Giana nodded. "Yes. That is what one generally does with books."

He frowned. "I'm aware of that."

She extended her arm to encompass the space around them. "Then you must also be aware of the fact that one generally reads in the library because it is the room where all the books are kept." She paused. "*This* room is the library at Larchmont Lodge."

Adam glanced at floor to ceiling shelves filled with books, then rolled his eyes. "So it is."

Giana laughed. "You are surprised? I am not like other chambermaids. My parents and the Countess of Brocavia value an education."

He shook his head. "Not surprised, just foolish. I didn't realize chambermaids could read." He turned away from her and began scanning the titles on the shelves, noting in passing that several of the volumes that should have been shelved in alphabetical order were not. "What were you looking to read? Milton? Shakespeare? Sir Walter Scott?"

"Newspapers," she answered, focusing on the stack on his desk.

"Newspapers?" he parroted.

"My duty may be to work as a chambermaid, but I like to improve my mind by keeping recent on events."

"Current," Adam translated automatically. "Current on events."

Giana blushed at the mistake. "Current," she repeated. "So I would like to borrow your newspapers. If you have concluded your reading of them." She held her breath.

"I haven't started my reading of them." Adam frowned again. The words sounded strange to his ears until he realized that his speech was beginning to sound like George's.

"Oh."

Adam smiled at her. "But I'm not likely to have a chance to read them before I leave—"

"Leave?" She interrupted. "You are leaving Larchmont Lodge?"

"I'm leaving for London in the morning," Adam confirmed. "So feel free." He walked over to his desk, gathered the stack of newspapers in his arms, and handed them to her. Unable to keep from touching her, Adam lifted her chin with the tip of his index finger. "Don't look so stricken, George. I received a letter from my sister in London—"

"Sister?" It was Giana's turn to repeat his words.

Adam gave a little self-deprecating laugh. "I have a sister," he told her. "Actually, I have four sisters and a mother." He gently tapped the tip of her nose with his finger. "That's right, George. I have a mother and three sisters back home in America and another sister in London. Did you think I crawled from beneath the cabbage plant fully grown?"

"What about your father?" she asked.

Adam shrugged. "I suppose he's in London, too."

"With your sister?"

"Nope," he replied. "With his wife and children."

Giana wrinkled her brow, and Adam reached over and soothed them away with the pad of his thumb. "I never knew the man. He met and married my mother, a widow with four daughters, in America, then returned to England before I was born. When he learned of my birth, he sent for us, but my mother refused to give up her farm and her independence. Several years after that, he had their marriage annulled so that he could marry someone else."

"You never saw him?"

"No."

"And he never saw you? His son and heir?"

"Not to my knowledge."

"How sad for you!" she said. "And how sad for him! I cannot imagine never knowing my father. He was"—Giana caught herself—"is a great man."

"Don't be sad on my account, George," Adam told her. "I've done all right growing up with a mother and four sisters." He grinned crookedly. "One of whom I'm going to visit." He leaned closer and brushed her forehead with his lips, breathing in the scent of orange blossoms and George. "But I'll be back before you know it." Adam took three steps back, then gently turned Giana around and headed her toward the door.

"And George—"

"Yes?"

"Try to keep your beast off my bed and out of my room while I'm gone. He ate the toe from one of my slippers this morning."

Chapter 19

The Bountiful Baron is a man who knows who he is and what he wants from life. He is as comfortable in a roomful of rough miners as he is in a mansion full of millionaires.

—THE FIRST INSTALLMENT OF THE TRUE ADVENTURES OF THE BOUNTIFUL BARON: WESTERN BENEFACTOR TO BLOND, BEAUTIFUL, AND BETRAYED WOMEN WRITTEN BY JOHN J. BOOKMAN, 1874.

The train trip to London took ten hours from Glasgow. The first leg of the journey, the trip from Glasgow to Edinburgh, was the slowest, taking nearly four hours. The second leg from Edinburgh to London aboard an express train took a mere six. They traveled in relative comfort in first-class coaches, and Adam said a silent prayer of thanks that the express train they rode had been newly fitted with steam heat.

After pulling into the London station, Adam and Murphy traveled by hansom cab to Lord Marshfeld's Mayfair town house. Although Kirstin had written to beg Adam to come to London as soon as possible, his visit would not be allowed to interrupt the Marshfelds' social calendar. Adam's arrival coincided with an evening musicale and reception hosted by Lord and Lady Marshfeld for the cream of London society. Adam and Murphy O'Brien arrived in time to bathe and dress for dinner.

"And there he is now," Kirstin Marshfeld announced as Adam descended the main staircase of the Mayfair town house and entered the drawing room. "My brother, America's famous Bountiful Baron!"

She beamed at Adam, then at her society friends as they crowded around, politely applauding his approach.

"Christ!" Adam muttered beneath his breath. "Now it's reached London."

Murphy laughed.

Adam greeted his sister, leaning down to kiss her cheek. "I see you're up to your old tricks, sister mine." He stepped back and studied her, peering past the subtle application of cosmetics and rice powder coating his sister's beautiful face. "Has His Lordship been up to his?"

Kirstin glanced at her husband, who had moved aside when Adam entered the room. "He's treated me like a queen since my return to England—especially after the Bountiful Baron stories began to appear." She turned her loveliest smile on her brother. "You are quickly becoming the toast of London nearly as famous as one of Sir Walter Scott's dashing heroes. When my friends started telling me about *The True Adventures of the Bountiful Baron: Western Benefactor to Blond, Beautiful, and Betrayed Women,* I couldn't believe it!" she gushed. "In fact, I arranged this little soirée and invited you here because I knew I was the only hostess in London who could do so. Oh, thank you, Adam, for helping to make my party such a success."

Kirstin turned to O'Brien and cast some of her reflected glory his way. "With the exception of the members of the royal family, I am now *the* premier hostess in London." Kirstin was so pleased with her success that she glowed almost as brightly as the diamonds she wore. "You should be proud of me for discovering a way to increase my stature in London society."

O'Brien winced at Kirstin's thoughtless comment and braced himself for the explosion he knew was coming.

"Proud of you?" Adam was seething, but he kept a smile plastered on his face and spoke to his sister through clenched teeth as he lifted two glasses of champagne from a passing waiter's tray. He handed one to his sister and kept one, leaving O'Brien to fend for himself. "You want me to be proud of you for tricking me into coming to London? And for worrying me half to death, just so you can increase your stature in London society?"

Kirstin squeezed out two perfect tears and allowed them to glisten on her eyelashes before she blinked them away. "I didn't work so hard to become the premiere hostess in London for my benefit alone," she told him. "I did it for Marshfeld and for you as well."

Adam took a long swallow of champagne. "Would you mind explaining how you came to that conclusion?"

"Marshfeld wishes to move in higher circles. Several members of his club have asked him to join them in forming a company to buy and sell forests and mines in other countries. As his wife, it's my duty to help him in any way I can."

"Really? In exchange for what?" Adam whispered. "His promise not to hit you again?"

"He only hit me once."

"He didn't hit you, Kirstin. He beat the hell out of you."

"He lost his temper."

"So what?" Adam demanded. "I lose my temper. Murphy loses his temper. But we don't go around beating women."

"You're not married."

"And you shouldn't be either, if you think marriage gives your husband the right to beat you."

"But it does, Adam. I belong to him."

"You belong to yourself. He belongs in hell and that's where he'll be if he touches you again in anger."

"He won't, Adam. He's changed. He promised he wouldn't hit me again." Kirstin told him what she thought he wanted to hear, but she couldn't bring herself to look her younger brother in the eyes. "He's been so nice to me since the prince began to take an interest in me."

"What prince?"

"Prince Victor of Karolya," Kirstin replied. "He and Marshfeld have business together."

"Christ, Kirstin, you're married. Don't start anything with a prince," Adam warned. "He'll be worse than an English lord. And don't think he'll give you any more consideration than Marshfeld. Because he won't."

Kirstin shrugged her shoulders. "The prince is very nice. A true gentleman." She lifted her chin a bit higher, smiled at Adam and deliberately changed the subject. "My friends are so excited to have you here. Is it true that you're planning a preview of your lodge during Regatta week?"

"Where did you hear that?" Adam demanded.

Kirstin ignored his question and asked one of her own. "Is it true? Because I'm so looking forward to seeing it."

"You won't be seeing it," he told her. "It's a gentleman's club. No women allowed."

"Adam!" She nearly stamped her foot in frustration.

"All right," he said. "I'll make an exception for you because you're my sister." He glanced at Kirstin and then over at Marshfeld. "But be careful, Kirstin. I hope Marshfeld's changed, but I don't think he has. A polecat doesn't change its stripe. The only reason he isn't hitting you is because he has more reason to fear me than he can find to hit you. But make no mistake about it, Sis, if he ever feels he no longer has reason to fear me, then you'll become the target for his anger once again."

Kirstin's eyes flashed fire at him. "Despite what you may think of me, Little Brother, I am not an imbecile. Whether you know it or not and whether you like it or not, you need these people."

Adam glanced at the ladies and gentlemen milling around the room. "I need these people?" He lifted his eyebrows at her. "Unlike Lord Marshfeld, I won't need to marry for money in order to keep myself in the manner to which I've become accustomed."

"That may be true," she shot back, "but you are in the process of renovating a hunting lodge in the wilds of Scotland. And if you want to have paying guests when the lodge opens, you need to cultivate a few of the most influential people here tonight."

"She got you there, boyo," O'Brien butted in.

"Stay out of this," Adam warned.

"And another thing . . ." She smiled brightly as Lady Carstairs walked by. "I don't need you to remind me that my husband married me for your money, Adam McKendrick. I may not have known what kind of man Marshfeld was when I married him, but I know what he is now."

Adam reached down and lifted Kirstin's chin with the tip of his finger so he could look her in the eye. "Do you love him, Kirs?"

"I did once," she admitted. "I don't now."

"Then why do you stay with him?" Adam didn't understand.

"Because he's my husband and I stood in a church and promised I would," she said. "For better or worse."

Adam smiled at the childish simplicity of her statement. "I don't believe God expects you to put your life and health at risk in order to keep a promise to a man who hasn't kept his promise to love and cherish you."

Kirstin looked stunned. As if that idea had never occurred to her. "Do you really think so?"

He nodded. "Yes, I really do."

She smiled. "Except for Marshfeld's temper, I like my life here, Adam. I dreamed about living like this all my life." She glanced around the glittering drawing room. "I won't allow him to hit me again—ever. But I will fulfill my obligation as Lady Marshfeld—including inviting the famous Bountiful Baron to my party."

"Understood." Adam nodded. "And I'll play along for tonight. But watch yourself. Don't be like the little boy who cried wolf."

Her eyes widened in surprise.

"He lied and cried wolf to get attention so many times that the villagers didn't believe him when a wolf did appear."

"I don't have to worry about that," she replied in a haughty tone of voice. "Because the Bountiful Baron never refuses a woman in need."

"Where did you hear that nonsense?"

"In the *First Installment of the True Adventures of the Bountiful Baron: Western Benefactor to Blond, Beautiful, and Betrayed Women*," she said with a smirk.

"Don't believe everything you read," Adam retorted. "Even the Bountiful Baron gets tired of being used."

"I'm your sister," Kirstin reminded him. "And you love me."

"You're my sister," Adam agreed, "and I love you dearly.

But," he teased, "I have three other sisters who all look like you. I'm not likely to miss the most troublesome one."

Adam kept his word to his sister. For the rest of the evening and long into the night, he acted the part of the perfect gentleman guest of honor. He listened to a Miss Johnstone sing arias from the latest opera and escorted a Miss Caldwell into the midnight supper. After supper he and Murphy donned smoking jackets and joined Marshfeld and a dozen other gentlemen in the smoking salon, where conversation centered on politics and business and fox hunting as well as a dash of society gossip.

As much as he hated to admit it, Kirstin had been right. He did need these people to help make the lodge a success. These men were the power behind the Crown. They were the leaders of government and industry, and Adam hoped that in a few months, they would be making Larchmont Lodge a favorite stop during the Season.

"McKendrick."

Adam glanced over as Lord Bascombe sat down beside him. "Bascombe."

"It's a pleasure to see you again," Bascombe said. "I've heard that you've decided to stay at the lodge."

"Yes."

Bascombe shuddered. "I assume you received my note and the keys to the place and that you found everything in order?"

"The keys arrived safely tucked inside your letter, and everything was exactly as you've described it. Except the staff in residence—" Adam smiled. "The staff came as a surprise."

Lord Bascombe's smile mirrored Adam's. "If there was a staff in residence, it comes as a surprise to me as well. All of the permanent staff of Larchmont Lodge except Gordon Ross was pensioned off two years ago."

"I telegraphed Ross before I arrived and asked him to begin hiring a staff," Adam told him.

"Was he successful?"

Adam nodded. "He hired his sister, Isobel, as housekeeper and her husband, Albert, as butler."

"So Isobel has returned home from Karolya," Bascombe said. "I'm glad to hear it. She's always loved the lodge. She'll take very good care of it."

"She already is," Adam replied. "Tell me, sir, how long was the lodge in your family?"

"Since the reign of Queen Anne. But it wasn't a lodge then," he said. "It was the home of Clan Moray. The earl of Moray was my grandfather."

"Your mother was Scottish?"

"Aye," Lord Bascombe said in his best Scots burr. "A Highland Scot."

"And she married an Englishman?"

"No, she married a Scot from Edinburgh whose family lands lay on both sides of the border," Lord Bascombe explained. "And what of your heritage? McKendrick is a Scottish name, is it not?"

"The surname may be Scottish, but my father was an Englishman."

"And your mother?"

"My mother was born in Sweden. She immigrated to Kansas from Stockholm as a young bride. Three years later she was a widow with four small daughters."

"Four?"

Adam chuckled. "That's right. I have four sisters. My mother is rather extraordinary. She's given birth to two sets of twin girls."

"Then Lady Marshfeld is a twin?"

"Most definitely. Astrid and Erika are the oldest, then Greta and Kirstin. Lady Marshfeld's twin lives in Kansas on a farm near my mother's."

Lord Bascombe did some quick mathematical calculations. "Your father must have died before you were born."

"No," Adam corrected. "My sisters' father was killed in a farming accident. My father met and married my mother while he was visiting America as part of his Grand Tour."

"He settled with your mother in America?"

Adam shook his head. "He returned to England before I was

born. He later dissolved his marriage to my mother and married someone else."

Lord Bascombe cleared his throat. "I'm sorry."

Adam frowned. Lord Bascombe was the second person in as many days to express his sorrow over the fact that he had grown up without a father. "Don't be," he told the older man. "As you can see, I've done quite well for myself."

"You are a credit to your father's name."

Adam met Lord Bascombe's gaze. "I didn't work to accomplish everything I've accomplished so I would be a credit to my father's name. As far as I'm concerned, he's the bastard, not me. I don't give a damn about being a credit to his name, I just want to be a credit to mine."

Lord Bascombe seemed momentarily taken aback, but he looked at Adam and nodded in agreement. "Quite right." He snipped the end of his cigar, lit it, then inhaled and slowly expelled the smoke. "Your sister, Lady Marshfeld, mentioned that you've been renovating the lodge?"

Adam welcomed the change of subject. "Nothing major," he said. "The structure was sound. The roof over the servants' quarters leaked, so we replaced it. We also rearranged the women's quarters, and we're installing plumbing and adding running water and water closets throughout the house."

Bascombe whistled. "That's quite an improvement. Tell me, Adam"—he paused—"may I call you Adam?"

Adam nodded.

"Tell me, Adam, are you planning to take up permanent residence in Scotland, or will you be returning to America?"

"I imagine I'll eventually return to Nevada in order to be closer to my mother. She's getting older, and even though my other sisters and their husbands live nearby, I don't like the idea of having an ocean and most of a continent between us."

"Might there be a chance that your mother would leave her home in Kansas and join you if you decided to remain in Scotland?" Lord Bascombe asked.

Adam gave a short laugh. "It's not very likely. She may be getting older, but my mother is as independent as ever. She'll never leave the farm. It's the only thing she's ever had that belonged solely to her. She will never give it up and I will never try to force her. If that means returning to Kansas one day to look after her, so be it."

Lord Bascombe stared at him. "Your mother has brought up a son who would make any mother and father proud." He finished his cigar, then stood up and held out his hand. "I'm very pleased to have the opportunity to get to know you, Mr. McKendrick." He grinned. "Very glad to have lost my hunting lodge to you."

Adam stood up and shook hands with Bascombe. "Likewise, Lord Bascombe." As he shook hands with the man, Adam realized that he had finally found an English lord he genuinely liked. It was only one man, but it was a start. If Lord Bascombe's friends were anything like him, the opening of the lodge would be a success. "Tell me, Lord Bascombe, don't you feel any bitterness toward me for winning the lodge that has been in your family for generations?"

Bascombe laughed. "Not at all. I wouldn't have wagered it, if I wasn't willing to part with the place. We used to spend the hunting season and Christmas there. I preferred our house in London, so I always hated going to Scotland. To me, Larchmont Lodge was always dark and cold, and aside for the hunting, grindingly boring."

"I sincerely hope I can change *that* situation," Adam said, meeting Lord Bascombe's gaze. "How do you feel about the game of golf?"

"I may live in England, but I'm a Scot as well as an Englishman. I haven't golfed in years, but I was once quite good at it."

"I'm building a golf links on the grounds of the lodge," Adam told him. "And I'd like very much to have you come up and try it out one day."

Lord Bascombe clamped Adam on the shoulder. "Adam, my lad, I'd be delighted."

Chapter 20

The Bountiful Baron always maintains his control, never betraying his anger, disappointment, or discomfort.

—The Second Installment of the True Adventures of the Bountiful Baron: Western Benefactor to Blond, Beautiful, and Betrayed Women written by John J. Bookman, 1874.

"I thought Lord Bascombe had a reputation for being an Englishman of few words," O'Brien commented as he and Adam shared breakfast just after daybreak the next morning.

"I suppose so," Adam replied, slathering a slice of freshly baked bread with jam before taking a sip of his coffee. "Why?"

"You and he spent a great deal of time huddled in the corner of the smoking salon last night talking." O'Brien attacked a rasher of bacon, four scrambled eggs, and half a loaf of bread.

Adam looked up at his friend and grinned. "Jealous?"

"Yer bloody right I'm jealous!" O'Brien retorted. "I had to listen to Marshfeld trying to impress the likes of Lord Carstairs and that dunderhead Viscount Shepherdston while you and Bascombe seemed to get on famously." O'Brien shot him a dirty look. "What was he doing? Trying to talk you into letting him buy the lodge back?"

Adam shook his head. "He doesn't want it back. He had heard I was renovating the place, and he was interested in what I was doing."

"And you gave him a detailed report," O'Brien guessed again.

"I summarized," Adam said. "We talked of many things and . . ."

"And?"

Adam gave another little laugh. "Everything I've learned about Bascombe would lead me to believe that he's smart enough to hang on to his estates."

"Yeah, that puzzles me, too."

"And as surprising as it may sound, I like him, Murph. And so will you."

"When will I have the opportunity to make his acquaintance?" O'Brien asked.

"Sooner than you might think. I invited him up to play golf as soon as we finish building the links."

"Bloody hell, Adam! We're already up to our necks in foreign servants who look down their noses at me for being Irish and you for being a provincial American, and now you want to go and invite Englishmen—the most arrogant bastards who ever walked the earth!"

Adam shrugged. "I liked Lord Bascombe. I didn't find him to be arrogant."

"Well, good for you," Murphy retorted. "But if you don't mind, I'll reserve judgment. Who was it that told his sister last night that a polecat didn't change its stripe?"

"Guilty." Adam raised his hand. "Do you think I was too hard on her, Murphy?"

"No," Murphy answered honestly. "You were a bit more blunt than you probably should have been, but Kirstin is a headstrong young woman. She was wrong to have lied in order to get you down here or to use you for her personal glory."

"She used me to show off for her friends." Adam was still angry about that. But anger was no excuse for cruelty, and he was afraid that he'd been deliberately cruel to Kirstin, who, though selfish and thoughtless, wasn't normally malicious. "I should have showed more understanding. I should have kept my temper and my patience. I know Kirstin. . . ." Adam poured himself a second cup of coffee.

"We both know Kirs—Lady Marshfeld—and we both know she could try the patience of a saint."

"Yes, but I grew up with her. I know her strengths and

weaknesses. She can't help being drawn to the cream of society any more than a moth can help being drawn to the flame. I love my sister, but that doesn't make me any less angry with her. Still, it was thoughtless of me to remind her that her husband married her for my fortune first and her charms second."

"It didn't hurt to remind her," Murphy said. "Marshfeld wears a layer of polish, but he's a savage underneath." O'Brien waited until Adam finished his coffee before asking, "Are we going to wait for Lady Marshfeld to come downstairs so you can apologize to her, or are we boarding the morning train and returning to Scotland?"

"We're going back to Scotland." Adam pushed his chair back from the table and stood up.

"Oh, well." O'Brien gave a dramatic sigh. "It's back to being your manservant instead of simply being your friend."

"I'm truly sorry about cutting your holiday short," Adam told him. "And you're welcome to stay if you wish, but I've had all of my sister's hospitality I can stand. She's already invited a half dozen of her lady friends to drop by this afternoon in order to take tea with the Bountiful Baron."

"I'm going with you." O'Brien got up from the table. "Bloody hell! Kirstin is either the most courageous or the most foolhardy woman I've ever met. I'll say that for her."

"At the moment she appears to be the most foolhardy," Adam said. "Because I'm not in a very forgiving mood."

"In order to save Lady Marshfeld's life, it would be best if we got moving before she comes down for breakfast."

"Yes," Adam agreed. He briefly scanned the front page of the newspaper, then folded the copy of the morning edition of the *Times of London* and slipped it in his coat pocket. There was no need for him to rush to read it before the other guests arriving downstairs for breakfast interrupted him. He had ten hours to read it at his leisure on the train. "That would be best."

The return train trip to Scotland took just as long as the first one. Adam did his best to catch up on the hours of sleep that he'd lost the night before, but this time the coach carried its full capacity of six passengers. Sleeping in a coach full of strangers was out of the question.

By the time they arrived at the Kinlochen station and boarded a carriage to Larchmont Lodge, Adam's head ached from hunger and lack of sleep and from inhaling the soot from the smokestack on the train, and his arse ached from too many hours seated on the hard seats of the coach.

He was in a foul temper and not a man to be trifled with. Adam stared out the windows as the carriage made its way from the station through the village of Kinlochen along the post road, where traffic forced the carriage to crawl at a snail's pace.

A throng of people crowded into the tiny village as laborers whitewashed cottage walls and rethatched leaky roofs. A group of carpenters were building fences between the village green and the golf links, and painters were painting signs advertising the local tavern, cobbler shop, bakery, greengrocer, and butcher shops.

Adam was amazed at the transformation of the village. It was bustling with commerce and life. Down the street Old McElreath advertised golfing clubs and gentleman's golfing clothing, and village boys signed their names to slate boards posted beside the stables and the railway station listing themselves as caddies for the golf links at Larchmont Lodge.

Adam nudged O'Brien's ankle with his foot. "Wake up and look at this."

Murphy sat up. "It's the village."

Adam leaned forward. "Those workers painting the front doors of those cottages look familiar. Are they ours?"

O'Brien nodded. "They're all yours."

"From the lodge?"

"Aye." O'Brien smiled. "Didn't you know? Crews of laborers come to the village to work every day."

"On whose orders?" Adam demanded.

"Yours, I thought." O'Brien read the surprise in Adam's face. "Gordon organizes work crews every morning. I thought you knew and approved." Murphy shrugged. "The good Lord knows the lodge has made a difference in this town."

"The lodge hasn't opened yet," Adam reminded him. "Who is financing this?"

"They are." O'Brien nodded toward the men and women in the village. "Now that they have work, they have money to spend, and they see the potential for new business once the lodge opens. But no one wants to holiday in a poor village with nothing to offer. Like you, the villagers of Kinlochen are gambling on the belief that the lodge is going to be a huge success."

"If it ever opens," Adam grumbled. "It's no wonder we're behind on our renovations. Our workers have been renovating everything else."

"Aye," Murphy agreed, "and it's worth it." He shrugged. "Besides, it all belongs to you. The village and the lodge."

He knew it was true, but Adam didn't want to hear O'Brien sing the villagers' praises, or admit that he hadn't given any thought to the village that accompanied the lodge or its commercial potential. All he could think about was crossing the threshold of the lodge and climbing the stairs to his bedchamber, where he planned several hours of uninterrupted sleep.

But opening the front door of the lodge and stepping over the threshold was like stepping into a world gone mad.

The lodge had undergone as much of a transformation in the last twenty-four hours as the village. Workmen were neatly dressed, their clothes pressed and their boots cleaned and polished. They doffed their hats to the maids when they walked by and a chorus of *please*s and *thank-you*s and *pardon me*s echoed throughout the building. It was as if the rough-and-tumble laborers had all been magically transformed into choirboys.

And that wasn't all. Albert greeted them at the door, relaying the news, in a combination of broken English and French, that the plasterers were working on the ceiling of the main salons and that afternoon tea had been moved to the library. Afternoon tea for whom? As far as he knew, the lodge wasn't yet opened for guests. Adam looked to O'Brien for answers, but Murphy looked as bewildered as he was.

"Who is taking tea in the library?" Adam asked.

"The women," came Albert's reply.

"What women?" Adam asked again.

"All of them." Albert turned and led the way. "Follow me, sir."

He hadn't planned to go to the library until after his nap, but curiosity was a force stronger than sleep. Adam had to see it with his own eyes. And seeing was believing because the thing he had sought to avoid in London—a late-afternoon tea party—was in progress, and every maid in the house and every woman from the village looked to be in attendance. And this was no ordinary tea. His sanctuary, his library, had been turned into a ladies' salon where Brenna arranged the hair of a woman seated on the leather sofa while Isobel and George and eight other women sat in nearby chairs plying their needles on several baskets of mending, exchanging recipes and offering advice on fashion and the latest cosmetics.

The remnants of afternoon tea littered the massive library table—at least he thought it was the library table. Covered, as it was, in white linen, crystal and china, and an overflowing vase of flowers, it was difficult to tell.

Adam removed his hat and wiped his eyes with the back of his hand. "Am I seeing what I think I'm seeing?" he asked O'Brien, who had followed him in the front door and now stood at his elbow viewing the scene. After almost no sleep and ten hours on the train, Adam was too tired to judge.

"I'm not sure," Murphy admitted.

"What does it look like to you?"

"It looks like every man's fantasy. Or every man's nightmare." He frowned. "It's a hen party."

"I can see that," Adam growled, "but what the devil is it doing in here?"

"Good afternoon, sir," Isobel greeted cheerfully as she saw Adam and Murphy hovering in the doorway. "Have you just come from the station?"

"Yes," Adam replied.

"Have you had your afternoon tea?" she asked.

"No."

"Would you like to join us? There's plenty."

Adam glanced at the tea table. There was indeed plenty of delicate little sandwiches and light, buttery scones and an array of little cakes and pastries to make a man's mouth water. "No, thank you," he answered, but his stomach growled, loudly betraying him.

Isobel got to her feet. "Here, sir, let me make you a plate," she offered.

Adam shook his head. "I'm going up to my room to lie down until supper, but before I do, I'd like to know the occasion for your gathering and why you invaded—uh, selected—the library."

"The workmen are replastering the ceilings in the main salons," the housekeeper answered.

"What about your room?" Adam demanded. "Isn't the housekeeper's room generally used for the purpose of entertaining staff?"

"Aye, sir," she confirmed. "But the workmen are wallpapering in my room."

"On whose orders?"

"Yours, sir."

"Mine?" Adam was genuinely surprised.

"Aye." Isobel smiled at him. "You told me to do whatever was necessary to make the housekeeper's room my own. I decided to wallpaper."

"I told you that weeks ago."

"Aye, you did," she agreed, "and I decided to wallpaper."

"When? Yesterday?" Adam was trying hard not to raise his voice or lose what remained of his temper.

"It seemed like a perfectly reasonable solution," Isobel told him. "After all, the plasterers were going to be working anyway."

Adam didn't understand the logic in that. What did plasterers have to do with paperhangers? He tried again. "Would you mind explaining the occasion?" He gestured toward the room full of women. There were two new faces, but he recognized the others, having met them when they were hired as kitchen helpers, scullery maids, and laundresses.

"There is no occasion."

"I don't understand," he admitted, looking to O'Brien for

help. But Murphy simply shrugged his shoulders as if to say the answer to the riddle lay somewhere beyond his reach.

"We take tea every afternoon, sir."

Adam was nonplussed by Isobel's reply, and O'Brien fought to keep from snickering. Adam elbowed him in the ribs. "I suppose you do. I just didn't realize everyone did." He nodded toward the two women he didn't recognize. "I don't recall meeting those two ladies."

"You've a good memory for faces, sir." Isobel was impressed. "You haven't met them yet, but they are Martha on the left and Sally on the right." The women got up from their seats and bobbed polite curtsies.

"And what do they do here?" he asked.

"I hired them to help Giana."

Adam automatically turned his gaze on George. She glanced up at him for the merest second before returning her attention to the embroidery in her lap. "I see."

"There is quite a bit for a chambermaid to do," Isobel reminded him. "Giana couldn't do it all alone, and besides . . ." She lowered her voice to a whisper. "I thought it might be a good idea to let someone else dust the breakable items and handle the china."

"Leaving George free to do the hard physical labor . . ." Adam didn't want to admit the idea bothered him as much as it did. But there was no getting around it. He couldn't stand to think of George laboring to clean his house. He'd rather have her break a fortune in china than to have her scrubbing the floors and cleaning fireplace grates.

"I assure you that Giana can manage it," Isobel hastened to reassure him. "She is tall and quite capable."

"What of Brenna?" he demanded.

"You just won't let go of that bone, will you?" Murphy hissed.

Isobel looked at him in surprise and replied, "Brenna is a lady's maid."

"Who arranges the hair and clothing of the other female employees."

"She must keep up her skills else she will be out of practice," Isobel said.

Adam narrowed his gaze at Brenna. How he had ever thought he could prefer her to George simply because of her height and the color of her hair and eyes was beyond him. But she was safe. He knew that. With Brenna, there would be no surprises. One day would be very much like the next. All safe and quiet and dull. Adam exhaled. There was no doubt that she would be the better choice for him if all he wanted was safe and quiet, if all he wanted was a woman who would always defer to his greater knowledge and better judgment. Brenna was shy and retiring, the kind of woman who would never question his choices or push him to greater accomplishments.

Brenna Langstrom was all he'd ever thought he wanted in a helpmate, yet he wasn't the slightest bit attracted to her. She was pretty enough, in a quiet colorless way, while George sparkled with light and color—despite the fact that he'd never seen her in anything except black and white. What was it about George? What was it about her that made him go against his better judgment and want her? She was everything he'd always said he didn't want in a woman, and yet, she was everything he'd always admired. Christ, but he was tired. Adam raked his hand through his hair. Too tired to be debating with Mrs. L. or contemplating the mysterious attraction he felt for George. "Heaven forbid that Brenna get out of practice," he muttered, "even though there's no lady in residence to worry about."

Adam hadn't realized he'd spoken loud enough for Isobel to hear until she answered. "There will be a lady in residence one day, and I'm sure that lady will be pleased with Brenna's skills."

"Of course she will," Adam replied. "How could Brenna displease anyone?" *Except me.* "Now, if you'll excuse me, ladies, I'm going up to my room before I say anything more." His stomach growled again, louder this time.

"What about tea?" Isobel asked. "Shall I have O'Brien take you a plate after he deposits your luggage?"

Adam glanced over at Murphy who was carrying both traveling valises and who was every bit as tired and hungry as he was. "O'Brien has been traveling just as long as I have today. Please see that plates are sent up for both of us."

"I'll send Martha and Sally up directly."

Adam almost requested that she send George but thought better of it and changed his mind. There was no point in embarrassing George if she did break more china. And no point in tempting fate. He was tired and his defenses were weak. He might not be able to keep from kissing her if he had her alone in his room.

"Fine." He backed out of the library and turned toward the stairs with Murphy following close on his heels. Max caught up to them as Adam and O'Brien reached the marble entrance hall.

Adam groaned.

"Good afternoon, sir," Max acknowledged Adam, but typically ignored the fact that O'Brien was standing directly beside him.

"Please, not now, Max. I haven't had more than a couple of hours' sleep since I left here and I'm on my way up to bed."

"Understood, sir," Max empathized. "I simply wanted to inform you that you've nothing pressing on your desk to worry about. I've taken the liberty of handling your correspondence—"

"You what?"

"I've taken the liberty of handling your correspondence with the exception of the personal letter from Lady Marshfeld, of course, since you took care of that one on your own," Max explained.

"You're reading my mail?" Adam was shocked by the idea.

"Of course, sir. And I posted the letters you left on your desk. That is one of the duties of a private secretary. I've separated it for you into matters that must be handled right away and matters that can wait. I've also taken the liberty of rearranging your social calendar and weeding through the various requests for funds from myriad charities. I've made a list of the ones with which I am familiar and the ones I deem most worthy. We shall have to go over the others together—until I become more familiar with your activities and your routine correspondence." Max outlined the tasks he'd performed in Adam's absence, omitting the fact that he hadn't posted the advertisements Adam had written for all of the major American and European newspapers. "Is there anything else you require of me before you retire for your nap?"

Adam frowned. He hadn't required anything of Max to begin with. And he certainly hadn't required that Max imply that he was a doddering old fool who needed a nap every afternoon. He didn't need anyone to manage his correspondence or arrange his social calendar or tend to his charitable requests. "We'll discuss it later."

"Quite so, sir." Max clicked his boot heels together and bowed before withdrawing from the entrance hall.

"What do you make of that?" O'Brien asked as they climbed the stairs leading to their bedrooms.

Adam took his traveling valise out of Murphy's hands. "I can't make sense of it," he admitted. "This is either a bad dream or the whole damned place has turned upside down."

Chapter 21

A Princess of the Blood Royal of the House of Saxe-Wallerstein-Karolya is always a gracious guest. She never seeks to cause her host or hostess any discomfort. She never makes unusual demands or allows any members of her retinue to do so.

—Maxim 483: Protocol and Court Etiquette of Princesses of the Blood Royal of the House of Saxe-Wallerstein-Karolya, as decreed by His Serene Highness, Prince Karol V, 1641.

Downstairs in the library Giana patiently continued sewing as she mentally counted the minutes. She heard Max waylay McKendrick and O'Brien in the marble entrance hall on their way to the stairs and had seen Max walk by minutes later on his way to the room he had appropriated as his office—the room that had once belonged to the bailiff who oversaw the estate. "One thousand thirteen, one thousand fourteen, one thousand fift—"

"Miss Langstrom!"

His roar seemed to shake the rafters, echoing as it did off the marble floors. Giana expected it to rattle the windows in their casements, and knock the fresh plaster from the ceilings.

She looked up and met Brenna's gaze. Giana nodded and Brenna dropped her hairbrush and ran out of the library and across the marble entrance hall. They had worked out a plan. Unless he was specific in his request for her, Giana had decided that Brenna should answer the call. Adam McKendrick had instructed her to stay away from him on more than one occasion, and that was exactly what Giana intended to do for as long as she could.

"Not you!" Adam's shout stopped Brenna at the foot of the stairs. "The other Miss Langstrom. George!"

Giana set her embroidery aside and rose from her chair.

"Take this." Isobel thrust a plate full of sandwiches and tea cakes into her hand. "It might just soothe the savage beastie." Giana glanced down at the plate in her hand. While she appreciated the gesture, she knew it would take more than a few sandwiches and cakes to soothe this savage beastie, but she did not know what that something was.

She met Brenna just inside the doorway of the library and smiled her thanks for Brenna's willingness to beard the lion in his den, then straightened her spine, lifted her chin, and stepped outside the library door. Giana's heels clicked against the marble floor as she crossed the entrance and began the climb up the stairs.

Adam took the plate out of her hand as soon as she reached the landing and pointed through the open door. "What is the meaning of this?"

Giana winced as she peeked inside the doorway. Wagner had been lying in the center of Adam's bed. That much was clear. The pillows and the bedclothes bore the impression of his head and body, and so did the shredded remains of a stack of London newspapers he'd been lying on, but Wagner was nowhere to be found. "What is the meaning of what?"

Adam set the plate on the bedside table and grabbed a square of sandwich. Rather than talk with his mouth full, he shot George a meaningful look that told her he knew she wasn't that stupid. "Try again." He motioned her into the room.

"Wagner?"

"I thought I told you to keep him out of my bed."

An unspoken "or else" hung on the end of his sentence, and Giana decided to challenge it. "Does this mean you are going to flame us?"

"*Flame* us?" Adam wrinkled his brow in frustration. "What the devil does that mean?"

"If you are unhappy with our work, then you must flame us."

Understanding dawned. "I'm not unhappy with your work,"

he told her. "And I'm not going to *fire* you. I just want you to control the beast and keep him out of my bed."

Now that she knew her position and the positions of her "family" were secure, Giana decided to overlook the fact that Adam insulted her by referring to her pet as a beast. "Wagner is not in your bed."

"He was."

She surveyed the room and its furnishings. "Where is he?"

"He was sleeping like a baby with his head on my pillow, his body sprawled across my bed and with all four feet in the air until I shouted. Then he disappeared."

"He hates loud noises," Giana said. She knelt and looked under the bed.

"He *dislikes* loud noises," Adam corrected. "He hates me."

"Oh, no, he likes you." She looked behind the bedroom door and beneath the writing desk.

"That's debatable." Adam snorted. "What isn't debatable is the fact that he continues to like my bed. Tell me, George, did you sleep here in my absence?"

"No, of course not!"

"Just checking." He grinned. "I thought maybe you missed me."

"I did miss—" Giana could have bitten out her tongue for that slip. Well, she decided, there was nothing to do except brazen it out. "I may have missed you," she clarified. "But not enough to sleep in your bed while you were away."

"Just enough to allow Wagner to do it for you," he accused.

The dog whimpered at the sound of his name, and Giana followed the sound to the open door of the armoire. Wagner lay huddled in the bottom. "Wagner?"

He scrambled to his feet, sat up, and thrust his nose through a row of Adam's dark wool suits, peeking out at them. Giana couldn't help but smile, and even though he struggled hard to hide it, she thought she might have caught a shadow of a smile on Adam's handsome face.

"I did not allow Wagner into your room," she answered truthfully, gently caressing the top of Wagner's head. She had instructed Isobel to let Wagner into Adam's room. "It is all right, boy, Adam did not mean to frighten you."

"Adam *did* mean to frighten him, if it meant getting him off my bed," Adam corrected. "Adam is dead on his feet and not at all inclined to sleep with a hundred-fifty-pound canine." He winked at George. "Now, Wagner's master is another story all together. . . ."

Giana bit her bottom lip, unable to decide what he meant.

"Never mind," Adam said. "Just don't let him in here again."

"I did not let him into your room," Giana repeated.

"If you didn't let him into my room, how do you explain the tiny bits of newspaper scattered all over it?" he demanded. "I distinctly recall giving the newspapers to you because you asked to read them."

"I returned the newspapers to your bedchamber after I finished reading them."

Adam watched her as she answered his questions. He knew she was telling the truth because she was so transparent; it was impossible for her to lie. "Why here? Why not the library?"

"I did not finish reading them until late this morning." Giana found it hard to concentrate on his questions or on her answers. She would not be surprised if she heard herself blurting out the truth at any moment because she found herself watching his mouth as he formed his words. Watching. Wondering how it would feel to kiss him again. Wondering if he wanted to kiss her again as much as she wanted him to. "I brought the papers here and placed them on your writing desk because Is—my mother—was readying the library for afternoon tea. He was not in here then, but any one of many people could have let him in," she said. "It is easier to keep Wagner out of your bedchamber than it is to keep him away from the tea table."

"Is it? I hadn't noticed."

She knew she deserved it, but still, his sarcasm cut like the shards of china that had sliced her hand. Giana bowed her head and stared down at the tip of her shoes. "I was wrong," she said. "I am sorry." And she was. Sorry she had to deceive him. Sorry she had allowed Wagner to destroy his property even though the property was only a bundle of newsprint that could jeopardize her future. "I am not the only person who comes into your room during the day."

"You are from now on."

Giana didn't answer or acknowledge that she'd heard what he'd said. She kept her gaze on the floor.

"Hey." Adam reached over and lifted her chin with the tip of his index finger. "I'm sorry, too."

This time she looked at him, and Adam saw the shimmer of tears in her eyes.

"Don't cry," he said softly.

"Do not be impractical," she admonished. "Everyone knows that pri—people in my position never cry."

"Oh, really? Why not?" *Impractical?* Adam searched for a word that meant "impractical" as he wiped a tear off her cheekbone with the pad of his thumb. *Silly. Do not be silly.*

"Because we cannot afford to," she answered. "Besides, crying does not change anything."

"Sometimes it makes you feel better," he told her.

"It does not," she replied. "It makes your eyes and your throat burn, stuffs up your nose, and makes your head ache."

"Sometimes it makes you feel better inside. And how do you know so much about what it does on the outside if people like you never cry?"

Giana gave him her haughtiest, most regal look. "I did not say that I had never cried," she said. "Like everyone else, I cried as a child. And I remember how uncomfortable it was and how little it solved. That is, of course, why I no longer do it."

Adam caught another teardrop with his thumb and nodded. "Of course. It's why I no longer do it, either." He made a face at her and Giana laughed. "There, that's better."

"Is it?" She leaned toward him.

He rubbed his thumb across her mouth. He wanted to kiss her. He wanted very much to kiss her, but Adam was learning just how dangerous to his peace of mind that could be. He had to stop this madness before he was lost. "Yes. I'd like to oblige you, but . . ." Adam shook his head. "At the moment I'm not much of a companion, much less a lover. . . ."

Giana opened her mouth into a perfect circle of surprise.

"It's all right," he told her. "You don't have to say or do

anything. And you don't have to worry about me. I'm not going to do anything. Now, just take Wagner and go."

She tried. She honestly tried. But after a quarter hour of commanding and coaxing and pleading, even bribing with morsels from Adam's plate, Giana was forced to admit failure. Wagner, normally the most obedient and faithful of companions, disobeyed and disappointed her. He simply would not come out of the bottom of Adam's wardrobe. Finally Giana leaned into the opening and attempted to lift Wagner out of his cozy den.

"Oh, no, you don't!" Adam placed an arm around her waist and pulled her back against him. "He's too big and heavy. You'll hurt yourself." Although he'd only meant to prevent her from hurting herself, Adam enjoyed the way his arm pressed against the underside of her breast and the way her bottom fit snugly against his front. They were like spoons stacked atop each other with all the dips and curves and lengths fitting perfectly, complimenting each other.

"Then you must try—"

"Not me." Adam reluctantly let go of Giana, breaking contact as he stepped away and shook his head. "This may seem cowardly to you, but I'm not risking my back or any other part of my anatomy on him." He stared down into the dog's soulful brown eyes. With his big head, expressive eyes, and jeweled velvet collar, Wagner didn't look dangerous, but they weren't called wolfhounds for nothing, and anything that could chase and kill a wolf deserved respect.

"What shall we do?" she asked.

Adam could think of dozens of things he would like to do—all of them with her as a willing partner, but those weren't the kind of suggestions Giana had in mind. Unfortunately for him, they were the only kinds of expressions that sprang to mind. He had no previous experience with removing a recalcitrant dog from a wardrobe, and Adam was quite sure he could do without gaining any. "Leave him where he is."

"Pardon?"

Adam smiled. "You heard correctly. I suggested that we leave him where he is for the night."

"You are certain?"

"Not at all," he replied. "But as long as he stays put, he's not going to bother me tonight." He smothered a yawn with his hand, then turned Giana and headed her toward the bedroom door. "Good night, George."

Giana glanced at the window. It was still light outside.

Adam saw the direction of her gaze. "I intend to sleep through supper and, hopefully, the remainder of the night." He opened the bedroom door and steered her though it. "Bring my breakfast, a pot of coffee, and the morning newspaper when you come to get the dog."

"He goes out quite early," she warned.

"As long as he goes out," Adam said. "And, George, if he does any damage in there—"

Unwilling to listen to any more threats, real or implied, Giana cut him off. "I know," she answered. "Do not concern yourself. If he does any damage, I will pay."

Chapter 22

A Princess of the Blood Royal of the House of Saxe-Wallerstein-Karolya must always be an asset to her name and to her house. She must never do anything that would bring scandal or ruin upon them.

—Maxim 10: Protocol and Court Etiquette of Princesses of the Blood Royal of the House of Saxe-Wallerstein-Karolya, as decreed by His Serene Highness, Prince Karol I, 1432.

Giana arrived at Adam's bedroom at half-past five the following morning carrying a butler's table containing his breakfast, a pot of coffee, and one slightly scorched morning newspaper. She was grateful that Karolya's missing princess was no longer front-page headline news but had been relegated to a small column on page three. Giana had ironed it herself, putting into practice the skill she had learned so long ago in Karolya. It had been seven years since she'd earned her Sixteenth, and she was quite relieved to know that she only had to iron one paper and to burn only one small section of it. She was also grateful that she was up before the other members of her household. The only members of the staff she had to face were the kitchen staff and Mrs. Dunham, and Henri, who now shared the responsibility of breakfast. If they wondered why she had requested a breakfast tray, they didn't mention it, and Giana thought that might be because the pot of coffee made the answer quite clear. Only three people at Larchmont Lodge drank coffee instead of tea, and those three were: Adam McKendrick, Murphy O'Brien, and Henri Latour. She wasn't taking the chef breakfast in bed, so she could only be taking it to McKendrick or O'Brien. And since most everyone in the household had heard McKendrick shouting for her yesterday afternoon, he was the man most likely to have made such a demand of her.

Giana shifted the butler's table to one hip, then tapped on the door. She tapped a second time, and when there was no answer on the third knock, she turned the knob and eased the door open and discovered that Adam McKendrick was still asleep.

And that he did not sleep in a nightshirt. Or anything else.

His broad back, baked a golden color by the sun, was bare. And Giana wanted to reach out and touch him—to place her palm against his shoulder to see if his skin was as smooth and as warm as it looked.

She glanced around the room. Adam's shirt, waistcoat, jacket, and trousers were draped over the back of the wooden chair of the writing desk and his hat crowned the top of the pile. Giana tiptoed into the room and carefully set the butler's table on the floor beside the nightstand.

One of his tall black leather boots lay beside the cast-iron bootjack where he'd tugged it off. The other lay on the floor beside the footboard of the bed. The toe of that boot, while essentially undamaged, was a bit less glossy than its counterpart and sported recent scuff marks that Giana was certain would match the teeth of the wolfhound that lay curled atop the covers beside Adam.

Giana picked up his boot. There was no disguising the scuff marks on the toe. No hiding the fact that they were there or that Wagner had made them, but she might be able to keep Adam from noticing for a while longer. She studied the boot for a moment, then began polishing the toe with the hem of her apron. The musky odor of mink oil used to waterproof the boots filled her nostrils. She finished polishing and set the boot down beside its mate only to find that the pristine condition of the leather of the right boot made the scuff marks on the left one more noticeable. So Giana put the boot back where she'd found it, placing it on its side on the floor near the foot of the bed. There was nothing to be done about it except to pay for the damage. She unbuttoned the top buttons of her dress, then turned her back and reached inside her corset cover and pulled at a piece of jewelry stitched inside. She thought she had grabbed one of the diamond earrings she had sewn there, but what she pulled out was a gold ring set with a huge black pearl from the South Seas and surrounded by small diamonds. Giana sighed. She had always admired the ring. As a child, she had stood before the portrait of her ancestor, Princess Rosamond, and practiced her counting by counting the circle of diamonds. There were sixteen of them.

Acting quickly, before she could find reason to stop herself, Giana reached down, righted Adam's boot, then dropped the ring inside, shaking it down to the toe, before returning the boot to its place on the floor. Feeling the hot sting of tears, she bit her lip to keep from crying. It was done. She had paid for Wagner's crime and the part she had played in it with a small part of her heritage. She hated that it was one of her favorite parts, but she cared far more for Wagner than she did for a pearl ring. Any pearl ring. And Wagner could not help it.

He was a dog. He could not help being attracted to the scent of mink any more than a bee could help being attracted to the scent of nectar. Any more than she could help being attracted to the man in the bed. Giana sighed. She knew she should not stare at him—especially when he slept, but she simply could not deny herself the pleasure.

He lay in the center of the bed. The cotton sheet draped across his lean hips and over his firm buttocks was the only thing covering him, and the white fabric drew her gaze back to the bed. Lying there, he appeared much younger than he did when he was awake. His hair was tousled in sleep, his jaw shadowed by the stubble on his face. His thick dark eyelashes fanned against his face. But there was nothing boyish about him. The tiny wrinkles marking the corners of his eyes, the powerful muscles of his shoulders and back, and the ridge of a long-healed scar, proclaimed him fully grown. Adam McKendrick was a gloriously healthy man in the prime of his life, and although it seemed to Giana that sleep should have given him a harmless appearance, the opposite was true. He looked dangerous instead. Dangerous to her peace of mind. More dangerous than she'd ever imagined.

Giana bit her bottom lip and clenched her fists to keep from giving in to the wicked, almost overwhelming urge to throw off her clothes and climb into bed beside him. Her whole body quaked with the effort to control it. Heat rushed to her face. Her lips ached to be kissed, and her body begged to be touched.

She wanted to watch him open his eyes, to see those blue eyes darken with desire to a deep indigo. She wanted to feel him run his hands over her naked breasts and on the smooth skin of her thighs the way he had that day on the leather sofa in the library.

Until this moment she had not realized that the desire to hold someone and to be held in return could be so powerful. Living as she had in a sheltered world, she had not understood that such desires truly existed. But now she knew. Now she recognized the urgency—the desire—the need to be with a man. And not just any man, only this one. Only Adam McKendrick. The man who had filled her with these desires. The man she loved.

Loved. Giana shook her head, trying to push the unbidden, unwanted thought aside. Not love. She could not be in love with Adam McKendrick. Princesses did not marry for love. They married for the good of their families or their countries. And she knew that better than most, for she was a princess hiding from the man who wanted her in his bed or dead. Either one, so long as he gained possession of the Karolyan State Seal.

Adam McKendrick was a self-made man. An American. She could not be foolish enough to fall in love with Adam McKendrick. It was desire, she told herself. What she felt for Adam was desire, pure and simple. Lust. Healthy, animal lust. But if that were true, she asked herself, why was it that she had never desired other men, handsomer men, nicer, more suitable men? Giana suddenly began to quake for real. When had she taken the tumble? When had she fallen in love with Adam McKendrick?

"Wagner!" She whispered his name as she quietly made her way around the bed and tugged on his collar. "Time to go outside."

The wolfhound opened his eyes, stretching and yawning, as he stepped off the bed and onto the floor, where he promptly trotted over to the boot lying near the foot of the bed, sniffed, and then pawed at it.

"No!" she hissed.

"George?" Adam murmured her name.

Giana's heart seemed to catch in her throat at the sound of it. Her heart increased its beat, and it seemed that she could hear it rapidly telling her to: follow her heart, follow her heart, follow her heart . . . "Yes?"

He wrinkled his nose against the pillow. "Is that coffee I smell?"

She smiled. "Yes. I brought your breakfast, a pot of coffee, and the newspaper just as you instructed."

"Where are you going?"

"I must take Wagner out before he lifts his leg and christens your bedpost."

Adam rolled onto his back. "Are you coming back to join me?"

Giana watched in fascination and disappointment as the sheet rolled with him, keeping the mysterious part of him covered while allowing a tantalizing view of an arrow of dark hair boldly pointing the way toward the part of him that stood out against the sheet. "Do you want me to?"

He opened his eyes and smiled at her. "I don't think there is any doubt as to what I want. Do you?" He glanced down at the sheet barely covering the lower half of his body

Giana blushed as she followed his gaze. "I am not sure."

Adam frowned. "Not sure you understand what I want or not sure you want the same thing?"

"I do not understand what it is you want exactly," she answered truthfully, "but I know it is something I should enjoy."

"How do you know that?" Adam teased.

Her answer was low and husky, barely above a whisper, "Because I enjoy your kisses."

His erection throbbed beneath the thin sheet, and Adam found himself fighting to maintain control. "Then put the dog outside and come over here so we can share a few kisses and see where they lead. . . ."

Giana bit her bottom lip as she stared at the dark arrow beneath his navel.

"Don't worry," he soothed. "We can start with kisses. And then, I'm open for suggestions."

"Then I will return." She snapped her fingers and Wagner trotted to her side. Giana glanced at the boot near the foot of the bed. The toe was pointing in the opposite direction from the way she had left it, but the ring was still secreted inside.

"Hurry back," Adam replied as he stretched his arms over his head, then yawned, and lay back against the pillows—pillows that carried the faint odor of musk. Adam raked his hand through his hair. No wonder he had awakened hard and as randy as a billy goat! It wasn't enough that he spent the night dreaming erotic dreams filled with images of George in various stages of undress and various stages of arousal. Awakening to the mingled scents of musk, orange blossoms, and coffee were practically guaranteed to do the trick. "And we'll discuss our options and decide the best way for me to negotiate a treaty with the beast."

"You can start by not calling him the beast."

"He's a dog," Adam said. "He doesn't know the difference."

"*I* know the difference." She favored Adam with her mysterious princess smile, then walked to the door. "And he recognizes the tone of your voice."

"Hey," Adam complained. "Aren't you forgetting something?"

"Your breakfast and your coffee are on the table beside your bed."

"And the newspaper?"

"It is on the tray beside your plate." She nodded toward the butler's table.

"You carried that all the way up here by yourself?"

"Yes," she answered proudly. "And your plate and your cup and saucer remain in the single piece."

Are still in one piece. He translated the idiom automatically. "Thank you."

"You are welcome." Giana opened the bedroom door.

"I trust the dog stayed in the wardrobe and behaved himself

last night." Adam knew he was pushing his luck when Giana didn't answer right away.

"George?"

"Wagner, come!" She issued the command, then hurried through the door and quickly closed it behind her.

Adam groaned at her choice of words. He listened for the sound of footsteps and of canine toenails clicking against the floor, but there was nothing until he heard her voice.

"We regret the damage to your boot," she said softly. "He was attracted to the mink oil. We hope you will accept our apology and the payment."

"What happened to my boot?" Adam practically leaped out of bed and across the floor to the door. "George!"

Giana and Wagner were halfway down the corridor when she glanced back over her shoulder and saw Adam McKendrick standing in the door of his bedchamber in all his naked male glory.

Giana swallowed the lump in her throat. The sight of Adam McKendrick standing in front of her as naked as the day he was born practically took her breath away. Her imagination hadn't done him justice. He was beautiful! As beautiful as the statue the cardinals in the Vatican had draped upon her family's last state visit.

She hurried down the stairs to keep from flinging herself at him.

"George!"

She began counting, not daring to look back until she heard his bedroom door slam and open again. "Five, six, seven, eight . . ."

"Wagner! You beast! These boots are handmade! They cost three hundred dollars a pair!"

But Wagner had already disappeared, bounding down the stairs, through the kitchen door, and out into the garden, startling laborers as he hurried to escape Adam's wrath and to relieve himself by the garden gate.

Chapter 23

The Bountiful Baron is a proud man. A confident man. A bold man. Sure of his every move.

—The First Installment of the True Adventures of the Bountiful Baron: Western Benefactor to Blond, Beautiful, and Betrayed Women written by John J. Bookman, 1874.

She wasn't coming back.

It didn't take three quarters of an hour to let the dog out.

Adam arrived at that brilliant conclusion three quarters of an hour or so after he last saw George hurrying down the stairs as if she feared a lunatic was after her. And the truth was that he had behaved like one. Shouting at her. Shouting at that blasted dog. Standing in the corridor outside his bedroom at six in the morning shouting to wake the dead while wearing nothing but a scowl on his face and his pride of the morning. Good God! How could he blame her for not coming back? He wouldn't if he were in her shoes.

"Adam?"

He looked up to see O'Brien opening his door.

"I knocked but you didn't answer."

"Sorry," Adam muttered a halfhearted apology. "I didn't hear you."

O'Brien chuckled. "That much is obvious." He set the tray he carried on the foot of the bed. "I suppose you've got a lot on your mind. I brought fresh coffee."

"Thanks." He held out his empty cup and saucer, and O'Brien filled it from the fresh pot.

"You're in trouble, my friend." O'Brien didn't waste time getting to the point or mince his words once he got there. "*She's* trouble."

"Yes, I know," Adam agreed.

"The other one would be better for you," Murphy continued. "And she's more your type—the kind of woman you've always said you wanted."

Adam squeezed his eyes shut, then opened them again and looked around the room as if hoping to find it had miraculously changed. He gave a derisive laugh. "Christ! You're not telling me anything I don't already know. There's no doubt that Brenna would be much better for me. Better than George in every way. Less talkative. Less stubborn. Less complicated. Less everything. What I wouldn't give to be able to take Brenna to bed and scratch the itch I'm feeling! What I wouldn't give to get it out of my system. . . ." He let his words trail off as he turned toward the door. "Did you hear that?"

O'Brien shook his head.

Adam shrugged. "I thought I heard something."

O'Brien walked to the door. It was ajar. He pushed it shut, leaning against it, waiting for the latch to click into place. But it didn't click into place. It couldn't because there was a fold of black satin caught between the door and the jamb. He eased the door open and nudged the fabric out of the way, then stealthily pulled the door completely closed. "The little lady's maid, Brenna, is very easy on the eyes."

"She is that," Adam agreed.

"She's petite and ladylike and she has curves in all the right places. Any man would be pleased to have her on his arm."

"I can't argue with that."

"She would make you a much better wife than the Amazon."

"If I were looking for a wife," Adam pointed out. "Brenna is the type of woman I'd want. . . ."

O'Brien gave a low, appreciative whistle to cover the sound of a sudden, sharp intake of breath and the sound of footsteps hurrying down the hall.

"But I'm not dreaming about Brenna. I'm not compromising my morals over Brenna. I'm not having any trouble keeping my hands off Brenna." Adam set his cup and saucer down, then got up from his chair and stalked to the window. "And I'm not making a fool out of myself over Brenna."

"There is that," Murphy agreed.

"Have you ever known me to forget to make sure I was dressed before I ran after a woman?"

O'Brien shook his head. "No." The fact was that Murphy O'Brien had never known Adam to run after a woman. Any woman. At any time. He'd known him to offer assistance or ask them to leave—as the case may be—but he had never run after one before. And not when he was bare-arsed naked. "Can't say that I have, but I'm very happy to see you rectified your mistake."

Adam snorted. He was clean-shaven and fully dressed except for his boots. "It was the least I could do after the show I put on this morning. Jesus, Joseph, and Mary! What a mess! I must be losing my mind," Adam muttered.

"Just your perspective," O'Brien corrected. "And if it makes you feel any better, Georgiana and I were the only ones who witnessed the display, although some of the others may have heard the shouting."

"It doesn't. But thanks anyway." He crossed the room and retrieved his cup and saucer.

"Well, just so's you know, I've seen far worse things than you in yer birthday suit," O'Brien said in his best Irish brogue.

"Yes, but has she?" Adam made no attempt to hide his thoughts.

O'Brien smiled. "She had a slightly different view," he pointed out. "My view was of yer fuzzy arse. And I'd hazard a guess that you probably made a bigger impression on her."

"Yeah," Adam said. "Proud enough to give an innocent young virgin nightmares."

"Or tweak her curiosity . . ."

Adam took one final swallow of coffee and set his cup aside. "As you can see, she hasn't returned."

"She probably has more sense than you." Murphy paced the length and breadth of the room, tidying as he went along. "I take it the dog ate your boots." He changed the subject.

"He chewed the toe of one," Adam confirmed, pointing his foot at the boot in question.

"That's all?" O'Brien bent to get a closer look at the damage.

Adam gave his friend a sheepish look. "I'm afraid my temper got the best of me."

"That's an understatement," O'Brien told him. "Especially when a little boot black and a coat of paraffin should cover the scuff marks."

"What do you use as waterproof?"

"I don't." O'Brien grinned. "*I* pay one of the stable boys to polish your boots as well as mine."

"What does he use?"

O'Brien lifted the undamaged boot and sniffed. "Smells like mink oil."

"That's what I thought," Adam agreed. "Tell the boy not to use it."

"Why not? You can't beat it for waterproofing."

"How about dog-proofing?" Adam looked over at his friend. "He's a male dog. The musk is attracting him."

"Makes sense," O'Brien commented. "Do you want me to have the boy polish it now or wait until Wagner chews the other one?"

"Wait." Adam sighed. "At the rate he's going, it shouldn't take long." He glanced over at the mantel clock. "I was right to get dressed," he announced. "Because she isn't coming back."

"She's probably trying to give you time to eat your breakfast, to cool off, to drink your coffee, and to read the paper you insisted she bring." O'Brien paused long enough to place the silver covers over the dishes on the butler's table, hiding the remains of Adam's breakfast.

"You don't have to do that," Adam told him. "Don't you remember? You're a Pinkerton detective, not a valet."

"Boyo, the first thing you learn as a Pinkerton is to become whatever role you're playing. This is the role I've chosen to play, and as long as I'm at Larchmont Lodge, I'm your gentleman's gentleman." O'Brien picked up the neatly ironed and folded newspaper and tossed it to Adam. "I see she managed to make it up here without breaking the china and that she brought you your newspaper. Since she went to the trouble of ironing it for you, the least you can do is open it."

"How do you know she ironed it?" Adam shot O'Brien a nasty look before unfolding the newspaper. "Never mind," he added before Murphy had a chance to answer.

Adam held the paper up so O'Brien could see the triangular shape of the iron for himself, then shook his head. Two columns on the third page were scorched so badly they were unreadable. "I don't know what her parents were thinking when they trained her as a domestic," he said. "I'm sure she has other talents, but housekeeping isn't one of them." He refolded the paper, tossed it on the bed, and burst out laughing.

O'Brien looked at him as if he was afraid Adam was about to repeat this morning's outburst. "What's so funny?"

"That!" Adam pointed to the paper. "I haven't had the opportunity to read a newspaper since I got here."

"I don't believe it!" O'Brien exclaimed in mock horror. "Adam McKendrick? The man who lives and breathes the financial pages?"

"Believe it," Adam said wryly. "I've been trying to read a newspaper since I got here, but something has happened to all of them. Wagner shredded the batch I got last week, and George's attempt at ironing has ruined this one."

But Murphy O'Brien didn't find the matter amusing. "Have you ever thought that someone might not want you to read the newspaper?"

Adam stopped laughing and focused his attention on O'Brien. "What do you mean?"

"What I mean, me boyo, is that I don't believe in that kind of coincidence." He stared at Adam. "Do you?"

"No, I don't." He met O'Brien's gaze. "Hand me my boots, please."

Murphy handed him the boots.

Adam pulled on the right one, then stepped into the left. "What the devil?" He took his foot out and turned his boot upside down, shaking it a bit until he dislodged the object stuck in the toe. It rolled out of his boot and thudded onto the carpet. "Son of a bitch!"

Beside his foot lay a ring. Adam reached down and picked it up. It was heavy gold and set with an enormous black pearl surrounded by a circle of diamonds. He wasn't a jeweler, but he'd spent years mining silver ore, and he knew quality when he saw it. The ring he held in his hand was worth a fortune. It could only be a family heirloom, and only one person could have placed it in his boot.

Murphy whistled in admiration. "I've never seen anything like it."

"Me either," Adam told him. "Except on the fingers of kings and queens and of the popes in portraits in museums." He stopped. "What would George be doing with a ring like that?"

"She is a chambermaid," O'Brien reminded him. "The obvious answer would be that she stole it."

"She didn't steal it from me," Adam said.

"The countess of Brocavia?" O'Brien asked.

"It's possible," Adam admitted, "but I don't think so. If she stole it, why would she put it in the toe of my boot where I would be sure to find it?" He scratched his jaw. "Besides," he added, "I don't believe there was a countess of Brocavia. I think it's just a name and a story they made up to get the job here."

"How did you come to that conclusion?" O'Brien asked, and Adam related the incident in the library when George had mistakenly called the woman the countess of Brocadia. O'Brien listened to Adam's argument and nodded in agreement. "They lied about the countess. But why?" He looked down at the ring in Adam's hand. "Where do you suppose they came from?"

"Karolya," Adam answered automatically.

"Karolya?" O'Brien frowned. "Is that where . . ."

"Lord Bascombe said that Isobel and Albert had lived in Karolya." Adam handed the ring to Murphy and walked over to his wardrobe, where he began rummaging through the pockets of his overcoat. "There is one newspaper left in this house." He waved the paper triumphantly. "The one I picked up yesterday in London. The one I stuck in my coat pocket to read on the train. But I didn't read it." Adam unfolded the paper, frowning as the ink smeared his hands. "I read the front page and the financial pages and glanced at a few other headlines. But I quit reading when my head began to ache. Still, I thought I remembered seeing something about . . . There it is."

Adam read the headline aloud: " 'Karolyan Princess Missing. Feared Dead.' " He read the rest of the article, studying the small photograph beside it. It was hard to tell, but the picture bore a striking resemblance to George. Adam shoved the paper at O'Brien.

"Do you think it's possible?" O'Brien asked, shocked.

"Yeah, it's possible," Adam replied grimly. "It's not very likely, but it's possible." He gritted his teeth. "Unfortunately, there's only one way to find out."

"Adam?" Murphy's voice was filled with concern. "Are you going to ask her about the ring?"

"In a roundabout way."

"What does that mean?"

Adam exhaled. "If she's that missing princess, she's lied about everything since she arrived. And she obviously has her reasons for hiding here and for lying, but tell me, Murph, what are the odds that she'll trust me enough to tell the truth?"

"If she's that missing princess, she's desperate to remain hidden or she wouldn't be at Larchmont Lodge working as a chambermaid."

"Exactly." Adam met O'Brien's gaze. "But how desperate?"

"Don't," Murphy warned. "Please, Adam, cut your losses. If she's a princess, there's no hope for it. And believe me, boyo, it would be better if you don't have those memories to carry around."

Adam managed a lopsided smile. "I wish it were that simple."

Chapter 24

A Princess of the Blood Royal of the House of Saxe-Wallerstein-Karolya never shows strong or upsetting emotions. Her subjects must never see anything other than a pleasant countenance.

—Maxim 217: Protocol and Court Etiquette of Princesses of the Blood Royal of the House of Saxe-Wallerstein-Karolya, as decreed by His Serene Highness, Prince Karol I, 1432.

He found her alone in the newly refashioned women's quarters, lying on her side in the center of her bed, her knees drawn up to her chin, her back curved into a protective posture. Wagner lay beside her.

Adam had half-hoped that he wouldn't find her. And if he did find her, he imagined her looking up and smiling at him or running to meet him, welcoming him with hot kisses and open arms—eager to pick up where they'd left off. But George didn't look up when he entered the room or give any sign of having heard him.

As he drew nearer, Adam saw the movement in her shoulders and recognized the sound echoing hollowly in the empty room and realized why she hadn't heard him. She was crying as if her heart would break. Or as if it had already broken.

Adam's stomach tightened and his heart seemed to catch in his throat. He stopped in his tracks, then silently retreated into the shadows, momentarily stunned, unsure of what to do. Her tears made him uncomfortable, anxious, and willing to do whatever he could to end them. Perhaps because they were unexpected and private. His sisters cried at the slightest provocation. They used their tears or the threat of them to wheedle gifts and favors from him. He was accustomed to those kinds of tears. This was something else.

Only last night George had informed him that people in her position did not cry. *Do not be impractical, she had admonished. Everyone knows that pri—people in my position never cry.*

But she was crying now. And the sight of it tore at Adam's heart. He wanted to sweep her up in his arms and hold her. He wanted to cuddle her close and promise her everything would be all right. He wanted to tell her that her secret was safe with him. He wanted . . . He wanted . . . her. The woman he had come to know and admire. George Langstrom, the chambermaid with the pale blond hair, fierce pride, and determined glint in her eyes.

Adam walked toward the bed.

Wagner growled, low in his throat, as he approached. Adam ignored him and closed the distance between them. He walked over to George's side of the bed and sat down. "George?"

"Go away." She didn't look up but kept her face buried in the pillow.

He tried again and this time he called her by her name instead of the pet name he had given her. "Giana?" Adam placed his hand on her shoulder.

She shrugged it off. "You do not have permission to put your hand upon my person."

Adam snatched his hand back as if she had bitten it, taken aback by the rancor he heard in her voice. He wasn't sure if his shouting at her had brought it about or if there was another cause, but George was definitely in a fine fettle. Having four sisters had taught him to recognize the signs and to know when to advance and when to retreat and when to do both. But he was rapidly running out of options. "Are you crying?"

Giana scrubbed the tears from her cheeks with the heels of her hands, then rolled to her side and sat up. "Do not be absurd. We never cry in front of strangers."

"You give a good imitation of it," he said. "But since I'm no stranger, I think it's fair if you indulge."

"You think not?" she challenged.

"No," he answered gently. "I'm not." He smiled at her. "How can I be a stranger to you when I'm the man who gave you your first kiss?"

"When he had nothing better to do," she retorted. "When he would rather be kissing someone else."

"I don't know where you get your ridiculous notions or what kind of man you think I am. But I am not in the habit of kissing one woman when I would rather be kissing someone else." Adam was stunned by the way she looked at him. Tears glistened on the surface of her blue eyes—eyes that were red-rimmed and bloodshot. Her angry gaze flashed fire at him, and when she spoke, her voice was full of venom. He stood up and began to pace.

"We received our notions from you!"

"From me?" His surprise was rapidly giving way to anger.

Giana wanted him to go away so she could curl up in a tight ball of shame once again with only Wagner for company, but she could not take the coward's way out. "We heard you," she murmured. "We heard you talking to your manservant."

"When did *we* hear that?" Adam demanded, stepping up to the challenge and issuing one of his own just to see how she would react. "And is that we you and Wagner or the royal one?"

"Wagner and I." Giana looked him in the eye, daring him to question her veracity. "We—I—returned to your bedchamber. I heard you speaking with your gentleman as I waited outside the door."

"I was waiting for you. Why didn't you make your presence known?" Adam asked.

"For what purpose? Having already assisted you with your toilette, your manservant was going about his duty, tidying the room as you spoke. My presence was not necessary."

Adam knew he was about to tread on thin ice, but he was willing to risk it. "Your presence was very necessary in order to continue what we started—"

"That is what you say now," she accused.

Adam raised an eyebrow in warning. "Twice you've implied I misled you regarding my intentions. Let me clarify things for you. I may not always speak my mind, but I'm not in the habit of misleading women in order to get them to share my pillow. I may not have said it at the time," he conceded, "but I don't believe you mistook my intentions." He glanced at her. "I don't believe I left any room for doubt."

"Humph." She sniffed in disdain.

"Careful, George."

She ignored his warning. "You left no doubt that you wanted someone to share your kisses and your pillow. But I was not that someone. I heard O'Brien say that Brenna would be better for you. You agreed with him."

"Son of a—" Adam raked his fingers through his hair in a show of frustration. "Yes, I agreed with him," he told her. "And it's true."

Giana's heart and all of her lovely dreams of kissing and being kissed, of holding him and being held by him, shattered. His words inflicted so much pain she couldn't speak. She sucked in a breath and fought to keep the fresh onslaught of tears stinging her eyelids from sliding down her cheeks.

"It's true." He twisted the dagger in her heart. "Brenna would be a better choice for me."

"Then go to her!" Giana shouted at him. And the sound of it startled them both. But not for long. Once she found her voice, Giana discovered that shouting could be very invigorating. Very liberating. She tried it again, louder this time. "Find her! Kiss her! You have my permission. But go away and leave me alone!"

"Damn it, George!" he swore. "I don't want Brenna!"

"You said—"

"I know what I said," he snapped. "I agreed with O'Brien when he said that Brenna would be better for me. And do you know why I agreed?" He didn't wait for her to answer. "Because I knew this would happen! Because I knew there was no danger of me falling in love with your sister. She's the image of everything I ever thought I wanted in a woman, and I feel nothing for her. Nothing." He shook his head. "While you make me crazy! You turn me into a raving lunatic! You're shouting because I don't want you. I'm shouting because I do. Damn it, George, I don't dream about Brenna. I don't compromise my morals over Brenna. I don't have any trouble keeping my hands off Brenna." He pointed a finger at her. "And you should have known that. Have you seen me kissing Brenna? Have you seen me chasing after her?"

Giana shook her head.

"That's right. You haven't. And you know why? Because I don't want to take Brenna to bed. I don't want to make love to Brenna. I want to make love to you!" He turned and stalked toward the door. "But you do whatever you want. Run away. Hide. Cry. Feel sorry for yourself. I'm not apologizing for telling the truth. And I'm through explaining."

Giana snapped her fingers and pointed toward the door. "Wagner! *En garde*!"

Before he knew what was happening, Wagner was sitting in front of the door. Adam found himself facing a hundred and fifty pounds of snarling wolfhound. And there was no doubt that the threat was real. If George snapped her fingers and ordered Wagner to attack, the dog could have Adam's bed and his boots all to himself.

"Call him off," Adam ordered.

"No." Giana climbed off the bed and crossed the room to stand beside the dog.

"This isn't funny, George," Adam gritted out.

"No," she agreed. "But I do not want you to leave."

"You told me to go away and leave you alone," he reminded her.

"I was mistaken," she said. "That is not what I want."

Adam eyed her warily. "Then, what do you want?"

"I want you to kiss me and see where it leads."

Her answer sucked the fight right out of him. But her blue eyes were smoldering with desire. "I know where it will lead," he said. "The question is whether or not you'll want to go there."

"Kiss me," she ordered, moistening her lips with the tip of her tongue in preparation. "And I will follow wherever you lead."

"Will you follow if I lead you to bed?" he asked.

Giana moved closer and closer still, until she was able to loop her arms around Adam's neck and press her body to his.

"Kiss me and find out." She followed her invitation with action, pulling his head down so she could kiss him.

Adam returned the kiss. Kissing her thoroughly until one of them came up for air. "I'm not playing games, George. I want to make love to you." He shrugged out of his jacket and let it fall to the floor, then he untied his tie, removed his collar, and unfastened his watch chain, dropping them on top of his wool jacket.

"I want you to do so." She licked the seam of his lips, hoping to encourage him to resume his soul-stealing kisses.

"Then put the dog out," he directed.

"He will not harm you," she told him. "He is simply guarding the door as he was taught to do. His presence ensures us that no one will interfere."

"*He's* watching." Adam smiled. "*His* presence will interfere."

"Oh," she said.

"Send him out," Adam said. "He can guard the outside of the door as well as the inside of it."

Giana snapped her fingers, and Adam opened the door as she issued the command, "Wagner. Outside. *En garde.*"

"Thank you," Adam breathed the words against her lips, before he covered them with his own and proceeded to show her just how thankful he was.

Desire arced between them like a flash of lightning.

Adam bent at the knees and lifted George into his arms, stepped over his garments, and carried her to her bed. Giana thrilled at the feeling. No one had carried her since she was twelve years old and had fallen from her horse and broken her leg. She thought that if it were possible to love him more, she loved Adam for that. She stood nearly six feet tall in her stocking feet, and he carried her as if she were Brenna's size.

Adam placed her on her bed, then followed her down atop the coverlet. He reminded himself that she was a virgin. She deserved gentleness. She deserved tenderness. She deserved his undivided attention, so Adam devoted himself to giving George everything she deserved. He nibbled at her lips, tracing the texture of them, before he touched the seam between her lips with the tip of his tongue, showering Giana with pleasure as he tasted the softness of her lips and absorbed the feel of her mouth; poring over every detail, every nuance of her lips and mouth and teeth and tongue, with the same single-minded determination that had taken him from the bowels of the Nevada silver mines, digging for ore, to Larchmont Lodge in Scotland and a bank account worth millions of dollars.

He leaned into her, pressing the lower part of his body against the cradle of hers and Giana opened her mouth and parted her legs to grant him access. Acknowledging her generous offering, Adam reached up, tangled one hand in her hair, and unpinned the twin coronets of braids, then pulled the ties from the bottom of the braids. He raked his fingers through them, loosening the plaits and breathing in the scent of her as he pulled her closer. He deepened his kiss, delving his tongue into the lush sweetness of her mouth.

Giana's tongue mated with his, mirroring his movements, as she plundered the depths of his mouth, retreating, then plundering again. She sank against him, shivering in delicious response as Adam left her lips and kissed a path over her eyelids, her cheeks, and the bridge of her nose. He brushed his lips lightly over hers once again before continuing his trail of kisses until he reached the pulse that beat at the base of her throat.

There were many times in her life when Giana despaired of the position to which she had been born, but now she was glad of it. Being a princess had taught her how to lead and how to follow, and she discovered that in Adam's arms, she was thrilled to do both. He had much to teach and she had a great deal to learn. And she was a little bewildered to learn that she enjoyed having someone else take the lead for a while. She enjoyed relinquishing her authority, finding incredible pleasure in letting go, becoming an enthusiastic slave to her desires.

Adam rubbed his nose into the hollow below her ear. He inhaled the fresh orange blossom scent of her as he laved the spot where her pulse throbbed with his tongue. He nibbled and teased and coaxed his way from her mouth to her throat, to the dainty pink shell of her ear and back again with a finesse he'd almost forgotten he possessed. A fierce longing flowed through him, making him shudder with the need to touch all of her, to taste all of her.

He remembered the way her breasts had looked beneath the fabric of her nightgown the first time he saw her, remembered the way their pink tips tightened beneath his gaze, and he ached to caress them.

Giana lay back on the bed, watching as he unpinned her apron. He tossed the pins on the night table and pushed the bib down. Sliding one hand beneath her bottom, Adam untied her apron strings and pulled the garment from around her waist. Her dress buttoned in the front, and once he dispensed with her white apron, Adam began unbuttoning the row of tiny jet buttons that held her bodice closed.

Adam opened the bodice of her dress, then cupped her breast with his hand, pushing it up and out of the confines of her black lace corset so that only the fabric of her chemise and corset cover separated her breasts from him. Her chemise, he noticed, and her corset cover were also black. He swallowed hard. He had expected white undergarments and was surprised to find her wearing black.

He felt the tightening in his groin as his erection throbbed against the front of his trousers. Adam smiled. He had never cared much for black lingerie. It held no special attraction for him. He always looked at the woman first and then her undergarments, but this . . . He gritted his teeth. Her choice of lingerie had nothing to do with seduction and everything to do with life and death. Adam hadn't realized, until that moment, that the black dresses George habitually wore had nothing to do with her position as a housemaid. She was in mourning.

Adam ran his hand over the front of her, and all of his worst fears were confirmed. A dozen or more hard lumps and bumps marred the fabric of her corset and corset cover. Suddenly he realized that the black pearl ring wasn't the only family heirloom George kept hidden. And Adam knew that if the ring was anything to go by, she was wearing a fortune in family heirlooms while working as chambermaid in a hunting lodge.

He took a deep breath to help steady his racing pulse, then slowly exhaled. As much as he wanted to undress her, as much as he wanted to caress her breasts, he wanted—no, needed—to allow her a few secrets.

Adam kissed the hollow of her throat, along her jaw, and back to her ear.

"Would you like to remove your corset and corset cover or shall I?" he whispered, his hot breath caressing the sensitive lobe of her ear.

Giana squirmed against him, eagerly seeking his lips and the feel of his hands on her. She started as Adam rubbed the pad of his thumb over the tip of her breast until it hardened against the fabric, then moved lower, stroking a place to the right of it, a place where she had sewn a pair of diamond earrings. . . .

"Oh!" She opened her eyes, and Adam knew the moment she realized what he was stroking. He smiled at her, then kissed his way from her ear to her lips.

"Be my Amazon," he urged in a deep husky voice that sent chills down her spine and hot liquid pooling between her thighs. "Bare your breasts for me." Adam covered her lips with his, kissing her hungrily, thoroughly, before pulling away and adding, "Show me your hidden charms."

She nodded and Adam gently tugged her into a sitting position.

Giana pulled her arms from the sleeves of her dress, then took hold of the hem of her corset cover, lifted her arms, and skimmed it over her head. She tossed the garment on the floor and reached for the back of her corset. It proved more difficult, and Giana was forced to seek help.

"Hooks," Giana gasped as he took advantage of her open bodice and traced the tips of her breasts with the pads of his fingers. "The hooks are hidden beneath the back flap."

"Hidden?" Adam muttered. "What's the point of hiding them? You know they're there. And it isn't as if you get to show all of this beauty off . . ." He didn't have to understand the fine points of ladies' fashion to unhook it, so Adam dutifully reached behind her and felt beneath the flap, groaning when he encountered a hundred or so tiny hook-and-eye closures. "Judas Priest!"

It took a few moments. Adam sighed with relief as he finally unhooked the contraption and freed her. Giana scrambled to her knees, then reached down and grabbed hold of the front of her corset and flung it into the air. It landed with a thud near the equally heavy jewel-laden garment she'd worn to cover it.

Her tight-fitting bodice was still buttoned at her waist, so Giana unbuttoned it and let it fall to the bed. Adam sat back on his heels and enjoyed the view as George tugged the hem of her chemise from the waistband of her skirts, pulling it up and over her head, leaving her gloriously naked above the waist.

She smiled at him.

Adam stared in awe. If he lived to be a thousand, he would never forget the sheer beauty of the sight of George's perfectly shaped breasts or the wonder of her smile when she looked into his eyes as she revealed them to him.

He pushed himself to his knees and reached for her, but George danced away. Guessing her game, Adam lay down on his back and waited for her to come to him. He didn't have to wait long.

Moments later Giana leaned over him. Adam raised his head and licked the rosy peak of her breast with his tongue.

Fire, like the fire of a glass of brandy on an empty stomach, shot through her, only this fire was a thousand times better than anything alcohol induced. Giana gasped as the warmth of his breath against her breast made her nipple swell and harden until she ached in the dark mysterious recesses of her body.

"Again," she ordered. And Adam obliged.

"More?" he asked.

Giana nodded.

"Then come closer."

She responded, leaning over him, dangling her exquisite globes above his face, like forbidden fruit.

Adam licked one breast and then the other.

Giana arched her back and moaned.

He reached over, placed his hand on either side of her waist and lifted her atop him, placing her legs on either side of his so that she was pressed against him, straddling him.

She leaned forward and Adam began lavishing her nipple

with attention. He suckled at her breast and thought how much he wanted to touch her, and taste the sweet hot essence of her. He wanted to bury his length inside her warmth and feel the heat of her surrounding him as he throbbed and pulsed within, and he wanted to capture her lips and swallow her cries as they careened toward the heavens on an intimate journey where two became one, where desire and passion were forged like iron and carbon melded into steel, to form an exquisite blend of love and faith and trust.

Adam worked his way from her breasts back to her lips. He plundered her mouth with his warm rough tongue, then slipped a hand beneath her skirts, negotiating a path through the sea of petticoats until he felt the lace of her drawers.

He reached beneath the lace ruffle at her knee and ran his hand up her silk-clad thigh as far as the give in the fabric allowed, then frustrated by his lack of progress, he withdrew his hand from the leg of her drawers and began again. His second foray yielded better results as he ran his hand over the top of her thigh and down into the valley between her legs. Locating the opening in the fabric, Adam gently eased his fingers inside it, caressing the nest of silken curls, finding the damp swollen flesh hidden beneath them.

"Adam!" Giana nearly shouted his name as she thrust her hips against his incredibly talented fingers. Adam traced the contours of her flesh and teased the tight little bud hidden within the folds.

She gasped, unable to describe the myriad delicious and forbidden sensations she felt as Adam worked his magic upon her. He slid his skilled fingers into her petal-soft folds, and Giana felt the impact of those sensations deep inside her womb. Longings she never dreamed she possessed shot to the surface and raged in a most unprincesslike fashion.

Giana knew she should be scandalized by Adam's familiarity with the forbidden places on her body, but he stroked and probed her secret places with such infinite tenderness and such agonizing care that she couldn't be outraged. How could she be shocked and angry when all he gave was pleasure? Incredible pleasure?

"Please . . ." She murmured the entreaty in such a heartfelt tone of voice that Adam couldn't tell if she was inviting him to continue or begging him to stop. He deepened his caress and wiggled his fingers. Giana immediately pressed her legs together in reaction, before opening them again to give him access. And Adam had his answer.

Giana squirmed as pleasure—hot and thick and dangerous—surged through her body. She thrust her hips upward as she moaned her pleasure and gasped out his name in short frantic little breaths.

Adam kissed her, gently at first, then harder, consciously matching the action of his fingers to that of his tongue as he caressed her. He knew she was close, and his body chafed beneath his self-imposed restraint. Adam ached to join her in blissful release, but he took his time, pressing his thumb against her, soothing her aching core with the sweet honey she lavished on his fingers.

George sighed against his lips, then shuddered deeply as her fragile control shattered and she collapsed upon his chest.

Chapter 25

A Princess of the Blood Royal of the House of Saxe-Wallerstein-Karolya must possess virtue beyond compare.

—MAXIM 15: PROTOCOL AND COURT ETIQUETTE OF PRINCESSES OF THE BLOOD ROYAL OF THE HOUSE OF SAXE-WALLERSTEIN-KAROLYA, AS DECREED BY HIS SERENE HIGHNESS, PRINCE KAROL I, 1432.

She opened her eyes and looked up at him with such an expression of sheer wonderment and joy that Adam's breath caught in his throat. He was humbled by the look in her eyes and rewarded tenfold for his unselfish restraint.

Emotion shimmered in her eyes as Giana reached up, placed her palms on both sides of his face. "Thank you," she said simply as she pulled his face down to meet her lips.

"It was an honor," he whispered seconds before he captured her mouth with his own.

Adam kissed her again—this time with all the pent-up passion and frustration and longing he'd been holding in check so long. He kissed her until her breasts heaved with exertion, until her bones seemed to turn to jelly, until all she could do was cling to him while she fervently returned his kisses measure for measure. Adam's mind reeled from the flood of sensations she evoked as her tongue mated with his.

Shaking with need, he pulled away.

"What's wrong?" she asked.

"Nothing's wrong," he answered.

"Then why did you stop kissing me?"

"Because I want you." Adam leaned his forehead against hers and drew a shaky breath. "All of you."

"You have all of me." She looked down at him.

He shook his head. "Not really. Technically, we could stop this now and you would still be a virgin." Adam stared up at her.

Her eyes widened. Adam had kissed her, touched by her in places she had not known existed. How could it be that technically, she remained untouched?

"Do you understand what I'm trying to say?" he asked.

Giana shook her head.

"I'm saying that we could stop what we're doing right now, get dressed, and go our separate ways, and it wouldn't matter for you."

She frowned.

"It wouldn't matter *for* you," he repeated, lifting himself on his elbow so he could kiss her. "My greatest hope is that this will matter *to* you for as long as you live," he said. "But at this moment you can walk away and marry another man or take another lover and no one, except you and I, will ever know what happened in this room between us."

Giana did not understand exactly what he meant, but she knew Adam was allowing her to choose. She was a princess, and she knew that while her parents' marriage had been a true love match, it was also incredibly rare. Royal marriages were arranged for the good of the nations. Princes and princesses understood, almost from birth, that love was not part of the arrangement. Giana sighed. It was her duty to save herself for marriage to ensure a secure succession to the throne. Princess Giana must go to her future husband untouched. But Giana, the woman, wanted Adam McKendrick to continue his love-making until no part of her remained untouched. The fact that a match between them was impossible didn't matter. She wanted to be loved for herself. Just once before she was required to fulfill her duty.

Giana decided to forget that she was a princess and decided that for today, she would be only a woman, free to choose, free to love Adam and be loved in return. She reached for Adam and smiled. "I do not want to be untouched. Technically or otherwise."

That was all the encouragement he needed. Adam unhooked

her skirts, untied the waistbands of her petticoats, and unbuttoned her lacy drawers, then untied her frilly black garters. When everything was unfastened, he peeled the garments and her black silk stockings down her slim thighs to where they pooled at the bend in her knees.

"What's this?" Adam fingered a length of thick gold chain encircling her slim waist. A heavy gold ring hung suspended from the chain. He had seen belly bracelets on Egyptian dancing girls in Paris, but he had never seen anything like this one. It was locked around her waist. George couldn't remove it without a key. He wondered, suddenly, who had put it there. There was no doubt that the ring had belonged to a man, for it bore a motto and a coat of arms. "A new kind of chastity belt or a memento from a knight in shining armor?" He kept his hands on the chain, steadying her as she lifted each leg and kicked free of her clothing. He wasn't sure what it was, but it had its uses and there was a certain erotic cachet to making love to a woman with jewelry around her waist.

Giana glanced down. She had forgotten about the seal! Except for the locket she wore around her neck and the gold chain bearing the Seal of State around her waist, Giana was completely nude. "My father gave it to me. It has been in his family for years."

Adam snorted. If her father gave it to her, it had to be some sort of chastity belt. Luckily, for him, it didn't seem to work properly.

Giana blushed bright red and squeezed her eyes shut.

"Open your eyes, George, and see how beautiful you are," he whispered.

She did as he asked, opening her eyes to see if the expression on his face matched his tone of voice and was instantly gratified to see that it did.

"You take my breath away."

She blushed.

"What happens now?" she asked.

Placing the palms of his hands on the undersides of her firmly rounded bottom, Adam urged her up onto her knees, then he grinned as he slid her forward, up his chest. Giana felt the soft, cool satin of his waistcoat and the linen of his shirt against her inner thighs as he moved her forward until her bottom rested against his collarbones. "Now you allow me to see if you taste as good as you look."

Giana looked down and met his unerring gaze.

"Trust me," he said.

And she did. Even so, the feel of his hot breath came as a complete surprise. Giana clamped her legs together. Adam lifted his head and looked at her. "I'm not going to hurt you, George," he said. "I'm only going to love you. If you'll let me."

When he looked at her like that, Giana found she couldn't deny him anything—didn't want to deny him anything. He was the teacher and she, the student. He was the sculptor and she was the clay. As long as he kept his promise to love her, her body was his to do with as he pleased. "Proceed," she ordered.

"My pleasure."

Giana thought she had achieved the greatest level of pleasure when his fingers caressed her, but when Adam pulled her to him, and began to taste the places his fingers had explored, she knew that there was greater pleasure to achieve.

He drove her to the brink of rapture and beyond, then gently rolled her to her side and cradled her beside him, capturing her cries with his mouth as she shuddered back to the earth in his arms. He brushed her damp hair off her flushed face, wiped the tears from her eyes, and murmured love words of praise and encouragement in her ear.

Giana opened her eyes to find Adam staring down at her. "Have you touched me completely?"

He moved his head from side to side on the pillow and laughed. "You're a lot less untouched," he told her. "But a virgin you remain."

"There is greater pleasure?"

"There's a great deal more pleasure," he explained, "as well as a small amount of pain. But the pleasure far surpasses the pain."

Giana eyed him warily. "Pain for whom?"

"You."

"Oh."

Adam leaned over and nipped her bottom lip, catching it

between his teeth, before soothing the bite with his tongue, and kissing her again, making her forget the momentary pain. "What's a little bit of pain compared to this?"

She nipped his lip. "Show me."

"Good Lord!" He laughed. "An autocrat!"

Giana looked shocked and then, dismayed. "I am not an autocrat," she informed him. "I am a constitutional monarchy."

Adam laughed harder. "And I'm a standard-bearer for democracy," he said. "But we'll save that debate for later." He sucked in a breath as his body tightened and the bulge in his trousers threatened to pop his buttons. "At the moment, I have a more pressing problem to discuss with you. . . ."

"What?" She kissed him again.

"The fact that one of us is wearing too many clothes . . ."

She smiled a wicked little smile that played about the corners of her mouth. Her blue eyes sparkled with merriment when she reached for the top button of his shirt. "May I?"

He favored her with a devilish grin and turned her earlier words around on her. "Since you asked so nicely, you have permission to put your hands upon my person."

"I have never before undressed a man," she confided, unbuttoning all of the buttons on his shirt and pushing it open and away from his chest.

"You're doing such a fine job, no one would ever know that you're only a beginner," he praised her.

Giana slid his shirt off his shoulders, down his arms, and over his hands, exposing the hard muscles of his chest and stomach. She rubbed her hands over the mat of hair on his chest, then indulged herself by allowing the tips of her breasts to rub against it.

Adam's blood rushed downward. The hard male part of him throbbed with each beat of his heart. He ached to sheathe himself in George's warmth. He ached to end his exquisite torment.

Wrapping his arms around her waist, Adam gently rolled her onto her back. Giana followed the line of his spine, sliding her hands down his back and over his tight buttocks, then back to the waistband of his trousers. She followed the strip of fabric from his back to the front of his trousers. Adam groaned aloud as she brushed her fingers against him.

She located the buttons of his trousers and carefully undid each one. Adam kicked free of his pants, moaning his immense satisfaction as the hard jutting length of him spilled into her waiting hands. Giana caressed him, marveling at the velvety soft feel of his flesh, and she would have continued her exploration if Adam hadn't gently lifted her hands from around him, then guided her legs up over his hips, and pressed himself against her, gently probing her entrance.

Lost in a frenzy of need, Giana locked her legs around his waist and pulled him to her.

Adam pushed inside her. He closed his eyes, threw back his head, and bit his bottom lip as he sheathed himself fully inside her warmth. His entire body shook with the effort as he fought to maintain his control.

Giana cried out as he entered her and tried to pull away. Adam, realized, too late, that she was no longer a virgin and that he'd just ruthlessly pushed through the veil of her innocence. He held on to her to keep her from squirming and causing herself more discomfort as he soothed her with his words and kissed away the salt of her tears. "It's all right, Giana, the worst will be over in a moment. Lie still. Let me kiss you."

She gasped, then bit his lower lip, hard enough to draw blood. "That was not a little pain."

Adam grunted as they exchanged a bit of his blood for hers. She was entitled. "Sweetheart, the first time for a woman always hurts, but the pain will go away soon, and I promise you, the pleasure will be worth it."

He didn't lie. Her pain gradually disappeared and as it did, Giana began to experiment, moving this way and that, testing to see if it would return. Adam lost his battle to maintain control as her movement forced him deeper inside her. He began to move his hips in a rhythm as old as time. Giana followed, matching his movements thrust for thrust, clinging to him, reveling in the weight and feel of him as he filled her again and again, gifting her with himself in a way she'd never dreamed possible.

She squeezed her eyes shut. Tears of joy trickled from the corners, ran down her cheeks, and disappeared into the silk of her hair. And as she felt the first tremors flow through her, Her Serene Highness Princess Giana of Saxe-Wallerstein-Karolya surrendered to the emotions swirling inside her and gave voice to the passion with small incoherent cries that escaped her lips as Adam rocked her to him and exploded inside her.

He brushed his lips against her cheek as he buried his face in her hair. He tasted the saltiness of her tears, then lifted his head, and looked down at her face. God, but she was beautiful! Adam shuddered as a rush of emotions raced through him. He should have spoken words of love instead of words of passion. He should have cherished her and treated her tenderly instead of using her to slake his raging desire. He'd known she was a virgin. . . . She deserved a wedding night. . . . She deserved to be . . .

Scolded or spanked or . . . loved. . . . Adam sighed. The incredible satisfaction of release also brought the first wave of guilt. Damn it to hell! She had allowed him to seduce her. To take her virginity when she'd had every opportunity to change her mind. What the hell had he done? What the hell had they done? And how would they ever manage to undo it?

Adam stared down at her—into blue eyes shimmering with emotion—and was lost. He wouldn't think about the future. He wouldn't question his good fortune or ask for more than she could give. He'd simply love her while it lasted.

Leaning closer, he touched his mouth to hers in a kiss so gentle, so loving, so precious, it brought fresh tears to her eyes. "Thank you, Adam."

"You're welcome, *Princess*."

Chapter 26

A Princess of the Blood Royal of the House of Saxe-Wallerstein-Karolya should never expect wedded bliss. Such a thing does not exist for royalty. Joy must be found elsewhere, but joys found beyond the boundaries of marriage always come at a terrible price.

—MAXIM 517: PROTOCOL AND COURT ETIQUETTE OF PRINCESSES OF THE BLOOD ROYAL OF THE HOUSE OF SAXE-WALLERSTEIN-KAROLYA, AS DECREED BY HER SERENE HIGHNESS, PRINCESS DARIA, 1782.

"*You knew?" she asked.*

"Not until a moment ago," he admitted. "I suspected, but I didn't know for sure until I looked into your eyes and saw the truth." But he had *known* it. Some part of him *had* known George was different. But he had never suspected how different until he'd discovered the pearl ring and the newspaper. There had been clues all along. So many things that hadn't made sense—the way she talked, the things she said, the way her "family" treated her.

"I can explain."

"Explain what happened or why it happened?" he asked. "Because I know what happened. What I don't know is why it happened." Adam raked his hand through his hair. "You're a princess, for God's sake! I gave you every chance! You were supposed to stop me! You were supposed to say no!" He rolled out of bed and crossed the room. "Damn it! I'm an American. We don't have royalty! I don't even know what I'm supposed to call you!"

"We—I—am Her Serene Highness Princess Georgiana Victoria Elizabeth May of Saxe-Wallerstein-Karolya. I am styled

'Her Serene Highness.' In public you would address me as 'Your Highness' and in private, you may call me George," Giana answered softly, watching as he bent to collect his scattered clothing. "I did not say no because it is not what I wanted to do. I did not want you to stop. Nor did you try very hard to stop yourself."

Adam looked at her and saw that her heart was in her eyes. "You're right. I didn't try to stop myself at all."

"The question is why not?" She pulled the sheet over her breasts and anchored it beneath her arms.

He shook his head. "I don't know. Maybe it's because I wanted the fairy tale. Maybe it's because I wanted to be the prince who saves the beautiful princess. Or maybe it's because for a while there, I truly believed in happy-ever-afters."

A stream of silvery wet tears glided silently down George's face. "You cannot save me from my duty, Adam. Or protect me from my fate." She tried to smile at him and failed miserably. "But you have given me a wonderful gift. A gift I can carry with me for the rest of my life."

"I may have given you more than a gift, Princess," he said bluntly. "It's possible that I gave you a child."

Giana blanched.

"An obviously unwanted child," he remarked cruelly.

Adam wanted to kick himself as soon as the words came out of his mouth. It wasn't her fault. She'd been a virgin. He was the one who should have been prepared. No, he was the one who should have had better sense than to make love to a princess in the first place!

George had enough to worry about without worrying about having a baby. And he could have prevented it, Adam reminded himself, if he'd been thinking with his head instead of that other part of his anatomy. But that was no excuse, and if George were to find herself with child, he'd have to find some way to take responsibility.

"How dare you think that I would not want our child?" Giana threw the pillow at him. It landed squarely, hitting him in the face before bouncing onto the floor.

"You turned as white as the sheet you're wearing," Adam told her.

"Perhaps that is because I forgot such a thing is possible. In my country, children are seldom born beyond the bonds of marriage," she informed him.

"Children are born beyond the bonds of marriage in every country," Adam said. "And royalty is no exception." He carried his clothes back to the bed. "And you're right. I was being unnecessarily cruel, because I was angry, not at you, but at myself." He leaned down and kissed her forehead. "Forgive me."

She nodded. "You are not angry at me?"

"Not for not realizing our lovemaking could have unexpected results," he answered honestly. "That was my fault."

"But you *are* angry at me for the other things." She looked up at him. "Yet you want to kiss me."

"I'd want to kiss you even if I hated you," he said wryly. "Kissing you doesn't mean I'm not angry, it just means that I crave the pleasure you give me."

"Are you still angry about Wagner and the china?"

Adam shook his head. "I believe you paid for Wagner and the china." He reached into his waistcoat pocket and pulled out the pearl ring. "With this." He tried to give it to her, but Giana refused to accept it.

"It's yours," she said.

"No," he corrected. "It's yours or else it belongs to the people of Karolya, in which case, you've no right to give it away." He pressed the ring in her palm and closed her fingers around it.

Giana held it to her heart. "I do not have enough coin to pay for the damages."

"It doesn't matter. I don't want your coin." Adam covered her hand with his. "And I certainly don't require any of the Karolyan Crown Jewels as payment."

Giana looked up at him, and this time he saw that her eyes were full of love and gratitude. "This ring was not part of the Crown Jewels," she told him. "It was part of Princess Rosamond's personal collection, but it has always been one of my favorite pieces." She smiled. "I practiced my counting by counting the diamonds." She proved it by counting to sixteen in half a dozen different languages. "There are . . ."

"Sixteen of them." He leaned over and kissed her tenderly. "I speak French," he reminded her. "And enough Spanish, German, Swedish, and Mandarin to get by."

Giana kissed him back, holding on for dear life. "Mandarin?"

He nodded. "Chinese. I made my fortune building railroads and mining silver. Over half the workers were Chinese, and the other half were Irish." He made a face at her. "Tell me, Princess, how did you come by your fortune?" He pointed toward her corset and corset cover.

"I inherited part of it upon my birth, and I inherited the rest the night my parents were murdered."

"I'm sorry," he murmured sincerely.

"So am I," she said. "They were murdered together in their bedchamber at Christianberg Palace in the capital city of Karolya after retiring from the state dinner celebrating the opening of Parliament." She recited the facts in a calm, unemotional tone of voice. "The palace was overrun and servants loyal to my father were slaughtered."

"By anarchists?" Adam repeated what he'd read in the paper.

But George shook her head. "No, by my cousin, His Highness, Prince Victor of Saxe-Wallerstein-Karolya."

"Your cousin?" Adam struggled to breathe as surprise pushed the air from his lungs. "The man searching for your kidnappers? The man who has been running the country in your absence?"

"The same."

"Son of a bitch!"

"Indeed," Giana said.

"There were no anarchists? Or kidnappers?"

"There may well be anarchists in Karolya," she answered, "but they did not kill my mother and father. Victor was inciting the young men of the ruling class, encouraging them to denounce my father's support of a new constitution and a Declaration of Rights for the Masses. Victor promised estate grants, titles, and funds in order to gain the support of the younger sons of the aristocratic families. He convinced them to become traitors by telling them that my father intended to reward the *bourgeois* for their support by granting them landed estates of the rich. My father and mother were shot and stabbed several times, and Victor ordered it done."

"Why?"

"Greed," she answered simply. "He wants control of Karolya's rich iron ore deposits and its vast acreage of virgin timber."

It took a moment for Adam to comprehend what she was saying. "Your cousin killed your parents to gain control of iron ore and timber?"

"It is a great deal of iron ore and timber," she informed him. "Papa explained the value of the iron ore and the timber to me when other governments began approaching him with offers to secure the rights to them, but I did not understand the role Victor played in the attempts to secure the rights until Max explained it to me after my parents' deaths. Papa refused to sell or lease the rights. Refused to even consider doing so. He believed that Karolya's natural resources belonged to the people. His role as prince of Karolya was to protect those resources for future generations of Karolyans. Karolya is a wealthy country. We do not need to rape the countryside to provide money or jobs for our people."

"Does Victor need money?" Adam asked.

Giana shook her head. "No. Victor needs power. Max told me that Papa learned Victor had made agreements with men of other countries to supply them with Karolyan iron ore and the timber without Papa's consent."

"What did your father do to Victor?"

"I do not know." Giana looked up at Adam. "But Victor asked for my hand in marriage and Papa refused." She dropped the black pearl ring on top of the sheet covering her lap, stared down at her lap, and began twisting the cotton fabric in her hands. "But that will not matter now. Victor will not stop until he finds me."

"Here, let me take that." Adam retrieved the pearl ring and placed it on the nightstand to keep it from being lost among the bedclothes. George surrendered it without a second thought. Adam gave a half smile. He wouldn't have to worry about providing her with expensive jewelry for their anniversaries in the years to come, because George had more than she would ever need and she didn't seem to care. The only jewelry she wore, outside of the fortune sewn into her undergarments, was the locket around her neck, the bracelet around her waist, and a pair of tiny gold earrings. And there was a pin somewhere. He remembered seeing something silver pinned to her chemise. No, George wouldn't require jewelry. She would probably rather have puppies—or children. Lots of children and dogs.

He didn't know Prince Victor, but he had known men like him, and he could well imagine the man's fury when he was forced to give up the iron ore, the timber, and George. And now that he had had the privilege of sharing her bed, Adam knew without a doubt that, even without wealth and power, she was the greater loss. "How did you escape?"

"I was not home," she answered. "My father was afraid for me, so he sent me to our summer palace in Laken." Giana looked up at Adam and spoke in a tiny forlorn voice that first took him by surprise, then frightened him. "I should have been there. I should have been there when they died. I should have been there with my mother and father. I should have died with them, but he sent me away. My father sent me to safety while he and my mother faced their enemies alone. . . ." She began to shake, then burst into tears.

Adam gathered her up in his arms and held her. "Oh, no, my sweet, you should not have died with them. Your father loved you, and because he loved you, he did exactly as he should have done. He sent you to safety, so you would live. So you would marry and have children and continue his line. I would have done the same."

"But they left me. They left me alone!" she cried.

Adam shook his head. "They didn't leave you of their own free will, sweetheart. They had no choice. You were their baby. Their precious daughter and the future of their country. They sent you away because they loved you, because they could not bear to watch you die. And you would have died, George. Make no mistake about it. If you had been home, you would have died and there would be no one to look out for the people of Karolya. You did exactly what your parents expected you to do," he told her, smoothing her hair away from her face, brushing his lips against her forehead. "You survived."

"I survived because no one knew where I was except the staff at Laken."

"Let me guess—Max, Isobel, Albert, Brenna, and Josef."

"No, Max was at the palace in Christianberg with my parents."

Adam took a deep breath. "The article I read in the *Times of London* hinted that Lord Maximillian *Gudrun*, your father's private secretary, masterminded the plot to overthrow Prince Christian and engineered your kidnapping."

"Lord Maximillian Gudrun saved my life," she announced, her voice ringing with pride. "He was wounded in an attempt to save my parents. My father gave Max his Seal of State and charged him to bring it to me and to get me out of Karolya to a place of safety." Giana glanced down at her waist.

Adam reached over and traced the outline of the gold chain at her waist through the sheet. "I take it that this is the Seal of State of Saxe-Wallerstein-Karolya."

"Yes."

"When you said your father gave it to you, I thought it might be some kind of chastity belt," he teased, his blue eyes twinkling with mirth.

"Until I am crowned ruler of Karolya, the Seal of State cannot leave my person. That is why we placed it on a chain and why I locked it around my waist."

"Where's the key?"

"I threw it in the ocean," she said. "We could not risk having the seal lost or stolen, nor could we risk having it recognized. This was the safest place to keep it," she said. "Because no one but Max and Brenna knew of its whereabouts."

"Until today." Adam reached across the bed and retrieved her chemise and handed it to her.

She smiled at him, then let go of the sheet and pulled her chemise over her head. "Until today."

"And now that I know," Adam teased, "I suppose my life is forfeit?"

Giana shook her head. "Not yours. Mine."

Chapter 27

The Bountiful Baron values truth foremost. He does not take well to surprises.

—The First Installment of the True Adventures of the Bountiful Baron: Western Benefactor to Blond, Beautiful, and Betrayed Women written by John J. Bookman, 1874.

"What?" Adam was paralyzed with terror at her calm pronouncement.

"In order to succeed the throne of Karolya, Victor must produce the Seal of State and my body or marry me within one year of my father's death." She reached over and caressed Adam's cheek. "Even if I would accept my father's murderer, Victor will never marry me now that I am no longer a virgin."

Her words, spoken in that calm, matter-of-fact way, sent Adam spiraling into anger. "He'll kill you." Adam got up from the bed and began pulling on his clothes. "Jesus Christ! George! This place could be crawling with Victor's spies. If he finds out we made love . . ." He let his words trail off as he stepped into his trousers and shrugged on his shirt. "And it's not as if we have tried to be discreet. We've been missing all morning and anyone who cares to investigate could find us." Adam began buttoning his shirt. "Wagner is posted outside the door. What the devil was I thinking?" He shot her a frustrated look as he tossed her chemise on the bed. "What were you thinking?"

Giana pulled her undergarment over her head. "I was thinking that I did not want to die or to go into another man's bed without knowing what it was like to be in yours," she told him.

His knees gave way and he sat down, abruptly on the edge

of the bed. "You knew? You knew and you were willing to forfeit your life to share my bed?"

"I am a princess, Adam. I do not know if there is such a thing as a happily-ever-after for people in my position. My parents were the only royal couple in Karolya's recent history to marry for reasons of love, instead of reasons of state and a member of their family murdered them. I do not know if I will be able to marry for reasons other than for reasons of state. I only know that if I could choose, I would choose you to be my Prince Consort." She looked at him. "Whatever should happen, please know that for the rest of my life, I choose you."

I choose you. Adam's heart began a rapid tattoo, his breath caught in his throat and the sudden rush of tenderness he felt for her made his legs go weak in the knees. *He loved her*. The unexpected realization struck him like a bolt of lightning from the blue sky. He loved the way she made him feel. The way she touched him. And for now, his love would have to be enough. "Choosing me could cost you your life."

"It will have been worth it."

"Giana, I—"

Giana reached out and placed two fingers against his lips to stop the words she did not want to hear. "George," she corrected. "From you, I prefer George."

Adam gave her a sheepish look. "It doesn't sound very regal."

"I have many regal titles, but you are the only person besides my parents who has ever called me by a pet name."

"Really?" He was surprised and genuinely pleased.

"Yes."

"What did they call you?"

"My mother called me Fleur, but my father called something far more endearing, but not nearly as flattering."

"What did your father call you?" he asked.

"Her Royal Highness, Princess Monkey."

"Princess Monkey?" Adam was intrigued in spite of himself.

"Because I was all arms and legs."

"I think I would have liked your father," Adam told her.

"I think so, too," Giana said. She reached up and fingered

the locket on the thin, gold chain around her neck. "Would you like to see them?"

Adam nodded.

Giana unhooked her gold-and-diamond locket from around her neck, then opened it and held it up for Adam to see.

He stared at the portraits inside the locket.

"This one is my mother's father and mother, the marquess and marchioness of Barracksford." She pointed to the portrait on the left side of the locket. "It was copied from their official wedding portrait. And this one is"—she pointed to the other portrait—"my father and mother and me on my christening day."

"His Serene Highness Prince Christian, Her Serene Highness Princess May and Her Royal Highness Princess Monkey." Adam made a face at her.

Giana giggled.

"Nice portrait," Adam said. "Nice family."

"Yes, we were," she agreed. "I have always loved the expressions on their faces as they looked down on me." Giana's lower lip trembled. She swiped at a tear with the back of her hand and managed a wistful smile.

"You were greatly loved," he said, studying the portraits again. "And who is this?" He touched a tiny clasp at the bottom of the locket and the portrait of her grandparents slipped out to reveal another portrait—one of a handsome gentleman dressed, like her grandparents, in the style of the Regency.

"You have discovered my family's skeleton in the armoire," she told him. "George Ramsey, the fifteenth marquess of Templeston."

"Who was?" Adam remained unenlightened.

"The man who gave my mother life."

Adam raised an eyebrow at that.

"My grandmother was French. A Parisian actress and a commoner. She married very young, to her childhood sweetheart. When she was twenty and he was twenty-two, Grandmama's husband went off to war. He died in Russia fighting for Napoleon and my grandmother found work as an actress on the stage in Paris. She met George Ramsey when he went backstage to present her with a bouquet of flowers and to ask her if she would join him for dinner. Grandmama always said it was love at first sight. Grandmama fell deeply in love with Templeston and he with her. He set her up in a house in Paris and she prayed every day that he would marry her, but Templeston had promised his late wife he would never remarry. And he kept his word. My grandmother ended their affair when she realized that no matter how much George Ramsey loved her, he loved the memory of his late wife more. The marquess of Templeston returned to London and Grandmama returned to the theatre.

"Soon afterward, Grandmama was introduced to another titled Englishman by one of the ladies in the chorus. The marquess of Barracksford was much older than Grandmama. He had never married, but was considered quite a catch and quite a ladies' man. He frequently traveled to Paris on business and for pleasure and was welcomed at all the fashionable Parisian salons. Lord Barracksford fell in love with Grandmama and pursued her. Grandmama tried to discourage him by telling him that she was still in love with George Ramsey, but Lord Barracksford did not care. He continued to court her until my grandmother agreed to marry him." Giana paused, trying to gauge Adam's reaction.

"What happened to Lord Templeston?" he asked.

"He died in a boating accident off the coast of Ireland before my mother was born. He never knew my grandmother was carrying his child."

"Did Barracksford know?"

Giana nodded. "Grandmama told him as soon as she discovered it. She thought Lord Barracksford would change his mind about wanting to marry her, but he did not. Barracksford was in love. He willingly accepted my grandmother and her unborn child as his own. He and Grandmama married and settled in Paris. After my mother was born, Lord Barracksford moved the family to London. George Ramsey had died and his oldest son and heir had become the new marquess of Templeston. My mother was a girl so there was no need for anyone to know the truth of her paternity. Lord Barracksford brought my mother up as a daughter of the house and loved her as dearly as his own, but he was not her father. Lord Templeston was."

"How did you learn of this?"

"It was the story my grandmother told my mother when she gave her the locket and the story my mother told me when she gave me the locket. You see, Lord Templeston made provisions for his mistresses and their offspring in his will. If ever they were in need, they were to present this locket to the current Lord Templeston." Giana smiled. "My grandmother and my mother were fortunate to have married for love and been well provided for. There was never any need to present the locket." Giana knelt on the bed beside him and watched as he replaced the miniature of her grandparents, hiding the likeness of the marquess of Templeston, before he handed it back to her.

"Why haven't *you* presented the locket to the current Lord Templeston?"

Giana fastened the locket around her neck. "I intended to," she answered. "As soon as I reached England, but the newspapers were full of stories of my disappearance and Victor's accusation that Max was responsible." She looked up at Adam. "The papers kept reporting that Queen Victoria's government was assisting Victor in the search for me and the apprehension of Max and his band of anarchists, and that the queen had appointed her adviser, the marquess of Templeston, to act as liaison between the Court of St. James and the Court of Saxe-Wallerstein-Karolya. I was afraid to present the locket until I knew Max was safe and until I discovered if the British government wanted the iron ore and timber more than it wanted me on the Karolyan throne. I could not be sure the marquess would believe my claim or that he was not in league with my cousin . . ."

Adam reached out and touched the gold locket, then the silver pin on her chemise. "Until you are safe, we can never do this again." He turned to kiss her.

Giana looped her arms around his neck and returned his kiss with a passion equal to his own. "And once I am safe, we may never be able to do this again."

"I know," he said, "but nothing is worth risking your life.

Or the life you may be carrying within you. Agreed?" Adam pulled on his waistcoat and jacket.

"Yes." George inhaled, then placed her hand on her abdomen.

He smiled at her and their gazes met and connected. Desire sparked and Adam regretted his earlier words.

"Adam?" she asked, almost as if she had read his mind. "Have you any regrets about this morning?"

He shook his head.

Her eyes sparkled with a sheen of unshed tears. "I apologize for our deceptions and for the delays we caused to the lodge. But we knew we were safe here and we had no where else to go." She walked him to the door.

"There is no need for you to go anywhere," he said. "You can stay here where we can protect you."

Giana gave him a sad smile. "I can only stay until Queen Victoria comes to Balmoral on holiday. She is my godmother. I shall need to see her and explain. Max will not be safe until I've spoken with her . . ."

Adam nodded his understanding.

"I cannot ask anything of you . . ."

"Yes, you can," he answered. "You can ask anything."

"Then, I have two requests."

"Name them."

"I should like to continue our stay here until the queen arrives in Scotland. Their positions here have given the staff a purpose and work to do, something to keep their minds away from the fear and the desire to be home instead of far away in Scotland."

"Done." Adam scratched his chin. "But you might as well know that there are many times when I think your staff leaves a lot to be desired. I've seen you working harder than any of them."

Giana chuckled. "Only because they are barred by Karolyan law from performing any task that might interfere with their traditional duties to the sovereign. While they may work for wages, they must attend to my needs before anything or anyone else."

Adam made a face. "I suppose that explains why my schedule is never followed."

She nodded. "When royalty is in residence, the household staff must attend to them first and to everyone else second."

"Royalty does have its rewards," Adam teased.

"Those rewards always come at great personal sacrifice. Everything has a price."

"And your second request?" Adam asked.

"Will you give thought to my offer?" she asked. "I may not be able to choose, but if I am able to choose, I would choose to have you by my side."

"George, I don't thi—"

"Shh!" She put a finger to her lips. "Do not answer yet. Take the time to think about it. There is much to consider. And your sacrifices would be enormous . . ."

"Are you asking me to marry you?"

She smiled. "I am asking you to accept the role of prince consort of Karolya if I am able to offer it to you . . ."

"I'm a commoner and an American. Is that possible?"

Giana shrugged her shoulders. "It should not be impossible, but I am a woman and it will not be easy . . ."

She sat on the little stool in front of the dressing table staring into the mirror long after Adam left.

Giana thought that she must be losing her mind. She had asked Adam McKendrick to marry her. She could not imagine what she had been thinking to do such a thing. Giana frowned at her reflection in the mirror. That was a lie. She had known exactly what she was thinking when she asked Adam to consider her offer to become her Prince Consort. She had been thinking how nice it would be to wake up in his arms every morning for the rest of her life.

She had been selfishly thinking only of herself. Not of Adam. Giana reached up and touched her lips with her fingertips. How could she ask him to give up his home in America and the Scottish hunting lodge he was working so hard to make a success? How could she ask him to forfeit his businesses in order to take on her problems? How could she ask him to give up his freedom, his way of life, to accept the yoke of a lifetime of obligation and duty to the people of a country not his own?

Giana sighed. She knew better than anyone, the sacrifices Adam would have to make in order to build a life with her. Marrying her would force him to give up everything he loved. Would she be enough for him? Could she give him enough to make up for all he would lose if he decided to accept her offer?

She would be making a sacrifice as well. But Adam didn't know that. And she didn't want him to know. There would be plenty of time to tell him later—if he decided to accept her offer of marriage. Giana bit her bottom lip. She would be heartbroken if he didn't take her offer, but she refused to relinquish all her pride and bribe him to marry her.

Although the Karolyan Charter had abolished the Salic Law prohibiting females from ascending the throne, members of Parliament had added provisos that limited her power to rule.

According to Karolyan law, the heir-apparent had to be married in order to ensure succession. But a princess lost power in the marriage because Karolyan law granted her husband legal jurisdiction over her. By virtue of their marriage, Giana's husband automatically gained equal rights, and in some cases more rights, to everything his wife owned except the hereditary title of Prince. Adam would become prince consort, but a prince consort with more legal rights than his wife.

If she married Adam, Giana risked losing her power over her own country. She wanted to tell him about the Female Provision in the Karolyan Charter, but she was afraid. Afraid that knowing he could gain control of her country might induce Adam to agree to marry her.

Giana didn't know if she could live with the knowledge that the man she had chosen, the man she loved, wanted the role of Prince Consort more than he wanted her. How would she ever know?

Chapter 28

A Princess of the Blood Royal of the House of Saxe-Wallerstein-Karolya must never doubt that the decision she makes is right. She must never show hesitation or weakness.

—MAXIM: 519: PROTOCOL AND COURT ETIQUETTE OF PRINCESSES OF THE BLOOD ROYAL OF THE HOUSE OF SAXE-WALLERSTEIN-KAROLYA, AS DECREED BY HER SERENE HIGHNESS, PRINCESS ROSAMUND, 1782.

"*Okay, boyo, it's time for a talk.*" *O'Brien* burst into the library later that afternoon; waving a newspaper he'd gone into Kinlochen to buy. He found Adam seated behind a desk covered with papers.

Adam shook his head. "Not now."

"I'm beginning to think you've found another boon companion," O'Brien teased, "and are avoiding me."

"It's nice to know that you can take a hint." Adam frowned at him. "Besides, I've got work to do."

O'Brien walked over to the desk and picked up one of the papers Adam was laboring over. "I thought you sent out invitations to the private opening of the lodge two weeks ago." He tossed the letter back on the desk.

"I did," Adam confirmed. "And now I'm sending out more."

"Announcing that the opening of the lodge has been postponed?"

"Not postponed, just rescheduled." Adam held up a letter. "I've written to invite the queen," he said. "I hear she'll be coming to Balmoral soon."

O'Brien frowned. "I thought you'd decided—"

"I did. But now, I've changed my mind." He glanced around to see if any of the workers were working close by.

O'Brien followed Adam's gaze to where one of the paper-hangers working in the room across the hall, hovered beside the door of the library. He slapped his thigh. "I met Josef as I was returning from the village, sir, and he asked me to ask if you intended to ride out today."

Adam stood up and grabbed his hat. "I could use some exercise," he said. "And I need to take a look at the progress on the links."

A half an hour later, Adam and O'Brien rode out of the stable yard.

"Where are we headed?" Murphy asked.

"The links," Adam answered. "We can talk there."

They rode in silence until they reached the eighteenth hole of the golf links. They dismounted near the clubhouse and allowed their horses to graze as they walked about what would soon become the putting greens.

"Is she or isn't she?" O'Brien asked, unable to contain his curiosity any longer.

"She is."

O'Brien nodded. "That's the rumor in the village as well. The news of her disappearance didn't mean much to a tiny Scottish village, but now that the renovation on the lodge is under way, people are beginning to put the pieces of the puzzle together." He paused. "The people we've hired to work in the lodge are keeping pretty closemouthed, but there are others who are beginning to believe that the princess is being held hostage against her will at the lodge. And it doesn't help that Prince Victor of Karolya has offered an enormous reward for information leading to her safe return. It won't be long before someone decides to claim it."

"Prince Victor wants her dead."

"Prince Victor is the one paying for her safe return," O'Brien corrected.

"Prince Victor committed regicide," Adam told him. "He wants George returned so his assassins can finish what they started. The only reason she escaped them the night her parents were murdered was because she wasn't in the capital city. Her father got wind of an assassination plot and sent his heir to safety. Nobody except Maximillian knew where she was."

"Shit!" O'Brien took off his hat and began fanning the air with it.

"That about covers it," Adam responded, dryly.

"The newspapers are pointing a finger at Max," Murphy said. "They've named him as the man who organized the anarchists and engineered her kidnapping."

"There were no anarchists and there was no kidnapping. Victor made it all up so nobody would look too closely at what he was likely to get out of having his uncle and his uncle's family murdered."

"What does he get out of it?" O'Brien asked. "As far as I can tell, he's acting as regent for Princess Giana because he can't inherit."

"Control," Adam answered. "Control of George and control of Karolya's iron ore deposits and thousands of acres of timber. He's already trying to broker deals. And the reason Victor is eager to identify Max is because Max witnessed Prince Christian's murder. He recognized one of the assassins as one of Victor's followers." Adam related the story Giana had told him.

"That may all be true, and Max may be entirely innocent of the crime Victor's accusing him of, but how long do you suppose it will be before someone decides to turn Max in?" O'Brien exhaled slowly. "Prince Victor has covered his tracks very well. And Princess Giana is correct. The papers are reporting that the British government is helping him in the search. Although the queen refuses to recognize him as ruler, my sources tell me that Karolya's prince regent is in Scotland to meet with Her Majesty."

"What?" The idea sent a shudder through Adam.

"I telegraphed the New York Pinkerton office for information and received word that the German papers carried the story that the Karolyan government is announcing that His Highness Prince Victor, regent of Saxe-Wallerstein-Karolya has left Karolya in order to pay a visit to Great Britain. There's speculation that the queen has given up hope that Princess

Giana is alive and will use this visit as an opportunity to recognize Victor as Karolya's rightful ruler."

"Damn!" Adam swore. "Part of the reason George has been hiding here is because Queen Victoria is her godmother. George was planning to use the queen's holiday at Balmoral as an opportunity to present herself and explain the circumstances of her disappearance."

O'Brien shook his head. "She can't go to Balmoral. Not if Victor has taken it upon himself to pay the queen a visit." O'Brien paused, then stared at Adam. "You did say Victor wanted to sell Karolya's iron ore deposits?"

"Yes, but Prince Christian opposed it."

O'Brien was silent for a moment. "I heard several men at your sister's reception talking about buying iron ore."

Adam felt a sinking feeling in the pit of his stomach. "Marshfeld. Kirstin mentioned it and Prince Victor, but I didn't connect it with anything at the lodge."

"Marshfeld isn't the only one. There are others. They were forming a business whose sole purpose was to provide a market for the imports."

"Son of a bitch! I can't help feeling that this is all my fault," Adam admitted. "They were safe at the lodge until I arrived and began a massive and very public transformation of the place from an isolated hunting lodge to a fashionable gentlemen's club."

"You couldn't have known that a princess on the run for her life would choose to hide in the hunting lodge you won from a rich Englishman in a poker game," O'Brien pointed out. "And they couldn't have known ownership of the place would change hands or that you would decide to use the property for anything other than what it had been used for. It was fate, my friend. And you can't change fate."

You cannot save me from my duty, Adam. Or protect me from my fate. Giana's words came back to Adam in a rush of emotion. "She wasn't fated to die, Murphy. If she had been fated to die Max wouldn't have been able to save her from her cousin's assassins. No matter how it happened, the fact is that she was safe until I showed up. My job is to keep her safe."

"This Bountiful Baron business has gone to your head, my friend," O'Brien told him. "I know this one is blond and beautiful, and she's definitely been betrayed, but she is also a princess. You're in over your head, Adam. You cannot save them all!"

Adam stared at his friend. "I have to save this one. She's my future."

"Not necessarily," O'Brien protested. "You said it yourself, Adam, and you were right. This one may be the death of you."

"So be it." Adam caught O'Brien's gaze and held it with his own. "I would gladly die for her. She's worth it. But if that happens, promise me you'll keep her safe." He looked around—at the clubhouse situated at the end of the golf links, then back at O'Brien. "This is the safest place on the estate. It's stone and it has a wine cellar. If Victor should happen to find her, bring her here and keep her safe. Promise me you'll stay with her as long as she needs you."

"We're not just talking about protecting a princess here, are we?"

Adam shook his head. "We're talking about protecting the woman I love."

He loved her. Adam had no trouble coming to terms with that. But he couldn't help wondering: would his love be enough?

She had asked him to think about taking on the role of prince consort, if she was able to offer it, but Adam wasn't sure that was something he could do no matter how much he loved her.

One morning of loving did not make a marriage—no matter how wonderful it was. And marriage to a princess came with a set of problems all its own. Even when the prospective bridegroom was a prince—and Adam was no prince.

Marriage to the sovereign head of a nation required a huge sacrifice on the part of the spouse, and Adam knew that in some ways his sacrifice would be greater still because it meant giving up his homeland. It meant leaving everything that was

Adam McKendrick behind and becoming someone else. It meant giving up his freedom.

And giving up his freedom was a sacrifice Adam wasn't sure he could make. He wasn't the same man he was a month ago. He was different and the new Adam McKendrick had fallen madly in love with a woman of incredible strength, love, courage, and an awe-inspiring loyalty to the people she loved. But even the new Adam McKendrick quaked in his boots at the thought of everything he would have to give up in order to be with George.

But he couldn't ignore his responsibility to George any more than she could ignore her responsibility to her country. He knew that in order to offer George some measure of protection, he ought to marry her, but marriage to the heir apparent of a country is not something any man with a healthy measure of self-respect and self-preservation would choose. And he had both. Marrying George meant forfeiting his American citizenship, and giving up control of everything he had worked so hard to gain. It meant allowing someone else to manage not only his property but also his life. Adam frowned. It meant living in Karolya, far away from his family and friends, giving up everything he'd ever known in order to occasionally stand at George's side, but more often than not, it would mean standing in the background, playing second fiddle to George and to any children they might have for the rest of his life.

Could he give up his way of life for George? Could he live with himself if he did?

"*You were correct in your assessment, my lord.*" The marquess of Everleigh stood before his friend and mentor, Andrew Ramsey, the sixteenth marquess of Templeston, in the private study of Lord Templeston's London home and related the details of his audience with His Highness Prince Victor of Saxe-Wallerstein-Karolya.

Templeston frowned. "I'm sorry for that." He looked up at Ashford Everleigh. "I fear, sometimes, that I have lived too long. That I have outlived my usefulness. The world is changing, and I don't envy you the challenges with which you will have to contend." He sighed. "I've seen so much greed and envy and malice—within families and among friends—that I am never surprised anymore." He looked sad, remembering. "We are about to enter the last quarter of this century," he said. "When it began, we were fighting Napoleon—and now, we have this young pretender to the throne of Karolya to defeat."

"Prince Victor is no Napoleon, sir," Everleigh pointed out.

"That is true," Templeston agreed. "Ambitious geniuses like Napoleon appear but once in a lifetime." He propped his elbows on his desk, steepled his fingers together in thought, and breathed a heartfelt prayer. "Thank God. But petty tyrants like Prince Victor are just as dangerous as men who aspire to conquer and rule the world—perhaps even more dangerous."

"How so?" Everleigh studied his mentor. He had known Lord Templeston all of his life, having been at school with Templeston's son, Kit. There wasn't a finer man in all of England, and Everleigh was proud to be among the few chosen to work with him. Templeston still had a great deal of knowledge to share, and Everleigh was eager to absorb it.

"Men like Prince Victor are cunning and subtle and devious. They present a charming face to the world and to the people around them. They are evil disguised as angels. People rarely see them for what they are and most people would deny it if you told them. There was nothing subtle or devious about Napoleon. He was straightforward. He set goals and did what was necessary to attain them, but he was a soldier and everyone recognized that. He was a tyrant—a charming tyrant—but the whole world knew him for what he was. He amassed armies and proclaimed that he would conquer the world, and the worlds he would have conquered knew that the only way to keep from being conquered was to form an alliance and defeat him. Napoleon was a large, lone rogue wolf. Prince Victor is a wolf in fashionable sheep's clothing." He turned to Everleigh. "Do we know if Princess Giana is still alive?"

"No, sir. But I took the liberty of requesting a copy of the Karolyan Charter through our ambassador, Lord Sissingham. I learned from reading it that a coronation must take place within a year following the death of the reigning prince. In order to be crowned, Prince Victor must possess the Karolyan Seal of State and proof of Princess Giana's death. And he must marry. Our sources in Karolya tell us that Prince Victor offered for his cousin's hand in marriage, but Prince Christian refused."

Lord Templeston smiled. "Then she's still alive. Prince Christian has been dead for more than five months. The planning and execution of even a small coronation will take the better part of six or seven moths. If Victor had the Seal of State, he would most certainly have produced it by now. If he doesn't have it, it must be because someone else has it. You investigated the murders and followed the trail of the anarchists. Any sign of them?"

"No."

"No declaration of grievances against Prince Christian's government. No manifestos? No demands? No threats of violence against other royal families?"

Everleigh shook his head. "Nothing. It's as if they disappeared from the face of the earth. Just like the princess."

"The difference is that we know Princess Giana existed," Templeston reminded him. "We cannot say the same of the supposed anarchists. I suspect Prince Victor forgot to complete the fiction. Forgot that anarchists must leave a trail."

"That's because he's accused Lord Gudrun."

"Who also existed and who also disappeared from view." He thought for a moment. "What of the kidnappers? Have we heard from them?"

"No," Lord Everleigh replied.

"So all we have is Prince Victor's version of the story."

"That is correct."

"And, sir, I know Maximillian Gudrun. He did not murder Prince Christian and Princess May or incite anyone else to do it. He was as loyal to his prince as I am to you. He did not kidnap their daughter. Nothing would ever induce Max to betray his prince or his country. Certainly not forests of virgin timber or vast iron ore deposits."

"Ah, the rights to the timber and iron ore deposits. Who has them and who wants them?" Templeston mused. "They should belong to the people of Karolya. They should be held in trust and protected by Princess Giana. But we cannot find her to ask, so we need to ask who is in a position to sell them and who is willing to pay to get them?" He glanced over at his younger protégé.

"His role as regent gives Prince Victor the power to sell them—provided Princess Giana fails to return to Karolya and claim her throne," Everleigh answered.

Lord Templeston clapped his hands together. "All right then, let's look at Prince Victor. Do we know his plans? Where he is going and where he's been?"

"He's here in London," Everleigh reported. "He left Karolya shortly after I did."

The sixteenth marquess of Templeston grinned. "Yes, I read in yesterday's papers that he was planning a trip to Scotland to see the queen. Tell me, Lord Everleigh, since Prince Victor did not announce his arrival in London through the proper diplomatic channels or request an audience with Her Majesty, who is he visiting and why did he come?"

"He's visiting the viscount and viscountess Marshfeld," Everleigh replied, also grinning. "Just down the street. And our sources tell us that the viscount Marshfeld's name was recently added to the roster of businessmen who have formed a consortium in order to purchase and import raw materials necessary for the building of railroads—including virgin timber and . . ."

"Iron ore." They spoke in unison.

"Why Scotland?" Templeston asked. "What, or shall we say, who, does Prince Victor want to see in Scotland?"

"Besides the queen?"

Templeston nodded.

Everleigh shrugged. "I haven't the foggiest."

"We need to find out," Lord Templeston said. "For I suspect she has done a Margo."

"Pardon?"

"Princess Giana has done a Margo." He looked at Everleigh, expecting him to recognize the name and when Everleigh failed to do so, Lord Templeston explained. "Years ago my wife had a pet fox named Margo. She had reared Margo from a kit, and Margo was as tame and nearly as well mannered as a pet dog. That often made it hard for us to remember she was a fox. But whenever Margo felt cornered or threatened, she behaved as any threatened or cornered fox would behave. She went up a tree or to ground. Now, if our missing princess sought to escape her enemies by going up a tree, she would have turned to her godmother, our gracious queen. But if for some reason, she couldn't go above her enemies, she would have to go to ground, to hide and bide her time. Princess Giana has gone to ground."

"How do we go about clearing the way for the princess to come out of hiding?" Everleigh asked.

"We kennel the hounds," Templeston answered. "Pay a visit to the Marshfelds and extend an invitation to visit the queen at Balmoral. She begins her Scottish holiday in a sennight and Victor won't be able to resist an opportunity to present his case."

"Sir?"

"Don't worry," Templeston said. "I'll arrange it with Her Majesty. Just remember that any kenneling we do must take place on Scottish, rather than English soil."

Lord Everleigh frowned. "The Act of Union unified England and Scotland as Great Britain, a single nation under one rule—the rule of our gracious queen."

"That's true," Lord Templeston agreed. "Our gracious queen rules Great Britain, but she is first and foremost, Queen of England and the Queen of England must not be perceived by other countries, or the sovereign heads of those countries, as meddling in Karolyan affairs or assisting in the overthrow of Prince Victor's government. He may be a murderer and a thoroughly despicable male specimen, but the rest of the world isn't privy to that information. The rest of the world only knows that Prince Victor is the last surviving male member of the Karolyan royal family, acting regent, and heir presumptive to the throne. We cannot kennel the hounds in England, but Scotland retains a measure of autonomy in its domestic laws and policies, religious practices, and its system of education that can be used to our advantage."

"Meaning?"

"That a usurper like Prince Victor is guaranteed a certain level of protection under English law that does not necessarily have to be extended to him in Scotland."

"What about Princess Giana?" Everleigh asked.

"As the queen's goddaughter, Princess Giana will be guaranteed protection throughout the whole of Great Britain." Templeston sighed. "Provided we locate her before Victor does."

Chapter 29

In years to come, women of the West will sing the praises and tell the tales of the Bountiful Baron the way Englishmen sing the praises of King Arthur and his knights of the round table.

—The Second Installment of the True Adventures of the Bountiful Baron: Western Benefactor to Blond, Beautiful, and Betrayed Women written by John J. Bookman, 1874.

It had been three days since he held her in his arms. Three long miserable days he had given himself to consider her offer.

He tried to stay away, to give himself time to think about her proposal, but Adam couldn't look at George without wanting her. He couldn't pass her in the corridors without wanting to kiss her, to take her in his arms and promise her everything would be all right. But he had no right to make promises unless he intended to keep them.

"Sir?"

Lost in thought, Adam looked up to see Max standing beside his desk. "Yes?"

"A telegram marked urgent was just delivered from the village." Max held out the telegram.

Adam frowned. Max's manner had become distinctly cold and distant during the last three days. There could only be one reason and Adam decided now was as good a time as any to broach the subject. He set the telegram aside.

"Your pardon, sir, but the telegram from London is marked 'urgent'," Max repeated.

"It's not as urgent as the topic I need to discuss with you." Adam smiled. "Close the door, Max."

Max did as instructed.

"I want to thank you," Adam said. "You have my undying gratitude for saving Princess Giana's life."

Max turned so white, Adam was afraid the older man would faint from lack of blood.

"S-s-sir?" Max stammered, not quite certain if Adam were fishing for information or if the princess had confided in him.

His worst fears were confirmed when Adam replied, "George told me what happened."

"Happened, sir?" Max's voice trembled.

"In Christianberg," Adam told him.

Max groped for the leather chair in front of Adam's desk as his knees threatened to give way.

Adam stood up, rounded his desk and ushered the older man onto the seat. "What I say to you now goes no further than this room. If as Giana says, Victor's spies are everywhere, I cannot promise that some of them aren't working here now. I can promise you that I haven't spoken to anyone about this except O'Brien—"

Max groaned. Why was it that gentlemen felt compelled to tell their secrets to their tailors and valets?

Adam meant to set the older man's mind to rest, but may have succeeded in upsetting him further, so he hastened to add, "—who is not a valet, but is my closest friend and a detective with the renowned Pinkerton National Detective Agency in America. Murphy O'Brien is the very soul of discretion."

Adam paused, allowing Max a moment to digest that bit of information. "She told me everything. I know about Prince Victor and Prince Christian's dying request that you take the Seal of State of Karolya to Giana and that you protect her with your life. I want you to know that I have seen the Seal of State suspended from a gold chain that encircles your princess's waist."

Max leapt from the chair. "You have seen . . ." He sputtered. "How is that possible?

Adam lifted one eyebrow.

"You, sir, are a scoundrel!" Max's body shook with outrage. He removed one of his white gloves and slapped Adam across the face with it. "You deliberately set out to *seduce* an innocent!"

Adam didn't flinch at the insult. He didn't move a muscle. He simply accepted the old man's right to demand satisfaction. The way Max said it, seduced sounded shoddy and lecherous. Something of which to be ashamed. But he wasn't ashamed. Seduced was a word that had nothing to do with what had happened between him and George. "No, sir, I did not."

"How would you characterize it?"

I made love to her. The thought popped into his brain, but Adam wisely kept it to himself. He straightened his shoulders, pulling himself up to his full height. "However I characterize it, it is between Princess Giana and me." Adam looked the older man in the eye. "I'm not defending myself or excusing my actions. What's done is done and I will not embarrass your princess by discussing the intimate details of our relationship with you—except to say that I did not know she was a princess until after . . ." Adam let his words trail off, then cleared his throat and tried again. "Had I known, I could have prevented . . . But there was nothing I could do after the fact."

The older man gasped and turned even paler. "She revealed her identity after she allowed you to . . . ?"

Adam nodded. "Now that you understand, shall we face off with pistols or sabers drawn at dawn? Or will you help me?"

Max began to pace and wring his hands. "You do not know what you have done." He stared at Adam. "Prince Victor will kill her if he finds out."

"That's why I came to you," Adam told him. "I need you to help me make damn sure Cousin Victor doesn't find out—until after she's safely married and beyond his reach."

"Married?" Max was stunned. "Princess Giana cannot get married."

"Why not?"

"Prince Victor will never allow her to marry anyone except him and Princess Giana would never marry her parents' murderer."

"Why does she need Victor's permission to marry?" Adam asked.

"Because she is female. Under Karolyan law, females may not marry without the consent of their nearest living male relative," Max explained.

"Even princesses?"

"Especially princesses. Because there is so much more at stake."

Adam swore beneath his breath. "What if there is no living male relative? Who grants consent?"

"The Ecclesiastical court. But everyone knows that Princess Giana has a living male relative in Victor."

"Victor is her cousin, right?" Adam knew the answer, but he needed confirmation.

"Yes."

Adam smiled. "Tell me, Lord Gudrun, what do you know about George Ramsey, the marquess of Templeston?"

Max was genuinely shocked. Only Princess May, her parents, Lord and Lady Barracksford, Prince Christian, the fifteenth marquess of Templeston and he had known the truth about Princess May's conception. Princess May had insisted that her future husband be told before they married and Lord and Lady Barracksford had complied with the request. As Prince Christian's private secretary, Max had been asked to record the audience and to file the papers in Prince Christian's private archive. In the unlikely event that anything happened to Prince Christian to force Princess May or any of her children to request assistance from the marquess of Templeston, she would have the locket as proof, but she would also have a document to prove to the Karolyan people or government or any other court or government that Prince Christian had been made aware of her heritage before he married her. Max had retrieved that document from Prince Christian's private archive the night the prince was murdered. He had kept the bloodstained document hidden safely inside the heel of his boot in the event that the princess needed it.

Max had never breathed a word of what he knew and everyone else who had known was dead. Except, it seemed, Princess Giana. Max was stunned. He had had no idea that the princess had known. "There is a likeness of George Ramsey, the fifteenth marquess of Templeston inside the locket the princess wears about her neck."

"That would mean that the fifteenth marquess of Templeston was her maternal grandfather and that the current marquess would be her uncle."

"That is correct."

"An uncle who could grant her permission to marry?"

"Yes," Max confirmed.

"Where do we find him?" Adam asked.

"In London. He is one of Queen Victoria's most trusted advisors. But having permission to marry is not the only requirement our princess must meet in order to marry. If she chooses to marry any member of a royal house, Princess Giana must undergo a doctor's examination confirming that she is a virgin." He looked Adam in the eye, challenging him. "As she is no longer a virgin, who can we find who would marry a princess knowing that she is not a virgin, knowing that she may be carrying someone else's heir? What man would be willing to give up his personal identity in order to marry a princess who would have complete and utter jurisdiction over him?"

"I will," Adam said.

"You do not possess a title, sir," Max told him. "Under Karolyan law, the princess may marry a titled commoner, but not an untitled one."

"Will a baron do?"

Max frowned. "A baron ranks below a viscount, an earl, a marquess, a duke, and a prince in the order of precedence. On state occasions, a baron would be required to walk behind all personages above his rank."

"I don't care about any of that," Adam said. "Can she marry a baron?"

"Most assuredly. The style of baron is an ancient and honorable one." Max faced him, his expression, unreadable. "What baron did you have in mind?"

"The Bountiful Baron Adam McKendrick."

"I'm sure that will be most acceptable."

"To you? Or to the people of Karolya?" Adam asked.

Maximillian, Lord Gudrun, grinned. "I was charged with one last request by the late Prince Christian. A request I was not certain I could manage. But Princess Giana came to me two nights ago and told me that while she was quite prepared to do her duty to the people of Karolya, if her proposal went unanswered, she wanted me to help her find a way to follow her heart. When I asked what she meant, she told me that she had chosen you to be her prince consort and that if you wanted the position, my duty would be to convince the Karolyan government to accept you. If you refused her offer, my duty was to find a way to help her abdicate, for you were her heart and she was bound to follow you." Tears sparkled in Max's eyes as he faced Adam. "Her father's, Prince Christian's, last words to me were: *'Tell Giana never to be afraid to follow her heart. Promise me, Max. Promise you will help her find a way.'* " He smiled a satisfied smile. "I have fulfilled my promise and done my duty."

Max picked up the telegram and handed it back to Adam. "I took the liberty of sending a telegram in your name to the marquess of Templeston yesterday morning. You received this reply this afternoon."

Adam opened the telegram and read: "The marquess of Templeston will be arriving at Balmoral, Scotland, as a guest of Her Majesty, Victoria Regina, by the Grace of God, Queen of England in two days time. He invites you and the members of your senior household to travel to Balmoral under the protection of Her Majesty, the Queen, where you will be granted an audience. He is most eager to view the locket, your documentation, and discuss your request. Signed Ashford, Marquess of Everleigh." Adam looked over at Max.

Max stood at attention and clicked his heels together in the military fashion. "I should like to accompany you, sir."

Adam smiled. "I should like that as well," he said, gently, "but I'm afraid it's not possible."

"I am a senior member of the household," Max said.

"You are, indeed," Adam answered. "But you are also the only witness to the murders. We cannot risk your life. You must stay here with the princess where it's safe."

"Who will you choose to accompany you, sir?"

"Gordon," Adam answered, "and Josef."

Max gave a quick nod, then sat down on the leather chair. "You will require this documentation, sir." He propped his left foot on his right thigh, then bent and twisted the heel of left boot. It swung open to reveal a hollow compartment filled with bloodied parchment paper. Max carefully lifted it out and handed it to Adam. "Might I suggest that the princess also compose a letter of introduction for you that contains her signature and official seal?" He didn't have to mention the seal still locked around Giana's waist to convey his intent.

Adam understood. "Her official seal might be hard to manage," he answered.

Max met his gaze. "I am sure she and we, may rely on your discreet assistance."

Giana joined Adam in his bedchamber later that evening. Adam looked up as she entered the room. She was fresh from her bath and the scent of orange blossoms clung to her hair and to her nightgown.

Wagner entered silently behind her. He, unfortunately, did not smell entirely of orange blossoms, but of a more pungent odor of orange blossoms and wet dog. Adam wrinkled his nose at the smell.

"I bathed him, but it is raining outside. He will smell better once he dries."

Adam wasn't as certain, but he pretended he believed her.

She looked at him. "I tried to stay away," she said. "But I could not."

"I'm glad you didn't," he said.

"I promised myself I would not try to persuade you into accepting my proposal, but . . ." She glanced down at her bare toes, unable to finish her sentence.

Adam reached out, took hold of her hand and pulled her toward him. "It's all right, Princess," he said, kissing her eyes and cheekbones and throat before finally kissing her lips with a passion that left her breathless. "I've made my decision."

Giana was so nervous her breath caught in her throat. "Have you?"

He nodded.

"And . . ." She prodded.

"And as a result, I've been invited to Balmoral for the weekend," he said.

"Why?"

"I've a meeting with the current marquess of Templeston."

Giana gasped, then waited on pins and needles, for Adam to continue.

"I've decided to accept your offer, George, and I'll need your locket so Templeston can authenticate it." Giana didn't reply. She simply stared at him until he reached over, gently took her face in his hands, and leaned down to kiss her. When he finished kissing her, he said, "I'll also need a letter of introduction with your signature and seal. After my meeting, Victor won't be able to hurt you, and you won't have to worry about him anymore."

"You want to be prince consort?"

She stared at him.

He grinned. "If the offer's still open."

She wrinkled her brow. "Are you certain, Adam? Are you certain you wish to take on the responsibility? I have yet to secure my throne," she babbled. "I may have to fight to secure it. And it is possible that I will not succeed it securing it at all. Do you understand?" She stared into his eyes. "If I do not succeed the throne, I cannot keep my promise and reward you with the title."

"Are you trying to talk me out of it?" he asked. "Because I warn you that it won't do you any good." Adam shrugged his shoulders. "Until I met you, I never cared much for people with titles."

Giana opened her mouth to speak, but words failed her. Her mouth formed a perfect O of surprise.

Adam took advantage, leaning down to kiss her once again. "I want to marry you. The only promises I'll hold you to are the ones you make on our wedding day."

"Oh, Adam!" Giana unfastened her locket and handed it to him and promptly burst into tears.

"Is that a yes?" Adam dropped the locket into his pocket for safekeeping moments before Giana wrapped her arms around his neck, pressed herself against him and kissed him again and again until he was dizzy with the scent and feel of her.

He wiped her tears off her cheek with the pad of his thumb. "You know I've heard it said that genuine princesses never cry."

"Who is crying?" she demanded, taking his hand in hers and leading him toward the bed.

"You are, Princess."

Giana shook her head. "Those are not tears," she answered. "They're exclamations of joy."

"In that case . . ." he whispered in her ear, "spread the joy. Let's consummate this deal."

Adam followed her down onto the mattress, then rolled over to find Wagner resting his head on bed. He watched as the dog lifted a paw, and attempted to settle in beside them.

"Oh, no, you don't," Adam said. "Off!"

Giana giggled as Wagner retreated ever so slowly and walked around to the foot of the bed. "I think you hurt his emotions."

"Feelings," Adam translated. "I may have hurt his *feelings*, but he is not sleeping with you tonight. He'll have to learn to get used to it."

"We are not going to be sleeping," she informed him. "We are going to be practicing."

"Practicing what?" he asked, curiously aroused by the inflection of her words.

"The skills I learned the last time we shared a bed."

"You're going to be a very busy woman," he said. "For it takes time to perfect those skills."

"Wagner is going to be very busy as well," she said. "As soon as you issue his orders."

Adam snapped his fingers and pointed to the door. "Wagner! *En garde*."

Wagner trotted to the door and lay down in front of it.

"That is better," Giana said, lifting the hem of her nightgown and pulling it over her head. The light from the lamp reflected off the gold at her waist and around her neck as she crawled onto Adam. "Have you any orders for me?" she teased.

Adam snapped his fingers and pointed to the member that was already standing hard and erect. "Princess! *En garde*!"

Chapter 30

The Bountiful Baron is the ideal American. He journeyed west to find his fortune and succeeded where others failed. He is a self-made man. A millionaire, a gentleman and a frontier hero.

—The First Installment of the True Adventures of the Bountiful Baron: Western Benefactor to Blond, Beautiful, and Betrayed Women written by John J. Bookman, 1874.

Four days later, Adam boarded the express train from Kinlochen to Balmoral for a journey that would take half as long as the journey to London. O'Brien had wanted to accompany him, but Adam asked him to stay behind and look after George. Just in case.

O'Brien had agreed, so Gordon and Josef went in his place.

The three of them were escorted off the train at the station and driven to the castle. They departed the coach at the front door where they were allowed admittance by a butler.

"How do you do, Mr. McKendrick? I am Lord Everleigh, Lord Templeston's associate." Everleigh greeted Adam at the door, then led the three men to the marquess of Templeston's temporary office.

Gordon Ross and Josef Sommers remained outside the room, waiting beside the door to Lord Templeston's office while Lord Everleigh ushered Adam inside.

"I shall be down the hall should you require my assistance, sir," Everleigh spoke to the gentleman seated at the massive desk, then quietly withdrew, leaving Adam alone with the other man.

"Good afternoon, Mr. McKendrick. It's a pleasure to meet you."

Andrew Ramsey, the sixteenth Marquess of Templeston, was a big man, older than Adam expected, and still quite handsome and youthful despite his advanced years. He pushed himself to his feet and came around the desk to shake Adam's hand.

"Likewise, sir." Adam sketched a low bow.

"You have come about the missing princess." Lord Templeston returned to his chair.

"Yes, sir," Adam replied. "I have come on her behalf."

"Princess Giana is claiming to be a granddaughter of my late father?" Lord Templeston's inquiry was more statement than a question.

"Yes"

"I suppose you have proof?"

Adam reached into his waistcoat pocket, retrieved the gold-and-diamond locket, the document Max had given him, and the letter George had written and affixed with the State Seal of Saxe-Wallerstein-Karolya. "Her Highness sent this to you and a note for her godmother, the queen. She asked that you read her letter first." He handed the letters, the proof Max had given him, and the gold locket to Lord Templeston.

The marquess studied the wax seal binding the edges of the letter together, then opened it and read:

My lord Templeston, I have entrusted my most precious possessions and my life to the man you see standing before you in hopes that you will grant me my heart's desire. He carries my locket—a locket I am certain you will recognize. My grandmother presented it to my mother when my mother came of age and my mother, Princess May of Saxe-Wallerstein-Karolya, presented it to me along with instructions to present it to the sitting English marquess of Templeston or his representative should I ever find myself in need. I send Mr. Adam McKendrick to present it to you today, because I find myself in desperate need of assistance in regaining my homeland.

You may know that my mother was born Lady Caroline Frances Alexandra May Barracksford, daughter of the marquess and marchioness of Barracksford. What you may not know is that, my grandmother, the marchioness of Barracksford, was once a Parisian actress . . .

Lord Templeston closed his eyes, vividly remembering the day he had stood in the study of his London town house and listened as his father's solicitor, Martin Bell, had explained the terms of the codicil to his father's will. It had happened so many years ago—more years than the young man standing before him had been alive—but the memory was as fresh in Lord Templeston's mind as if it had happened yesterday.

"There is a codicil to your father's will. He named several. There were more than one."

"More than one what?" Drew had asked.

"Ladybirds." Martin cleared his throat.

"On the yacht?" His father and his father's latest mistress had died in a yachting accident and Drew remembered wondering how many more mistresses he might have aboard and how many more of his father's mistresses might need to be buried in the family cemetery.

"Oh, no," Martin reassured him. "On land."

He had breathed a sigh of relief. "How many?"

"He mentioned five. In addition to the young opera singer, there's a milliner in Brighton. An actress in Paris. A seamstress in Edinburgh. And a young woman in Northamptonshire."

The young woman in Northamptonshire had turned out to be Kathryn Markinson Stafford, the current marchioness of Templeston, and the love of Drew's life. The actress in Paris had married another English marquess—the marquess of Barracksford—and had given birth to a daughter who had married a prince and who had given birth to a daughter of her own—Princess Georgiana of Saxe-Wallerstein-Karolya.

The daughter of his half-sister. A daughter who had been given a feminine form of his father's name. Georgiana. Drew opened his eyes and turned his attention back to the letter the princess had written.

I have known for some time that I had family in England, but my grandmother's, mother's, and my own, great source of pride was that we had never needed to call upon you for assistance. Were it not for the murder of my parents and the situation I find myself in today, I am quite certain that I would never have called upon you and would have carried this family secret to my grave. But today, dear sir, I require an extraordinary favor. Karolyan law requires that a Princess of the Blood Royal receive permission from her closest living male relative in order to marry.

As my uncle, you are my closest living male relative, and today, I ask that you grant me permission to follow my heart and marry the man I have chosen to be my prince consort—Mr. Adam McKendrick. Such a marriage would fulfill the requirements set forth in the Female Provision of the Karolyan Charter and would allow me to fulfill my duty and obligation to my country by reclaiming my rightful place on the throne of Saxe-Wallerstein-Karolya.

Her Serene Highness Georgiana Regina
Princess of the Blood Royal of the House of Saxe-Wallerstein-Karolya.

Beneath her signature was the wax impression of the Karolyan Seal of State.

Lord Templeston carefully refolded the letter and laid it on the blotter beside the letter addressed to the queen and picked up the remaining letter. All three letters bore the wax impression of the Karolyan Seal of State, but only one carried the signatures of the late prince and princess. Only one was stained with blood.

Lord Templeston raised an eyebrow in question.

"Lord Gudrun assured me that the blood was his," Adam said. "He secreted the letter inside his waistcoat pocket after he was injured and unfortunately, bled on it. He transferred it from his waistcoat pocket to a hollow compartment in the heel of his boot during the journey from Christianberg to Laken and it remained there until he presented it to me."

Templeston read the document from Prince Christian's private archives. It confirmed everything Princess Georgiana had written. The only thing left to authenticate was the gold-and-diamond locket. Lord Templeston scooped it off the desk and opened it, revealing the tiny likenesses of the marquess and marchioness of Barracksford and of Prince Christian and Princess May and the infant Princess Georgiana. It came as no surprise to Drew to discover that the marchioness looked enough like his mother to be her sister. All of George Ramsey's mistresses bore a striking resemblance to each other and to his dead wife. Drew studied the likenesses, then carefully slipped the portrait of the Barracksfords aside and found himself staring into the handsome face of his father, George Ramsey, the fifteenth marquess of Templeston. He looked down at his father's face, then carefully closed the locket and turned it over, searching for the jeweler's mark he knew would be there. "I haven't seen one of these in a very long time. It's authentic." Lord Templeston closed the locket and handed it back to Adam, then removed a document from a sheath of papers on his desk and gave it to him as well. "This is a copy of the codicil to my father's will. Please give it to my niece."

Adam glanced at the document. "May I?"

Lord Templeston nodded. "Please do."

Adam finished reading the codicil and looked up at the marquess. "He must have been an exceptional man."

"Yes, he was," Templeston agreed. "As you can see, Princess Giana is entitled to a substantial sum of money and . . ."

"She isn't interested in the money, sir, just in the permission," Adam told him.

"Permission granted," Lord Templeston said. "I'll put it in writing in case the question of permission arises once she returns to Karolya. Good luck to you, my boy," the older man said. "I'd gladly give my permission to protect Princess Giana from the likes of Victor—even if she weren't my niece. You're in luck, you know, because you're in Scotland. You can be married right away. Today if you like by the local vicar."

"Thank you, sir."

"My pleasure, my boy. Welcome to the family." Templeston

stood up, walked around his desk and clamped his hand on Adam's shoulder.

"If there is anything I can do—" Adam began.

Templeston smiled once again. "Before you go, there is someone who would like to speak to you." He rose from his desk and walked across the room where he opened a door, then stood back to allow a small, round figure completely dressed in black except for her lace collar and widow's cap to enter.

A tall, brawny Highlander entered with her. Adam watched, in fascination, as the Scotsman moved into position, towering over her as he stood a few steps behind her, quite obviously guarding her back.

Lord Templeston closed the door, then bowed to the queen, and made the introduction. "Your Majesty, may I present Mr. Adam McKendrick?"

The queen held out her hand. "Mr. McKendrick."

Adam bowed over her hand and briefly touched her fingers the way he'd seen Lord Templeston do. "Ma'am."

The queen walked over to a chair and sat down, then motioned for the gentlemen to do likewise. Once they were seated, she wasted no time in getting to the heart of the matter. "You are an American?"

"Yes, ma'am."

"From Texas?"

Adam shook his head. "From Nevada Territory, ma'am."

"We understand that you have gained ownership of a hunting lodge here in our beloved Highlands."

"Yes, ma'am," Adam answered. "Larchmont Lodge near the village of Kinlochen."

"I see." She studied Adam for a moment. "We understand that Princess Giana sought sanctuary in your hunting lodge before you took up residence there."

Adam nodded. "Yes, ma'am."

"As an American, you had no idea she was a princess?"

"No, ma'am. She was disguised as a chambermaid."

Queen Victoria laughed at the idea of Princess Giana disguising herself as a chambermaid. Once, many years ago, before she became queen, she had delighted in disguising herself and appearing for dinner dressed in all manner of costumes. "So, you have come to Balmoral as her representative?"

"Yes, ma'am," Adam acknowledged. "She asked me to deliver this letter to you." He glanced at Lord Templeston who retrieved the letter George had addressed to the queen from the desk before presenting it to her.

The queen didn't open the letter, but held it on her lap while she looked at Adam, and asked, "How is our goddaughter?"

"She is an extraordinary woman, ma'am," Adam answered.

The queen smiled. "Of that I've no doubt. But how is she, Mr. McKendrick? How is she coping with her terrible bereavement?"

Adam stared at the tiny woman, still grieving for her husband, still wearing her widow's weeds and white mourning cap and understood what the queen wanted to know. "Her Highness is coping as well as can be expected in light of her tremendous loss—of her parents and of her homeland. She dresses all in black, ma'am, as she mourns her loss. But she bears her grief as one would expect of a princess and sheds her tears in private."

The queen nodded her approval, then broke the wax seal on the letter, unfolded the paper and read the note Giana had written. When she looked up again, she pinned Adam with her sharp, no-nonsense gaze. "Tell me, Mr. McKendrick, do you know what is in this letter?" She tapped the paper against the edge of her chair.

"No, ma'am."

"How do we know this note is from Princess Giana? How do we know you did not write the letter and seal it with a stolen seal? How do we know you are not in league with her kidnappers?"

Adam met the queen's steady gaze. "You've only my word, Your Majesty, and the word of Princess Giana."

She smiled at Adam, then glanced at the note again, and laughed. "Princess Giana's message was as well-chosen as her messenger. She, alone, knew that we would understand."

The queen turned the letter so Adam and Lord Templeston could see it.

Adam was clearly surprised. The letter wasn't a letter at all. It was a drawing. A pen and ink sketch of Wagner asleep in the center of Adam's bed—head comfortably pillowed, back curved, and all four paws pointing toward the ceiling. A cloud-like bubble above the dog's head contained sketches of a tea table, complete with cakes and whole salmon, and bore the caption: *Wagner Dreams of Iced Teacakes and Salmon, 1874. To Our Beloved Teacher, V. R from her grateful student. G. R.*

"We taught her to draw and paint when she was no more than four or five," the queen explained. "And we have continued to exchange drawings from that day until this one. Mostly of dogs and horses." She looked over at Adam and at Lord Templeston. "Princess Giana excels in the drawing of dogs. When she visits, we pack picnic lunches that always contain salmon as the main course and teacakes for dessert. We drive out onto the moor and sit together for hours in companionable silence, with our trusted Mr. Brown looking out for us." She nodded toward her Highland Servant. "While we sketch."

After carefully refolding the drawing, Queen Victoria rose from her chair and walked over to the Scotsman. He nodded once, then rang the bellpull suspended from the ceiling. When the maid arrived, the Highlander repeated the queen's request and waited at the door until the maid returned with the queen's latest sketchbook and a box of pencils, and a small silver-framed photograph of the late prince consort.

The Highlander presented the sketchbook and box of pencils to the queen and kept the framed photograph in readiness as he returned to his position at her back.

"Please sit, Mr. McKendrick, as we shall return Her Highness's message in kind."

With those words, the queen took out a pencil and began to draw.

When she finished, she presented Adam with a sketch of Wagner wearing a top hat and tails and a much more elegant female wolfhound wearing a veil and a wreath of orange blossoms. There was a Gothic arched window above the canine pair bearing the Karolyan coat of arms and a circle of bulldogs, wearing the emblem of queen's Coldstream Guards, stood guard around them.

Adam was amazed by the queen's talent and by the symbolism of the drawing. The caption read: *Long life and felicitations from H.M.V.R. to H.S.H. G. R.* He looked up from the drawing and met the queen's sparkling gaze.

"We kept our drawings secret," she explained. "Sharing them as a form of secret code known only to us. Something special to be exchanged between a royal godmother and a royal goddaughter." She handed Adam the other drawing.

It was an amazing likeness of him signed by the queen.

She smiled at him and Adam caught a glimpse of the young woman she had been.

"To thank you," she said. "For providing comfort and shelter to our goddaughter."

"It has been an honor, ma'am," Adam said.

The queen turned to Lord Templeston. "We should like to send a number of our own Coldstream guards to Mr. McKendrick's hunting lodge to escort Her Serene Highness and Mr. McKendrick back to Balmoral. If you have no objection." She looked at Adam. "We should like to see you married. We shall arrange for the ceremony to be held here at Balmoral in two days' time. You shall honeymoon here as my guests—"

"But, Your Majesty," Lord Templeston interrupted. "Lady Templeston and I were hoping that Princess Giana and Mr. McKendrick would spend time with us at Swanslea Park."

The queen turned her attention to her adviser. "You and Lady Templeston shall join us here. It's been too long since we have seen our dear Wren and we so much enjoy our art lessons."

Templeston nodded.

"Two days, Your Majesty?" There was no way to disguise the note of uncertainty in Adam's tone of voice. "What about Prince Victor?"

The queen frowned. "We shall handle Prince Victor," she said. "We shall take great pleasure in seeing that particular royal usurper squashed like a bug." She motioned for her Highland Servant. "And we shall take great delight in arranging the princess's wedding while we await her arrival. Please give these to our goddaughter with our great love and tell her that it would please us greatly for her to wear the cameo our dear Albert gave to us." Queen Victoria reached up and unpinned a black onyx and mother of pearl cameo from her lace collar and handed it to her servant who handed the pin and the silver-framed photograph to Adam.

"Thank you, ma'am," Adam replied.

"You are most welcome." The queen rose from her chair.

Adam and Lord Templeston bowed as she walked past. Moments later, she and her servant had disappeared through the massive doors.

Adam stood staring until Lord Templeston clapped him on the back: "Congratulations, my boy! The queen doesn't present a photograph of Prince Albert to everyone. The fact that she did means she approves of you and of the marriage."

"I don't care about the queen's approval," Adam said. "We don't require her approval—only yours."

"Her approval of your marriage will go a long way in dissuading Prince Victor from continuing his pursuit of the princess."

Adam shrugged. "As long as the princess is safe."

"She will be now," Templeston told him. "Prince Victor would have to be insane to defy the British Empire."

"A sane man would not commit regicide," Adam reminded him.

"Quite right," Templeston agreed. "But now, Prince Victor has more to lose."

"How much more?" Adam asked.

"His life should you decide to end it." Lord Templeston's reply was matter of fact.

"You're granting the princess permission to marry me and granting me permission to kill the royal cousin?"

"If needs be." Lord Templeston met Adam's gaze. "And neither I nor the queen are condoning murder," he said. "We are simply reminding you that you're an American. While Her Majesty's government would frown upon its soldiers or citizens taking arms against a member of a royal family who happened to be visiting our country, it would certainly understand if you, an American citizen residing in Scotland, found it necessary to protect yourself—and your bride, Her Majesty's own goddaughter, from Prince Victor's murderous wrath."

"I see," Adam said.

"I thought you would," Lord Templeston answered. "You can't touch him. Even to protect the princess."

"The Coldstream guards can protect the princess, but they cannot kill Prince Victor in order to do so, whereas you . . ."

"Can do whatever I need to do to protect Her Highness from harm."

Lord Templeston nodded. "Quite right."

"The idea of waiting two days to get married makes me uneasy."

"Then don't wait."

"But the queen said . . ."

"Yes, she did," Templeston agreed. "But there's no law that says you can't have multiple wedding ceremonies. You can marry the princess when you get home and marry her two days from now here at Balmoral."

"I can't thank you enough—" Adam began.

Lord Templeston cut him off. "We'll be here when you arrive for your second wedding." He grinned. "In the meantime, I'll set things in motion by telegraphing the vicar in Kinlochen. I'll have him waiting at the lodge when you arrive."

The journey home was uneventful, but Barchmont Lodge was in chaos when Adam arrived. Lord and Lady Marshfeld and entourage had arrived for a surprise visit four days before the date of the postponed preview of the lodge and the household had been thrown into disarray.

Adam knew something was wrong when Henri, dressed in his best imitation of a butler's suit, opened the front door. "Good evening, sir, it's nice to have you home again."

Adam stared at him. "Where's Albert?"

"Gone," Henri replied. "They're all gone."

"What do you mean gone? Gone where?"

Henri shrugged. "They left. All of them. Including Mr. O'Brien who was very disappointed not to get a game of golf in. He said he particularly liked the eighteenth hole."

Adam looked askance at Henri. Murphy didn't play the game of golf. He did, however, know where the clubhouse was and the clubhouse had wine cellars. "What about Ma—?"

Henri shook his head and put a finger to his mouth to signal Adam to shut up, then spoke in rapid French. "Lord and Lady Marshfeld have arrived with a gentleman from London and the Prince Regent of Karolya."

"Bloody hell!" Adam said.

"Adam! Surprise!"

He turned around to find his sister Kirstin gliding the main staircase. "What are you doing here?"

"We decided to surprise you." Kirstin was bubbling with excitement. "We were invited to Balmoral and decided to surprise you."

"We?"

"Marshfeld and your father and Prince Victor and I."

Every word she spoke fell like a hammer blow to his heart. "Marshfeld, Prince Victor, and my *father*?"

"Yes," Kirstin said. "Isn't it exciting? I've found your father!"

"Who the hell asked you to meddle in my affairs? Who the hell asked you to find my father?" Adam demanded.

"I did."

Adam turned. "Lord Bascombe, what are you doing here?"

Bascombe smiled. "I came to play golf with my son."

The world seemed to be spinning the wrong way on its axis. Adam sat down on the nearest chair to keep from falling. He looked at Bascombe "You?"

Bascombe nodded.

"Why?"

"It was a chance for me to get to know my son."

"You son of a bitch!" Adam jumped to his feet, raked his hands through his hair, then drew back his fist and punched Lord Bascombe in the nose. "You had twenty-eight years to get to know your son! Where the hell were you when I was growing up? Where the hell were you when I was labeled a bastard and forced to fight to defend my mother's reputation?" Adam shouted, standing over Bascombe, looking down on his long lost father. "I needed you then! I sure as hell don't need you now!"

Bascombe pushed himself to his feet and wiped the blood from his nose with a white linen handkerchief, wiggling the cartilage to see if Adam had broken it. "Maybe not." He stared at Adam. "But your sister does."

"What?" Adam looked from Kirstin to Bascombe.

"Prince Victor, Adam. You warned me about Prince Victor, but I . . . I . . ." Kirstin began to cry.

"What is it, Kirstin? What has he done?" Adam demanded.

"His Royal Highness Prince Victor of Saxe-Wallerstein-Karolya has designs on your sister," Bascombe told him. "She came to me because she was afraid you'd think she was crying wolf and because Marshfeld is encouraging her to pursue a—shall we say—friendship with the prince."

"M-M-Marshfeld w-wants me to go to Karolya with Prince Victor and pretend to be that missing princess," Kirstin sobbed. "But something happened to her and I'm afraid that if I go with the prince something bad will happen to me . . ."

Adam blanched. His face lost all color as he turned to his father. "Oh my God!" He shoved Kirstin into his father's arms. "Where's Victor?"

"When we arrived your wolfhound was in the garden. Prince Victor said the dog reminded him of home. He said he'd been confined long enough and he wanted to see the countryside. He borrowed a horse from your stables and rode out. Marshfeld went with him," Bascombe answered.

"Where's the dog?"

"Prince Victor followed him toward the golf links."

"Jesus!" Adam nearly panicked. "If anything happens to that dog, George will kill me. I've got to go!"

"Adam!" Kirstin shouted. "Who's George?"

Adam didn't answer. He simply took off in the direction of the golf links. Bascombe and Kirstin exchanged looks and ran after him.

Adam's long legs ate up the distance to the golf links. He ran the entire way, approaching the eighteenth hole only to find it empty. There was no one about. He turned toward the clubhouse and caught a flash of light from the window.

Murphy O'Brien unlocked the clubhouse door and allowed Adam entrance, but slammed the door in Kirstin's face.

She pounded on the door, loudly voicing her displeasure until Adam reluctantly nodded to Murphy to open the door.

"You're in," Adam snapped when Kirstin and Bascombe entered the clubhouse. "Now, stay the devil out of my way." He turned to Murphy. "What happened?"

O'Brien glowered at Kirstin. "Lady Marshfeld and her guests took us by surprise," O'Brien admitted. "But Josef recognized Prince Victor when he came into the stables demanding a mount saddled. Josef hurried to the lodge and warned us. Gordon went for help."

Isobel, Albert, Brenna, Josef, and Max stood before him—Max, resplendent in full dress uniform and sword—but George was no where in sight. "Where's George?" Adam demanded.

"She's fine," Murphy assured him. "We've been watching for you. What took you so long?" He pocketed his watch as Adam entered the main room of the clubhouse. Adam realized that the flash of light he'd seen had been the glint of sunlight off the cover of O'Brien's silver watch.

"I had an audience with Lord Templeston and the queen," he answered. "Where's George?"

"She's fine," Murphy repeated. "Are you armed?"

Adam shook his head.

O'Brien opened his jacket. He was wearing a holster and a Colt revolver buckled around his hip. He made a clucking sound with his tongue, then removed a small revolver from his jacket pocket and handed it to Adam. "We collected Georgiana and the rest of the family and brought them here to wait for you. How the hell did he find her?"

"He didn't," Adam said. "He was invited to Balmoral as a ruse in order to trap him. He arrived early because Kirstin decided that as long as they were in Scotland, they should surprise us with a visit."

O'Brien frowned. "I thought you told her the lodge was for *gentlemen* only," he joked weakly.

"You know Kirstin," Adam reminded him. "She never listens to me. Where's George?" he asked again. But this time, nobody answered.

Wagner trotted over and nudged Adam's hand.

Adam looked over at O'Brien. "Wagner's here?"

"Of course he is. He goes where I go."

Adam turned around to find Giana dressed in black except for the wreath of orange blossoms in her hair coming up the stairs from the wine cellar. He forgot about his sister and his father. He forgot about Wagner. He forgot about Prince Victor. He forgot about everything except George. She was so beautiful she took his breath away. Adam looked at her and said what was in his heart. "I love you."

George burst into tears and threw herself in his arms. "And I love you."

"Where were you?" he asked.

"Downstairs with the vicar," she said.

Adam breathed a sigh of relief.

Giana stared at him. "Oh, Adam! Victor is here!"

"Don't worry, Princess," Adam told her, holding her close to his heart. "Everything will be all right. You're safe here. I promise."

The vicar came up the stairs. "I thought I was invited here to perform a wedding."

Adam ignored the vicar and stared down at George. "Are you ready?"

She nodded.

Adam turned to the vicar. "We're ready."

They exchanged vows in the wine cellar.

"Do you—" the vicar looked at him.

"Adam McKendrick," Adam said.

"Do you, Adam McKendrick, take this woman to be your lawfully wedded wife?"

"I do."

"And do you—" The vicar looked to Giana.

"Georgiana Victoria Elizabeth May."

"Georgiana Victoria Elizabeth May, take this man to be your lawfully wedded husband?"

"I do."

"Do you have rings?" the vicar asked.

Adam turned to O'Brien. "Jesus, Joseph and Mary! I forgot the ring!"

"I have them," Giana said. "I have rings." She turned her back to the vicar.

Realizing her intent, Adam turned with her, protecting her from prying eyes as she reached inside the bodice of her gown and produced the black pearl ring and the Karolyan Seal of State she had hidden in her bodice since the night Adam had cut the chain from around her waist so that she might use the seal to seal her letters.

"Your undergarments are no longer the safest place to keep your jewels, Princess, now that you've given me access to your hidden treasures," he whispered. "However, I do have a strong steel safe in the library. You might consider keeping either your jewelry or your undergarments in it."

"I may need my jewelry to pay for Wagner's damages," Giana replied.

"Then you'll definitely be securing your undergarments in the safe, because you won't be needing them."

Giana refastened her bodice and turned to face the vicar.

They exchanged rings. Adam placed the black pearl ring on the third finger of George's left hand and she placed the State Seal of Karolya on Adam's finger.

"I now pronounce you husband and wife."

Giana had told Max of her decision to give the State Seal to Adam for safekeeping, while they were waiting in the wine cellar for Adam to arrive, but Max still paled when she placed it on his finger. Giana glanced at her Lord Chamberlain and feared he might faint.

"It's all right, Max," Adam assured him. "I'll give it back to her when she asks for it. And I'll die before I'll allow Victor to get his hands on it." He grinned at Max. "And if I die, George will be a widow and Karolya will be safe from an American usurper."

"That may be sooner than you think."

Wagner growled low in his throat and moved to stand beside Giana.

Adam and Giana whirled around. Prince Victor and Lord Marshfeld stood in the doorway, pistols in their hands.

"Prince Victor, I presume," Adam drawled insolently.

"In the flesh," Victor retorted. "And you must be Adam

McKendrick." He turned his cold gaze on Giana. "Congratulations, Cousin, you nearly succeeded in outmaneuvering me."

"I have outmaneuvered you," Giana cried. "Adam and I are married."

"Not quite."

She gasped as Victor aimed the small silver pistol at her.

Adam moved to stand in front of Giana, but Victor stopped him. "I'll kill her," he warned, moving the derringer closer to Giana to show that he was serious.

"You can't kill her," Adam growled. "You need her."

"I did need her," Victor admitted, "before I met your sister. Now, all I need is the Seal of State. Hand it over."

"What does my sister have to do with this?" Adam demanded.

"She bears a strong resemblance to the princess, does she not? Strong enough to fool the Karolyan people from a distance," Victor said. "And luckily for me, the altar of the Christianberg cathedral is a long way from the pews. Once she dons a veil no one will know the difference."

"I will know the difference," Giana snapped.

"And so will I," Kirstin cried, tears starting to run down her face.

"It won't matter," Victor told them. "Because you'll be dead," he nodded toward Giana. "And you will be within my reach." He nodded at Kirstin, who shuddered.

Adam studied the prince regent. He was shorter than George by an inch or two and although there was a family resemblance, Prince Victor's looks were a pale imitation of his cousin's. Adam snorted in contempt. Prince Victor was dressed in an immaculate uniform complete with dress sword, but his only distinctive feature was the dueling scar that bisected his cheek.

Adam tensed, every muscle ready to spring, as Victor cocked the hammer of the derringer.

Wagner reacted instantly, leaping at Prince Victor's wrist. Adam followed on his heels.

Victor fired as the dog reached him. Wagner yelped in pain as the first shot grazed his side and Adam swore as the second one burned a path across his upper arm.

"Adam!" Giana screamed and rushed toward the fighting. "Wagner!"

Victor shoved Giana aside and pulled his sword. "Come, McKendrick!" Victor taunted. "I'll slice you to ribbons."

"I'm unarmed," Adam told him. "Will that even the odds for you?"

Victor glanced at Max. "Give him your sword."

Max looked to Adam for confirmation.

Adam nodded. "Give me your sword, Max."

Max unsheathed his sword and handed it Adam.

Adam glanced at O'Brien. "Whatever happens, remember your promise." Turning back to Victor, Adam invited, "Shall we?"

Although dueling was forbidden under English law, Scottish law prevailed. "If you're ready to die," Victor replied.

Victor backed out of the clubhouse and onto the lawn. Adam followed.

"Keep her safe," Adam ordered.

"No!" Giana protested, but O'Brien did as Adam ordered.

"Come with me, ma'am," O'Brien told her. "He has to know you're safe or he won't be able to defend himself." Giana resisted, but Murphy hooked an arm around Giana's waist and lifted her bodily out of the main room and carried her down to the wine cellar, then he went back for Kirstin, who was weeping noisily, and the wolfhound. The rest of the household, with the exception of Max, followed.

"Wagner?" Giana sucked in a ragged breath as O'Brien carried the wolfhound down to the wine cellar and placed him on the stone floor. He took off his jacket and placed it under Wagner's head while Isobel inspected the wound.

"He'll be fine, Your Highness," Isobel told her. "The ball scraped his ribs, but it didn't enter."

Reassured that Wagner would live, Giana rushed to the small cellar window, frantically looking for Adam.

"Give me the seal, McKendrick," Victor ordered, "and I'll kill you and my cousin quickly."

"You won't kill us at all," Adam retorted.

"I'll kill you," Victor boasted. "I am an expert swordsman."

"Good for you." Adam sneered. "Because you're a lousy

shot." Adam knew he was taking a chance in taunting Victor. He wasn't a fool. He'd understood the significance of the dueling scar on Victor's cheek, but he wasn't a novice. He'd studied fencing during his tour of Europe. Only this time, they would be fencing with swords instead of foils and to the death instead of until first blood. Adam had no doubt about that. Victor would give no quarter. "Choose your second."

"Marshfeld." Adam's brother-in-law stepped up and accepted the role of Prince Victor's second.

"Be careful of the company you keep, Marshfeld," Adam warned. "Live by the sword. Die by the sword."

"I will serve as McKendrick's second." The earl of Bascombe stood at Adam's side.

"En garde!" Victor shouted the traditional warning, seconds before he attacked.

Adam reacted quickly as the blade of Prince Victor's sword sliced through his jacket and barely missed cutting into his side. He was bleeding in a dozen places within minutes. Christ! A gun would have been better. He was a good shot and he'd have a better chance. And having Victor shoot him was preferable to being sliced to ribbons.

"Adam!" Lord Bascombe shouted. "Don't try to overpower him. Dance with him. Listen to me. Thrust! Parry! Feint! Move!" Bascombe called out the commands, desperately trying to anticipate Victor's moves, in order to keep his only son from being sliced to bits.

"O'Brien! Do something! Victor is killing him!" Giana could feel Murphy struggling with his promise to keep her safe and his anguish for Adam, and she knew she could no longer just stand by and wait for Adam to die. Before Murphy could react, Giana reached inside Murphy's jacket, grabbed his gun and began firing at the two men dueling on the lawn.

"Son of a bitch!" Adam shouted as a shot glanced off his thigh.

Victor roared in pain as a shot hit him high in the shoulder.

Giana cringed when she realized that she'd accidentally shot her husband, but gave a triumphant little squeal when her next shot found a mark on Victor's shoulder. She turned the gun on O'Brien. "Let me out of this room."

"I can't," he said, simply. "Adam will kill me."

"*I* will kill you if you do not," she retorted. "For if we do not stop him, Victor will kill Adam."

Hands slippery from the blood running down his arms, Adam lost his grip on the sword hilt and dropped his weapon. It was over. He had failed her and now he was about to pay for that failure with his life. Thank God for O'Brien. He would take care of Giana. He would make certain Giana gained her throne.

But Giana wasn't safe. Adam looked up and saw her running across the green, a silver Colt revolver in her hands.

"Roll!" Bascombe ordered, snatching up Adam's sword.

Bascombe blocked Victor's thrust and another as Adam rolled out of danger. But Victor outmaneuvered the earl on the third thrust and the blade sliced into his shoulder.

"Move!" This time, Adam shouted the warning to his father. He drew his revolver and fired as Victor lifted his sword for a final thrust. Giana did the same. She raised O'Brien's gun, took aim, and squeezed the trigger.

They would never know who killed him, but as Adam, suffering from blood loss staggered off the green, supported by the earl of Bascombe, Giana rushed to support his other side. "Adam, you are hurt!"

"Yeah," Adam agreed, grimacing in pain. "And you shot me."

"You were already hurt," she protested. "That is why I shot you."

Adam stared at her.

"I could not help it," she explained. "I have never fired this kind of weapon before."

Adam managed a slight laugh. "Well, you're a damn sight better shot than your cousin." He slipped to his knees, took hold of George's hand and slipped the State Seal of Karolya onto her thumb. "I love you, my princess George. I will love you, walk behind you, and defend you until the day I die."

"Which will be today if we don't get you taken care of."

The earl of Bascombe lifted Adam to his feet and helped Giana carry him into the clubhouse.

"How's the beast?" Adam asked when he was lying safely ensconced in his bed at the lodge, allowing Isobel to tend his cuts.

"He'll be fine," Giana assured him.

"He can sleep on the bed from now on," Adam said.

"No, he cannot," Giana protested.

"But he saved our lives," Adam said. "Prince Victor was wearing a ring like the seal. He intended to kill us and use Kirstin as a substitute for you whether he got the real seal or not." He looked over and saw O'Brien, Bascombe, and Kirstin standing at the foot of his bed. "Thanks, Murph, for protecting my wife."

O'Brien shrugged. "I only protected her until she began protecting you."

Adam grinned at his friend, then turned to his sister. "How are you, Kirs?"

"I want a divorce from Marshfeld," she said. "As soon as possible."

"I'm sure that can be arranged. Can't it, sir?" Adam looked at the earl of Bascombe.

"It can indeed."

"Thank you, sir, for acting as my second and for saving my life."

"I helped give you life," Bascombe said. "I wasn't about to let Victor take it." He shrugged his shoulders. "Besides, it was the least I could do for the infamous Bountiful Baron—and my son."

Adam groaned. "Oh, Jesus, you know about those stories?"

"Of course I do," Bascombe told him. "They're what led me to Nevada, what led me to seek you out. I read about the first adventure of the Bountiful Baron and I knew I had to find you. And Baron is a misnomer. As my son, you are entitled to be called Viscount Kennisbrooke. But the Bountiful Viscount doesn't have quite the same ring to it."

"How does your family feel about that?" Adam challenged. "Because if you are who you say you are, I'm your bastard son. The product of your annulled marriage to my mother, remember? And as far as I know being a bastard doesn't give me any rights to your titles."

"My family approves," Bascombe said. "My wife died six years ago and my two daughters—" He looked at Adam. "Yes, that's right, you have two more sisters, each of whom have sons of their own—urged me to find you and make things right. I drew up papers to make you my legal and legitimate heir when my wife died. Like it or not, you are the Viscount Kennisbrooke."

"I knew you were a bloody English lord the first time I laid me eyes on ya." O'Brien burst out laughing. "The only one I ever liked. Until now."

"I am Adam McKendrick." Adam narrowed his gaze at the man who claimed to be his father. "I'm not quite sure who you are, but my father was Benjamin McKendrick."

"I *am* Benjamin McKendrick," Bascombe told him. "It's our family name. I didn't become Viscount Kennisbrooke until my father inherited the title of earl of Bascombe and I didn't become Bascombe until he died eleven years ago."

"Nobody had ever seen or heard of the Bountiful Baron when I met you."

"I had," Bascombe smiled at him. "Because one of my American holdings publishes those dime novels."

"You're John J. Bookman?"

"No, that's the *nom de plume* of one of my correspondents." He winked at Kirstin. "I'm the man who pays those correspondents to create legends. One of those legends turned out to be the son I never knew." He stared down at Adam. "Ask your sister, she'll tell you who I am. My sincerest hope is that you will allow me to get to know you."

Adam hesitated, but Giana did not.

"It may take time, of course, but Adam will learn to forgive you. He has a most generous heart and our children will have great need of a loving grandfather." She rushed to Lord Bascombe and hugged him.

"Will you?" Bascombe asked, staring at his son.

"It won't be easy," Adam admitted, "but I'll try."

"Thank you."

"It's the least I can do for the man who made me the Bountiful Baron and helped me win a princess." He extended his hand to his father and when Bascombe shook it, there were tears in both men's eyes.

"That is enough," Giana said, shooing everyone out of the room a few minutes later. "We are on our nectar moon and Adam needs to rest."

"Honeymoon," Adam corrected gently. "And resting has nothing to do with it."

"But you are hurt."

"Yes, I am." He took hold of her hand and pulled her down for a lingering kiss. "And if you're a very good princess, and take very good care of me, I'll allow you to kiss me until everything is all better."

Adam and Giana celebrated two more wedding ceremonies and two more honeymoons before they settled down to life at the palace in Christianberg in Karolya.

The second wedding, held at Balmoral, two days after the duel on the golf links, was a small, intimate affair that took place in the chapel under the watchful eyes of the Queen of England, the marquess and marchioness of Templeston, the earl and countess of Ramsey, the marquess and marchioness of Everleigh, and the earl of Bascombe and Lady Marshfeld as well as all the members of the staff of Larchmont Lodge and the contingent of Coldstream guards who had escorted the couple to the queen's Scottish castle.

The second honeymoon also took place at Balmoral, but fortunately, the wedding guests did not expect to catch more than a glimpse of the participants or to have any say in the proceedings.

The same could not be said of their third wedding ceremony. Held in St. Vincent's Cathedral in Christianberg, four months after their original wedding, the state wedding fell subject to all the rules of etiquette and protocol and contained all the pomp and circumstance, all the spectacle any princess bride could ask for.

Thousands of Karolyan citizens, kings and queens, princes and princesses, dukes and duchesses, heads of state of sixty-eight countries, and the groom's mother, father, and five sisters and their families, attended.

Murphy O'Brien stood as best man in all three weddings and Brenna Mueller served as maid of honor. Archbishops performed two of their three weddings and a local vicar performed the other one. Crowds of commoners rubbed elbows with royalty as they packed the cathedral to witness the exchange of vows between Her Serene Highness Princess Georgiana Victoria Elizabeth May and Adam McKendrick, Viscount Kennisbrooke and Baron Bountiful in a ceremony that lasted over two hours.

At the conclusion of that ceremony, the royal couple journeyed to the palace at Laken where they spent a good deal of their honeymoon recovering from the wedding.

And they needed the time to rest and recover, for the planning of Princess Giana's coronation and preparations for the birth of the heir began immediately after the wedding.

Adam sold the Queen City Saloon and Opera House, and the Queen City Hotel to Murphy O'Brien, but kept Larchmont Lodge. It had, after all, been in his father's family for centuries. It became a world famous gentlemen's club and golf resort except for the one month in August each year, when Adam and Giana and their family and friends gathered for a holiday.

Epilogue

A Princess of the Blood Royal of the House of Saxe-Wallerstein-Karolya deserves a happily-ever-after. Her birthright should always be the love and respect and protection of her family first and then of her people. She is her family's and her country's greatest asset for she is the future and the future should always be filled with love and happiness.

—MAXIM I: PROTOCOL AND COURT ETIQUETTE OF PRINCES OF THE BLOOD ROYAL OF THE HOUSE OF SAXE-WALLERSTEIN-KAROLYA, AS DECREED BY ADAM I, PRINCE CONSORT TO HER SERENE HIGHNESS, PRINCESS GIANA, 1875.

Christianberg Palace, Karolya
ONE YEAR LATER

Adam finished noting his suggestions for revisions to the Female Provision of the Karolyan Charter, a document only a tyrant could love, and set them aside. He picked up the blue leather-bound volume Max had placed on his desk and leafed through the gilt-edged pages. "What the devil are these?"

"What?" Giana looked over at him from her position in the middle of their massive bed. She sat propped against the headboard, a mound of pillows behind her back as she held their infant daughter, Caroline Alexandrina Margaret, to her breast.

Adam held the book up so she could see it.

"You must be looking at the maxims in the book of *Protocol and Court Etiquette of Princesses of the Blood Royal of the*

House of Saxe-Wallerstein-Karolya. They are the rules by which a royal princess must abide."

"Christ, I thought the Female Provision was bad, but this . . ." Adam flipped through the pages once again, stopping to read several before tossing it aside. "Why didn't you tell me?"

"Because you got so upset when I told you about the Female Provision," she answered.

Adam had to admit that he hadn't reacted well to the news that marrying him had limited her ability to govern her country. "Where are the rules for Princes of the Blood Royal?"

"There aren't any," she answered. "Princes of the Blood Royal are beyond reproach."

"The hell with that!" Adam burst out, unable to keep from shuddering at the memory of the last Prince of the Blood. If Victor had been a product of that philosophy, there was plenty of room for improvement.

"Adam!"

He got up from his desk and moved to sit on the edge of the bed. Leaning over, he kissed George on the lips and touched his daughter's cheek with his finger. "If Princesses have rules, then Princes must also," he said softly. "We can't allow one sex to rule over the other. Not when they've equal attributes and strengths to offer." He smiled down at the baby. "At the moment, Alex is the heir presumptive to the throne because she's a girl. If she's our only child or the eldest of a palace full of girls—which, in our families, is likely to be the case—" He gave a little laugh. "There is no problem. As first-born or as an only child, she inherits. But according to the Karolyan Charter, if we have a son, he inherits." He paused to catch his breath and swallow the lump in his throat as Princess Alex reached up and grabbed hold of his finger. Adam stared at the woman he loved more than life itself and the daughter they had created. "That doesn't seem fair to Princess Alex or to her father. What about her mother?"

Giana thought for a moment. "I think she should have the right to choose. She did not ask to be born or to have this responsibility thrust upon her—nor will she have any say as to whether she has brothers or sisters, so I think that as firstborn, she has earned the right to choose whether or not she wants the job of running the country. But," Giana cautioned her husband, "we do not have the power to change the order of succession. Only Parliament can do that."

"Right," he agreed. "But as sovereign, you *do* have the power to rewrite the Female Provision."

Giana laughed. "Actually, *you* have the power to rewrite it."

"Exactly." He snapped his fingers. "And that's what we want to change. You are the hereditary princess, you should have more rights in your own country than I do, but because you're a woman, you don't. I want that changed, George. And I intend to work to see that it's changed . . ."

Giana shook a finger at him. "I warn you," she teased. "You will have only yourself to blame when you limit the powers you have over me."

"I don't intend to limit all the powers I have over you," Adam said, in the deep, husky rumble that sent shivers of anticipation up her spine. "Only the constitutional ones." He traced the top of her breast with the tip of his finger. "And I fully intend to exercise all my other powers as soon as you grant me permission to do so."

Giana giggled as he waggled his eyebrows at her and gave her his cat-that-ate-the-cream look.

"I want to make the changes, George," he continued. "So that Alex will never have to worry about losing her inheritance simply because she chose to marry. I want her to be safe."

"So do I, my love." Giana shifted against the pillows and leaned close enough to touch his lips with hers. Sometimes she couldn't believe her good fortune in finding Adam McKendrick. And although she hated to think of Victor and the murders he had committed in order to gain control of the crown, she couldn't help but think that if it hadn't been for him and his incredible greed, she would never have met Adam or fallen in love and married him and she would never have given birth to the miracle that was Alex. One day, she hoped to find it within her heart to forgive Victor for the destruction he'd wrought, but until that day arrived, she said a prayer for his soul along with her prayers for the souls of her parents. And she gave thanks for the gift of Adam. And for the love he gave her. Victor had many crimes for which he must answer. But she had much for which to be grateful.

In the end, Giana supposed it all balanced out. Victor had taken the lives of the two people she loved most in the world but his actions had made it possible for her to have two other people to love most in the world.

"George?"

"Hmm?"

"Pay attention. This is important."

She smiled at his serious expression. "I was thinking of something more important," she told him.

"Oh?" He raised his eyebrow in the gesture she loved so much.

"I was thinking of you and Alex and how very much I love you and all the reasons I have to be thankful."

"I know," Adam agreed. "And that's why we've either got to revise the current version of the Karolyan Charter—especially the Female Provision—to make it more equitable or come up with a book of maxims for princes."

"Does it have to be either or?" she asked.

Adam grinned. "You're the hereditary ruler of this country, you tell me."

"Let's do both."

Four days later, in a ceremony to celebrate the coronation of Her Serene Highness Princess Georgiana Victoria Elizabeth May of Saxe-Wallerstein-Karolya and the birth of the heir-presumptive Her Highness Princess Caroline Alexandrina Margaret of the House of Karolya-Kennisbrooke-McKendrick, His Highness, Adam, the prince consort, declared before the people of Karolya, and his family and friends, that the Female Provision of the Karolyan Charter would be revised in order to limit the powers of the husband over the hereditary ruler.

The hereditary princess, he declared, should be granted the singular right to reign over her country, her subjects, and her husband, with courage, wisdom, and love. Especially love. For love is the saving grace of all husbands and princes.

Turn the page for a preview of

Almost a Gentleman

The next novel in the
Marquess of Templeston's Heirs series

Coming soon from Jove Books.

Prologue

Continuous as the stars that shine
And twinkle on the milky way.

—William Wordsworth, 1770–1850

Inismorn, Ireland
Summer 1824

The stars sparkled like finely cut diamonds spread out on a background of black velvet. A solitary figure huddled against the wall of the crumbling tower of Telamor Castle. She sat with her back pressed to the rough, moss-covered stone and her neck tilted at the optimum angle for stargazing through the battered crenellations. Below the tower lay the beach and she could hear the low roar of the ocean and the occasional sound of voices, but she ignored them. Her attention was focused on the heavens as she studied the array of constellations visible in the northern sky, reciting the fanciful names her mother had taught her. She stared at the brightest star, then breathed a reverent sigh as one of its lesser companions streaked across the heavens.

"I wish that when I grow up I can marry a rich, handsome prince and live in this fine castle," Mariah Shaughnessy prayed with all the fire and fervor a six-year-old could muster. "That I can have dogs and cats and ponies to ride and that I can sit in the tower and eat cakes and biscuits and look up at the stars every night until I die." She took a deep breath before continuing her litany of wishes. Falling stars were rare. They didn't happen every night and Mariah had learned to make the most of their magical powers. "And . . ."

"You'll get fat if you eat cake every night."

Mariah sat up straight and stared into the night. A boy stood holding a lantern on the top step of the spiral stairs that led to the tower.

"No, I won't." Mariah stuck out her bottom lip and dared the intruder to contradict her.

"Of course you will." He left the top step and walked over to sit beside her. He leaned his back against the stone wall and slowly slid down it until he was sitting beside her. He trimmed the wick on the lantern so the light wouldn't interfere with her stargazing, but he kept the light burning low. "And then no prince will marry you."

Tears welled up in her eyes. "But I like cake," she replied.

He gave her a disgusted look. "Everyone likes cake."

She sighed again. "It was good."

"That's why they call it cake," he told her. "If it tasted awful they would have called it turnips."

"Will I get fat if I just wish for cake and biscuits every night?"

He shook his head. "No," he promised. "Wishing for cake won't make you fat. Only eating it."

She shrugged her shoulders. "Can you get fat from eating it once?"

"No."

"Then I guess I'll never get fat."

"You've only had cake one time?" He was genuinely surprised.

She nodded.

"How come?" he asked.

"The sisters don't believe in spoiling us."

"How many sisters have you?" he asked.

She giggled. "I don't have any sisters."

"But you said . . ."

"The sisters at St. Agnes's Sacred Heart Convent where I live."

The boy shuddered. He knew what convents were. But he had always thought they were reserved for nuns and old ladies.

He had never heard of little girls living in there. "You live in a convent?"

"Yes," she answered. "Down the hill and beyond the wall. I come here after evening vespers so I can look at the stars. See there!" She pointed through the hole in the ancient stonework. "That's Draco, the dragon."

"Why don't you just look out your window?"

"My room doesn't have windows."

"Oh." He was thoughtful once again, almost unable to comprehend the idea of a room with no windows to look out. "How do you get out?"

"It has a door, silly," she replied in a tone tinged with superiority. "I'm very good you know. And very quiet. As long as you're quiet no one pays much attention to you, so I sneak out after everyone else goes to bed."

He eyed the little girl with new respect. To sneak out of a convent and come all this way without a lantern was an enormous feat of bravery.

"Where are your mother and father?"

"I don't have a da," she told him. "And my mummy's in heaven. She's a star. See that one up there? The shiniest one?"

He nodded.

"I think that one must be my mummy 'cause she used to wear lots of sparkly things." Tears welled up in her eyes once again and her voice quavered with emotion.

He reached over and covered her small hand with his own, stunned by the magnitude of her loss. Life without his mother and father was unthinkable. "I'm sorry."

She sniffled, then wiped her nose with the back of her other hand.

"Here, take this." He reached into his pocket and pulled out a clean handkerchief.

"Thank you."

He shifted uncomfortably against the wall. "Is that why you come—to wish on the stars?"

She nodded once again. "My mummy said that if you wish on the stars God hears your wishes and if you wish on a shooting star God grants the wish."

"Do you always wish to marry a handsome prince and live

in this castle eating cake and biscuits every day?"

She shook her head. "No," she answered truthfully. "Most of the time I wish for my mummy to come back down from heaven and get me. But sometimes I wish that I'll grow up and marry a handsome prince and live in this castle and have cake to eat whenever I want it." Her voice broke and she quickly covered her mouth with her hand.

"A handsome prince might marry you," he said, offering what comfort he could. "And give you cake to eat. As long as you don't eat it *every* day."

"My wish won't come true now," she answered softly.

"Why not?"

"They don't come true if you share them with someone else. They only come true if you keep them all to yourself."

"Kit!" A loud masculine shout echoed through the ruins from the ground below. "Your mother's finished. Time to go."

The boy shot Mariah an apologetic glance. "Papa's calling me," he told her. "I have to leave now. My mama and papa were collecting sea creatures from the beach for my mama to draw. Papa only let me come to the ruins because the groundskeeper swore they were safe. We're going home tomorrow and I wanted to see the old castle."

"Oh."

She sounded so bereft that his heart went out to her. "Will an earl do?" he asked.

"Huh?"

"I'm not a prince," he explained. "I'm an earl. But my mama says I'm handsome, and one day when I'm all grown up, I'll come back and marry you if you like."

"Truly?" she breathed. "You would come back and marry me?"

"Sure," he answered with a nonchalant shrug of his shoulders. "I have to marry someone. It might as well be you."

"All right." She smiled up at him.

He pulled her close and planted a kiss on her lips the way he'd seen his papa do to his mama. "Then it's settled," he pronounced.

"Kit!" His father's voice sounded louder, closer. "Son, where are you?"

"Coming, Papa," he called down the stairs, then glanced back at the girl. "I have to go."

"You won't tell anyone about this?" she asked. "If the nuns find out . . ."

"I won't tell." He turned and started down the stairs.

"Wait!" she whispered urgently. "You forgot your lantern." She picked it up and held it out to him.

"You keep it," he said. "And use it to find your way to and from the tower in the dark." He smiled at her once again. "Now that we're betrothed, you have to take care of yourself."

"You won't forget?"

"I won't forget," he promised.

He waved once more and then he was gone.

Chapter 1

A mother's pride, a father's joy.

—Sir Walter Scott, 1771–1821

SWANSLEA PARK
NORTHAMPTONSHIRE, ENGLAND

"*Talk him out of it, Drew. He's too young.*"

Andrew Ramsey, the sixteenth marquess of Templeston, stared down at his wife. Tears shimmered in her beautiful eyes and her voice held a barely discernable note of panic. Kathryn was on the verge of bursting into tears at any moment and Drew felt powerless to stop it. He had been her husband for nineteen years and he ached to see thc pain in her eyes. Thcre were streaks of silver in Kathryn's hair, but she was every bit as beautiful to him today as she had been the first time he'd seen her. And he loved her more than he thought possible, but he loved Kit, too, and Drew would not—could not—forbid Kit to pursue his destiny. He didn't have that right. Not even for Kathryn. "He's old enough to know his own mind, Kathryn. Older than you were when I first proposed to you."

His words and his tone of voice sent shivers of anticipation up her spine. After nineteen years of marriage, he still had the power to take her breath away and to reduce her to a mindless, quivering mass of anticipation without so much as a touch. All he had to do was speak her name. *Kathryn*. Only Drew called her Kathryn. The rest of the world called her Wren. "That's beside the point," she insisted.

Drew shook his head. "It *is* the point, my love. Kit is two and twenty years old. He's not a child anymore. He's a grown man and he wants and needs a place of his own."

"He can have a place of his own here," she said. "He needn't go all the way to Ireland for that."

Drew laughed. "Are you suggesting I give him Swanslea Park just to keep him at home?"

Swanslea Park, the country seat of the current marquess had been handed down to Drew from his father, the fifteenth marquess of Templeston, who had gained possession of it through his marriage to Drew's mother, the only child of the earl of Munnerlyn. The Ramsey family estate lay farther north, too far from London for convenience and the fifteenth marquess and his wife had chosen to live and raise their son at Swanslea. Drew and Kathryn had continued the tradition.

"I would if I thought it would do any good," Wren admitted.

"Well, forget it." Drew laughed again. "Because I'm not ready to turn over the keys to Swanslea just yet." The title of marquess of Templeston and the keys to Swanslea went hand in hand and although Drew had already given Kit his lesser titles of earl of Ramsey, Viscount Birmingham and Baron Selby, he intended to keep Swanslea Park awhile longer.

"But, Drew, Swanslea Park is Kit's home, too. And it's large enough to accommodate his desire for privacy." She looked at her husband. "He can have the whole east wing to himself and come and go as he pleases. It has a private entrance."

"Yes, it does," Drew agreed. "And a household staff who will note his private comings and goings as they go about their daily activities and those remarks will reach Newberry's ears who will report them to me even though I've no wish to infringe upon Kit's privacy." Drew reached out and enfolded his wife in his arms, hugging her close. "I'm the marquess, Kathryn. Everyone answers to me and nothing goes on at Swanslea Park without my knowing about it. He wants to go to Ireland, Kathryn. He delayed his departure for a year because he didn't want to upset you, but he's eager to take possession of his inheritance. Kit needs to be his own man and the lord of his own domain in a place where the staff answers to him instead of to me."

"I wish Martin had never delivered that letter to Kit," Wren said.

He frowned at her. "You don't mean that."

"Yes, I do," she replied. "If Martin hadn't delivered that letter, we all would have remained in blissful ignorance and Kit wouldn't be moving to Ireland."

The letter their solicitor, Martin Bell, had delivered to Kit on his twenty-first birthday, was a letter informing him that he was the sole inheritor of Telamor Castle and the surrounding estate in the village of Inismorn in County Clare through his maternal grandfather. Drew and Wren weren't Kit's natural parents. Kit was born the illegitimate son of the fifteenth marquess of Templeston, half-brother to Drew and twenty-eight years his junior. Kit's natural mother, the fifteenth marquess's mistress, had died shortly after giving him life and his father had died in a yachting accident three years later.

George Ramsey, the fifteenth marquess, had taken his infant son to Wren Stafford and given Kit to her to rear as her own. Drew had married Kathryn and adopted Kit, making Kathryn the marchioness and Kit, the twenty-ninth earl of Ramsey, the marquess of Templeston's legal son and heir. They were the only parents Kit had ever known and neither of them had been aware of Kit's inheritance.

Castle Telamor had come as a surprise. When he died, the Irish earl of Kilgannon had left it to his only living heir—Christopher George "Kit" Ramsey. Martin Bell, a lifelong family friend and solicitor had held it in trust until Kit reached his majority. Martin had presented a letter from his maternal grandfather and the deed to the castle and the estate a year ago and Kit was eager to inspect his Irish castle and set up housekeeping on the property.

"Swanslea Park came to us through *my* mother," Drew reminded his wife. "You are Kit's mother. There is no question about that. You are the woman who's loved and nursed him and molded him into the wonderful man he is today. Fate robbed Kit of one mother's love, but it granted him another's when my father loved him enough to place him in your care. Nothing will ever change the way Kit feels about you, but he carries the blood of the woman who gave birth to him in his veins. He wasn't granted the opportunity to know that woman, but he has a chance to know the place she called home. Shouldn't we, the parents who love him the most in the world, give him the wings he needs to fly and encourage him to use them?"

Wren choked back a sob and nodded her head in agreement. "But I don't want him to go. A lot of things can happen in a year. And I'll miss him so much."

"I know you will," Drew soothed. "So will I. But we always knew this day would come some day."

"It's come too soon, Drew," she whispered. "I thought I would be ready, but it's come much too soon."

"He won't be gone forever and we'll still have each other and the girls. The time will pass faster than you think." He planted a kiss against Kathryn's forehead. "Remember that Iris has her London Season coming up." He reminded his wife that they had two other children—daughters, seventeen-year-old Iris and twelve-year-old Kate—to think about. "And you have paintings to complete for the new exhibit at the museum. There will be lots of things to keep you busy and before you know it, Kit will be back to visit."

"What if he doesn't come back?" she asked, giving voice to her deepest fear. "What happens if he decides to remain in Ireland?"

"Ah, my darling . . ." Drew leaned down to kiss her soundly and to chase away the tears. "If Kit decides to stay in Ireland, then we'll visit as often as he will allow."

"Allow?" Kathryn wrinkled her brow and narrowed her gaze at the suggestion that Kit might not welcome them with open arms every time she felt the need to pay him a visit. "Why wouldn't he allow his parents to visit?"

Drew wanted to bite his tongue, but it was too late. Kathryn had latched on to his promise to visit with all the tenacity of a terrier on a rat. He had expected that. But he hadn't expected her to balk at the idea that Kit might not appreciate long visits at regularly scheduled intervals. "What's the point of setting up housekeeping and becoming lord of your own castle if you have to answer to your mother and father while doing it?" He reached out and tilted Kathryn's chin up with the tip of his index finger so that she was forced to meet his gaze. "We have to let him go, Kathryn. We must let him become the man he's meant to become. *We* need it and more important, *Kit* needs it."

"*You* didn't move to Ireland to escape your father's realm of influence in order to become the man you were meant to become," she said.

"That's true." Drew's voice took on the harder tone. "But only because *I* went to war. I joined Wellington and went to Belgium to fight Napoleon." He caressed Kathryn's cheek. "My character was refined by heartbreak, betrayal, and war. I became the man I am today because I survived the horrors of war. I would rather Kit build and refine his character in the relative safety of the Irish countryside as lord of Telamor Castle. Wouldn't you?"

"Of course, I would!"

"Then do your best to pretend to be excited and happy for him." Drew grinned. "For heaven's sake, Kathryn, the boy inherited a castle!"

"A crumbling castle," she retorted.

"The tower may be crumbling, but I was told the new castle is quite livable. But Kit won't care if it's old and crumbling, too," Drew said. "It's his castle. Just as Lancelot was his pony. Remember?"

Wren smiled in spite of herself. Lancelot was Kit's first pony. A shaggy old Shetland with a white blaze on his face and black coat mottled with flecks of white and gray. Lancelot had been destined for the rendering pot when Drew bought him. Kit had loved him instantly and the two had become constant companions. Even now, Kit refused to part with Lancelot. The ancient pony still held the place of honor among the thoroughbreds in Drew's magnificent stables. "What should I do?"

"Help him pack, wish him Godspeed, and don't let him see you cry."

Kathryn lifted herself up on tiptoe and pressed her lips against Drew's. "How did you get to be so wise?"

He smiled. "My father was an excellent judge of character. I inherited the gift from him."

"Is that so?" she teased.

"Yes, indeed," he answered. "You see, I once fell in love with a woman thought to be a most notorious mistress."

"Was she?"

Drew laughed. "Of course she was. That's why I married her."

Chapter 2

Bliss was it in that dawn to be alive,

But to be young was very heaven!

—William Wordsworth, 1770–1850

Inismorn, Ireland
One month later

Kit Ramsey, the twenty-ninth earl of Ramsey, topped the rise in the road that led to the tiny village of Inismorn and gazed out over the land surrounding it. Standing in the irons, he surveyed his inheritance. Everything except the village and the convent was his. All of the land as far as the eye could see—twenty-six thousand acres of it—including the castle rising above the mist in the distance belonged to him. His land. His castle. His place. And by Jove, but it was beautiful!

He grinned. The tower to the right of the castle, perched on the edge of the cliffs, was all that remained of an ancient Norman fortress. A newer, more modern castle had been built farther inland, but the tower remained to mark the spot of the original castle and to serve as an observation post and guardian for the new castle. There was a clear view of the beach below the tower and of the miles of ocean stretching beyond it. And although it was currently shrouded in clouds and mist, Kit knew that it was possible to look through the holes in the massive moss-covered crenellations and see the stars sparkling in the night sky like finely cut diamonds spread out on an infinite background of black velvet.

Kit smiled at the memory. A few miles down the hill, inside the wall, facing the coast road sat the slate-roofed gables and spires of St. Agnes's Sacred Heart Convent. Once, long ago, one of the residents of St. Agnes's crept out of her room every evening after vespers, climbed over the stone wall surrounding the convent grounds and made her way up the hill along the coast to the crumbling tower of Telamor Castle in order to wish upon the stars. And once, long ago, an eight-year-old boy had accidentally discovered her hiding place and impulsively proposed marriage.

HOT CHOCOLATE

BJ 2/02

HOT CHOCOLATE

Suzanne Forster

Lori Foster

Elda Minger

Fayrene Preston

JOVE BOOKS, NEW YORK

HOT CHOCOLATE

A Jove Book / published by arrangement with
the authors

PRINTING HISTORY
Jove edition / February 1999

For information address: The Berkley Publishing Group,
a division of Penguin Putnam Inc.,
375 Hudson Street, New York, New York 10014.

Visit our website at
www.penguinputnam.com

ISBN: 0-515-12452-4

A JOVE BOOK®
Jove Books are published by The Berkley Publishing Group,
a division of Penguin Putnam Inc.,
375 Hudson Street, New York, New York 10014.
JOVE and the "J" design
are trademarks belonging to Penguin Putnam Inc.

PRINTED IN THE UNITED STATES OF AMERICA

13 12 11 10 9 8 7 6 5 4 3

CONTENTS

Not Abigail!

Suzanne Forster

ONE

"I'll also need a prospectus on Intel, their current price-earnings ratio, a couple of aspirins, and a wife."

Abigail Hastings's rolling ball pen left a black blotch where it came to a halt on her yellow legal pad. She'd been dutifully taking notes while her boss, Max Gallagher, president and CEO of The Gallagher Group, paced his spacious office and dictated the to-do list for that day.

Nothing unusual about that. This was how they'd begun each day since Abigail came to work for the San Francisco–based investments titan nine years ago. Granted, he'd asked her to do some strange things in that time, including baby-sit his senior varsity college football trophy so his best friend couldn't kidnap it.

But she *couldn't* have heard him right just now.

He was still deep in concentration as she looked up.

"Excuse me, Mr. Gallagher?"

He turned with an expression of mild surprise on his handsome face. Abigail smiled inwardly, fondly tolerant of her boss's eccentricities by now. He'd obviously zoned out for a moment and forgotten she was there.

Max Gallagher, whose chiseled jaw was a Renaissance sculptor's dream, and whose irises were as midnight blue as the pinstripe in the Italian suit she'd picked out for him, had a focus like the Eximer Laser. He was a one-track thinker, and nothing else existed except the express train he was riding. He still called her Ms. Hastings after all this time, but not out of an excess of politeness. He couldn't seem to remember her first name from one day to the next.

Abigail had stopped being offended a long time ago. It was common knowledge that if you wanted to get Max Gallagher's attention, you had better be a hot stock market tip.

"Excuse you, Ms. Hastings? For what?" he asked.

"I wasn't sure I heard you right."

"Oh, that." He frowned and pinched the bridge of his nose. "Surprised me, too. I can't remember the last time I had a headache."

"No, not the aspirin—" But Abigail had already lost him. He was pacing again, absorbed in his thoughts and the financial coups that lay ahead of him that day.

"Would you alert Research to keep their eye on the dollar/yen rate this morning?" he said. "I'd like an update every fifteen minutes. Oh, and tell them I'm still waiting for the results of my blue-chip timing model."

Abigail went back to taking notes, despite her confusion. She wouldn't dream of interrupting him. This was the man they called Midas Max. He'd knocked the international financial world on its keister with his deceptively simple investment policies and made himself impossibly rich. He'd amassed his first billion by age thirty, more than doubled that by thirty-five. Now he was coming up on forty and there didn't seem to be any limits to what he could accomplish.

"Read the list back to me, would you?" he said.

This was part of their routine, too. Every morning he gave her his list, and every morning he wanted it read back to him, perhaps several times while he juggled goals and strategies in his mind.

Abigail went through the first nine items. When she got to the last one, she hesitated. "And number ten . . . find you a wife?"

"Yes, right. Good." He checked his watch. "Think you can get all that done today?"

"You want me to find you a wife, sir? Today?"

"Oh, no!" He laughed as Abigail stared at him in shock. "You can have until the fourteenth on that, which is my fortieth birthday. That shouldn't be any problem, should it?"

Abigail was speechless. February fourteenth was two weeks away, Valentine's Day, but even if it had been two light-years away, she would have been speechless. She'd heard him right, but it must have been a Freudian slip. He meant find him a life, a steak knife? Maybe a drum and fife?

His phone rang before she could ask him to explain.

"That's probably Daniel Kim from the Asian office," he said as he strode to his desk and hit the speaker phone button. "Looks like the bottom's dropped out of the electronics sector, and it's time to buy."

A liltingly accented male voice came on the line, and Max gave Abigail the sign that it was going to be a long, involved conversation. There was no point sitting and waiting, anyway, she knew. She had a busy day ahead of her as well. She would catch him later, and he could clear up the misunderstanding.

But when she stood, she had the sensation that the floor had mysteriously been tilted a few degrees during the last couple of moments. Her office adjoined his, and she might have walked into the half-open door if he hadn't called out to her.

"Oh, Ms. Hastings, I forgot to tell you—"

"Yes?" Abigail spun around and got even dizzier. She just

knew that he'd finally realized what he said and now they would have a good laugh over it. *Wife? I meant wine! I'd like you to pick out a case of really good Merlot to send to Warren Buffett for the stock tip.*

Abigail was all ready with a big smile. Another great Max Gallagher story to share with Mavis, the receptionist who'd been with him even longer than Abigail. But he was still embroiled on the phone. He'd picked up the receiver, and he was covering the mouthpiece with his hand as he whispered to her.

"I'm having lunch with Jeff at the athletic club today," he said. "Could you make sure we get a table that's not by the steam room door? You know, the smell—"

He gave her a thumbs-up, and she nodded dumbly.

"Can do," she whispered back, words she had uttered so many times they were automatic. And then she turned around and walked headlong into the door.

"What's wrong with you, Abbie? Sugar?"

Abigail looked up from her brown study to see Mavis Swan standing in her office doorway. Her hands were propped on her ample hips and her shoulders tick-tocked to the bluesy music that was playing from earphones she wore looped around her neck like jewelry.

"Nothing," Abigail insisted. Perhaps a little defensively she added, "Why do you ask?"

"Because you're playing in your paper clip tray again."

"I am not." Abigail glanced down and let out a sigh. Caught in the act. Her desk drawer was open, and she'd organized the tiny silver clips into two neat rows with the long loops down. There was one in her fingers right now. She dropped the evidence and shut the drawer.

"Nothing wrong with having things in their place," she insisted. "That way they don't get lost."

"Sometimes it's good getting lost," Mavis chided. "How else is anybody going to find you, girl?"

Officially, Mavis was the executive row receptionist, but she was far more than that. The gleaming marble counter that fronted Abigail's and Max's offices was Mavis's domain, and she claimed to have come with the lease when Max moved in. She answered phones, directed traffic, and dished out advice that usually turned out to be right. She was the company's lifestyle guru, and even Max admitted she ought to have her own talk show.

Nobody could tell you how to "live large" like Mavis could, and lately, Abigail had been the focus of her efforts. The receptionist swore there was an "Abbie" hidden inside Abigail Hastings. Abigail wasn't sure which frightened her more: whether Mavis was right or wrong.

"Lord, girl, what's that red knot on your forehead?" she asked, peering at Abigail.

"I got lost and the door found me," was all Abigail would say.

"You need some of my Gramma Swan's comfort rub." Mavis mmmm-bopped up to Abigail's desk, moving with the music.

There were times when Abigail wished she had half the receptionist's sense of self. Mavis knew who she was and made no apologies for the generosity of her body or her personality. She was a big, beautiful woman, and you either dealt with it or you got out of her way.

This morning, she wore palazzo pants in blue and green madras silk that flattered her café au lait skin tones and a long, sheer overblouse to match. Peeking out from beneath the blouse, a turquoise tube top had its work cut out for it, reining in her voluptuous breasts.

Abigail felt sparrowlike in her tailored beige suit and no-fuss do, a French braid she usually coiled into a knot at the nape of her neck, because it was the quickest way to subdue her heavy, wayward, light brown hair.

Mavis set a bag the size of a small suitcase on Abigail's

desk, rooted through it, and found a colorful tin of salve, which she handed over with a pleased look.

"Heal thyself," she said.

Abigail felt the stinging ease immediately as she daubed some of the clear goo onto the tender bump.

Mavis could have opened a pharmacy of her Gramma Swan's home remedies. There were headache cures, natural antidepressants, bust developers, and herbs to enhance fertility. She even claimed to have a love potion, which she slipped to her man, Harry, every once in awhile, when his "eye got to wandering."

It was a rich Jamaican chocolate concoction, laced with something that looked like marshmallow cream. She'd brewed some up in the office coffee room once but wouldn't let Abigail near it. "I could not be responsible for what might happen," she'd warned ominously.

Abigail thanked Mavis for the ointment and tried to give the tin back, but the receptionist insisted she keep it.

"Everyone needs some comfort rub in their medicine cabinet," she declared. "Now, tell me what the real problem is, sugar. My gramma's salve will take away the sting, but it won't heal the wound—and you've been sighing like there's no tomorrow."

Abigail picked up the legal pad and handed it to the receptionist, making an effort not to breathe heavily. "Mr. Gallagher's to-do list. That's the problem."

Mavis scanned the list with great interest. "Intel prospectus, P/E ratios," she murmured. "Aspirin?"

"Keep reading. He wants me to find him a wife."

Mavis's brown eyes goggled like a ladybug's. "If I wet my pants, it's your fault, girl! You can't be serious."

Abigail massaged the bump on her forehead. "I keep thinking *he* can't be serious. But he's pretty much always serious."

"This is true. Somebody gave him a soap on a rope for Christmas one year, and he thought it needed to be fed."

"He wants a wife, and he wants her by Valentine's Day."

"Well, there's your answer," Mavis said with a rich chuckle. "Ignore the silly man, and he will have forgotten all about it in two weeks. He can't remember what he did yesterday, unless there was a stock option involved."

"I don't think he'll forget this. It's part of his twenty-year plan."

"Come again?"

The bump on Abigail's head had opened a memory trace. When Max had interviewed her for the job all those years ago, he'd told her about his long-range goals and handed her a rumpled sheet of paper he'd had with him since college. Scribbled on it were his five-year plans through age forty. At twenty-five, he wanted to have launched his own business, by thirty he wanted to be a millionaire, by thirty-five he wanted to have gone public, and by forty he wanted to have found the perfect woman and be married.

"Do you have any thoughts on how to help me accomplish these things?" he'd asked Abigail.

She'd taken him quite seriously at the time, because he'd already achieved the first two, and then some. His deep blue eyes had sparkled like sapphires. She'd found herself staring into their mysterious facets and promising to do everything in her power to help him. She'd only been twenty at the time, and just out of college with no job experience, but her enthusiasm must have sold him. She was hired on the spot.

She explained all that to Mavis with another huge sigh. "I didn't pay much attention to the 'perfect woman' stuff back then, and I never dreamed he'd actually ask me to help him find her." Her shoulders lifted. "Why in the world would he want *me* to pick out a wife for him?"

"Well, you pick out his ties, don't you?"

His ties, and everything else, Abigail thought. She was a bit of an organization freak, which was exactly what Max Gallagher needed. When he'd seen how efficient she was, he'd gradually turned over his entire life to her, including his penthouse apartment, which was one floor above his office and connected by a private elevator.

Abigail had redecorated the rooms for him, and she still picked out pieces occasionally. Before she left work each day, she popped up there to lay out an array of vitamins and pills, select a Healthy Gourmet meal from his freezer (she'd found a service that provided a week's worth of delicious microwavable meals at a time) and make sure any clothes he needed for an evening function were ready to go.

"Oh! Who's that manhandling me?!"

Abigail was jerked out of her thoughts by Mavis's shrill squeal. She stared in shock at the pair of male hands the receptionist was screeching about. They'd snaked around Mavis's body from behind and were clearly bent on fondling her pillowy breasts.

Mavis squirmed and slapped at the hands, but the shocked smile on her face gave her away. Abigail didn't know what to think, until she got a glimpse of the attacker's mop of wavy chestnut hair.

"Mr. Weston," Abigail said sternly. "Are you going to stop molesting Mavis, or do I have to call Security?"

The hands froze, then sheepishly crept away.

Mavis straightened her clothing and stepped aside, revealing Jeff Weston's expression of total innocence. The tall, gangly head of The Weston Fund was Max's best friend from college and his fiercest competitor in everything from mega business deals to the everyday trivia of life. Abigail had seen the two of them bet on whether a fly would light on the windowpane of Max's office.

"A hundred bucks says that fly touches down by the time I count to ten," Jeff had said. "Two hundred says it doesn't," Max had replied, and started counting. Max had won. He usually did, but Jeff was always the instigator, always the Pan to his Apollo.

"I was just trying to say hello, ladies," Jeff protested. "What's everybody screeching about?"

"Next time you say hello to my face," Mavis huffed, trying not to giggle.

"Next time I'll meet you in the conference room, we'll lock the door, and you can say hello to *my* fac—"

"Mr. Weston," Abigail admonished. Someone had to keep lover boy in line, and clearly, it wasn't going to be Mavis. "If you behave," she told him, "I'll let Mr. Gallagher know you're here."

Jeff grinned wickedly and pulled a stock report from inside his suit jacket. "Tell him it's the genius who just beat the pants off him on our stock-picking bet."

Abigail picked up the phone and waved at Mavis, who'd grabbed her carpetbag from the desk, waggled her fingers at both of them, and was on her way out.

Jeff blew Mavis a kiss and headed straight for Max's door.

"I'll surprise him," he told Abigail.

"Wait!" But Abigail couldn't stop him, and when her intercom buzzed moments later, she was playing with the paper clips again.

"Ms. Hastings, could you come in here a moment and bring your notebook?"

Abigail assumed by their heated conversation that they were discussing a business deal or some new wager, but to her astonishment, they were talking about women when she walked into her boss's office.

"You're never going to find one by Valentine's Day," Jeff was crowing. "You can kiss the trophy good-bye, Max, my man."

"Don't put it in your display case yet," Max warned him. "I just bought ten million dollars' worth of stock in one sixty-second transaction on the phone. How hard could it be to find a woman in two weeks?"

"The *perfect* woman," Jeff reminded him. "And if you recall the criteria we set down when we were twenty, you know she doesn't exist. Where is a woman who can dance topless on the coffee table at halftime *and* throw a spiral pass like John Elway? Where is she? Point me to her."

"What are you two talking about?" Abigail said faintly.

"Oh, Ms. Hastings—" Max hesitated, turning to look at her. Only this time he didn't wave her in and go right back to his conversation. He stared at her for a moment. He even seemed to draw in a breath while he was reflecting.

Abigail felt as if he were seeing her for the first time. His eyes were on her legs, the hem of her skirt, which was a perfect three inches above the knee, and the cropped jacket, which fit her like a glove. He also took in her startled expression and her sandy brown hair, which had been even more unmanageable than usual this morning, leaving her little choice but to braid and coil it.

Other than that, there was nothing unusual about the way she looked today, only about the way he was looking at her. Jeff seemed to notice it, too. Abigail could see him watching the two of them, curious.

"Abigail," Max said, and then caught himself. "Do you mind if I call you that? It's about that wife situation. Remember, I told you I needed one in two weeks? Well, I do."

He exhaled, and Abigail could feel the pressure of it from across the room. It wasn't like him to be tense about anything. Intense, yes, but never tense.

"Have you made any progress?" he asked her.

"Well, no, I wanted to talk to you. I wasn't sure you were serious."

"Oh, he's serious." Jeff took up where Max left off. "He's never been more serious. To make a long story short, Abigail—Do you mind if I call you Abbie? If your boss isn't married by Valentine's Day, I keep the wrestling trophy for life."

Abigail glanced from one man to the other and ended up with Max. "You're getting *married* to win a bet with Mr. Weston?"

"Call me Jeff—" The other man fell backward into the chair behind him, chuckling. "God, I love to win."

"It's more than a bet." Max shot Jeff a dark look. "I'd always planned to be married by forty."

"I see," Abigail said stiffly. She was aware that their senior varsity wrestling trophy had been going back and forth between them since college, when Max won it from Jeff in the state competition. Later, in grad school, Max had mapped out his future, and Jeff had bet him the trophy that he wouldn't make his five-year goals.

This time, Jeff had been right. Max had kept the trophy until his thirty-fifth birthday, when he lost it to Jeff for not having met the deadline to go public. One simple form had been overlooked, causing The Gallagher Group's stock offering to be delayed an entire month. Jeff had had the trophy ever since, and Abigail had always felt partially responsible for Max's losing it.

"If I may ask?" she said. "What *is* the perfect woman?"

"You may ask." Jeff fished a tattered piece of notebook paper from his pants pocket and made a show of snapping it open. "I just happen to have the list we made up when we were twenty—"

"And twisted," Max broke in.

"True," Jeff admitted. "I probably shouldn't read it in mixed company."

"Read it." Abigail could barely keep the impatience out of her tone. "How am I supposed to find this paragon of womanhood if I don't know what I'm looking for?"

Jeff glanced at Max and got a nod.

"Okay, here goes," Jeff said. "Not necessarily in this order: Big bazoo—er, magnificent mammaries, rarely speaks above a sexy whisper, serves pizza, beer *and* dances topless on the coffee table at halftime, and last, but definitely not least, throws a mean spiral pass."

The room fell silent when he was done, and Abigail hoped it was because the two of them were seriously ashamed of themselves. Magnificent mammaries? It sounded like they wanted a milk cow who would waitress and play football.

"Such are the dreams of frustrated twenty-year-old economics grads," Jeff intoned quietly.

"And now that you're both forty?" Abigail asked hopefully.

Jeff shook the list. "This still pretty much does it for me. How about you, Max?"

With nary a moment of reflection, Max nodded. "Who wouldn't want a woman who could throw a spiral pass?"

The rolling ball pen bent nearly double with the pressure of Abigail's grip as she added another item to her to-do list: "Call the animal service and have them both neutered."

TWO

"You look like you bit into a pickle," Jeff observed, studying Max's expression. "Something wrong with your sandwich?"

Max hadn't realized he was making a face—or that his friend was watching him. "What could be wrong? It's tuna. I love tuna. I've always loved tuna. *Back off.*"

"Hey, okay, man. Chill. I just wondered why you were making that weird face."

"I wasn't making a weird face. I was chewing. Some of us like to do that before we swallow."

Jeff dropped his sandwich and pretended to duck. "What's got you so edgy? It couldn't have anything to do with your quest for the perfect woman, could it?"

Max started to protest again, then thought better of it. Heads were already turning in the small, trendy bistro where they often grabbed something to eat after working out, and Max wasn't anxious to end up in the tabloids. It was a private health club and restaurant, and the security was tight, which was the main reason Jeff had convinced him to join—that and the "buff babes," as his friend put it. But it was also a celebrity hangout, and the paparazzi were not above bribing the staff.

Besides, something did have Max edgy, but he wasn't sure what it was. He wasn't even sure he liked tuna, to be honest. Abigail could have told him. She could have told him what he normally ordered when he came to the club and saved him all this trouble. She'd made a science of what he liked and disliked. Hell, she knew everything there was to know about him, including his cholesterol ratios, his resting blood sugar, and probably his sperm count. It was her they called with the results of his yearly physicals.

"Stock deals I understand," Max admitted. "Women I don't."

"Woman are easy! Give 'em presents and tell them they're beautiful." Jeff tipped his beer to Max with a knowing smile. "Advice from the master. And by the way, if you ask me, the perfect woman for you is right under your nose."

Their waitress had stopped to refill Max's coffee, and Max checked her out as she sashayed away from the table. She looked shapely and fit, probably in her midtwenties. Max wasn't sure about the purple hair and the tattoo in the hollow of her throat, but otherwise, she seemed nice enough.

"Probably too young," he told Jeff. "She looks like a college coed."

"I'm not talking about the waitress." Jeff clunked down his beer and laughed. "I'm talking about your assistant."

Max had to think for a moment who he meant. "Abigail?"

"Right, the woman who sharpens your pencils. She's perfect."

"Not Abigail!"

"Why not Abigail?"

"Well, because she *does* sharpen my pencils, and sets out my clothes, and—come to think of it, she does everything for me. To be honest, I'm not sure I could function without her. I don't want to lose Abigail."

"You wouldn't be losing her, you'd be marrying her." Jeff gave him a lascivious wink. "She could still sharpen your pencils, if you know what I mean."

Max didn't like Jeff talking about his assistant that way, although he wasn't sure why.

"Abigail has a boyfriend," he said as if that were the end of it. Max had discovered this little-known fact when he'd made a half-assed attempt to ask her out a few years back, and she'd gasped as if he'd suggested sex on his desk. All he'd done was mention lunch, but she'd started to hyperventilate and had to sit down. When he asked what was wrong, she'd mumbled something about it being Wednesday and she'd brought egg salad from home. He offered to put her brown bag in the company fridge, but she kept shaking her head, and finally she got it out. "I can't," she'd whispered. "I have a boyfriend."

"A mystery lover?" Jeff said, intrigued. "Can't say I'm surprised. There's something about Abigail. She's still waters, you know. I've sensed the currents, sucking and churning down there, pulling on a man's . . . imagination."

He sat back and smiled, as if he were thoroughly enjoying the image he'd created. "And I do love a woman with wild, curly light brown hair."

"Wild and curly hair?"

"Yeah, she probably pulls it back because that's the only way she can handle it."

Max started to say, "Not Abigail," again, but stopped himself. He wasn't sure what was bothering him. Was it the idea of Abigail being wild? Or that Jeff had noticed it before he had?

He looked his friend straight in the eye. "Can you see Abigail Hastings dancing on the coffee table at halftime? Tell the truth."

"Okay, maybe not. You have a point. But that was on *my* list of criteria for the perfect woman. You had your own list."

"I did? Where is it?"

"How would I know, Max, my man? It was your list."

Max tossed the sandwich down, disgusted that he couldn't even remember what he normally ate when he came here. It didn't make him any happier that there was a movie clip playing through his own head that he couldn't tune out. It was of Abigail—his Abigail—her wild, curly light brown hair blowing in the breezes as she threw a perfect spiral pass. She looked like a nymph, dancing around with bare feet in a dress that he could see through because it was so sheer, and because the sun was behind her.

Max had never entertained such a fantasy, but none of it would have surprised him too much, even the spiral pass, if there hadn't been one thing that confounded him. Abigail didn't have light brown hair, did she?

"What's that you're chewing on? Looks naaasty."

"Pnnnnahbrrrrrnnn—" Abigail nearly choked on the wad of bread that lodged in her throat. Mavis had just wandered into the coffee room, and the receptionist was poised in front of the small conference table where Abigail sat, giving her one of those when-are-you-going-to-get-a-life looks.

"It's the same thing I have every Tuesday," Abigail explained once she'd washed the lump down with some low-fat milk. "It's a peanut butter and banana sandwich, and it's not at all nasty, thank you, *unless* someone asks me a question while I'm trying to swallow."

Mavis pretended to gag with a finger in her mouth. "I'm off to the Big Easy Café for some blackened catfish. Why don't you come with me," she coaxed. "Come on, ditch that peanut butter sandwich and live dangerously."

But Abigail already had another mouthful and couldn't talk. She picked up the brown paper sack that contained her celery and carrot sticks and her blueberry yogurt, and gave it a shake. Can't, she was saying. Look at all this nutritious food I have to eat. Got all four of the basic food groups right here.

Mavis rolled her eyes. "Girl, you need to get your bad self out of here once in awhile."

It was a struggle to chew and smile at the same time, but it amused Abigail that Mavis actually thought she had a bad self.

Their conversation was interrupted when a payroll clerk from down the hall in Accounting dashed into the coffee room to use the Coke machine. Abigail took advantage of the break to swig some more milk. Eating peanut butter was proving to be plenty dangerous enough.

"Here's an idea," Mavis said when the woman had left. "If you won't come to lunch, why don't you come with me to my dance lesson tomorrow night?"

"Would I have to dance?"

"No, you'd have to park cars. Of course, you'd have to dance, but this isn't the ballroom stuff. It's different."

"Different how?"

"You know . . . interpretive dance. Great exercise." She laughed and twirled around, her great bosoms bouncing along with the rest of her. "As you can plainly see."

Abigail set down her sandwich, weary from all the chewing. "You do live large, Mavis. I wish I had your confidence."

"What *are* you talking about, sugar! Confidence? Where do you think Mr. Max Gallagher would be without you? Lost in space, that's where. And who ever said you weren't a knockout with all that curly hair?"

"Curly hair?" Abigail couldn't imagine what Mavis meant until she reached up and felt the wisps corkscrewing around her head like a halo. Her hair was so naturally curly she had it straightened every few weeks when she got a trim. She must have forgotten the last time.

"No wonder I'm having so much trouble with it," she mumbled, talking to herself.

Mavis bent over the table to get her attention. "Sweetheart, your hair is staging a prison break, and so should you. You need to dance. You need to move. You need to *get down.* Tell Mavis the truth. Have you ever had a man?"

"A what?"

"I rest my case. You don't even know what they are."

"Yes, I know what a man is—and yes, I've had—you know."

"Are you sure now?"

"Of course, I've had a man! If I had a nickel for every man I've had—"

Mavis cocked her head. "You'd have a dime, right?"

"Something like that." Actually, Mavis had just inflated the count, which was a pitiful comment on Abigail's social life. A sour taste crept into her throat as she stared at her lunch and thought about all the years she'd devoted to The Gallagher Group and its eccentric genius of a CEO. Some people would say she'd sacrificed her personal life for her job, but she'd never regretted a moment of it . . . until now.

"There is a bad taste in my mouth," Abigail admitted. "But it's not the sandwich. I found out why Max—Mr. Gallagher," she corrected. She'd always thought of him as Max, but couldn't seem to bring herself to call him that, probably because he still called her Ms. Hastings. "I found out why he wants to get married in such a rush. He'll lose the wrestling trophy to Jeff if he doesn't."

"Men." Mavis's disdain spoke for women the world over.

"He and Jeff have a perfect-woman list." Abigail shuddered. "They want sports with some T and A thrown in during halftime. Can you believe it?"

"Actually, I can." Mavis settled herself on the edge of the table, clearly about to dispense some wisdom where the male gender was concerned.

"Men have got this thing about trophies and team mascots and such. You know how they run around before the big game, trying to steal each other's mascot. They'd do anything to win, including nearly getting themselves killed in the process. And you know what that trophy symbolizes, don't you?"

Abigail winced, trying to think how to put it delicately. "The male member?"

Mavis grinned. "You do know. But did you know that a car is a penis and a job is a penis and a credit card is—" She didn't wait for an answer. "That's right! Everything in a man's life is a reflection of his male prowess, and he's got to have it to prove himself, but not to us, to other men. Poor babies have to play the mine-is-bigger-than-yours game their whole lives, just like bighorn rams have to butt heads for a little female companionship."

"But, Mavis, Max and Jeff aren't bighorn rams. They're both forty now."

"True, but their brains are still twenty, and their privates never made it past thirteen. You do know why men give names to their penises, don't you?"

Abigail hadn't the faintest idea.

"They hate having a complete stranger make all their decisions for them."

Abigail was grateful she didn't have any peanut butter in her mouth. She would have choked. "Poor Max," she said, laughing. "I should have a talk with him, don't you think? He's about to make a terrible mistake."

"You can talk, girl. That doesn't mean he'll listen to you over the noise his glands are making."

Abigail gave that some thought and decided she had to speak up, anyway. She'd been with Max Gallagher nearly a decade, and she couldn't pretend not to notice that he was about to do something he might regret the rest of his life. Even if Mavis was right about men like Jeff, her bighorn ram theory didn't necessarily apply to Max. There was very little Abigail didn't know about her boss—

She pursed her lips to keep from smiling. Except what name he'd given his penis.

THREE

Max Gallagher's Pacific Heights penthouse was a reflection of the man. But it was Abigail's reflection more than it was Max's. She'd been given carte blanche to do whatever she wanted with the dozen rooms that made up his high-rise address, and after careful observation of his habits, she'd decided to make him a refuge as well as a castle.

She wanted it to be warm and welcoming, a place where a man could escape from the daily pressures of multimillion-dollar transactions that rocketed around the globe in a split second. She'd picked overstuffed chairs and couches, upholstered in gray striped silk, hoping to coax him to relax. And she'd accented them with black lacquered pieces that were both masculine and soothing.

Richly painted Oriental screens added color, and thick Tibetan carpets covered the hardwood floors. There were fireplaces in the living room, library, and bedrooms, and fragrant fresh-cut flowers everywhere, white tulips when she could get them, or daisies, which she adored.

Very little money was spent, considering Max's wealth, but she did splurge on two matching sixteenth-century bronzes of erotically entwined Roman gods. She hadn't been able to take her eyes off the statues in the antique shop, and finally she'd had to buy them. They still gave her the shivers every time she looked at them, and she often wondered what effect they had on Max. Or if he even knew they were sitting on his mantel.

Her one other indulgence was an antique French love seat, designed for more than just sitting, according to the shop owners. She'd asked about the oddly positioned armrests and was informed they were leg rests. They'd described the settee's intimate possibilities in such shocking detail that Abigail had left the shop flustered and had vivid dreams all night.

The next morning, wishing she'd never set eyes on the wickedly beautiful thing, she'd crept back to the shop. She'd bought it surreptitiously, the way a user makes a drug deal, but there'd been nowhere to hide it in Max's place, so she'd decided on a bold move and had it placed in front of his fireplace.

She pretended ignorance when he asked about the angle of the armrests. "Maybe they had back problems in the French court?"

He'd given it an intent look and cleared his throat. "If not before, afterward," he said.

Tonight, she was finishing up in the kitchen when she heard the penthouse door open. She glanced at her watch, aware that he was early. Usually, she was gone before he came up. This might be as good a time as any to talk to him, but she'd planned to wait until tomorrow morning. It was easier discussing personal things in an office setting, where there were clear boundaries.

Abigail was a big boundary person. She liked to know where the lines were that defined a relationship, and with Max it had been easy to establish an unspoken understanding. They rarely invaded each other's personal space, except by accident. Someone like Jeff, of course, would be constantly trampling all over one's lines. Very unnerving.

But this was a little unnerving, too, she realized. The penthouse was Max's personal space, despite the fact that she'd decorated it, and she could feel her pulse quicken as he came up behind her.

"I was just putting out your pills," she hurried to explain.

She was standing at the island in the middle of the large, low-lit kitchen. She hadn't turned on the overhead lighting because she'd been planning to leave, but all at once the room was brighter, and he was standing beside her at the counter.

She continued to screw lids on pill bottles without looking up. She really ought to do this more efficiently, she thought. Make up little packets or something, enough for a week at a time, but then she wouldn't have to come up here every night.

"There's a pan of eggplant lasagne in the microwave," she said, wondering why he hadn't spoken. "Five minutes on HIGH should do it. I could make a salad before I leave, if you'd like."

She gathered up the bottles to put them away, but he was so quiet she finally had to look at him. He was leaning against the counter, facing her, his arms folded, and his brow was knit in concentration. He looked a little perplexed, but very, very intent on whatever had caught his interest.

"Mr. Gallagher?"

"You're not blond," he said.

"Blond?"

"Your hair. It is curly, though. Has it always been?"

"Blond? No, it's never been blond."

He smiled, and she felt like the one who was lost in space. Why was he so interested in her hair? Why was *everyone* so interested in her hair? She liked it better when people barely noticed her. It was easier to function that way.

"You don't have to leave yet, do you?" he asked. "I was hoping we could talk."

He took the pill bottles out of her hand and set them down. Abigail felt naked. That was the problem, she realized. There were no boundaries in this kitchen. She didn't know where her space ended and his began, and he didn't seem to, either, because he was standing unusually close.

"I'm glad you're still here," he said. "I had a feeling you misunderstood about the wife thing."

I hope so, she thought. *I certainly do.*

"Jeff made it sound like I'm looking for a *Sports Illustrated* swimsuit model with sunshine for brains, which is probably what he's looking for."

"But you're not?"

He shook his head, still intent on her hair. "Interesting. There are blond shimmers when you angle your head a certain way, and the light catches those curls. Maybe that's what Jeff was talking about."

She felt her cheeks heating up and didn't know what to do. "Is it you who likes blonds? Or Jeff?" she asked.

"I like women who blush."

This was not the Max Gallagher she knew and understood. She had no idea who this man was, but he was invading her space in every possible way. Her boss of nine years had been predictable. She could count on him to forget she was in the room. This man was close enough to count the times her nostrils flared in a minute—and she was probably setting records.

Abigail couldn't think of a thing to say, and as the silence lengthened, the heat rose in her face. Her pulse was ticking like a schoolhouse clock, and one of her eyelids had begun to flutter uncontrollably. Her body seemed to be taking on a life of its own, which might not have concerned her so much if she hadn't been afraid she might hyperventilate.

No, please! Not that.

"Are you all right?" he asked. "Abigail?"

She nodded, but consciously slowed her breathing. Was his voice really that deep and melodious? She'd never noticed. It seemed to be vibrating inside her head, like piano chords played tremoloso, low and powerful. Her name had sounded like music.

She needed to speak, tell him she was fine. But she didn't dare look at him yet. He would see how *not* fine she was. Her cheeks were on fire and, as she tried to imagine herself frozen in a block of ice since prehistory, she felt his fingers on her face. Actually felt him *touching* her.

Had that ever happened before?

Not like this, her mind responded. If she hadn't known better, she would have sworn one of them was drinking Gramma Swan's Luv Potion.

"Your face, it feels so hot. Could you be running a fever? Are you ill?"

"I'm fine," she croaked. At least she could talk. She thought he understood about boundaries, but obviously not. They were standing toe to toe and he was caressing her cheek with the back of his hand. It was the sweetest, lightest touch imaginable, but if he didn't stop, she would faint. Right in front of him.

"Are you sure? You're very warm."

He blew lightly, scattering the curls on her forehead, and she closed her eyes helplessly. His breath was spearminty and cool. It made her think of mouthwash, which made her think of his mouth. He had a good mouth. She'd always liked a man with a good mouth.

"Abigail?"

There was a strange urgency fizzing in her throat like seltzer bubbles. When he said her name, it did something to her, and she wanted to make funny noises. It felt like a moan building, but that was unthinkable.

She took a breath, and something caught. To her horror, she began to cough, and it wasn't a pretty sound.

"Abigail! Are you choking?"

He grabbed her by the shoulders, and she was afraid he was going to spin her around and start pounding on her back. Or worse yet, the Heimlich.

She backed away, waving him off until she could catch her breath. "I'm all right, really. Sw-swallowed wrong. So embarrassing. Don't know how it happened."

"Should I get you some water?"

She shook her head.

"Would you like to lie down then? I could help you into the living room."

The living room. The love seat.

"Don't be silly. I'm fine." She thumped her chest and took several careful breaths, determined to convince him that all was well. But once the wheezing noises had subsided, things grew quiet again. At least there was some distance between them now. He was across the room from her. Mentally, she drew a line dividing the kitchen. *Your side. My side. Now, stay there.*

But he was staring at her with such intensity, she knew no imaginary line was going to hold him, no matter how badly she wanted it to.

She straightened her jacket, patted her hair. Once she got herself back together, he would see that there was no need for concern. Everything would be exactly as it always had been. There would be no more confusion about who stood where, even here in his kitchen.

"You're going to laugh," she said, "but I actually thought you were serious about getting married by Valentine's Day. You really had me going, Max—Mr. Gallagher—"

"I *am* serious about getting married by Valentine's Day."

She looked up, the heat draining from her face. "But sir, you can't be."

"Why not?"

"Because—well, because giving yourself two weeks to make a lifetime commitment is crazy. You're not a bighorn ram, and your wrestling trophy is not a penis. It's just a trophy."

His mouth fell open in surprise.

That was when Abigail realized what she'd done. He'd startled her so badly, she'd said exactly what was on her mind, word for word.

"I'm sorry," she whispered. "I shouldn't have said the P word. I overstepped." His pills were still on the island, and she gathered them up. "I'll just put these away and leave."

He remained quiet as she went to the refrigerator and opened the door. *Probably stunned,* she thought. She had no idea why she was putting his vitamins and the rest of it in the refrigerator, she just wanted to finish her business and get out of there.

But when she turned, he was standing right where she'd left him, and the look on his face made her realize she couldn't run off. His lips were parted in surprise, but there was a flicker of curiosity in his gaze. *No more boundaries, lines, or hyperventilating,* she told herself. She had to stay here and face this, deal with him. Unfortunately, she wasn't quite sure who she was dealing with.

She had always been able to read Max Gallagher, his moods, his wants and needs. But that seemed to have changed, and she didn't know which one of them was different now, him or her. He looked the same—a dark-haired dreamboat with a visionary's eye on the future. There wasn't anyone sexier in a snow-white dress shirt, tucked neatly into his tailored slacks, than her broad-shouldered boss. She had the feeling he wanted to say something, but the words had escaped him. She knew what that felt like.

"I'm truly sorry," she said. "I have no business telling you how to run your private affairs."

"No, you're right, Ms. Hastings—Abigail. You're right about all of it. Basing an important decision on a bet is a stupid move. But there's one thing you're forgetting."

He hesitated, and so did her heart.

"What's that?" she asked.

"I'm forty. It's time."

He was completely sincere. She could see it in his expression, hear it in his voice. This wasn't a man under the influence of a love potion. This was a man who wanted a relationship. He was ready to share his life. No one knew better than she that it got lonely living by yourself, even when your home was your refuge. Most people wanted a companion, a lover and partner to celebrate the good times and ease the ache of the bad.

"Something happens inside a man when he knows it's time to settle down and start a family," he said. "I can feel that happening inside me. It's time. I can't explain it any better than that."

"You don't have to. I understand."

"Then you'll help me?"

She turned away from him, spoke to the kitchen cabinets. It didn't help to close her eyes, even for that one moment, but she did it anyway. "Of course."

"Thank God. I couldn't pick the perfect woman if my life depended on it. But you can. You know exactly what I need. Ms. Hastings? Abigail?"

She was grateful she'd put the pills away. They would have been all over the floor. Yes, she understood his needs. But she didn't understand how she was supposed to set aside her own in order to do this for him. Some sacrifices were too great to make. There were things you couldn't do, not even for love, because they turned love into something else. They made your heart grow cold. It seemed she was about to find out what those things were.

She turned to him and managed a reasonable smile. "Of course, I'll help you. Haven't I always, no matter what it was you asked for?"

He sighed with relief. She could have predicted that. He was Mr. Gallagher again, with his bold schemes and dreams, his gambler's lust to beat the odds, and she was Ms.

Hastings, the woman behind the man, but never standing by his side. She wanted to cry. But, of course, that was unthinkable.

"You've always been there," he acknowledged, "a far better assistant than I deserved. I can't tell you how much I appreciate the way you take care of things, Abigail, the way you take care of me. You're like a mother who sleeps with one eye open at night in case her child should cough."

A one-eyed mother? That was the way he thought of her? A shadow fell over her heart, and she could feel its chill. She could hardly miss the message hidden in his gratitude. It sounded as if he were trying to tell her she'd taken over too much of his life, that she was smothering him like an overpossessive parent.

"I honestly didn't realize how much I depend on you until recently," he said. "I've been thinking that it's time to relieve some of that burden and let you have a life of your own. There must be things you want to do . . . like spend some time with your boyfriend?"

"Oh . . . yes." She looked at him sharply, wondering if he was teasing her. She didn't have a boyfriend. She'd invented one in a pinch and then was too embarrassed to uninvent him. Max had suggested lunch not long after he'd hired her, but Abigail had been in total awe of him, and too overcome to accept. Odd that he'd never tried again in all these years. She'd always thought if a man was really interested in a woman, he persisted. He'd persisted his whole life to hang onto that silly trophy.

Another one of those terrible silences was falling around them, and Abigail knew she couldn't endure it. She went to the microwave oven and tapped in the numbers on the control panel.

"Five minutes on high," she said. "Be careful of the steam when you open the lid."

"Thanks, but I won't be needing the frozen dinner. I'm going out tonight."

"You are?"

"I may have forgotten to tell you. Marcia Walters is throwing me a little prebirthday dinner party."

"But I didn't—" She started to explain that she hadn't laid out his clothes, and then she realized that he might prefer it that way. Maybe that was the point. He wanted her to back off. He was getting married, undoubtedly to someone beautiful and accomplished like Marcia Walters, whom he'd dated on occasion and who was as glamorous and charming a woman as had ever lived. He didn't need a one-eyed mother hovering about.

"Did you tell him to go to hell yet?"

There was no ignoring Mavis Swan, Abigail realized despairingly. The receptionist had decided to make herself at home in Abigail's office, and she'd done a fine job of it. She was tilted back in the chair, her feet up on the desk, and she was giving Abigail the once-over as she straggled into work that morning, an hour late.

"We spoke," Abigail informed her, "if that's what you mean."

"And did you set him straight?"

"I reminded him that he wasn't a bighorn ram."

"That's my girl." Mavis tweaked at the sleeve of her cranberry-red angora sweater, removing a pill. "Did that bring him to his senses?"

"Not exactly." Abigail unloaded her purse and briefcase on the desk, then took off her blazer jacket and tossed it at the coat tree by the door. It caught on the hook but slipped to the floor in a pile of hunter green wool. Abigail didn't bother to pick it up. That was the kind of mood she was in.

"What does that mean?" Mavis asked suspiciously. The chair crunched and scraped as she sat forward.

The third degree, Abigail thought. Any minute now the lights would go out, a spotlight would hit her in the eyes, and Mavis would start circling her, demanding a full confession.

"It means I'm going to find him a wife," Abigail said. "He wants one. And I'm going to find him one. That's my job."

"Your job? Excuse me? Where does it say wife-mongering on your job description?"

"It doesn't say one-eyed mother, either, but I do that—maybe too well."

"One-eyed mother?"

Abigail's quick head shake said never mind, *just never mind.*

"Well, you don't have to do this," Mavis persisted. "You just go in there and tell him you won't do it. And then you tell him why."

"Why?"

"Yes, tell him why—because you're in love with him."

Abigail gasped. She wished Mavis weren't sitting in her chair, because she needed it. The floor was tilting again.

"That is the most horrible thing you could possibly say to me, Mavis Swan. And it's the last thing I want to hear this morning. You don't know what I went through last night with him telling me how much he appreciated me and how he couldn't possibly find the perfect wife without me. I can't help it that I'm not as beautiful and effervescent and accomplished as Marcia Walters."

"Who's Marcia Walters?"

"That wench who keeps inviting him over to her home to dinner parties." Abigail could hardly believe she'd used the word *wench,* but she was too upset to stop and apologize. "I barely slept. I haven't eaten."

"That bad, huh?"

"Just because I've given up my entire life for the man doesn't mean I'm in love with him."

"Yes, it does."

Abigail clutched herself. Her eyes welled with tears. "All

right, it does. I'm in love with him. I love him, okay? So what? I'm his assistant, and that is all I will ever be to him. He made that painfully clear last night."

Snapping fingers caught her attention and she turned to see Mavis humming a tune with a faraway look in her eyes.

"What are you doing, Mavis?"

"Thinking; this is how I think . . ."

"But you're humming 'Lonely Teardrops.' "

Mavis held up a hand as inspiration struck. "Maybe Max is waiting for his devoted assistant to tell him how she feels?"

Abigail let her exasperation be known. "If he thought of me as the perfect wife, then he wouldn't be asking me to find him one, would he? Hmmm?"

"You don't know until you ask."

"Never. I have more pride than that."

"Then I will—"

"No! You do that, and you can wave good-bye to me *and* your Walkman. We'll be on a flight to Beirut. I hear the weather's fabulous there, and they want us back, as tourists."

Mavis resumed humming, and a moment later, finger snapping. Abigail could see the cogs turning in Mavis's head. She was scheming, strategizing, calculating, and hatching plans.

"Mavis, what are you cooking up now?"

"Nothing, nothing." She hushed Abigail, rather rudely, Abigail thought, but it was the gleam in her eye that had Abigail nervous.

"You are coming with me to the dance class tonight, aren't you?" Mavis asked.

"Do I have a choice?"

"Not if you want to keep your secret love a secret."

Abigail regarded her darkly. "Okay, but get out of my chair. I have work to do. I'm going to come up with a list of candidates for the perfect wife, present it to Mr. Midas

Touch in there, with my best wishes for his happy future, and then I'm getting out of here, maybe for the rest of the day, maybe for good."

Abigail swung around the desk and pulled the chair back as Mavis scrambled out of it. The receptionist was quicker and more agile than she'd realized.

"Do we have a deal?" Mavis asked.

"Sure, I'll come to your dance class," Abigail muttered. "A girl never knows when she's going to need a new job skill."

"Brooke Stuart?" Max swung around in his chair to look at Abigail. "Do I know her?"

So far, he hadn't recognized any of the names on Abigail's list, and when she'd refreshed his memory, he'd nixed every one of her candidates for what she thought were rather trivial reasons.

She hadn't expected this reaction, but she liked it.

"Brook is the daughter of J. B. Stuart, the New York textiles magnate," she told him. "You met her at the White House last year, and then again, I believe, at the David Hockney exhibition in Los Angeles. She's in her early thirties and will inherit the business when J. B. retires."

"Right, the one who wears nothing but green. She's a rain forest activist, isn't she?"

Abigail read through her research notes and nodded. "Animal rights, too. She even spent some time in jail."

"I like that—" He rubbed his chin, then shrugged. "No chemistry, though."

"Alice Fitzwater, the cookie heiress? She does charity work, mostly horsey stuff. You went riding with her at that equestrian event in Gladstone last fall."

"Sure, Alice. Nice gal. She does love those geldings of hers."

He made a throat-cutting gesture, then flashed Abigail a grin. "Think I'm being too picky?"

I think you're impossibly spoiled, she shot back, hoping he could read her mind this once.

"Is that it?" he asked. "The end of your list? That can't be all the women in the world who are far too good for me."

"Well . . . there's Marcia Walters, of course."

"Of course." He stared off into space, thinking. "That was a good dinner last night. Salmon poached in white wine, asparagus vinaigrette, and of course, dessert."

A smile crept across his face, and Abigail froze. Froze solid. He liked her. Abigail knew it. He liked Marcia Walters. He wanted her. *Maybe he'd already had her.*

"Marcia," he murmured.

"There could be one little problem," Abigail said, hating the desperate feeling that rose inside her. Hating herself for what she was about to do.

"A problem with Marcia?"

She nodded and tucked her hand into the folds of her skirt, where she crossed her fingers. "There's talk of a . . . " She hesitated so long that he began to stare at her intently. "Social disease," she whispered.

FOUR

Abigail knew she was in trouble when she saw the name of the dance studio, if it *was* a dance studio. The one-story, windowless building looked like a military bunker.

She pulled her car into the parking lot and turned to Mavis. "The Gee Spot? They teach interpretive dance here?"

Mavis patted her hand reassuringly. "Yes, sugar, every Thursday night. It's better than your standard studio because there's a stage and lights, a great sound system and a DJ—everything you need. The girls love it."

"Shouldn't I have brought a leotard, some slippers?"

"Relax, there's gear inside. It's like a bowling alley, you know, where you rent balls and shoes. Oh, pull over! There's valet parking."

The "valet" who took Abigail's compact car looked like he'd eaten a Honda Prelude for breakfast that morning. He had muscles on his muscles, but it was his lack of front teeth that made Abigail nervous. He was a bouncer, she was sure of it. And this place was a nightclub.

The moment they were inside, Abigail's suspicions were confirmed. The low-lit room was dominated by a spotlight and a runway stage, where a cluster of female students were gathered, listening to a woman Abigail assumed was their dance instructor. She was done up like a forties screen siren. Her floor-length gown was spangled and slinky. She wore elbow-length gloves, and her long blond hair completely hid one side of her face.

What caught Abigail was the total confidence the woman exuded. She didn't exhibit a moment's doubt as she described a move to her students and then demonstrated it. Everything she did said "I am beautiful, sensual, utterly desirable."

Abigail wondered what it would feel like to be that confident and in control. It had to be empowering on some level to believe that you were ravishing. She also realized it must be a state of mind more than anything else, because when the dance instructor swept her hair back, Abigail could see that the woman wasn't a beauty. What she exuded came from inside, and it was very powerful.

"It's all in the knees, ladies," she told her rapt students. "When you bend, it's from the knees. Watch," she said, executing a roll of her hips and what looked like a deep knee bend at the same time. "Even when you're doing glove work, it's all about staying loose and flexible."

Glove work? Abigail glanced at Mavis, who was as riveted as the other women.

"Now, I'll demonstrate the entire sequence," the instructor said. "Music!"

Background music magically swelled to fill the room. Abigail hadn't recognized the sexy, pulsing beat until the volume came up. It was "The Stripper," and it rocked the walls. The instructor began to stride down the ramp, very gracefully, considering the length of her skirt. Every so often, she stopped to rotate her hips and pluck at the fingers of her gloves. When she had one all the way off, she whipped it around like a lasso and flung it.

"What's she doing?" Abigail whispered. "That looks like a striptease."

"It's burlesque," Mavis explained. "It's back in style. All the posh clubs are adding burlesque acts. It's very hot right now."

"I'll bet," Abigail said under her breath. If this was interpretive dance, Abigail had been going to the wrong recitals all these years.

"Every woman is a sex goddess," the dance teacher told them when she'd finally rid herself of both gloves and stopped rotating. "She simply has to know it and show it. That's the secret, ladies. Know it and show it!"

The music came up again, and she began to bump and grind for real. Satin straps slipped up and down seductively as she worked first one shoulder and then the other. The students applauded and swayed to the music. Abigail found it almost impossible not to move herself.

The instructor shed her dress like a proverbial snake coming out of its skin. It was very impressive, and when the gown was in a glittering heap around her feet, she stepped out of it and bowed her head to great applause. Abigail was relieved to see that she was dressed underneath in a shimmering white body stocking.

"Now for the important stuff," the instructor said. "Wear comfortable shoes. They're the only thing you're *not* taking off when you do this for real. And never forget that Velcro is a girl's best friend."

That got her some laughter and more applause.

"That's Justine Divine," Mavis said reverently. "We call her Just Divine for short. She's the most famous stripper in the country. She taught Demi Moore."

"I thought you said this was burlesque?"

"Oh, it is. The girls who work here dress only in white,

they never bend over all the way, and nothing touches the floor except the soles of their feet. Those are the rules. Very classy stuff."

Never bend over *all* the way? What did that mean?

"Mavis, I want to go home."

"You can't. The Incredible Hulk took your car."

"I can't do this," Abigail said through clenched teeth. "I don't look like Demi Moore with my clothes off."

"Who does? Have a look around, child. Do you think any of these ladies does? Even Demi Moore doesn't look like Demi Moore."

That reassured Abigail only slightly. But she did have a look around, and what she saw surprised her. There were several senior citizens, one woman who appeared to be pregnant, and another in a wheelchair. The common denominator was enthusiasm. They all seemed to be caught up in the exhilaration of the music and the forbidden art form that some people believed celebrated the female body rather than exploited it. It all depended on who was dancing and who was watching, she supposed.

Many of the students were already going through racks of feathery, slinky outfits and picking out their favorites. Abigail saw cat suits, baby dolls, men's tuxes, corsets, and sequined bustiers.

"Come on," Mavis coaxed. "Let's get over there before all the good stuff is gone!"

She grabbed Abigail's hand and dragged her over to the costumes. "There are rooms in the back for changing, and they have bodysuits for the faint of heart," she explained. "Even Just Divine wears one, so you shouldn't feel squeamish."

But Abigail did feel squeamish. Very squeamish. "I can't take off my clothes and dance. I can't even dance."

"That's what you're here for, girl. To learn."

"Oh, look at this!" Mavis pulled an outfit off the rack that was nothing but gloves, hot pink boa feathers, and a nude body stocking.

She held it up to her ample figure and sighed. "Be lucky if I could get my big toe in this thing. If I had your bony little body, hon—"

"Costume up, ladies," the instructor called out. "It's your turn to shine."

Mavis winked at Abigail and handed her the outfit. "Slip into those feathers and try it."

All Abigail had to do was touch the clingy material and she knew this wasn't going to work. The boa feathers would make her sneeze and the bodysuit was made out of the same stuff she wrapped her sandwiches in.

"Not in a million years," she told Mavis. "Not in a *billion.* You are never going to get me into this getup, Mavis Swan. I wouldn't do it if the heavens opened up and a thunderous voice commanded me to. It will show every pimple and dimple! I might as well be naked."

"Bah bah ba boom, chicky boom . . . chicky boom boom boom."

Abigail hummed to herself as she finished reorganizing her research files the next morning. That darn dance class music was contagious. She hadn't been able to get it out of her mind all night. She felt as if she'd been strutting around, doing "feather work" in her sleep.

At Mavis's instigation, the students had ganged up on her and made her join in the fun, but Abigail hadn't regretted it.

She'd loved all the great old songs. Just Divine had taught the class how to take it off to everything from Motown to Irving Berlin tunes. They'd disrobed to "Lullaby of Birdland" and "Lonely Little G-String."

But Abigail had liked the traditional music best. She couldn't get "The Stripper" out of her head.

"Boom, chicky boom boom boom—"

Mavis's favorite was "Big Millie from Philly," and she'd

been quite a showstopper with her routine. She'd done a takeoff on the famous Blaze Starr performance, where the stripper ends up on the floor, writhing like a fish out of water. For the grand finale, Mavis had actually rigged it so chemical smoke would rise from her hips and rippling red ribbons would make it look like she was on fire.

She'd proudly taken her bows after that one.

Abigail had stopped the show once, too, when she'd fallen off the ramp. That was when Just Divine started paying particular attention to her, taking her under her boa feather wing, so to speak. Abigail had improved a good deal by the end of the lesson. She even got some applause herself.

She smiled now, remembering the instructor's chant.

"Rock the shoulders, swivel the hips, now give it a twist and shimmy down." That was where the girls all squealed and performed a sexy little knee bend, shaking their way toward the ground and back up again.

"Rock, rock, swivel, swivel," Abigail murmured, trying the move where she stood. "Now give it a twist and shimmy—"

"Ms. Hastings? Is there a problem?"

Abigail froze. It was Max. He'd come in through her office door instead of his own. He was behind her, but she had no trouble imagining him standing there, watching her switch and twitch, like a horse swatting flies with its tail. Why he'd called her Ms. Hastings, she didn't know. Unless he'd forgotten her name again. He must be shocked.

"Are you all right?" he asked.

She nodded and mumbled, "Yes."

"Is it your clothing?"

"Clothing?"

"It looked as if something were caught . . . somewhere."

"No, I'm fine." Apparently, he thought she needed to adjust her underwear.

"You're sure?" he persisted.

"Yes—" How did one explain the shimmy down? "My back," she said. Her voice was breathier than she intended, but it was crucial to make him understand because that unavoidable moment was coming when she would have to turn around and face him.

"I had an itch," she said. "You know how that is, when your back itches and you can't reach it."

"Yes, I do know how that is."

It seemed a safer excuse than having to use the facilities, but Abigail had picked up something in his voice. It sounded a little husky and thick.

Her pulse quickened as she imagined what must go through a man's mind when he watched a woman do the things she was learning last night. It might be highly arousing. Highly.

"Where . . . does it itch?" he asked.

Tell him the itch is gone. There is no itch.

"Nowhere special." She wriggled her shoulder blades. "There."

He cleared his throat, and the next thing she knew, he was right behind her. "I can reach it," he said. "I can do that easy."

Abigail said nothing, which was the same as inviting him to go right ahead. Which he did. Oh, and how. She'd had her share of fantasies about her sexy, absentminded boss, but she'd never imagined him scratching her back. She *couldn't* have imagined how incredible it would feel as he gently raked his fingernails between the wings of her shoulder blades and then buzzed down the entire length of her spine.

Lord, have mercy. Nobody'd told her what it was like to have a man set your skin to shivering right through your clothing, and then slowly rub it out with the palm of his hand. Rake and rub. Rake and rub. She felt like a kitten getting scratched and petted.

Such slow, sensual vertical strokes. Such lovely warmth. When he switched to a horizontal mode, it made her want to move her hips the way she'd been taught to last night. But she couldn't do that. What would he think? She had to hold still.

"Is that better?" he asked as he slowed.

"Oh . . . much." Her whole body must be down around her toes in a puddle.

"Should we get started then?"

"Started . . . ?"

"With the to-do list?"

"Oh . . . sure."

"I'll be waiting for you."

His voice was thrillingly low and rough. It had a quality that made her think of a hairbrush, soft and bristly and very stimulating.

When she was sure he was gone, she turned and stared at his office door, aware that she needed to do more than adjust her underwear. She needed to change it! She couldn't go in there with him. Even if she'd had the courage to face him the way her body was melting into rivulets, her legs wouldn't work!

What was she to do? The man was her boss, but he made her weak, and there was no hiding that anymore. No hiding the ache in her heart or the yearning in her eyes. No, she couldn't go into his office and sit there calmly taking down his damn to-do list, not feeling like this. She wasn't sure she could ever do that again.

Her purse and briefcase were sitting on the chair where she'd left them. She quietly closed the file drawer and gave in to a sudden crazy impulse, one she probably should have given in to a long time ago.

Hurry, she told herself, *before you change you mind.*

A moment later, she dashed past Mavis's station, hoping the receptionist was on the phone and wouldn't notice her.

Abigail knew she couldn't stop without bursting into tears. And she didn't stop, not even when Mavis called out to her.

"Where are you going in such a rush, sugar?"

I don't know, Abigail thought. *I don't know where I'm going, and for once it doesn't matter. Anywhere is better than here.*

FIVE

Max heard a tap on his door and looked up. He'd been expecting Abigail, but it was Mavis standing in his office doorway. She had her hands planted firmly on her hips, and there was fire in her eyes. Not a good sign.

"I'd like a word, Mr. Gallagher."

"Come on in." He stood up, but she marched into his room with such bristling force, she almost knocked him back down. Now he knew why they gave female names to hurricanes. There was definitely something going on with the women in his office today. Abigail and Mavis were both acting strangely. Maybe he'd missed some special occasion like Secretary's Day or a birthday.

"Was there something you wanted to ask me about Abigail?" Mavis demanded.

Max stared at her as blankly as if she'd asked him to explain relativity. "Ask you about Abigail? Is she all right?"

"Wrong question."

"I guess that means she's all right. I was just in her office, scratching her back—" That didn't sound right. "Is this Secretary's Day?"

"*Wrong* question."

The receptionist clearly had some direction she was headed with this. Max had never been good at guessing games, but he wasn't about to mess with Mavis Swan. For all he knew, she could be one of those women who headed for the cutlery drawer when they were suffering from PMS. Maybe that was the problem.

"Is Abigail having female trouble?" he asked. Now he was really groping. "Bad hair day?"

"Wrong, wrong, wrong! Ask me about that boyfriend of hers."

"What about that boyfriend of hers?" *Damn good question,* he thought. He was curious about that.

"There *is* no boyfriend," Mavis announced. "He's long gone."

"Really? They broke up?"

She glared at him. "There never was any boyfriend, you nincompoop. Now, ask me what's going to happen if you make that poor girl find you the perfect wife?"

"What's going to happen?"

"*She's* long gone." With that shot to the heart, Mavis Swan did an about-face and marched out the way she came in, through his door. Over her shoulder, she fired one last salvo. "And so am I."

Max felt as if he needed CPR. He must be bleeding from the eyes after that. It was a quarterback sack, but he had no idea what had provoked it. Mavis was furious with him, and it had something to do with Abigail's boyfriend, who apparently didn't exist.

Max was already on his feet. It seemed a natural enough thing to walk to Abigail's door and ask her how she was doing. Maybe he'd upset her when he was scratching her back. He'd felt some sparks at being that close to her. To be honest, he'd felt a brushfire, but he hadn't been able to tell about her. He could never tell about Abigail.

She wasn't there, he realized as he opened her door and looked inside. That didn't seem possible. Abigail was always there. He couldn't remember a time when she wasn't. He had no idea what to do, but it felt like he should do something. Calling the police seemed a little extreme, especially if she was coming right back. Maybe she'd gone to the ladies' room. Something told him women did that when they were upset.

He entered her office and stood there in her domain awhile, pondering the mysteries of the female sex in general and one Abigail Hastings in particular. No answers came to him, but a question flashed repeatedly through his thought processes.

There was no boyfriend?

Max was ready to call the police by the time he got up to his penthouse that evening. He strode into his living room, tossed his jacket onto the first piece of furniture he encountered—the odd-looking antique settee Abigail had picked out—yanked off his tie, and went to the bar to fix himself a drink. He'd lost a bundle today, but that wasn't the problem. He'd get the money back tomorrow. He didn't know *how* to get her back. He didn't even know where she was.

She hadn't shown up by quitting time, and she'd never missed a day's work in all the years he'd known her. He was certain of that because he would have remembered. If he'd ever gone through a day like this before, he would have remembered.

The pencil sharpener had bitten him, he'd misplaced his Day-Timer, the Intel file had disappeared, and every phone call he made was answered by a disembodied voice that read off an endless list of choices, scolded him for not choosing viable options, thwarted him at every turn, and more often than not, disconnected him. Abigail had always made those phone calls.

The Scotch he'd just poured tasted like car exhaust.

He took another swallow, forced it down, fumes and all, and left the glass on the wet bar. He needed to keep moving, even if it was laps around his own apartment. He'd never felt this restless in his life. Mavis had talked him out of doing anything rash. She'd insisted that Abigail would want to be left alone, but she wouldn't explain what she meant. She'd said too much already, that was all she would tell him. But the look in her eyes had told him he ought to know why.

He didn't. He didn't understand at all.

Why did women make up boyfriends that didn't exist except to ward other men off? If Abigail had been trying to ward him off, which she clearly had, then why should it bother her that he'd decided it was time to get married? Maybe he shouldn't have asked her to pick out his wife. Okay, maybe that was pushing it, but hell, she did know him better than anyone else, better than he knew himself.

There'd been a couple of occasions when he'd asked her to accompany him to functions in the capacity of his assistant. They were black tie, and she would have had to dress formally, but it wouldn't have been a date. It was business, but she'd always had a reason she couldn't, and he'd assumed it was the boyfriend.

He rolled his neck and listened to the cracking sounds. He was tense enough to open screw caps with his teeth. What was worse, he had no idea how to unwind. He got tired once in awhile, sure, but never uptight. He was only edgy when he didn't understand things. Right now, he didn't understand anything.

She could have explained all of this to him in a minute, but she wasn't here. *Not here?* he thought, looking around the place. She was everywhere. That was why her absence was inescapable. She picked out his clothing, his food, the furniture.

He fell into one of the overstuffed couches and wondered how she'd known that he would have chosen this exact piece of furniture himself. Gray was a depressing color. There couldn't be that many people who liked it. Somehow she'd known that he did.

He sank back and closed his eyes, but he couldn't release the thoughts cluttering his head. They kept springing back at him like the rubber belt of a slingshot. He was up again, immediately, wandering around his own living room, seeing things he'd never noticed before. He felt like a man coming out of a deep sleep, a man who'd been dreaming his way through life.

There was a statue on the mantel—actually there were a pair of statues, one on each end. They weren't identical, but based on the one Max was looking at, there were definitely two people involved, and one of them was a contortionist. He could see arms and legs, a naked buttock— What were they doing?

The longer he looked, the more he was certain it was a man and woman in the throes of animal lust. Did Abigail like erotic art? His Abigail? She blushed when he stood close to her. He was beginning to wonder what was going on under those buttoned-all-the-way-to-the-top blouses she wore.

What else didn't he know about his assistant?

He looked at the statue again and saw her this time, naked and arched, gasping as her powerful partner bent himself to her breast and braced her high-flying leg with his shoulder. He was bearing down on her welcoming body at an angle that would have challenged a gymnast. It was a woman being ravished. She was in total ecstasy, Max realized with a flash of jealousy. Who the hell was that naked guy?

Interesting that he was having explicit fantasies about Abigail when he'd never thought of her in those terms. She wasn't the type men got crazy in the head over. She was the type you came to rely on so heavily you couldn't breathe when she wasn't around.

The kitchen was where he'd always felt her presence most. By the time he got there, he was pretty sure he was suffocating. There was no dinner in the microwave, no pills laid out. He wasn't hungry, but the pills had him worried. He took them every night, but he had no idea why. He could have a fatal illness and not even know it.

"For Christ's sake, woman," he said to the empty room. "Are you going to let me die?"

He stalked the wall phone with his eyes. "I could call her," he thought aloud, feeling as guilty as a kid planning a prank. "Ask her how she is . . . and where my pills are. Yeah, I could do that. She doesn't have a boyfriend."

He paced the kitchen, trying to convince himself to pick up the phone, but he ended up doing just the opposite. "I'd be intruding on her privacy. Mavis said she wanted to be alone, and I should respect that."

The truth was, he didn't know what the hell to do. There was only one thing in life he was good at, and that was making money. It was Abigail who was good at everything else.

God, he hated all this confusion and emotional turmoil. Maybe by tomorrow it would all be gone. Abigail would have returned, and everything could go back to the way it was. They would start their day with the to-do list, and she would lay out his pills.

Tomorrow everything would be fine. If he lived that long.

SIX

Abigail was in the ladies' room, staring in the mirror with something like fierce concentration, when the brassy beat of a Latin salsa band announced Mavis's entrance. The receptionist was carrying a boom box and a mug of coffee as she came through the door.

The sight of Abigail brought her to a stop.

"Is this where you've been since yesterday?" Mavis asked. "Hiding in the john?"

Abigail shook her head and watched little frizzlets pop out of her braided tresses like sprigs from a tree. Her hair was impossible. She would have to have it straightened before she could leave the bathroom. She needed a hair stylist who did emergency house calls.

"I just got here," Abigail confessed. "I couldn't face him, Mavis. I can't go in there."

Abigail's overriding sense of responsibility was the only thing that had brought her into work today. The Gallagher Group newsletter had to be ready for the printer by that afternoon. She'd never missed a deadline, but she'd realized on the elevator that she could not pretend it was business as usual. She was tempted to ask Mavis to smuggle the work to her in here.

The salsa band became background music as Mavis set the boom box on the stainless steel tray, along with the coffee mug. "He's not in there, sugar. He's gone to some big network taping today, poor baby. Kept mumbling about his pills."

"His pills—" Abigail had forgotten all about Max's pills, his dinner, his clothes for *Money Talks*, a weekly television show that brought together some of the country's best financial minds to discuss the current state of the market. She could only imagine what Max was wearing.

"The hell with him," Mavis said with a pointed sniff. "Are you all right? You were out the whole day."

More curls sprigged as Abigail nodded. "I was walking on the beach, trying to decide what to do."

"Did you give any thought to what you *want* to do?"

"I know what I want, Mavis. I made the craziest, most momentous decision of my life yesterday, but then I had to abandon it."

"Really? What crazy, momentous decision was that?"

"I want him. I want Max."

Mavis stared at her without blinking. "That may come as a surprise to you, sugar. But it doesn't to me."

"No, it's not what you're thinking. I *want* him, but only for a night."

"One night . . . like all night? An all-night stand?"

"Yes, exactly that. If I can't have Max Gallagher for a lifetime, then—" She drew in a breath and just as suddenly, a wave of emotion overtook her. Perilously near tears, she said, "I want him for a night. One perfect night."

"Oh," was the only word that came out of Mavis.

Abigail knuckled away the wetness on her lashes and frowned at her unkempt appearance. "Crazy, huh? Look at me."

Their gazes met in the mirror.

The other woman cocked an eyebrow. "You do look a little ragged around the edges."

"And this is as good as it gets. I've been working on this bramble bush all morning, trying to get the curl under control. It's hopeless."

"That's the problem right there," Mavis intoned. "You're going at it backward. My gramma always said, 'Free the hair and free the soul.'"

"Would that be Gramma Swan?"

"It would. Tishanda Swan, the flyest woman in Macon County, Georgia."

"Your grandmother was fly?" Abigail didn't know exactly what that meant, but she knew it was good.

"Still is. What that woman didn't know about freeing the soul." Mavis's smile turned nostalgic. "When my mamma skipped town for kiting checks, just two steps ahead of the sheriff, Tishanda took me in and raised me. She savored every morsel of the buffet life laid out for her, that woman. She partook with an appetite, and she didn't believe in frustrating a child's natural appetites, either, which is why I'm so natural, I guess."

Interesting. Abigail's grandmother had been the daughter of a Presbyterian deacon who believed in frustrating natural appetites at every opportunity with a birch switch.

"Come here and let me free that hair," Mavis ordered.

Abigail was probably too trusting a soul, but she had little to lose at this point. She put herself totally in Mavis's hands, and within moments, the rubber bands and bobby pins were history. Mavis combed her fingers through the tight, kinky locks, "redistributing the natural oils," she said, and then she seduced them into loose ringlets with a wire pick and plain tap water, which she sprinkled like holy droplets.

She also hummed while she worked, and every so often, she stole a sip from her coffee cup. The way she smacked her lips made Abigail wonder what she had in there.

"That's remarkable," Abigail said, admiring the dark gold riot of curls that materialized as Mavis tweaked and spritzed, finishing up with hair spray.

Abigail was ready to go out and conquer the world, but Mavis wasn't finished with her. "Something has to be done with that face," she said, digging through her makeup bag.

When she'd picked out the tubes and brushes she wanted, she set to work, using a pale blue shadow that made Abigail's eyes look as if they were set in a misty lake and a cherry red lip gloss that made her mouth look like succulent fruit. Her cheeks were dusted with roses, and her earlobes adorned with Mavis's pearl and diamond studs.

Abigail had expected it to take a crew of cosmeticians, working around the clock, but Mavis had transformed her from a spriggy tree branch into a seductive siren with very little effort.

It embarrassed her that all she wanted to do afterward was gaze at herself in the mirror. But Mavis seemed to understand.

"Now, that's Abbie," her friend declared.

Abigail nodded in complete agreement. "I think I could seduce a man, looking like this," she said softly.

"Seduce a man *and* ruin him for any other woman."

"Well . . . that would be nice." Abigail grinned, and was ashamed of herself.

"You're not only fly," Mavis said with a brisk nod of approval, "you've had strippin' lessons. You can dance your way into his bed."

Abigail's spirits sank like a rock. "The only thing I can dance myself into is the emergency room. You saw me tumble off the stage."

Mavis tapped the boom box and gave the volume a boost. "Feel that beat? Hear those bongo drums? All you have to do is relax and let the music soften your brain, sugar."

She held up the mug she'd been sipping from. "And what it can't do, this will."

"Caffeine? That makes me nervous."

"This is not coffee, child. No coffee could ever free your soul the way Gramma's potion can."

"Is *that* the infamous love potion?" Abigail was intrigued. She tried to get a peek, but Mavis covered the cup with her hand.

The other woman's smile was indulgent. "First you have to say it right, with feeling. It's not *love,* the way you sign a letter. It's *luv,* the way you feel when the lights are low and the music's blue and your man is doing you right."

Well, *that* must be some feeling. "Can I try it?"

Mavis looked shocked. "At nine in the morning? You want to get yourself arrested?"

"You're drinking it."

"That's because it's Friday, and I plan to have myself a fine weekend. I've built up a tolerance over the years, but you're a baby. It'll go straight to your head."

The other woman held out the mug and let Abigail take a look at the sinfully rich, sinfully dark and creamy brew.

"It smells like hot chocolate."

"It is hot chocolate." Mavis took a sip, closed her eyes, and shuddered. "Lordy, watch out. You watch out now. I'm goin' be dangerous by quitting time."

Her lids slowly fluttered open, but Abigail could see that her eyes were dreamy and unfocused, the pupils dilated.

"What's in that stuff?"

"I can't honestly remember. Gramma sends me packets in the mail. There are special cocoa leaves from Jamaica, a splash of raspberry nectar, a pinch of orange zest, whipped cream for garnish, if you want to get fancy. And horn of unicorn, of course.

"Just kidding—" she winked. "I've got the recipe somewhere, but the trick is in the brewing."

"Raspberry nectar? That sounds good."

"Good? This is elixir of the gods, and don't you forget it!

With all due respect to Just Divine, she was wrong. Velcro isn't a girl's best friend, Gramma Swan's Luv Potion is."

Max thought he was in the wrong apartment when he walked into his living room that night and saw a woman standing by the windows. *What is this?* he asked himself as he came to a stop with his coat in one hand and his bulging briefcase in the other. Not just a woman. This was a vision, and there was only one explanation. He had to be dreaming.

Either that or he really was a dying man.

He couldn't see her face because she was looking out, gazing at the lights that twinkled over the city like a string of crystal chandeliers. But she had a glorious head of hair that was dizzy with curls, and the candle glow seemed to sheen every ringlet with gold and bring it to life.

Candle glow?

His fireplace mantel was dotted with flickering tapers, the lights had been dimmed, and soft music was playing.

No question about it. He was dying. He had some fatal disease, and this was a near-death experience.

The dress she wore shimmered with anticipation. It was as alive and electric as her hair. The shoulder straps gave it the look of a long, translucent slip, but that could have been a trick of the iridescent material. The way it clung to her curves made you think you were seeing legs and other female secrets, when you really weren't.

Max had convinced himself he was hallucinating when the vision in white actually turned and looked right at him.

"Mr. Gallagher? I didn't hear you come in."

He was staring, but it couldn't be helped. The voice sounded exactly like his assistant's, but the face, the dress, the elbow-length gloves. This stunning creature couldn't be Abigail. Not that Abigail wasn't attractive in her way, but this woman was—a vision!

"Are you all right, Mr. Gallagher?"

"Abigail? Is that you?"

She laughed, a bright sound that made him think of bracelets with charms. "Of course, it's me. Who else would it be?"

Her gown rustled like music as she turned toward him. He couldn't tell what was her and what was the fabric, but things were moving and bobbing and shimmying. He wasn't sure she had on anything at all under the dress, and it was making him as dizzy as her curls.

Who was this woman?

"What are you doing here?" He qualified the question. "Dressed like that?"

"I thought you'd like me to lay out your pills."

"Oh . . . yes . . . thank you."

That must be what he needed, his pills. Maybe it was a mental condition. He was delusional without them. This had been the second worst day of his life. The worst was yesterday. All day long, his head hadn't stopped pounding or his gut churning. Now he wasn't sure how he felt, but there was some seismic activity in the center of his chest. Something in there was shifting like the earth's plates.

"Can I get you a drink?" he asked her.

"I have something, thank you."

That was the first time he noticed the long-stemmed crystal cup in her hand. It was the kind they served Irish coffee in, and the way she brought it to her lips told him the brew was a hot drink rather than a cold one. She closed her eyes when she sipped, and her gloved fingers lightly held the delicate stemware.

For some reason, the sight made his stomach feel hollow. It was entirely possible that he was hungry. He hadn't eaten anything but some rubber chicken for lunch.

He still couldn't figure out what she was doing in his living room, dressed like a movie star, a vamp, an angel. Take your pick.

"Are you going somewhere tonight?" he asked. "A date?"

She looked startled, and the widening of her eyes made

her even more beautiful. "You didn't forget, did you? There's a charity benefit at the Performing Arts Center tonight."

"Charity benefit? Are you sure? I don't think it's in my Day-Timer."

"Oh, I'm sure I put it down. It's a very important event, and I never forget that sort of thing. Don't I always make it a point to have your clothes ready?"

She glanced over at the conversational grouping by the window. Max had to look twice to make sure he actually saw the black-tie outfit she'd draped over the couch. Another non sequitur. Why had she laid his clothes out in the living room? She couldn't be expecting him to change in here.

He rubbed his jaw, felt the stubble. "I thought I'd shower and shave first."

"Now that's a lovely thought. It really is, but I doubt if we have time."

"We . . . ?"

"Oh, don't you want me to go along? You've asked me to accompany you to these functions before—in a strictly professional capacity, of course—and tonight I thought I would. But if you prefer that I didn't, well . . ."

She let the thought hang in the air, gave him a wounded glance, and then cast her gaze down at the carpet. A little sigh slipped out, and her lower lip seemed to double its size. Was she pouting? He thought she might be, but he couldn't make himself believe it. Abigail Hastings didn't pout. She barely breathed she was so restrained.

He'd often thought she would pop like a soap bubble if he touched her. Pop and disappear. Maybe that's why he'd never gone too close. He'd been afraid she would disappear.

"Of course, I'd like you to go," he said.

Wherever the hell it was they were going.

She smiled, beamed, actually, and took a sip from her cup.

The transformation she underwent whenever she drank from that thing was amazing. The liquid seemed to shiver through her whole body. He could almost trace its path, and the pleasure that came over her expression was something to see.

She closed her eyes, tilted her head back, and held the cup close to her throat. Gloved fingers caressed it lightly, lovingly, as if she were clinging to a man's arm. Max's own biceps tugged at the thought. It was an unbelievably sensual sight. His jaw was so tight it felt like someone had run a wire through it. He could feel sparks all the way to his groin.

When she opened her eyes, she looked a little dazed and dreamy-lidded. A soft sound caught in her throat as she stared at him. But it only took a moment for her gaze to darken and connect with his. The seismic activity dropped to his groin when he registered her intent. She was homing in on him like a fluffy white kitten going after its very first mouse. He could almost hear her purring as she gave him the once-over.

He had to be delusional.

This could not be Ms. Hastings, the woman who sharpened his pencils.

She consulted the diamond watch on her wrist, which she wore over her glove. "You're going to need some help getting ready, or we'll never make it, sir."

"I don't think—"

But she'd already set her cup on the mantel and started toward him. He couldn't take his eyes off the way her hips moved, the way everything moved. He would never have guessed that her legs were that long, but there was a hell-to-pay slit running up the side of her dress that proved it. He didn't have a clue why she wanted to help him undress in the living room, but apparently, he was going to find out. And who was he to deny her?

He was still holding his coat, and the first thing she did was reach inside it like a sexy little pickpocket and snatch his Day-Timer. She tossed it away with an innocent smile, and then she patted his face with her gloved hand.

"You're not going to need that silly old appointment book, sir. I've got everything under control."

Her touch was cool and satiny against his overheated skin. Max wanted to groan it felt so good. God, he'd missed her. Where had she been the last couple of days? In some alien spaceship being transformed into this curly-haired seducer of earth men? Maybe she wanted to have his baby. Maybe that was what this was all about.

"You don't look well, sir," she said. "Are you all right?"

That brought him back to reality. His heart was pounding like a sledgehammer and his mouth was dry.

"I don't know, Abigail, am I? I haven't taken my pills in a couple of days."

She blinked at him and laughed, but he was serious. "You can tell me," he said. "Do I have some kind of medical condition?"

"No! Those pills are vitamins and minerals. There is one for your tummy, which the doctor said tends to produce a little more acid than it should—"

She stopped and gave his belly a rubadub, which was probably meant to reassure him. It made his eyelids twitch.

"Do we have a cute little tummy ache?" she asked.

Baby talk. Was that how alien females seduced their abductees these days? What was he, breeding stock?

God, he hoped so.

"I'm fine," he said. "Are *you* all right?"

She popped up unexpectedly, brushed a kiss over his mouth and gave him a dithery smile. "Of course, I am, silly!"

Max did nothing but stare at her. He could feel the wire twisting his jaw, only the sensation wasn't limited to that area anymore. She'd run another one right through his groin. The woman was killing him. He needed his pills.

"Now, let's get these naughty old buttons undone and give you some air," she crooned.

Her fingers teased and tickled his Adam's apple as she undid things, and then they delved into more dangerous territory—dangerous for both of them. She flitted and flirted with his chest hair as she freed several more buttons.

"Look at all this lovely dark fur," she exclaimed, making wanton circles and creating little tufts in the darkness that graced his pectorals and belly. Her hands smoothed across his chest and forced a deep sigh out of him.

God, he was going to die. He'd never known anything could feel as good as the way she was touching him.

"You must have been awfully warm in there," she said, gazing up at him. "Doesn't it feel better with your shirt open? Hmmm?"

His "Yes," sounded like a moan.

"Oh, poor baby, you are in a bad way. Here, I have just the thing. This will make you all better."

She left him standing there, half dressed, half nuts, with his shirttail hanging out, as she strolled away from him. He'd never seen anything swing quite the way her backside did. There were strippers who couldn't sell it that well. Where had she learned to walk like that?

There was another cup of whatever she was drinking next to hers on the mantel. She brought them both back with her and handed one to him.

"This'll cure whatever ails you," she said. "I solemnly promise."

She was about as solemn as a fireworks display on the fourth. But if the stuff would make him as happy as it was making her, what did he have to lose? He took a drink, rolled it around in his mouth like wine, and swallowed. It was delicious. It tasted like she had when she'd kissed him.

"Reminds me of hot chocolate."

"Yes—" She giggled. "It does, doesn't it. Now, drink it all up like a good boy."

She took a sip of hers, then asked him to hold her cup, too, while she finished with his "silly old shirt."

Max had his hands full—literally—as she continued to help him undress. There was nothing he could do to stop her antics, and she was taking every advantage of the opportunity. He couldn't suppress a smile while she worked her way down the front of his shirt, cooing about how strong he was and what lovely, big muscles he had. He didn't know about lovely, but he'd pumped up since he'd been working out at the club. And there was one muscle in particular that was getting plenty of exercise since she started in on him.

If she got those pants off him, she was going to be in for a *big* surprise. And he was damn sure going to spill some hot chocolate.

He drank the stuff as she worked her wiles on him, mostly in a futile attempt to distract himself. But he had to admit that it was tasty. Something was making him feel better. His headache was fading, and his stomach had settled down. But his body was alive with sensation everywhere else.

"Oh, my goodness," she whispered when she undid his belt, "look at you. You must have drunk all the potion."

"Potion?"

He sucked in a breath as her hands brushed against him. Maybe it was unintentional, but she was touching him all over the place as she searched for snaps, hooks, and zippers. Her fingers dithered and danced. And finally she found that zipper.

Yes! Pull it down, ease my pain.

"Mr. Gallagher," she whispered.

"Call me Max," he groaned.

He couldn't hang onto the cups. They were tipping every which way when suddenly she bobbed up and spirited both of them away from him. She set them on the coffee table and gave him a coy glance through her curls. Her expression said, *You haven't seen anything yet, sir.* Before he could respond, she had arched up and languidly shook her head. Her hair caught the light, shimmering like a halo.

What the hell was she doing?

"I've been taking dance lessons," she announced. "Would you like to see what I've learned?"

He wanted her to finish what she started! But something about the sound of that intrigued him. Dance lessons?

"Show me," he said.

She glanced over her shoulder and produced one of those pouty smiles as she strutted to the fireplace and spun around like a showgirl. She rocked her shoulders, sending a dress strap skittering down her arm, but she paid it no heed. With her hip cocked provocatively, she bent from the waist, opening the slit of her dress all the way up. Apparently, there was something on the floor, but she was in no damn hurry to pick it up.

She rocked her hips and smiled at him, clearly curious about his reaction. When he refused to smile back, she pursed her lips and made a kissy sound.

She was teasing him. It wasn't enough that she left him with his pants undone and his loins aflame. The little vixen wanted blood.

The thing she'd made such a production of picking up from the floor was a boom box. When she had it on the fireplace mantel, she touched a button, and sultry music pulsed throughout the room. Her next move was to fix her gaze on him and rotate her hips. The song was Sonny and Cher's "I've Got You, Babe."

She pointed a gloved finger at him and did several more rotations. "You," she whispered. "I've got you, babe."

He mouthed the word, "Me?" and thumbed his naked chest. He wanted to laugh, but he couldn't. This was too wild. She was too wild. He couldn't imagine another woman in the world doing this—and he certainly couldn't imagine Abigail Hastings doing it. But he wasn't dreaming.

He'd *been* dreaming.

His whole life.

He'd been walking around in a daze, completely oblivious to the woman who worked beside him every day. He'd never had an inkling there was a blue-eyed, hot-blooded vixen in Abigail Hastings. He had a feeling Mavis knew about this side of his assistant. Even Jeff had noticed her wild, curly hair. But when Jeff had mentioned it, Max Gallagher's brilliant response was "Not Abigail!"

That was sad. That was a crime.

Max didn't know what to do, but she didn't leave him in doubt for long. She started toward him, swinging her shoulders, and every few steps, she stopped, cocked her hip, and began rotating again. She repeated that little number several times, and if he thought she'd been working it before, he *hadn't* seen anything.

She was halfway across the room when she plucked off a glove, gave it a toss, and landed it right on his head, a three-point shot. With a husky little moan, she bent forward and shimmied, giving him an eye-popping look at breasts that were as ripe and plump as fruit hanging on the vine.

His jaws ached at the thought. He was hungry for the smell, the taste, the essence of a woman's sweet, tart flesh. God help him, this woman. He wanted to nibble and suck, eat and drink, until he was sated. She was dripping with juice, and he was a thirsty man. A dying man.

When she had the other glove off, she surprised him by hooking it beneath her fanny and using it like a bath towel. She rocked to and fro, swishing her hips and peeking at him through the fringe of her lowered lashes. At least she had the decency to blush.

"Well, what do you think?" she asked.

"Say what?"

Breathless, she jigged a little curtsy and walked up to him. "That's as far as I got. I've only had one lesson."

This woman had no idea how close he was to giving her a lesson she would never forget. If he didn't rein himself in, and quickly, Abigail Hastings would be down on the floor with her legs in the air, being plundered as thoroughly as the woman in the statue.

"One lesson? Is that right?" He couldn't hide the thickness in his voice.

"Should we finish undressing you?" she asked.

Her breasts rose and fell, shimmering wantonly beneath her dress. The damn fabric hid nothing and accentuated everything.

Ripe fruit, he thought. *Ready to be plucked, licked, and sucked. Savored* would be the polite way to put it, but he wasn't feeling very polite.

He yanked his shirt free of his pants and let it hang open. "One lesson?" *Let's go for two, babe.*

He could see her breath go quick and shallow as he stared at her. If she couldn't see the animal lust in his eyes, then she had vision problems in addition to all the other trouble she was in. A sound caught in her throat when he closed the short distance between them. She clearly wasn't expecting him to break formation. She'd been making all the moves up to now, and he'd been standing on the sidelines like a thunderstruck kid. She probably felt safer that way. She *was* safer that way.

"I wonder what the second lesson would have been?" He was close enough to lift a tendril of her hair with his breath.

"Maybe some glove work?"

"Works for me." He hooked the curl with his finger, playing in its springy warmth. The glove she'd thrown was draped over his shoulder.

"Or strap work," she allowed.

"Are we talking about this strap?" He brushed his thumb lightly over the single satin ribbon that held up her dress.

She said nothing while he coaxed the strap off her shoulder, but he could see the way her flesh quivered. The bodice descended with the strap, but the sheer fabric clung to the tips of her breasts.

One breath and it would be gone, he thought.

She glanced up at him, a hint of anguish in her exquisite blue eyes as she gave her shoulders a little shake. The fabric slipped and she was naked to the waist. Her nipples peaked yearningly, and he hadn't even touched them yet.

She made his guts twist, she was so desirable.

He knew she would be beautiful. What he hadn't known was that she would so willingly expose herself to him. All he wanted to do at the moment was look. This woman was a feast.

"You make my mouth water," he said under his breath.

She started to back away, her breasts bobbing. That was when he knew for a fact that he was going to make love to her. He had to. Her succulent body was crying out to him, but hormones were only part of the reason. There was no doubt in his mind that he would die if he didn't make love to her, but he also felt as if he'd just come alive. He was in the process of discovering who she was and what life was all about. Perhaps he'd drunk too much of that sweet chocolate brew, but it felt like he could discover it all tonight. With her.

He pulled the velvety glove she'd tossed at him off his shoulder and stretched it out in front of him, measuring its length. That should do fine, he thought.

"Come over here, Abigail," he commanded.

"Why?" The vulnerability in her voice was irresistible. But then so were her bared breasts.

"Because I'm going to make love to you."

He saw her gulp and her eyes widened like saucers, but all she said was, "In that case, I think you should call me Abbie."

SEVEN

Abigail knew the minute Max tied her to the love seat with one of her own gloves that she was in trouble. He'd only bound one of her wrists to the arm of the settee, but it was a very effective way to make sure she stayed put. And, considering where her heart was, she might not have if he hadn't restrained her.

Her heart was in her mouth.

The love potion was wearing off, but he was just getting started. Abigail desperately needed to be a little drunk. She did. She truly did. She must have been drunk to end up this way, bare-breasted and tied to a couch, with a darkly powerful man standing before her, gazing at her as if he had every intention of doing unspeakable things to her.

"Let me have some of the drink," she said. *"Please."*

"Open your legs for me," was his low, husky, startlingly sexy answer.

His eyes were dark as fire as she complied. It must be the potion compelling her to do such things. There was no other explanation. Still, she could hardly watch as he sank to his knees and began a breathtakingly slow and sensual assault of her lower body.

He was completely absorbed in what he was revealing as he stroked the silk of her gown up her legs. A breath caught high in her throat as his hands dropped back to her ankles. His thumbs circled, tickling delicate bones, and electric tendrils of pleasure touched her inner thighs, making them ache. Possessively gentle now, he smoothed the back of her legs with his hands, warming her calves.

She closed her eyes when he had the dress up to her knees. It was too much. But her senses had already memorized the fantastic, nearly surreal moment of lying back while Max Gallagher undressed her in this forbidden way. There was something utterly erotic about being bare-breasted while he bared the rest of her.

It was too erotic for a woman named Abigail. *Much.*

She had no underwear on at all except a tiny G-string with a pink satin heart that just covered her opening. Mavis had suggested she wear only the dress, but Abigail had needed something. Now she was glad she had.

She peeked out from between lowered lids and saw him kiss the inside of her knees. It sent an ache through her that cried out for release. Her dress crept upward as he coaxed her legs farther apart. Abigail watched in breathless shock as he slowly descended on her. He brushed his lips along the inside of her thighs, and she sighed, wondering what she would have done if he hadn't tied her down.

That beautiful mouth of his was every bit as soft and warm as she had always imagined it would be, although she hadn't allowed herself to imagine it down there! He placed tiny kisses along her flesh, each one a footstep on the path toward the glorious throb that overwhelmed every other sensation.

A startled sound escaped her. She couldn't hold it back when he pressed his mouth to the pink satin heart and kissed her there. Beneath the silky material, her petals moistened and fluttered as he ran his lips up and down the seam. Abigail arched her back, pressing herself toward him. She couldn't help it. What had been the loveliest kind of torment was quickly becoming more than she could bear.

Unable to stop herself, she used her free hand to move the satin heart aside. Her fingers stole beneath his heated breath and shyly she opened the way to him. She had to know what it would feel like. His lips on hers. Their flesh, touching, with nothing to separate them. Her whole body sang with that need.

His gaze darkened as he looked at her, and the sound he made resonated with wonder and satisfaction. He understood that she was offering herself, and he slipped his hands beneath her to lift her to his mouth. At the first touch of his lips, she gasped. It was that wild and wondrous.

He kissed her there gently and deeply. And then he did something with his lips that made her think of butterfly wings drumming against delicate flower petals. When he did it again, she nearly screamed with the sweetness that pooled and flowed through her.

He opened her with his fingers, exploring her in a way that was more tender and loving than she could have imagined, yet totally demanding and possessive of her. Again, he glanced up and stunned her with the naked pleasure in his eyes. She wouldn't have believed his enjoyment could be as great as hers, except for the brilliance of those dark sapphire irises.

This is how I do glove work, he told her silently.

"Oh, Mr. Gallagher," she whispered, catching a glimpse of his tongue before it slipped inside her. "Sir!" She moaned as her head lolled back and the most glorious sensations filled her body.

She could do nothing but shudder and sigh. This was not pleasure. It was much, much more.

When she roused herself, she saw that he was standing—and in acute discomfort. There was an enormous bulge pressed at an impossible angle against the inside of his slacks. She watched in silent fascination as he slid his hand along the hardened member and tried to shift it.

"Let me," she said impulsively.

For a moment, she wasn't sure if he would come to her or not. When he did, her pulse roared with excitement, and she stared at the jutting steel for a moment. She placed her hand on him and felt him respond violently. His hands balled into fists as she curled her fingers around him and deepened the pressure. Finally, all caution gone, she bent forward and kissed the place she had just held, kissed him through his clothing, and felt him quiver and leap to her caress.

That was all he could humanly take. He told her so as he pressed her shoulders to the couch and gazed at her, his chest heaving.

"It's taking all the control I have not to love you right here," he said, struggling for his own breath. "But I can't do that, Abbie. I have to have you underneath me in my bed."

He untied her then, lifted her into his arms, and bent toward her. Her mouth opened under his, crying out to be filled. A moment later, they were in his bed, and it was her legs that were opening under his, crying with the same need. He pressed down on her, sweetly drowning her in the mattress with his weight, pressing everywhere, legs, belly, mouth. And then he pressed into the heart of her with one deep and thrilling stroke.

He was large and there was the fleeting pain of possession, but it was gone in an instant as she intuitively positioned herself to accept him. She'd never thought of herself as greedy in any way, especially this one. But she was now. She had to have every second, every breath, every sweet, tormenting inch of him. There would never be another time.

"I don't want to hurt you," he whispered. But her deep sobs and clutching fingernails told him how fulfilling it was to surrender herself. She couldn't have told him any other way. She was speechless with joy.

When the shuddering began again, she gave herself over to it completely and fell back in his arms, crying.

"Abbie," he whispered, "forgive—" But the rest of it was lost in his rushing breath. Her senses sparked as she tried to hear what he was saying. He was murmuring something about being awake for the first time, about never wanting to sleep again. It sounded as if he were telling her that he didn't want to dream anymore. But that didn't make sense, and she knew it must be the potion he'd drunk. He was as intoxicated as she was.

His body began to rock into hers until a powerful shudder stopped him. He groaned out something she didn't understand. But it was her name on his lips as his essence flooded into her like a healing balm.

"Don't leave—" He shook his head, and the sound in his throat might have been laughter, but there were tears in his eyes. "Don't let me fall asleep, Abbie."

Abigail touched his face, touched his lips, hushing him. She had no idea what he was trying to tell her. She only knew it was breaking her heart.

Deep in the night, Abigail stirred in the arms of the man who'd made such sweet, unbridled love to her. He'd asked her not to leave, but she had to. She couldn't be there when he woke up and the drug wore off. She couldn't go back to being Abigail Hastings again, not with him. That would kill her.

"Where are you going, sugar?"

Mavis came around the counter as Abigail burst through the front doors the next morning, headed for Max's office. The receptionist threw her body into the breech, blocking Abigail's path.

"Is Max in there—I mean, Mr. Gallagher. I mean—" Abigail heaved a sigh. "Is *he* in there, Mavis?"

"Yes, he's in. But you're *not* going in until you tell me what happened last night."

Abigail didn't know where to begin. She stared at her friend, slowly shaking her head. Her feelings about the evening were deeply conflicted. The beauty of it was tainted by her guilt, but there was no denying that it had been the most amazing experience of her life.

Mavis watched her, searching her features with concern, and Abigail couldn't lie.

"It was unbelievable, Mavis. Un—be*leeeev*able."

"Is that good or bad?"

Abigail let out a little squeak of disbelief and clapped her hand over her mouth, aware that she could easily become hysterical.

"Tell, girl, tell!" Mavis shook her. "Did the potion work?"

"Like a dream." Abigail gave out another squeak. "I was so good, Mavis. I stripped and everything!"

"Yeah? What did he do?"

"He went nuts. And I *do* mean nuts. That's why I have to talk to him. I can't let him think he really felt that way. It was the potion."

"Sweetheart—"

"No, Mavis, I have to confess. I couldn't live with myself if I didn't."

"Abigail, you didn't do anything but give him a little bit of love and some hot chocolate."

Abigail shook her head, and curls flew everywhere. She'd made no attempt to get her hair back under control. What was the point when her life was shot to hell?

"No, I took advantage of him. I took advantage of that sweet, trusting, passionate man, and I can't live with myself."

Mavis was smart enough to know she wasn't going to win

this one. She stepped aside and waved a hand toward his door. "Do what you must."

Abigail had thrown on a casual blazer, a T-shirt, and slacks, not her usual working garb, but then, who knew whether she was going to be working here after today. She crunched a handful of hair in her hand, knowing it was pointless. And stared at his door.

It wasn't that she didn't intend to go through with it. Her nerve hadn't failed her. It was just that she—

Couldn't do it! It was more than guilt. She felt embarrassed when she thought of all the outrageous things she'd done last night and had done to her. How did one face a man after that? At least she could blame the dancing on the potion. She could never have pulled that off sober.

Pulled it off, she thought. *Bad choice of words.*

"You need a little push?" Mavis asked.

"I need a forklift."

But Abigail was compelled by her conscience. She tapped on the door and heard him tell her to come in. He was sitting at his desk when she entered, looking over the newsletter proof she'd put together yesterday. He always wrote a President's Letter for the inside cover, and he liked to read what she'd done first.

He seemed calm and composed, focused. That surprised her, since she was anything but. Maybe the evening hadn't been as traumatic for him as it had for her. Was that possible?

"Mr. Gallagher— Max, I—"

He tilted back in the chair and looked her over, his gaze sharpening as he took in her appearance. Unless she was mistaken, a mysterious sparkle had sneaked into his sapphire eyes.

"I think you should go back to calling me sir, Abbie," he said. "It turns me on."

Abigail hesitated, confused. Was he still under the influence of the potion? Maybe it took longer for men to shake off the effects than it did women. Before she could get going with her confession, Mavis had entered the office. She was carrying a tray with a cup on it, which she set on Max's desk.

"What is that?" Abigail asked. She was immediately suspicious of Mavis's motive, but the receptionist shrugged and moved out of eyeshot, back by the door.

Max smiled and picked up the cup. "It's the hot chocolate we had last night. I liked it so much I asked Mavis if she knew where I could get some. Turns out it was her grandmother's recipe. But I guess you already knew that."

He smiled and bent to take a sip.

"Stop!" Abigail came out of her chair. She couldn't let him drink it. Mavis shouldn't have done it. "Don't drink it, Max—sir. It's drugged!"

"What are you talking about? It's hot chocolate."

"No . . . it's a potion. Mavis can tell you." Abigail turned around. "Mavis?" The receptionist was nowhere to be seen. She'd sneaked out. "Mavis!"

"She didn't say anything about a potion, Abbie." He took a sip. "It's delicious, and it's the only thing that gets rid of my headaches."

"But, sir, you can't . . . Please! It'll make you—"

He held the drink in both hands, close to his lips, smelling the richness and fondling the cup with his long fingers. "Make me what?"

It was too late, Abigail realized. She had wanted to ruin him, and she had. He was addicted to the chocolate, and probably to her. There were no rehab centers for that.

"You didn't answer my question, Abbie. By the way, you look incredibly beautiful this morning, although I don't know why that should surprise me. You *are* beautiful."

"Sir, you don't mean that. You're only saying it because I drugged you with that hot chocolate last night."

"With this, you mean?" He tipped the cup and then drank deeply.

"Yes, sir, you were under the influence last night. And now you're drinking more of it, and I wish you wouldn't. I can't swear that it's not addictive."

"I can swear," he said huskily, "that *you're* addictive."

He was gazing at the rather snug white T-shirt she was wearing, and Abigail was thinking about how he'd bared her breasts the night before. She wrung her hands, not knowing what to do.

"It's the hot chocolate talking, sir."

He settled back in the chair and smiled at her, his dark eyes dancing. "Mavis gave me a copy of the recipe so that I can have some of the drink made up for my headaches. Would you like to know the ingredients?"

She nodded sheepishly. "Opium, I suppose?"

He read the list. "Jamaican cocoa leaves, ground to a fine powder, a pitcher of sweet milk, raspberry nectar to taste, orange zest for flavor, and *Myristica fragrans.*"

"What's *Myristica fragrans?* That must be it, right? The drug?"

"*Myristica fragrans* is Latin for nutmeg, Abbie."

"But that can't be . . ."

He brought the recipe with him as he rose and came around the desk. "Have a look," he said, sitting on the desk while she read.

The ingredients were exotic, but not magic elixir material.

"Nothing but nutmeg? You mean I wasn't under the influence of anything when I did those things?" She gazed at him, too weak to breathe.

"You weren't, and neither was I."

"You mean—"

"That's exactly what I mean. We weren't high, Abbie, except with wanting each other. And I still want you, so bad I can taste you. You're more delicious than the potion."

Abigail couldn't take it all in. "But what about the wedding, the trophy? What about Marcia Walters?"

"Marcia Walters?"

"You like her. She was on my list of candidates, and you smiled when I mentioned her name."

"Oh, yeah." He smiled again, remembering. "I was thinking about how her eyes cross when she's pretending to be interested in what you're saying. Ever noticed that?"

No, Abigail hadn't. She'd never noticed anything but how beautiful and accomplished the woman was.

"As far as Jeff goes," Max was saying, "he can keep the trophy with my blessings. And as far as my personal list, the only thing on it now is the woman who makes me forget the stock market exists." He cleared his throat. "That's you, Abbie. All I want is you, that is, if you'll have an absent-minded dreamer like me."

"Oh, Max . . . oh, sir, I—"

"Come here," he said raggedly. But he didn't wait for her to get there. He went to her chair, the one she'd been sitting in for nine years and diligently taking down his to-do lists. The chair where all of her secret yearnings began, and now, it seemed, would be fulfilled.

"Stop calling me sir and kiss me, Abbie," he said, pulling her into his arms.

She wanted to kiss him more than anything in the world, but there was something she had to say first. "Yes, sir. I'll stop calling you sir, but only if you'll keep calling me Abbie."

She pressed a hand to his lips and managed a shaky smile. "*Not* Abigail."

TANGLED SHEETS

Lori Foster

One

She refused to spend her twenty-sixth Valentine's Day as a virgin.

Despite her circumspect upbringing, despite the well-meaning strictures of the maiden aunt who'd raised her, she was ready to become a woman, in every sense of the word. And Cole Winston—bless his gorgeous, sexy soul—was offering her the opportunity she needed to see her plans through.

Sophie Sheridan scanned the flyer again as she hesitated just inside the door of Cole's bar, previously called The Stud by some macho former owner, but changed to merely the Winston Tavern after Cole bought it. Heaven knew, the bar's reputation was notorious enough without a suggestive label. Though, to Sophie's mind, The Stud was pretty apropos, given what the Winston men looked like, Cole Winston especially.

All the neighboring shops had received a flyer inviting women to take part in a new Valentine's Day contest. Not that the Winston men needed an incentive to draw in the female crowd. Women loved to come here, to see one of the four brothers serving, tending bar, simply moving or smiling. They were a gorgeous, flirtatious lot, but Sophie had her eye on one particular brother.

The door opened behind her as more patrons hustled in, allowing icy wind and a flurry of snowflakes to surround her. For just a moment, intrusive laughter overwhelmed the sound of soft music and the muted hum of quiet conversation. Distracted, Sophie stepped farther inside the bar, then headed for her regular seat at the back corner booth, away from the heaviest human congestion. Since she'd met Cole some seven months ago after buying her boutique, he'd gone out of his way to accommodate her, to make certain her seat was available for her routine visit each night. He did his best to cater to all his customers' preferences, which in part accounted for his incredible success at the bar. Cole knew everyone, spoke easily with them about their families and their problems and their lives.

But he was so drop-dead sexy, Sophie spent most of her time in his company trying to get her tongue unglued from the roof of her mouth. It was humiliating. She'd never been so shy before; of course, she'd never received so much attention from such an incredible man before, either. Cole made her think of things she'd never pondered in her entire life, like the way a man smelled when he got overheated, so musky and sexy and hot, and how his beard shadow might feel on the more sensitive places of her body.

She shuddered, drawing in a deep breath.

While Cole believed she was timid and withdrawn, and treated her appropriately, Sophie had concocted some sizzling, toe-curling fantasies about him. Now, thanks to his contest, she just might be able to fulfill them.

Heat slithered through her, chasing away the lingering cold of winter, coloring her cheeks. Unfortunately, Cole chose that moment to set her requisite cup of hot chocolate in front of her. He'd put extra whipped cream on the top, and the smell was deliciously sinful. Almost as delicious as Cole himself.

"Hello, Sophie."

His low voice sank into her bones, and she slowly raised her gaze to him. Warm whiskey described the color of his eyes, fringed by thick, black lashes and heavy brows. She swallowed. "Hi."

Slow and easy, his grin spread as he looked down to see the flyer clutched in her hand. "Good." There was a wealth of male satisfaction in his rough tone, and his gaze lifted, locking onto hers, refusing to let her look away. "You going to enter?" he asked in a whisper.

Here was the tricky part, the only way she could think to gain her ends. Their relationship, already set by her tongue-tied nervousness, was hard to overcome. She couldn't merely go from reserved to aggressive overnight, not without confusing him and risking a great deal of embarrassment.

Her aunt Maude had drummed the importance of pride and self-respect into her from an early age. If she gambled now, and lost, she'd also lose the comfort of coming to his bar every night, the excitement of small conversations, and the heat of her fantasies. If he rejected her, she wouldn't simply be able to pick up and carry on as usual. Something very precious to her—their relationship—would have been destroyed. Everyone she loved, everyone she felt close to, was gone. She didn't want to risk the quiet, settling camaraderie she shared with him in the atmosphere of his bar.

But if she won, if she was able to interest him for even a short time, it wouldn't last. Cole was reknowned as a die-hard bachelor; he simply didn't get overly involved with anyone. At thirty-six, you had to take his dedication to living alone seriously. The man obviously *liked* being a bachelor, had worked hard at staying that way.

His rejection could put a distance between them she wasn't willing to chance. So she had to use deception.

"I couldn't," Sophie said, laying the colorful flyer aside. She licked her lips in nervousness and toyed with the cup of hot chocolate, making certain it sat exactly in the center of her napkin. "I'd feel silly."

Cole's smile was indulgent and blatantly male. He pulled a chair over from the next table rather than sitting opposite her in the booth. He straddled it, his arms crossed over the back. "Why?" He sat so close, Sophie could smell his scent, cologne and warm male flesh, a combination she hadn't appreciated or even noticed until meeting Cole. She breathed deeply and felt her stomach flutter, as if his scent alone could fill her up.

Cole tilted his head at her, cajoling. "All you need to enter is a photo. I can even take your picture here at the bar. There will be dozens of other pictures up, too, you know. Already, we've had around twenty women sign up. I'll hang all the pictures in the billiard room, and on Valentine's Day, we'll vote on the prettiest picture."

"There's no point in it," Sophie said, though she hadn't meant to. She wasn't fishing for a compliment, but she realized that was how it sounded when Cole made a tsking sound.

His hand cupped under her chin, lifting her face, and his look was so tender, so warm, her heart tripped over several beats, making her gasp. "You're very pretty, Sophie."

Oh, to have him mean that! But Sophie had seen Cole treat everyone in the bar in the same familiar way. He was simply a people person: open, solicitous, and friendly. He teased the older women until they blushed, left all the younger women giddy with regret, and the men, regardless of whether they were businessmen, laborers, or retirees, all liked and respected him. They gathered around him and hung on his every word. Cole liked people, and he made everyone, male and female, young and old, feel special.

The heat from his hand, the roughness of his palm, was a wicked temptation, inciting sinful thoughts. She wondered what it might feel like to have that hard palm smoothing over other parts of her body, places no one had ever seen, much less touched. Her breathing quickened and her hands shook.

Clamoring to get her thoughts in order, Sophie held up the flyer and tried for a bright smile. "I think this might be more suitable for my sister. I don't photograph well, but she's in town for a brief visit and might like the idea."

For an instant, Cole froze, then he dropped his hand and studied her. "You have a sister?"

"Yes. A twin actually." The words slipped easily past her stiff lips. "Though we're not that much alike in personality. Shelly is much more . . . outgoing."

"Outgoing?" He looked intrigued. Shifting slightly, he said, "A twin," and his tone was distracted, low and deep. "Tell me about her."

Sophie blinked at him. "Um, what's to tell? She looks like me, except she's not so . . ."

That small smile touched his mouth again. "Buttoned down?"

"Well, yes, I suppose." *Buttoned down? What did that mean?* "Shelly was always the popular one in school."

Suddenly, he shook his head and his dark, silky hair fell over his forehead. Sophie loved his hair, how straight it was, the slight hint of silver at his temples, the way it reflected the bar lights. She wanted desperately to smooth it back, to touch him, to see if it felt as silky and cool as it looked. She clasped her hands tightly on the table.

"You should both enter. Maybe even together. The judges would love it."

"Who . . ." She had to clear her throat. Cole suddenly stood, and his size, his strength, always sent her brain into a tailspin. She peered up at him, liking the differences in their sizes, imagining how they might fit together. There was just so much of him to appreciate, to tempt. "Who are the judges?"

Now his grin was wicked. "Me and my brothers. I think it's justice, given the way the media has taunted us this last year. Did you see that most recent article?" He snorted in amusement. "My brothers ate it up."

Sophie smiled, too. All the Winston brothers were superb male specimens. Cole owned the friendly neighborhood bar, but his brothers, Mack and Zane and Chase, helped work it. Mack was the youngest, and still in college, but at twenty-one, he had the quiet maturity of a much older man. Zane, at twenty-four, was the rowdiest and split his workload between his own computer business, which was still getting off the ground, with the sure paycheck from his brother. Chase, at twenty-seven, only a year older than Sophie, shared all the responsibilities with Cole. Though Cole owned the bar, he consulted with Chase on all major decisions. Chase, unlike Cole, was quiet, and more often than not, worked behind the bar, handing out drinks and listening, rather than talking.

In the seven months since she'd first met them, Sophie found the brothers got along incredibly well, and combined, they were enough to send the female denizens of Thomasville, Kentucky, into a frenzy.

"They actually suggested we should go topless," Cole said.

Sophie covered her mouth in an effort to hold back her mirth. The local papers had a fine time with their good-natured taunting of the Winston men. They teased them for their good looks and their overwhelming female clientele, constantly soliciting them to do an article on their personal lives. The brothers always refused.

Cole sounded disgruntled, but Sophie thought the idea had merit. Heaven knew, even with the business they had now, their popularity would likely double if the Winston men strutted around bare-chested. It was an altogether tantalizing thought.

"Zane has been threatening to take his shirt off all day," Cole added, "and the women have been egging him on. Knowing Zane, he just might do it. I have to make sure he doesn't end up doing a striptease and get us shut down."

This time there was no stifling her laughter. She, too, could picture Zane doing such a thing. He flirted outrageously, and like the other Winston brothers, had his share of admirers.

"You don't laugh very often."

Sophie bit her lip. His look was so intense and intimate, her belly tingled. He had the most unique effect on her, and she loved it. No other man had ever listened to her so attentively, shown such interest in her thoughts and ideas and feelings. He made her feel so special. She had no idea what to say, then didn't have to say anything as his concentration was diverted by Mack, who had sauntered up to his side. "The delivery guys are here."

Looking back at her, Cole nodded. "I'll be right there." He waited until Mack had turned away, then leaned down, one large hand on the booth seat behind her, the other spread on the table. "Enter the contest, Sophie."

His breath touched her cheek and she jerked. She stared at the table, her hands, anywhere rather than meet that probing gaze at such close proximity. She'd likely throw herself at him if she did. "My sister will be in later tonight. She'll enter."

He straightened slowly and she heard him sigh. "All right. I'm not giving up on you, but you can tell her to come see me when she gets here. I'd like to meet her."

Sophie watched him walk away, loving his long-legged stride, the way his dark hair hung over his collar, the width of his back and hard shoulders. As he maneuvered around the tables, women watched his progress, their sidelong looks just as admiring. He stopped to speak to many of them, leaving laughter and dreamy smiles behind, and Sophie knew he'd convince them all to enter. That was just the way he was, attentive to everyone, easy to talk to.

He'd meet her sister, all right. Sophie could hardly wait.

"Here."

Cole started in surprise as Chase shoved the icy cold can of whipped cream into his hand, drawing his attention away from Sophie. He raised a brow. "What?"

"You've been standing there salivating ever since she lifted her spoon. I always wondered why you put so damn much whipped cream on her chocolate. Now I know."

Cole didn't bother to deny the charge. Hell, he'd been half hard since Sophie had lifted the first spoonful to her mouth. Such a sexy mouth, full and soft and—he was obsessing, damn it.

He remembered the very first day he'd met her, when she'd bought the boutique a few doors down and across the street. She'd come in after work, looking prim and proper and very appealing, and she'd ordered hot chocolate, of all things, even though the weather in July had been steamy. Amused, he'd put an extra dollop of whipped cream on top, then watched in sensual appreciation while she'd savored it, her small tongue licking out over her upper lip, her eyes closing with each small taste. She'd been unaware of his scrutiny, and for seven months he'd been allowing her to torment him nightly with the ritual.

"Since she's finished that up, you want to go for broke and give her more?"

Cole shook his head, choosing to ignore the jest. "Too obvious. If she had any inkling how much I enjoy watching her, she would never order hot chocolate again."

"Or maybe she'd put you out of your misery and take you home with her."

Cole slanted his brother a look. Usually, Chase was the

quietest, but he was damned talkative tonight. "Any particular reason why you want to annoy me right now?"

Chase grinned. "Other than the fact you're hiding over here in the corner, staring at her like a kid in a candy store with a pounding sweet tooth but no money to buy anything? Nope. There's no other reason."

"She refuses to enter the contest."

"Well damn." Chase stepped away for a moment to fill an order, then came back to Cole's side. "You couldn't talk her into it?"

He shook his head, distracted. "She has a twin."

"Oh ho, *two* Sophies. Now that sounds interesting. They're identical?"

Cole elbowed him. "Yeah. And get your mind out of the gutter."

"Too crowded, what with yours already being there?"

"Something like that. She says her sister will enter, but she doesn't want to." He sighed in disgust. "What is it about Sophie that makes me start fantasizing all kinds of wild things?"

"You tell me."

Crossing his arms over his chest and leaning back against the wall beside the ice chest, Cole considered her. "She's so buttoned down, so serene. Not once in the seven months I've known her has she ever missed a night, which means she must not be dating at all." He studied her dark brown hair, parted in the middle and hanging to her shoulders with only the gentlest of curls. It looked incredibly soft; he wanted to bury his nose against her neck, feel that silky hair on his face, his chest, his abdomen.

He wanted to see it fanned out against his pillows as he covered her with his naked body, wanted to see it tangled and wild as she reached for the pleasure he'd give her.

He shuddered in reaction. "Damn."

"Care to share those thoughts?"

"No." Narrow shoulders, but always straight and proud,

posture erect. Her skin could make him nuts, so smooth and pale. He wondered if she was that smooth all over, the skin on her thighs and bottom, her breasts, low on her belly. She would smell so sweet—he'd be willing to bet his life on that. Sweet and warm and sexy, just like the woman herself.

"Maybe her sister will give you a break. If they look the same, you could do a little imagining."

"I don't want her damn sister. I want her." He watched Sophie lift the mug of chocolate to her mouth now that the whipped cream was gone. She sipped, then patted her lips with a napkin. "It's more than just how she looks. It's *her*. She smiles at me, and all I can think about is warm skin, heavy breathing, and tangled sheets."

"You've got it bad."

"Damn it, I know it. But she shies away from me every time I try to get close. She's just plain not interested." He could easily picture the way her wide blue eyes would skip away, avoiding his, how her hands would twist together, how she'd bite her lip. God he loved how she bit her lip.

"Ask her why."

Cole glared at his brother. "Yeah, right. I can't even get her to enter the damn contest. How am I going to get her to open up her head to me?"

"There's a couple of days left. But if she doesn't enter, what are we going to do?"

Cole shrugged, angered by the prospect. "We'll pick a different winner. It's still a good contest. All the local papers have picked it up, so it's a great promo, even if we didn't need the publicity. And it'll only cost us drinks for a month."

"It'll also cost you a night on the town, lady's choice, because none of the rest of us are dumb enough to open that bag of worms. You're liable to find yourself with a permanent female escort."

Truth was, he wouldn't mind a permanent escort, if it was Sophie. He'd spent the better part of his life raising his younger brothers after his parents' deaths. He didn't regret the time he'd devoted to his brothers, just the opposite. Their closeness was important to him. But raising three boys, when he wasn't much more than a boy himself, had been a full-time job with no room for other relationships. He'd had to be content with fleeting female pleasure, the occasional night of passion.

Now Mack was in his last year of college, all the brothers were settled and secure, and Cole was finally free to live his own life. He wanted more. He wanted Sophie.

Damn her for her stubbornness, and for trying to pawn her sister off on him.

Cole walked away as Chase got sidetracked again with customers. He had some paperwork to do and might as well get started, but again, he paused in the hallway leading to his office and stared at Sophie. His plan had been so simple. Valentine's Day was a time for lovers, so therefore perfect for a contest that would bring the two of them together.

She was a shoe-in to win because his brothers knew how he felt about her, though they were amused because they thought it was mere lust. They didn't know he spent the better part of his day looking forward to seeing her when she closed her shop, when she'd spend a quiet hour sitting in her favorite booth, talking to him about everything and nothing. They didn't know he was obsessed with a woman for the first time in his life.

The winner of the contest not only got drinks at the bar free for a month, she would also have her picture taken with all the Winston men. The photo would be prominently displayed on a wall, and each year, another photo would join it as the contest became an annual event.

But best of all, the winner got a night on the town of her choice. Cole had visions of Sophie choosing a nice restaurant for dinner where they'd have plenty of time to talk without the bar's audience, followed by a little slow dancing where he'd be able to hold her close, move her body against his. He'd feel her thighs brushing his, her belly moving against his groin, her stiff nipples hot against his chest. And they'd eventually end up in bed with those tangled sheets he couldn't help seeing in his mind.

He didn't want to meet her sister. But at the same time, his curiosity was extreme. A woman who looked like Sophie, but wasn't. A woman who could be Sophie, but who wouldn't be so shy with him. He shook his head even as his body stirred. At that moment, Sophie looked up and their gazes locked. Even from the distance separating them, he felt linked to her, a touch that kicked him in the heart and licked along his muscles, a feeling he'd never experienced with any other woman.

Damn, he wanted her.

He wouldn't give up. Sooner or later, he'd get Sophie Sheridan exactly where he wanted her, and he'd keep her there for an excruciatingly long, satisfying time.

TWO

Mack gave a long, low whistle that effortlessly carried through the closed office door. "Will you take a look at that."

Cole glanced up from his desk and paperwork, wondering what had drawn his brother's attention. It had been a long, frustrating night, and his eyes were gritty, his head leaden.

"Hubba hubba. Who is she?" Zane asked as he, too, came to loiter in the hallway. Cole frowned and pushed away from his computer.

"Don't you remember her? I'll give you a clue. Cole is going to choke on his own tongue—once he gets it back in his mouth."

"No!" There was a considering pause, then, "Well, yeah, I suppose it could be her. But what did she do to herself?"

"Hell if I know. But she looks good enough to—"

Cole shot out of his chair, his curiosity too extreme to repress. He'd been determined to ignore the sister if and when she showed, and considering it was well after midnight, he figured he wouldn't have to worry about it.

He jerked the door open and Zane, who'd been leaning on it, almost fell on the floor. Cole helped to right him, then followed Mack's gaze across the room. Every muscle in his body snapped into iron hardness. He couldn't move. Hell, he could barely breathe.

Like a sleepwalker, he let go of Zane and started forward. He could hear his brothers snickering behind him, but he ignored it. God, she looked good. His heart punched so hard against his ribs he thought he might break something—and he didn't care.

As he got closer, she looked up, and her smoky blue gaze sank into his. She trembled, her chest drawing deep, quick breaths, and then she smiled.

"Sophie?"

A husky laugh sent fingers of sensation down his spine. "Of course not. I'm her sister, Shelly. And you must be the big, gorgeous owner Sophie's told me so much about." Her gaze boldly skimmed down his body, like a hot lick of interest, then back up again. "My my. I have to say, Sophie didn't exaggerate."

Cole was floored. Oh, he was interested; after all, he wasn't dead, and the woman standing in front of him, dressed all in black, was a surefire knockout. But she wasn't Sophie.

She could be Sophie, he thought, unable to keep his gaze from roaming all over her from head to toe, but the words out of her mouth were words he'd only imagined, not something Sophie would ever actually say to him. She held out her pale, slender hand, and he took it, painfully aware that he had all three of his brothers' rapt attention.

"Cole Winston," he said, and his voice sounded deeper than usual, huskier. Arousal rode him hard, making it difficult to form polite conversation. "Sophie told me you might want to enter our contest?"

Her hand lingered in his, small and warm and fragile. It felt just like touching Sophie, sent the same rush of desire pounding through him, and he felt like a cad, like he'd somehow betrayed her. Only Sophie's touch had ever sizzled his nerve endings this way, but now her sister's was doing the same.

"Yes."

That was all she said, and Cole stared. Amazingly, he could see her pulse beating in her slim throat, the fragile skin fluttering as if she were nervous. *Or excited.*

They were still holding hands. Cole cleared his throat. When he started to pull his hand back, she held on, stepping closer to him. She brought with her the scent of the fresh evening air, brisk and wintery, mixed with the warm, feminine scent of her skin, a scent he recognized. His nostrils flared.

"I didn't realize Sophie had a sister until today."

Her gaze lowered, and a wry smile curved her lips—lips the exact replica of Sophie's lips. His muscles twitched.

With a slight shrug, she whispered, "My sister is a little shy."

The urge to taste her rushed through him. He hadn't felt this primal, this turned on, in a long, long time. Even though she wasn't Sophie, she looked the same, only wilder, more attainable, and his beleaguered male brain reasoned that she likely even tasted the same. He couldn't seem to stop himself from pulling her up to his side, wanting to feel her close, wanting to see how her body lined up to his. "Why don't I show you the rest of the bar?"

Very slowly, her thick lashes lowered. "I'd like that."

Long-repressed desire for Sophie twisted in his guts. Every image he'd ever formed in his mind slammed into him at once. Slumberous, sated blue eyes, taut nipples and trembling breasts, open, naked thighs. *Tangled sheets.* He stifled a deep groan and put his hand on her narrow waist through her coat.

They turned, and all three of his brothers jerked around, running into each other, tripping, trying to pretend they were busy doing something besides staring. He could feel their cautious glances as he led Shelly to the back room where the billiard tables were housed, but it was a peripheral awareness; all his attention was on the petite woman beside him, the sound of her anxious breaths reaching his ears above the din of normal conversation and music. There were few people still in the bar so late on such a cold and snowy night, and the two men playing pool took one look at him, grinned, and put down their sticks. They left the room without complaint.

"Can I take your coat?"

Shelly smiled, then slipped it off her shoulders. As Cole stepped behind her to take it, he leaned close, breathing in the scent of warm woman. His stomach muscles knotted and he locked his knees. He tossed her coat—black leather, long and sexy—over one end of a pool table. She turned to face him again, slowly, expectantly. Her sweater was black, emphasizing her pale skin and the richness of her chestnut hair, now pulled on top of her head with a gold clasp, showing her vulnerable nape and small ears, little wisps of baby-fine hair. He wanted to press his mouth there, to watch her shiver in sensation.

His gaze dropped to her breasts, lingered, and amazingly, her nipples puckered, thrusting against the soft, fuzzy material of the sweater. Cole didn't dare look at her face, knowing he'd be lost, his vague control shot to hell. A few glossy curls had escaped the clasp, and one curved invitingly just above her breast, taunting him, forcing him to imagine her without the sweater. Her breasts were small, but they tantalized him, looking soft and sweet, and he knew her skin would be very pale.

Unable to help himself, he stepped closer. With the coat gone, he saw she was wearing the skinniest pair of black jeans he'd ever seen, jeans that hugged her bottom and showed the long length of her legs. He'd often wondered on the details of Sophie's build. Her clothing was always somewhat concealing, so that while he knew she was slim, he couldn't detect all the curves and hollows of her woman's body.

Shelly's outfit left little to the imagination, and he wondered if Sophie was built the same, so slight, but so damn feminine. His hands shook.

"Do you play?"

It took a second for his brain to comprehend the words, and when he did, his body stirred. He could easily imagine playing with her, spending long hours toying with her body, learning every little secret, every ultrasensitive spot. He would explore first with his hands, and then with his mouth. He gave her a hot look that made her eyes widen and her lashes flutter. In nervousness? Not likely, considering her bravado.

She stammered slightly. "Pool, I mean. I've . . . I've never played, but I've often wondered . . ."

"I'll teach you," he heard himself say, even though he knew he should get away from her. She wasn't Sophie, no matter that he was so turned on he could barely breathe. He couldn't imagine Sophie ever being so coy, teasing a man in such a way. *Damn, he liked it.*

"Are you good?"

He'd turned away to move her coat and rack the pool balls, and now he froze, his eyes closing, sexual innuendoes tripping to the tip of his tongue. Hell, he could banter with the best of them, make sexual sport of any conversation, no matter how mundane, but he didn't want that with this woman. If he ever hoped to make headway with Sophie, if he ever hoped to have her body under his, open to him, accepting him in all ways, then he had to curb his desire now.

He wasn't a horny kid incapable of maintaining control. He was a grown man and he wanted Sophie, not just for a night, though that was his most immediate craving, but possibly for a lifetime. He wanted to sleep with her every night and wake with her beside him in the morning. He wanted to know every inch of her, heart and soul.

As tempting as he found Shelly, she still wasn't Sophie. It was the way she looked, being the mirror image of Sophie, that was playing havoc with his libido. Nothing more.

So he summoned a calm he didn't feel and turned to face the sister. Determination made his guts twist in regret because at the moment, despite all he'd just told himself, he had an erection that throbbed in demand, and it wouldn't be going away anytime soon.

"Actually," he said, keeping his gaze resolutely on her face, "I'm a little rusty."

Her eyes, turning a darker blue, held his. "Then maybe we can warm up together." Before he could find a retort, she selected a pool cue and came to stand very close to him. "How do I hold the stick?"

With his heart thumping in slow, hard beats, Cole turned her so her back was to him, then guided her to lean slightly over the table, positioning the cue, placing her hands just so. She took her first shot, and barely disturbed the colorful balls. One rolled about an inch. Shelly chuckled. "Sorry. I suppose I didn't do it hard enough?"

Cole felt as if he were dying by slow degrees as he once again racked the balls. "Try again, and this time, follow all the way through."

He straightened and she whispered, "Show me."

Damn. If he hadn't wanted to so badly, he could have said no. But for some reason, Shelly drew him as no other woman had, except for Sophie. It didn't make any sense. He hadn't even looked at another woman in a sexual way once he'd really gotten to know Sophie and realized how perfect they'd be together.

He walked behind her again, and this time, she bent without his instruction, her small bottom pressing into his lap while his body curved over hers. She wiggled, a soft sound escaping her, and he froze. Almost without his permission, his hands moved, from folding over her hands, to slowly slide up her arms to her elbows, then inward to hold her waist. She was so narrow, so warm. His palms rubbed over the softness of the fuzzy sweater, then higher, feeling her ribs and then the warm weight of her breasts against the backs of his hands.

He hurt; his stomach knotted, his chest felt tight, his erection throbbed. He had to stop or he'd totally forget himself. With a stifled groan, he straightened away from her and took two steps back. Slowly, Shelly laid the cue stick aside and turned to face him.

She tilted her head, eyes wide; something in her gaze looked almost desperate. He ignored it and drew on his nearly depleted control. "Maybe it would be better if I got one of my brothers to instruct you."

Distressed, Sophie felt her stomach give a sick flip at his words. He didn't want her, even with her being so obvious, even with her making herself more appealing, he didn't want her. She turned away and bit her lip to keep him from seeing her hot blush of mortification. She didn't blush well, never had. While another woman might get a becoming pink flush to her cheeks, Sophie could feel hot color pulse beneath her skin, from her breasts to her hairline, turning even her nose and ears red. Her skin was so fair that any blushing looked hideous, not attractive.

Zane stuck his head into the room. His gaze skimmed her, his brows lifted curiously, then moved on to his brother. He spoke quietly. "Mack left a while ago. The bar is nearly empty, and Chase is ready to give the last call. I'm going to head on home."

She felt Cole approach behind her. "All right. Drive careful. I hear the roads are crap from all the sleet and snow."

With escape uppermost in her mind, Sophie turned to face

Cole again, a smile planted firmly in place, her blush hopefully under control. He was closer than she'd suspected, and she took a hasty step back. "Oh, I'm sorry." A nervous laugh bubbled past her lips. "I, ah, suppose that settles the pool lesson. I should let you men finish up here and go home."

Cole looked cautiously undecided. Good manners won out. "We have about half an hour. Enough time for you to enter the contest if you're still interested."

He kept watching her, his golden brown eyes direct, almost probing. Sophie prayed he wasn't suspicious. If he figured her out now, she'd just die. To that end, she sidled close once more, doing things Sophie had always wanted to do but would never have the nerve to follow through on.

One hand splayed over his chest, and she was stunned by the feel of his hard muscle, of the heat emanating from him in waves. There was no need to deliberately lower her tone; it emerged as a husky whisper as her body seemed to soak up his nearness. "Of course."

He covered her hand with his own, paused, then carefully removed it, holding it to his side. "The camera is in my office. You can wait here—"

"I'd rather just come with you." Self-preservation warred with curiosity. She needed to get away from him, to accept the pain of his rejection in solitude. But she'd always wanted to see his office, an extension of the man, knowing it would reveal so much about him.

He had a thick, overstuffed couch in his office. Many times she'd heard one of the brothers joke about taking a nap, especially Mack, who had his schoolwork to contend with but insisted on carrying his weight at the bar. Cole had done such a fabulous job with the brothers. They were all exceptional, responsible men.

So many times, Sophie had pictured him in that office behind the thick wooden door, dozing on the couch or sitting at his desk going over papers. She now wanted to know if the reality was the same as the fantasy, since the fantasy was evidently all she'd ever have.

Reluctantly, Cole nodded. "All right." He released her, putting his hand at the small of her back and guiding her forward. Just that slight touch, so simple, made her think of other things. His spread hand spanned the width of her waist. He was large all over, his hands twice the size of hers. With a small shiver, she imagined those large, rough hands on her body, covering so much of her skin with each touch. Her breasts throbbed and an aching emptiness swelled inside her.

The light was out in his office, and the cool dimness enveloped her as they stepped inside. She didn't quite know how she managed it, but she turned as he closed the door behind them and their bodies bumped together. Her feet seemed glued to the floor.

"Shelly . . ."

His voice was husky, not at all unaffected. She didn't need to breathe deep to inhale his hot male scent, not when she was already close to panting, her lungs expanding in sheer excitement at the touch of his hard-muscled body against hers.

Slowly, unable to resist, she went on tiptoe and nuzzled her face into his warm throat. God, it was as wonderful as she'd always imagined, his smell brisk and hot and stirring, his skin warm to the touch.

His hands clasped her upper arms, his fingers wrapping completely around her, biting into her flesh. "The light is on the desk," he muttered, but he sounded desperate, the words shallow around thick breaths.

Sophie tried to pull back, knowing this wasn't what he wanted, struggling to accept her defeat, but he lowered his head, cursing so softly, and his jaw brushed her temple. She swallowed hard at the near caress, aching for something she'd wanted for so long now. Sexual craving was new to her; she'd never experienced it for anyone but him, and the overwhelming need to indulge the craving and answer the burning in her body was making her crazed.

He shifted slightly and then her belly brushed his lower body and she felt the iron-hard length of his erection like a thunderclap. It burned into her, solid and unmistakable and with a small gasp, she pushed closer, her body seeking out more contact, reassured by the discovery.

Cole cursed again. In the next instant, his hand turned her face up and he groaned harshly, even as his mouth covered hers. Devouring, eating, holding her steady for the frenzied assault of his tongue and teeth. She'd imagined a kiss, but never this carnal mating of their mouths. Her heart rapped against her breastbone, her stomach curled tight. Helplessly, she opened her lips and accepted his tongue, all the while pressing into him, loving the feel of his excitement, the way his erection ground into her.

He pulled his mouth away, but it wasn't to stop.

"Cole," she whispered as his lips burned across her jaw, her throat, nipping and licking. His hands slid down her back, roughly grasped her bottom, and lifted her into his pelvis, his fingers plying her flesh as he moved her against him.

She held onto his shoulders, dizzy with a building urgency and a tender relief. *He wanted her.*

She moaned as he adjusted his stance, pressing her legs open to make room for his long, hard thigh, pulling her higher so she rode him. Embarrassment couldn't quite surface, even with the newness, the intimacy of it all. This was Cole, and this was what she'd wanted since the first night she'd met him. He was all the things her aunt Maude had ever warned against, every temptation imaginable wrapped up into a gorgeous package of throbbing masculinity. But he was also the most incredible man, gentle and proud and caring. Strong in all the ways that counted most. Every sinful fantasy she'd ever had winged through her mind, and she wanted every one of them to come true with him.

His open mouth pushed aside the neckline of her sweater so he could suck her soft skin against his teeth. Sophie wondered if he'd leave his mark, and hoped he would. She tilted her head to make it easier for him, and her toes curled inside her shoes at the delicious sensation of his warm mouth and tongue.

He groaned. "Damn . . ."

Somehow, he seemed to know how her breasts ached, and keeping her close with one hard hand on her buttocks, he lifted his other hand and enclosed her breast in incredible heat, his palm rasping deliberately over her nipple until she gave a raw moan of pleasure, then cuddling the soft mound gently. His mouth found hers again, swallowing her broken gasp when he lightly pinched her nipple, tugged and rolled. His tongue, warm and damp, slid into her mouth and she greedily accepted it.

They were leaning against the door, the heat thick around them, the darkness shielding, when the knock sounded and they broke their kiss, both of them panting for breath.

"I've locked everything up and I'm taking off. Just wanted you to know." There was a low chuckle, then Chase added, "Carry on."

Cole's chest moved like a bellows. Her feet were completely off the floor as she straddled his thigh, her arms tight around his neck. One hand still held her behind, and it contracted now as he seemed to fight some inner battle. She could see the white gleam of his eyes in the darkness, could feel his scrutiny.

No, no, she begged to herself, holding the words inside with an effort. But then she was being set back on her unsteady feet and moved a good distance away—the entire length of his long, muscular arms. She felt cold, denied his body heat, and she wrapped her arms around herself. One of his hands still held her, making certain, she supposed, that she couldn't close the distance between them, while he raked his other hand through his hair. She heard Cole's head hit the door as he dropped it back, then twice more. His frustration was a palpable thing, shaming her, making her want to run.

He abruptly moved away from her and opened the door. He stepped out into the hall, and she could hear the murmur of voices as he spoke to Chase.

She wasn't at all surprised when Cole came back to tell her, his tone steady and detached, "It's time to go. Come on, I'll see you to your car."

He didn't touch her again, and she felt defeated. Until she remembered how wildly he'd responded to her. He wanted her. But for some reason, he didn't want to want her. Maybe, her thinking continued, it was because he feared she might require a commitment. Did he think because she was *Sophie's sister* he might be obligated to pay if he played? Did dallying with a friend's relative imply ties she hadn't considered? She'd led such a solitary life, she had no idea of the codes involved in male/female social relationships.

Sophie thought maybe he was only fearful of being trapped, and she felt newly encouraged.

The silence was almost oppressive as they slipped on their coats and Cole finished up a few last-minute things. The bar was pitch dark as they left, but when they stepped outside, the bright glow of a streetlamp lit the entire front of the building. Cole managed several locks, then turned toward her, and when Sophie glanced at him, again taking in his incredible body, she had to struggle for breath.

Cole was still excited. She could read it on his face: the color high on his cheekbones, the clenched jaw, the heat that burned in his eyes. Her gaze skimmed lower, beneath the hem of his coat, and she saw his erection still plainly visible beneath his fly. Oh, he wanted her, all right. All she had to do was reassure him, to make certain he knew there would be no repercussions to their lovemaking.

He took her keys from her and opened her car door. For the first time since leaving his office, he spoke. "You're driving Sophie's car."

Bolstered now by new confidence, Sophie smiled. "She insisted. We live on different schedules, with her an early bird and me a night owl, so there isn't a conflict. And," she added deliberately, hoping to entice him, "I won't be in town that long. Not more than a few days."

He didn't take the bait. "I see. Well, good night. It was . . . nice meeting you."

She almost laughed at that inane comment and the irony in his tone, but his face was hard, set in stone, and she didn't want to anger him. "Oh, we'll see each other again. You forgot to take my picture. I'll be back tomorrow night, okay?" Playfully, trying to be bold to insure the credibility of her ruse, she reached out one leather-gloved finger and stroked his chest. "Maybe then we'll be able to stay on track. Or then again, maybe not."

His jaw locked, and as he turned away, she heard him mutter an awful curse. Sophie closed her door and started her car. Her heart was still beating too fast, her breasts still tingling, and there was a pulling sensation deep inside her, an acute emptiness that demanded attention. It felt delicious, and she wanted more. She wanted everything.

She wanted Cole Winston.

THREE

It had been an awful night. Cole sipped his coffee and tried to order his thoughts, but lack of sleep and extended, acute sexual frustration made his brain sluggish, hampering his efforts. The events at the bar, the sensual overload, and then the smothering guilt had conspired against him to make him toss and turn in between dreams of making love to a woman who looked and felt and tasted like Sophie but reacted like Shelly. Every so often, the two had combined to provide dreams so damned erotic he'd awake with his own raw groan caught in his throat, his body sheened in sweat, every muscle hard and straining.

He could still taste her, still feel the damp heat of her lips and tongue, and the warm softness of her mound as she'd worked herself against him. Her breast had felt perfect in his palm, small and sweetly curved, the nipple thrusting, eager for his mouth. And he'd wanted so badly to suck on her, to draw her deep until she begged for more.

He swallowed hard and closed his eyes, heat washing

over him in waves. His hands trembled as he groped for his coffee mug and took a scalding gulp.

He had to talk to Sophie. When he admitted to her how he felt, how damned attracted he was to her, how badly he wanted her, she might bolt. If she wasn't interested in him, he could lose her friendship, and that wasn't something he even wanted to contemplate. But at least his confession should take care of Shelly, removing her as a temptation. He couldn't go through that again, couldn't chance the strength of his control. Hell, he'd been a hair away from laying her across his desk and stripping those damn flesh-hugging jeans down her long legs. He would have taken her hard, in a hot rush, and he had a feeling she'd have liked it.

But he couldn't exchange one woman for another; it wouldn't be fair to any of them. And the simple truth was, he wanted Shelly because she was the exact image of his Sophie. But she wasn't Sophie, and he didn't want to blow a chance with Sophie by missing that distinction.

He glanced at the clock as he finished his third cup of extra-strong coffee. He was seldom up this early, not with his hours at the bar, but sleep had been impossible. The caffeine hadn't kicked in yet, but it was almost nine-thirty, and by the time he got to Sophie's boutique, she should be there. Shelly was right about that, Sophie was an early bird. He'd better go before he lost his nerve.

That thought made him laugh because no woman had made him nervous since he'd turned sixteen. But then, no woman had ever mattered like Sophie did. He'd been waiting seven months for her. Ridiculous. It was time he put an end to things.

A half hour later, Cole opened the oak and etched glass door of the boutique, hearing the tinkling of the overhead bells. It was a classy little joint, filled with feminine scents and at the moment, lots of Valentine decorations. A small blonde-haired woman was perched in the corner, preparing to dress a nude mannequin in an arrangement of filmy night wear. She glanced up, looking at him over the rim of her round glasses.

"I'll be right with you," she said around a mouthful of straight pins that she held in her teeth.

"I came to see Sophie. Is she in?"

The woman straightened with new interest and quickly folded the garment in her hand, laying it aside and placing the pins on top. "No, I'm sorry. She's running a little late today. She called to ask me to open for her. Was she expecting you?"

Cole shook his head. It wasn't like Sophie to be late, and a flash of concern hit him broadside. "She's not ill?"

"No, I gathered she's just extra tired today." The woman smiled. "I'm Allison, her assistant. Aren't you the oldest Winston brother who owns the Winston Tavern? I saw your picture in the paper recently."

Cole twisted his mouth in a wry smile, well used to the feminine teasing. "Guilty. I hope you ignored the article. The paper loves catching me and my brothers unaware."

Allison's grin spread as she gave him a coy, slanted look. "It was a very nice shot. I saved the article."

Her blatant flirting didn't bother him; he'd deflected plenty of female interest in his days, gently, so he wouldn't ever hurt a woman's feelings.

Unfortunately, he hadn't deflected Shelly very well.

Cole abruptly changed the subject. "Do you know when Sophie will be in?"

"Sorry, I don't. She just said *later* around a very loud yawn. I think she's zonked and getting a late start this morning, judging by how she sounded."

"She was probably up late with her sister." He frowned with the thought. What if Shelly had already related the events of the evening to Sophie? What if she'd told Sophie how he'd kissed her . . . and more? They'd probably sat up all night gossiping about him and his cursed lack of control.

Damn it, Shelly had no business interfering with Sophie's rest. He knew Sophie worked long hours, and if anyone was going to disturb her sleep, he wanted it to be him.

Allison laughed. "Nope, that couldn't be it because she doesn't have a sister. Sophie is an only child."

Cole was surprised that Allison didn't know her employer any better than that, but then he thought of how private Sophie was, how little she talked, and he understood. "Shelly is her twin. She's in town for a short visit."

Allison shook her head and put her hands on her hips. "I don't know who's been pulling your leg, but Sophie is all alone. She lost her folks when she was just a kid. Her aunt took her in and raised her, but she died, too, about a year ago."

His heart flipped, then began to slow, steady thumping. Every nerve on alert, Cole asked, "Are you sure about that?"

"Positive."

Bombarded by a mix of feelings, most of all confusion, Cole braced his hands on the countertop and dropped his head forward, deep in thought. *No twin.*

"Hey, are you all right?"

He nodded. Hell yeah, he was all right. He was damn good. It was just that . . . He looked up at Allison again, trying for a casual expression to hide the emotions slamming through him, most of all sexual elation.

He felt off balance. On top of the carnal images crowding his brain, a swelling tenderness threatened to overwhelm him. Sophie was all alone in the world, not a single relative around. He'd lost his parents, too, so he knew how devastating that could be. But he'd always had his brothers, and they were closer than most complete families. He wanted to protect Sophie, to comfort her, to tell her she'd never be alone again.

His mind immediately skittered onto more profound thoughts, like the heat and sexual urgency of the night before. A hot rush of searing lust forced him to grip the counter hard. If Sophie didn't have a sister, then his entire day was about to take on a new perspective. Anticipation churned low in his abdomen. "You know Sophie well?" He was careful to keep the question negligent, not to arouse suspicions.

Allison shrugged. "Sure. I've been with her since she bought this place, around seven months now."

"I remember when she opened it." Cole could feel the heated, forceful rush of blood in his veins. His body hardened, pressing against the rough fly of his jeans, but he couldn't help himself. He shifted uncomfortably, remembering last night, how he'd touched Sophie, kissed *Sophie*. He knew what her breast felt like, how it nestled so perfectly in the palm of his hand. He knew the texture of her tight little derriere, the taste of her skin.

And he knew that Sophie Sheridan, actress and fraud, wanted him—enough to pretend to be someone else. His knees nearly buckled.

He cleared his throat twice before he could speak. "Sophie and I have gotten to know each other pretty well. But I could have sworn she told me she had a sister."

"No." Allison, bursting with confidences, perched on a stool by the cash register and leaned her elbows on the counter. "Her aunt was all she had, and they were really close. They've always lived together because the aunt got sick and Sophie had to take care of her. But then she died last year. It was an awful blow to Sophie and she took her inheritance and moved here, away from the memories." Allison tilted her head. "You interested in her?"

Oh yeah, he was interested. He knew his eyes were glittering with intent as he smiled down at Allison, making her blush. "We've been close as friends, but I was hoping to give her a surprise for Valentine's Day, something a little more . . . intimate. Could you do me a big favor, and not mention that I was here or that I asked about her? I don't want to ruin the surprise."

Eyes wide, Allison made a cross on her chest with an index finger. "I won't say a word. Sophie deserves a little fun."

Oh, he'd give her fun, all right. He mentally rubbed his hands together in sizzling anticipation. Sophie Sheridan was about to get what she wanted.

No, not sweet shy Sophie, he thought, remembering how she'd refused to enter his contest, how she froze every damn time he touched her. The sexy Shelly. Cole grinned, already so aroused he didn't know how he'd get through the day. Only the thought that the night would be an end to his frustration kept him on track with his plan. He'd deal with Shelly tonight—and then Sophie would deal with him in the morning.

He'd give her a Valentine's surprise she wouldn't soon forget.

Sophie was dragging by the time she'd gotten off work. The combination of the late night, the stress of deception, and the anticipation of starting it all again had her weary, both in mind and body. Aunt Maude had believed in early to bed, early to rise, and Sophie had always adhered to the philosophy, happy to do her best to please the aunt who'd raised and loved her. Yet she'd been up till almost two A.M. last night, and even after she'd gotten to bed, she hadn't been able to sleep, too filled with repressed desire. She wasn't used to the churning feelings that had kept her awake, and rather than sleep, her mind kept wandering back, remembering the delicious feel of Cole's hard, warm body pressed close, his muscled thigh between hers, his rough palm on her breast. She shivered anew. It had been a long, disturbing night.

Allison had been helpful, but too cheerful all day, smiling and humming, and Sophie had been endlessly relieved when she finally hung the Closed sign in the front window.

Despite her tiredness, she was anxious to see Cole, now

that they shared a measure of carnal knowledge. She knew what his body felt like, how ravenous he was when kissing, his heady taste.

When she walked into the bar, shivering from the icy night, Cole immediately looked up at her, snaring her in his golden brown gaze. She had the feeling he might have been watching for her, and her heartbeat tripped alarmingly. His smile was different somehow, warmer and more intimate. Sophie wondered if it was Shelly's effect that made the difference.

For an instant, she was jealous of herself.

When Cole picked up a mug to fill with hot chocolate, releasing her from his gaze, she went to the back booth. Her belly tingled and her breasts felt heavy as she waited for him to serve her. She'd be herself, she thought, keeping her conversation to a minimum, drinking her hot chocolate without exception.

Only he didn't just give her the chocolate and leave after a few polite words. He set the cup in front of her, then seated himself opposite her in the booth, propping his chin on one large fist and smiling directly into her stunned eyes. He surveyed her until she squirmed, all the feelings from last night seeping into her muscles like an insidious warmth until her breath came too fast and shallow and her nipples puckered almost painfully tight. She hunched her shoulders in an effort to hide them.

Cole grinned, his gaze still a little too warm, too intent, slipping over her face as if he'd never seen her before. Just to break the tension, Sophie nodded at the steaming mug. "Thank you. I've been looking forward to this all day."

"Hmmm. Me, too."

She paused with the spoonful of whipped cream halfway to her open mouth. His tone had been a low hungry growl. "Cole?"

He reached across the table and his large hand engulfed hers, then gently guided the spoon to her mouth. His gaze stayed directed on her lips, expectant, and like a zombie, Sophie obediently accepted the whipped cream. Slowly, Cole pulled the empty spoon away from her closed lips then laid it aside, his eyes so hot she could feel them touching on her. Using his thumb, he carefully removed a small dab of the cream from the corner of her mouth, and the gesture was so sensual, Sophie experienced a stirring of need low in her abdomen. His rough thumb idly rubbed her bottom lip, and for a few seconds her vision clouded and she had to close her eyes to regain her equilibrium.

She felt nervous and too tense. Much more of this and she'd be getting light-headed, fainting at his feet.

He pulled away, and his voice was low when he spoke, almost a whisper. "Have you ever dated, Sophie?"

His hands rested flat on the table, and she watched him shift, those long fingers coming closer to hers. She tucked her hands safely into her lap. If he touched her again, she'd be begging him for more, ruining her entire charade. "Why do you ask?"

"Oh, I don't know." His wicked smile was too sexy for words, but also playful. "Meeting your sister last night made me wonder why the two of you are so . . . different."

"You liked Shelly, then?" She already knew the answer to that. If Chase hadn't interrupted them, she had an inkling their intimacy might have become complete. What they'd done had been so satisfying in a way, but also very frustrating. The incredible feelings he'd created had been escalating, building, and she wanted to know what would happen, what the fullness of it all would be. She wanted to feel his body bare of clothes, to trace the prominent muscles she'd felt with her fingertips, skin on skin. His scent was stronger at his throat, and she wondered how it might be in other places, across his chest and abdomen, and where that thick erection had thrust against her.

Her breath caught and held as Cole reached across the

table and fingered a curl hanging over her shoulder. "Yeah, I liked Shelly. But I like you, too."

She made a croaking sound, the best she could do with her thoughts so vivid and him looking at her like that. His knuckles brushed her cheek as he continued to toy with that one loose curl. "Well? Do you ever date?"

"No. I . . ." She tried a slight smile, but her face felt tight and strained. "You know how it is, how busy a business can keep you."

He nodded. "I raised my brothers, you know. Keeping them out of trouble and in school took up most of my time. I've just gotten to where I can have a serious relationship."

Sophie wanted to run away as fast as she could. Was he hinting that he wanted a relationship with Shelly? Good grief, she'd have to find a way to dissuade him of that notion.

Her jealousy swelled.

A smile flickered over Cole's mouth as he gave a playful tug on her hair. "Why don't you and Shelly get your picture taken together? I can't imagine anything prettier than that."

"Together?"

"Mmm. I could almost guarantee you'd win. And since you come in here every night, you could get your hot chocolate on the house."

And he could get his night on the town with Shelly. Words escaped her, so she merely shook her head. Winning the contest had never been her intent. She'd merely wanted to spend more time with Cole under the pretense of entering, using it as a way to introduce him to Shelly—on a temporary basis.

"All right. Suit yourself. But could you do me a favor? Ask Shelly if she can come in a little later tonight. Closer to closing. I have a lot of things to take care of and when she's here, I don't want to be distracted with work. Could you do that for me?"

Her mind raced. She'd probably have time to go home

and catch a nap. She was absolutely exhausted, and as excited as she was about seeing him again, kissing and touching him again, she could barely keep her eyes open. A little sleep would refresh her and sharpen her flagging wits. "Yes. I'll tell her. There . . . there shouldn't be a problem. Her time is pretty free right now."

"Good. And Sophie?" He grinned, waiting for the questioning lift of her brows. "If you change your mind and decide to enter the contest, just let me know."

She could feel the embarrassed heat rushing to her cheeks and barely managed a nod. God, she hated it when she blushed. "Yes, all right. Thank you."

He walked away, whistling, and Sophie stared at her chocolate in abject misery. Most of the whipped cream had melted.

Well heck. She was horribly afraid her plans had just gotten irrevocably twisted.

Cole made it sound as though he hadn't stayed single by choice but rather by necessity. He'd even hinted that he wouldn't mind getting involved with a woman now.

And here she had stupidly given him over to her make-believe sister. Sophie covered her face with both hands. *The best laid plans,* she thought.

She finished up her hot chocolate and literally fled.

"You're grinning like the cat who just found a bucket of cream."

"Yeah." Cole turned to Chase and grinned some more. He'd been grinning all night, and with good reason. Damn, he felt good. *Sophie wanted him.* He kept reminding himself of that, but every time, it thrilled him all over. If he hadn't already known about her ruse, her last blush before rushing out would have done it. No one blushed like Sophie. He wanted to see her entire body flushed that way, hot for him and how he could make her feel. He'd been thinking and planning for hours now, ever since Sophie left, knowing that Shelly would return.

"So, what's up? You and Ms. Sunshine finally hook up, or was it that little rendezvous with the sister? That lady looked like she could put the grin on any guy."

Cole and Chase had always been as much like best friends as they were brothers, possibly because they were the two oldest, even though nine years separated them. They'd pretty much always confided in each other, but even so, if he'd had a choice, Cole would have kept Sophie's secret to himself. Problem was, Chase already knew she supposedly had a twin, so an explanation was in order. He sighed. "There is no sister."

Chase paused in the act of polishing a glass. "Come again?"

Damn, but he couldn't seem to stop grinning, the satisfaction almost alive inside him, bursting out. "Sophie doesn't have a sister." He said it slowly and precisely, relishing the words. "She's an only child."

Cole waited while Chase sorted that out in his mind, then a dumbfounded look spread over his face and he laughed out loud. "Well, I'll be." He gave a masculine nudge against Cole's shoulder. "Aren't you the lucky one?"

Relieved that Chase was going to view the circumstances in the same way he had, Cole nodded. "Damn right. But no one else knows."

"Not a problem. Mack and Zane were so busy tripping over themselves yesterday trying to figure out what was going on with you two, I just left them to their own imaginations. It's not often they get to see you tongue-tied around a woman."

Cole slanted him a look. "It wasn't my tongue that was knotted up. Hell, I think the Inquisition could have been easier than last night was."

"But tonight will be different?"

"Oh, yeah." Tonight he had no reason to resist Shelly's

invitation. That expanding tenderness gripped him again, and his resolve doubled. When he thought of what Sophie was putting herself through, the elaborateness of her plan, he wanted to whisk her away and spend days showing her how unnecessary it all had been. Almost from the first day he'd seen her, he'd wanted her. All she had to do was smile, or order hot chocolate, and he was a goner. "If I don't miss my guess, Sophie is trying to get one thing without losing another."

"And you're both of those things?"

He nodded. "She's lived a sheltered life with an elderly aunt, and she hasn't ever dated much. She doesn't want to risk the comfort of coming here every night, which I gather is the sum of her social life, by causing an awkwardness between us. If we have an affair, things might change, at least that's how she likely sees it. But once I explain it all to her, she'll know how silly she's been."

"So you're going to admit to her you know she's an only child?"

"Hell no!" Cole scoffed at the very idea. Sophie, in all her innocence, was offering him a fantasy come true, and no way was he going to mess up her little performance. Besides, he wanted to see exactly how far she'd go with it. "I intend to show her that I want her, no matter who she is."

"Sounds like a dumb, hormone-inspired plan to me. And one guaranteed to tick the lady off."

"Like you're the expert?" Chase did even less honest dating than Cole. The death of their parents had hit him hard, and he'd been mostly reclusive ever since. Not that he was a monk, just very selective, and always very brief. Cole couldn't think of a single woman Chase had ever seen more than three times.

Chase shook his head. "It doesn't take a genius to figure out she'll be embarrassed. And women can be damn funny about things like that. You can accidentally bruise her while horsing around with some rough play, and she'll forgive you that. But hurt her feelings, and she'll never forget it."

Since that wasn't what Cole wanted to hear, he shrugged off the warning. Sophie had two sides, that was apparent now, and he intended to appease them both.

At that moment, she walked in, and incredibly, she looked even better now than she had last night. Of course, now he was looking at her with new eyes. This was his Sophie, so shy and sweet, yet now looking so sexy his teeth ached. The combination was guaranteed to blow his mind.

She wore the long, black leather coat again, this time over a loose, white blouse that buttoned down the front, tucked into a long black skirt and flat-heeled black shoes. She looked sensuously feminine and good enough to eat.

"Here comes Mutt and Jeff, so you better get your eyes back in your head and your tongue off the ground."

At Chase's muttered words, Cole pulled his gaze away from Sophie—*Shelly*—and turned to his brothers.

Mack was the first to speak, though he kept his fascinated gaze on Sophie. "What's going on with her lately? She's looking too damn fine."

"I'll say," Zane added. "Not that she wasn't a looker to begin with, but she never seemed aware of it before. She was always so . . . understated. Now her sex appeal is kind of up front, right in your face." He chuckled. "I like it."

Cole didn't bother responding to either brother. "I'm going to take her picture, so I'd appreciate some privacy while I'm in my office with her."

Mack's grin was so wide, it lifted his ears a fraction of an inch. "You need privacy to take her picture?"

Zane slugged him, which gained a disgruntled look, and a reciprocal smack. As Zane rubbed his shoulder, he said, "Don't tease him, Mack. Hell, I'm just glad to see him finally cutting loose a little." To Cole he remarked, "You act more like a grandpa than a big brother."

"Gee thanks."

Mack chuckled again. "We promise to give you all the leeway you need. In fact, given it's Friday, I can close up with Chase if you like."

"I was going to ask. Thanks."

"Sorry I can't stay too, Cole, but I already have plans. If you'd warned me—"

Chase gave his brother a distracted look. "Zane, you always have plans. What's her name this time?"

Unabashed, Zane straightened in a cocky way and said, "I never kiss and tell."

Cole figured Zane was more than old enough to manage his own love life, so he thumped him on the back and said, "Have fun," as he walked away to meet Sophie. She was still standing in the middle of the floor, and he realized she wasn't certain where to sit. From the beginning she'd always taken the back booth, which was the most secluded. But tonight, right this moment, she wasn't supposed to be Sophie and she didn't know how to act.

Someone turned on the jukebox just as Cole reached her and he had to yell to be heard. "I see you got my message."

She stared at him, devouring him with her eyes, and now he knew how to interpret that look. His lower body tightened in anticipation.

"Yes. Uh . . . Sophie told me to make it a little later. How soon will you close up?"

"Chase will give the last call in a few minutes." A couple shuffled past them, clinging to each other, barely moving their bodies as they feigned an interest in the music. Cole grinned. "Do you dance?"

As he asked it, he caught her hands and tugged her closer. She blanched. "Ah, no I don't. . . . That is . . ."

"No one is paying any attention," he cajoled. He pulled her into his arms, at the same time looking over her shoulder and seeing the rapt faces of his brothers. No attention, indeed. He frowned and shook his head at them. They all three nodded back, displaying various degrees of humor and curiosity.

Sophie tucked her face into his shoulder. "I've never danced much."

"You're doing fine." He nuzzled her temple, enjoying the feel of her warmth and softness so close, breathing in the sweet, familiar smell of her. She brought out his animal instincts, and he wanted to somehow mark her as his. His arms tightened and his thoughts rioted with plans for the coming night. "I like holding you."

Shuddering slightly, she leaned back to see his face. "I like having you hold me. Very much." She bit her lip, hesitant, then blurted, "And I liked what we did last night. Why did you stop?"

Cole felt poleaxed by her direct attack. He hadn't expected it. Lifting one hand, he cupped her cheek. "It was time to close the bar."

Sophie shook her head. "No, it was more than that. You seemed angry." Color in her cheeks deepened, but she held his gaze. "I want you to know, Cole, just because I'm . . . Sophie's sister, that doesn't mean I'd expect any more from you than any other woman."

"Oh?" *Silly goose.* She was so sweet and innocent, he wanted to pick her up and carry her away someplace private, then spend the long night reassuring her, making love to her, tying her to him. He knew his brothers were all watching, all alert, so he controlled himself. "What do other women expect from me?"

She swallowed audibly, but those smoky blue eyes never wavered, and he realized he admired her guts as much as everything else about her. Carrying out her plan couldn't be easy on her, and it directly indicated just how badly she wanted him. Lord help him, he'd never make it through the night.

"Nothing more than a nice night or two together, I suppose. I won't . . . won't be in town long. For the few days I am here, I'd like to share your company. But you don't have to worry about me hanging around afterward. I have my own life to live and I'm not interested in complicating it with a relationship. You don't have to worry that I'll make a pest of myself."

His chest tightened with some strange emotion he'd never experienced before. He brushed her bottom lip with his thumb, then whispered, "Come into my office where we can talk. I'll have Chase bring us something to drink."

She looked more than a little relieved by his offer and smiled her thanks before taking the hand he extended to her. Her fingers were still chilled from the outdoors, and he gently squeezed, giving her some of his warmth. His body thrummed with excitement.

He turned and caught the flurry of movement as his brothers quickly found something to do. Zane was pulling on his coat, ready to leave. Mack was red in the face, studiously inventorying their stack of shot glasses. And Chase merely smiled, giving them both a brief nod.

As Cole passed him, he said, "A couple of drinks, Chase?"

"Sure thing." There was so much wickedness in Chase's tone, Cole felt obliged to add, "Colas please." He didn't want to give Sophie a hot chocolate, thereby giving up the game by showing her he knew her preferences. Beyond that, he wasn't at all certain his control was up to it right now. The way she drank hot chocolate was better than an aphrodisiac.

Luckily, Sophie didn't notice the byplay. Her gaze remained on her feet as they entered his office. This time, he'd left the light on. He wanted to see every small expression that might pass over her face. He locked the door and smiled at her. "Come here."

Slightly startled, her eyes rounded and her sweet mouth opened just before he covered it with his own. He vaguely heard Chase announcing the last call, and he felt his muscles tense. Soon they'd be alone; he'd have her all to himself, with all the privacy he needed to see about fulfilling every single wish she'd ever had.

He folded her closer, one hand cupping the back of her head, his fingers tangled in her silky hair, the other pressing low on her spine, urging her body into more intimate contact with his.

And just that easily, she melted. There wasn't an ounce of resistance in her. He parted her lips with his tongue, licking into her mouth, touching the edge of her small white teeth, stroking deep, claiming and exciting. Her hands fisted on his chest, pulling tight the material of his shirt.

"Cole . . ."

The knock on the door announced the arrival of their drinks. Cole took in her dreamy gaze, her flushed cheeks, and smiled to himself. "Don't move."

She merely nodded in response.

He opened the door and took the tray Chase handed him. "Thanks."

"Don't do anything I wouldn't do."

"What wouldn't you do?"

"Exactly." Chase slapped him on the shoulder and pulled the door shut.

When Cole turned back to Sophie, she was still standing in the same spot as if rooted there. He smiled, set the tray on the desk, and turned to her. He touched her cheek, her chin, smoothed her eyebrows. Her face was so precious to him. He kissed her again, then began maneuvering his way to the desk. She clung to him, following his lead, and when he lifted her to sit on the very edge, she did no more than sigh.

"I'm glad you wore a skirt, baby." He trailed kisses over her jaw and down her throat.

Breathless, she asked, "Why?"

He lifted his gaze, amused by her innocence, charmed by her heavy-lidded eyes and dazed expression. Slowly, he slid one hand down her side to her knee, then back up again, under her skirt.

"Oh!"

He grinned, but it cost him. Her slim thighs were warm, silky, and as his fingers climbed, he realized she wore stockings. He muttered a low curse and took her mouth, bending her back on the desk, hungry for her. With her skirt bunched up it was easy to nudge her legs apart and nestle his hips there. He gave up the exquisite explorations of her legs to cup one small, perfect breast. "I can feel your heart racing," he said against her mouth.

She pressed her face into his chest. "I love having you touch me."

"Then you'll love this even more." He slid the top button of her V-necked blouse free. She sucked in a breath, then held it. The next button opened, and he could see the silky-smooth flesh of her chest, the beginnings of her cleavage. He traced a finger there, dipping and stroking both breasts, moving close enough to a nipple to make her shiver in anticipation. "God, there can't be anything softer or sweeter on earth than a woman's breast," he said as he continued to tease her. He shaped and molded her breasts in his palms, pushing them up, marveling at the resiliency of her soft flesh.

Sophie gave a quiet moan.

He tugged another button free. Her bra was white lace, barely there, and the sexiest damn thing he'd ever seen. He wondered if it matched her garter and panties.

Their foreheads were together, both of them watching the slow movement of his dark hand on her pale, delicate skin. He opened the last two buttons and pushed her blouse aside, lifting both hands to cup her breasts in his palms.

"So pretty," he breathed.

Her breasts trembled with her deep breaths; he touched the front closure of her bra with a fingertip.

And the music in the bar died. Sophie lifted her head, startled.

"Shhh, it's okay. They're just shutting down. It's time for everyone to go home."

She blinked, and her lips quivered. "Do we need to go, too?"

"Not if you don't want to." He kissed her, a warm, featherlight kiss. "But I'd like to take you home with me, sweetheart. My apartment is only a few blocks away. My couch is okay for a quick nap, but I don't have napping in mind, and I don't want anything about tonight to be quick." He touched her face, his fingertips barely grazing her downy cheek. "I don't mean to rush you. I know things are progressing awfully fast." His mouth tipped in a small smile and he added, "After all, we just met. But I want you, and you obviously want me. Will you come home with me? Will you spend the night?"

Her eyes went wide, her lashes fluttering. He could see the wild racing of her pulse in her throat. "Yes." She swallowed hard, then smiled. "Yes, I'd like that. Thank you."

FOUR

Cole grinned at her perfect manners, wanting to tease her but unable to dredge up an ounce of humor.

The rigidity had left Sophie's shoulders by the time they were in his car, but she was far from relaxed. He'd barely managed to talk her out of driving herself to his apartment. He knew she'd wanted her car there as an avenue of escape.

He wanted her to trust him, to give him everything.

She remained silent as he parked the car and led her to the second floor of his apartment building. He didn't mind. The silence wasn't overly uncomfortable, but rather charged with tension and anticipation. Something very basic and primal inside him wanted to see Sophie in his home, on his territory, in his bed. He wanted to stake a claim, and he intended to do it right. He'd never been a barbarian before, but right now, he felt like howling, like slaying dragons to prove his affections.

She looked around as he unlocked the door and led her inside.

"My place is pretty simple. I'm not one for much

decorating, and until recently, one or more of my brothers lived with me. Mack only moved on campus this past year and he was the last to go."

He watched as her gaze skimmed over everything, the dark leather furniture, the light oak tables, the awards and trophies set on a table that one or more of his brothers had won in sports and academics.

The eat-in kitchen was barely visible through an arched doorway. The bedrooms were down a short hallway.

"It's very nice," she said.

He pulled off his jacket, then took her coat, tossing both over a chair arm. "Zane teases me about being a housewife, but I like to keep the place clean, and now, he's no different. Teaching those three to do laundry and mop floors and cook was a chore, but they finally picked it up. We used to have a regular cleanup day, and there were no excuses accepted for missing it. Well, except for the time Chase broke his leg. Then we let him off the hook."

He grinned at her, wanting her to relax, to get to know him better. He was telling her things he'd never discussed with any other woman, and truth be told, she looked fascinated.

"How old were you when your parents died?"

"Twenty-two. I'd just finished college. Mack and Zane were still in grade school, but Chase was in junior high."

"It must have been awfully rough."

He nodded in acknowledgment, unwilling to rehash the past and all the problems that had cropped up daily. "We got through it. They were good kids, just a little disoriented by it all. It took time to get readjusted, to get past the loss." He wanted to ask her about her own loss, but because he wasn't supposed to know about it, he couldn't, and it frustrated him. They should be using this time to build a closeness, not hiding behind secrets.

Abruptly, he asked, "Are you hungry? Or would you like something to drink?"

She hesitated only a moment and that intriguing blush turned her face pink. Then, suddenly, she launched herself at him. Her arms went tight around his neck, almost smothering him as he caught her. "All I want is to finish what we started at the bar." She pressed frantic kisses to his neck, his nose, his ear, making him laugh, and at the same time groan with an incredible rush of hot lust. "I want to lie down with you and touch you and—"

"Honey, shush before you make me crazy." To guarantee her compliance, he kissed her, holding her face still, thrusting his tongue deep, tasting of her, making love to her mouth. Her words had affected him, making his body ache in need.

He pulled her blouse from her skirt and quickly skimmed the buttons open, then pushed it off her shoulders. She helped, wiggling her arms free and trying to keep their mouths together.

Laughing again, he said, "Take it easy, honey. We've got all night. There's no rush."

He gentled her, stroking his hands up and down her bare back, placing small, damp kisses across her skin. Her hands clutched at his hips and he obligingly stepped closer to her, letting her feel his rigid erection, nestling it into her soft belly.

She made a small sound of mingled excitement and delight. "Cole?"

"Hmmm?" he muttered, distracted by the taste and texture and scent of her skin. The fact that this was his Sophie sharpened the pleasure to a keen edge.

"Will you take off your shirt, too?"

He hesitated, afraid he might lose control if she started touching him too much. But her eyes were soft and huge, inquisitive and excited, and he couldn't resist. His heart pounding, he unbuttoned his shirt and shrugged it off, then peeled his T-shirt over his head. He dropped them both on the floor. Sophie's gaze moved over him, warm and intimate.

"You can touch me, honey."

Still, she seemed timid, so he took her hand in his, kissed her palm, then laid it flat on his chest. Sophie licked her lips as she tentatively stroked him. "You're so warm and hard."

He laughed. Hot was a more apt description, and there was no questioning how hard he was. It felt like his jeans would split at any minute. He ruthlessly maintained his control and started on the side button to her skirt.

"Cole . . ." She stiffened, anxiety in her tone.

"I want to see you, baby." He searched her expression and read so much nervousness there, he paused. Cupping her face and leaning close, he whispered, "You're very sexy. I could spend a lifetime looking at you and it wouldn't be enough."

Her small hands curled over his wrists. "And we certainly don't have a lifetime, do we? I . . . I'm leaving in just a few days."

When would she give up that ridiculous tale? At this point, it almost annoyed him. It was so difficult not to call her by name, not to admit how much he cared. But this was her show, he reminded himself, and he was determined to let her play it as she chose, at the same time, helping to meet her goals, to give her everything she'd ever wanted. "Are you sure you won't be able to stay in town awhile?"

"No." She interrupted him quickly, firmly, then stepped against him to wrap her arms tight around his waist. "No, we can have tonight, but that's all I need. Just one night. An exciting experience for both of us, but no more than that."

His confidence started to dip. Had he misread her? Did Sophie truly only want a very brief affair?

Not even that, he thought, as her words *just one night* reverberated in his brain. Maybe, unlike him, she had stayed single by choice. God knew, the woman was more than attractive enough to draw men in droves. He'd seen the underlying sensuality beneath her quiet persona, so it stood to reason other men would have seen it as well. Even Zane had commented that she was a looker, and he was a connoisseur of women.

Anger washed over him. Her ruse no longer seemed so touchingly sweet, and he was met with a new determination, one to make her so deliriously satisfied, so sated with his lovemaking, she wouldn't be able to deny him ever again. He would give her what she wanted and more. Before the night was over, she'd be as addicted as he.

One night hell.

"Take off the skirt, sweetheart. Let me touch you." The growled words hung heavy between them until finally Sophie released her death grip on him and lifted her head. Cole stepped back just enough to allow her to move freely.

Her eyes looked more gray than blue as they held his, looking for reassurance. At his smile, she carefully released the button to the waistband of the skirt and slid the zipper down. It immediately dropped over her slim hips to layer around her ankles. Cole took her hand and she stepped out of it, leaving her shoes behind as well.

The dark, sexy stockings covering her long, slender legs were enough to make him groan, but it was the sight of her narrow waist, her flat belly, that shook his control. Her panties were pale, and the small triangle of chestnut curls could be seen beneath the sheer material, taunting him, making his palms burn with the need to touch her.

"Christ, you're beautiful."

He hadn't realized she'd been holding her breath until she let it out in a long shaky sigh. "I wasn't sure what you would think—"

"I think I'm one lucky bastard," he muttered, his tone none too steady. "Come here, honey."

He didn't mean to be rough, to startle her, but he didn't think he could take much more. He'd been imagining this moment for almost seven months, and the reality was much sweeter than any fantasy he'd dredged up. He supposed it was because he genuinely cared about her, because he liked and respected her, that sex between them seemed like so much more. To him, laying her down and burying himself in her would be more than physical, it would be emotional and mental, too, a bonding of more than just their bodies.

The softness of her skin drew him, and he touched her everywhere, his hands gliding over her shoulders, her waist, the back of her thighs above the stockings. He pulled his mouth away from hers as he slid both rough palms into her panties, cuddling her small buttocks. Sophie stiffened, and he kissed her ear, then nipped the lobe. She gasped and her fingers contracted on his arms.

"I like that," she whispered.

He smiled despite his roaring lust. "This?" he asked as he stroked her silky bottom again, "Or this?" His teeth closed carefully on her earlobe as his tongue teased. She arched against him.

"Yes, that."

"There are other places to nibble, you know. Places you'll like even more."

"Oh?" She was breathless, trembling all over. Keeping one hand on her bottom to hold her close, Cole slid the other hand back up her side until he reached her breasts. With only one flick, he opened her skimpy bra.

They both groaned as he cuddled the soft, delicate weight of one warm breast in his hand. She gave a rough purr of feminine pleasure but jerked slightly as he caught her stiff nipple between his fingertips and rolled.

"There's here, too." With that warning, he bent his head and caught the tip of her breast between his teeth, flicking with his tongue, just as he'd done to her earlobe. Sophie grabbed his head, her fingers tight in his hair as she cried out. Cole opened his mouth wide and drew her in, sucking strongly. His hands closed on her waist and he backed her to the nearest wall, then stepped between her thighs, deliberately forcing her legs wide.

His hand moved down her waist, over her belly, and his fingertips toyed with the edge of her panties. Sophie shivered and moaned and he knew he was tormenting her as much as himself. Just as his fingers dipped inside he kissed her again, swallowing her moan of pleasure.

She was warm, wet, her tender flesh swollen, and his fingers gently caressed her until she was panting, her face pressed to his throat, her fingers grasping his biceps.

"Right here, honey," he whispered as he used his middle finger to ply her tiny, swollen clitoris.

"Oh God . . ." Her body jerked in reaction, pressing hard against him.

Cole kissed his way back to her ear, his teeth once again catching the lobe. His tongue stroked just as his finger did, and Sophie wasn't too innocent to realize the parody of what he did. She clutched at him and her hips began to move in tandem with the rhythm he set.

Shc was close, and he knew it. It surprised him, her immediate, unsparing reaction to him. It also made him nearly wild with lust. He'd always assumed Sophie had hidden depths, that once unleashed, her passion would be savage and uninhibited. His entire body pulsed with each small shudder she gave, each deep, raw moan. And when he whispered, "You would taste so sweet. Can you imagine my mouth here, honey, my tongue touching and licking—" she gave a stifled scream and climaxed.

Cole held her close, keeping the wild pleasure intense until she whimpered and slumped into him, utterly drained. Blood pounded through his veins, roaring in his ears. He scooped her up and hurried into his bedroom. He lowered her to the bed, laying her on top of the cool quilts, his own body coming down to cover hers.

He kissed her long and deep, caressing her breasts, her thighs, her belly. He leaned back to look at her, then removed her open bra and finished stripping her panties down her legs. She turned her face away, breathing shakily.

"You're perfect, sweetheart." What an understatement. He'd never seen a woman who stirred him like this one did. He kissed her breasts, sucking and nipping, his mouth gentle, his tongue rough. Sophie's body seemed to be designed with his sensual specifications in mind. He felt a near frenzy of need, but Sophie lay sated and limp beneath him, one hand in his hair, idly stroking. He shoved up to his side, pulled a condom from his jeans pocket, then held it in his teeth while he struggled out of the rest of his clothes.

His shoes went across the room when he kicked them off. He stood to shuck his jeans down his legs, and then turned back to Sophie. She immediately protested.

"I didn't get to see you," she said with a sexy pout.

Despite his need, Cole chuckled and moved her thighs apart, situating her for lovemaking. "Whereas I can see you very well. All of you," he added in a low, breathless growl, looking at her damp, soft curls and the tender flesh they protected. She still wore her stockings and the wisp of a garter belt, and she was so incredibly sexy he nearly lost his control. His fingers stroked over her again, easily now with her recent orgasm, feeling her slick dampness, her heat. Her modesty was gone and she simply allowed him to look, to touch. The sight helped to curb his rush. He could look at her forever and be happy.

She wasn't willing to give him forever. Damn this game.

She stretched like a small cat and smiled at him. "It's hardly fair, you know. I've been very curious about your body."

"You'll see me soon enough." He tore the silver package open and slipped the condom on. "But not now because I can't wait."

He caught her legs in the crook of his elbows and bent low over her, leaving her totally exposed and vulnerable to his possession. Sophie grabbed his shoulders to hold on, her eyes wide and dark, her breath coming in small, anxious pants. He probably should have taken more care, treated her more gently, with more restriction. Instead, he held her wide open and watched as he entered her body, as her delicate flesh gave way to his, slowly allowing him entrance. His muscles clenched even more, his heart thumping heavily. She was tight, resisting him, and he flexed his buttocks, forcing his way forward.

She said his name on a low moan.

"God, you're snug," he whispered through clenched teeth, and his forehead was damp with sweat. Sophie tipped her head back, biting her lip and squeezing her eyes shut. A rosy flush spread from her breasts to her throat and cheeks, not embarrassment, but sharp arousal. It fed his own. And then he sank into her, her body finally accepting his, squeezing him like a hot, wet, hungry fist.

He knew, of course, that she wasn't overly experienced, that she was mostly shy and withdrawn and therefore probably not all that practiced with men. But he hadn't expected her to be like this, so tight that he had to wonder if any other man had ever had her. The thought that he was the first, that she'd waited twenty-six years for him, broke his control, overwhelming him with a tidal wave of feelings he couldn't name and wasn't ready to deal with.

He withdrew, only to rock into her again, slow at first, but then harder and faster. "I'm sorry, baby," he said between rushing breaths, "I can't wait."

With no apparent complaints, Sophie reached for him, drawing his mouth down to hers, kissing him with a hunger that matched his own. Her small, feminine muscles held him tight, resisting each time he pulled away, then gladly squeezing as he pushed deep back into her, milking him, making him wild. When she pressed her head back, groaning in another immediate climax, Cole followed her. His mind went blank, his vision blurred, and his body burned. He felt a part of her, her scent in his head, his heart. He pounded heavily into her slim body until finally, he stiffened and his body shook as he emptied himself. He stayed suspended like that for long moments, then slowly collapsed against her.

Their rapid heartbeats mingled, and he could feel her breathing in his ear, soft, fast breaths. *God, he loved her.* The possessiveness nearly choked him; he wanted badly to whisper her name, to tell her how their lives would be from now on. To make her admit she cared also.

He'd gladly given up his personal life to care for his brothers. In that time, no woman had really appealed to him, to tempt him from his duty. But now he was free, and Sophie was here, as if sent by fate just when he was ready for her and needed her most. He wanted her, now and always. But he held back the words of commitment, unsure of her and how she would take such a declaration when she'd been so insistent on their time limit.

Slowly, carefully, he untangled his arms from her legs and heard her moan as her legs dropped. He'd been too rough, moved too fast for her, but she hadn't complained.

He managed a kiss to her neck by way of apology, but his mind was too sluggish, too affected, to do more than that. Her fingers sifted through his damp hair, and he could feel her smile where her mouth touched his shoulder.

"I hadn't imagined anything like that."

How the hell could she form coherent words? Cole struggled up onto his elbows and looked down at her, still breathing hard. She appeared smug and very satisfied. "So you thought it was okay?" he teased.

"Incredible."

He felt like a world conqueror at her words. He brushed his fingertips over her swollen lips. "I'm glad. I think you're pretty damned special, too. I always have."

She stilled for just a moment, her eyes wary. Her tongue came out to touch nervously on her lower lip, and she accidently licked against his finger. They both shuddered in reaction. "We only met a few days ago."

He was still inside her, her naked breasts flattened against the hardness of his chest, their pulses still too fast, and she continued the ridiculous game. She should have been admitting the truth to him by now. He'd all but told her how he felt.

Unless, of course, she didn't feel the same. If what her assistant, Allison, had said was true, her life had been so quiet, so sedate, she may have just hungered for a quick bite of adventure. Did she truly want him as a one-night stand? He'd assumed she'd concocted the absurd plan because she was unsure of herself and him. But it was possible the opposite was true, that she didn't hope for more involvement, but rather a guarantee of less. His stomach cramped at the possibility.

"Cole?"

"I was just thinking. It seems like I've known you a long time."

"Maybe that's because you've known Sophie. But we're nothing alike."

He smoothed her dark hair away from her face, wishing there was some simple, magical way to figure her out. He'd never suspected that his Sophie might be so contrary and complex. "I don't know about that," he whispered. "Sophie is—"

She laughed, interrupting him and quickly changing the subject before he could say the words that he desperately wanted to say, words he hoped would reassure her and gain a reciprocal declaration. "Are you ever going to get around to taking my picture?"

Momentarily distracted, he teased, "Like this?" He looked her over leisurely, the wild tangle of her hair, her sated gaze, the way her limbs were entwined with his. His hand smoothed over her hip. "You'd be a winner for sure."

She smiled. "How about just a head shot?"

He pretended disappointment. "I suppose it'll have to do." He pulled away, letting his hand linger on her thigh for a heart-stopping moment. "Don't move."

"I'm not sure I even can." But she did turn toward him, propping her head on an elbow. "Where are you going?"

"I have a camera here."

Cole disposed of the condom, then slipped on his jeans before rummaging in his closet for the instamatic camera. He looked up to see Sophie posed there, her hair wild, the quilts rumpled beneath her, one long, stocking-clad leg bent, the lacy garter still in place. A new wave of heat hit him. She was his. One way or another, he'd make her admit it.

"I should have gone slower, played longer," he said as he surveyed the feast she made.

"Why didn't you?"

He shook his head and came to sit on the edge of the bed. "Because you made me so crazy I couldn't even think straight, much less wait very long. I meant to make our first time together really special."

She laughed. "You haven't heard me complaining, have you?"

He'd never imagined Sophie with that particular impish smile. He kissed her, loving her more with each passing moment. "So you feel satisfied?"

She stretched again. "Absolutely. It was more than I'd ever imagined. So stop worrying."

"All right." It was easy to convince him since he didn't want to waste a single second with her by debating the issue. The night was still young enough, he'd have plenty of time to prove his point to her.

He lifted the camera to his eye, sending her squawking and screeching, grabbing for the sheet. "Cole, wait! I have to comb my hair. I'm a wreck."

"No, you're beautiful." She crossed her arms over her breasts and laughed at him, and that's the picture he took.

When it slid out of the camera, he lifted it out of her reach, then stood to put it on his dresser.

"Don't you dare consider hanging that anywhere!"

"I'm keeping that one for myself."

She relaxed again and studied him, her expression going soft and curious. "Why?"

"So I can look at you whenever I want." That was the truth, though not nearly close to how deeply he felt about it. "Now, if you want to put your blouse on and comb your hair before I take the entry picture, that's fine, but I swear you don't need it."

"I'm going to do it anyway."

He chuckled at her show of prim vanity. "All right. I'll go get us something to drink. You have about three minutes."

He was back in two, and Sophie had just begun to untangle her hair. She still felt languorous and warm and sated. She wanted nothing more than to curl back up on the bed with Cole and do all those things they'd already done, plus more. The bed smelled like him, and she could have snuggled into it forever. She pondered the possibility of stealing one of his pillows, but knew she'd be found out. She glanced at the clock and wanted to cry over the amount of time that had already passed them by.

Though she was enjoying their easy banter and intimate conversation—something she hadn't expected—she hadn't had near enough time to explore his body. It fascinated her, his perfect collection of hard bone and strong muscle. The few quick looks she'd gotten had made her insides feel like they were melting. She literally wanted to kiss him all over.

"What are you thinking about? There's a wicked gleam in your eyes."

Startled, Sophie looked up at him. He set a tray with two mugs of hot chocolate and a can of whipped cream on the dresser. His chest was bare and as he moved, muscles flexed and rippled. His jeans hung low, thanks to the fact he hadn't buttoned or zipped them, and his bare feet were large, braced apart, the tops sprinkled with dark hair.

She wanted to groan in pleasure; she wanted to tell him to stand there for about a year or so and let her look her fill. "I was thinking of your body, and how unfair it is that I haven't gotten to touch you much."

He froze for an instant, then shuddered. His eyes narrowed and grew dangerously bright. "You'll get your turn, if you're sure you want it." He loaded one mug of hot chocolate with whipped cream, forming a small mountain, then carried it to her with a spoon. Sophie scooted up against the headboard and balanced the warm cup between her palms. Leaning forward, she licked at the cream, more than a little aware of Cole's gaze.

His hand touched the side of her face, smoothing her hair back behind her ear. "I'd like to make love to you until morning, honey, if you're sure you're up to it."

Dark color slashed high on his cheekbones and his eyes were bright, glittering. He looked very aroused, and Sophie set the mug aside on the nightstand to give him her full attention. "I'd like that, too. I want this night to be enough to last a long, long time."

"You're not too sore?"

Such a strong wave of embarrassment washed over her, she felt even her nose turn red. "Of course not." It was a partial lie; she did feel achy in the places she flatly refused to mention. But it didn't matter, not when compared with the pleasure of getting to hold him again.

"You were so tight," he whispered, his hands still touching her as if he couldn't help himself. "I know you haven't had much hands-on experience. No," he said, placing a finger over her lips when she started to object. "I'm not judging or asking for details. But I know women's bodies, babe. And you were either a virgin, or you've been a hell of a long time without a man. You were so damn tight

I almost lost my mind. But either way, I don't want to hurt you."

Sophie felt touched to her soul. He was so wonderfully considerate, so decidedly male. Protective and virile, and she could gladly spend a lifetime with him. He'd hinted several times that he wouldn't mind continuing his relationship with Shelly, and she was so very tempted. But how could she ever manage such a thing? Keeping up the game for only a few days had worn on her. Already, she'd missed more sleep than ever before. Her boutique demanded all her attention in the mornings, so she couldn't keep up the late hours with Cole along with her normal shift at the shop. And the longer she was with him, the more risk she ran of being found out. If Cole knew she acted out both roles, what would he think? She shuddered at the mere possibility.

Softly now, because tears were so close, she whispered, "I want anything and everything you can give me tonight. What little discomfort I have doesn't matter at all, not in comparison to how you make me feel."

The muscles in his shoulders and neck seemed to tighten even more. Abruptly, he stood and grabbed up the camera. "Give me a smile, honey."

She did, though she knew it was a weak effort. His obvious arousal triggered her own. Once the photo was taken, he looked at the picture, nodded in satisfaction, then put it and the camera aside. "Now."

Shakily, her smile barely there, Sophie asked, "Now what?"

"Now we finish our drinks—after you get rid of that shirt."

Once again, he unbuttoned her blouse, playing with her, kissing each spot of skin that was uncovered, teasing her. Sophie relished his attention to detail. He also knelt in front of her to remove her garter and stockings. "I want you completely naked," he explained, and she hadn't cared to argue with him, too excited by the husky timber of his voice.

To her surprise, once that was done, he didn't attempt to make love to her again but instead wanted to assist her with her mug of hot chocolate. Sophie giggled every time he carried a spoonful of whipped cream to her mouth, but he was persistent, cajoling, and before the drinks were done, she had caught on and teased him unmercifully, licking at the spoon and sometimes his fingers, making him groan in reaction. She'd never been a flirt before, but she liked it.

And judging by his reactions, he liked it, too.

She thought of all the nights she drank hot chocolate at his bar and knew she'd never be able to order the drink there again. The chocolate always gave her a boost to get through the rest of her evening after a long workday, sort of like the caffeine from coffee did for others. She drank it year round, but now, she would imagine this scene, and if Cole so much as looked at her, she would recall his touch, his kiss. Though this was happening to Shelly, Sophie would be affected. No, she would never drink hot chocolate in front of him again. But it was worth it to lose the one small, routine comfort, when compared with the excitement of their present play.

"God, the way you do this ought to be outlawed for the sanity of mankind."

She merely smiled.

"You're such a tease," he whispered.

To which she replied, "Me? You're the one who still has his jeans on."

He leaned forward and kissed her, his tongue smoothing over her lips, then dipping inside before he pulled away. "An easy enough problem to fix." He stood and unself-consciously shucked off the last of his clothes. Sophie caught her breath at the sight of him. He was already hard, thrusting outward, and her body warmed at the significance of that.

"I started something earlier that I didn't get a chance to finish."

She couldn't imagine what. Everything had felt very finished to her; her nerve endings all came alive as she remembered the ways he'd touched and kissed her. Her eyes rounded when he scooped her up and laid her flat on the bed, one of her legs across his lap, the other behind him. Without a word, he leaned over and very gently nipped her ear, his tongue touching, stroking. One hand closed on her breast, and his fingers smoothed over and around her nipple until she squirmed.

Her body thrummed in immediate excitement. She closed her eyes, thrilled by his touch, how quickly he could bring her to a high level of excitement. She'd never imagined anything like this in her life.

He moved from her ear to her throat, then her shoulder, which she hadn't realized was so sexually sensitive to his touch, but every time he kissed her skin, every little lick, sent a riot of sensation through her body, seeming to concentrate between her thighs.

"There's a lot of things I'd like to do to you, honey."

"Yes." Whatever he wanted was fine with her; he seemed to know things about her body she'd never guessed.

"You taste so sweet," he whispered as he neared her breasts. His breath was fast, his mouth hot as he covered her nipple and tugged. Her back arched, but he soothed her, murmuring to her until she relaxed again, though her heartbeat still galloped.

"Relax and let me make love to you, baby."

Relax? Her entire body felt too tight, too sensitive. Then his teeth closed on her nipple, just sharp enough to alarm her. He tugged and she cried out, but he didn't stop, gently tormenting her. She started to grasp his head, but he caught her hands in one fist and pinned them above the pillow. His rough, raspy tongue smoothed over and around her nipple until she cried, then he switched to the other breast.

He was in no hurry now and she could do no more than accept his unique brand of torture. Still, she tried to protest when he left her breasts to kiss her ribs, but he wouldn't be deterred. Sophie moved against him, wanting to feel him push inside her body, to fill her. She ached for him. The feelings were even stronger now that she knew what to expect, what to anticipate.

She stiffened when his mouth moved to the top of her left thigh and her breath caught in her chest. His fingers slipped between her thighs and cupped her. "Remember what I told you earlier, babe?"

One finger found her most sensitive spot and gently rubbed back and forth. Sophie couldn't find enough breath to answer him.

"Do you remember?" He lightly pinched her, tugged, stroked, and Sophie couldn't keep the long moan from escaping between her tightly clenched teeth.

"That's it. You do remember, don't you? Here, and here . . ." He kissed her ear again, her nipple. "And here." In the next instant, his mouth replaced the fingers between her legs and she couldn't believe it, couldn't control her reactions or her small screams. Her hands pulled free and knotted in his hair, keeping him close, and he moved closer still, tasting her, licking her, nipping with his teeth. He gently sucked as he worked one rough finger into her, then another. Pushing deep inside, slowly, adding to the building pressure and pleasure.

The contractions hit her hard and she screamed out her climax, vaguely aware of his hum of satisfaction, of the way he pressed his own body firmly against the mattress. Her hips bucked and he resettled her, his long fingers biting into her hips, holding her still. It seemed to go on and on and he wouldn't relent until she pounded on his shoulders and shuddered and begged.

Seconds later he was over her and he cupped her face

between his palms, his fingers still damp. "Look at me, Sophie."

She managed to get her eyes open though it took a lot of effort. His words were indistinct to her muddled brain, but she knew he wanted her attention. Cole looked fierce, his face flushed darkly, his nostrils flared as he struggled for breath. And then he drove into her and once again her body reacted, her heels digging into the mattress as she strove to get as close to him as possible. Her climax, so recently abated, so utterly exhausting, came back to her in a flash of undulating heat and pinpoint sensation. She clung to Cole while he ground himself against her, his eyes never leaving her face, their gazes locked. It was a connection that went beyond physical, that joined their hearts as well as their bodies.

He groaned harshly and cursed and then she felt him coming, knew he'd locked his legs against the intensity of his climax. And he said her name again and again, as if he couldn't help himself. "Sophie, Sophie . . ."

This time when he collapsed, he turned so she faced him on her side, sparing her his weight. One heavy thigh draped over her own. His body was damp with sweat and radiated heat. For long minutes neither of them spoke. They allowed their heartbeats to slow, their bodies to cool.

Something, some vague unease niggled at the back of Sophie's mind, but she was too drained to identify the cause. She tried to ignore it, but it remained, vexing her like a dull toothache, prodding at the recesses of her mind.

Cole kept her close, locked in his arms, and then he whispered, "Sleep." His fingertips touched her nose, her cheekbones. "You look tuckered out, honey. Give in. I'll wake you when it's time to go."

Sophie sighed, comforted by his scent and the leisurely way he stroked her. She felt safe, protected. He snagged the quilts and pulled them over her, tucking her in. Within minutes she could feel herself drifting off, the long, restless nights two days past suddenly catching up to her.

Cole's hand cupped the back of her head, his fingers kneading her scalp, and that was all it took. She was aware of one last lingering kiss to her forehead, and then she was asleep.

FIVE

At first she was only aware of warmth and comfort, a coziness she'd never experienced before. She'd never awakened in a strange bed, and doing so now momentarily disoriented her. She sighed, mentally forcing herself from the depths of the deep sleep she'd enjoyed. Cole's scent and warmth mingled around her, stirring her senses. Even without full awareness, things felt almost perfect, except for one tiny problem. She frowned and concentrated on getting fully awake.

But the second she opened her eyes, she knew what had gone wrong.

Oh God, he'd called her by name.

Sophie was afraid to move, almost afraid to breathe. Cole lay heavily beside her, his even breaths touching against her temple, disturbing the fine hairs there. He had one heavy thigh draped over her legs, one arm limp around her waist, the other cushioning her head. Their combined body heat had worked to glue their skin together and she knew, if she moved, he'd awaken.

Then the questions would begin.

She closed her eyes as dread filled her. *He knew!* The last time they'd made love, he'd called her Sophie, not just once, but over and over again. He knew she wasn't Shelly, but he'd made love to her anyway. She couldn't begin to comprehend the ramifications of such a thing. She was naked, in bed with the man she'd spent seven months fantasizing about, the man she'd slowly fallen in love with. They'd made love repeatedly and her body ached in tender places, reminding her just how new this all was to her, and how well he now knew her body.

Carefully, moving like a ghost, she turned her face to look at him.

His dark lashes cast long shadows on his cheekbones and beard stubble covered his lean jaw, chin, and upper lip. How long had they slept? His dark, silky hair fell over his forehead, and Sophie was amazed at how the sight affected her.

God, she loved him.

She closed her eyes as pain swelled inside her. Cole knew who she was, and now she had to deal with that. But she needed time. She couldn't sort out her thoughts with him so close, his naked body warming her own.

At that moment he yawned and stretched. Sophie froze, frantically praying that he wouldn't awaken. He put one arm above his head and rolled onto his back.

Her insides quivered in relief; she felt almost light-headed. Not daring to move, she waited several moments, but he slept on. He, too, was exhausted. And his normal routine was to sleep later, since the bar kept him out at night. Slowly, holding her breath, she slid one leg to the edge of the bed.

When he remained motionless, she moved her other leg. Luckily, his bed was firm and didn't sag or rock overly with her motions. It took her nearly three full minutes, but finally she was standing beside the bed, staring down at him. He muttered in his sleep, scratched his bare chest, then sighed heavily.

What had she done?

Escape was the only clear thought in her mind. She needed time, time away from him, from his magnetism. She had to think. On tiptoes, she gathered up her clothes and slipped out into the hallway. There she dressed hastily and grabbed up her coat. She didn't bother to look into a mirror, already knowing she looked a wreck. A night of debauchery had to leave a woman somewhat disheveled, but there was nothing she could do about it now, so she didn't want to dwell on it.

The lock on his front door gave a quiet snick as she slipped it open, and her heart almost punched out of her chest. But there were no ensuing noises, so she assumed he slept on.

She ran the few blocks back to her car still parked at the bar, the cold slicing into her, almost unaware of the tears on her face. Fortunately for her peace of mind, the streets were all but completely deserted. There was no one to witness her humiliation as she stumbled up to her car, then dropped her keys twice before finally getting the door unlocked.

She drove like a madwoman, anxious to be home in the comfort of familiar surroundings where she could sort it all out in private. When she finally pulled into the parking lot, her car was still cold and she was racked with shivers. It was almost six-thirty.

She couldn't bear the thought of working today, not sure if Cole would feel obliged to come and see her after the way she'd run off, more afraid that he wouldn't bother at all. The humiliation was too much. She called Allison and asked her to cover for her the entire day. It would mean paying the assistant overtime, but Sophie didn't care.

Once Allison had agreed, Sophie stripped off her clothes, took a warm shower, which did nothing to shake off the awful chill deep inside her, then she crawled into bed.

She had to decide what to do, how to explain, what excuse she could use for such a dastardly trick.

But first, she cried.

"So what's wrong with you? You've looked ready to commit murder all night. The customers are giving you a wide berth."

Without answering, Cole stalked away from Chase. He felt heartsick and so damned empty he didn't know how to deal with it.

Of course, Chase wouldn't let it go, following Cole as he headed for the office, throwing the door back open and walking in without taking the obvious hints. He pulled out a chair and sat down. "Give it up, Cole, and tell me what's wrong."

His eyes burned and his gut clenched. Furious, he turned to Chase and said, "You want the goddamned details? Fine. She walked out on me."

"Sophie?"

Cole threw up his hands. "No, the First Lady. Of course I mean Sophie."

Carefully, Chase asked, "So you went after her and stopped her and told her how you feel, right?"

Sending his brother a look of intense dislike, Cole said, "I was asleep. She snuck out on me."

"Oh."

"After I woke up this morning, I went to her boutique, but her assistant said she called in sick. I don't have her home phone number or even know where she lives." He laughed, the sound devoid of humor. "After seven months—*after last night*—I don't have her damned address."

"Ask the assistant."

He growled, then said in a mock woman's voice, "It's against policy to give out personal information, but I promise to tell Sophie you asked."

Chase scowled. "She refused to give you Sophie's number?"

"Yeah. No matter what I said, she wouldn't give in."

"So that's it? Hell, I might as well throw dirt on you. If you're giving up now, you're dead and buried."

"I'm not giving up, damn it! I just don't know what to do at this precise moment. Waiting doesn't sit right. I have no idea what Sophie might be thinking."

"All right. I'll take care of it." At Cole's incredulous look, Chase added, "I'll go over there and talk to the assistant. I'll get Sophie's number for you."

"And how, exactly, do you plan to do that?"

"Never mind. Just figure out what you want to say to her when you do call her. If you blow this, I'm going to be really disappointed in you."

Mack and Zane approached the office just in time to hear Chase's comment. "Disappointed in Cole about what?"

Chase left the office to fetch his coat and get on his way. The three brothers followed him like he was the Pied Piper.

"What's going on with you two? Where's Chase going?"

When they were all behind the bar, Cole turned to his brother Mack. "On a blind mission, though he doesn't believe that just yet. But he will, after he meets Allison."

Zane stepped up, a look of confusion on his face. "Who's Allison?"

"Sophie's assistant."

"Oh yeah. I remember her."

Both Cole and Chase turned to stare at him. They started to ask, but thought better of it. The details of Zane's love life were often too boggling to deal with. Mack snickered.

After a moment, while Chase tugged on his coat and gloves, Zane asked, "Did you and Sophie have a falling out or something?"

"It's none of your business, Zane."

He shrugged at Cole. "Fine. But I just wondered if there was some reason you weren't serving her. If you'd rather I'd take her a drink, just say so. But I don't like ignoring a woman."

Cole's head snapped up and he stared over at the familiar booth. There sat Sophie, hands primly folded on the table, her expression cautiously serene, though her face was pale and her eyes were red. His heart twisted, then lodged in his throat.

Chase asked, "How long has she been sitting there?"

"About ten minutes now. Usually Cole serves her right off, so I didn't know . . ."

His words dwindled off as Cole climbed over the bar instead of going around it, sending several customers jumping out of his way, awkwardly snatching up their drinks so they wouldn't get spilled. Cole's stride was long and forceful, his gaze focused on his approach to Sophie's table. With each step he took, his pulse pounded in his ears until he almost couldn't hear. When he reached her, she looked up and he saw her eyes were puffy. God, had she been crying? He searched her face; words, explanations, all jumbled in his mind so that he couldn't get a single coherent thought out. Finally he just leaned down and kissed her. Hard. Possessively. He kept one hand on the table in front of her, one on the back of her seat, caging her in, keeping her from pulling away.

But she didn't try to pull away. Her small hands came up and grabbed his shirt, tugging him closer still.

He heard a roaring in his ears and realized it came from the bar. Lifting his mouth from Sophie's, he looked around and saw a majority of male faces laughing and cheering—led by his damn, disreputable brothers, of course.

He grinned, then faced Sophie again. She started to speak, but he covered her mouth with a finger. "I love you, Sophie."

Her eyes widened.

He leaned closer still, speaking in a rough whisper. "I've waited seven months to spend the night with you, and it was worth it. But I'll be damned if I'll wait anymore. I love you, I want you. Now and forever, regardless of what name you go by, or how you dress. You're mine now. Get used to it."

He waited, but her big smoky eyes never wavered from his. She was completely still except for the pulse racing in her throat. Cautiously, he lifted his finger. "Well?"

She swallowed audibly. "All right."

By small degrees, his frown lifted and his mouth quirked. She'd said yes. "You want me, too?"

"I've wanted you since the very first time I saw you."

He kissed her again, then asked, "Why the hell did you run from me today? Christ, I almost went nuts when I woke up and you were gone."

"I'm sorry. I felt stupid—"

"Damn it, Sophie—"

It was her turn to shush him, and she used her entire hand. Their audience chuckled. No one could hear what was being said, but Sophie's actions were plain enough. Cole grinned behind her palm.

"I felt stupid for pretending to be someone else instead of just being brave enough to tell you how I feel. So I decided to stop being a coward. Aunt Maude always told me an adult should own up to what they do, to be responsible for their actions and accept the results. She also told me I should never be afraid to go after what I want."

Through her muffling fingers, he asked, "You want me?"

She nodded, tears once again in her eyes. "I love you."

His long fingers circled her wrist and he pulled her hand down. "I wish I could have met Aunt Maude. I have a feeling we'd have been good friends. Will you tell me all about her?"

She nodded, then forged onward. "I realized you must care about me, too, because you kept hinting about wanting a relationship. At first I thought you wanted Shelly. I was jealous."

His look was affectionate, full of love. "Goose."

"But then I finally remembered that you knew Shelly and I were the same."

"Not at first, and it almost made me demented. I wanted Shelly because she looked like you, made me feel like you do. I couldn't understand it because you're the only woman who makes me insane with lust and sick with tenderness." Then he growled, "Not to mention what you do to a mug of hot chocolate." He pulled her from her chair and swung her in a wide circle to the sounds of raucous cheers. "Will you marry me, Sophie?"

Very primly, she replied, "I was hoping you'd ask."

At that moment, Chase set two hot chocolates on the table. He winked at his brother. "Hey, might as well go for broke."

The Valentine contest went off without a hitch. Sophie was chosen unanimously by Cole's three desperate brothers, who wanted nothing to do with an arranged date for themselves. The local newspaper explained it away by saying Sophie and Cole had fallen in love during the contest, which put the perfect slant on the whole Valentine ambiance and gained them an enormous amount of publicity, some of it even covered by a local news station. Sophie, as the lucky winner, got incredible publicity for her boutique as well. Allison had her hands full fending off reporters who blocked the growing influx of new customers. She complained heartily, but Cole figured she was well up to the task.

Cole announced to the reporters that since he was soon to be a married man, next year one of his brothers would serve as escort for the winner. That brought about some bawdy comments from the women customers and some hearty groans from his brothers, who pretended to be terrified by the prospect but who nonetheless preened under the weight of feminine attention.

Sophie stood by Cole's side, elegant and serene and

beautiful. He felt like the luckiest man alive. The contest really had been the perfect idea for both of them, even if they'd each indulged in ulterior motives.

He glanced up and saw the contest photo on the wall. As per the contest stipulations, Sophie had posed with all the Winston men. Their much bigger bodies crowded around hers, dwarfing her petite frame. She was laughing, and all the men looked smug.

In his nightstand drawer at home was a different photo, the one he'd taken of Sophie while her hair was still tousled and her cheeks flushed from his loving. But that one was private, for his eyes only. Forever.

Next year, he thought, grinning as he watched his brothers give one interview after another, the contest might work out as the perfect idea for another Winston man. He wondered which of them would be the lucky one. Then Sophie nudged his side and he forgot about everything but her. He led her to his office where solitude awaited—along with a carafe of hot chocolate and a can of whipped cream.

Buried in Her Heart

Elda Minger

ONE

Abby Sheridan felt as if she were poised on the edge of the world.

Her plane had touched down at LAX just before noon on this cloudy February day. Seated in a cab in bumper-to-bumper traffic and looking out the window at the rainy, gray, windswept skies and at feathery palm trees swaying against that wind, Abby felt far removed from Evanston, the suburb of Chicago she'd called home for most of her twenty-nine years.

Her cell phone inside her purse rang, and Yoda, her fawn-colored Chihuahua, gave a worried grunt. She'd settled herself in Abby's lap, curled up tightly against the slight chill in the cab. Abby had draped her trench coat over her small pet, and only Yoda's nose peeked out. The little dog, who was usually so lively, seemed tired after the flight. But Abby knew she was only resting before she managed to get herself into another bit of mischief.

"Uncle Pat?" Abby said as she answered, knowing it had to be her uncle back at the family law firm in Chicago. He'd called her twice at O'Hare before her flight. Apparently there had been a mix-up at the hotel where she'd originally been scheduled to stay.

"How are the accommodations out there? Are you at the bed-and-breakfast yet?" Her uncle's voice sounded too full and rich to be restrained by the small cell phone she held in her hand. "Can you see the Pacific, Abby?"

"Not yet. We're in a taxi and on our way." As she spoke, Abby looked out the rain-streaked window of the cab and saw the enormous, impersonal, corporate hotel she was supposed to be staying at this week. The conference, which would cover many of the finer points of the law, was still why she was in L.A., but she wouldn't be staying at the hotel where it was to be held.

She'd had a reservation at that hotel, but at the last minute, she and her uncle Pat had been informed that the hotel had been overbooked. So her uncle had frantically checked around for another place for her to stay. Unfortunately, Southern California at any time of year was a vacationer's paradise and a conventioneer's dream, and quite a few of the giant hotels near the airport had been booked solid.

But her uncle had persevered and found her a small bed-and-breakfast out at Venice Beach, slightly north of the airport. The commute each day wouldn't be that bad. It would even be comparable to what she was used to every day at her job in Chicago.

"Rain out there, from what I hear on the news."

"El Niño strikes again." She paused, then decided to get down to business. "When's the first seminar scheduled?"

Her uncle cleared his throat. "That's what I'm calling about. Abby, there's been another complication. It seems that Mr. Cameron won't be able to fly out there until Wednesday night. Health problems. So nothing will start until Thursday morning."

"Oh." She'd flown out on a Saturday morning, gained

two hours of time, and decided to give herself Sunday to recover before starting the intensive educational seminar on contract law. Now she had a few more free days than she'd anticipated. "Should I come back? Do you need me for anything?"

Her uncle laughed, then said, "Consider these extra days a little vacation. Walk on the beach. Do some shopping. I can certainly hold down the fort here. How did Yoda like the trip?"

She had to smile at that. Her uncle adored animals, particularly dogs. Any breed, from an enormous Irish wolfhound to her tiny Chihuahua, received his undivided attention. And they loved him right back.

"She's fine. She charmed everyone in business class."

"That little rascal's so predictable. Well, give her a pat for me, and keep her out of trouble until the two of you come back."

"I will. And thank you for finding me this bed-and-breakfast. I'm sure it will be just fine."

"I thought you might like it. Didn't think the conference hotel would fill up so fast."

"I'm sure I'll like this a lot better." Abby wanted to reassure her gruff uncle, who had always wanted only the best for her and her brother and sister.

After saying her good-byes, she stuffed her cell phone into her purse, then sat back in the cab's seat as she scratched Yoda's ears. The little dog whined and looked up at her, and Abby had to smile.

How incredibly perceptive dogs could be. She'd been trying to deny her feelings, but Yoda, as always, had sensed something was wrong.

The driver had turned off Century Boulevard onto another street, and now the taxi started to pick up speed as they headed north, toward the water and the bed-and-breakfast. Abby closed her eyes, picturing the enormous, impersonal hotel she'd almost checked into and was suddenly glad her life had taken this unexpected turn.

She caressed Yoda's head, and the Chihuahua let out a contented sigh. Abby herself felt far from contented. If she was honest with herself, she hadn't been contented, or even happy, for a long time. And in the last six months, she'd decided she had to do something about it.

She was almost a classic case. A lawyer who, once finished with law school, had found out she really didn't want to practice law. What had seemed like such a good idea while she had been in school had turned into a routine that threatened to suffocate her.

"I really want out," she whispered to herself, and Yoda whined. Abby resumed patting the small dog as these thoughts raced through her mind.

Yoda was such good company when she found herself in this particular mood. One of the most wonderful things about dogs was that they never sat in judgment of you. Yoda simply thought she was wonderful, and Abby needed that kind of support at this time in her life. She didn't know why, but there were times when she thought she'd done absolutely everything wrong in the last few years. Wrong decisions, wrong actions, wrong, wrong, wrong. Her life felt wrong, and Abby had finally, in the quieter moments, admitted that it *was* wrong. For her.

"All set," the cabdriver said as he pulled the vehicle up to the curb.

She'd been so immersed in her problems that she hadn't even been aware of where they were. Now, she glanced first toward the beach, and it was glorious. Abby was a winter-at-the-beach type of person; she far preferred mist and fog to the blinding brilliance of a hot, summer sun. Then she turned her head; her gaze fell on the place where she was to stay—and Abby fell in love.

The gray-shingled beach house seemed to rise out of the fog like a welcoming ship on a stormy sea. Curtains were pulled back in the front window, and a single lamp gave off a soft, welcoming glow against the rather gloomy weather. A brilliantly painted sign, in total contrast to the weathered shingles, swung gently in the wind. *The Buried Treasure*, the letters said, their flowing shapes elegant against a bright red, painted banner. Below that banner, a painted brown chest overflowed with gold coins, and a brilliantly colored parrot, wings spread, perched on the trunk's open lid.

The beach house looked like the sort of dwelling a large, happy family might inhabit. She could picture young children running down the front steps and toward the beach, shouting with happiness as they carried pails, shovels, and toy boats to the beach while Mother and Father brought up the rear with sunscreen, hats, and a generous picnic basket.

Abby's eyes stung sharply for just a second, but she blinked the emotion back.

"This is the right place, isn't it?"

She realized the driver was waiting for her to get out of his cab.

"Yes. Thank you." Tucking Yoda securely beneath her arm and reaching for her purse and money for the driver, Abby then grasped the door handle and let herself out, hauling her suitcase and Yoda's carrier behind her.

Walking up the stairs, she examined the landscaping, her gaze taking in every detail. Brilliant impatiens—salmon, fuschia, and light pink—and a few strategically placed ferns added color to the walk. As she got closer to the sign, she noticed smaller writing at the bottom: Proprietress, Molly Dawson. Est. 1974.

Abby took a deep breath of the sea-scented air. It had been such a long time since she'd felt her life had the smallest element of adventure to it, such a long time since anything out of the ordinary had occurred. This little gem, this bed-and-breakfast, was definitely out of the ordinary. And in that instant, as Abby started up the front steps toward the front door and that welcoming light and warmth, she decided that just for a few days, she was going to pretend.

She was going to pretend she wasn't a lawyer.

She and Yoda swiftly settled themselves into their room. The Chihuahua always came with her on business trips; the tiny dog was small enough to travel in her own carrier in the main cabin.

Yoda had her own particular routine. As soon as the plane lifted off, she'd scratch at the small door, demanding to be let out and be a part of all the excitement going on. And if there wasn't any excitement, Yoda would create some. It was just the kind of dog she was.

"What shall we do now?" Abby asked the Chihuahua, perfectly at ease with talking to her pet as if she understood. And Abby was sure Yoda did.

Yoda jumped off the bed, ran over to one of the overstuffed chairs by the window, scrabbled against the glass, and barked sharply.

"A walk? In this weather?"

Yoda barked again, even more insistently.

Well, they were both from the Midwest, and perfectly used to rain. And it would feel good to breathe in the clean ocean air after the stale, recycled air on the flight. Abby dug into one of her bags for a leash, and within minutes, they were down the bed-and-breakfast's front steps, crossing the cement boardwalk, and sinking their feet into the sand, walking along in the drizzling rain and fog.

"Yoda, heel!"

How did one deal with a dog that weighed just under six pounds, yet insisted on acting like some sort of wolfhound? Despite plenty of obedience classes, Yoda sprinted well ahead of her, and Abby found herself running to keep up with the rascal.

"Yoda—" She stopped as the fog cleared and she saw her dog race toward a tangle of disgusting-looking seaweed.

"Yoda, *no,* I—"

She stopped. Something was in that seaweed. Something dark and furry.

Now Abby felt fear slide up her spine. The last thing she wanted to have happen was for Yoda to be bitten by some sea creature that had washed up on shore. They would investigate this carefully, see what had to be done.

Her pet raced up to the wet, matted tangle of fur, barked sharply, then stared at Abby with her dark, doggy eyes as if to say, "All right, what are we going to do?"

Abby knelt down, completely oblivious to the fact that she was encrusting her dark gray, wool pants with damp sand. She leaned closer, and what she saw tore at her heart.

The cat had the small, round face of a Persian, and the delicate ears. The long, thick, dark coat was soaked with seawater and matted with sand. Strands of seaweed, green and bulbous, wrapped around the cat's body, but it was the piece of fishing line wrapped tightly around its neck that caught Abby's eye.

Oh, no . . .

Gently, as gently as she could, she reached out and touched the shaggy little cat's head, that place right between its ears that cats so love to be scratched. She didn't even realize she was holding her breath until the cat opened tired, deep copper eyes and looked up at her. And Abby saw, the instant their eyes met, that this animal didn't expect much, and had just about given up hoping for anything.

A small crowd had gathered around her. A short, stocky Mexican man and his three children. Two young male surfers, one with long, red hair and a nose ring. A mother and her daughter, each with an ice-cream cone. When the mother saw what it was they were all looking at, she hurriedly distracted her young daughter, and they headed down toward the waves in their matching raincoats.

Where were her gardening shears when she needed them? Abby glanced around at the people surrounding her. "Does anyone have anything that can cut wire?"

"I do," said a man who stepped to her side, knelt down, and seemed to size up the situation immediately. The bedraggled cat didn't even have the energy to struggle as the stranger took out an efficient looking set of clippers and gently cut the loops of lethal fishing line.

"We've got to get him to a vet," Abby said, taking off her scarf and wrapping it around the cat's body as the man gently lifted the animal and disentangled it from the seaweed.

"I have a car, and know a good vet," the stranger said.

"Fine."

They were inside his car, the heater on high, on the way to the vet's, the cat on Abby's lap and Yoda at her feet, before the stranger, never taking his eyes off the rain-slick road, said, "My name's Jack."

"Abby," she replied, then turned her attention back to the cat.

Jack found a vet in record time; they burst in, and were let into one of the examining rooms immediately. The vet, a tall, white-haired man with extremely gentle hands, examined the cat thoroughly. And Abby finally had a chance to study her stranger.

He was tall, easily five eleven to her five four. He had dark brown hair, lively hazel eyes, high cheekbones, and a strong jaw. For some reason, he seemed like the sort of man who would smile easily, but now his attention was as tied up in this animal's fate as hers was. Then he caught her looking at him and smiled down at her, his expression one of total reassurance.

Something peculiar squeezed the region right around her heart.

She still couldn't quite believe she'd gotten into a strange man's car and raced off to the vet's, but she'd always believed in her gut reactions. Instinct told her that most serial killers didn't take the time to clip a tangled fishing line off a half-dead cat.

"She'll need fluids," the vet was saying. "And a good antibiotic. We'll give her a bath, and may have to shave off some of that fur."

"What happened to her?" Abby had to know. She had to understand how something like this could have happened.

"My guess is that she stayed with a family until she was no longer a kitten, or too much trouble. Someone abandoned her, or perhaps she was stolen. There's a good chance that someone threw her into the water, as most cats won't go near a body of water like the ocean. Once she was in, she got tangled up in some loose fishing wire, then washed up on the beach. She was lucky the two of you found her." As the vet talked, his voice soothing, he gave the cat several shots, then clipped away some of the worst of the matted, tangled fur in order to examine her neck.

"How old is she?" Jack asked. Abby found that she liked the sound of his voice, deep and reassuring.

"Not even a year." The vet had carefully examined the cat, cleaned out a few cuts and scrapes. One of the technicians, a young woman with blond hair pulled back in a French braid and wearing a blue smock and pants, came into the examining room and took the cat from the vet, carrying her into one of the back rooms for a quick cleanup.

"When can I pick her up?" Abby asked.

"I'd like her to remain here overnight so we can keep an eye on her. Why don't I phone you in the morning?"

"I'm staying at The Buried Treasure bed-and-breakfast, right on the beach," said Abby. "I'll leave the number with your receptionist—" She caught Jack's eye. He was grinning.

"What's so funny?"

"I'm staying at the Treasure, too."

"Really."

"I just checked in two days ago. I'm in The Garden Room. Which room do you have?"

"The Juliet Room. The one with the balcony that faces the ocean."

They walked out into the reception area, Yoda at their heels. She had sat patiently on a plastic chair throughout the cat's entire exam, and now wagged her little tail delightedly as she trotted along behind them.

"I'll bet it's a great view when it's not so foggy," Jack said.

"It was beautiful today. I like the fog."

They made a quick stop at the receptionist's desk, and before Abby realized what was going on, Jack had put the entire bill on his credit card.

"I can't let you do that!"

"I'm the one who brought her here."

"But I was the one who insisted—"

"There's a way you can solve this entire problem," he said as he looked down at her, just a hint of laughter in his eyes.

"What would that be?"

"Have dinner with me tonight. I haven't been disappointed with the Treasure's dining room."

She hesitated. Meeting a man had not been on the agenda for this trip. But then again, Jack wasn't like any man she'd ever met.

"All right."

The started toward the front glass double doors, and it was only then that Abby realized it had begun to pour, the rain slanting down in sheets. She glanced around for Yoda, then realized Jack had picked up her pet and tucked the tiny dog securely beneath his jacket, where she would remain warm and dry. Yoda barely exposed her nose, and her dark eyes clearly expressed her delight with this new friend.

"I can bring the car around," Jack said.
"I don't mind a little rain."

"What to wear for dinner," Abby said to herself as she studied the clothing she'd brought West for her business trip. It seemed as if everything she owned was far too stuffy and conservative for dinner with a man like Jack.

Stuffy and conservative seemed to fit her present life.

When she dreamed, Abby was far from the person she normally was. When she dreamed, she wasn't a contract lawyer, working for Uncle Pat's law firm. She didn't wear conservative suits—sometimes with skirts a little too short—and skim her straight brown hair off her face into a conservative twist. She didn't carry a briefcase to work, didn't sit at her desk occupied with legalese, and she didn't wear clear nail polish. She didn't take brief lunches and even briefer breaks.

No, when Abby was dreaming, she was cooking. Her idea of heaven was attending cooking school in Paris, or one of those two-week travel packages in Italy that included a thorough study of the foods and cooking techniques of the region. *Gourmet, Bon Appetit,* and *Cooks Illustrated* were her guilty pleasures, magazine subscriptions waiting patiently in the pile of mail by her apartment's front door, vying for her attention.

Abby devoured cookbooks as if they were murder mysteries. She could never walk past a cooking store, a Williams Sonoma or a *Sur La Table*, without going in and investigating the gleaming copper pots and pans, the exotic spices, and infused oils.

Heaven would be cooking for a group of twelve sailing a ship around the Caribbean. Or catering for a wedding, birthday, or anniversary. Or perhaps the dream she quietly held dearest to her heart, that of being a chef in a tiny little restaurant by the sea. A place where regulars came, candles flickered, incredible aromas wafted out from the kitchen, and the specials always changed, depending on what foods were in season.

She knew exactly how she had become a lawyer. What she didn't know was exactly how she was going to get out and become something else.

Abby was both a dreamer and a realist. That, she thought as she lay back down on the comfortable, queen-sized canopied bed next to Yoda, was what had gotten her life into this mess in the first place.

She'd done well in high school and college, and had had no trouble getting into law school. She'd graduated at the top of her class and knew within a year of working at her uncle's firm that the law wasn't something she wanted to devote the rest of her life to.

There were no dark secrets in her family. Her mother and father had loved each other deeply. Abby had been born within two years of their wedding day. Her fraternal twin siblings, a brother and sister, had arrived eight years later, and life had been blissful for a time. She'd grown up with so much love.

She'd lost both her parents in a plane crash that first year she was at her uncle's law firm. Her brother and his twin sister had been seventeen years old and were absolutely destroyed by the news. It had been all she could do to get them through their high school graduations and convince them both to go on to college. Abby had desperately tried to keep as much of their lives the same as before the accident. She wanted her siblings to have some sort of emotional security, and if that security had been her determined presence in their lives, then that was the way things had to be.

It hadn't been the time to strike out on her own, even if she'd always wanted to go to cooking school. She couldn't have left her family. Not then.

So she'd waited. Bided her time. Desperately tired to keep her dream alive. Abby's mother had taught her how to cook, and she thought of her mother every time she sliced an onion, mixed up a cake, or poached a salmon. So Abby took a few professional cooking classes on carefully planned vacations from the firm. She read every professional article she could get her hands on.

But most of the cooking she did was in the realm of preparing her own dinner in her apartment's small kitchen when she got home from work. Many an evening had been spent eating with one hand and holding a phone with the other as she talked to one of her twin siblings at college, offering encouragement.

Three years after the accident, she still missed her parents. Each and every day. The twins were stable now, in their junior year at school, each at different colleges, doing well, and filled with the enthusiasm that only someone on the verge of graduating and beginning to conquer a brand-new world possesses.

And Abby felt old.

Her uncle Pat and aunt Mary had done their best, but with five children of their own, Abby had instinctively known it was up to her to keep her family together. Her uncle had offered her a job at the family firm directly out of school, and she'd taken it. She worked harder than anyone else there, lived frugally, and invested her money. Though her father and mother had left small trust funds for the twins' educations, Abby had known that it was up to her to provide them with the stability to see that education through to the end.

But every so often, it felt more and more like she was the one who was dying.

The most horrible part of it, the part she almost kept secret from herself, was that as the months passed, it became harder and harder to envision herself doing anything but working at the family firm. Abby knew what was happening to her. She was becoming very used to her comfort zone, that nice, comfortable rut that would ensure that nothing ever happened to her.

Nothing she wanted to happen.

Twenty-nine was an extremely scary age. *Almost thirty.* When she remembered the last few months she'd spent in law school, when she'd started to have doubts about her chosen profession, and when she remembered all the dreams she'd had, and where she'd thought she would be at thirty—

The soft knock on the door startled her out of her thoughts, and she swung her legs over the side of the bed, walked over to the door, and opened it.

Molly Dawson, the fiftysomething proprietess of The Buried Treasure, entered the room with a grand flourish and a tray in her hand.

"Tea time!" she announced.

The woman stood just barely over five feet, with short-cropped gray hair, lively blue eyes, a round face, and an even rounder body. Today she was dressed in an outrageously colored caftan, the design rather African and executed in purples, pinks, and golds. Her face was flawlessly made up, her sandals an exotic design of leather straps and beads, her toenails painted a brilliant fuschia. A light, sparkly scent trailed in her wake. If Abby had possessed only one word to describe the woman, that word would be *flamboyant.*

"You *must* try these, Abby," Molly said as she placed the tray on a small antique table next to a bay window. Abby sat down in one of the chairs across from Molly and saw the colorful ceramic plate of homemade cookies and a comforting pot of tea.

"I don't want to spoil your appetite for dinner, but what with the chocolate convention starting Monday morning, I thought you might like a little preview of what we'll be offering."

"Chocolate convention?" Abby said, reaching for one of the cookies. The flavors exploded in her mouth as she bit into it, a glorious mingling of butter and coconut, with just a hint of rum flavoring. Abby, with her passion for good food and everything that went into that food's preparation, was in heaven.

"An entire week devoted to chocolate! We'll have classes in candy making, and how to temper chocolate, and outrageous cakes. There's also a contest for the best chocolate chip cookie recipe, and some truly outstanding hot chocolate drinks—"

"Can I come to the first part of the convention, before my law seminars start?"

Molly beamed. "I made a special deal before I agreed that The Buried Treasure would sponsor the convention. Any of my guests get to attend up to three seminars, free of charge."

"That's more than fair."

"Excellent. So I'll see you downstairs, joining in on the fun bright and early Monday?"

"You couldn't keep me away."

"Now," Molly said as she whirled through The Juliet Room. For such a small, round woman, she moved with the grace of a ballerina. "Just one more thing, and then I'll leave you alone. Would you like dinner sent up, or will you be joining us below? The weather's taken a nasty turn tonight, with all that rain, but if you'd like a list of some of the restaurants in the area, I can bring that up as well—"

"That won't be necessary, I'm eating in the dining room."

"Splendid. My son-in-law is an excellent chef, but I can't quite remember what the special is tonight." Molly started toward the door, all sparkly energy. Before she reached it, she turned. Stopped. Wrinkled her forehead.

"Is there something wrong with your dresser drawers, dear?"

"No, not at all."

"Do you have enough room for all your clothes?"

Abby glanced around her room and realized that every single outfit she'd packed was spread out on the room's chairs, on part of the bed, and on the large table in the comfortable sitting area.

"Oh, no . . . you see, I have a dinner date tonight, and—"

"Someone I know?" Molly's bright blue eyes twinkled. "I just adore romance!"

"Jack. Jack—" Abby flushed, realizing she didn't even know her mystery man's last name.

"Jack Hayes? Our Jack? How wonderful!" Molly dashed over to a chair, sat on its overstuffed edge, and studied Abby, her friendly blue eyes gleaming with pleasure. "Did the two of you meet here, in the parlor?"

Abby thought of how her uncle would have loved that expression; it sounded so quaintly old-fashioned.

"No." Briefly, she explained the events of the day, their cat rescue, and the ride home in the rain.

"Well." Molly was grinning now. "That Jack's a good man to have around in an emergency, but I guess I don't have to tell you that." She eyed the wild profusion of outfits all over the bedroom. "And you don't know what to wear."

Abby nodded. "I packed for a week of corporate seminars, not a vacation."

"I have just the thing!" And with that, Molly shot out the door and disappeared down the hall.

Abby could only wonder. And wait. And sip her hot tea as the February rain continued to fall steadily outside her window.

"Isn't it just the perfect dress?" Molly said.

And it was. While all of Abby's corporate suits were tailored just so, draped and cut to subtly flatter her body without revealing too much, this dress was the absolute essence of femininity, romance, candlelit dinners, and English country gardens. Silk chiffon, in a brilliant cherry red, it slid over her body like a second skin and felt incredibly good.

"I knew you were the same size as my daughter. She bought this, got it home, and decided she didn't want it, after all. It's not the right color for her, but it looks fabulous on you."

"I'll pay her for it, of course."

"Sold. It still even has the price tag on it."

Cost was the least of Abby's worries. This was a dress she never would have bought for herself. But the minute she'd tried it on, she'd known this was the dress the "other Abby" would have worn. The Abby who had longed for evenings sitting in a café along the Seine, drinking red wine and dancing until dawn.

For some reason she didn't want to examine too closely, she wanted to be that woman with Jack. The thought of wearing one of her carefully tailored suits and twisting her hair back was too unbearable.

She'd brushed her hair and let it fall simply around her shoulders, then been a little more daring with her makeup.

"Fabulous!" Molly said of the final results as Abby walked out of the bathroom. For some reason, the older woman had wanted to see her transformation, and Abby hadn't had the heart to not grant that particular wish.

Besides, she'd wanted the opportunity to pump her for information about Jack.

"What does he do?" she'd asked as she applied her foundation.

"Some kind of businessman. But he's really excited about this newest venture. He's bought a little restaurant down the street, and he's planning on totally gutting the place, remodeling it, and creating a little café by the ocean. I think it's going to be darling."

Abby stopped in the middle of applying eye shadow, not believing she was hearing her long-denied dream.

"Does he cook?" She picked up her mascara wand.

"Cook?" Molly bent over with laughter. "Jack loves good food but can't cook worth a damn. Oh, he can do all the regular bachelor stuff, scramble an egg, make a sandwich, that sort of thing. But when it comes to cooking, he says he's simply going to hire the best."

Her heart gave the smallest of flutters as it picked up speed.

"What kind of food?" She closed her eyes, unable to look in the mirror.

"California French. You know, really fresh ingredients and a menu that changes seasonally. I keep telling my son-in-law, 'Harry, get some new recipes together, this man is going to give you a run for your money!' And the wine cellar Jack talks about creating, well, I can tell you, he'll be on the top of my list of recommended restaurants!"

Her eyes still closed, Abby pictured Jack the way he'd looked at the vet's. Strong, sure, and capable. Unafraid. Unafraid to dream.

Not at all like her. At twenty-nine, there were times when she simply felt too old to remake her life into something she really wanted.

She applied a rosy lip gloss, then stepped out of the bathroom and toward her bed, where she slipped on her high heels.

"Don't you look fantastic!"

Molly so effortlessly gave her all the confidence she needed.

"What are you going to use for a wrap?" the older woman asked.

"I thought maybe—I just have a trench coat—"

"I know just the shawl." Molly bounded out of the room as Yoda yapped happily. Abby couldn't help smiling. She felt as giddy as a girl getting ready for her first dance.

He'd been impatient to see her all day, since he'd said good-bye to her in the foyer and watched as she climbed the stairs to The Juliet Room. He'd examined the flyer Molly Dawson kept by the front desk, seen the luxurious room with its rose, moss green, and stone décor, the fireplace, the huge windows, the large, canopied bed, the balcony. . . . He'd thought of her in that room, with a little dog for company, thought of her getting ready to have dinner with him.

Jack had sensed a loneliness in her, a sort of quiet desperation. That had been after he'd been knocked almost senseless as the small crowd on the beach had parted and he'd taken his first good look at her.

Delicate features. He'd seen absolute concern in those clear gray eyes. Her straight brown hair had been pulled back in a swift braid, several strands escaping to brush against her flushed cheeks.

She hadn't given a damn about her clothing; the fine wool pants had been crusted with wet sand. That image had reminded him of his mother, down on her hands and knees in her garden, her Yorkie following her everywhere she went.

Then he'd gone to work on the cat and hadn't been able to take another look at Abby until their feline friend had been safely out of danger. Abby had seemed a little shyer then, and he'd gotten the distinct impression that she didn't have a whole lot of experience with men. Or perhaps with men who moved as quickly as he did.

He'd had to. At the time, he hadn't known how many days she had at the bed-and-breakfast, and he'd wanted to ensure they spent as much time as possible together. Tonight's dinner was simply a means for him to discover all he could about her, find out where she lived when she wasn't vacationing by the Pacific Ocean, and ensure that she found him as charming a companion as possible.

At The Buried Treasure, guests met for tea at four every afternoon in the flower-filled brick patio with a white gazebo. White chairs were placed around round tables dressed in pink tablecloths and set with china with a delicate strawberry pattern. Obviously, with the cold, gray winter rain still coming down heavily, tea outside wasn't an option. But tea would still be served in the large front parlor, where a buffet was arranged and waiting for guests.

The cookies baked for today's tea had been the first scent that had greeted Abby as she had pushed open the door to the bed-and-breakfast, Yoda tucked securely beneath her arm.

Chocolate chip cookies. And something with coconut. And nutmeg.

Her first impressions had been swift and instinctual. The atmosphere was easy, a very homelike feeling. Also, as she glanced around, she thought about how amazing a house could be, how different it was from the ordinary when a building of wood and glass was loved like a member of the family.

She'd been tired after her time on the beach and at the vet's, so she'd been thankful that Molly had thoughtfully brought her first tea up to her room. Being ruthlessly honest with herself, Abby knew she didn't want to see Jack before dinner, no matter how cozy and inviting tea in the parlor could be, with a roaring fire in the fireplace and no doubt several fascinating guests sitting on the comfortable sofas and chairs.

Now, as she came down the carpeted steps and stepped into the parlor to wait for Jack, she found that she was looking forward to that glass of sherry by the fireplace in order to steady her nerves.

Even though she was twenty-nine, she hadn't dated a lot. She'd been rather shy in high school, and law school hadn't left much time for fun. Then her parents had died, and her siblings had needed her, and she'd gone right to work. Her uncle had frowned on coworkers dating, so Abby could actually count the number of bona fide dates she'd gone out on with both hands.

She had several good male friends and wasn't totally

tongue-tied with the opposite sex, but she'd never really met anyone who had made her heart race. And even though she knew in her heart that she'd settled in her career choice, Abby was absolutely determined never to settle in her choice of a life partner.

Well, that wasn't actually true, about never having met anyone who made her heart race. Her heart had been doing funny little flutterings, like flip-flops, the entire time she'd been with Jack. Those same flutterings had ensured she hadn't made it down for tea.

Her heart seemed to be working overtime. Abby glanced up from her chair by the fire as Jack entered the room and started straight toward her.

TWO

He looked absolutely wonderful.

She'd only had time for quick glances, the quickest of assessments, as they'd both rushed the cat to the vet's. Afterward, Abby had been so upset by the thought of anyone abandoning an animal that, other than the scary little fluttering of her heart, she hadn't been able to really focus on the man now in front of her.

There was a quality about him, an indefinable quality that made her think she would always have a good time with him. He knew how to have fun; she saw that in his eyes and the way his mouth seemed always on the verge of a smile. Yet he didn't seem like the sort of man who was only out to have a good time. She knew he was a caring man, that much had been proven by their time together at the beach. She also knew, from what Molly had told her upstairs, that he was an extremely hard worker. Not just anyone attempted to open his or her own restaurant.

She liked the direct way he looked at her, the way his hazel eyes lighted with pleasure as he caught sight of her. So many of her girlfriends, calling late at night, would ask the same questions over and over about the men they were dating. "Do you think he cares for me? Do you think he likes me? Do you think he'll call?"

Jack Hayes was a very authentic person. He liked her very much, and he didn't bother to hide the fact. She responded to that immediately.

He sat down next to her, taking another chair by the parlor fire.

"You look beautiful," he said, and she found her stomach tightening at the sound of his voice. How could one man's voice, so dark and soft, have that effect on her?

"Thank you. So do you."

He'd dressed in a dark suit, well cut and made of a gorgeous material. He even smelled good, a spicy after-shave that didn't overpower, simply made her all the more aware of him. That strong jaw was clean-shaven. He was smiling as he looked at her, as if he couldn't believe his luck.

Jack made her feel very special.

"This," he said softly, "will be fun."

Dinner at The Buried Treasure was often served out in the garden, the round tables lit by candlelight, the smells of Arabian and night-blooming jasmine filling the air, the sound of a waterfall coming from the natural-rock fountain in one corner. In the summer, Molly had told Abby, they often hung vivid Chinese paper lanterns among the tree branches or little white lights in the shrubbery. But lately, the strong wind and rains had made both of those options impossible.

In inclement weather, the dining room came into use. An enormous room, with polished wood floors and windows that looked out over an ocean view, the dining room was part of the house's legacy that remembered a time when families were larger and all ate together in a rather formal manner. Molly encouraged her guests to talk and get to know one another, an easy feat, considering the large dining table they would all share.

Abby had found herself yearning for the garden, for a small, round table lit by candlelight in the midst of scented, night-blooming flowers. She'd found herself wanting a little romance with Jack, and as they walked toward the large dining room, she realized she didn't want to share her time with him with the other diners.

She was surprised when he took a different turn and led her to a small room on the first floor, down the hallway from the dining room, with windows that offered an incredible view of the garden.

"It's not the ocean," he said as he stepped up to a small, linen-covered the table directly in front of those windows and pulled out her chair, "but I thought it might give us more of an opportunity to get to know one another."

She couldn't believe that part of her private fantasy was about to come true. With slightly wobbly knees, she lowered herself into the chair just as a familiar little canine head peeped out over the table from a third chair.

"Yoda! What are you doing here?"

"I invited her," Jack said. "I asked Molly if it was all right, seeing as it's just the two of us in this room. She didn't have a problem with her eating with us."

"Not on the table, I hope!"

"Oh, no. She'll have a bowl next to her chair, then a comfy rug by the fire."

Abby had been so surprised by the small, private room that she'd neglected to notice the other details. Fresh flowers, white and light peach-colored roses, graced both the table and the small, marble fireplace's mantel. An Oriental rug in shades of scarlet, gold, and jade green covered most of the polished wood floor. The walls were that same shade of rich scarlet, with gold accents that glowed softly in the flickering firelight.

The dining table and chairs were clearly antiques, though Abby couldn't say from which period. She just knew they looked old and well cared for, with the soft, mellow glow of good wood that has been polished many times.

A small shelf of hardback books caught her eye, adding to the cozy appeal of the room. The sparkle of beveled glass reflecting firelight along the windows that looked out into the darkened garden gave the private room an almost magical glow. This was a cozy little nook, the perfect place for an assignation with a loved one. The perfect place to get to know Jack Hayes better.

One fat candle glowed on the tabletop, and she was glad there weren't that many distractions between the two of them. She'd always disliked restaurants where the table was so fussy you could barely see the person you were eating with.

"Harry will be here in just a moment to take our order," Jack said, and Abby realized their menus were right in front of them, hand lettered in delicate calligraphy. Molly had told her that her son-in-law was a seasonal cook, and the choices offered by his kitchen reflected that fact.

When Harry arrived, Abby chose the crab cakes with a creamy lobster sauce, while Jack selected the salmon. The true test of her willpower would come with dessert, but Abby had already decided she was going to indulge herself as much as possible while she stayed at this wonderful house by the ocean. Half the fun for her was truly savoring the food, and then asking herself if she would have prepared it the same way or done something different.

She admired the way Harry attended to each detail, explaining the various items on the menu before they'd made their choices, then helping them select a wine to go with their dinner. A tall, thin man, with gangly arms and legs, a rather bony face, and a shock of carrot-red hair, Harry's face was saved from utter plainness by his eyes. They were beautiful, thickly fringed, and a clear, brilliant green. She wondered if he wore contacts to enhance their color.

His personality was perfectly understandable to her, as he was passionate about food.

"Molly said you were out here for some sort of legal convention," Jack said as Harry filled their wineglasses, "so I'm assuming you're some sort of lawyer."

"Yes."

"Your specialty?"

"Contract law."

"Do you like it?"

The question caught her off balance, for it was one that was rarely asked of her. Grateful for the wine in her mouth allowing her a slight delay, she swallowed the excellent California vintage, then said, "No."

"Really?"

"I knew within a year of starting to practice that it wasn't for me."

"How long has it been since that realization?"

She hesitated. With anyone else, she would have feared condemnation. With Jack, he seemed truly interested. She decided to take an emotional chance.

"Three years."

He took another sip of his wine, and she sensed he was thinking.

"It's not too late to start over, Abby."

Conversation with this man had become incredibly personal incredibly quickly. Jack clearly wasn't the sort of person who liked wasting time on small talk.

"I know that . . . in my head. But sometimes, it feels so incredibly hard."

"Fair enough." He was silent for a moment, then said, "If you could do anything in the world, anything at all, what would that be?"

She started to laugh, then reached over to pat Yoda, who

had been quietly watching their interaction with her gleaming, dark eyes.

"You're going to laugh."

"Trust me, Abby. I won't."

"It's almost too much of a coincidence."

He smiled. "Coincidences happen for a reason."

Their salads arrived, sparing her the necessity of answering him immediately. Once Harry left, she fiddled with her fork, then blurted out, "I wanted to be a chef. To cook for people. Not a caterer, but to cook every single night for a small group of people in a little café by the sea." She could feel her cheeks reddening, and for just a moment regretted the impulse that had allowed her to confide in him.

"That's amazing."

She'd been afraid to look at him, and now that she did, she saw that smile she so liked was firmly in place.

"Why is that?"

"Because I'm looking for a chef."

"I wasn't asking you for a job."

"I know that. Don't get defensive, Abby. I just find this little coincidence pretty delightful. I can't think of a person I'd rather have in my kitchen than you."

She started to laugh. It was so wonderful; it made the breath in her chest feel so very light, to talk about dreams this way. "You don't even know if I can cook!"

"Call it gut instinct. Call it intuition. I have a feeling you'd be excellent in the kitchen."

She took a tentative bite of her salad, tasted it, chewed. Excellent.

"How did you learn to cook?"

"My mother. I can still remember standing on a chair by the stove, one of her big aprons wrapped around me, learning to scramble eggs."

"That's a wonderful memory. Does your mother do a lot of cooking?"

No matter how many times she was asked a question, any

question about her mother that assumed she was still alive, Abby still found it incredibly hard to answer. This time was no exception. Though she'd lost her parents three years ago, she could still call up the memory of the moment she'd been told. Abby could still feel those feelings, that moment when her heart had stopped, her feelings had frozen, and the only part of her brain that had worked rationally had gently penetrated her state of shock to let her know things would never, ever be the same.

"My mother passed away three years ago." She took a deep breath, let it out slowly. "She and my father died in a plane crash, coming home from a convention."

He was silent for a moment, and in a strange way, she was glad he didn't feel he had to rush in and fill the silence with words.

"How old were you?"

Something in his tone of voice almost made her want to cry.

"I'd just turned twenty-six."

"How horrible."

She liked the fact that he didn't try to cover up what had essentially been the most painful time of her life with platitudes.

"Do you have other family, Abby?"

Briefly, she told him. He guessed the rest.

"So," he said as their salad dishes were cleared away, "you felt you had to give your siblings the stability they needed at the time."

She looked at him, shocked at his perceptiveness. "How could you have known that?"

His smile, so slight, so gentle, touched her. "I was with you today on the beach."

"Oh."

"Any woman who wouldn't care about getting sand on her pants is the sort of woman who would put others first.

You did what had to be done." He reached across the table and touched her hand. "I can understand that."

She simply looked at him and realized that he could.

Dinner was incredibly good. On Abby's private food scale of one to ten, this particular evening rated a ten. And not just because of the company. Harry was a genius in the kitchen. The crab cakes had been light, the cream sauce sublime. Their vegetables hadn't been overcooked, and the rice that had come with both entrées had been delicately spiced. Of course, they'd traded tastes, and Jack's salmon had been cooked to perfection.

"Why did you order fish?" she asked him.

"In my opinion, it's the hardest thing to cook. A minute too long and you can ruin it, fish is so delicate." He lowered his voice and leaned toward her. "I'm checking out the competition, and with Harry just down the street from my restaurant, it's fierce. The Treasure is lucky to have him."

"I agree."

Abby didn't even agonize over dessert and went straight for her favorite, crème brûlée.

"Good choice," Jack said, studying the menu. "What do you recommend?" he said, asking Harry, who hovered over them, clearly wanting this dinner to be memorable.

"I'm experimenting with some chocolate desserts, getting ready for the convention."

"Which one do you like the most?"

"Oh, the mousse is excellent."

"I'll have that." Jack handed him the hand-lettered dessert menu and sat back in his chair.

Abby glanced around their small, private room. The fire burned merrily in the fireplace. Yoda, sated after her dinner, lay sprawled by the fire on a plump cushion, snoring softly. She could hear the distant sounds of conversation and laughter coming from the main dining room, but they didn't seem to touch her. All her awareness was centered on this room, this man, this evening. This moment.

"So, what are your plans for tomorrow?"

Jack's question caught her off guard. She'd been planning to devote Sunday to resting, in preparation for a grueling ten days of seminars. Now, since she'd arrived at the bed-and-breakfast just this morning, her life had taken some different turns. She didn't even have to think about the law until Thursday, and she had a chocolate convention to attend.

"The only thing I have planned is to call the vet first thing in the morning."

"That sounds like the beginning of a plan. Have you ever visited Venice Beach before?"

"Never. I've flown in and out of Los Angeles, but most of what I saw was the inside of my hotel room. Views of downtown."

"All work and no play makes Abby a dull girl."

"Tell me about it."

"We'll have to remedy that. How about if I take you on a grand tour?"

Her heart lifted. Their evening had gone so well, she felt so close to him. There were some people with whom you talked on a deeper level from the moment you met them, almost as if you'd known them before. Jack was one of those people for her, and now she knew he felt the same way. He wanted to spend more time with her.

"I'd like that." She thought of something else. "Even if it rains?"

"Even if it rains."

Harry came bustling into the room again, all arms and legs, bearing a tray with two white coffee-sized cups.

"If the two of you might indulge me for a moment, I'd like you to give me your opinion of this." He set a cup down in front of each of them, and Abby could smell the rich scents of chocolate and milk. Both drinks were topped with whipped cream, and she knew they were in for quite an indulgence.

"You see," said Harry, "the conference here is sponsoring a contest for the best hot chocolate drink, and I thought I might try my hand at it. Enter this particular recipe." He eyed them both. "Give it a taste and tell me what you think."

"Of course." Jack raised the cup to his lips.

Abby did the same.

"Be critical, now," Harry warned.

Abby closed her eyes, better to concentrate on the flavor as it bloomed in her mouth. Harry had used an excellent quality of chocolate, and obviously, whole milk. No two percent stuff for a treat like this! It was simple, and subtle, and stirred the senses. Chocolate, milk, rum, whipped cream. Just a touch of sugar. Delicious.

Sometimes the simplest recipes were the best. This was a drink to make one think of swaying palm trees, trade breezes, and warm sand beneath one's feet. The total opposite of today's rainy day.

"Wonderful," she breathed.

"Ditto," Jack said.

"But something's missing," Harry answered them, his long face worried, his brow furrowed. "It's simple, yes, but I want it to be a show-stopper."

"Give me a moment," Abby said, thinking.

"I'll let you two work," Jack said, leaning back with his mug of hot chocolate. "I'll just enjoy."

Harry hovered anxiously until Abby said one word.

"Nutmeg," she whispered.

"Nutmeg!" Harry said. "Of course!"

Abby opened her eyes and looked at him. "Freshly grated, just a sprinkling over the whipped cream. None of that already-grated stuff."

"Never!" Harry reacted with true horror. "Don't drink any more; I'll be right back." He turned toward Jack. "I'll want your opinion, as a—" He stopped, searching for the right word.

"Noncook," Abby said gently.

"Yes. That works. Stay right there. Don't go anywhere, I'll be right back." Muttering to himself, the chef left the private dining room.

"As if I planned on going anywhere, without my mousse," Jack said, and Abby had to laugh. She liked the way she laughed with Jack, the way he looked at life. Things seemed just a little brighter around him.

Harry returned with a whole nutmeg and a tiny nutmeg grater.

"Just so!" he said, grating a touch over both fluffy mounds of whipped cream. "Now, taste it and tell me what you think."

They did.

"Harry," Jack said, "you've got a winner. It makes me think of pirates and buried treasure, so it's perfect for this place."

"Yes," Abby said slowly, the flavors still on her tongue. "The nutmeg is the perfect touch. It balances the flavors out. And you used quite a good rum."

"Only the best," Harry said. "Now, for your mousse and crème brûlée, and then you can both use this room for the rest of the evening," he said, indicating the comfortable love seat in close proximity to the crackling fire.

Their desserts finished, they retired to their seats in front of the fire.

Yoda raised her head, gave them a look, then yawned, closed her eyes, and settled her head between her tiny paws. She snorted once, then went back to sleep.

"Where did you find her?" Jack asked.

"I was on a business trip to Dallas. It was raining, and I wanted to take a walk, so I headed for this enormous mall. There was a pet shop, and Yoda was sitting in the front window, on sale, just a puppy and looking extremely unhappy at being cooped up. I watched her for a while, kept walking past her sad little face as I exercised, and on the third time around, I just went inside and bought her. I couldn't stand to see her trapped there."

"I can't understand how someone didn't just snap her up."

"Oh, there was some nonsense about her being disqualified from the breed's standards, or something like that."

"What's wrong with her?"

"Her tail is too short."

Yoda whined in her sleep, shifted her head. Abby smiled at her pet.

"But don't tell her that. She has no idea she's not a champion."

Though she loved talking to Jack, the combination of her long day, the plane flight from Chicago, her comfortably full stomach, the wine, and the little bit of rum in the hot chocolate drink served to make Abby's eyelids heavy. She felt like the little girl she'd been so long ago, standing at the head of the stairs in her family home, sneaking out of her bed even though she'd been so sleepy. Knowing that the most magical things always happened at night.

"You need to go to sleep," Jack said.

She blinked and realized her head had been resting on the back of the love seat.

"I'm so sorry. It's not you—"

"I know." He stood up, moved easily, picked a half-asleep Yoda up, and then reached for her hand. "Let's get you to your room."

He saw her to The Juliet Room, and they stood in the hallway for a moment. As tired as Abby was, she felt what happened mere seconds before it did. Jack lowered his head so gently toward hers, the gesture felt so right as his mouth touched hers in a very soft, very gentle kiss.

His instincts were fabulous. Anything more than that, and she might have resisted. But she didn't resist this, the meeting of their lips, that certainty, that lack of awkwardness that made it seem so right. As if they'd been waiting for each other.

She knew he sensed it, too.

She stared up at him for just a moment, then turned, suddenly self-conscious, and unlocked her door. Yoda, still in Jack's arms, gazed adoringly up at him, wagging her stubby little tail. He handed the dog to Abby.

"Good night," she whispered and wished that she had the courage to risk another kiss.

"Good night, Abby. I'll see you in the morning."

She listened against the closed door as he started down the stairs to The Garden Room on the first floor.

She barely had the energy to get out of her glorious red dress, wash the makeup off her face, and slip into her nightgown before she fell into an exhausted sleep, Yoda curled up on one of the plump pillows beside her.

Her dreams, what she could remember of them, were of Jack.

The following morning, a soft knocking at her door disturbed her dreams. In that delicious state between waking and sleeping, Abby wrinkled her nose as the knocking became more insistent, then groaned as she heard Yoda leap to the floor and start yapping as she approached the door.

Opening her eyes, Abby reached for her robe, swiftly tied the sash around her waist, and, not even bothering with her slippers, approached the door and opened it.

Jack stood in the doorway, the handle of a plastic pet carrier in his hand.

All thoughts of more sleep left Abby's mind as she saw the shy little Persian cat face peeping out from the carrier.

"Come in! How is she? What happened?"

Jack entered her room and set the carrier down on one of the overstuffed chairs.

"I went out for an early-morning run, then thought of our

feline friend and called the vet from a pay phone. They were just about to call you, and had no trouble with my picking up our cat and taking her back to The Treasure."

Our cat. She liked the way he'd said that.

"What's the verdict?"

Jack laughed. "She's fine. The only thing that's going to take a little time to heal are the sores around her neck from the fishing line. I held her at the vet's, and it's clear she was someone's pet, she was so eager to be loved. Can I let her out?"

"Of course!" Abby scooped an excited Yoda into her arms, where the tiny Chihuahua wriggled desperately and tried to escape her grip. "Yoda, give her time to get acclimated." She glanced at Jack. "What about a litter box?"

"I have supplies out in the hallway."

Molly was right. Jack was a good man to have around, in an emergency or not.

They fixed a cat box in the bathroom, set up both water and dry food in one corner of the bedroom, and both watched as the Persian made a tentative look-see of the bedroom before she jumped down from her carrier onto the lush carpet. Her gorgeous fur seemed to float behind her.

Yoda wriggled madly, but Abby held firm.

Other than looking slightly peculiar from clumps of her long, thick fur having been shaved, the cat was absolutely gorgeous.

"Look at that fur," she whispered to Jack.

"A black smoke Persian, that's what they called her at the vet's."

The contrast between the fine white undercoat and the black tipping on each strand of silky hair was striking.

"They gave me a cream for the sores on her neck, and some medication." Jack grinned. "Do you have much experience giving cats pills?"

"I've never had to do it before."

"You're in for a treat. I'll help you."

Yoda yipped once in excitement, and the cat turned her broad head, then gazed at the tiny dog with quiet copper eyes.

"She doesn't seem that frightened," Abby whispered.

"Yoda isn't exactly a two hundred pound terror. Does she like cats?"

"Yoda loves everybody. She wants to be friends."

"Let's give it a try," Jack said softly. "Who knows, maybe a little animal company would be good for both of them."

Abby, holding her breath, set her dog down and watched as Yoda made a beeline for the Persian. The Chihuahua pulled up just short of his new pal at the frightened look in those copper cat eyes. Yoda stopped, then wagged her short, stubby tail, then cocked her head to one side, her dark, liquid eyes beseeching.

"Careful, Yoda," Jack said.

One delicate step at a time, the little dog closed the distance between herself and the fluffy cat. Abby watched, still holding her breath, as Yoda's pink tongue flashed out, lapped at the cat's nose. The Persian looked slightly startled, but held her ground.

Yoda wagged her tail, her fawn-colored body quivering.

The cat raised a paw, claws completely sheathed, and patted Yoda's face, then turned and trotted toward the bathroom, Yoda following.

"I'll be damned," Jack said.

"Maybe there was a dog in her life, somewhere in her past," Abby said. "She doesn't seem too scared."

"They're going to get along just fine." Jack looked down at her, a teasing glint in his eyes. "So, how does it feel to be the proud new owner of a cat?"

Abby's first breakfast at The Buried Treasure was one she wouldn't forget soon. The garden sparkled after the rain, the colors of brilliant flowers blooming in profusion. Chairs and tables had been wiped down and set for the morning meal, as weather reports predicted a clear Sunday and even prettier Monday.

"I can't decide between the peach cheese French toast or the artichoke quiche," said Abby.

"Have both. I'm treating you today, and that way, I can take a taste of each and size up my future competition."

"All right." She studied the breakfast menu. "Oh no, strawberry crepes!"

They ended up ordering all three, along with an egg-and-cheese casserole, and two generous slices of homemade coffee cake.

"I'm in serious trouble," Jack said.

"The restaurant?"

"No. My waistline."

She laughed at that. They finished their breakfast with excellent coffee, freshly ground and spiced with just a hint of cinnamon.

"I couldn't eat another bite," Abby whispered after she finished her last sip of coffee. "Why is Harry coming out with a basket of freshly baked blueberry muffins?"

"I think it's a form of torture unique to The Treasure. Ready for that walk I promised you?"

"We're going to have to walk all the way up the coast to Malibu to make up for this breakfast."

He laughed, then said, "Did you enjoy it?"

"Everything was fantastic."

"Then that's all I'm worried about."

They pushed back their chairs and grabbed sweaters and jackets as he said, "Can you cook that well?"

She thought about being modest, but it didn't seem like a day for false modesty.

"Yeah."

"Then you'll have to work for me, just to ensure that my restaurant gets off the ground."

She glanced up at him as they headed out the door and down the stairs. Bright sunshine glinted off the ocean, causing Abby to squint and reach for her sunglasses. "Does this café of yours have a name yet?"

"Not yet. I name businesses totally intuitively. I'll know it when I feel it."

"Hmmm."

"It's not a bad method of making one's way through life."

"I didn't think it would be," she said.

The morning passed quickly. Between the beach, the boardwalk, various shops, and all the tourists, there was plenty to do and see. Abby admired the people on Roller-blades, privately wishing she had enough nerve to try the sport herself. They listened to a one-man blues band, watched a man who swallowed dipsticks, and even attended one of the shows by a man who had christened himself The Texas Chain Saw Juggler.

Abby had to close her eyes through most of his show. She could barely watch a grown man juggling chain saws, though she knew by the size of the crowd this juggler gathered on the boardwalk that he had to be making excellent money and must have been doing this particular show for a long time without any loss of life or limb.

Around lunchtime, they drove in Jack's car up the coast to a restaurant that overlooked the ocean. They feasted on fish and chips and threw some of their French fries to the gulls that wheeled overhead.

"I'm serious about your coming to work with me," Jack said suddenly, out of the blue. They'd finished their meal, with no dessert in deference to their incredibly hearty breakfast, and were now walking along the shore in their bare feet, shoes in hand.

"I'm seriously thinking about it," Abby replied, but inside, she trembled. It was such a huge change. From Chicago to Los Angeles. From a quiet law office to the noise and delicious smells of a professional kitchen. From solitary days going over clauses in contracts to a small crowd of customers in a café.

From a life that was sometimes too lonely to a life working side by side with a man like Jack.

And that kiss . . .

That was the real change. That was what she truly feared. Abby was no fool when it came to emotions. She felt the subtle, humming current that existed so effortlessly when she and Jack were in the same room. What would happen if she took the job he offered her, and something went wrong with their relationship? Could she continue to cook in his café, night after night, and not have serious regrets about the choice she had made?

Either way, she couldn't remain in this particular limbo. A decision had to be made.

"Jack," she said softly, her voice barely audible above the pounding of the waves.

"Yes?"

She stopped. Looked up at him, certain he could see the trepidation in her eyes.

"Would you show me your restaurant?"

THREE

The property was located only six doors down from The Buried Treasure. In between, she counted a French bakery with glorious pastries in its glass-fronted windows, a gourmet coffeehouse currently packed with customers, the fragrance of freshly ground coffee beans spilling outside into the misty air, and a clothing store with tie-dyed slip dresses and brilliant T-shirts. She also spotted a small newsstand beneath a dark blue awning, a card shop with spinning racks of colorful postcards, and a gourmet pizza stand that sold the incredibly tasty smelling pies by the slice.

Each of the storefronts faced the cement boardwalk, which was filled with people walking their dogs, Roller-blading, or hurrying to various destinations.

As Jack unlocked the massive double doors, Abby could already visualize what the restaurant could be.

The ceilings were high, the three separate rooms large, but they still had a feeling of intimacy. There was room for tables out on the generous balcony that overlooked the boardwalk and the ocean. As she studied the area, she could picture tubs of bright flowers outside, spilling over their terra-cotta pots, and the walls painted a beautiful cream to contrast with the reddish tiles on the roof. The building had a Mediterranean feel to it, which seemed absolutely perfect for the food Jack planned to serve, the ambiance he wanted to create.

"It's a wonderful old building," she said as she walked around. He wasn't so much studying the building as he was watching her. She was aware of his gaze as she explored, taking it all in.

"I like it," he said. "I like the location even better."

She knew what he meant. Restaurants were one of the riskiest businesses to open. So many of them, even with wonderful food and excellent management, went out of business after less than a year. Location was everything, yet that still couldn't guarantee success. But Abby had no doubt that Jack would succeed, situated as he was in a tourist locale and right down the street from an extremely successful bed-and-breakfast.

"Do you want to see the kitchen?"

She nodded, knowing exactly what he was up to, and followed him into a large room in back. The area was absolutely immaculate, equipped with two professional stoves, three huge, stainless steel refrigerators, and incredibly large sinks. Pots and various utensils hung everywhere. Even though Jack couldn't cook, and it certainly wasn't his goal to prepare the food in his restaurant, he clearly understood the kind of professional equipment his chef would need.

For the fleetest of seconds, Abby wanted to be that chef.

"What do you think?"

"It's wonderful." She followed him through several other rooms clearly designed for storage, to one particular back room that opened out on to an alley and had a loading dock.

Clearly, Jack had thought of everything.

"When do you see yourself being open for business?"

"Another six weeks at the latest." He glanced down at her. "But you'd be cooking the entire time, because we'd be working out the menus and setting up the wine cellar. I'd want a working partnership with you, Abby. You'd have just as much say in what was served as I would."

If he had taken her most secret dream and created an entire blueprint of it, this restaurant, the kitchen, the location, and the chance to truly create a distinctive menu would have been it. Her dream had suddenly come to life. And Jack Hayes was offering it to her.

Conflicting feelings froze any decision. Overwhelming happiness was followed by a crushing fear. Standing in the empty building, her fingers restlessly twisting the strap of her leather purse, Abby came to a sudden and not-so-happy realization about herself. Her decision to create stability for her younger siblings had been an extremely creative and convenient way of making sure she never had to go out on a professional limb, go after what she really wanted, and risk failure.

Now Jack was offering her a chance to try again, before it was too late, before she became truly entrenched in her law office back in Chicago. But a part of her, the part that was scared of change, of the unknown, wanted to get on the next flight back to the Midwest and walk into her office the following morning, forgetting this trip and this man had ever happened to her.

Because the man, on one level, was ever so much more frightening than the dream.

Stalling, she said, "Did you give any thought to music?"

"You read my mind," he said. "Los Angeles is so full of talent, I thought I might set up a small stage area near the bar and highlight local musicians. Give them a chance to play for the joy of it, pay them very well, and let the patrons enjoy a little live music."

"It sounds great."

"But," he said, taking her elbow and guiding her into the

large kitchen, "I still need a chef, and I still want you to consider taking the job. It could be a lot of fun, Abby."

Jack was the only person she knew who could consider something as risky as opening a restaurant "fun." He was like no one she'd ever met. Yet she knew if she went along on this particular venture, it *would* be fun. The chance of a lifetime.

"I need a little more time to think about things," she said, hedging.

"Take all the time you need. I just hope your answer is yes."

She knew he was talking about more than the restaurant when he pulled her into his arms and kissed her again. Their second kiss. Just as gentle as the first, and she didn't feel at all uneasy, alone with him as she was. It felt perfectly right, being in his arms.

So perfectly right that it scared her. How could something that felt this right happen this fast?

He didn't pressure her for anything more than that simple kiss, and Abby was grateful. Jack locked the door after them, and then they walked back to the bed-and-breakfast, talking the entire way.

"I have this theory," said Jack as they strolled along. Somewhere along the way, he'd taken her hand, and Abby discovered she didn't mind. "It's a wonderful thing, being lazy, and totally undervalued in this culture. I think we all work too hard to begin with, don't you?"

She thought of the phones ringing at the law firm, her hurried sandwiches at her desk, the late nights with the city sparkling outside her windows as her eyes burned from reading fine print. And the headaches as she fell asleep most nights, totally drained.

"Yes. I know I do."

"This café is going to be a respite for people, a place where they can go to relax, be with friends and family, enjoy a good meal, great conversation, some music, and a bottle of wine. I want it to be a place that creates happy memories."

"You could call it the Memory Café," she said, as they started up the stairs of the gray-shingled beach house that was The Buried Treasure.

"It doesn't sound right. Like I said, I work intuitively when it comes to names. I'll know it when I feel it."

Back at the bed-and-breakfast, Molly enlisted both of them into helping her decorate for the chocolate convention that was to begin tomorrow morning.

"We need to string lights in the garden," she said, reminding Jack of a petite general, totally in command. "Thank God they aren't predicting any more rain for a while." Molly said this while handing those lights to Jack, who took them from her with a good-natured smile and motioned for Abby to help him.

He thought furiously as they worked together.

He'd done everything he could to convince her to stay and give the restaurant a chance. Once he had more time with her, he'd convince her to give him a chance, as well.

But maybe he was going about this all wrong, Jack thought as he carefully wound another string of little white lights around the branches of the trees surrounding the patio area. Maybe what he should be doing was convincing Abby that they would make a terrific couple, that he could see them together for the rest of their lives. It didn't really matter to him if she cooked in his restaurant or not. Abby could be a beachcomber and he would still want her in his life.

Yet he sensed that this new approach would scare her even more. But if he didn't lead with his heart and tell her the truth concerning how he felt about her, Jack had a feeling she would get on that plane after her legal convention was over and head back to Chicago as quickly as possible.

Back to a job she wasn't happy with, but a routine she found very comfortable.

He'd watched his uncle, who he had adored, do exactly the same thing, finally breaking out when he retired to do all the things he'd dreamed of. But illness had claimed him within two years of his retirement. Sitting in the sunny hospital room with his uncle, Jack had vowed never to make the same mistake.

So what if there were rough times and unpredictable highs and lows? Those came with the territory called life. Everyone had problems, but they were much more bearable if you followed your heart and at least worked at making dreams come true.

He started, then glanced down and saw Yoda at his feet. The Chihuahua had jumped up on the chair he was standing on, and now stared up at him, those dark eyes so very wise. Jack glanced across the courtyard, where Abby was talking with Molly and obtaining another string of the twinkling white lights.

He made eye contact with the little dog. "You know, you're probably the only laughs she's had in years."

Yoda whined and wagged her stubby tail anxiously. Jack reached down and petted the little dog, his fingers caressing the tiny, tawny head.

"I wish I had a magic word that would make her stay. That would take that little crease of worry and wipe it off her forehead, that would take that anxious look out of those beautiful gray eyes. But I'm working on it, pal."

Yoda whined again.

"Hey, I know. You don't want to go back to Chicago any more than I want to see the two of you go. I can't imagine you negotiating snowdrifts when you could be running on the beach and chasing seagulls. And what about your new friend upstairs? What's going to happen there, huh?"

The Chihuahua sat up on her hind legs and scrabbled against the legs of his well-worn, most comfortable jeans.

Jack set the strand of lights aside and picked up the little dog, who promptly wriggled with glee and licked his face furiously, grunting and whining.

"We'll work as a team," Jack whispered, his attention on Abby as she started to cross the back patio. "We'll figure this out, Yoda. Because we can't let her go back home."

They had dinner together, going over the chocolate conference pamphlet Molly had given each of them and trying to decide which of the many seminars they were going to take.

"It's a great deal, three free seminars for each of the guests," Abby said as she studied her pamphlet. "Which ones are you going to take?"

Whichever ones you are, Jack wanted to say, but wisely refrained. As someone who knew he was barely competent in a kitchen, he'd already decided to leave the selection up to Abby.

"Listen to this one. The Best Chocolate Chip Cookies You'll Ever Make! That sounds like a winner."

"Cookies are always popular," he said. "It wouldn't hurt to get the recipes for the café."

He watched as her gray eyes darkened, and that little worry line reappeared between her eyebrows. And Jack could have kicked himself. He'd wanted this evening together to be fun.

"Let's take that one," he said, deciding to get her back into thinking about which seminars to take. "And how about this one? Chocolate Quick Breads, Muffins, and Waffles."

"Chocolate waffles. It boggles the mind."

She was smiling again, and Jack was glad.

"And," said Jack, "we have to attend the seminar on hot chocolate drinks, because at the end of the session, they're going to announce who won the competition, and I'm hoping it's Harry with that rum concoction of his."

He watched as she marked her pamphlet, then set her pen down and sighed.

"I wish I could take all of them. You know, that one track that allows you to take any seminar you want."

"Why don't you?"

She didn't answer him, and he knew why. The answer hung in the air between them. As of Thursday, Abby would be at her legal seminar, and all thoughts of chocolate would have to be banished from her mind.

"It's just a thought."

"What are you going to do, Jack?"

"I'm going to sign up for the grand tasting tour of all the exhibits, and when I find something that makes my mouth sing and my eyes weep, I'm going to get down on my knees and try to finagle the recipe out of the person who created it."

She started to laugh, and it made his heart glad.

The following morning, Abby woke up with a keen sense of anticipation. She showered and dressed quickly in a short, cotton, flowered dress she'd managed to sneak off and buy at one of the little boutiques near the boardwalk. It was nothing at all like what she usually wore, a riot of color with a distinctly playful feel, yet the dress felt exactly right.

She couldn't help smiling as she saw Yoda and her cat curled up together in the window seat, the two of them snoozing in the bright sunshine. And it struck her that her dog had probably been lonely a great deal of the time, as she'd been left alone while Abby was in the office.

Abby's eyes stung as she thought of how happily Yoda had greeted her each night as she'd unlocked her apartment door. Now, with a furry friend, she wouldn't be as lonely. Until this moment, she hadn't realized that Yoda might need a little company.

And you could say the same for yourself.

She couldn't push the thought away. A part of her was glad that Jack hadn't moved in like some kind of player, smooth and sophisticated, trying to get her into bed within moments of their meeting each other. She liked the fact that he was giving her time to get used to him. She liked his kisses. If they had been dating, this morning would have been their third date, not counting their meeting on the beach. That first dinner, Saturday, would have qualified as their first official date.

They'd spent all day Sunday together, touring Venice Beach, seeing his restaurant, helping Molly set up, and having dinner together. He'd asked her to come with him to the chocolate convention, so this was their third date. Yet she felt as if she'd known him for a much longer time than that.

Back in the bathroom, she studied her appearance. For once in her life, she wanted to look as far removed as possible from that corporate lawyer from Chicago. This dress did the trick. It was a style a woman would wear for a very casual afternoon, as were the sandals. She'd pulled her shoulder-length hair back into a high ponytail and kept her makeup simple.

After giving Yoda and her cat each a pat, she locked the door behind her and started down the stairs.

Abby looked absolutely wonderful. Playful and cute and ready to have fun.

"I like that dress," he said as she came down the stairs. She didn't have to know that he'd been sitting in this chair at the bottom of the stairs waiting for her since just around sunrise. And thinking.

"Thanks."

"Breakfast?"

She laughed. "Not like yesterday. I have a feeling we're going to be eating a lot of chocolate today."

"Then lead on."

They ate out on the flower-filled patio, among all the other guests who were thrilled about the chocolate convention. Jack ordered an omelet, juice, and toast, but Abby went for coddled eggs and a blueberry-bran muffin.

"This is interesting," she said, after they'd both shared a few bites. "I would think a spinach omelet could have the potential to be extremely boring, but I can't quite figure out what Harry did to make it so good."

"He's not going to be giving away any of his secrets to me, not with my opening a restaurant so close by. Maybe you can get it out of him."

"I'll give it a try. Now, this is a case of presentation being everything. I love these porcelain cups my eggs are served in. Jack, you should remember this for breakfasts."

"I'll remember to tell my chef," he said, resisting the urge to tell her that she was the only chef he wanted.

They sat in on the first seminar, free to the public, which was essentially a history of chocolate and how it had been used throughout the centuries. And Jack made Abby laugh when he said that at least two good things had come from Mexico: chocolate and Chihuahuas. Then they went straight to the class on spectacular, gourmet, one-of-a-kind cookies. This was a hands-on cooking class, and even though Jack had sensed Abby was a good cook, her expertise in the kitchen was amazing.

They were paired as partners, and he watched as she swiftly incorporated the flour, baking powder, and salt into the creamy brown sugar, butter, egg, and vanilla mixture. The woman teaching this particular seminar started with a basic cookie recipe, then gave at least twenty-five variations. By the end of the seminar, all of the participants were eating cookies hot out of the oven.

"You see, Abby, we make a great team. You bake cookies, and I eat them."

She had to laugh at that. Then Jack saw his chance.

She took a bite of an exquisite chocolate chunk cookie, and the still-warm chocolate smeared slightly around her lips. Trying not to think too hard, Jack gently cupped the back of her neck with one hand, pulled her close with another, then lowered his mouth to hers and kissed her.

Really kissed her.

Time literally stopped.

Oh, she'd heard the expression before, but never really believed it.

She'd been kissed before, but never really believed those kisses, either.

Now, with Jack's arm around her, his other hand cradling her head, his lips covering hers, Abby found she couldn't think, couldn't move, could barely breathe. It wasn't that she was scared. It was that something extraordinary was happening to her, something that would rock her world, whether she wanted her world rocked or not.

She'd never really understood what people meant when they talked about chemistry, because it had never happened to her. But now, this feeling of rightness coupled with an emotional reaction so strong it almost started her trembling—this was what poets had written about since time began.

They broke apart, their lips still close. She could barely hear the noises of people cleaning up their work areas, the bustle that ensued as they packed their cookies in boxes the teacher had provided. All Abby could see was Jack's face, mere inches from hers.

His hazel eyes seemed concerned, and she realized he was waiting for her reaction.

"Jack," she whispered, knowing her face had to be revealing all she felt for this man. She'd never been one who had wanted to play games when it came to loving someone.

He smiled down at her. "I couldn't resist."

She knew he wasn't talking about the chocolate.

They made it through one more seminar, on spectacular, show-stopping desserts, before Abby took Jack's hand and walked upstairs with him to her room. She slipped the DO NOT DISTURB sign on the door, locked it, and walked over to the large bay window and closed the curtains.

Nothing in her life had ever prepared her for this moment.

It was on the tip of her tongue to say, "I've never done this before, been this intimate this fast," but she realized that words were meaningless. Jack wouldn't care. It was obvious to her that he felt it, too, that he had been just as shaken by the brief contact of their lips. And that he wanted more, wanted to know more.

She knew all the rules one usually followed in creating a relationship, but found that none of the rules applied when someone like Jack came along. And more than anything else, she knew that even though she might not be capable of staying in this beach town with this extraordinary man, she wanted the memories. She didn't want to end her life and never have an experience like the one she was sure they were about to have.

Yoda and the cat were curled up together, fast asleep on the window seat. After she closed the drapes, she looked at Jack from across the room. Closed the distance between them. Stood in front of him, then raised her hands and tentatively touched his broad shoulders. And the moment she touched him, she knew.

How could your heart feel so at home with another's? How could she feel, just before his lips touched hers, that she'd finally come home? Abby didn't question the emotions that flooded her as Jack kissed her. She simply held on, and when he broke that second kiss, she couldn't tell if she was trembling or he was.

"This is different for me," she managed to whisper as their lips parted. Then she rested her forehead against his chest and listened to his heartbeat.

"Me, too," he said, his voice low and slightly rough with emotion. And she smiled at the sound of it, and raised her head for another kiss. One blended into another, so smoothly, so swiftly, letting excitement build until he picked her up in his arms and carried her to the canopied bed.

The upstairs floor was so silent, the only thing she could hear was their breathing, their heartbeats. She still sensed hesitancy in Jack and kissed his cheek just below his ear. "Touch me," she whispered. "Jack, I want you to touch me."

He did, and the sensations that shot through her body were indescribable. No one had ever touched her so deeply before physically touching her, so now that they were in the realm of the physical, it simply made it all the better. She found herself unafraid, wanting his touch, moving toward it, and totally at ease as he slipped the dress off her body, the sandals off her feet, and she found herself lying in bed with Jack with only her white lace underwear on.

She started to laugh as he unhooked her bra with one hand.

"What?" he whispered, then kissed her.

"I knew you'd be good at this," she whispered back.

"Because of you," he said.

Then his hand closed over her breast and she forgot everything except the sensations evoked there. She wanted him to move faster, she couldn't get close to him fast enough, a part of her was shocked at how much she wanted this man. She cupped his head in her hands, running her fingers through his thick hair, then urged him down her body until he took her nipple in his mouth. The warmth and wetness and gentle tugging made her catch fire, caused a flushing heat to pool between her legs where she wanted him even more desperately.

Her hands went to his shirt, her fingers seeking the buttons, wanting his naked body against hers, not even wanting the thin barrier of cotton cloth. He sat up in bed long enough to shrug out of his shirt, then slip off his shoes and socks, then unzip his pants and skim them down over his hips. He left his boxer shorts on, and she knew that even though he wanted her, he didn't want to rush her.

She didn't care. At this moment in her life, she wanted to dive off that cliff, to take that leap of faith. She'd denied herself for so long, denied that deepest part of herself, that now she wanted it all. She wanted Jack.

"I want you naked," she whispered. She, who would have laughed out loud if anyone had told her she would say those words to a man, let alone a man she'd met only two days ago, told him what she wanted. But she didn't stop to question it, didn't give herself time to be afraid.

He raised an eyebrow at her, then smiled the most seductive smile, just for her, as he hooked his thumbs in his boxers and shimmied them off his hips.

And he was beautiful. So beautiful that her breath hitched in her throat as he took her hand and pulled her gently toward him. He had a beautiful body, muscled and firm, those muscles now taut with excitement. That humming energy had turned into an intense crackling; she couldn't take her eyes off him. It was obvious he wanted her, he didn't have a way of hiding his intense desire, and it made him slightly vulnerable in her eyes, which made her want him all the more.

"Jack," she said, touching his chest, running her fingers through the hair on the warm, muscled surface. "You're so beautiful." She didn't stop to question the note of wonder in her voice. He stunned her, this man in her bed. He'd totally caught her by surprise, from the first moment they'd met on the beach.

"You're the beauty here," he said, then eased her down on the bed.

Somewhere along the line, he removed her lace panties. And somewhere farther along, when she was flushed and almost helpless with desire, when he rose up over her and eased her legs apart, then started to enter her body, she knew she'd lost her heart.

His eyes held hers as he established that sensual rhythm, their gazes locked. His intense, hers so filled with wonder that he suddenly smiled.

"Abby," he said so softly before he kissed her, and she knew she'd never heard her name spoken that way before, and that no one would ever say it the same way Jack did.

She couldn't speak, she felt so full of emotion. She closed her eyes, feeling the way he took possession of her body, the way he built sensation, escalating it to an almost painful point, to the brink.

Her eyes flew open, she gripped his shoulders tightly, her head went back, and she heard him whisper, "Yes, yes, *yes!*"

Then she heard nothing at all. Muscles contracted, she felt that intense release, but it was so much more than the physical. She reached out to Jack as she climaxed, grabbing his arm, her eyes closed, her mouth open as if in pain. She held on to him, knowing that she had to take him where she was going, that it didn't mean anything at all without this man who had already given her so much.

"Jack!" she said, for just an instant worried she'd lost him. Her fingers dug into his forearm, her other hand reached up and grabbed his muscular shoulder, then she felt his body shudder, felt his surrender. And it completed her, knowing she could give him that. Knowing that they could create something this beautiful together. Her fingers clenched, almost spasmed as she kept hold of him, knowing in her heart that she couldn't bear to ever let him go.

Her eyes came open and she saw he was watching her.

"How long did I sleep?"

He smiled, then kissed her. "Does it matter?"

She thought about that for an instant. "I guess not."

"You needed the rest," he said, pulling the covers up around her bare shoulders. And Abby realized that sometime while she slept, he'd tucked her in. The thought filled her with a warm pleasure.

"There is something serious we have to talk about, though."

His tone surprised her. "What?"

"You have to give this poor feline a name. We can't continue calling her Yoda's cat for the rest of her life."

She laughed at that and moved closer toward him until her head was resting in the crook of his shoulder. Down by her feet, she could feel both Yoda and the smoke-colored Persian cat.

"You name her," she said. "I haven't a clue."

"I've been thinking about this," he said, playing with a strand of her hair. "We could go with something out of the classical world, her having been tossed up out of the sea like Aphrodite. But that seems like an awfully big mouthful for such a delicate little cat."

"I agree."

"Then I thought of something simple, like Smoky, because of her coat. But it seemed too simple for a cat like her."

"I know exactly what you mean."

"How did you name Yoda?"

Hearing her name, the Chihuahua made her way up through the tangled bedclothes and settled herself on Jack's chest.

"It should be obvious. She looks so much like the character in *Star Wars*. I also thought she was wise that way. She's a smart little dog."

"I agree. So you've already thought of giving this cat a name from the trilogy?"

"Leia just didn't cut it."

"No," Jack said. "She doesn't look like a Leia."

"And definitely not something like Wookie. What were those fluffy things in the forest, that looked like teddy bears?"

"The Ewoks. Not a particularly flattering name."

"I'm tapped out." She turned into his shoulder and

sighed. "I leave it up to you, or this poor cat will go throughout life without a name."

"Callista," he said. "Greek for 'most beautiful.' You could call her Callie for short."

"That's very pretty." Abby raised herself up on one elbow and glanced down at the fluffy cat curled up at the foot of the canopied queen-sized bed. "Callie? Do you like that name?"

The Persian raised her head and gave a soft meow.

"Yoda?" Jack said. "What do you think?"

The little dog vigorously licked Jack's face until he started to laugh.

"All right. Callista, it is."

By mutual agreement, they showered and made their way downstairs to the chocolate convention, where Jack surprised Abby by revealing that he had bought them each a Master Taster ticket that entitled them to attend any of the seminars for the rest of the week. She found herself totally touched by his present.

"You're trying to tempt me to be very bad," she said, as they wandered the sampling room and tasted first chocolate candy, then fudge, and then small pieces of cake.

"I'm trying to tempt you to have fun," he said. "Until Thursday, at least."

He bought her a chocolate necklace, then a small box of Champagne truffles.

"What's your favorite candy?" he asked.

"I like buttercreams. There's one made with white chocolate and lime that this one candy store makes back in Chicago—"

"I'll find something similar."

They attended the seminar on Gourmet Hot Chocolate Drinks and watched as Harry claimed second prize with his rum hot chocolate. First prize went to a contestant who created a very decadent drink flavored with hazelnut liqueur.

Harry wasn't disappointed. "Second prize! And this was a nationwide contest. First, second, and third prizewinners get to name their drinks, and their pictures and the recipes are going to be printed in a national cooking magazine! It'll be wonderful publicity for this place!"

"Excellent," said Jack. "What are you going to call it?"

"I was thinking of Chocolate Grog, in keeping with the pirate theme, and with it being created here at The Buried Treasure. But I have another few weeks to come up with a name."

Abby could feel Jack eyeing her. "Well, I know how hard it can be to come up with the perfect name," he said. "There was a cat I once knew who almost had to do without."

"Very funny," she whispered, as Harry hurried back into the kitchen.

"I thought we might have dinner tonight, in my room."

Her heart sped up at the thought of more time alone with Jack. Abby saw no reason to be coy with him. After all, they only had a few days left to spend together before she went back to her law seminar, and ultimately, to Chicago.

She would enjoy what time she had left with Jack.

"I'd like that," she said.

"Around seven, after the convention closes down for the night?"

"I'll be there."

He frowned. "I hadn't really planned on letting you out of my sight today."

"Okay."

"You're all right with that?"

"Of course I am." She reached up and tapped his brow. "Don't frown. Let's live for the moment." She consulted her brochure, then said, "There's a wonderful seminar on chocolate ice cream coming up. Are you game?"

"For anything."

FOUR

He'd lost her somewhere along the line, only he didn't know where.

They attended the ice cream seminar, then had dinner in his room. Jack had enlisted Harry's aid in pulling out all the stops. His room had been filled with flowers and candlelight, there had been an excellent bottle of champagne on ice, the five-course meal would have made angels weep, even the dessert had been spectacular. He'd requested her favorite, crème brûlée, thinking Abby might like a break from all that chocolate.

Afterward, she'd gone into his arms and they'd made love again. She'd fallen asleep in his bed, and he'd watched her sleep, all the time feeling that she'd put up a thin wall between them, so sheer it could barely be seen. But it was there, nonetheless. And he didn't know how to tear it down. He felt like one of the princes from the storybooks his mother had read to him as a child, who had to tear away at the wall of thorns surrounding the castle in order to get to the princess inside and rescue her.

Only in this case, it wasn't as simple as taking a broad-sword and slashing away at a few pesky enchanted thorns. The wall he had to surmount was firmly in place within Abby's emotional makeup. It would have to be her decision, and hers alone, whether or not she chose to let him any closer.

He'd been so elated at the fact that they'd made love this afternoon that he hadn't noticed when she'd slowly started to put her guard up. Now, studying her as she slept, he noticed the little furrows marring the smoothness of her forehead, even in sleep. She was worried about something, he could tell. And it didn't take all that much deduction to figure out that he was the cause of her worries.

She'd come out here for a simple legal seminar, and he'd offered her a chance to completely change her life. On the spot. No real time to think, just make the decision, move two thousand miles to the edge of the Pacific Ocean, and help him open his café. A restaurant, one of the riskiest business ventures of all. And she had a law degree and an office in a very old and prestigious law firm that was run by her uncle.

Talk about security.

Well, Jack had had just about enough of security. He'd seen what searching after security had done to his own uncle. He'd heard his last words in that sterile hospital room, the yearning in the older man's voice for dreams not attempted, journeys not taken. And he'd sworn to himself after he'd left the room, after his uncle had taken his last breath, that his own life wouldn't turn out like that.

Not even close.

So far, he'd been incredibly fortunate. Lucky, some people would call him. But luck wasn't the word. Just because he took chances, it didn't make them totally insane chances. He'd waited for this particular building to come up for sale, this particular location, for almost three years. Then he'd acted quickly, bought the property, and put his plan into effect.

Not for him, the slow death of an office and the nine-to-five corporate world. He'd had a taste of that, thank you very much. He hadn't much liked it. His uncle's passing had sealed his views on that particular subject. Life, for Jack, was an incredible gift, and not to be wasted. Failure didn't scare him.

But Abby Sheridan did.

How could a grown man, thirty-four years old, be ready to commit incredible amounts of money to a restaurant and not be afraid? A business venture that could—despite careful planning and research—possibly go belly up? How could he be ready to do this and not be as frightened by that decision as he was by the thought of laying his feelings on the line for one woman?

It boggled his mind.

He thought about waking Abby this instant, getting down on his knees, asking her to marry him. If that was what it took to get her to stay here with him and not go back to Chicago, he'd do it. Come to think of it, marriage to Abby wasn't that bad an idea. Jack was just afraid she'd think he was crazy. They'd known each other only three days. Not enough time, in most sensible people's estimation, to make one of the most important decisions of one's life.

But he knew. And strangely enough, he'd known from that first moment on the beach, when she'd turned an anxious face to him as she'd bent over their cat, Callista, in the sand.

How did you tell someone, "I just had a feeling?" Jack based most of his actions on feelings, because he'd seen where thinking got people. He'd seen where it had gotten his uncle. A nice, sterile hospital room and enough regrets to last the rest of his life—which hadn't been that long.

He studied Abby in the firelight, the play of flickering firelight over her delicate cheekbones. The way her eyelashes rested on her cheeks. She looked exactly like the princess in those storybooks his mother had read to him, for Jack knew he was nothing if not a romantic.

Now his only problem was how to convince Abby they were meant for each other, and she was meant to stay in this beach town and was the only person he could even think of hiring to cook in his restaurant. And the only woman he could ask to share his life.

Jack sighed as he stared at the ceiling, his arms behind his head. He had only six more days to convince Abby—four of which she would spend out of his sight.

The phone started to ring just as Abby entered her room. She'd wanted to check on Yoda and Callista, but seeing that they were curled up cozily in their favorite window seat in a little patch of sun and sleeping peacefully, she answered the phone.

"All ready for that seminar?" her uncle Pat's voice boomed over the long-distance line right after she said hello.

"Yes," she said. The legal seminar that had been delayed was set to start tomorrow morning.

But the truth was, she'd never felt closer to just skipping the whole thing. If Abby could have played hooky from her own life, she would have forfeited the seminar and attended the rest of the chocolate convention with Jack. But how could she say that to her conservative uncle without sounding as if she'd completely lost her mind?

"Hmmm, I wish I could be there myself. I hear Cameron's going to put on quite a show."

Abby clutched the receiver as if it were a lifeline. Somewhere along the line, she didn't know how, she'd lost her taste for law and everything that applied to it. She didn't care if Jonathan Cameron gave the most brilliant lecture on law in the history of mankind. She would have been quite happy if she'd never read another legal brief, another contract, in her life.

She tried to think of the words that would make her uncle understand what she was going through, but he led the conversation down another path.

"I talked with Katie the other day," her uncle Pat said, referring to Abby's little sister. "She told me she's considering taking a year off and traveling around Europe once she graduates."

Abby hated the quick flash of envy this announcement produced. She had a quiet code of honor about such feelings. You could feel whatever sort of envy or jealousy you wanted to. But you could never act on it, never try to hurt the person in question.

She'd never want to hurt her sister. But for just a moment, Abby wished she'd had a similar opportunity given to her at an age when she could have done something with it.

Isn't Jack offering you an opportunity? All you have to do is have the courage to take it.

"Abby? Abby, are you still there?" Her uncle's voice sounded concerned.

"What? Yes, I . . . I think I'm just getting a headache, that's all."

"Take a walk in that clear, ocean air. Breathe deeply, and that should clear all the cobwebs out of your head."

It would take more than a walk to help her deal with this mess.

"I will, Uncle Pat. Say hello to Mary for me."

They talked barely a minute more, then Abby hung up and walked quietly toward the balcony that ran the entire length of the room. No wonder Molly had christened it The Juliet Room. Knowing how soothing just sitting out in the sunshine could be, Abby opened the door and stepped out onto the balcony that overlooked an incredible view of the Pacific.

Even though it was a Wednesday afternoon, there were plenty of people on the beach and the boardwalk, sunning, drinking sodas out of coolers, Rollerblading, and walking in the surf. Abby stared out over the expanse of beach and wondered if any of them had ever wrestled with a problem like hers. Or had they all been born footloose and free?

Somehow, when it came right down to it, she knew she didn't believe she had the right to certain dreams. She'd never been able to understand how these things were so effortless for some people and such agony for her. Many women would have jumped at the chance to be Jack's new chef and would have moved out to the West Coast without a second thought about the consequences of their actions.

She wasn't many women.

She felt torn between what her head told her she should want and what her heart was trying to tell her she did want. For just a moment, she had the craziest urge to call her uncle back and tell him she'd decided to quit the firm, and she was going to stay in California for the rest of her life with a man named Jack.

The phone rang, and, thinking it might be her uncle, Abby went inside and picked up the receiver.

Jack.

"Hey, I thought I'd call and see if you'd care to have dinner with me tonight."

Abby hesitated. It was becoming harder and harder to spend time with Jack, knowing she was just going to have to return to the Midwest. In another week, the time she'd spent here would seem like a dream. Part of her wanted to spend every waking hour with this man, while the more cautious part of her was afraid, and wouldn't have minded leaving right now.

"I . . . I can't. I have a really early seminar tomorrow, and I've got to do some reading."

Jack was silent. She waited for him to put an end to the conversation, say good-bye and hang up, but instead he said, "Tell me a time you're taking a break. I'll give you one of my world-famous shoulder massages and bring you up a treat from Harry's kitchen."

Tears filled her eyes, though she struggled to keep them out of her voice. "That would be wonderful. How about around eight-thirty?"

"I'll be there."

This was getting serious. She was pulling away from him. Jack knew he had to do something before Abby decided to run back to Chicago and never return.

It wasn't that hard to figure her out. While she'd struggled to give her younger siblings a sense of security after their parents had died, no one had thought to do the same for levelheaded Abby. She'd been hurting inside, but if he knew her as well as he sensed he did, she'd toughed her way through it, shown the world a hard little exterior, and never given anyone a clue that her soft heart was dying.

She'd done what was expected, been a good soldier. And it was making her miserable.

"We'll have to put a stop to that," he said, talking with Yoda as they walked along the beach. "She doesn't even know how unhappy she is."

He'd stopped by Abby's room to take the Chihuahua for her evening walk so Abby could prepare herself for the legal seminar tomorrow. In Jack's opinion, the finer points of contract law didn't sound one bit as fascinating as the chocolate seminar on fantasy cake decorating that was being held in The Rosebud Room the same morning.

Of course, the chocolate seminar wouldn't be any fun at all without Abby there.

"She saw that you were unhappy in a cage. Why can't she see the same thing for herself?"

Yoda barked as she strained against her leash, determined to run after a seagull that had stolen a piece of hot dog another bird had found on the beach.

"Ah, you're no help," Jack said as he sat down near the shoreline. Yoda immediately ran up, jumped into his lap, and smothered his face with kisses.

"Okay, okay, I apologize." Jack stared out over the ocean, watching the sun as it began to make its slow descent, washing the sky with brilliant purples and pinks.

"She's in that room, Yoda, and she should be out here, watching the sunset with us, a glass of wine in her hand. We should all be walking along the beach, and she should be laughing, not studying. She's done enough of that to last a lifetime."

Yoda whined, then snuggled deeper into his lap.

"Four days. I've got four days, and I've got to make them count."

Yoda licked his face reassuringly, then cocked her head and whined.

"The grand gesture, you say? Throw out all stops? Well, you know Abby better than I do."

The tiny dog quivered with excitement and started to bark.

"I'll do it." Jack reached into his pocket and took out a baggie filled with doggie treats. He broke off a piece and handed it to Yoda.

"Thanks, buddy. I owe you one."

The keynote speaker was deadly boring.

Abby had more fun the evening before when Jack had knocked on her door and proceeded to wheel in a tea cart filled with delicacies. An entire high tea for two, courtesy of The Buried Treasure, complete with several bracing cups of tea guaranteed to keep her up for the few more hours she needed to gain a complete understanding of the material they were going to cover tomorrow.

They'd feasted on cucumber sandwiches, egg salad sandwiches, freshly baked scones, strawberry preserves, Devonshire cream, and slices of lemon cake that were a tart relief from all the chocolate they'd both been sampling.

That, and the shoulder massage, and she'd been in ecstasy. Callista had enthusiastically eaten her share of the cream, and Yoda had begged and begged and danced around on her hind legs until she'd been given some bits of scone.

Abby had to bring herself back to the present with a start as everyone in the vast hotel ballroom, seated at their rows of tables, turned the page of their handout at the same time. She'd doodled with her fountain pen while the main speaker had droned on and on. Now, as she glanced down at the legal pad in front of her, she realized she'd been sketching Jack's face, his high cheekbones and well-defined jaw.

He was all she could think about.

This wasn't just a case of a lovesick woman throwing over her career for love. She hadn't wanted to practice law for years. Abby didn't want to be in this hotel ballroom cum lecture hall. She had never, in her entire life, wanted so badly to be anywhere else than she did right now. Covertly glancing at the other conference attendees, she saw their rapt attention directed at the speaker.

For an instant, it seemed to Abby as if she were reliving the moment she'd seen the announcement of the plane crash on television. No survivors. She'd known the number of her parents' flight, and as she'd sat perfectly still and numb in front of the television screen, she'd finally understood the meaning of that old saying: *Life is too short.*

She felt the same way now. Glancing at the sketch of Jack, she thought that there were many ways a person could die. She'd been drowning, and he had tried to toss her a lifeline.

Her heart picked up speed as she thought about what she really wanted to do. She almost felt sick to her stomach. The speaker must have finished, because people were rising to their feet, clapping their hands, smiling at each other.

She saw it all as merely background noise as she grabbed the strap of her leather purse, closed her notebook, and quietly left the hotel ballroom.

• • •

Abby would have loved this lecture, Jack thought as he watched the woman creating an intricate cake for a child's birthday party. A pirate ship, perfect for a little pirate prince or princess. The instructor's creativity was simply astonishing, and he knew Abby would have appreciated this baker's talent far more than he did. He'd simply get the woman's card and hire her. Abby would want to know why and how, and would probably create a fantasy ship all her own, with different flavored cakes and frostings.

The instructor was just finishing up the last details on the ship when Jack saw the door in the back of the dining room open. He gave the late attendee no more than a cursory glance, until it registered in his brain that this attendee was Abby.

His heartbeat sped up as he left his seat and approached her.

"What happened?" he asked, his voice low, not wanting to disturb the last few moments of the presentation.

"What happened was that the lecture was unendurable. I've never been as bored in my life, so I decided to play hooky for the rest of the day." She pulled the chocolate seminar brochure out of her leather bag. "How does Creating Your Own Gourmet Truffles sound?"

Jack couldn't remember the last time he'd felt this happy. If she was willing to forfeit the legal seminar, then perhaps the next step could be trying to convince her to make Southern California her home on a permanent basis. At this rate, anything was possible—including a marriage proposal.

"Sounds great." He pulled his own brochure out of his jacket pocket, glancing at it and trying for a light tone. "Then, after lunch, how about Winning Tarts and Tea Time Treats?"

She smiled up at him. "I'll take tarts over torts anytime."

• • •

She never went back to the law seminar.

Abby decided that if she had to go back to Chicago and bury herself in stuffy law books, she was going to take the rest of the week for herself and let that other Abby out. She'd already arranged for a set of the legal seminar tapes to be sent to her office as soon as possible after the lectures had been taped. If anyone wanted to know what had been talked about in those lectures, she could simply smile and hand them a tape. She might even listen to one or two on her daily commute.

But not now. Not when she was living in a magical house on the edge of the Pacific and had met the most wonderful man. Not when she wanted to be baking brownies or sampling European chocolates or learning the secrets of making hand-dipped candies look utterly professional.

For just this moment in time, she wanted to be who she really was. And if it was only for a few days, and if that was all she could manage, she still wanted this time and these memories. They would be hers, and no one could take them away from her.

So she and Jack attended the rest of the seminars he'd signed them up for. The chocolate convention did not disappoint her. It had been billed as "A Mouthwatering Celebration of Chocolate for Chocoholics Everywhere," and as Abby happily melted and grated and chopped and tempered what she came to call the food of the gods, she felt a lightness in her heart and a renewed sense of energy.

She was happy.

She found that she had a real talent for decorating cakes, from making chocolate leaves to shaving off curls and creating delicate filigrees. As she and Jack made their way through rich layer cakes, pies and tarts, sauces and fillings, and easy snacks, she encouraged him to cook more instead of simply watching and tasting. By the end of the chocolate convention, both of them were molding chocolate flowers, feathering, marbling, piping, and making waves and baskets.

Saturday evening, at the final banquet, there was a contest for the best chocolate creation, and Abby entered a box she'd made out of semisweet and white chocolate. She'd feathered it so it appeared to be made out of marble and filled it with truffles made of white chocolate and lime, her absolute favorite.

She was sitting with Jack when her name was called as winner of the grand prize.

"I didn't think . . . I never thought . . ." She couldn't seem to let go of his hand as all eyes turned toward their table and people began to applaud.

"Don't think. Just get up there and take a bow." Jack gave her a kiss on the cheek, then gently disengaged her hand from his and gave her a gentle nudge in the back, sending her on her way toward the front of the brick patio, where a dais had been erected, along with a microphone and several chairs.

She didn't remember anything about the presentation of her award, other than saying a few words into the microphone. She answered the usual questions: How long have you been cooking? Where are you from? How did you hear about our convention, and what made you decide to attend?

But the final question, and the one that she remembered most, was when the portly old man who ran the entire convention asked her, "Now Abby, what is it that you do for a living?"

Without a second's hesitation, she said, "I cook."

They had their own private celebration in Jack's room later that night.

"I can't accept these," he said when she tried to give him the chocolate box. "Besides, these are your favorite truffles, not mine. A very clever trick, Abby, one that I noticed and appreciated."

She laughed. "I can't believe I won first prize!" Never that competitive by nature, she'd simply poured hours of sheer love into the project. In some ways, that little chocolate box represented all the creativity she'd been denying herself. She wanted to give it to Jack because she wanted him to know how much she appreciated him seeing her as a chef and not a lawyer. How much she appreciated him bothering to get to know the real Abby, the woman she had come to know that waited, hidden, stifled in her corporate suits and sleek shoes.

The real Abby would cook all day, step out of the kitchen and greet her customers, ask them how they liked their lunches and dinners. The real Abby would take breaks and walk on the beach with Yoda.

The real Abby might even get up the nerve to go Roller-blading, and race down the boardwalk as fast as the seagulls that wheeled overhead.

"Jack?" Her heart started pounding even before she asked the question on the tip of her tongue.

He turned his head toward her. He'd been admiring the little chocolate box, but now his full attention was on her.

"If that job's still open—"

She didn't even get the chance to finish the sentence before she was enveloped in the tightest, warmest hug. He held on to her as if he never wanted to let her go.

"Yes! Yes, of course it is." He released her, just slightly, and smiled down at her. "Though I don't mind telling you that you can negotiate ferociously for a higher starting salary, because I happen to know that you've spent the last few days improving your dessert skills."

She started to laugh. "Wouldn't that chocolate mousse in a chocolate shell be terrific? I mean, if we're going to serve fish, and make people eat healthy stuff, then we have to have some desserts that are absolutely decadent."

"I couldn't agree with you more. And speaking of decadent," he reached for the chocolate box, took one of the truffles out, then brought it to her mouth. "Abby, it's time to enjoy your creation."

She bit into the truffle, the fine, white chocolate shell breaking and exposing the whipped ganache inside, the butter and cream and white chocolate spiked with just a hint of lime.

"I think I like these better than the ones I buy in Chicago," she said, just before he kissed her.

Chicago, he thought as he kissed her. *She said Chicago, not back home, and that has to have some significance. With any luck, she's starting to think of this beach town as home.*

He knew he had to play his wildest card tonight. Saturday night. Abby had a plane ticket for Sunday at ten in the morning, a nonstop to Chicago. Jack had a feeling that if he let her get on that plane tomorrow, he'd never see her again. She'd never see herself again, and that might be the more crucial battle.

He'd known this woman exactly one week, from that Saturday afternoon he'd first seen her on the beach, bent over a soggy little cat with fishing line around its neck, to this Saturday night, when he'd seen a woman glowing and vibrant with happiness step up onto a dais and receive first prize for a chocolate creation absolutely exquisite in its execution.

She had no idea how good she was. That tore at his heart. For Jack was a firm believer that people should be allowed to fly free, to meet their destinies. And since that first moment on the beach, when she'd looked up at him with those compassionate gray eyes, he'd known that Abby Sheridan was his destiny.

He tried to put that feeling into the kiss, tried to make the lover's gesture as filled with emotion as he could. She trembled in his arms, and he could feel that same trembling inside him. What this woman did to him made him feel incandescent, as if lit from within. At the same time, it humbled him, brought him to his knees. He only hoped, as he lowered her to the bed, that she felt the same way.

Intuition told him she did. And it also told him he could move a little faster with her now, because she trusted him. He could make their time together more playful, or more erotic, or even funny. The list was endless, as he hoped their time together was.

"Abby," he said, smiling down at her face, searching her eyes. "Abby, will you marry me?"

Now she understood another of those old sayings: *Time stood still.*

She would remember this moment forever. The two of them lying in Jack's bedroom, the French doors open to the private garden outside, the fragrance of jasmine coming in and mingling with that warm scent that was Jack's alone.

The pressure of his body on hers, the way she felt so safe with her body sunk into the comfortable mattress. The fire that he'd lit before he'd poured them each a glass of celebratory champagne. The lilac and green Chinese rug, the antique vase on the table in the far corner. All these impressions strengthened for the length of a heartbeat, then blurred until all she could see, all she could focus on was his face above hers. So close. So anxious.

Probably less than a few seconds had passed before she smiled up at him and whispered, "Yes."

And she was glad her first and only proposal had taken place in this room, with its fluffy goose-down comforter, the fine linen she knew they would sleep on tonight, and the intimate view of the garden right outside.

Jack got up from the bed, went into the bathroom, and retrieved a fat, white candle. Lighting it, he placed it on the bedside table, then turned off the lights. Only the glow from the fireplace remained. She watched as he poured them two more glasses of champagne, then came back to the bed.

"Thank you, Abby," he said as he handed her the crystal flute. "I'll try to make you happy."

"You already do."

"You don't have to take the chef's job if you want to do something else."

"What else would I do?"

"Oh, I don't know. Take more classes, just walk on the beach for a while. I get the feeling you don't have a whole lot of practice being a beach bum."

She laughed. "Nope. You can't exactly walk in the sand wearing high heels. Or lie in a hammock in an Armani suit."

He leaned forward and kissed her. "You need to go barefoot for a while."

"I want to go Rollerblading. Do you know how to do that?"

"We can go tomorrow. I'll teach you."

She set her glass of champagne down, then reached for his. Delighted at this new side to her, he let her place both their glasses on the bedside table, then felt his heart lodge in his throat as she cupped his face in both her hands and kissed him.

"Jack, I want to go Rollerblading and I want to be your chef. I want to work with you and help you get your restaurant off the ground. I want to be your partner in every sense of the word. And . . . and I want to thank you."

"For what?"

"For seeing the real me, instead of the me that I usually present to the world."

He knew exactly what she meant and saw no reason to deny it. "You're very welcome." He took hold of her hand and pulled her closer. "Now, I have a little plan for both of us that includes a few more of those spectacular truffles, another glass or two of champagne, and neither of us getting much sleep tonight. How does that sound?"

Without any protest, she went into his arms.

FIVE

That night, nothing existed for Abby but the man in her arms.

Something changed in the lovemaking between a man and a woman when the thought of marriage came to the relationship. The emotional potential existed for something so much deeper and sweeter, so binding and yet at the same time, so freeing.

He told her that he'd known from the moment their eyes had met on the beach that Saturday afternoon. She confessed that she'd known something was happening but had been hesitant to put a name to it. Now, knowing that he loved her and wanted to spend the rest of his life with her, she knew that what they had found together was nothing short of extraordinary.

Even though the wind changed and grew cooler, even though a light rain began to fall, they left the French doors open, wanting the scents from the flowers, and that wonderful smell just before a storm. Then the rain, coming down, created its own rhythms, pounding down, drowning out first Abby's sharp cries of fulfillment, then the soft sound of their talking, tucked into the king-sized bed. But close together, arms and legs entwined.

She couldn't seem to get enough of him, couldn't look at him enough. His cheekbones were softened by the candlelight, his eyes darker and mysterious. When he kissed her again, mere hours later, her body responded as if it had a will of its own. And Abby realized that in a way it did, for her body had known, long before her mind had given up its stubborn control, that Jack was the man she was meant to be with.

"How lovely it will be," Jack said now as he kissed his way down her body, "to know that you'll always be in my kitchen, where I can come in and see you any time of the day."

She could barely catch her breath to answer him; excitement tightened all her muscles.

"And you'll be out front, meeting and greeting, making sure everything runs smoothly."

"Unloading boxes," he whispered as he cupped her breast, "checking that you have all the supplies that you need."

Their dream seemed to blend with their partnership, and as Jack kissed her stomach, then rested his head there for just an instant, Abby wondered at the fact that he'd been looking for a chef and she'd been longing to be one. She didn't have quite enough formal training, but he'd assured her they would work things out.

"Jack," she breathed as she relaxed further into the big bed. As he slid down her body and kissed his way up her legs until her entire body was shaking, until she didn't protest when he kissed her feminine heart, made her hips rise, made her fingers clench the cool cotton sheets until she cried out, finding her release in that sensual spiral of hot, trembling fire.

He gave her no time to recover, no time for her mind to

think, only for her body to respond. He was over her, covering her, his weight on his forearms. As she looked up into his face, she was glad of the intense expression, of the way each supple movement made so clear the urgency with which he wanted to be inside her.

Then he was, and that first moment of joining thrilled her, brought heat flooding down where they were one, where he moved with an urgent, almost desperately inevitable rhythm, pushing her deeper into the mattress, thrusting into her as if he would never, ever get enough. She answered those movements, reaching up to his thrusting down, rocking with him on their mattress, knowing she had to take this journey with him to the very end.

She didn't know whether it was his scent, the way he moved his muscled body, the rough texture of his chest hair against her breasts, the feel of his hands, strong and sure. It all came together in one man, and that man so effortlessly created anticipation, desire, excitement, and total fulfillment for her. She felt that spiral coil tightly within her as she moved beneath him, desperate to set it free. Then that tight build, that sense of climbing, and finally that glorious, sharp break. Everything inside her seemed to shatter, though it was a shattering she willingly let happen, knowing that when all the pieces came back together, she would be at peace.

She felt his own completion, within a minute after hers. When he finally rested upon her, his head on her shoulder, his chest expanding with the deep breaths he had to take, Abby put her arms around Jack and knew nothing in her life had ever felt as right as this.

She woke early the following morning to the sound of rain pouring down, and to the sense that everything was completely wrong. Much later, she would wonder what would have happened to her if Jack had been there in bed with her, warmly curled around her body. If she hadn't come awake to find a note on the table by the bed, the fire in ashes, the candle blown out, and weak, watery sunshine coming in through the window.

Abby lay in bed and knew she couldn't do it.

Any of it. The marriage, the move, the job. How could she have ever thought that she could be the chef in Jack's restaurant? His dream. She'd ruin it.

So she loved to cook. So what? That passion for creating meals was no assurance she would be able to maintain the menu for the type of restaurant Jack Hayes wanted to create. It was impossible.

The chocolate convention had been like something out of a dream. So had the man. But looking at both in the watery morning light, unsoftened by candlelight and champagne, Abby wondered what she could have been thinking. What terrified her most was that nothing would hold up in the day-to-day world. In reality.

She reached over and picked up the note on the bedside table.

Sleep in, beauty. I'm taking a run on the beach, but I'll bring us back some hot croissants. Then, on to Roller-blading.

Love,
Jack

She told herself she was doing the right thing for both of them as she quickly dressed, then gathered all her things and ran up the stairs two at a time to the sanctuary of The Juliet Room. Once there, she packed in record time, stuffing a surprised and indignant Yoda into her airline carrier, then juggling dog, purse, and large suitcase as she careened down the stairs and raced toward the desk near the entrance-way where she met Molly Dawson's startled gaze.

"Checking out this early? But you said your plane doesn't leave until late morning."

"I have to get out of here now." The words were said with a quiet finality. "Oh, and Molly, there's one favor I have to ask of you."

"Of course, dear." But those wise blue eyes were worried.

"Would you give this note to Jack?" She handed the woman the brief note she'd composed up in her room. "And would you tell him that Callista—the cat we rescued—is still there? I want her to stay with him." She choked back a sob on the last request, then half-laughed. "I guess that's two favors, isn't it? I'm sorry, Molly, to leave the cat in the room, but—"

"Dear, I'm worried about you. Are you quite sure you know what you're doing?"

"Yes, no, I—there's the cab, I have to run, Molly. I had a wonderful time, I want you to know that." She grabbed her bag, the carrier, her purse, and before the woman could look at her with that sadly puzzled expression a moment longer, Abby banged her way out the door and into the rain, not caring that her hair was getting soaked, not caring that her gray trench coat was half on, half off, just knowing that she had to get away before Jack found out, tried to stop her, and in the process ruined both their lives.

He knew the moment he opened the door. Molly's expression as she turned toward him was a dead giveaway. Jack had to stand in the foyer for a moment, just to catch his breath and get his bearings.

"She's gone."

The woman cleared her throat, handed him a simple white envelope. "She left the kitty in the room upstairs. Said she wants you to have her." She hesitated, then said, "I'm so sorry, Jack."

He sat down on one of the chairs in the foyer, feeling as if he'd been sucker punched. There had been moments during their week together when he'd thought this might happen. But he'd thought after last night . . .

What hurt the most was that he'd thought Abby had felt safe.

Slowly, not even caring that Molly was watching him, he opened the letter.

Jack,

I don't know why, but I just can't do it. Please don't come after me. But please know that I wouldn't have given up my week with you for anything in the world.

I do love you,
Abby

He sat, staring at the small piece of paper with its handwritten message until the pain lessened, just a little. Then he became aware of Molly studying him.

"What are you going to do, Jack?"

"Well, I'm going to respect her wishes and not go after her. Not right away, at least."

"That's the way!"

"I'll go get Callista and take her to my room."

"Oh, pish-posh, I can do that for you! Go on to your room, take a hot shower, and start formulating a battle plan to get her back!"

"For that," he said, unfolding the top of the white paper bag, "you deserve at least a croissant. Chocolate or almond?"

Abby wasn't even five miles from The Buried Treasure bed-and-breakfast before she knew she'd made a terrible mistake. As the taxi had pulled away from the gray-shingled beach house, and as its familiar outline had been obscured first by rain and then fog, she'd felt a terrible tightness around her heart.

Even Yoda, irrepressible Yoda, always a dog who looked at the bright side, gave her a puzzled expression, whined, then curled up in her carrier on the seat next to Abby in a manner designed to present Abby with her disgusted rear end.

"I couldn't have done it," she muttered to herself. "I made the right decision. I would have botched the job, and he would have ended up replacing me in the kitchen, and it would have put a strain on our relationship."

"Lady, what time did you say your flight was?" The cabdriver looked to be about twenty-eight, clean-shaven and probably one of the thousands of young men and women who worked their day jobs and wrote screenplays or studied scripts for acting auditions by night.

"Ten."

"Oh, you'll make it easy." He glanced out the window. "But there may be a little bit of a delay with this fog."

"That's all right. As long as I'm at the airport, I can wait."

Yoda whined, the doggy sound filled with anguish.

"That dog okay?"

"She's fine."

"They let you take her on the plane?"

"I wouldn't have it any other way."

"She looks like that little guy on those Taco Bell ads. Great ads, huh?"

She nodded her head, lost in thought. What hurt the most was thinking of Jack coming back after his run, croissants in hand, expecting to find her in his bed. Instead, a note from Molly and a Persian cat. And a week's worth of memories.

She touched the back of the front seat and for an instant almost asked the cabdriver to take her back.

Yoda whined hopefully, her back still turned.

Abby slowly sat back, straightened her spine. Well, at least she'd learned one valuable thing on this trip. It wasn't the circumstances of her life that had made her, it was her inability to take risks.

Jack would have been good for you.

She pushed the thought out of her mind.

You would have been good for each other.

She pushed harder.

The driver exited on Century Boulevard, turned right, and Abby knew they weren't far from the airport. And she decided that once she was sitting in business class and had a copy of the *Wall Street Journal* in front of her, and the flight attendants had made their first rounds and served juice and drinks, well, then she would indulge herself in a good cry.

But not until she made sure she got on that plane.

"The Honeymoon Suite's already taken," Molly said, studying the guest book in front of her as Jack looked on. "A couple just checked in last night. Cute as could be."

"What's left?" His reservation was up as of today, he was supposed to be on a plane to New York City this afternoon, but Jack knew he couldn't leave. Not yet. He had to wait and see if Abby changed her mind. A long shot, yes, but it was the only one he had.

"Not much. You were going to leave The Garden Room today, so the only place I can put you is . . ." She ran her fingers down the page until they rested on a blank square. "The Crow's Nest."

"The Crow's Nest?"

"It's way at the top of the stairs. A little cozy for two, but the view makes up for it, especially of the mountains." She frowned. "Of course, in this fog, you're not going to see much of anything." Her expression brightened. "Maybe her flight will be grounded, give her a little more time to think, you know?"

"I'm hoping." Jack had already decided that he couldn't go after her. Not after reading that note. Abby was fighting a peculiarly inner battle, and he couldn't be the one to take that decision away from her. It had to come from Abby. It had to be what she wanted, she had to take that leap of faith or else things would become poisoned down the road.

"Did you tell her about the sign?"

He sighed. "A little premature of me, don't you think? No, I didn't."

She shook her head. "I don't know if it would have made any difference. All of us have our demons driving us, Jack. I don't think it was about you."

He knew the effort she was making for him, and it touched him deeply.

"Thank you, Molly. I'll remember that."

She made it to her gate in record time, only to find out that all the airline's flights were backed up because of the thick fog and she would be lucky if they left by noon.

Not happy with this knowledge, she walked over to a bar, ordered a soft drink for herself and a hot dog for Yoda.

The Chihuahua glared at her through the mesh and ignored the usually much-loved snack. Abby was treated to a long-suffering whine, a sigh, and another look at her dog's indignant backside. How one small animal could put so much emotion into her body language was beyond Abby.

"All right," she whispered, "so maybe it was a bribe." She took a bite out of the hot dog, chewed, swallowed. "But you've got to understand that this is the only way it could be. I'm not the adventurous type. I'm always scared, Yoda, *always.*"

The dark, liquid eyes were patently disgusted before Yoda closed them and turned away. And Abby's eyes teared up as she remembered the way she'd had to disentangle Yoda from her feline friend. The two had become used to snuggling up to each other, and the quietly puzzled look in Callista's copper eyes had almost torn Abby's heart out.

But her fear had been so much stronger.

Abby gulped down her soda, threw away the rest of the hot dog she really had no stomach for, then picked up her purse, her upset dog in her carrier, and her bag. She'd be sitting in a hard plastic chair for a couple of hours, but she could buy a few magazines to while away the time.

Anything to distract herself. Anything not to think of Jack.

Three and a half hours later, she found that Jack was all she could think about.

She'd been half-reading an article that assured women of thinner thighs and happier sex lives when she overheard an elderly woman's anxious voice.

"There haven't been any cancellations?"

The woman behind the desk responded in a muted voice, and Abby would have turned her attention back to a rather ridiculous diet except that she caught sight of the elderly woman's face. The woman seemed truly frightened.

"Can I help you?" she said, getting out of her chair and offering it to the woman. With flights backed up, every single hard plastic chair was occupied

"Thank you." The woman sat down and put her head in both her hands for a moment. Abby just let her be, recognizing another's despair and confusion because she was still dealing with her own. She didn't expect Jack to come running to her rescue like a knight-errant. She'd meant what she'd said in the brief note.

No, she'd taken responsibility for this decision. There was no turning back now. Even if she wanted to, Jack would think she was a total flake, changing her mind as easily as most people changed television stations.

The woman raised her head, wiped her eyes.

"Can I help?" Abby asked again, kneeling down beside her.

"It's my . . . granddaughter," the woman said, barely able to get the words out. "She lives in Chicago with her husband. She's pregnant with their first child, and . . ."

Abby remained silent, knowing there was more. Yoda, in her carrier on the floor, was facing front, her tiny face intent on this new development.

"And something doesn't seem to be going right," the

woman said, letting the words out in a rush. "Her husband is away on business for another week, she's all alone, and won't contact him because she doesn't want to scare him. He wants this baby so badly. She called me, and I told her I would get there, one way or another." She raised watery eyes to Abby. "So I'm waiting to see if there are any available seats so I can get there as soon as possible."

"I'm sorry," Abby said softly.

"So am I," the woman said, then took a deep breath. "And I'm scared to death to fly."

There are moments in life, Abby would tell Jack later that night, when everything becomes crystal clear, brought into a clarity so bright it's as if someone had taken your own personal little spotlight and shined it down on you. For Abby, this woman and her predicament was one of those moments.

She studied the woman. Nothing remarkable about her. She could be anyone's grandma in her navy slacks, navy and white overblouse, lace-up sneakers, hip-length jacket, and beautifully crocheted scarf. But what made her stand out in Abby's eyes was the expression of determination on her face when she said, "I told her I would get there one way or another."

Yet she was scared to fly.

Abby blinked furiously against the sudden stinging in her eyes. She could see Yoda jumping and scratching against the door of her carrier, her stubby tail wagging. Perhaps animals could read their humans' minds, because Abby had the funniest feeling that her little dog knew exactly what she was about to do.

"What's your name?" Abby said.

"Gracie."

"Gracie, I'd like to give you my ticket."

The woman looked up at her with hope. "I can pay you any amount you'd like."

Abby laid her hand on the woman's arm. "No, you don't understand. I'd like to give it to you."

As the woman stared at her and began to protest, Abby walked over to the ticket counter, had a few words with the young man behind it, then walked back to the grandmother, still sitting in that plastic chair almost frozen in shock.

"He can do it for us, Gracie. Right now."

"I don't understand," she said, rising to her feet.

"I want to do this for you because you made me see something I should have seen a long time ago. Does that make sense?"

"No," Gracie said honestly.

"It doesn't have to," Abby replied. She paused as she heard the voice over the loudspeaker announcing that their flight would be boarding very soon, and would people with children or the elderly please move to the head of the boarding line.

"We've got to do this now if we're going to do it," Abby said, guiding Gracie toward the young man behind the airline counter.

"Let me do something for you," Gracie protested as Yoda barked and wagged her tail.

"What do you like to eat?" Abby asked as they reached the counter and she gave the young man her ticket and nodded her head. He smiled.

"I love a good omelet, but it has to be vegetarian. My doctor doesn't want me eating a lot of red meat these days."

"Gracie," Abby said, "when you get back, I want you to go to a place a few doors down from The Buried Treasure bed-and-breakfast on Venice Beach. A new restaurant, it'll probably be called Jack's Café. You ask for me, Abby, and I'll fix you the best spinach omelet you've ever tasted."

Gracie had pulled a tiny spiral notebook out of her purse and was furiously scribbling. "I'll find you!" she said, as the man behind the counter handed her the revamped ticket.

"Don't worry about anything but that granddaughter of yours. And that grandbaby."

"Thank you!" Gracie picked up her carry-on bag and was almost at the head of the boarding line when she called out to Abby, "But where are you going?"

"Home!" Abby called back.

She reached The Buried Treasure in record time, and Molly didn't even seem surprised to see her come barreling in the door. This time, Abby had the weirdest sense of déjà vu as she entered the beach house. Again, that atmosphere, that easy, homelike feeling. Again, the smell of baking cookies rich in the air for afternoon tea. Lemon, cinnamon, and something that smelled like roasted pecans.

"Where's Jack?" she said as she blew in the door, her hair damp and stringy, Yoda grumbling as she was rocked around in her carrier, trying to dig a toehold into the blue towel on the bottom of her cage.

"I'll take those things," Molly offered, grabbing Abby's bag and the dog carrier. "He's down at the restaurant doing some painting."

"Thank you!" Abby reached toward the carrier, unlocked the door, scooped up her pet, tucked her beneath her trench coat, and let herself out into the rain.

He closed all the windows, started a fire in the enormous fireplace in the main dining room, and stepped back to see the results of his work, paintbrush in hand. Jack liked it. He liked it a lot.

He'd needed to be alone after Abby had left, and now the combination of the soothing sound of rain beating down on the roof, the snapping and hissing of the fire, and the smells of the paints he'd laid out were working their peculiarly hypnotizing effect. That and a glass of wine–make that two glasses—made him feel almost mellow.

He was absolutely certain he was hallucinating when he

felt familiar little doggie claws scrabbling at his pants legs. He glanced down and saw Yoda, quivering so hard she looked as if she might explode.

"Yoda?"

Then he glanced up and saw her.

She was standing in the doorway, and even though Abby was an absolutely bedraggled mess, she'd never looked more beautiful to him. He started toward her, not sure if it was rain or tears on her face, and then she was in his arms, with Yoda running in circles around the two of them, and Jack knew he would have waited an entire lifetime for this exact moment in time.

But better sooner than later.

"I got scared," she whispered into his shoulder.

"Ah, but you came back. And that makes all the difference."

She started to cry, and he simply held her.

She saw the sign he'd been painting after she sat down and he offered her a glass of very good red wine.

"Abby's Café?"

The sign was an absolute masterpiece, her name in elaborate lettering that would have looked right at home on a pirate's map. In one corner, she saw a more than decent representation of Yoda, and in the other, a smoky colored Persian with copper colored eyes sat washing her paws.

"I knew it the moment I saw you. Some people might even say I have an instinct for these things."

"But Jack's Café has a nice ring to it."

He kissed her cheek. "But Abby will be in the kitchen."

She cleared her throat. "I might make some mistakes—"

"Oh, I'll be counting on it, they're what makes life interesting."

"And if it seems like I'm doing the restaurant more harm than good—"

"I doubt it, but we'll figure something out."

The rain still sluiced down in sheets, and Abby glanced up as thunder rumbled. "Do you still have your room at the B and B?"

As they walked out of the dark building that would one day be Abby's Café, Yoda tucked securely under Jack's coat, Jack said, "Oh, I still have a room. There's a nice little adventure in store for us tonight, Abby."

As he locked the door, Jack thought, *The rest of our lives . . .*

He carried her up all three flights, Yoda following, yapping excitedly.

"It'll get me in shape for our wedding night," he said.

She called her uncle and explained that she wasn't coming back for a while, then told him a little about Jack. Surprisingly, her uncle Pat thought her decision was a splendid one.

"You sound happier than you have in a long time, Abby. I hope I'll get a chance to meet this young man of yours."

"I want you to."

"You know, it was that way with my Mary, and we've been on a honeymoon that's lasted forever. A grand adventure."

Abby's throat tightened. He understood. She couldn't speak, she was so filled with emotion.

"I knew you weren't happy," her uncle said quietly. "But I didn't know what to do. I would have done anything for you, Abby, to ensure your happiness."

"But it had to come from me," she said.

"That's the truth of it."

"You'll like him," she said suddenly.

"I'm sure that I will. Now, I'll work some magic on the firm's schedule, and you just let me know when you want to come back and pack. Take your time; we can handle things here."

"Thank you," she whispered, then gently hung up the phone.

The Crow's Nest was a delight, small enough that they kept running into each other, but no one minded. Yoda and Callista greeted each other like long-lost friends, then promptly curled up together in a new window seat. There was no fireplace, so Jack lit several of the dozen candles Molly had placed around the room, along with strategically placed vases of white roses.

It looked like it was going to be a cold, wet day, and Abby was thankful for the extra pillows and blankets and the coziness of the little room with its sloping ceilings and warm wood accents and beams. The only room on the large beach house's fourth floor, she felt as if they were in a little world all their own.

Now, alone with Jack, she felt suddenly shy. A little self-conscious of how frightened she'd been, how foolishly she'd behaved.

"What now?" she said.

"Now," said Jack, "I'm going to come back inside the room and find you in bed, and we're going to go on with our Sunday as if nothing ever happened." He frowned. "Except for the Rollerblading, because it's kind of nasty weather for that."

She started to smile. "All right."

He hesitated at the door. "That's not to say that I wouldn't someday like to know what happened to make you leave."

"I'll tell you," she said. "And I'll tell you right now that I'm never going to leave you again."

"Well, that's good," he said. "Imagine me, running Abby's Café and Abby nowhere in sight."

He let himself out the door as she laughed.

He phoned to let her know that he had a surprise for her, and that it might take a little more time than a bag of croissants.

"You can take a bath or something," he said. "Just relax. Give me about half an hour."

So she filled the gilded, claw-footed tub with hot water, threw in some expensive bath salts, and soaked for a while, then slipped on a beautiful white nightgown that looked like something a bride might wear. She'd bought it almost six months ago on an impulse. The delicate silk and lace concoction had called out to her more adventurous, romantic side. Afterward, in her apartment, when she'd brought the nightgown home and taken the tissue-wrapped garment out of the shopping bag, Abby had felt that it wasn't really her.

But she'd packed it for this trip.

And now it felt—and fit—exactly right.

She was sitting up in bed, the pillows plumped all around her, when Jack let himself in the door, a silver tray in his arms.

"Now this is the breakfast we should have had!"

They feasted on a cheese and egg frittata and blueberry pancakes, along with pecan waffles and thick French toast with chunky applesauce.

"The competition," Jack said, leaning back after his last bite, "gets tougher all the time."

The pièce de résistance was a mug of Harry's Chocolate Grog for each of them.

"I'll weigh in the hundreds if we keep eating like this," Abby warned him.

"More of you to love," he replied, tickling her foot.

Yoda, eating the last of a blueberry pancake, snorted softly.

"It wasn't you, Jack," Abby said softly.

"I knew that."

They were silent for a time, then Abby told him about the grandmother she'd met at the airport, a woman determined to take to the skies even though she was terrified.

"People do the most extraordinary things out of love," Jack said, and as Abby stared at him, her eyes suddenly welled with tears.

"Oh, Abby," he said and, setting down his hot chocolate, he took her into his arms.

After she'd cried herself out and he'd handed her countless tissues, Jack leaned back on his side of the bed and said, "There's a method to this madness. It may seem totally random and out of control to you, but I do have an ulterior motive."

"And that is?"

"As we no longer have the option of burning off all of those decadent calories Rollerblading down the boardwalk, I've thought of another physical activity I'm sure we'll both enjoy."

She started to laugh as he kissed her.

Yoda raised her head from her nap and glanced over at the comfy bed from her perch on the window seat. Satisfied that her two favorite humans in the entire world were safe and sound and out of the rain, she yawned, then turned her attention back to her nap.

Callista simply purred.

Jack and Abby's Chocolate Grog
(Hot Chocolate with Rum)

Serves four

¾ cup heavy cream
4 cups milk
3 tablespoons sugar
1 tablespoon dark rum (can use regular or spiced rum)
8 oz. bittersweet chocolate, finely chopped
Optional: nutmeg (fresh, not already grated—it makes a huge difference)

Whip the cream until soft peaks form. Set it aside.

Heat the milk in a saucepan until almost boiling. (Be careful not to let it boil over!) Remove from the heat and whisk in the sugar, the rum, and all but one tablespoon of the chocolate. The mixture should be foamy.

Pour the hot chocolate into four cups. Quickly spoon on the whipped cream and sprinkle with the remaining chocolate.

Variation: You can also whisk in all the chocolate, then grate a little fresh nutmeg over the whipped cream, like Jack and Abby did.

Enjoy! (Hopefully while relaxing by the sea in an exotic locale with a pirate of your own.)

Ecstasy

Fayrene Preston

ONE

"Ummm . . . ahhh . . . ohhh . . . oh, my God . . . ahhh . . . oh, heavens. *Yes.*"

Hayden Garrett watched with interest as the woman at the next table had an orgasm. Naturally he'd seen a woman have an orgasm before, but the woman was usually in his bed when it occurred.

In this case, they were in a public place—a café called Brenna's in an elite part of north Dallas—and he'd had nothing to do with the orgasmic woman at the next table. Furthermore, the orgasm had been going on for at least five minutes. It was enough to give any man an inferiority complex, he thought wryly.

At last he'd seen the phenomenon his sister Lois had been telling him about, and she hadn't been exaggerating.

Although a relatively small business, Brenna's reputation was rapidly growing. Word of its excellent catering service and baked goods was being spread. In fact, he'd heard that the café was actually having to turn away catering orders because there were just too many for them to handle, a fact that naturally made the clamor for Brenna's services even greater.

The only meal the café served was lunch and the menu was small—two different soups, two different salads–and each day there were new selections. An extensive list of pastries, sweet confections, and hot chocolate specialty drinks completed the menu.

But the one item that was putting the café on the map at the speed of sound was the item over which the woman at the next table was currently having an orgasm. It was a chocolate fudge called Ecstasy.

His sister Lois had been raving about Brenna's Ecstasy for months now, urging him to consider the business possibilities of the fudge. She'd even brought him several pieces and demanded that he eat one. He had, and though it hadn't sent him into raptures the way it did his sister and the women he'd seen here today, it had been good. But then he wasn't a good test for any kind of chocolate. He liked it, but it wasn't a necessity for him, unlike a lot of women he knew and obviously the ones in this cafe.

Still, Lois hadn't stopped nagging him until he'd agreed to look into the possibility of obtaining the manufacturing rights to the fudge recipe. And he hadn't gotten where he was today by passing up promising business ventures.

First, though, he'd sent several pieces to his top chemists to see if the recipe could be duplicated. They'd analyzed Brenna's fudge ten different ways from Sunday, and they had used the women who worked for him as samplers. But in the end, they'd had to admit defeat. Nothing they could produce even came close to duplicating the taste or the response of Brenna's Ecstasy.

After that, he'd sent one of his top executives here to talk with the owner of Brenna's about securing the rights to the fudge. When the man had returned in defeat, Hayden had sent another and then another, until finally, he'd become intrigued. What kind of woman would turn down so much money for a single recipe? So today, he'd managed to carve thirty minutes out of his schedule to come see this Brenna for himself. So far, she hadn't appeared.

An older, slightly overweight woman with flaming red hair who'd introduced herself as Cora had waited on him. The corn chowder and garden salad he was just finishing up had been delicious, but he was still waiting to see Brenna.

Just then, a woman raced through the door and rushed up to the counter. "I'll give you my firstborn child for a piece of Ecstasy *now*!"

Cora leveled an amused gaze on her. "Denise, you know I don't want your firstborn. I've got five of my own."

"Okay, then what about my BMW?"

"I don't know. What color is it?"

"Beige."

Cora tasked. "Too bad. I had my heart set on a red one."

"I'll get it painted."

Hayden had deliberately waited until the lunch crowd had thinned to come so that he could avoid the lines Lois had told him about. An added benefit to his decision was that he could hear everything that was being said. He could even hear the orgasms that had started four tables over from him—two women this time.

"*Please*, Cora. I'm in severe danger of going into withdrawal. It's been almost twenty-four hours, and I need my fix *now*!"

"Well, then, I guess I better get you a piece. I just hate like the very dickens whenever I have to call 911." Chuckling, Cora moved toward the display case where the fudge was kept.

A lovely young woman breezed out from the back of the shop, her long, auburn hair piled neatly atop her head and somehow tied with a green ribbon. He was too far away to see the color of her eyes, and because of the white smock she wore, he couldn't tell much about her figure except that she was slim. But everything about her was confident, bright, and alive. From Lois's description, the young woman had to be Brenna, the owner and chef of Brenna's.

When Brenna saw the woman waiting for the fudge, a smile lit her face. "Denise, for heaven sakes. You could save yourself a lot of misery if you'd simply buy a couple of pounds of the fudge to keep at home instead of coming here every day and buying one piece."

Denise rolled her eyes. "Listen, if I bought two pounds of Ecstasy, I'd have all of it eaten by the end of the day, and then tomorrow I'd be big as a house. No, this way is harder on my nerves, but it's much safer for my figure."

"Okay, but just out of curiosity, what do you do on Sundays?"

A serious expression crossed Denise's face. "It's not pretty. My husband goes golfing so he doesn't have to be around me. Listen, I don't suppose you'd consider opening for say an hour on Sunday? I could make it worth your while. I could—"

Brenna chuckled. "Sorry, Denise, but even God rested on the seventh day."

"Okay, then, what about if I put a locked box out front? There'd be only two keys and you and I would have them. On Saturday, whenever you left here for the day, you could put my Sunday piece in the box and I could pick it up on Sunday."

"But if you knew it was in the box on Saturday, could you really wait to come get it on Sunday?"

Denise groaned. "Good point." Dejectedly, she handed Cora her money and took the little white paper bag that held her one piece of chocolate fudge. "Thank you, Cora. Now, if you two will excuse me, I'm going to retire to my car and enjoy my Ecstasy in private."

Brenna chuckled. "Will we see you tomorrow?"

"Just *try* to keep me away."

As the door closed behind Denise, Brenna grinned at Cora. "What'd she offer you today?"

"The usual. Her firstborn, but this time she added her BMW."

"Why didn't you take it?"

"It was beige."

"Ah, right." Brenna nodded understandingly, then cast an expert glance around the café. Her gaze stopped on him.

Hayden felt his stomach tighten. Her gaze was coolly assessing, as if she were sizing him up and had come to an instant conclusion. He was accustomed to women looking at him as a man to whom they were attracted, but that wasn't the way Brenna was looking at him. No, he had the uncomfortable feeling that she'd sized him up and neatly inserted him into a category. He didn't even have to know the category to know that he hated it.

Brenna moved from behind the counter and made her way from table to table, stopping at each to smile and chat. She seemed to know most of the people in the café and those she didn't, she quickly made friends with.

She had a way about her, he thought, watching her—a genuine warmth and brightness that seemed to reach out to all those within her domain and pull them to her.

She was also sexy as hell—a sexiness that didn't come from her body but rather her attitude.

It was in her carefree smile that said she was happy with herself, her life, and her world, just as it was, and she had accomplished it all alone. And it was in her knowing, amused looks that said she understood people.

Her loveliness made his pulse rate quicken. Her smile intrigued him. Her attitude challenged him. And all his attention was now riveted on this one woman as she drew closer and closer to him. And in that moment, he decided he would have her.

"Hi," she said, finally reaching him. "I don't believe I've seen you here before."

Green. Her eyes were green, with tiny flecks of gold. And her smooth skin was ivory with a golden undertone.

"That's because I haven't been here until today." He stood and held out his hand. "Hayden Garrett."

"Brenna Woods. Are you enjoying your lunch?"

"Very much. My compliments. The soup and salad were delicious."

"Thank you." She glanced down at the table. "You haven't had your dessert yet. Did Cora tell you what we're serving today?"

"Yes, but I don't care for anything."

"Are you sure? Our fudge—"

"I don't really have a sweet tooth."

"No?"

He shook his head. "But I've *heard* the reaction to your fudge." Just then another orgasm started, this time from a woman in the far corner. "When I have an orgasm, I like for there to be only one other person with me."

Her knowing eyes held laughter. "Really? I would never have pegged you as a prude."

He smiled. "And you would be right *not* to." He gestured toward the empty chair at his table. "Please join me."

She gave the café another sweeping glance, then looked back at him. "I suppose Cora can do without me for a few minutes."

"Speaking of Cora, I overheard her telling you she'd turned down that woman's BMW because it was beige."

She settled into the chair he held for her, then waited while he sat. "That's right."

"And you seemed to think it was a reasonable decision."

"Sure. Cora hates beige."

"But a BMW?"

She laughed. "First of all, Cora really, *really* does hate beige. Secondly, when Denise cuts it as close, time wise, as she did today, she forgets that all she has to do is pay for the fudge. But more times than not, she'll rush in here, dying for a piece of Ecstasy, and before we know it, she's offering us any and everything." She paused. "You're Lois's brother, aren't you?"

"That's right. How did you know?"

"There's something of a family resemblance. Plus"—she smiled—"she was in earlier and told me you might be stopping by today."

He chuckled. "Lois has this notion that I can't manage my life without her, so she keeps trying to help me."

"And how is she at it?"

"Let's just say that if *trying* were an Olympic event, she'd win a gold medal."

Brenna laughed, all her warmth and sexiness encapsulated in that one sound. A man could endure a lot, even slay dragons, if he knew that at the end of the day, he would hear her laugh.

"Lois is a nice lady. She comes in here a lot."

"So she tells me. But please, if she has the same reaction to the fudge as some of these other ladies, I'd rather not know it. After all, she's my sister."

She laughed again, and he found himself tilting his head to try to catch more of the sound. "I understand, but you can rest easy. Not everyone has the same reaction."

"That's good to know, because your fudge has the potential to be quite dangerous."

"*Dangerous?* That's one I've never heard."

"Think about it. Your fudge might make women decide they don't need men."

She smiled. "Somehow I can't see that happening."

"Thank God," he murmured, staring at her. "Has Lois told you my life story from birth to the present?"

"No, not really." It was the truth, Brenna reflected. Lois had only told her that her brother was a bachelor and that she'd like the two of them to meet. A red flag had automatically gone up in her mind. She'd done her share of dating, but since she'd opened her cafe, she stayed incredibly busy and really had no time for matchmaking. Plus, at this point in her life, she was choosy and would much rather select her own dates.

But when the first executive of HGI had showed up—HGI was Hayden's company—she'd realized that she'd been wrong to think that Lois was into matchmaking. Rather, she'd simply given her brother a good business tip.

All other information she knew about Hayden Garrett had come from the business and social section of the Dallas newspaper. He was seen at one high-profile party after another, with one beautiful woman after another. He gave a lot of money to charity, but when it came to business, he took no prisoners.

None of her resources, however, had prepared her for the man in person. Tall and lean, he was sex personified.

His dark brown eyes were velvet pools of seduction. His jaw was strong, his chin square. His dark brown hair gleamed shiny and healthy and was cut collar length, long enough to make a woman's fingers itch to run through it, long enough to make a woman try to imagine what it would be like to clutch those same strands while he made love with her.

All in all, each of his parts came together to make up the best recipe she'd ever seen for walking dynamite.

She knew this, yet she could feel herself reacting to him. But he was here for one thing and one thing only, she reminded herself, and it wasn't her.

"I'm grateful Lois didn't decide you should know all the little details of my life. Frankly, you would have been bored to death if she had."

"Oh, I don't know about that. You're the founder, CEO, and president of the conglomerate HGI, which includes the manufacture and distribution of any and all types of food products. Plus, according to the newspapers, you keep gobbling up other companies at an astounding rate. If that tells me nothing else about you, it tells me that, at the very least, you've been busy."

He grinned. "It's kept me off the streets."

She put her elbow on the table and cupped her chin in her hand. "So, Mr. Hayden Garrett, what has brought you to my humble cafe this afternoon?"

"The same thing that prompted me to send three of my top negotiators over here, one by one. Your chocolate fudge, your Ecstasy. I want to buy the rights to the recipe."

Of course he did. Why else would a man such as Hayden Garrett be in her cafe? "Then you've wasted a trip, just as your three executives did before you."

"Everything has a price, Brenna. All you have to do is name yours."

"Sorry, but my recipe is not for sale, not to you or to anyone else, for that matter."

He stared at her for a moment, then pulled a notepad and a gold pen from his inside jacket pocket and wrote down a figure. After tearing off the piece of paper from the pad, he pushed it across the table to her. "Tell me you can turn that amount down."

She glanced at the figure, then calmly returned her gaze to him. "I can turn that amount down."

He studied her for several seconds. "What's it going to take?"

She slowly smiled. "Something you don't have."

Eagerly, he shifted forward. "Then there *is* something. Name it and I'll get it."

She burst out laughing. "Give up, Hayden. You buy and sell corporations every day. It's not going to ruin your career if you don't get my fudge recipe."

"That's not the point."

"Oh, *no.* You mean I've missed the point?" Mischief sparkled in her eyes.

His gaze narrowed on her.

She chuckled. "Hayden, you're just going to have to accept that you can't have everything you want in life. If you haven't learned that already, you need to learn it now."

"Well, I'll tell you, Brenna. There's not that much I want anymore, but I do want your recipe." He paused. "You must have some vulnerability. What about your employees? Have you considered that they might succumb to bribery?"

"It's been tried, but you might offer Cora a red BMW and see where it gets you."

"You don't look worried."

"The thing is, Hayden, my employees watch me make the fudge every day, and they tell everyone the same thing: They don't have a clue. As far as they're concerned, I wave a magic wand over the pans."

Three orgasms started simultaneously from another part of the café. She looked at him with laughter dancing in her eyes. "You don't really want to be responsible for women all over America doing that, do you?"

"You bet I do. And who said anything about limiting it to America? Our distribution is worldwide. Brenna, in case no one has pointed it out to you yet, this could eventually mean millions of dollars for you."

"I have a brain. I know how things work, and I also know how much money it could mean to me." She sighed. "Look, I owe you no explanation, but just out of curiosity, let me ask you something. What's so wrong with the way I'm doing things? I love my business, just as it is, and it's not about how much money I'm making. It's about having fun and knowing that my business is successful because of *my* talent and *my* energy. I don't want it to get any bigger. This size is perfect, because I can manage and oversee everything. This place is mine and no one can take it away from me unless I fail to make my monthly payment to the bank. And since you've no doubt already researched my financing, you know I've nearly paid off my note."

He nodded. "Your financial profile is very sound."

"Yes, it is, which also makes me happy."

"There's nothing wrong with all of this for most people,

Brenna, but it's not good enough for you. You have the potential to be gigantic."

"But I don't want to be gigantic. Who knows? One day I may want to expand. If so, and if the next-door space ever becomes available, I'll knock through a wall. But that's the extent of my expansion dreams. Trust me, I will never expand across America, nor will I ever go global."

"Okay, then here's something else you should consider. I know I'm not the first person who's come here to try to get the rights. The problem is, with so many people trying to get the recipe, you may lose control, and there'll be nothing you can do about it."

"What do you mean?"

"There are a lot of unscrupulous people in this business."

She shrugged. "I'm sure there are in any business."

He sat back in his chair and stared at her. "I'm not one of them, Brenna. Do you understand? You can trust me. Accept my offer, and I can protect you and your fudge."

"If I sign over the rights to my recipe, it will no longer be mine, and *that* is not acceptable to me. Now, it was a pleasure meeting you, but if you'll excuse me, I need to get back to work."

Before she could rise, his hand shot out to grasp her wrist. "Relax. Everything is under control with your café. In fact, it's perfect. Women are having orgasms at practically every table."

Now that she'd talked to him for a while, stared into the depths of his sensual brown eyes, the word *orgasm* coming from him made her feel warm and flushed.

Just for a moment, she allowed herself to wonder what it would be like to have an orgasm with him. In more than one respect, he was a powerful man. Something told her he wouldn't be satisfied with anything second-rate. He wouldn't stop making love to her until she had an orgasm that would necessitate his having to peel her off the ceiling. Just thinking about it made her toes curl.

"You *do* realize, don't you, that they're not actually having orgasms."

He smiled. "Let's just say I recognize an orgasm when I see one."

"I prefer the term orgasm*like*."

Slowly he smiled. "Why would you settle for *orgasmlike* when you could have a real orgasm? One that would take you to the stars and back."

"You misunderstood me." And he'd done so deliberately, she reflected darkly. He was trying to play with her like a cat with a mouse, and he wasn't going to get away with it. "I was talking about the way women respond to the fudge. I wasn't talking about myself."

"Oh, then, you *do* prefer to have a real orgasm."

She gritted her teeth. "That, Mr. Garrett, is none of your business."

"Maybe not right now. But when you finally realize what a good deal I'm offering you and we go into business together, then your business will be my business and vice versa. And what happened to calling me Hayden?"

She folded her arms beneath her breast and shook her head in amused amazement. "You really know how to twist things around to your benefit, don't you?"

"I didn't get where I am today *without* knowing."

"Uh-huh. Okay." She pushed up from the table. "It's been very interesting talking to you, but the answer to your offer is still no."

"Does that *no* apply only to my offer for your recipe? Or does it also apply to your preference for an orgasmlike orgasm?"

"I never said—" She shut her mouth before she could say something else that he'd take and use as fuel for the fire he obviously could make all by himself. "Good-bye, Hayden. If you're ever in this part of town around lunchtime and you're hungry, by all means drop in again. I'd love to take your money." She turned to walk away, but his last words stopped her.

"We'll definitely see each other again, Brenna."

His tone was so self-confident, she wanted to throw something at him. And for some odd reason, she wanted to turn around and look at him one more time. She didn't do either. She kept walking.

As soon as he pulled his car out into traffic, Hayden punched his sister's number on his car phone and waited impatiently for her to pick up.

"Hello?"

"Guess what?"

"Hayden, this is no time for guessing games. One of the twins just threw up on the Aubusson grandmother gave James and me as our wedding gift because he ate too many sweets at a neighborhood birthday party, and the other one is running buck naked through the front-yard sprinklers."

"Never mind them. I need to tell you something."

"Oh, *nice* concern over your nephews, Hayden. Nice."

"Lois, are either of them in any imminent danger?"

"It all depends on how I feel when I get hold of them. Oh, great. I just looked out the window and now the next-door neighbor's kids have taken off their clothes and joined Nicholas."

"Good. He has company. Now, what about Noah? Does he need you?"

"No. Now that he's thrown up, he's fine. It's the Aubusson I'm worried about. Besides, don't you dare hang up until you tell me how your meeting with Brenna went."

"It went fine."

"Fine? *Fine?* That's all you have to say?"

"Pretty much."

"You're infuriating. I want details, and I want them now."

"She didn't agree to let me have her recipe."

"I didn't think she would."

"But she also hasn't accepted any offers from other companies, which means I still have a chance." He thought for a moment. "Sooner or later, she'll accept one of our offers—she's too smart not to—and I'm going to make sure it's my offer she accepts."

"Ummm, I don't know, Hayden. Brenna has different values than the people with whom you're used to doing business. And I also might add different values from the women with whom you're used to dating. So, come on. Tell me. You liked her, didn't you?"

"I'd have to be dead not to, but don't start congratulating yourself. This is only going to be a business match." That and he was going to get her into his bed or die trying.

"Of course, Hayden."

He grinned ruefully. His sister knew him too well. "Lois, I need your help."

"My help? *Wonderful.* Does it involve Brenna? What do you want me to do?"

He grinned at her enthusiasm. "I want you to give a party Saturday night."

"Uh, in case you haven't noticed, this is Monday, which means it's very short notice. What kind of party?"

"A big party. At least two hundred."

"Earth to Hayden. Earth to Hayden. Come back to the real world. *No one* could pull off that big a party given this short amount of time."

"So you're saying you can't do it?"

"I'm not saying anything of the sort. Who do you want me to invite?"

"I want you to invite Brenna and whoever else you want."

"I don't know if Brenna will come, Hayden. Saturday night is a big work night for her. Besides, Valentine's Day is coming up, which will make her even busier. She caters parties, you know."

"So you *can't* do it?"

"Damn it, Hayden. Quit pushing my buttons. Of *course* I can do it."

"That's my girl. Brenna has a staff. Convince her to use them. I'm counting on you."

"Ummm, Hayden. By any chance, is there any other reason why you'd want to see Brenna again? Other than the recipe, I mean?"

"What other reason could there be?"

"Oh, I don't know. Maybe because she's genuinely wonderful."

"For once, Lois, you'll be happy to know that I agree with you."

"Ha! I knew it. I just *knew* it. I knew all you'd have to do was meet her, and you'd fall hard for her."

"Fall for her?" He frowned as he took a corner. "I didn't say anything about falling for her."

"You didn't have to. I heard it in your voice."

"Don't go there, babe. This is not about matchmaking. This is about business."

"I know, I know. So what did she think about you? Did she like you?"

"Like me?" He chuckled, remembering the way she'd walked away from him. "What's not to like?"

"Uh-oh. Something tells me you weren't on your best behavior with her. Listen to me, if you did anything to upset her—"

"Relax Lois. She even invited me back to have lunch there again."

"Uh-huh. But not with her, right?"

"Which is why I want an opportunity to see her again in different surroundings, one where she's not working. You better get busy and find someone who can clean that Aubusson before Saturday night."

Lois sighed. "And right after that, I'm going to call Mom

and ask her why she couldn't have given me a regular brother."

"A regular brother?"

"Yeah, one that would give me more than five days to pull off a party."

TWO

Brenna braked to a halt at a stop sign, waited for a car to pass from the other direction, then stepped on the accelerator to proceed. She'd never know exactly how she'd let Lois talk her into attending her party tonight. Dallas's high-powered, glamorous, social scene was something she'd never actually participated in. She simply catered the parties and then went home, and she liked it that way.

But she'd learned in the last few days that Lois was obviously related to her brother in more ways than the slight family resemblance. She had both his charm and his determination.

And somehow, Cora had gotten into the mix. When Brenna had showed reluctance to go shopping for something new to wear, Cora had threatened to go out and buy her a dress herself. The thought of what Cora would return with propelled her into her own shopping trip, and in the end, she'd lucked out and found something she liked at one of the many secondhand shops around town.

Her choice was a filmy dress in jade green. The fitted

bodice was held up by narrow straps that crossed her shoulders to the low back. The skirt's light-as-air layers drifted outward when she moved and ended at different lengths above and below her knees. She found a pair of high heels almost the same color and brushed out her hair to fall loose to below her shoulder blades.

Right before she'd walked out the door, she'd glanced at herself in the mirror and stilled. She was so used to seeing herself in the white smocks she worked in, she'd forgotten how she could look if she put a little effort into her appearance. Staring at herself in the mirror, she saw that she looked . . . different, definitely different . . . maybe even attractive . . . maybe even a little sexy.

A knot formed in her stomach. What was she doing? Why had she let Lois talk her into this party? She'd so much rather supervise the catering job that was booked for tonight. Normally, she put in a personal appearance at every event she catered, double-checking every detail. But Cora had assured her that she and the rest of their small staff could easily take care of everything tonight. And they could. After all, she'd trained them well.

But still, she felt off balance, and the reason wasn't because tonight she was going to be in front of the catering table instead of behind it. It was because of Hayden Garrett.

Since his appearance in her cafe on Monday, she hadn't heard anything from him: not a call, not a note, not a repeat visit. No reason why she should have heard from him, she supposed. *Except* she hadn't been able to get him out of her mind, and all week she'd been wondering if he'd be at tonight's party.

There was something definitely different about him, something that had made her linger at his table and give him more of her time than she'd given all the others who'd come with offers. He'd had charm and intelligence, but so had many of the others. He'd had sex appeal that if graphed would go right off the charts. He had those eyes. But most of all, she'd believed him when he'd said he was not unscrupulous.

Get a grip, Brenna. Even if Hayden were at the party, he'd more than likely have a date, and if he showed any interest in her at all, it would be because he wanted the Ecstasy recipe.

Just ahead she saw Lois's multicolumned, two-story, redbrick home. It was brightly lit and young men in red vests were running back and forth, doing a remarkable job of keeping up with the many gleaming, expensive cars clogging the driveway and the street.

She hadn't realized the party would be so big, but on the other hand, Lois hadn't been very clear about it, beyond mentioning it would be a Valentine's Day party. Seemingly, her only concern had been to ensure that Brenna would attend, and to that end, she'd called her at least twice a day.

Well, she was here now, Brenna reflected wryly. She might as well have fun.

The Cadillac in front of her drove into the circular driveway and she followed. Almost immediately, her door was opened by a red-vested young man.

He extended his hand to help her out of the car. "Good evening."

"Good evening." She relinquished her keys to him.

"May I have your name?"

"Brenna Woods."

The young man ran down a list on a clipboard, checked off her name, then scribbled her last name along with her car's make and model and her license plate number on a tag that he attached to her keys. At parties of this type, security precautions such as these were common.

"Listen, if my car dies on you, just wait thirty seconds and try again. Okay?" A new car was very low on her list of priorities. Every cent she made was plowed back into her business.

To his credit, his smile never slipped as he climbed into her eleven-year-old car. "No problem."

At the top of the steps, a handsome man with streaks of gray at his temples greeted her with a friendly smile. "Welcome. I'm Lois's husband, James, and you must be Brenna."

She returned his smile. "And you must be clairvoyant."

He laughed. "Not at all. But Lois told me to expect you, and she all but drew me a picture of you."

"Really? How nice of her to think of me when she has so many other guests."

"She said you might not know many people, and she wanted you to feel comfortable." He grinned. "Besides, you and your fudge are very special to her. I've heard a lot about that fudge. I've also eaten a few pieces."

"And?"

"It was very good."

She liked him. "How diplomatic. Listen, don't feel bad if you didn't like the fudge as much as Lois does. Men and women generally have a different reaction to it."

"Ah, maybe that explains it. I'm estrogen deprived, and so the gender that has it is often a mystery to me."

She laughed. "Testosterone sometimes presents the same problems for me."

He hooked her arm over his. "We're soul mates. Come on in. I'll get you something to drink and introduce you around."

"Thanks. That would be great."

"Allow me to take that particular job off your hands, James."

Brenna looked around to see Hayden strolling up, dark and elegant in a black suit and a white collarless shirt. Her heart gave a hard thud against her rib cage.

James chuckled. "Good grief, Hayden. What do you have? Radar? Brenna just this minute arrived and already you've found her, the prettiest woman at the party besides Lois."

Hayden smiled lazily at her. "What can I say? I'm blessed. Besides, even if I hadn't been lying in wait for her, I would have recognized her laugh. Hello, Brenna."

"Hello, Hayden."

James looked from one to the other of them. "You two know each other?"

Brenna nodded, having a hard time tearing her gaze away from Hayden. "We've met."

"And we've become fast friends." Flecks of humor danced in the depths of his eyes. "May I show you around? Get you a drink? Keep you all to myself?" He held out his hand for her to take.

"You're outrageous," she murmured but nevertheless took his hand.

"And you're breathtaking, really breathtaking."

His husky voice had a sensual quality about it that curled through her body, liquefying and warming a place low in her belly. But as Hayden was drawing her away, she did have the presence of mind to cast a look over her shoulder at James. "Thank you."

"I didn't really have a chance to do much, but if you need a break tonight from my very intense brother-in-law, come find me."

She smiled. "I'll do that." *Intense.* That was a good description for Hayden, yet still she wanted to spend time with him.

Snagging two champagne glasses with his free hand, Hayden drew her into the large main room where most of the people seemed to be. And she followed, as trusting as a child.

Foolish of her, but at least giving him her hand and following him had been a conscious decision on her part. She'd done so because she'd finally figured out why she'd caved to Lois's persuasiveness to attend the party. She'd actually *wanted* to see Hayden again. Being *knowingly* foolish was a new experience for her.

Just inside the big room, he turned to the right and pulled her along the wall and into an alcove that gave them a certain amount of privacy in the crowded room.

Standing in front of her so that his back was to the room and he was half-blocking her view of the party, he handed her one of the two champagne glasses, then chimed his against hers. "To getting to know one another better."

She smiled up at him. "And to surviving the process."

He put his hand over his heart. "Hey, I'm not that hard a guy to get along with."

"No, of course you aren't," she agreed. "Not as long as you get what you want."

He grinned at her. "You say that as if it were a bad thing."

She sipped at her cool champagne, savoring its taste as it slid down her throat. "An educated guess tells me it generally would be for the person from whom you want something."

"Why?"

"Because I doubt if you would ever quit trying to obtain what it is you want."

"Well, you're wrong. I look at each case separately and often decide that some things simply aren't worth the effort it would take to obtain them."

She was surprised. "That's nice to hear."

"Why?"

"Because it sounds like such a . . . normal, sensible thing to do."

He threw back his head and laughed. "You had doubts that I was normal or sensible?"

"I may be slightly wary on the subject. After all, you did come on to me like gangbusters on Monday."

"Ah, yes. And I'll warn you that you have every right to be wary, because in your case, I *still* want something from you."

His deep voice sent tingles down her spine. "Thanks for the warning. It's very sporting of you."

"That's me in a nutshell. Sporting."

She chuckled. "Why don't I believe that?"

"I have no idea. But believe this. Your hair—I love the way you're wearing it tonight." He reached out and lightly touched a strand. "You should always wear it loose like this, down around your shoulders."

"Thank you, but I can't wear it this way when I'm working. Health department rules."

"What a shame." Once again, he reached out to her hair, but this time, he closed his hand around a section and fingered it as if he were feeling a piece of fine, silken material.

Trying her best not to let his touch affect her, she took another sip of champagne and surveyed as much of the crowd as she could see with him standing in front of her. She was surprised to see that quite a few of the guests were customers of her shop. She also recognized the sound of the band that was playing. They were a wildly popular group, and had to be booked months ahead.

"This is a lovely party, but . . ."

"Trying to change the subject?"

She nodded. "Trying, yes. So, humor me. Lois said that this was going to be a Valentine's Day party, but Valentine's Day comes on the same day every year, and it seemed to me since she and I talked every day, that she was throwing the party together at the last minute. Is that right?"

He nodded. "Yes."

She was convinced that if a woman stared long enough into the velvet depths of his dark brown eyes, she'd melt into a warm pool of jelly. "But why would she do that?"

"Because of you."

She blinked. "I beg your pardon?"

"I asked her to give the party so that I could see you again."

"You mean this whole party . . . all the people . . . the band . . . ?"

"They're all for you—a prettily wrapped package to entice you to come."

"But that means she must have organized all of this in a few days. That's close to impossible. How did she get that band on such short notice?" Of all the things she could have asked, that question was probably the most irrelevant, but she was having trouble comprehending what he was saying.

"Lois has her ways. I've always found it better not to question her too closely."

"But why didn't you simply call me and ask to see me?"

"Because you would have said no."

"Yes, I probably would have, but you could have come to the café again."

"That's your place of business. I wanted our next meeting to be in a more intimate environment."

"You call this intimate?"

He slowly smiled. "So far so good."

She felt overwhelmed and off balance. Right now, a feather would be able to knock her over. People simply didn't do things like this. Except Hayden and Lois had. "This is a very elaborate method of getting to see a person."

He shrugged casually. "Yeah, but it's also a good party, don't you think? My sister never lets me down."

"But is this the way you usually operate? Having your sister throw a party whenever a woman says no to you?"

"Actually, this is a first. But then you're a very special lady."

"Why?" she asked, still scrambling to regain her balance. "Because I said no?"

He grinned. "Maybe that's part of it, but it's not by any means *all* of it."

"But it's most of it, right? You still want the fudge recipe."

"Absolutely. Make no mistake about that. I want that recipe, and I won't give up until I get it."

She shook her head. "I told you I won't sell the recipe, and I mean it. Please believe that, because I couldn't be more sincere. There's no reason for you to keep putting your time and effort into trying to get it, because you're doomed to failure. The recipe is one of those things you mentioned earlier that you should view as not worth the effort." And when he came to that conclusion, she reflected a bit sadly, he would disappear from her life.

"I hate to tell you, but you're wrong again. With the right handling, your recipe could end up being worth millions and millions, and when we're talking those figures, I don't give up that easily. *But* there's also another reason I asked Lois to throw this party."

Her mind was still on the fact that he'd just said he wasn't going to give up on trying to get the recipe when she realized what he'd said. "What is it?"

"You. The minute I laid eyes on you, I decided I wanted you."

Well, she'd asked. Taking another swallow of the champagne gave her a chance to think up a reply. He wanted her and, heaven help her, she wanted him, too. Men like Hayden didn't walk into her life every day—a man who charmed her, sparred with her, and effortlessly and continually tried to seduce her.

He reached out and closed his hand around a section of her auburn hair and brought it forward over her shoulder. Using his fingers, he combed it downward until it fell in loose waves over her breast.

She swallowed against a hard lump that had suddenly appeared in her throat. "You're a very direct man."

"I've never seen any point in beating around the bush."

"No, I can see that about you." Hayden was the kind of man who saw something he wanted and took it. If it was a company, he simply threw enough money at its board of directors or the owner, until it was his. If it was a woman, in most cases he probably only had to look at her and crook his finger. "Let me give you a word of advice, Hayden. Directness is admirable, but in some instances, you might want to try disseminating the information a little at a time."

"Funny. I thought you'd be able to take it."

"Funny. I thought so, too." She looked away, at this point willing to do anything rather than gaze at him. He was way too beguiling.

"But you're not scared."

"Scared?" Her attention was instantly regained, which was probably the whole idea behind his remark in the first place. "I hate to bruise your ego, but it would take more than you to scare me."

"Good," he murmured, concentrating on her hair, his fingers brushing against her breast every time they reached the end of the strands. "Good."

His fingers were scorching her skin. Worse, she could feel herself waiting with anticipation for the next time his fingers combed through her hair and lingered on her breast. "You know what? I'd like to go find Lois and say hello."

"Whatever you say."

Something in his tone put her on alert. He'd easily acquiesced to her wish, yet every line of his hard body clearly stated the power of his determination to have his way and to acquire both the recipe and her. He was a predatory animal and he didn't try to hide it as others might.

An odd thought occurred to her. If she asked him which he wanted worse, the recipe or her, what would he answer?

She decided she didn't want to know. Now now. For tonight, she planned to simply enjoy being with him. Reality would come soon enough. It always did. Hayden was an anomaly in her life. Very soon now, he'd leave with the same speed and abruptness as he'd arrived.

He put his arms around her and drew her against him.

"We'll dance our way over to Lois," he said huskily, then bent his head and pressed his lips to hers.

It was a light, undemanding kiss, but firm and vaguely possessive. She tried not to respond, but as light as the kiss was, it still carried heat, heat that took her by surprise and caused her to grip his shoulders for support. His lips parted, and so did hers. His tongue darted in and out of her mouth as if he were sampling some exotic dish.

As for her, he tasted like something new, erotic, and forbidden. It was a delicious, enticing taste that compelled her to try for more. But then he lifted his head, ending the kiss and leaving her feeling as if her world had just been turned upside down.

As if he had done nothing unusual, and nothing extraordinary had passed between them, he whirled her into the middle of the people who were dancing, leaving her to try to regain her composure, and worse, leaving her to try to get over her craving for more of his kisses. But with his arms around her, it wasn't easy.

Enveloped in his embrace meant she was also enveloped in his heat, his strength, his earthy, masculine scent. Then he drew their hands between their two bodies so that his forearm pressed against the side of her breast.

To her horror, her nipples hardened, and she was positive he knew everything he was doing to her. He was too experienced not to know.

A quiver ran through her. Her hand moved restlessly across his shoulder. She could feel his heart pounding as hard as hers.

He pulled her closer, making her aware of his hard thighs against her legs and his sexual excitement against her pelvis. At her back, his fingers spread over her bare skin. "Like satin," he whispered, his mouth near her ear.

She swallowed, unable to speak. And even if she could have, she didn't know what she would say. She wasn't even aware of her feet or of following his lead. Somehow, he was moving them across the floor and she was with him, floating on a cloud, encased in sensations of heat, weakness, and need. God, the need.

She looked around, but people were caught up in whatever they were doing so that no one seemed to notice that Hayden was practically making love to her on the dance floor. Or maybe that was just the way it felt to her.

"Hi, Brenna." All at once she found herself dragged from Hayden's arms and engulfed in a hug from his sister. "I'm so glad you were able to come. Are you having fun?"

In a daze, she nodded.

"Oh, good. Have you seen the job the caterers did tonight? It's nowhere near the job you would have done, but I refused to ask you to cater a party that you would be attending." She glanced between her brother and her. "Everything going all right?"

"Go away, Lois." Hayden's tone was good-natured as he drew Brenna back into his arms.

Lois smiled at Brenna. "That's my brother. Always so grateful."

"He confirmed that you only had a few days to bring this party together. I don't know how you did it."

Lois rolled her eyes. "I'm not sure myself. I'm at my best when working under a deadline, but let me tell you, I'll be owing people big favors into the next millennium."

"And I *am* grateful," Hayden said.

Lois gave her brother an overly sweet smile. "That's good, because you'll be doing *me* big favors way *beyond* the next millennium."

He grimaced. "You'll get roses tomorrow. What color would you prefer?"

"Sterling."

"Of course. They're the hardest to find."

"And a diamond bracelet wouldn't be a bad idea either."

"Should I ask how many karats?"

"Don't bother. I'll pick it out and send you the bill."

"You're so thoughtful."

"Thank you, and by the way, those things are just for starters."

Brenna was enjoying the byplay between Hayden and Lois, but Hayden kept distracting her. With one arm around her waist, he held her firmly against him. Occasionally, he would run his hand up to the bare skin of her back in a light caress, and each time he did, a fire would shimmer through her.

"James and I have been wanting to get away together for quite a while. I'm thinking the Caymans for us and the twins for you."

"*What?* You expect me to baby-sit those little monsters?"

Laughing, Lois turned to Brenna. "Actually, he adores them and they know it. They're only four and already they can get him to do anything they want."

She looked up at Hayden, trying to see him as a loving uncle, taking care of a pair of four-year-olds. Nope. She couldn't see it. She could only view him as a seducer, because it was what he was currently doing to her with such expertise.

"Excuse me, Hayden, but may I cut in on you and have a dance with Brenna?"

Brenna turned toward the voice to see Robert Ramsey. He was tall, tanned, and in his early forties. He was also the head of one of the companies who had contacted her about buying the rights to her fudge recipe. He'd talked to her several times about it, but unlike Hayden who would probably still be trying to get her recipe on the day she died, Robert had eventually taken her refusal with good grace. "Hi, Robert. How nice to see you again."

He smiled at her. "My feelings exactly. Lois's parties are always fun, but seeing you here tonight is an added bonus I wasn't counting on."

Hayden addressed Robert, but kept his gaze on his sister in silent query. "I didn't know you'd be here, either."

Robert laughed. "I'm not on the official guest list. I had invited Christine Marshall out to dinner tonight, and since Christine is your sister's best friend and had an invitation to the party, I tagged along with her."

"Christine always brings the nicest people," Lois said to him with the finesse of a born hostess, "and I hope you know you're always welcome."

"Thank you, Lois." Robert turned to Hayden. "Well? May I?"

"No."

"You don't have to ask him," Brenna said. "I'd love to dance with you."

"Wonderful."

A quick glance at Hayden showed her his face looked like a storm cloud. *Too bad.* Robert was exactly the antidote she needed against Hayden's intense and seductive ways. She slipped from Hayden's arms into Robert's.

"Hayden didn't look at all happy about relinquishing you to me," Robert said as they danced away.

"It doesn't matter. *I* wanted to dance with you."

Robert smiled. "Gee, why am I not surprised that you have such an independent spirit?"

She laughed. He was easy to dance with, holding her loosely in his arms, and he was easy to talk to since he had no ulterior motives. "Could it have anything to do with the fact that I kept turning down your offers?"

He laughed. "And the lovely young lady wins the prize."

"Well, don't worry. I know Hayden is one of your competitors, but he's not going to get the recipe, either. No one is. So you'll never be put into a situation where you have to go up against my fudge."

"That's a relief. If your fudge ever did go into mass production, there'd be nothing my company could come up with that would come close to beating it."

"I'm not sure about that, but thanks anyway." As casually

as possible, she scanned the room to see if she could find Hayden. He was nowhere to be seen.

"But what about you?"

"What about me?"

"Have you ever thought about getting your own backing and putting it out on the market yourself?"

"No."

"You're a remarkable woman, Brenna. You're sitting on a mountain of money, and you don't seem to care."

She sighed. "Please, could we talk about something else? I'm getting very tired of the subject."

"I can understand that. Okay, how about I tell you how beautiful you look tonight?"

She laughed. "Great subject."

She gave the room another scan. Still no Hayden. She must be crazy. Minutes ago, she willingly and eagerly walked out of his arms. Now she missed him. She *was* crazy.

"I know. Let's go over to the buffet tables. I want to see what kind of job my competition did for tonight's party."

He laughed. "Normally, I'd be wounded to think that a girl would prefer to look at a buffet table rather than dance with me, but since it's you, I know better than to take it personally."

"Thank you, Robert."

Ten minutes later, Robert was with his date on the dance floor and Brenna was at the buffet table, her plate filled with samples of food and surrounded by several ladies who frequented her shop.

"Don't worry, Brenna," one of them was saying quietly, so as not to be overheard by the servers. "These people can't hold a candle to the work you do."

"I don't know about that," she said, eating a shrimp ball. "This is extremely good."

Another woman stepped closer, her voice low and confiding. "There's very good, and then there's excellent. Your food is excellent. Believe us. There's no comparison."

Brenna smiled at them. "I thank you all for your loyalty." At that moment, she happened to glance up and saw Hayden, watching her with intent in those velvet brown eyes of his.

Suddenly the women noticed him, too, and to Brenna's amusement, the women she knew to be otherwise smart and sensible turned into flirtatious vixens.

"Oh, hi, Hayden."

"It's good to see you again, Hayden."

"You look extremely handsome tonight, Hayden."

"Hello, ladies. My, but don't you all look beautiful."

The women giggled like little girls. Two of them were married, but it didn't seem to matter. Mentally, Brenna marveled at Hayden's effect on them, but she couldn't condemn them. She knew all too well how he could turn a normally sensible woman into someone who practically melted at a simple touch from him.

He looked over at her. "May I have another dance?"

The thought of dancing with him again and being held close against his body set her pulse racing with excitement. Amazing. It didn't even take the fact, only the thought.

Either she was incredibly easy or he was very good. It took only a moment to decide both things were true.

THREE

Out on the dance floor, Hayden once again took her into his arms, and she was surprised to discover his arms felt achingly familiar and, in an odd way, comfortable, almost as if they were a place where she belonged.

"Did you enjoy your dance with Robert?" His mouth was pressed to her ear as he asked the question, and his warm breath stirred her hair and feathered into her ear. Pleasurable sensations shivered through her.

"Yes, I did."

"I gather he's one of the people who contacted you about your recipe?"

She nodded. "But unlike you, he took no for an answer."

"Did he? That's interesting."

"How so?"

"Because taking no for an answer doesn't sound like the Robert I know."

Already her body was molding itself to his, her blood was heating, and an aching emptiness was growing in her lower body. If she stayed in his arms much longer, she would give in to her desire and agree to make love whenever and wherever he wanted.

Once again, he pressed his mouth to her ear. "I *hated* watching you dance with him." His tone was suddenly rough as he pulled her hard against him.

"I didn't see you," she said, gasping at the new closeness. Fire sparked between them and the intensity excited her, making it hard for her to breathe. "I thought maybe you'd left."

"Why would I leave when *you* were still here?"

If the scene with the three ladies hadn't reminded her, her body's reaction to Hayden did. He knew exactly how to play a woman to gain a desired effect.

The trouble was, she believed him when he said he wanted her, and the wanting had quickly become mutual. In this case, though, she had to remember that he also wanted the recipe. Maybe he figured he'd kill two birds with one stone, make her fall for him so hard that she'd go to bed with him and, at the same time, simply hand over the recipe.

Suddenly she felt exhausted. From the moment Hayden had walked up to her this evening, her senses had been under siege. She wasn't sure she had even tried to fight against the intense hunger he could so effortlessly evoke in her.

And she definitely didn't want to leave the circle of his arms. She loved the way they moved together, and she loved the feel of his hard, muscled body against hers. In fact, she'd love nothing more than to go on dancing with him into the night, which was a problem, a big one.

Because she'd also love to lie naked and sweaty with him in bed, their arms and legs entangled with one another while they made love together. Instinct told her she needed to protect herself, but she didn't want to heed the warning. Yet another big problem.

God, her head was beginning to hurt, trying to consider all the angles and stem her growing craving for him. It took all her effort, but she pushed against him. "Please excuse me. I need to go home now."

Instantly, he pulled back and looked down at her, a frown creasing his brow. "What's wrong? Was it something I did or said?"

She shook her head. "No, I'm just tired. It's been a long week." She surveyed the crowd. "I don't see Lois right now, but will you please thank her for me and tell her I had a lovely time?"

He eyed her with concern. "Are you sure nothing's wrong? Do you feel ill?"

He was truly worried about her. She almost laughed. Hayden had been straight with her from the first. He was a business shark who wanted something she had to make his business grow even bigger. He also desired her. And now she honestly believed there was nothing on his mind other than a sincere concern for her. This man was going to be the ruination of her yet. "Nothing's wrong."

"Then stay, at least for a little while longer."

His smile was incredibly persuasive, too persuasive. "No, I'm sorry, but I'd rather not."

"Okay, then if I can't change your mind about staying, let me take you home."

"I brought my own car."

"Okay, then I'll walk out with you."

He fell into step beside her, and she just had to laugh. "I've never met a man who dislikes the word no as much as you do."

He seemed surprised. "I wouldn't have thought *anyone* liked it."

"I suppose not, but you just never stop pushing."

Outside, she gave her name to the same red-vested young man who had parked her car for her earlier in the evening. He jogged off down the street in search of her car.

With his brow still creased, Hayden was silent for several moments, but strangely enough, as if she were connected to him in some way, she could almost hear the wheels turning in his head.

"If my pushing bothers you, Brenna, I'm sorry. In fact, I'm incredibly sorry. I could tell you I will try to change and I'd give it my all, but truthfully, I'm not sure how successful I'd be. Pushing is just my nature. It's how I got where I am today."

Now it was her turn to be surprised. What was he saying? That he'd actually try to change for her? She took a deep breath. "You know, I never actually said it bothered me."

"But it's got to be bothering you or you wouldn't have mentioned it." Casually, he slipped one hand into his trouser pocket, then captured her wrist with his other. "At this rate, I'm going to run you off, and believe me, that's not something I want to happen."

He was talking on a personal level, not a business level. Just as she was assimilating that piece of information, he lifted her hand and pressed his mouth against the sensitive underside of her wrist where the delicate blue veins traced a pattern beneath her almost translucent skin. She was sure he could feel her pulse race beneath his lips, and she couldn't control the shiver his touch evoked.

"Hey," he said softly, so softly she looked up at him. "I'm truly sorry if I've given you a hard time."

A hard time? What should she say to that? He'd made her laugh. He'd made her feel incredible heat and need. He'd made her forget for minutes at a time that his bottom line was the recipe. He'd made her aware of herself as a woman, something that hadn't happened for far too long. All in all, it had been one of the most interesting and enjoyable evenings she'd spent in a long time.

"You haven't," she murmured, then saw the young man jogging back to them.

"I'm afraid your car won't start, Miss Woods."

"Did you wait thirty seconds and try it again?"

"Yes, ma'am, but it wouldn't turn over."

"Okay, just tell me where it is, and I'll go get it started."

The young man handed her the keys and gave her the directions.

"I'm coming with you," Hayden said. "Maybe I can help."

"It's not necessary. My car can be cranky, but as my mother always says, it's just a matter of holding your mouth right."

He chuckled. "I can't imagine you holding your mouth wrong, but okay, that's fine. I'm still coming with you. I don't want you alone on some side street, stuck with a stalled car."

His protectiveness startled, then touched her. During the evening, her emotions had run the gamut. How could she ever survive Hayden? Then again, could she really survive without him? She wasn't sure, but it was a question that took her aback. It was also a question she needed to think carefully about.

At her car, he frowned. "*This* is your car?"

She laughed as she unlocked the door and slid in. "Come on, it's not that bad. My parents gave it to me when I graduated from high school."

"So that makes it what? Ten years old?"

"Give or take a year, but it gets great mileage and is usually pretty dependable."

"If you say so."

She rotated the key in the ignition. It turned over, but it wouldn't catch. She waited thirty seconds and tried a second time. Once again it turned over, but wouldn't catch. "This is strange."

"It sounds as if it's something serious."

She shook her head. "Sometimes it just gets cranky. I'll wait another thirty seconds and try again."

"Okay."

He was standing patiently beside her, his elbow propped on the open door. This Hayden Garrett didn't seem like the high-powered president and CEO of his own company who had come to see her on Monday. Rather, he seemed like a man who had nothing better to do than stand on a quiet side street on a moonlit night and wait to see if her car would start.

She tried it again. It wouldn't catch. Again. Same result. She wasn't doing any good, she realized, plus she was running down her battery and at the same time flooding the car.

With a sigh, she slid out of the car and stood staring at the car's hood, turning various possibilities over in her mind.

"Sounds as if you need a good mechanic."

She nodded, still thinking. Finally she said, "Okay, normally it would have started by now. I'll have to find a garage and get it towed."

"Look, it's almost midnight on a Saturday night. Tomorrow is Sunday. You're not going to find a garage open."

"I know, but I can go back to Lois's, call for a tow truck, have the car towed to the garage I normally use, then take a cab home."

Gently he took her arm, maneuvered her free of the car door, then closed and locked it. "I'll take you home, arrange for my mechanic to come look at it tomorrow and, if necessary, he'll tow it to his place. He won't mind working on a Sunday. He should have your car up and running by tomorrow afternoon."

"Uh, no. I can't afford Sunday rates. Besides, I've got a mechanic I use. I'll take care of the details."

He opened his mouth as if he were going to argue with her, then closed it again. As they strolled back toward the house, he reached for her hand. "I'll take you home."

"That's not necessary."

He looked over at her, a wry smile curling his lips. "No, it's probably not. But you see, I want to."

She didn't offer any further objections. With him in this

gentle, relaxed mood, he was a hard man to resist. Actually, in any mood, he was a hard man for her to resist.

Built in the thirties, her house was a one-story, two-bedroom redbrick with a covered front porch and a large maple tree in the front yard.

Hayden walked around his car, opened her door, and extended his hand to help her out. "I like your house."

"You do?" Some things she'd found she could intuit amazingly well about him. Other things came out of left field. Liking her house was one of those things.

"Why are you so surprised?"

"It's just that I would have thought your tastes ran to something grander, something like your sister's place, for instance."

"Actually, my place is larger than Lois's, but just because something is larger doesn't always mean it's better."

She smiled at him. "That's the way I've always felt, too. It's how I feel about my cafe and my fudge."

He chuckled. "I walked right into that one, didn't I?"

"You certainly did."

"Gloating doesn't become you."

She laughed. "Maybe not, but it sure is fun."

As they drew closer to the door, she found herself becoming nervous. Was he going to kiss her good night? They'd already kissed, so another kiss shouldn't be any big deal. Was she going to ask him in? Surely there'd be nothing wrong with that. A cup of coffee, music on the stereo, nice conversation. No, there wouldn't be anything wrong with that.

Who was she kidding? He'd practically made love to her on the dance floor. There was no telling what would happen in the privacy of her home.

At her door, she inserted her key into the lock and opened the door into the hallway. Then she turned back to him. "Please tell Lois I had a lovely time at the party."

His smile was unnervingly gentle. "You've already asked me to do that."

"Oh, right. Well, thank you for bringing me home." She glanced over her shoulder down the long, dark hallway, then looked back at him. "I'd ask you in, but—"

"Thank you, I'd love to come in."

"No. That is . . . Yes. That would be nice. Come on in and I'll make us something to drink."

"Wonderful."

Wonderful, she silently repeated with a tad of sarcasm directed solely at herself. In the end, she'd done exactly what she'd wanted to do.

"Would you like coffee or maybe some hot chocolate?" she offered.

"Hot chocolate?" There was a hint of amusement in his eyes.

"Yes. The caffeine hit of hot chocolate isn't as intense as it is in coffee. I like it better at this time of . . ." Her words trailed off when she saw the devilish expression on his face.

"Does it have the same effect on women as your fudge?"

Her mouth went dry at his husky tone. "On second thought, maybe we should just stick to coffee."

She hadn't left many lights on, but her hallway wasn't wide enough for furniture, so she wasn't afraid Hayden would trip. Besides, he was following very close behind her. "If you'd like, you can wait in the living room while I get the coffee under way."

"I'd rather be wherever you are."

She glanced back at him. He looked sexy and sophisticated and his expression was calm and assured as if walking into a woman's home was an everyday occurrence to him.

She stopped and turned toward him. "Okay, it's time I admit something to you. I'm a little nervous here, because it's been a long time since I've invited a man into my home."

"Then I'm honored to be the one you asked. I'll also

admit that I'm extremely happy there hasn't been anyone in your life for a while." He smiled in the dim light of the hallway. "It's a macho thing, I suppose, a man wanting to think he's not one of many."

Something she was sure he couldn't say about her. "You must be a pro at this sort of thing—being in a woman's home."

"Being in a woman's home is not a pro event, as far as I know."

"You know what I mean."

"Yes, I do." He folded his fingers around her upper arms and gently pulled her to him. "There's no reason for you to be nervous. Nothing is going to happen that you don't want to happen. Do you believe me?"

"Yes," she whispered. She trusted him, but she wasn't so sure about herself.

"And if at any time you decide you want me to leave, just tell me. Okay?"

"Okay." It sounded so simple, she thought, but there was nothing simple about the way she was feeling about him. Common sense was clashing with a need that became stronger every time she looked at him.

"Good. Then let's explore another subject for a minute. Did you seriously consider *not* inviting me in?"

"No."

He released one of her arms to comb his fingers over her hair. "Do you know why?"

She cleared her throat. "Because I didn't see anything wrong with it."

"And because you wanted to?"

"That, too."

"Do you know why?"

"I . . ." She couldn't think of anything to say that wouldn't tell him more about herself than she wanted him to know right then.

"It's all about chemistry, Brenna, and you and I have it in spades."

His voice was low and raspy, and it touched every nerve ending in her body. She was a believer.

"Something powerful and volatile ignited between the two of us from the moment we met, and it wasn't only all those orgasms going on around us." His fingers closed around a section of her hair, and his hand rested just above her breast. "During this past week, I couldn't forget you. In fact, I didn't even try. How about you? Could you forget about me?"

"No." Her lungs felt congested with heat. Her knees felt weak.

"And then, when we saw each other tonight, it began again. And with every minute I held you in my arms, the chemistry grew more powerful, more volatile, until it's a wonder we didn't set something on fire."

"I know," she whispered.

"Then let's forget the coffee for now and do something we'd both rather be doing. Let's make love."

He'd never know how badly she wanted to say yes to him, but there was something keeping her from saying it—the knowledge that the term *making love* meant different things to each of them.

To Hayden, their coming together would be sex, no matter how hot and wonderful it was. But for her, it would be so much more. Once she agreed to make love with him, there would be no turning back for her. She would be totally committed to him, heart and soul.

She gave a shaky laugh. "There you go again, being direct."

"Too much?"

She could feel the heat coming off his body. Or maybe it was her body that was burning to the point of danger. "No, it's not too much. You're not pushing. But for now, I'd really just like to have a cup of coffee."

He reached out his hand and gently caressed her face, his palm cupping her cheek, his thumb lightly stroking her skin. "Then that's exactly what we'll do."

At times he had a way of knocking the breath out of her and this moment was definitely one of those times. "You know what?"

"What?"

"You're a nice man."

He chuckled again. "You mean, all reports to the contrary?"

She smiled. "And expectations."

Slowly, he lowered his head until his mouth was hovering just above hers. He was giving her every chance to pull away, but she couldn't seem to move. So she waited, her lips parted, her breathing shallow. And when their lips finally touched, something detonated inside her, creating a huge fireball that sent its heat to every part of her body.

His tongue flicked in and out of her mouth, invading, exciting, demanding. And just like that, her world began turning at an ever-increasing speed. She clung tightly to him, returning his kiss with all the pent-up emotions she'd been trying to hold in: the hunger she had for him, the need that was deep in her bones, the passion that was so strong it threatened to implode within her.

How could she control these feelings? How could she fight their chemistry and her spinning world? She didn't think she could.

Slowly, Hayden drew away. "You said something about wanting to have a cup of coffee?" His breathing was ragged, his eyes dark with desire, but his voice remained even.

She gazed up at him, confused, dazed, and engulfed in a haze of heat. "Yes, yes. I did." She put a hand on the hall wall to steady herself. "Thank you for remembering."

She couldn't decide whether her thank-you was sincere or not. She'd been very close to letting herself go completely. Her body reacted to his slightest touch, to his every spoken word, and there didn't seem to be anything she could do about it. Their lovemaking was just a matter of time. Why not let it happen now when they both wanted it so badly?

"Uh, come into the kitchen, and I'll make us that coffee."

She turned away from him, away from his seductive warmth, and went into the kitchen. But just inside the door, she came to an abrupt halt. Close behind her, Hayden nearly ran into her.

"Brenna?"

"Something is wrong," she whispered, surveying her kitchen and willing her mind to make sense of what she was seeing. "Someone's broken in."

Drawers were pulled out and overturned, her pantry and cabinets were bare, their contents carelessly scattered on the floor. A great many of the dishes were broken. Her shelf of cookbooks had been emptied and the cookbooks were nowhere to be seen. There was broken glass by her kitchen door, where one of the panes had been knocked out.

"I'd better check the rest of the house."

"No." Hayden took her hand. "Come on."

"What?" She couldn't seem to take it all in. Her normally well-organized, immaculate kitchen was ruined. Who would do such a thing? And why?

"We're going to my car to call 911, and we're going to wait there until the police come. The person who broke into your house could still be here."

FOUR

An hour later, the police had come and gone, and Brenna stood in the middle of her living room, staring at the chaos. She knew she needed to start straightening and restoring, but at that very moment, she couldn't seem to do anything but try to control the tremors racking her body.

While the police had been there, taking a statement from her, they'd received a call that Brenna's had also been broken into. Whoever had trashed her home had also done the same thorough job at her cafe.

The two places she felt the safest in the world, the two places she cherished most, had been violated. And she still didn't know why.

Drugs? She might have a bottle of aspirin somewhere, though she wasn't sure where. Money? She rarely carried more than thirty dollars in her purse. Most of the time she simply wrote checks. But maybe whoever had broken in had thought she would have to keep the cash from the cafe's Saturday sales until Monday morning. If so, they'd forgotten about night depositories.

A few feet away from her, Hayden hung up the phone. "Okay. There's a policeman guarding your café for now."

"Why? According to the police report, whoever broke into the cafe did a thorough job the first time. Why would they want to come back?"

"It's a precaution against looters, Brenna."

His tone had been very gentle. Still, she felt the last remaining color in her face drain away. She hadn't even considered looters.

"I've got a crew already on their way over there. They should be there in about thirty minutes and will replace him."

"Crew? What do you mean, crew?"

"Men who work for me in various capacities. They have instructions to change all the locks and replace the glass that was broken. I also told them to do what they could about the mess."

"Thank you, but just have them secure the café. I'll do the rest." She looked around her a bit helplessly. "I'll do what I can here tonight, then go over to the cafe tomorrow." Just thinking about the work that would be involved in getting Brenna's up and running by Monday morning staggered her.

"Don't worry. My people will see to all that."

For the first time since she'd walked into the kitchen and seen that someone had broken in and trashed her home, she truly focused on him. "That's very kind of you, Hayden, but there are things only I will know what to do about."

"That's true, but there are many other things my people can do. If they see a bag of flour poured out on the floor, they can sweep it up, go out, and buy you another bag. Same with sugar. They can also wash your pots and pans, since I'm sure you wouldn't want to use them again until they're thoroughly washed. Same with your linens."

She nodded, wondering at how he understood her feeling that everything possible needed to be washed or dry-cleaned before she could feel good again about her home and cafe.

"You know, everything you've ever heard about a person viewing a break-in of their home as a violation is true."

"I know." He walked over to her and took her hands.

To her chagrin, she felt her eyes well with tears. "I don't even know where to start." She felt helpless and lost, and she didn't know how to handle it, but still, it startled her to hear herself say such a thing. It was so uncharacteristic of her not to even know how to map out a course of action.

"You're in shock, Brenna. Come home with me. Then, after a good night's rest, I'll come back with you tomorrow and help you clean all this up."

"That's very kind of you, but no."

"There's no need to keep telling me I'm being very kind. I wouldn't be here offering to help if I didn't want to."

She nodded an acknowledgment that she'd heard him. "I'm staying here tonight. No one is going to run me out of my own home. If you'll just help me put the mattress back on the bed in my bedroom, then I can do the rest." She drew her hands from his and wrapped her arms around herself. "I'll need to change the sheets," she added in a low tone to herself.

"Hold on for a minute." In what seemed like lightning speed to her, he zipped around the living room, his long arms picking up cushions, throwing them on the couch and chairs, righting the tables, the lamps, and finally the rocking chair.

"That was my grandmother's rocking chair," she murmured. "Is it okay?"

"It looks fine. I don't see a scratch on it."

With all the furniture righted, he went back to the couch and chairs to put order into the cushions. If he didn't get the cushions exactly as she'd had them or even where, he had at least made it so that there were places to comfortably sit and the floor was cleared for walking.

At last he stopped moving. "Coffee," he said firmly. "You

should have coffee." He waved a hand toward the couch. "Sit down. Try to relax. I'll be right back."

She glanced at the door through which Hayden had just disappeared, then looked back at the sofa. She wasn't accustomed to being waited on. Furthermore, she couldn't even imagine that Hayden could find what he needed in the mess to make coffee, much less know how to make it. But at the moment, she couldn't find the energy to go and help him.

She dropped down on the sofa, leaned her head back, and closed her eyes. Someone had broken into her home and her café and torn up both places, yet nothing had been taken. Her TV, VCR, microwave, and computer were all still here. And as for her cafe, the policeman who had spoken with her on the phone had said if anything had been taken, it wasn't obvious, which meant all her appliances were still there.

She opened her eyes as she heard Hayden return.

"The coffee is brewing. Do you take sugar or cream?"

"All of this was done because of my fudge recipe, wasn't it? Someone broke into both of my places, trying to find it."

He dropped down beside her. "Yes." With a hand, he turned her face so that she was looking at him. "But it wasn't me. Do you believe that?"

"Yes. It's not your style."

He expelled a pent-up breath she hadn't noticed he was holding. "Thank God you know that. I was afraid—"

"Hayden, I never for a second considered that it was you. Whoever did this is underhanded and hits below the belt. You, on the other hand, have never been anything but direct with me."

As if something she'd said bothered him, he glanced away to stare at a watercolor painting of flowers that was lying on the floor at an odd angle. "Do you know whether or not the person got the recipe?"

"They didn't get it. The recipe is somewhere quite safe."

"How can you be so sure? Have you looked? Maybe the cafe—"

"The recipe is in my head, Hayden, and has been ever since I was a little girl. When I opened up my cafe and started selling the fudge, my lawyer suggested that I write down the recipe and put it in my safe-deposit box, but somehow it didn't seem right to me."

"Why not? Putting it in a safe-deposit box sounds like a reasonable precaution to me."

"Remember that first day you came to the café and I said you didn't have what it takes to get the recipe?"

A grin flashed across his face. "How could I forget? You wouldn't tell me, and I couldn't guess."

"Well, here's your answer. The recipe has been handed down through the women in my family for generations. The only way to get the recipe is to be born into my family and to be a female."

He stared at her. "So none of us who have come knocking on your door for the rights have ever had a chance?"

"That's not true. When it is passed on, there are no stipulations attached. We're all free to do what we want with it."

"Then there's still a chance."

"If I were so inclined to sell the recipe, yes, but I'm not."

"Unless someone can change your mind." Instantly, he grimaced. "I'm sorry. This isn't the time."

"No, except I want you to understand that you will never get the recipe from me, so you might as well put yourself out of your misery about it. The recipe came to me from my grandmother. She tried to interest my mother in the recipe, but my mother is blatantly uninterested in cooking. On the other hand, I've always loved to cook and literally learned how at my grandmother's knee." She paused. "I'm the first person in my family to ever sell the fudge. Now I almost wish I hadn't."

He reached for her hand and squeezed it. "Don't let

someone else's dishonesty ruin it for you. I've seen you in your cafe. You love what you do. I know that right now, everything you have to do to set things right again must seem insurmountable, but it's not. We'll simply take things one step at a time. And the first step is to get some color back in your cheeks." He pushed himself up from the couch. "The coffee and sandwiches are probably ready by now."

"Sandwiches?"

"I thought you should eat something, since I doubt if you ate much at the party."

She looked after him. What would she have done without him? He'd been wonderful. He'd helped her deal with the police. He'd also made arrangements for her café to be guarded and repaired so that, at least for tonight, it was one thing she didn't have to worry about. And just now as she'd talked to him about the recipe and her family, she'd felt warmth returning to her body, and the awful shock she'd been feeling beginning to recede.

And he'd known what he was doing. He'd gotten her to start talking, to think, to focus, and the helpless feeling that had kept her immobilized had gradually gone away.

Hayden strolled back into the living room carrying a tray. "Since I couldn't find any sugar, I decided you took your coffee black."

"I do. Thank you."

Using his foot, he pushed the ottoman in front of the sofa, then he placed the tray on top of it.

"Melted cheese sandwiches?" she said, gazing at the tray. "I still don't know how you managed to make coffee in that mess in there, much less make the melted cheese sandwiches."

He handed her a cup of coffee and a napkin. "First of all, there's sort of an order to the chaos. For the most part, everything's in the proper area, it's just been torn apart or turned upside down. And as for the melted cheese sandwiches, Lois once showed me in case I got hungry and my housekeeper wasn't there. I've found they're nearly impossible to screw up, especially when you have a toaster oven, which you do."

She smiled and was aware it was the first time she'd smiled since she'd discovered her home had been broken into. "Yeah, I suppose it is."

"Besides, I've always found melted cheese sandwiches to be a comfort food. And don't look so surprised. CEOs occasionally need comforting, you know."

"Remind me to send you a teddy bear."

"What makes you think I don't have one?"

"Do you?"

"You'll have to come over to my house and see for yourself."

She laughed. "Does that line work for you often?"

"You wound me, Brenna. Deeply."

She smiled again. "Thank you, Hayden."

"Don't thank me, yet. You haven't tasted the coffee."

"It doesn't matter. My thank-you is for everything you've done for me tonight, including the laugh you just coaxed out of me."

He took her hand. He was always taking her hand, she realized, as if he didn't like to go too long without touching her, even if it was only her hand. "It would be a crime if you never laughed again, a crime I'd find hard to bear. Now, have a sip of that coffee and tell me how it is."

She did. "Ummm . . . uh . . ."

"It's not that bad, is it?"

Her brow crinkled. "Hayden, do you make coffee often?"

"I've never made coffee in my life."

"I see. Well, I feel awful having to tell you, but quite honestly, this is the worst coffee I've ever tasted."

"It is?"

He looked so astounded, she broke into a peal of laughter. "Don't worry about it. There was bound to be something you weren't good at."

"I suppose." He looked at her for several moments, and she could tell his mind had left the coffee far behind. After a few moments, he smoothed her hair back from her face. "If you won't come home with me, Brenna, then I'm staying here with you tonight."

"Hayden—"

"Don't worry. I'll sleep on the couch, but I'm not leaving you here alone. Whoever did this didn't find the recipe, and they may decide to come back."

A chill swept through her. "I hadn't thought about that."

Brenna flipped from her stomach onto her back. She couldn't seem to get comfortable, and it wasn't the bed. Hayden had put the mattress back on its box springs and helped her make it up with fresh sheets. He'd also insisted on helping her put her bedroom back in some kind of order.

She hadn't wanted him sorting through her panties and bras, though she'd had the sure feeling he would have done it without blinking an eye. But in the end, she'd given him the less intimate job of hanging up her clothes that had been thrown carelessly to the floor. Some clothes had been torn, and at her direction, he'd tossed those garments into a pile so that they could be taken to a seamstress.

If she had her way, she'd throw every single item out that had been touched by the people who had broken in, but that wouldn't be practical. She didn't have the money to replace every stitch of clothing she owned, much less the personal items and the pieces of furniture it had taken her a long time to collect. She'd simply have to be content to get everything washed and dry-cleaned that she could.

She rolled over on her side and punched her pillow. By rights she should be exhausted, but she was wide awake and restless. She couldn't turn off her mind or relax her body.

Part of the reason, of course, was that her house still looked as if a tornado had whirled through it, and her mind kept making lists of the work it would take to get it back as it had been.

Also, she'd decided her café had to be her first priority tomorrow and, as much as she hated the idea, she was going to have to let her house go until she had more time. The thought depressed her because it meant that every evening she'd have to come home to visual reminders of the break-in.

With a heavy sigh, she turned over on her back. If she didn't go to sleep soon, she'd be so tired in the morning she wouldn't be able to accomplish anything.

Was Hayden asleep? she wondered. Or was he awake, having trouble going to sleep as she was? It seemed strange and unsettling in certain ways to have someone else spending the night in her home. Yet somehow it also seemed very right.

If Hayden hadn't been with her when she'd discovered the break-in, she would have managed. She would have still gone into shock, but she would have come out of it in her own time and then she would have swung into action. And if he hadn't already done quite a bit of work in the house that made it possible for her to face what was left to do without breaking down, she would have still managed just fine.

But he had been there for her, and he was here now, and it felt very, very good.

In reality, she knew so little about him. Where had he been born? Where had to gone to school? What kind of sports did he like? What kind of movies? Colors? Music? She didn't know any of those things, yet she wasn't disturbed because, oddly enough, she felt she knew him in all the ways that mattered.

When it came to his business, he was a driven, focused man. And she wasn't fooling herself. He still would do just about anything to get her fudge recipe, but he wouldn't do anything dishonest. She believed that with all her heart.

There was a noise. Her heart leapt and she sat straight up in bed. The noise had sounded as if it were just outside her window. Stilling, barely breathing, she waited to see if the sound repeated itself, but it didn't. Little by little her nerves unknotted. Probably a tree branch scraping against the house, she decided, as she lay back down and allowed her thoughts to return to Hayden.

There was another side to him beside the driven businessman. He'd been kind and compassionate to her this evening. He'd made the melted cheese sandwiches, which had been a success, and the coffee, which had been a disaster. But the point was, he'd tried. And he'd even volunteered to spend an uncomfortable night on her sofa to make sure she would be safe.

And there was one more thing. She'd fallen hopelessly, helplessly, completely in love with him.

She didn't know when it had happened, and at this point, it didn't seem important. Her heart was leading her and—

The noise came again. She sat bolt upright, and her gaze flew to the window. A shadow of a man's figure moved across her curtain. Someone was outside her window.

Before she had time to think about it, she slid off the bed and flew down the hall. *"Hayden. Hayden!"*

By the time she reached the living room, he was on his feet and his outstretched arms caught her. "What? What is it?"

"There's a man outside my bedroom. I saw his shadow against the curtain."

"Let me check." Holding her against him with one arm, he used the other to reach for his cell phone and punch in a number. "Brenna said she saw the shadow of a man outside her bedroom. What's going on? Uh-huh. Okay, anything else to report? Great. Thanks." He closed the cell phone. "It was one of my men checking the backyard. I'm sorry he frightened you."

"What do you mean, one of your men?"

He swung around and turned on a lamp, then put his hands on her shoulders and bent down so that their eyes were level. "The last thing I want to do is frighten you even more than you already are, but I'm still worried about the people who did this. Since they couldn't find the recipe, they may decide to go right to the source: *you.* So after you went to bed, I called a couple of my security people to come over and keep an eye on the place so that you and I could get some sleep."

"Oh."

"Are you okay?"

She nodded, suddenly self-conscious. She was wearing cotton boxer shorts and an old, soft T-shirt, her usual far-from-glamorous sleeping attire. As for him, when he'd moved to grab his cell phone, she'd seen that all he had on were the trousers he'd worn to the party. His chest, arms, and feet were bare.

Her fear had receded, but her heart still raced. Their situation was charged with intimacy. They were half dressed, their voices hushed. Everything was darkness save for the one pool of light from the lamp.

He took her into his arms and held her comfortingly, rocking her back and forth. "I'm sorry that you were frightened, Brenna. I was trying to do the opposite."

"It's all right." She now realized that the main reason she hadn't been able to sleep was because she'd wanted to be with him. And if it hadn't been the shadow, she would have made up another reason to come down the hall to him.

The thrill of knowing that she loved him filled her to overflowing. She would have been happy to simply watch him sleep in the dim light and listen to him breathe. But he was awake and she was in his arms and at this moment there was no place on earth she'd rather be.

"I would have told you about the men except I thought you were asleep," he murmured.

"I haven't been able to sleep."

He relaxed his hold on her and smoothed his hand over her hair as he seemed to like to do. "Why didn't you come in here and we could have talked until you got drowsy?"

"Because I thought you were asleep."

He chuckled. "No. I've been too busy thinking."

"Me, too."

He took her hand and drew her over to the couch. "Then come and sit down here with me. Maybe if we tell each other what's been keeping us awake, we'll be able to put each other to sleep."

She chuckled. "Believe me, what I've been thinking about is not dull." He'd probably run screaming from her house if she told him she'd fallen in love with him.

"Sounds interesting. Tell me."

"I'd much rather hear what you were thinking." He seemed in such a serious mood, she really wanted to know.

"Okay." He sat forward slightly and leaned his forearms on his thighs, and in the pooled light, she could see his muscled back and the broad width of his shoulders. "I've been thinking about a lot of things, starting with who could have done this to your home."

"Any conclusions?"

He nodded. "Whoever did this is after your fudge recipe, which means he and I are in the same business. More importantly, it means I know him."

"Hayden, there are a lot of people in the food business."

"Yes, but there's only a small number who would do this."

"Really?"

"Oh, yeah."

"Do you have an idea who it might be?"

He sat back and looked at her. "Robert Ramsey."

The man she'd danced with that night. "You must be mistaken. Robert wouldn't do anything like this. He's entirely too . . ."

"What? Friendly? Polite? Remember when I told you that taking no for an answer wasn't the Robert I know?"

"I remember."

"Well, it's not. The Robert I know is a snake, but his camouflage of civility is so good, no one sees it unless he wants them to."

She shivered, remembering that she'd been in Robert's arms just hours before, and that more than likely, he had known at the time that his men were wrecking her house and café.

"My guess is that as soon as he saw you there at the party, he got on the phone to some of his more unsavory associates and sent them to your two places." He shifted around so that he was facing her. "But now listen to me, Brenna. This is not something you should worry about. If I'm right, the police will find out. If I'm not right, they'll still find out whoever's responsible. And in the meantime, you're safe, and tomorrow we're going to put everything to rights both here and in your shop." He smiled. "So you see, there's really nothing bad enough for you to be losing sleep over."

"No, I suppose not." If she lived to be a hundred, if she never saw Hayden again after tomorrow, she'd still remember this moment, she reflected. Sitting in the dark with him, a man who unknowingly now owned her heart, she felt vibratingly alive and happy. The darkness no longer threatened. The night no longer seemed too long and full of danger. He didn't love her, but it didn't matter. He obviously cared for her, and for now, that was good enough.

He rested his hand on her bare knee. "Do you think you could go back to your room and fall asleep now?"

"No."

He chuckled, a sound that resonated deep inside her. "Okay, do you want me to tell you what else I was thinking about?"

"Sure." She'd gladly listen to him as long as he wanted.

"I was thinking about *you*."

She laughed. "You mean, how you met me on Monday and offered me more money than I'll probably ever see in my entire life and how I turned it down? And then how by Saturday night you're here, trying to sleep on my couch in my torn-up house?" She chuckled again. "I'm sure you've never met anyone who has given you more grief in such a short amount of time than I have."

He reached over and encircled her neck with his hand. "You have the most beautiful laugh."

She hadn't expected the compliment or his touch. "Thank you."

"Before you came in here," he murmured, "I was lying here, thinking about how you laugh. How you fit into my arms when we dance. How you taste when we kiss. And how I started out wanting that damned recipe of yours and ended up wanting you as well."

"Really?" she said, swallowing hard against his hand that still encircled her throat. "You were thinking all of that?"

"And more." He paused. "Do you want to hear it?"

She nodded. She wanted to hear it almost as much as she wanted to draw her next breath.

He shifted closer until their thighs touched, her bare skin against the fine material of his trousers. "I thought about how it would be if I walked down that hall, slid into bed beside you, undressed you, and made love to you." Slowly, his hand skimmed from her throat down to one breast, and with his thumb he flicked the nipple back and forth, teasing it, her, inflaming her entire body. Then without releasing her breast, he leaned forward and took her mouth with his in a long, sweet, hot, kiss that had her moaning.

She slumped against him and slid her arms around his neck, deepening the kiss, pressing her breasts against his bare chest.

She'd never been in love before, and she'd had no idea of the way it would make her feel. It was as if she was an entirely new person, capable of a love that felt as if it had actually expanded her heart and given her a desire so deep and profound it touched her soul.

His hands slid beneath her T-shirt and up her back, his palms smooth, his fingers strong. Then, before she knew it, the T-shirt was off, his hands were all over her skin, and his mouth found her nipples, licking and nibbling them one by one.

She cried out and threaded her fingers through his hair, holding his head to her breasts. Fiery ribbons of pleasure circled through her, tying knots of need and desire as they went.

With an agonized sound, Hayden abruptly stopped. "*Wait.* We can't do this."

She couldn't believe what she was hearing. "What? What are you talking about?"

He pushed her away from him. "We've got to stop." He plowed shaking fingers through his hair. "What happened tonight . . . the break-ins. You've been traumatized, and by doing this, I'm only taking advantage of you."

She drew in a deep breath and attempted to gather the remnants of her composure around her. "Yes, I'm upset at what has happened. Who wouldn't be? But, Hayden, have I ever struck you as a woman you could take advantage of, even when traumatized? Besides, I *want* you to make love to me. I want it in the worst possible way."

His breath all came out in a rush. "Are you sure?"

"Please, Hayden. Let's go to bed."

He looked at her for a moment, then everything seemed to happen at once. She was on her feet, and he swept her into his arms. There was blurring movement as his long strides ate up the distance. Then they were in the darkness of her room.

In a fever, she peeled off her boxers and lay back on her bed, completely ready for him. She could hear his rapid breathing, smell his hot skin, hear the whisper of material as he stripped off his trousers and shorts.

"I've never wanted any woman as badly as I want you," he said harshly, roughly, kicking away his clothes.

"I don't have near your experience, but—"

He came down to her, aligning the long length of his naked body beside hers, and put a finger across her lips. "Ssh. What I said was the truth. For me, you're unique in every way, and I've never wanted this way before. But I misspoke, and I'm sorry. I should have said that nothing before tonight counts, because it's also very much the truth. Brenna, it's only you and me who matter. For us, it's all new."

For once in her life, she didn't know what to say, but it didn't matter, because his mouth closed over one of her nipples and suckled, her womb contracted, and all the excitement she'd felt before came rushing back.

She gave up the effort of thinking and skimmed her hand over his body, savoring each new angle, curve, and muscle she found, learning him so that she would also remember. He was magnificent, all power, strength, and grace. And when her hand worked its way down to his erection and closed around him, a fierce, primitive groan escaped him.

"I feel as if I've wanted you my whole life," she whispered, uncaring that what she'd just said probably made no sense to him. It made perfect sense to her, and the thing she wanted most in the world was about to happen.

In the softness of her bed, they came together, hot and wild and without restraint. Flesh against flesh. Arms and legs tangled together. Lips and tongues everywhere. And then he pushed deep into her.

An indecipherable satisfaction shuddered through her and she lifted her hips and took him deeper.

Then he pushed again and he was as deep as he could get. She wrapped her legs around his hips, holding him tightly inside her.

She felt whole, and she hadn't even realized she'd been incomplete. She felt wanton and realized that before now, she hadn't even known how amazing and exciting making love could be. Every cell and muscle in her body was involved. Flames scorched her insides. She strained against him as he drove again and again into her.

"Hot velvet," he muttered roughly. "And so tight. Tight. *God.*"

An animalistic sound rumbled up from his chest. Frantically, he began driving in and out of her with a force that shook her with its impact. At the same time, he kissed her face, her ears, her throat, then pulled her tongue deep into his mouth. What he was doing was nothing short of taking complete and absolute possession of her, devouring her, ravaging her.

Tension coiled and wrapped and twisted within her. Frenzied, she lifted her hips up to meet his in perfect rhythm, thrusting back at him, matching his wildness and his intensity with her own. Then her fingers gripped his back as a great swelling of pleasure rolled through her like thunder—electric, powerful, and endless, with a sweetness that was flammable and an ecstasy that was volcanic.

With a cry, she arched up to him, just as she felt a shudder course through his body and into hers. He drove once more into her, deep, deeper. The assaulting sensations were overwhelming to her, and she felt tears flow down her face. Then there was an explosion and she shattered into a thousand white-hot pieces.

The final, ultimate release was like riding a shooting star that was rocketing her high into the heavens. Holding tightly onto him, she rode the climax out until finally she returned to earth, to her home, to her bed, to Hayden, who still held her.

Brenna lay on her back, her body quivering, her lungs hurting as she fought for breath. "That was fantastic."

"It was more than fantastic," he said, his voice a harsh rasp. "In fact, I don't think they've invented a word yet for what just happened." After a minute, when he had his breathing more under control, he rolled his head on the pillow and grinned at her. "I don't suppose it was fantastic enough that I can have your recipe now?"

If she'd had the strength, she would have hit him with a pillow. Instead, she giggled. "No, but if you'd like to keep trying, please feel free."

He laughed and lifted his head to press his lips to her forehead. "I didn't know how much I really wanted you until we started, and then it was like . . . like I'd been hungry for you for a long, long time. Except . . ."

"Except we've only known each other for a short time."

"Yes. *Exactly.* And I *still* want you."

"I'm not going anywhere," she murmured and gave a soft moan as he pulled her to him.

He was puzzled about his feelings, but she couldn't help him figure them out, she reflected, as he drew her back into the firestorm of passion. She didn't know what his answer was. She only knew hers. She loved him. And she also knew that after tonight, she'd never again be the same.

FIVE

At dawn, Hayden awoke with Brenna in his arms, her long, auburn hair spread across his chest, her arms and legs inextricably entwined with his. They'd filled the night with each other until finally they'd been too tired to do anything other than fall asleep.

So what was he doing awake this early? He should have slept a couple of more hours at least. He angled his head so that he could see her face. She was deep asleep, her face beautiful and serene, her breathing even. He didn't have to think twice to know that *she* was the reason he'd awakened early. Incredibly, he was starving for her once again.

But he had to leave her alone. She was going to need as much rest as she could get. Even though he planned to do everything in his power to make the day ahead as easy as possible for her, it was still going to be hard.

Damn that bastard Robert Ramsey. If he got the chance, he would personally and happily tear him apart limb from limb. And as long as he was handing out blame, he couldn't overlook himself, although his sin couldn't begin to touch

Ramsey's. Still, very soon now, he was going to have to tell Brenna what he'd done.

He looked down at her again. In fact, he could barely take his gaze off her. He closed his eyes and tried to concentrate on relaxing, but it didn't help. He could see Brenna in his mind, and with her wrapped around him, his body was already betraying him.

He tried to think of business, the more mundane the better, but his mind kept going back to her. It was no good. He was hard to the point of pain. In her sleep, she stretched against him and he silently cursed. He couldn't take it any longer.

Carefully, so as not to wake her until the last possible moment, he shifted until he was over her. Then slowly, millimeter, by millimeter, he sank into her heated, velvet depths. Deeper and deeper he went until he had to grit his teeth against the fiery sensations that were bombarding him.

Still asleep, Brenna moaned and lifted her hips. He paused, but the effort of being inside her and not moving was enormous, excruciating. Sweat broke out on his forehead.

Her eyes fluttered, then opened, and she smiled slowly up at him.

He was lost. He let himself go, pounding into her again and again until his brain was fogged. His release came quickly. It was blistering and powerful, and he poured everything that was him into her.

When he woke again some time later, the first thing he smelled was chocolate—hot chocolate—then something else that made his taste buds water. He reached for Brenna, but she wasn't there. Rubbing his eyes, he sat up in bed and looked around. "Brenna?"

"Just a minute," she called from another room.

He reached for his boxers and pants and had just finished putting them on when Brenna swept into the room, carrying two mugs filled with the most wonderful smelling hot chocolate.

"Wait just a sec." She set the mugs on her dresser, then quickly pulled the comforter over the bed and threw the pillows against the headboard. "There. Sit back down and we'll have our chocolate in bed. I feel like giving myself a bit of luxury, because I have a feeling the rest of the day is going to be brutal."

For a moment, all he could do was look at her. She'd slicked back her hair into a ponytail and donned a small, white T-shirt and an old pair of jeans. Both fit her like a second skin. Her face looked as if it had been freshly scrubbed, and parts of her hair were wet. She was a long way from the glamorous woman he'd been with last night but, if possible, she was even more beautiful this morning.

"You've had a shower?"

She nodded, handed him one of the mugs, then pointed to the pillows. "Prop yourself up there."

He did as he was told, and she plopped down in the center of the bed, facing him, her legs crossed, her hand lifting the mug to her lips for a sip.

"Listen, I need to apologize to you. I wanted you to sleep as long as you could, but a couple of hours ago, I woke up and you were in my arms and—"

Smiling, she lifted a hand to stop him. "I didn't mind at all. It was a marvelous way to wake up, and afterward, we both went back to sleep. I haven't been up long."

"Then I feel better."

He also felt awkward and uncertain. Usually, when a woman spent the night with him or vice versa, he knew exactly what to do when they awoke. If he wanted to see her again, he would kiss her good-bye, then have his secretary send her two dozen roses, perhaps with a dinner invitation attached. On the other hand, if he *didn't* want to see her again, he would play it cool. Then, when he arrived at his office, he would have his secretary send four dozen roses with a card that said something to the effect of, *It was fun. See you around.*

But with Brenna, he was bewildered as to what to do about her. He definitely wanted to see her again, on that point he was determined. But at the moment, he didn't know how to act. He felt unsettled because she made him feel so many emotions at once.

Each time they had made love, he'd lost control with her. It wasn't just odd, it was absolutely amazing, because it had never happened before. What's more, having sex with a woman once, at the most twice, was always enough to sate his appetite. But with Brenna, he'd wanted her again and again. Hell, he still wanted her.

And now she was sitting cross-legged on the bed, all bright and fresh, just as if last night hadn't happened between them. She looked untouched, a look, startlingly enough, that he hated.

She grinned at him. "By the way, I figured out what you did wrong last night when you made the coffee."

"What?"

"You didn't use a filter."

"I was supposed to use a filter?"

She nodded. "On my kind of coffeemaker, you need to."

"I probably saw some filters but didn't know what they were." He took a sip of his chocolate. "This is *delicious.*"

"Thank you. I have to admit, though I doubt if my hot chocolate has ever given anyone an orgasm. But let me know if you feel one coming on."

The look he sent her sizzled all her nerve endings. "Oh, I promise you'll definitely know if I have one, but I don't believe we'll need any help from your hot chocolate—or your fudge."

Her grin widened. "I also have a couple of trays of cinnamon rolls baking. They'll be ready in about twenty minutes."

"How did you manage that?"

"It was as you said last night. Things were in the general area where they were supposed to be. It just took a little digging."

"You shouldn't have gone to all that trouble."

"Cooking is never any trouble to me. Besides, I figured the men who watched the house all night deserved a treat. I've already taken them coffee."

"I'll go out there in a few minutes and tell them they can go home as soon as their replacements get here."

"Replacements?"

"Until they catch whoever did all this, I want you protected."

A frown creased her forehead. "Do you think we'll hear from the police today? I mean, do you think they've had enough time to get a lead on who did this?"

He nodded, trying to be as encouraging as possible. "Sure. After something like this, the police usually canvass the neighborhood. It's entirely possible one of your neighbors saw something."

"I hope so." She paused. "You know, I vaguely knew that all sorts of espionage and dirty tricks went on in business, but I thought it always happened on your level of business, not mine."

"You underestimated the desirability of your product."

She smiled ruefully. "I guess I owe you a great big thanks."

"For what?"

"After we discovered the break-in, you didn't say that it wouldn't have happened if I had aligned myself with one of the big, powerful companies such as yours."

"To tell you the truth, the thought never entered my mind. I was too concerned about you."

"Then thank you for that and for everything else, too. I can't tell you how much I appreciate all you've done for me."

He leaned forward and briefly squeezed her hand. "Doing

for you is easy. And right now, I want to do something else for you that will protect you from this ever happening again."

"What?"

"I want to strongly suggest—no, make that *insist*—that you call your attorney right now and have him come over as soon as possible this morning."

She looked at him blankly. "Whatever for?"

"He needs to register your fudge recipe for a trademark. If he'd had the sense to suggest that you put a copy of your recipe in a safe-deposit box, then he should have had enough sense to also get a trademark for it. If he had, the break-ins would not have occurred."

"I think he did say something about a trademark, but he's not a trademark lawyer, and I would have had to go to someone else." She shrugged. "And at the time, I was so busy opening the café that it simply slipped my mind. Plus—"

"Well, don't worry about it. That's something we're going to correct first thing today."

"You didn't let me finish. Plus . . ."

He waited, but when she didn't go on, he prompted, "Plus what?"

She eyed him steadily. "Let me ask you something. Did you by any chance have your lab guys try to analyze and duplicate the fudge?"

"Yes, I did."

"But you didn't get the same result, did you?"

"Not even close."

"That's because there's a little trick that all the women in my family are taught. Hayden, you can watch me make the fudge a hundred times. You can even write down everything I do. But you'll never get the same result that I get."

His brow creased. "So you're saying it can't be duplicated by anyone but you?"

"Oh, sure it can. It can, that is, if I told everything, but I'm not. Not even for the trademark attorney."

Wiping his hand over his face, he gave a mild curse and thought for several moments. "Okay, this will still work. Just give the trademark attorney the basic ingredients of the recipe, and don't tell *anyone* that there is a trick, or whatever the hell it is. That way, you'll still be protected, because as soon as the less-than-honorable people in my profession learn you've applied for a trademark, they'll lose interest in using their tough tactics. Companies may still come after you to try to *buy* the rights, but they'll never again try to find the actual recipe, nor will they try to get it out of you, since the recipe will be protected as well."

She nodded. "Sounds good."

"Now, I could recommend a lawyer to you, but since my intentions regarding the fudge are less than pure, I'd feel more comfortable if the recommendation comes from your lawyer."

"Okay. I'll call him tomorrow."

"Today. You'll call him *today*. In fact, this morning. I want that trademark lawyer over here before noon."

"*Hello?* Hayden, lawyers may drop everything and come running when you call them, but they don't for me. I have to wait until I can get an appointment."

"As soon as we finish our chocolate, you call your lawyer and get the recommendation. *I'll* call whoever he recommends. Okay?"

She sighed. "Okay, you're right. If you're worried enough about my safety to put guards on me, then it's important. I just hope my lawyer's home number is listed."

"If it's not, there are other ways we can find it."

She glanced at her watch. "The rolls have another ten minutes to go. Since I have no idea where my telephone book is, I'll call information when I get up to check on them." She tilted her head and looked at him. "Thank you once again. You're quite wonderful."

He grimaced. "Not really." He couldn't put it off any longer. He had something to confess to her, and he prayed like hell she wasn't going to hate him. If he could get away with it, he wouldn't tell her at all, but he knew that he wasn't going to be able to find any peace within himself until he did.

"No, it's true. After our first meeting, I was intrigued with you, though I really didn't think I'd see you again. But somehow, even then, I knew you were a straight shooter. And now I know the extent of your honesty and your compassion and nothing you can say will make me change my mind about how wonderful you are."

He took another gulp of hot chocolate, then set the mug on the nightstand. "I have something I need to tell you that just may do the trick."

"What? What is it?"

Once again, he wiped his hands over his face, dreading this moment. "Actually this is a confession."

"Okay, but unless you're about to tell me you really were behind the break-ins, or that you're married, I'll tell you in advance that you'll be in the clear."

She smiled at him, and it made him feel even worse. "No, it's neither one of those things. Remember last night when your car wouldn't start?"

Suddenly she straightened. "Oh, damn! I forgot to call the tow truck! That's another thing I've got to do as soon as I go back into the kitchen."

"You won't have to call for a tow truck."

"Why not?"

"Because I know exactly what's wrong with your car and I can fix it. While you were dancing with Ramsey, I went outside and slipped one of the valet parkers some money to disconnect the coil wire on your car. I wanted to spend more time with you, and I was hoping that if your car didn't work, you'd accept a ride home with me."

Her mouth fell open in amazement, her eyes widened.

"You—" She began to laugh, a clear, crystal sound filled with humor and happiness.

He was totally astonished. He'd imagined her reaction might be anger or even disappointment, but he'd never imagined she'd laugh. "Wait. Why are you laughing? You've told me I'm frank and forthright, but I just told you I sabotaged your car so that I could get you to accept my offer of a ride home."

She wrapped her arm around her middle because she was still laughing so hard. Finally, she shifted off the bed and placed her mug on her dresser, then returned to the bed and wiped the tears of laughter from her eyes.

"Hayden, that car is over ten years old. Just about everything that could go wrong with it has, which means I've had to learn some things about my car. All the basic stuff, plus a few of the not so basic. The point is, I'm perfectly capable of raising the hood on that car and checking things out myself. I've done it a hundred times, and I've learned that there are several things I can do, even if it's only temporary, to make the car run. For instance, did you know that you can make a temporary belt out of panty hose?"

He frowned. "Wait a minute. You're saying you *knew* what I did?"

"I didn't have a clue, but I stood there and stared at the hood, trying to decide if I wanted to go to the trouble of lifting the hood and checking things out or leave it be. In the end, I made the deliberate decision *not* to look under the hood."

"I don't understand."

She chuckled. "For a smart man, you're being pretty dumb about this. Hayden, I made that decision so that I could take you up on your offer to drive me home."

He stared at her for several moments, then reached for her arm and pulled her to him. "You're incredible," he said gruffly and crushed his mouth down on hers.

• • •

Hayden grinned at his sister who was diligently vacuuming Brenna's living and dining rooms. She'd tracked him down on his cell phone, and as soon as he'd told her about the break-in, she'd hurried right over to help. He moved closer to her so that she could hear him over the sound of the vacuum. "I don't think I've ever seen you run a vacuum cleaner before."

She straightened. "Oh, like I've ever seen you run one."

He shrugged. "Can I help it if Mom is a clean freak who believes no one can clean her home as well as she can?"

"Exactly. And thank the Lord. And now I have a housekeeper because my twin brats keep me running, and what energy I have left over at the end of the day, James wants. Again, thank the Lord. But as it happens, you have an exceedingly smart sister who can figure out most things, including how to run a vacuum cleaner if necessary."

He grinned "I just wish I had a camera. In certain circles, I bet I could get good money for a picture of you vacuuming."

"Never mind." She waved her hand in the air as if she were erasing the subject of vacuuming. "Listen, do you think I should call for more help? I know at least a dozen women who would do anything for Brenna. All I'd have to do is call them."

"Bad idea. Last night, she accepted my help because she was in shock. Today, I had to really talk fast to get her to let me stay and help." After the night they'd spent together, he had assumed she would want to spend more time with him today, but she'd done her best to get him to leave. It was as if she'd already forgotten their lovemaking or that it simply wasn't important to her. He was more than disturbed about the idea.

"Then it's a good thing I simply showed up instead of asking her if I could come over."

"Brenna's accustomed to doing things on her own, and

it's hard for her to accept help." He glanced at his watch. "The only reason she's still here is because she's waiting on that lawyer. But as soon as he's gone, she's going to want to go over to the café. I told her I had some people working over there, but she doesn't know the full scope of what they're doing, and I'd like to keep it that way until they're through."

"What are they doing?"

"If I have it my way, by the time she gets over there, she won't have to do anything but come back tomorrow morning and start cooking."

Lois glanced around. "Is she still in her bedroom?"

"Yes. Apparently there are some feminine things in there that she feels she should put away herself."

In a conspiratorial manner, Lois stepped closer to him. "I have to tell you, I find this whole thing very interesting."

"What? And by the way, why don't you turn the vacuum off?"

"Because I don't want Brenna hearing this."

"Hearing what? And what do you find interesting? Cleaning a house?"

She hit his arm. "No. *You.* To be more precise, *you with Brenna.* I've never seen you react to a woman like you react to her, and it's just fascinating."

He frowned. "What do you mean? How do I react?" Since Lois had arrived, he'd gone out of his way to avoid doing anything that would give away the fact that he and Brenna had spent practically the whole night making love. As far as he was concerned, he didn't care who knew, but he definitely did not want Brenna to be embarrassed.

"First of all, you're very protective of her. Secondly, when she walks into a room where you are, you react as if she's a magnet. If you don't go to her, which most of the time you do, your body sways in her direction. And if she's not in the same room as you, you constantly check on her.

And one last, extremely telling thing: You can't take your eyes off her."

"Your imagination is working overtime."

"Uh-uh. I'm right. You forget how well I know you. But even so, I'm afraid a complete stranger could read you today."

"I don't remember doing any of the things you're talking about. You're wrong."

She grinned. "I'm always right. You know I am. And I have to give myself a great big pat on the back and say that this whole thing has worked out really great."

"Okay, okay, I'll admit it. This time you really outdid yourself with your matchmaking."

Her grin widened with satisfaction. "And you don't even know yet how well I've done."

"What are you talking about?"

"You're in love with Brenna."

"No, I'm not in love . . ." Oh, God, she was right. Why hadn't he realized it before? He was a smart man. Some even called him brilliant for the way he'd built and structured his businesses. But he hadn't been able to see what was right in front of his face.

He loved Brenna, and it explained so much. His obsession with her. His inability to get enough of her. His overwhelming need to help and protect her. His desire to be with her all the time. The fact that he was upset because she'd tried to get him to leave.

"Earth to Hayden. Earth to Hayden."

"What? Oh." He grabbed his sister and gave her a big kiss. "Lois, you're *brilliant.*"

She laughed. "Well, of course I am. Did you really think you were the only one with any brains in our family?"

He grinned. "Yes."

She hit him again. "How soon should I wait until I offer to help Brenna with the wedding plans? I'm thinking something small and intimate. Five hundred people at the most, maybe in my backyard."

He pointed a stern finger at her. "Don't say a word until I tell you it's okay."

The phone rang, and Hayden reached to turn off the vacuum. In the other room, he heard Brenna pick up the phone.

"Hello?" A pause. "Yes? Uh-huh." Another pause. "Oh, that's great. *Really?* Okay, so what's going to happen now?"

Minutes later, Brenna hung up the phone and made her way into the living room, her face pale. "That was the police. You were right, Hayden. It was Robert."

He went to her. "What did they say?"

"They were canvassing the neighborhood after they left here last night and discovered that Mr. and Mrs. Johnson who live five doors away from me saw a strange car parked in front of their house. They're part of our Neighborhood Crime Watch committee, and they wrote down the license number as a precaution."

"What a lucky break," Lois said.

"Whose car was it?" he asked.

"A man named Johnny Philips. The police tracked him down early this morning. In the course of questioning him, he admitted that Robert Ramsey had hired him and two of his friends to find the recipe."

"That son of a bitch," Hayden muttered.

"Robert? Good heavens. I wonder if Christine knows about this." Lois looked at Brenna. "Have they picked Robert up yet?"

She nodded. "But the policeman who called said as soon as he's processed, he'll more than likely be released on bail."

Hayden let loose a stream of curses.

"Brenna, did the police indicate you might be in any danger?" Lois asked worriedly.

"No." She looked at Hayden. "What do you think?"

"Now that the police know that Ramsey was behind the break-ins, I don't think he'll take any further action. If something were to happen to you, Ramsey has got to know that he'd be number one on the police suspect list."

She nodded, but her expression was vulnerable. "That's reassuring. If I end up injured or worse, at least I'll know Ramsey will go to prison for it."

Hayden crossed to her and was just about to take her into his arms when her doorbell rang. She jumped.

"Hey, everything's fine. I'm sure that's the lawyer I called, and once he gets rolling on your trademark, your recipe will be protected, and so will you."

She exhaled a long breath. "I'll let him in."

"I want to thank you for everything, Hayden."

He groaned teasingly. "Do me a major favor and *please* don't thank me again. That's practically all you've done today, and frankly, I'm tired of it." They'd just returned to Brenna's home after spending time at the café and then eating dinner at a restaurant he'd insisted they stop at.

"I know, but the cafe . . . I can't get over how wonderful it looked. If I hadn't known for a fact that it had been broken into last night, I would never have believed it. I mean, I couldn't even tell if anything had been broken or not. Everything was in its place, and all my supplies were in order. I'll never know how your people did it, but by the time we got there, there was nothing for me to do."

He chuckled. "But you still had to stick your nose into every cabinet and drawer and rearrange a pan or two."

She whirled on him, her expression suddenly stern. "I expect a bill from you. Make it itemized, and don't leave a thing out. I want to pay for everything that had to be replaced, plus the hours your people put in. I mean it, Hayden."

He nodded, a smile in his eyes. "You'll get a bill." But the total wouldn't even be close to what it had really cost. His people had performed a miracle, and because of it, there would be a nice, fat bonus in their paychecks this week.

"And this house! Last night, when I first saw the kitchen, and then the rest of the rooms, I thought it would take me a couple of weeks to get it back in some sort of shape, but it's all done."

He smiled. She looked like a different person from the one who had viewed the carnage of her home last night. She was tired, but she was also happy and relaxed. "Your thanks have been all-inclusive, so don't thank me again,"

"Okay, but I can still thank Lois. She insisted on staying here and working while you and I went over to the cafe."

While Brenna had consulted with the lawyer at her kitchen table, he'd taken Lois outside and arranged for her to get her housekeeper, along with two others she knew of, to come over and give the house a thorough cleaning and washing. Lois was so efficient that by the time he took Brenna out the front door to drive her to the cafe, Lois was letting her crew in the back door. A couple of hours later, Lois had called him on his cell phone to tell him the house was shining from top to bottom. Brenna didn't need to know that he also planned to pick up that bill. She'd been through enough. She didn't need to worry about money, too.

"Before this, I knew Lois was nice, but now I know she's also remarkable. Who would have thought she could have the house looking like this by the time we returned?"

"We'd already done most of the work," he said to mitigate her suspicion. "And between you and me, I think she might have recruited her housekeeper to help her." He knew Brenna was too smart to believe Lois had done everything by herself. "But yes, I agree with you. She is remarkable."

"Normally, I would be angry that she brought a stranger into my house, but right now, all I can think of is how relieved I am that I won't have to come home from work every night to try to put my house back together little by little. How am I ever going to be able to thank her?"

"Just keep her supplied with Ecstasy for the rest of her life and help me baby-sit the twins while she and James go to the Caymans. Believe me, she'll consider you even."

Brenna fought against reacting, but he'd just casually suggested she help him baby-sit as if he planned on the two of them seeing each other again. During the last twenty or so hours, she'd been so anchored in the present with her problems and falling in love with Hayden, that she hadn't even thought about a future with him.

But somehow all of her problems had been taken care of in a remarkably short amount of time, and now she could actually sit down, draw a deep breath, and consider the most important thing of all that had happened to her this weekend: the fact that she'd fallen in love with Hayden.

"Unless, of course, you can't stand kids," Hayden added, watching her closely.

"Kids? Oh, you mean the twins. Actually, I love kids."

"Then you will have Lois's eternal gratitude right along with mine. When those twins get me alone, they can be merciless. By the time they're through with me, I'm ready to give them anything they want."

She smiled at him. "I can't wait to see that."

He went over and dropped down on the sofa, which reminded her that she hadn't even asked him if he wanted to stay a while.

Up to this point, they'd had one thing after the other happen, and they'd had to deal with it all: the party, the break-ins, the guards, making love all night, cleaning up the house, Lois, the lawyer, the cafe, the restaurant. But now it was just the two of them.

"Could I make you some coffee?"

He laughed. "Isn't this where we came in?"

She grinned. "Yes, I think it is."

"What I want more than anything is for you to come over here and sit beside me."

"I think I can manage that," she said, her tone deliberately airy. So far, their relationship had gone at the speed of light, but now that they had a chance to slow down, she didn't know what would happen between them. But she did know that she hadn't been mistaken last night. She definitely, positively loved him. As for him, she wasn't sure.

During the weekend, Hayden had stayed by her side and had done an incredible amount for her. Despite the babysitting comment, he now needed to know that he could go if he wanted.

He put his arm around her shoulders and drew her against him. "You must be tired."

"A little." She paused, running various scenarios through her mind.

He reached for her hand and held it. "Hayden, I need to say something to you."

"Am I going to like it?" he murmured, idly playing with her fingers.

"Probably. Most men would."

"So tell me."

"This is not another thank-you, but the fact is, you've done so much to help me this weekend and we've gone through a lot. We've become . . . close. We, uh . . . we made love last night, and it was wonderful."

He looked over at her. "Why do I think there's a *but* coming?"

"Because there is, but it's a good *but.*" She drew away from the shelter of his arms. "I want you to know that as far as I'm concerned, I won't be upset if you'd like this to be the end of the line for our relationship." She saw him stiffen and hurried on. "In other words, I don't expect anything else from you. Nothing."

His expression turned thoughtful. "I'm not sure where you're going with this, Brenna, and I'm also not sure I like it."

"Look, all appearances to the contrary this weekend, I'm not one of those clinging vine type of women. If you'd like to go out with me again, fine. I'd like that, too. But if you don't, that's fine, too. I promise I won't cry or beg or turn into a stalker."

"A stalker, huh?" He nodded, humor returning to his eyes. "Well, I suppose that *is* good news."

"I'm serious, Hayden."

"I know." He looked down at her hand in his. "You've obviously given a great deal of thought to this, but have you considered the opposite happening?"

"I'm not sure what you're referring to."

"That you might be ready to end the relationship and that I might turn into a stalker."

"Hayden, I told you I was serious."

"And so am I, Brenna." He blew out a long breath. "I'm not ready to end our relationship. In fact, I can't even fathom *ever* wanting to end it." He smoothed his hand over her hair. "I've fallen in love with you, Brenna. Hard. It's a wonder when I fell I didn't make an imprint in the ground or cement walkway. Actually, I probably did, except I couldn't tell you when or where it happened. I love you, and if it were up to me, I'd never leave your side."

Her mouth had fallen open and with a smile, he gently shut it. "But since we both have jobs we love, I'm going to have to be content to see you every morning when you wake up and every night right before you go to sleep. And then there'll be the weekends and—"

"Wait a minute," she said shakily. "What are you saying?"

"I'm trying to gracefully segue into asking you to marry me, and if you hadn't interrupted, I think I would have gotten there in another minute or two." He chuckled. "Will you, Brenna? Will you marry me?"

"Yes!" She threw herself at him and caught him off balance. He fell backward onto the couch, and she went with him, raining kisses all over his face. *"Yes. Yes. Yes!"*

He was laughing, and then she started laughing. He

wrapped his arms around her and held her to him as they both laughed and kissed each other. It took a while for him to regain his breath, but as soon as he could talk again, he asked, "When?"

"Yesterday, tomorrow, I don't care."

"Would it scare you off if I told you that Lois is already planning the wedding?"

She grinned. "Not a bit. Would you change your mind if I told you that marrying me still will not get you the fudge recipe?"

"No, because I'm convinced I'll eventually get it."

She sat up and he did likewise. "*How?* There's no way."

"There is too a way."

"What? I'm not going to give it to you and, thanks to you, the recipe is going to have a trademark that will protect it from sharks like you. Plus, there's that small trick I told you about."

"So what? It will still be passed down in your family through the women, right?"

"Right . . . Oh, I get it. You think if we have a girl, she'll give you the recipe."

"That's right," he said with a wide grin. "After all, she's going to be Daddy's little girl."

Her green eyes sparkled. "Maybe so, but she's also going to have her mother's love of cooking and baking, and she's never going to want to see her family's recipe distributed worldwide."

"She might."

She playfully swatted at him. "You're so sure of yourself. What if we have boys?"

"Then we'll just have to keep trying until we have a girl."

"I wouldn't mind that at all, but if I were you, I still wouldn't get my hopes up about the recipe."

"Why not?"

"Because you've already told me you're a marshmallow

when it comes to your nephews, and you'll be even more so when it comes to your own children."

"I don't know about that."

"Oh, give me a break, Hayden. One look at your baby girl, and she'll have you wrapped around her little finger."

"Oh, yeah?"

"Yeah."

"Yeah," he whispered and reached for her. "Just exactly like her mother."

The parking lot of Von's Supermarket was all but deserted at ten P.M. and the January air held a sharp nip. Worse, Carlie was still in high heels and her black winter silk suit. She'd stayed long after the speech, answering questions and expecting to talk with Jo Emily, only to discover that her heckler had slipped out without anyone noticing.

Carlie had been deeply concerned. She'd called campus security, and while they scouted the grounds, she'd checked the auditorium and the ladies' rest room, but without success. Jo Emily was not to be found, and there was nothing Carlie could do but hope that she'd picked up a flyer at the door and would show up at a support group meeting.

Right now, her arches aching and bone-tired from the day she'd had, Carlie faced two overflowing cartfuls of groceries. Everything had to be loaded into the back of the Explorer, and it had already taken about as much heft as she had to raise the hatch door. Naturally there wasn't a bag boy in sight.

"Tote that bale." Trying not to break nails or anything else, she power-lifted several slippery plastic bags of bottled water, one after another, and reminded herself that tomorrow at this time she would be in her mountain hideaway. She'd had the quiet little weekend trip planned for months now, and just the thought of it had helped to keep the crazies at bay.

The last year had been the most thrilling of Carlie's life, but the pressure had been relentless. Two ten-city book tours alone would have crushed most ordinary mortals by her estimation, and she'd also had to run her consulting business and contend with the demands of her new post as chair of the Stalker Violence Task Force. She was running on fumes, but wouldn't have changed one overwhelming minute.

She was fiercely proud of the book, and the presidential appointment felt like her greatest accomplishment. At times it was still hard to believe that her goal to see a nationwide support network for victims was actually being realized. The federal program included education, hot lines, and advocacy groups, and Carlie had the chief executive's personal promise of support. However, as optimistic as she was that the program would take many women out of harm's way, she was beginning to wonder if it might put *her* in the hospital.

The muscles of her arms were on fire. She still had half a cart to go, and a dozen bags alone had been bottled water, plus she had groceries for her house in Marina del Rey, as well as the mountain cabin. Fatigue was making her clumsy, but she was too tired to stop, if that made any sense. She just wanted to get home.

"Oh no!" Carlie gaped in horror as the plastic finger hooks got away from her. The bag she'd been lifting hit the cement, and an explosion of yellow-and-white muck sent her moaning to her knees. It was the milk and eggs!

"Not that bag, not tonight," she pleaded, but the gods of overwhelmed women weren't listening. She couldn't even get to her car. The seeping, gelatinous mass had blocked access, and for one horrible moment, Carlie thought she was going to cry. She was actually blinking away tears in a supermarket parking lot. *What was wrong with her?*

"Your book is at the top of all the best-seller lists," she told herself. "You're not allowed to get emotional over spilled milk."

It had to be stress, of course. Now that the immediate pressure was off, she could fall apart. But as she searched for a Kleenex in her jacket pocket, someone knelt opposite her and offered a white flag of surrender.

Actually, it was a man's handkerchief, and Carlie and her fellow croucher were almost knee to knee.

"Blow?" he said as she looked up.

Eyes that must have seen every heartache known to man gazed down at her from beneath kohl lashes. His irises were deep wells, but that wasn't what made her stare.

"Where did you get those lashes?" she asked. Hers had always been rather stubby and fair. His were the blackest she'd ever seen. Velvet pillow fringe, those lashes. This guy was killer. She didn't know how else to describe him.

"Thrifty Drugs," he said. "Manager's special."

She shot him a look, then laughed. "They came with the package, didn't they? A genetic freebie."

"'Fraid so, but it's not a body part a man likes to brag about." He surveyed the glop at her feet. "How about a salvage operation? I think the milk's totaled, but we might be able to save an egg or two."

Carlie wrinkled her nose. "Too slimy."

"Want some help with the rest of it? Maybe we can get the other bags in your car without another casualty. Think?"

"We can try." The right answer was no. No, I don't need

your help. I'm a freaking black belt in jujitsu, and I can handle a few measly bags myself. That was what she'd just advised her lecture audience to say. Carlie warned women about these conditions all the time. They were fraught with peril. It was late, the parking lot had emptied out, and her Good Samaritan was the worst kind, a stranger with a killer smile.

All the indicators were there, but for whatever reason, the thought of danger barely registered with this guy. Instead, Carlie was mulling the possibility that he might be one of the most appealing men she'd ever met. And even more improbable, considering her focus on dangerous strangers these days, she rather liked him.

"Let me," he said as she braved the mess on the pavement and reached for one of the bags. He loaded the car himself, all the while engaging her in light conversation. He was especially curious about her dozen one-gallon containers of drinking water.

"You planning to bathe in it?" he asked.

"It's for my tree house." She tried not to laugh as his head swiveled around. There was no way not to explain that her unique mountain hideaway lacked only for piped-in drinking water.

"Family land," she said. "With nothing on it but huge oaks and chestnuts. The conservationists begged me not to cut them down, so I built my dream cottage in the branches. I thought the height would bother me, but I love it up there in the ozone, me and the birds."

"Ever see that Hitchcock movie?"

She laughed out loud. "I could have written the script. They flock for my burned toast. Got my nose pecked once."

"Only once?" He gazed at her nose, her eyes, her mouth, lingering. "I'm trying to imagine that."

Oh yeah, she liked him. Fortunately she caught herself just as she was about to invite him up to check out her mountain retreat, and wondered what she could have been thinking about.

"Chilly tonight, isn't it?" he said. "Perfect weather for a hot cup of coffee."

Carlie didn't give him a chance to ask. "I really have to get these groceries home," she said. "The frozen yogurt will melt." Finally, the right answer!

He let her go with nothing more than a friendly admonition to drive safely, and moments later Carlie was whooshing down the street in her Explorer and congratulating herself on a narrow escape.

It wasn't until she pulled onto a little-used side street that she noticed the headlights behind her. It was the way the car hung back as much as the driver's tenacity that made her suspect she was being followed. When she slowed, the car did, too.

They were in a residential neighborhood close to her home, where streets were short and stop signs stood at every corner, so it was easy to confirm her suspicion. She negotiated a couple of unplanned turns, saw the lights still behind her, and quickly dug the pepper spray from her purse. She also placed a 911 call on her cell phone.

The intersection coming up was a well-lit street. Carlie's plan was to try to get a look at the car, but it was no longer behind her when she checked her rearview mirror. A couple more blocks convinced her that she'd lost him. Relieved, she headed for home. But as she pulled onto the street where her small gambrel-roofed house was located, she saw a flashing red light.

A police car had driven up behind her.

Carlie pulled over, hoping it was in response to her 911 call, but something bothered her about the car. It wasn't a black-and-white, and from what she could see of the driver, he wasn't wearing a uniform. Unfortunately, she already had the window down before she realized all this, another rule of safety shattered. So far tonight she'd managed to violate almost every word of caution in her own book.

Carlie stared in shock at the man who appeared at her window. It was the stranger with the good eyelashes. He was reaching inside the lapel of his jacket, but she didn't wait to find out why. She grabbed the pepper spray and blasted him before he could get to whatever was in there.

There had been something in his hand, she realized. She'd seen a flash of silver, but the object had already dropped to the ground with a clunk.

"Stay right there!" she shouted, holding him off with the spray while she got out of her car. She knelt to confiscate what she expected to be a weapon and realized it was a detective's badge. LAPD, RHD. She'd heard of the elite robbery and homicide division that dealt with high-profile crime, but she never would have imagined—

"A cop," she whispered. "I've Maced a cop."

CHRISTMAS IS ALWAYS

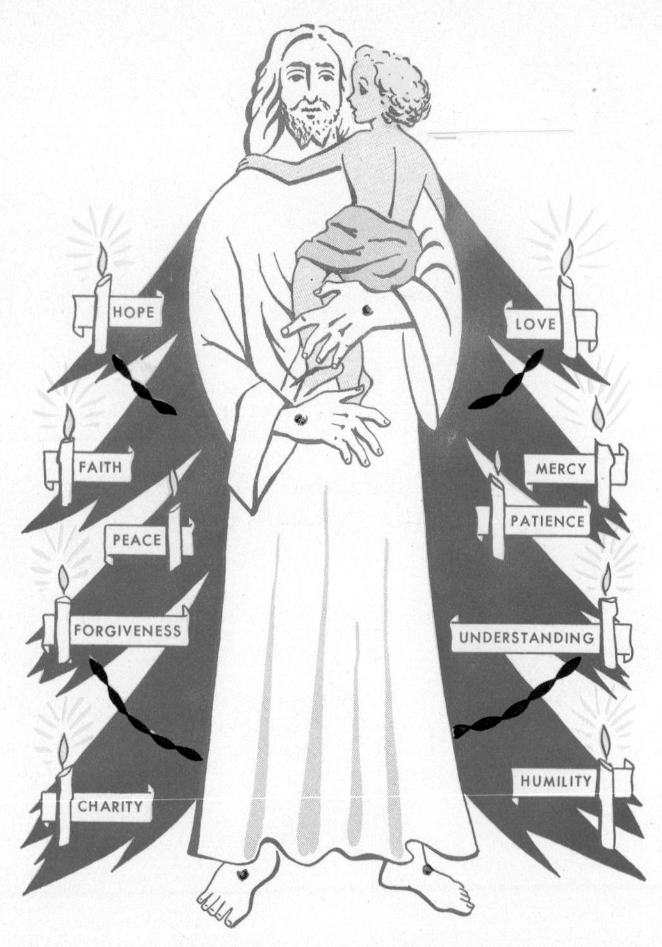

"... we adorn this tree with the gifts He brings to those who accept Him ..."

Dale Evans Rogers

Christmas Is Always

FLEMING H. REVELL COMPANY

Westwood, New Jersey
London E.C.4—29 Ludgate Hill
Glasgow C.2—229 Bothwell Street

Library of Congress Catalog Card Number: 58-13765

Printed in the United States of America

1.1

To

REVEREND HARLEY WRIGHT SMITH

with appreciation for his remarkable ministry to God's little ones

By Way of Introduction...

WE ARE TOO worldly-wise about Christmas, too sophisticated—and shoddy. Getting and spending in order to "give," we forget what was given us at Christmas; we have lost its deeper meaning and its joy; growing older, too many of us have not grown wiser about it, but only "adult." Christmas, we say, is for children.

Occasionally, throughout this little book, Dale Evans Rogers speaks to the children. "Christmas, my child, is always . . ." or

"This, my child, is a wonderful mystery." But the children to whom she speaks are aged seven to seventy; they are youngsters and grown-ups. She speaks thus to those who have had the courage to remain young in heart, to all who understand that "Except ye . . . become as little children, ye shall not enter into the kingdom of heaven." The age of her "child" means nothing; she speaks to the hearts of all who are arrested by the mystic mystery of Christmas, who know that it is something more than a present under a tree, who would approach in child-like (not child*ish*) faith to discover its nobler, deeper spiritual meaning. She speaks to all the yearning children of God, for whom God made Christmas. . . .

If you insist that Christmas is just a day, perhaps you had better not read this book at all. . . .

But if you can understand that Christmas

is always and has been always, that it is not a moment in time nor yet a date on the calendar but "a state of heart" . . . then perhaps you had better read it . . . slowly . . . again and again. . . . For here is Christmas as God meant it; here is the Incarnation that challenges the mind of man and warms and often breaks his heart, in such language and beauty as God might use in explaining it to His children. . . .

Here is Christmas, my child, perhaps as you have never heard it before, certainly as you shall never forget it. . . .

The Publishers

is always and has been always. That it is not a moment in time, nor yet a date on the calendar but "a state of mind" . . . then perhaps you had better read it . . . slowly . . . again and again . . . For here is Christmas as God meant it: here is the incarnation that challenges the mind of man and warms and often breaks the heart in such language and beauty as God might use in explaining it to His children. . . .

Here is Christmas as a child, perhaps as you have never heard it before—and now you shall never forget it. . . .

The Publisher

CHRISTMAS IS ALWAYS

Christmas Is Always

Christmas, my child, is always.

It was always in the heart of God. It was born there. Only He could have thought of it.

Like God, Christmas is timeless and eternal, from everlasting to everlasting.

It is something even more than what happened that night in starlit little Bethlehem; it has been behind the stars forever.

There was Christmas in the heart of God before the world was formed. He gave Jesus to *us,* the night the angels sang, yes—but the Bible tells us that Jesus shared a great glory with the Father long before the world was made. Jesus was always, too!

God's Spirit has always been, too; the Spirit "moved upon the face of the waters" at the time of the beginning of the world. And the Holy Spirit visited the mother of Jesus and brought forth our Lord as the Christ Child, in the manger. . . .

Christmas is always. It has been always. But we have not always understood it.

❄ ❄ ❄

When I was a little girl, the word "Christmas" was magic! It meant climbing into a railroad "sleeping car" and going from our home in Osceola, Arkansas, to my grandfather's home 'way down in Uvalde, Texas. It meant a happy family reunion with all my aunts and uncles and their children, under the great spreading Texas roof. It meant warm weather in the middle of winter. It meant loads of "goodies" spread on the long family table, with Grandfather at the head thanking God for His abundant blessings and asking that His grace be with us all. It meant a family gathering at an early bedtime around the huge fireplace in grandfather's bedroom, when we popped corn and ate fresh, luscious fruit and said our good-night prayers. I can still see that blessed room, with the well-thumbed Bible beside my grandfather's big wicker chair. It was quite a family.

But, of course, we were still children then, and we spoke as children, and we understood as children, and it was a long time before we grew enough spiritually to understand Christmas as God meant it to be. (Too many of us, I think, never grow out of our childish concepts of Christmas!)

heart of God. But we never find that unless we look beyond the presents under the tree. . . .

❋ ❋ ❋

Sometimes, when I was still a child, Christmas came for me in the summer, when we visited my father's folks in Mississippi. There I found the same warmth of family love. What a wonderful time we had in that old, rambling, two-story white house in Centerville, Mississippi. There were beautiful "summer Christmas trees" on the front lawn, adorned with velvety white magnolia blossoms. I remember the heavily-loaded fig tree just outside our bedroom window; I just reached out of that window, and touched it. This was Christmas, too, in our hearts, for there was an abundance of peace and love for God and each other.

I learned that Christmas could come on

a summer's day. Christmas could come at *any* season, if that sense of love were strong in the family.

Have you ever stopped to think that our Lord chose to come to earth as part of a family? He heartily approved of the family, as a social and spiritual unit. When we talk about the first Christmas, do we not always see the Holy Family in the humble manger? It couldn't be Christmas, without them there!

When we are careless about our family relationships, we are losing Christmas.

❊ ❊ ❊

Following my marriage with my first sweetheart in my 'teens, God blessed me with a wonderful spiritual child, my beloved first-born, Tom. It was Tom who gently led me to the feet of the Saviour, nine years ago, by his quiet and steady devotion to

Him in every area of his life. It was Roy's three motherless children and my feeling of spiritual inadequacy in meeting the problems of being a stepmother that made me look with longing at the serenity of Tom's face. I knew he had Someone he could depend upon, and I needed that Someone.

To Tom, Christmas was *every day*, for Christ was with him every day. Christ had been born *in him*. Every heart is, or can be, a manger in which the Lord is constantly reborn.

I have many wonderful Christmas memories, gathered as the years rolled by. . . . Perhaps the loveliest is the one of the second and last "earth" Christmas of Robin, our little angel. I wanted so desperately to see her enjoy, understand and really catch the spirit of Christmas, and I hoped that our carefully chosen little gifts would help and please her. You know, she looked just as though she belonged on top of a beautiful, glimmering Christmas tree. Her nurse used to call her "angel," and that Christmas day she really looked the part.

Robin was one of the greatest Christmas gifts of my life; she brought me into suffering and taught me to walk by faith with Christ through the deep waters to a new and clearer understanding of life. Through her I learned where abundant life is really to be—in the service of others through the Christ who lived, died and rose for all of us.

I remember the indescribable feeling of happiness as I watched Robin delightedly pound the little red piano that still sits on my window-sill . . . and I remember hearing a song in my heart. . . .

You little blue-eyed angel,
Heaven has sent you to me,
You little blue-eyed angel,

You belong on a Christmas tree.
Hair that is gold has my precious one,
That little smile is warm as the sun.
You little blue-eyed angel,
You belong on a Christmas tree.

. . . what a blessed Christmas experience that was! My soul grew much in understanding that day.

* * *

Then, the next Christmas, as we trimmed the tree for Cheryl, Linda, Dusty and our two "newest Rogerses," Sandy and Dodie, I picked up a little Christmas-tree angel, and inwardly saw little Robin's face. As I placed it on top of the tree, I suddenly knew that little Robin was very, very happy now and having a Christmas with the One who made it possible! Sandy and Dodie were ecstatic over the tree and their gifts, and we all felt warmly grateful to God for the two charming little strangers He had sent to take the place of our "angel unaware". . . .

There was the usual Christmas turkey with my favorite Texas corn-bread dressing, marshmallow-topped sweet potatoes, "ambrosia," and fruit cake—the Christmas dinner of my childhood. "Daddy Roy" gifted me with an electric organ on Christmas Eve, and its soothing notes proved blessed therapy to a heart remembering a little blonde head missing around the tree. It seemed the other children "outdid themselves" to help make this Christmas happy for "Mom"—because they knew I needed help. . . .

Children are "part and parcel" of Christmas. . . . Think how wonderful it would be if childless couples would "borrow" some orphans for Christmas!

The next time we had an addition to

Christmas at the Double R Ranch, was when Marion, our foster Scottish daughter, spent her first Yuletide with us. I shall never forget the glow of happiness on that little face as she helped trim the tree and opened her gifts. How that child relished oranges! Oranges are so plentiful in California that we are prone to take them for granted. But I do believe that child's Yule tree was the one in our front yard, loaded with oranges!

Then came the Christmas in Chatsworth, with another new "little pixie" hanging ornaments on the tall tree in the den, and piping a little "sing-song" Korean rendition of "Silent Night"—little Debbie! She and Dodie wanted, and got, shiny red "trikes" and little baby dolls that cried very wee wet tears. . . .

We had nine for breakfast that Christmas morning, around the huge, round oaken table, and of course, seven of them were too excited to eat! Tom and Barbara, Mindy and Candy, Grandma Smith, and "Uncle Son," my brother Hillman, and Mammy and Grampy Slye came for dinner and rounded out the family, as well as five of our old "stand-by," or "on-the-loose" friends—so the place was really jumping with joy. You need something like that, at Christmas; you need to share it with a *crowd.* The Bethlehem stable was crowded, you know: Christ was not born in obscurity.

As I watched little Debbie chatting happily with Dodie and busy with her toys, I felt a twinge of sadness for those countless other children in Korea, and I wished I might have them all here, too. But I thanked God that day for Dr. Bob Pierce and his World Vision, Inc., which makes Christmas really Christmas for those orphans of the storm by providing foster parents for them in America. Yes, Christmas is always . . . it goes on, and on . . . in people like this. . . . Christmas is always.

❋ ❋ ❋

One day we all took a ride on the ski lift on Mount Summit, riding in pairs in the little suspended chairs which scaled the mountain. The higher we got, the colder and more beautiful it became. Our ascent was very slow in comparison with the descent of those who went down on their skis, just under the cars in which we rode. What a parallel to life! To climb requires effort and persistence; to slide down, no effort at all. . . .

At the top we jumped out of the chairs and ran into a warm "sky house" where we drank hot chocolate and warmed our toes at the big, old-fashioned, round iron stove. The children were delighted with the little snow-covered "Christmas trees" which we saw on the way up—and there were so many! Roy said, "Wouldn't it be wonderful to have one like that for Christmas, with real snow on it?" I thought of the sixteenth verse of Psalm 147: "He giveth snow like wool: he scattereth the hoarfrost like ashes."

Giving. Always, God is *giving*. Not just on one day do His gifts arrive, but always . . . constantly . . . day by day . . . hour by hour. . . . He causes Christmas to happen with the spectacle of little snow-covered trees on mountainsides, in August and July; He trims them with a color and a glory that make our hearts leap up as we behold them. He gives unstintingly and constantly of Christmas beauty to us all, if we have but eyes to see. . . .

❄ ❄ ❄

So Christmas has been for me, so it has

grown and developed from my childhood days. So, I think, God intended it to be: an unfolding, growing lesson in love. And as I have grown, I have come to understand that this great love must be practiced not just on December 25, but every day in God's year.

Before me is a little story written by Robert Sylvester. It reads: "The Salvation Army always has a tough time getting the right pictures to be used for each coming Christmas and the blizzard in New York on the first day of spring this year gave them a wonderful break. The Army hurried out, found a pretty Salvation Army lassie and draped her in a red cape, broke out a standard tripod and kettle and set it up in the snow on Fifth Avenue with the sign, 'Give a Happy Christmas.' They figured to get some good advertising and promotion pictures for next Christmas. It got them. It also got two half-dollars, four quarters, three dimes, seven nickels and three pennies —a total of $2.68—from passersby still thinking of Christmas on the first day of spring."

❊ ❊ ❊

But . . . why?

Why should there be a Christmas at all? Why did God want to do all this for us, in the first place? Why? He didn't have to, you know!

You have to go back to the Bible to find the reason for it—and it isn't hard to find. This Bible was written by many men who believed in God, who prayed to God for help and understanding in their bitter, loveless world, and then listened quietly with all their minds and hearts for God to speak the truth to them. Now, God made their world and their earth with all its beauties; He was lavish with natural beauty as He finished it off, and when it was done it was perfect, and I'm sure He enjoyed looking at it. But He had something more than beauty to lavish upon His creation: He had love to give. He wanted someone like Himself, who could talk to Him, love Him and obey Him by enjoying this beautiful world in the way that God intended him to—and, of course, since God designed it all, He knew the best way. So God made man in the pattern of Himself and then told man that he could have this whole wide, beautiful world. What a Christmas present *that* was!

The reason God made man was that man might rule the earth, for God had all of heaven and He isn't selfish. This was a *real* Christmas.

God was so loving and generous that He gave man a mind like His, to think with and to decide things for himself; He gave man the superb, priceless gift of reason, for He wanted man to search for Him and love Him because he wanted to, and not because he didn't know any better. Man's mind is the gift of God.

Then God saw that man, in his perfect earth, was lonely—because, although man could hear God, he couldn't see Him; because God, His Son and the Holy Spirit could be heard but not seen. He had formed man of the dust of the earth, so man was "of the earth, earthy." But God was not content to leave him like that. He breathed His Spirit into man, and from that moment on, man was never again just "earthy"; he had within himself a Holy Spirit, and he was a living *soul*.

Then, seeing that man was still lonely for a mate in his earthly paradise, God made woman, so that man could be happier and so that God could enjoy them both!

Yes, Christmas is always. It was back there in Eden, with God giving, giving, giving. . . .

❄ ❄ ❄

Now the man and the woman were told by God that they could eat and enjoy the fruits of any tree in the lovely Garden of Eden, except one. God knew why it would be bad for them to eat the fruit of that one tree. But the man and the woman were not as wise as God, so they disobeyed Him. When they disobeyed they were not happy and God was not happy. You all know what happened after that. . . .

The years went on, and God peopled the earth with more men and women—but they were not happy, either, because the first man and woman had brought sin, or evil, into the world, with their disobedience.

But God still loved them; He has never

stopped loving us, no matter how evil we have become. From time to time, He would send certain men to earth who were filled with His Spirit, to try to get people straightened out and on the right path again. All He asked was that man love Him as He loved man. All He wanted them to do was to love each other. But, as usual, most of the people wouldn't listen to the men God sent; they were too busy having what they called " a good time." Finally, they became so wicked that God decided to clean up the world by washing it with a gigantic flood.

God is clean and holy; He wanted His people clean and holy too. He could not bear to look down upon a world grown filthy with evil. Yet, in His infinite mercy, He gave His people one more chance: He told them through Noah, His chosen spokesman, that He would spare anyone who would turn away from wrongdoing and do what was right, and worship Him. I'm sure that it grieved the heart of God that no one would listen to Noah, but no one would. So ". . . the rain descended, and the floods came . . ." until even the mountains were covered, and only Noah and his family and the animals in the ark were alive and safe.

When it was all over, God sent a beautiful present—a glorious rainbow in the sky, with colors more beautiful than any you ever saw on any Christmas tree. . . .

Things began all over again, and more people came to fill the earth. In time, they forgot all about the Great Flood, and they began to abuse the beautiful, rain-washed earth again with their wickedness. God kept sending special men to speak to them, to try to get them to turn back to Him and His perfect way of life. The people treated these prophets very badly: some they ridiculed, and some they threw into prison and some they killed. They were selfish, and cruel, and they wanted their own way. The prophets were good and great men—but they failed.

Finally God was so concerned, and He loved the world so much, that He decided to try once again, with the dearest possession He had: His own Son. He would send His own Son to earth; perhaps they would listen to Him!

He knew that His Son would have to be born like a human being, and live and look like a human being, in order to reach human beings. God wanted His Son to be accepted on earth; He also wanted to show the people of earth what the Father, our God, is like.

God looked the world over and chose a young and pure maiden named Mary to be the mother of His Son. Now, God could have put His Son Jesus Christ on earth in any way He wanted, but wasn't it an indication of His love that He chose to honor a human being in allowing her to be the mother of His Child? What a present that was for Mary!

God decided to make the arrival of His Son startlingly different from what the world expected. So, the night of His Son's birth, He sent a heavenly host of angels to announce the birth to humble shepherds on a hillside in Judea. What a present for *them!*

The world expected the Christ to arrive in a scene of dazzling splendor, like a king from heaven. But no—God planned it otherwise. He made the scene of the nativity radiant with the simplicity of a lowly manger, with Joseph, the husband of Mary, and the shepherds, and the beasts of burden in the stalls round about. Instead of princely robes of velvet and satin, our Lord was wrapped in swaddling clothes, and He lay in a bed of straw.

You can still see the spot where He was born, in a little rock-lined room cut into the hillside of Bethlehem. Thousands make their pilgrimage there every year, to stand in awe-struck silence for a moment—for the greatest moment of their lives. No one ever laughs there; many weep. To no other being ever to live upon our earth is such homage paid, after 1900 years. As we go in to see the manger-spot, we pass through a little door cut so low that we must bow to get through it. No man, woman or child approaches this holy spot without a bow.

No matter which day in the week you go there, it is Christmas. Christmas is always, in Bethlehem. . . .

❋ ❋ ❋

"As the heavens are higher than the earth,

so are my ways higher than your ways . . ." saith the Lord. Our Saviour's coming had been predicted by the prophets centuries before, and even the kings of the Orient, far from Bethlehem, were eagerly watching for a sign of His arrival. They were so vigilant in their watchful waiting that they recognized immediately the bright new star in the East and started down the long, long road that led to Bethlehem, to see this long-awaited Messiah. Imagine their surprise when they found Him in a stable!

But perhaps it made no difference, for in the pictures we have of them standing at the manger, we see no surprise on their faces. They stand there in their rich, royal robes, or they kneel there offering their finest gifts of treasure. One offers gold; hereafter, gold is good enough only to be thrown before the feet of Jesus Christ! Another offered frankincense—a sweet-smelling incense often burned at the altars of the temple; frankincense, as well as gold is useless now; it was not holy ritual but holy living that this Christ demanded. One offered myrrh; this Babe would die young, on a cross, and Mary, happy now, would need myrrh for the embalming.

These were the first Christmas gifts from human hands to God. Study them well: they have deep meaning.

Even then, God was saying to the wise and the mighty: "Except ye . . . become as little children, ye shall not enter into the kingdom of heaven." What did God mean by giving us this Babe, by this lowly birth? Was He not giving Him as a Christmas present to the poor, and as a rebuke to those who put their trust in riches?

As He grew to manhood, Christmas was everywhere that Jesus went. He gave lovingly to friend and foe alike. He gave of His divine nature to heal the sick, to raise the dead. He changed water into wine at a wedding feast, fed thousands on a hillside with a few loaves and fishes, made the blind to see, forgave guilty, miserable men and women and transformed them into new, victorious people by His matchless words. . . .

Imagine the joy of Jairus, a ruler of the synagogue, brokenhearted at the death of his twelve-year-old daughter, when Jesus took the dead child by the hand and lifted her up into life again! What a Christmas for that family!

Think of what must have gone through the hearts of Mary and Martha when their brother Lazarus walked out of that tomb after four days! That was really Christmas, for, you see, Christmas is giving and Jesus really gave of His divine strength to revive those loved ones from the sleep of death.

He has been doing it ever since: millions

have been lifted out of the sleep of unhappy, purposeless lives into abundant life by the gift of faith in this Christ. . . . On whatever day they accepted this gift from Him, that day is Christmas to them forever.

How much Christmas He gave! Remember the time when the mothers all crowded around Him with their little ones, and how He put His strong, tender hands on each of them in blessing and how His followers complained of His taking so much time for the little ones when there were so many weighty matters to be discussed, so many other more important things to be done? What did He answer? "Suffer little children . . . to come unto me: for of such is the kingdom of heaven." He was saying that Christmas is for the young in heart, and that only those with the simplicity of a child's heart can appreciate Christmas and His gifts. Those who become so wise in their own eyes that they think they need not Christ—these have lost the wonder, the true magic, the glory of Christmas.

❄ ❄ ❄

Yes, my child, Christmas is giving, in the name of Christ. But—Christmas is also *receiving!* Is that hard to understand? It shouldn't be. What would you think of the Christmas "spirit" of a friend who wasn't even grateful enough to thank you for a present? If he has the Christmas spirit at all, he will receive it with joy and gratitude and thanks, because of the love which prompted the gift. The Bible says that God so loved this world that He gave His only Son, and that "as many as received him, to them gave he power to become the sons of God. . . ." As many as *received* Him! When we understand that, we understand that receiving is even more important than giving, at Christmas!

Let me illustrate what I mean. Suppose a child had an overabundance of beautiful toys, and he saw a poor, ragged little fellow with no toys at all. He would feel sorry for the luckless youngster, and offer him one of the best toys he had, as a present. But—he says he doesn't want it! He still looks unhappy, when he says it. So the benevolent one picks out another, and offers that, and *that* one is rejected. He tries several times, and finally offers him his favorite toy, the one he loves best, the one he really wanted to keep forever. The other looks at it for a moment, shrugs, and turns away. This would be too bad, wouldn't it? This could have been a real Christmas for the boy, but he wouldn't receive the gift. . . .

Can you imagine how God feels when He offers us His only Son, and we reject Him, even crucify Him on a cross? You see, my child, to really receive Christmas you must receive Christ first; the rejoicing comes later. . . .

What does it mean to receive Christ? It means to understand that He came into the world to save sinners, and that we are all sinners by nature. We need to be saved from our sinful natures, or, as the Bible says, to be "born again." Or, if you will, "made over." When we receive Christ and take Him into our lives and let Him make those lives over, then we receive the Supreme Gift, for He comes into our hearts through His Holy Spirit and we experience the gift that is Christmas, the joy of union with God, and peace on earth and good will toward men.

Christmas is not just a date on our calendar; it is a state of heart.

The folks who have the best time on December 25 are those who have received Him, and who give in remembrance of Him. Suppose we set up a different Christmas tree this year! Suppose we set one up in our hearts. Suppose the tree is Jesus Christ, the True Evergreen, the Life Everlasting. Suppose we adorn this tree with the gifts He brings to those who accept Him—love, forgiveness, patience, hope, charity, peace, mercy, understanding, humility. Suppose we turn on the lights of this tree very brightly, and *keep* them on! If we do this, our "traditional" tree will take on a new and richer meaning.

❄ ❄ ❄

Speaking of the Christmas tree—trees, you know, have been historically recognized as symbols of everlasting life. That is, no tree ever dies: it leaves new life behind it, in seed and acorn. Job says that ". . . there is hope of a tree, if it be cut down, that it will sprout again . . ." and we are told in the first Psalm that one who loves the Lord "shall be like a tree planted by the rivers of water. . . ." It is all symbolic of the rebirth of Christ in the human heart. Every time a repentant and seeking heart says, "I believe . . ." the King and Lord of all is born anew in the humble dwelling of the heart.

The Christ Child in us must be allowed to grow, and we allow Him to grow, like an everlasting tree as we, His branches, bear fruit fit for His Kingdom.

This, my child, is a wonderful mystery, but it happens. I have seen it, and experienced it. . . .

The Bible says that the human heart is by nature deceitful, and desperately wicked. But Jesus wants His home there, so that His Spirit can change that heart. You know, when once I opened my heart to Christ in sincere faith, I was just like a little child seeing her first "Christmas tree." All of a sudden everything around me looked new and beautiful and shining. . . . I was like a new tree "planted by the rivers of water. . . ." It was the crowning Christmas of my life.

❊ ❊ ❊

The Christmas tree is traditional; so is Santa Claus. We've always had him around at Christmas; he's really a tradition!

But just what does Santa Claus have to do with Christmas, anyway? And how did *he* get into the picture?

Well, my child, the figure of Santa Claus is actually a symbol of the truly Christian spirit of giving, in spite of what some people say about him. He represents a man named Nicholas who, according to tradition, lived many, many years ago in Asia Minor. Nicholas' father was a very rich merchant who for years had no children. He and his wife prayed and promised God that if He would send them a child, they would train him to love and serve God. God answered their prayer and sent the boy, whom they named Nicholas. He was carefully and lovingly nurtured and well educated in the Christian faith.

His parents died, however, when he was quite young, and left him a great deal of money. The spirit of the Lord prompted Nicholas to give away all he had, with the exception of three small bags of gold, which at that time would have kept him nicely for the rest of his life.

One day he overheard the weeping of a neighbor's daughter, and he heard the father say to the girl that he was too poor to give her a dowry for her marriage. (In those days a girl could not marry unless she had a dowry, or a gift of money, to bring to her husband; if she could not do this, her father had to sell her as a slave.) There were three daughters in this family, and they all wept when they were told they could not have a dowry. The girl who was at the marriageable age wept loudest of all; she was the one Nicholas heard, and he couldn't bear it. He had all three bags of his gold at this time; he crept behind a bush under the window of the neighbor's home, and tossed one of his three bags of gold through the window. He did not want them to know who did it, for he remembered the words of Jesus: "When thou doest alms, let not thy left hand know what thy right hand doeth: That thine alms may be in secret: and thy Father which seeth in secret himself shall reward thee openly."

So the daughter was happily married. Then came the next daughter's turn. The father was still poor, and again Nicholas heard the weeping. Again he secretly provided the dowry by tossing his second bag of gold through the window.

By this time, the father was determined to know who their "angel of charity" was—so when it came time for the third daughter to marry, he stationed a watchman outside the house, to catch his wonderful benefactor. Sure enough! As Nicholas tossed in his last bag of gold, the man grabbed him and took him in the house, where a very grateful father thanked him for insuring the futures of three tearful but very grateful girls.

Of course, this became known in the town, which embarrassed Nicholas, for he was a modest young man; and since he loved to serve God and his fellow man, he decided to become a priest. When he had finished his studies, he decided to return to his home town of Myra, in western Greece. Myra was having quite a time of it, right then, trying to elect a new bishop to preside in their cathedral to take the place of the old bishop who had just died. The clergy just couldn't agree on the man to fill the vacancy so they decided to wait until the next out-of-town priest walked into their cathedral, and they would make him the bishop.

While all this was going on inside the cathedral, Nicholas came along the main street of the town; just outside the cathedral he found a crowd of little children and he stopped to talk with them (and, I like to think, even *play* a little with them!). Then he stepped into the cathedral—to be welcomed by the shouts of the clergy, who then and there proclaimed him the new Bishop of Myra.

Nicholas became known as "the patron of the children" for his untiring efforts to help them and teach them. Each year on his birthday, which was December 6, Nicholas would collect presents and distribute them among the children. This idea of presents for the children spread all over Europe, and it was always done in memory of St. Nicholas, who was such an outstanding example of the Spirit of Jesus.

The word "Santa Claus" is the Dutch name for St. Nicholas, and we adopted "Santa Claus" when the early Dutch settlers came to New Amsterdam, or New York, as it was called later. The English called him "St. Nicholas" and, sometimes, "old Kris Kringle," but whatever they called him, they always associated him with the giving of gifts at Christmas. In the town of Myra, after Nicholas died, the practice of giving gifts continued on December 6 for a long, long time before it was finally transferred to December 25.

The red robe of Santa Claus has a religious significance too; it represents the red "cope" (or cape) which the priests of the church wore at Christmas. The fur-trimmed hat and boots were adopted by the cold countries of the north; travel there would be very cold and very difficult for Santa unless he had a sled and some fast reindeer—so he got the deer and the big sled, and he became a jolly, round, old man distributing untold happiness to children everywhere. He was never meant to overshadow the celebration of the birthday of our Lord Jesus Christ, but only to supplement it, for it was the Spirit of our Lord that gave us "St. Nicholas."

❄ ❄ ❄

Someone is asking, "If Christmas is always, as you say, then why do we set aside December 25—just one day in the year—to celebrate it?" Well, there's a lot of tradition in that, too. We might answer that question by asking, "Why do we stop work one day a week—on Sunday—instead of on Thursday or Friday?" The answer is that God gives us that one day in the week to rest, to think about what happened last week, and what will happen next week, to renew our strength through prayer and meditation so that we can face whatever comes. We *can* rest on other days, too, of course, but having a special day set aside for this seems to impress upon us our need for refreshment, and for the remembrance that we need to stop and "take stock of ourselves."

The same thing can be said of December 25: it is the yearly reminder that our Lord loved us enough to become one of us, to sacrifice Himself for us so that we might understand once and for all *that God is, and always was, and always will be; that God is Love, and that love will win, even on a cross.*

Love is the greatest power there is, and love is the meaning of Christmas. This is why we need a day set aside for remembering the "earth birth" of our Lord, who was Love clothed in human flesh. Christmas is the day set aside for us to ask ourselves whether we honestly love God and man. We need this day of spiritual inventory to clean out the old worthless stock of indifference and to restock our hearts and minds with the spirit of the Christ, to receive Him and give ourselves.

Christmas, my child, is love in action. . . . When you love someone, you *give* to them, as God gives to us. The greatest gift He ever gave was the Person of His Son, sent to us in human form so that we might know what God the Father is really like! Every time we love, every time we give, it's Christmas!

❋ ❋ ❋

So let's put *our* love into action this Christmas.

How?

Wouldn't it be nice to visit Christ this Christmas by visiting those imprisoned by sin or sickness?

Wouldn't it be more Christlike for us to visit someone in need of food or clothes, instead of exchanging a lot of gifts and gadgets which have little use?

Somewhere on the plains of Kansas there is a humble little doctor who spreads the Christmas spirit in a chain reaction. As Christmas day comes closer and closer, the doctor writes every patient who owes him anything, canceling the bill as a sort of Christmas present! But . . . there is one little condition: the patient must contribute a similar amount to a worthy charity. The doctor writes the patient: "Send us their receipt and we will close your account." It is a four-way gift: from the doctor, to the patient, to the charity—and on to the unknown man or woman who benefits by it all! Why not try *that* this Christmas? Why not try a little actual forgiving of our debtors, instead of just mumbling it over in the Lord's prayer?

Instead of worrying about what we should or should not pay for a gift for a friend, how about a donation for an orphanage in his name? You could send him a card saying that he has shared in some Christian Christmas giving with you.

How about offering Christ your talent this Christmas, instead of some of your money? He wants the best you have to give, not the cheapest! Do you know the story of "Why the Chimes Rang"? It deals with a set of church chimes that rang only when someone offered a gift that came from the heart, at Christmas. The rich gave their gold—no, gave *some* of their gold—but the chimes were silent. The not-so-rich gave "what they thought they could afford"—and the chimes did not ring. Finally there came a lame boy who had no money at all; he laid his crutches on the altar—and the chimes rang! I've always had an idea that that boy walked out of the church with a new strength, leaving the crutches behind.

Sacrificial giving to God always rings the bell.

How about giving up a grudge or a grievance or an imagined hurt this Christmas, to get a little peace in your heart? "Peace on earth, good will toward men!" That heavenly announcement is printed on many of our Christmas cards. Do you know, my child, that many years before the Saviour was born, a prophet named Isaiah foretold the birth of Jesus and said that He would be known as the Prince of Peace? Later, this Prince of Peace told us that peacemakers are blessed—or happy. What He meant was that unless you have peace you can never be happy. Another time, He said that if we have anything against our brother, we should be reconciled (or make peace) with him before we offer a gift to God in His place of worship.

In Czechoslovakia, I am told, the people celebrate Christmas by visiting their friends and foes and forgiving any misunderstandings which might have arisen during the year; Christmas to them means the ending of old quarrels and the beginning of the new year among new friends. God must love that! He never gives us His peace until we have drowned every hate and grudge and bitterness in the great sea of His love and mercy. Only when we are at peace with others do we have Christmas in our hearts.

Or, you can gather up some of the things you don't use any more, get them to one of those organizations that mend and restore them and send them out to folks who are in need. Remember the joy each item brought you: wish the same joy to the one who receives it from you, and you will find out how blessed it is to give with such a wish. For wishes, like thoughts, are things; this way, you will be sending two things—a wish and a useful gift.

While we are at it, how about a real sacrifice this Christmas? Like choosing one of your most prized possessions, and sending it out to someone to express your love? God gave us not "something He could afford"—He gave His most precious possession in heaven, His own Son!

We need to see His Son beyond the gilt and gadgets of Christmas, need to see Him in the manger, in the streets, on the cross. Hilda W. Smith put it beautifully once:

The Carpenter of Galilee
Comes down the street again,
In every land, in every age,

He still is building men.
On Christmas Eve we hear Him knock;
He goes from door to door:
"Are any workmen out of work?
The Carpenter needs more."

Christmas is like that: like the walking of Jesus, like the moving of the Spirit from the days when time began to our own times, like the redemptive purpose of God working out its way in our lives through the One born at Bethlehem. . . .

Yes, my child, Christmas is always, for Jesus said, "Lo, I am with you alway . . ." and Christmas is Jesus!

THE

IBIZA

Rough Guides online

www.roughguides.com

Rough Guide Credits

Text editor: Fran Sandham
Series editor: Mark Ellingham
Production: Tanya Hall, Julia Bovis
Cartography: Maxine Repath, Ed Wright, Katie Lloyd-Jones

Publishing Information

This second edition published April 2003
by Rough Guides Ltd,
80 Strand, London WC2R 0RL

Distributed by the Penguin Group:

Penguin Books Ltd, 80 Strand, London WC2R 0RL
Penguin Putnam, Inc. 375 Hudson Street, New York 10014, USA
Penguin Books Australia Ltd, 487 Maroondah Highway,
PO Box 257, Ringwood, Victoria 3134, Australia
Penguin Books Canada Ltd, 10 Alcorn Avenue,
Toronto, Ontario, Canada M4V 1E4
Penguin Books (NZ) Ltd,
182–190 Wairau Road, Auckland 10, New Zealand

Typeset in Bembo and Helvetica to an original design by Henry Iles.
Printed in Spain by Graphy Cems.

A catalogue record for this book is available from the British Library.

ISBN 1-854353-063-5

THE ROUGH GUIDE TO

IBIZA

by Iain Stewart

with additional contributions by Martin Davies

We set out to do something different when the first Rough Guide was published in 1982. Mark Ellingham, just out of university, was travelling in Greece. He brought along the popular guides of the day, but found they were all lacking in some way. They were either strong on ruins and museums but went on for pages without mentioning a beach or taverna. Or they were so conscious of the need to save money that they lost sight of Greece's cultural and historical significance. Also, none of the books told him anything about Greece's contemporary life – its politics, its culture, its people, and how they lived.

So with no job in prospect, Mark decided to write his own guidebook, one which aimed to provide practical information that was second to none, detailing the best beaches and the hottest clubs and restaurants, while also giving hard-hitting accounts of every sight, both famous and obscure, and providing up-to-the-minute information on contemporary culture. It was a guide that encouraged independent travellers to find the best of Greece, and was a great success, getting shortlisted for the Thomas Cook travel guide award, and encouraging Mark, along with three friends, to expand the series.

The Rough Guide list grew rapidly and the letters flooded in, indicating a much broader readership than had been anticipated, but one which uniformly appreciated the Rough Guide mix of practical detail and humour, irreverence and enthusiasm. Things haven't changed. The same four friends who began the series are still the caretakers of the Rough Guide mission today: to provide the most reliable, up-to-date and entertaining information to independent-minded travellers of all ages, on all budgets.

We now publish more than 200 titles and have offices in London and New York. The travel guides are written and researched by a dedicated team of more than 100 authors, based in Britain, Europe, the USA and Australia. We have also created a unique series of phrasebooks to accompany the travel series, along with an acclaimed series of music guides, and a best-selling pocket guide to the Internet and World Wide Web. We also publish comprehensive travel information on our Web site: **www.roughguides.com**

Help us update

We've gone to a lot of trouble to ensure that this Rough Guide is as up to date and accurate as possible. However, things do change. All suggestions, comments and corrections are much appreciated, and we'll send a copy of the next edition (or any other Rough Guide if you prefer) for the best letters.

Please mark letters "**Rough Guide Ibiza Update**" and send to:

Rough Guides, 80 Strand, London WC2R 0RL or
Rough Guides, 4th Floor, 345 Hudson St, New York NY 10014.

Or send an email to mail@roughguides.com
Have your questions answered and tell others about your trip at
www.roughguides.atinfopop.com

Acknowledgements

Thanks to Tanya Hall for typesetting, Maxine Repath, Katie Lloyd-Jones and Ed Wright for maps, Sharon Martins for photos, John Sturges for proofreading, and Geoff Howard for helpful suggestions. The author would like to thank Martin Davies for expert support, Fran Sandham for editorial proficiency, the Wilson clan of Sant Agustí, Lenny Krarup, Jill Canney, Zuka people, Enrique, Kirk Huffman, Senyor Antoni Roselló, Saché, Martin Reilly, Michael Stuart, Roberta at Pacha, Gayle, Zumo FM, Jasmine Elias, Live Ibiza, the Charltons, and Demon Library.

Cover Credits

Main front Ibiza Town © Getty
small front picture Manumission Parade © Leelu Morris
back top picture Port de Sant Miquel © Robert Harding
back lower picture Sant Llorenç de Balasia © Axiom

CONTENTS

Listings

Contexts

MAP LIST

Maps at back of book

MAP SYMBOLS

Symbol	Meaning	Symbol	Meaning
	Paved road		Pine trees
	Dirt road		Vineyard
	Path		Fuel station
	Waterway	P	Parking
	Mountain range	★	Taxi/bus stop
▲	Mountain peak		Accommodation
	Airport		Restaurant/bar/café
	Point of interest		Post office
	Cave		Information office
	Lighthouse	H	Helipad
	Windmill		Church (regional maps)
	Viewpoint		National park
	Campsite		Beach
	Tower		Salt pan
	Archeological site		Building
	Historic house		Church (town maps)
	Statue		

Introduction

Ibiza is an island of excess. Widely acclaimed as the world's clubbing capital, it's a unique and almost absurdly hedonistic place, where the nights are celebrated with tremendous vitality. Thanks largely to the British tabloid press, the popular perception of Ibiza is of a charmless, high-rise party destination, but, while it's true that high-octane techno tourism is central to the local economy, there's much more to the island than the club scene.

Ibiza's scenery is captivating – dotted around its dazzling shoreline are more than fifty **beaches**, ranging from expansive sweeps of sand to exquisite, miniature coves beneath soaring cliffs. Many of the best beaches were insensitively transformed into functional holiday resorts in the 1960s, but plenty of pristine places remain. Ibiza's hilly, thickly wooded **interior** is peppered with isolated whitewashed villages and terraced fields of almonds, figs and olives. The cosmopolitan capital, **Ibiza Town**, has most of the island's architectural treats, including the spectacular walled enclave of **Dalt Vila**, and a historic port area with hip bars, stylish restaurants and fashionable boutiques. Within easy reach are the small beach resorts of Talamanca and Figueretes, pleasant enough places to spend a day by the sea.

However, for a better selection of beaches, head for the disparate **east coast**, dotted with family resorts such as Cala

Llonga as well as beautiful undeveloped coves like Cala Boix and Cala Mastella, and the slender sands of Aigües Blanques, a naturist beach. The east coast's main town, **Santa Eulària** is an agreeable but unremarkable place, though you'll find a decent restaurant strip here as well as historical and cultural interest on the Puig de Missa hilltop above the town.

The isolated, remote **northwest** is Ibiza's least developed region, with a rugged coastline ideal for hiking, the two small resorts of Portinatx and Port de Sant Miquel, and a smattering of spectacular coves including the cliff-backed bays of Cala d'en Serra, Benirràs and Portitxol. Inland, the scenery is equally impressive, dominated by the lofty pine-clad Els Amunts hills; between these peaks lie a succession of diminutive, isolated settlements such as Sant Joan and Sant Miquel, each with its own fortified whitewashed church and a rustic bar or two. Ibiza's bohemian character, rooted in 1960s ethics, remains particularly strong in the north of the island, where you'll find yoga retreats, ethnic bazaars and a large population of hippy-minded residents.

On the western coast, Ibiza's second largest town, **Sant Antoni**, is no architectural beauty, but can boast a dynamic bar and club scene, plus a selection of mellower chillout bars on its much-touted **Sunset Strip**, home of the legendary *Café del Mar*. Sant Antoni's beaches tend to get

CATALAN AND CASTILIAN

Though you'll often see and hear Castilian Spanish in the Pitiuses, the official language is Catalan, which has replaced Castilian on street signs and official documents in recent years. We've followed suit and used Catalan in this guide, giving Castilian alternatives where useful. For more on language, see p.334.

packed in high season, but west of the town, Cala Conta and Cala Bassa offer luminous water and fine, gently shelving sands. The wildly beautiful **south** of the island boasts over a dozen beaches, from tiny remote coves like Cala Llentrisca and Cala Molí to the sweeping sands of Salines beach and Es Cavallet on the outskirts of Ibiza Town – two of Ibiza's most fashionable places to pose.

"Pitiuses" is the general term used to refer to Ibiza, Formentera and their outlying islets; in turn, the Pitiuses are part of the Balearic archipelago, which also comprises Mallorca and Menorca.

Serene, easygoing **Formentera**, the other main island of the Pitiuses, is just a short ferry ride south of Ibiza. With few historical sights apart from some sombre fortress-churches and a few minor archeological ruins, Formentera's main appeal is its relaxed, unhurried nature and its miles of ravishing, empty sands that shelve into breathtakingly translucent water. Comprised of two flat promontories linked by a narrow central isthmus, the island is very thinly populated; even **Sant Francesc Xavier**, the attractive but drowsy capital, is little more than village-sized. Though Formentera is equally dependent on tourism, it's much less developed than Ibiza; its best **beaches** – Platja Illetes and Platja Migjorn – have barely been touched, and the sole resort, Es Pujols, is a pleasantly small-scale affair.

When to go

Ibiza and Formentera are at their **hottest** between June and late September, when cloudless skies are virtually guaranteed. The heat can get intense in July and August, but even at this time of year, cooling sea breezes usually intervene to prevent things getting too uncomfortable. Winter in the

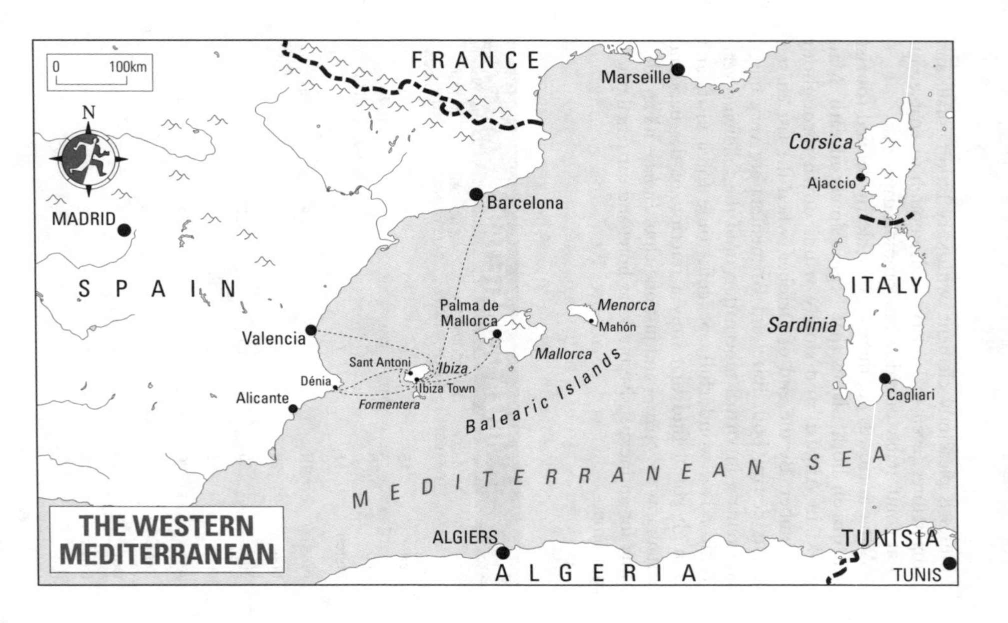
THE WESTERN MEDITERRANEAN
0
100km
N
MADRID
S P A I N
F R A N C E
Marseille
Barcelona
Valencia
Alicante
Dénia
Sant Antoni
Ibiza
Ibiza Town
Formentera
Palma de Mallorca
Mallorca
Menorca
Mahón
Balearic Islands
Corsica
Ajaccio
Sardinia
ITALY
Cagliari
M E D I T E R R A N E A N S E A
ALGIERS
A L G E R I A
TUNISIA
TUNIS

Pitiuses is pleasantly clement, with very little rainfall, and temperatures (even in January) high enough to enable you to sit comfortably outside a café on most days.

As far as crowds go, there's a very clearly defined **tourist season** on both islands that begins slowly in early May, peaks in August, and slowly winds down throughout September. By the end of October, when the last charter flights depart, both Ibiza and Formentera are very quiet, and remain in virtual hibernation until the following year. Winter is a wonderfully peaceful time for a visit, and though you'll find that only a fraction of the bars and restaurants are open – and just one club, *Pacha* – it's an ideal time for an inexpensive break, as hotel and car rental prices plummet.

IBIZA CLIMATE TABLE

	AV. DAILY TEMP (°C)	AV. HOURS OF SUN PER DAY	AV. NO. OF DAYS WITH RAIN	AV. SEA TEMP (°C)
Jan	15	6	5	14
Feb	15	6	4	13
March	17	7	3	14
April	19	8	4	15
May	22	9	2	17
June	25	10	2	20
July	28	11	1	23
Aug	29	12	1	25
Sept	27	8	3	24
Oct	23	6	7	21
Nov	19	5	6	18
Dec	16	5	5	15

BASICS

Getting there

By far the easiest and cheapest way to get to Ibiza and Formentera is to fly to Ibiza airport. If your final destination is Formentera, you'll then have to catch one of the regular ferries and hydrofoils that shuttle between the two islands.

Most people arrive on **charter flights** from the UK and Ireland, either as part of a **package** holiday or on a flight-only basis. You could also consider travelling **via mainland Spain**, from where there are plenty of flight and ferry connections; however, this may not be cost-effective, and is probably best considered if you want to explore other parts of Spain as well.

With no direct flights and a very limited number of tour operators offering vacations in the Balearics, Ibiza and Formentera are not major destinations for North Americans. However, plenty of travel agents can arrange flights to Ibiza, and many can book accommodation. Getting to Ibiza **from North America** involves changing planes in either Barcelona or Madrid. However, if you're flying from New York, you might want to take advantage of the relatively inexpensive flights to London, and pick up an onward flight from there (see pp.4–5 for details).

There are no direct flights **from Australia or New Zealand** to Spain, so you'll have to change planes two or three times in order to reach Ibiza. It's possible to get to the island within 24 hours if you travel via Asia, or thirty hours via the US – not counting time spent on stopovers – with flights routed through Asia generally being the cheaper option.

For more on getting to Ibiza from the rest of Spain, see pp.13–15 onwards.

Booking flights online

Many airlines and discount travel websites offer you the opportunity to book your tickets online, cutting out the costs of agents and middlemen. Good deals can often be found through discount or auction sites, as well as through the airlines' own websites.

W www.cheapflights.com Bookings from the UK and Ireland only. Flight deals, travel agents, plus links to other travel sites.

W www.cheap-ibiza-flights.com Cheap flights, packages and information on Ibiza.

W www.cheaptickets.com Discount flight specialists.

W www.expedia.com Discount airfares, all-airline search engine and daily deals.

W www.hotwire.com Bookings from the US only. Last-minute savings of up to forty percent on regular published fares.

FROM BRITAIN AND IRELAND

Between Easter and October, you should have no problem finding an inexpensive, direct **charter flight** from any of the main British airports or from Dublin. All the main tour operators fly to Ibiza, and even in August there are usually plenty of spare seats; however, bear in mind that there are no charter flights to Ibiza after October 31. The best place to start looking for a flight is either online via the websites list-

ed above, via Teletext (@www.teletext.com), or by using a good travel agent (see p.6) or tour operator (see p.8).

Fares are generally inexpensive. If you book two to three months ahead, a return ticket typically averages £160, while if you leave it to the last minute, rates often drop to around £100. Charter flights often lack flexibility (most of the carriers operate on weekly and fortnightly return schedules), though recently it's become a lot easier to visit Ibiza for a long weekend. Another possible drawback of booking a charter service is timing – many flights arrive in the early hours of the morning.

SCHEDULED FLIGHTS

Four airlines offer **scheduled flights** from Britain to Ibiza, and only no-frills airlines Go (from Stansted) and BMIbaby (from East Midlands) fly **direct** to the island, though during the summer season only. Iberia and Air Europa fly to the island all year round, mainly via Barcelona, Madrid or Palma. Iberia also offer daily scheduled flights from Dublin to Madrid and Barcelona, from where there are connections on to Ibiza.

It pays to **book well in advance** because, although flights to mainland Spain or Palma are easy to come by, connecting flights to Ibiza are frequently fully booked, particularly in the summer.

Scheduled **fares** vary considerably, and depend mainly on the flexibility of the ticket; you'll have to pay a little more if you want the freedom to change dates. Iberia usually have some good winter deals, with special offers from around £140 return, though £180–230 return is a more standard price. The cheapest tickets are usually out of one of the London airports.

Scheduled airlines

Air Europa ⓣ0870/240 1501, ⓦwww.air-europa.com. Daily flights from Gatwick to Ibiza via Madrid or Palma between May and October, plus limited winter connections.

BMIbaby UK ⓣ0870/264 2229, Ireland ⓣ01/242 0794, ⓦwww.bmibaby.com. Daily direct flights from East Midlands to Ibiza between May and September.

Go ⓣ0870/607 6543, ⓦwww.go-fly.com. Direct flights to Ibiza from Stansted, twice daily between May and October only.

Iberia UK ⓣ0845/601 2854, Ireland ⓣ01/407 3017, ⓦwww.iberia.com. Scheduled flights from Heathrow and Gatwick to Ibiza via Barcelona, Alicante, Palma, Valencia or Madrid. There are also flights from Manchester direct to Barcelona, and from Dublin to Barcelona and Madrid, from where there are regular flights to Ibiza.

Travel agents

All agents are UK-based unless stated.

Avant Garde ⓣ020/7240 5252, ⓦwww.ministryofsound.com/travel. Flight and villa rental packages via Ibiza Trips; quality apartments and tailor-made Ibizan holidays are also available.

AVRO ⓣ0870/036 0111, ⓦwww.avro-flights.co.uk. Specialists in discounted charter and scheduled flights.

Ibiza Sun Centre ⓣ0870/737 7222, ⓦwww.ibizasuncentre.co.uk. Good choice of hotel and flight options, with some very inexpensive accommodation deals outside high season.

North South Travel ⓣ01245/608 291, ⓦwww.nstravel.demon.co.uk. Excellent service and competitive scheduled flight prices. Profits aid projects in the developing world.

Spanish Travel Services ⓣ020/7387 5337, ⓦwww.apatraveluk.com. Spanish flight and package specialists.

STA Travel ⓣ0870/160 6070, ⓦwww.statravel.co.uk. Independent travel specialists, plus discounted flights.

Thomas Cook UK ⓣ020/7499 4000, Ireland ⓣ01/677 1721, ⓦwww.thomascook.com. Ibiza packages and flights.

Travel Bug ⓣ020/7835 2000 & ⓣ0161/721 4000, ⓦwww.flynow.com. Large range of discounted flights.

Usit CAMPUS ⓣ020/7730 3402 (for branches nationwide call ⓣ0870/240 1010), ⓦwww.usitcampus.com. Youth/student specialist.

Usit NOW Ireland ⓣ01/602 1600, N.Ireland ⓣ02890/324 073, ⓦwww.usitnow.ie. Inexpensive flights for students and young people.

PACKAGES

Most people travel to Ibiza, and to a lesser extent Formentera, as part of a **package holiday**, though the proportion of independent travellers is increasing steadily every year. All sorts of different deals are available, from simple self-catering apartments to luxury hotels. These package holidays generally represent good value for money, though accommodation is usually in rather soulless large hotels or apartment blocks in the main resorts. You'll also have far less flexibility to change your hotel or resort if you book a package holiday than if you make your own travel and hotel arrangements – though if you protest strongly enough to your holiday rep, alternatives can sometimes be arranged. It's well worth checking the independent reviews of Ibizan hotels used by package tour operators at the website ⓦwww.ibiza-uncovered.org.uk before you book anywhere.

On the plus side, package holidays are very convenient, with direct flights from all the main UK airports, inclusive airport transfers, and children's activities often laid on in the hotels. Package holidays can also represent exceptional value, with **prices** falling to almost absurd levels, especially if you travel early or late in the season. In May and October there are usually deals available from as little as £120 for a week, or around £160 for two weeks (based on two people sharing). At these prices, you'll almost certainly be allocated basic self-catering accommodation in Sant Antoni, as other resorts tend to be more expensive.

Listings of accommodation in Ibiza and Formentera start on p.214.

Tour operators

Astbury Formentera ⓣ01642/210 163, ⓦwww.formentera.co.uk. Formentera specialist offering a wide selection of villas, cottages and apartments.

Club Freestyle ⓣ0870/550 2561, ⓦwww.club-freestyle.co.uk. Inexpensive package holidays geared to the youth market, plus flight-only deals.

Clubbers' Guide Ibiza Trips ⓣ020/7836 1414, ⓦwww.ministryofsound.com/travel. Ministry of Sound's travel division has some decent clubbers' deals based in villas, apartments and hotels spread across Ibiza.

First Choice ⓣ0870/750 0465, ⓦwww.firstchoice.co.uk. Package holidays to all the major Ibizan resorts, and plenty of high-season charter flights from airports across the UK.

JMC ⓣ0870/758 0203, ⓦwww.jmc.com. Massive selection of charter flights and package holidays in Ibiza, from one of the UK's biggest tour operators.

Joe Walsh Tours Ireland ⓣ01/678 9555, ⓦwww.joewalshtours.ie. Inexpensive packages and flights.

Late Deals ⓣ0800/027 3157, ⓦwww.latedeals.com. Inexpensive packages and flights.

Magic of Spain ⓣ0870/027 0480, ⓦwww.magicofspain.co.uk. Up-market villas, and some four-star hotels, in both Ibiza and Formentera.

Mundi Color ⓣ 020/7828 6021, ⓦ www.mundicolor.co.uk. Limited selection of Ibiza hotel and flight packages in four- and five-star hotels.

Portland Holidays ⓣ 0870/241 3172, ⓦ www.portland-direct.co.uk. Packages to nine Ibizan resorts, including Figueretes.

Sunclubbers ⓣ 0800/073 0239, ⓦ www.sunclubbers.com. Clubbing holiday specialists with a number of deals in hotels in and around Sant Antoni.

The Real Spain (Citalia) ⓣ 020/8686 0677, ⓦ www.citalia.co.uk. Tasteful villas and apartments in prime Ibiza locations, with flights from Gatwick or Manchester.

Thomson ⓣ 0870/165 0079, ⓦ www.thomson-holidays.com. Vast selection of package holidays, plus flight-only deals.

FROM NORTH AMERICA

The best **fares** to Ibiza are usually found via the discount travel agents listed on p.10, though you could also contact the airlines direct and see if they have any special promotional offers. The cheapest regular tickets (APEX and special APEX fares) can also be competitive, although you'll generally have to pay in advance and are likely to be penalized if you change your schedule.

Iberia is the only company that flies **from the US** to Ibiza, via connecting flights from a mainland Spanish airport. Fares start at around $545 in low season and $785 in high season from the East Coast, and $660 in low season, $950 in high season from the West Coast. Alternatively, travel agents can often get similar rates by flying you from the US to Spain with one of the other airlines listed on p.10, and organizing a connecting flight to Ibiza with either Iberia or Air Europa.

There are no non-stop flights **from Canada** to Spain, so

you'll have to fly there via the US, or alternatively via a European capital, and then on to Ibiza. Round-trip fares to Ibiza start at around CAN$875 in the low season, or CAN$1100 in the high season from Toronto or Montréal via London or Madrid, and CAN$995/1780 from Vancouver.

Airlines

American Airlines ⓣ 1-800/433-7300, ⓦ www.americanair.com. Daily non-stop flights from Miami and Chicago to Madrid.

British Airways US ⓣ 1-800/247-9297, Canada ⓣ 1-800/668-1059, ⓦ www.britishairways.com. Flights from 20 gateway cities in the US and Canada, to Madrid and Barcelona, all via London.

Continental Airlines ⓣ 1-800/231-0856, ⓦ www.flycontinental.com. Daily non-stop flights from Newark to Madrid.

Delta Airlines ⓣ 1-800/241-4141, ⓦ www.delta-air.com. Daily non-stop flights from New York and Atlanta to Madrid and Barcelona.

Iberia ⓣ 1-800/772-4642, ⓦ www.iberia.com. From New York, Miami and Chicago non-stop to Madrid, with frequent shuttle connections on to Ibiza.

US Airways ⓣ 1-800/622-1015, ⓦ www.usairways.com. Four non-stop flights a week from Philadelphia to Madrid.

Discount travel agents

Airtech ⓣ 212/219-7000, ⓦ www.airtech.com.

Council Travel ⓣ 1-800/226-8624 or ⓣ 1-888/COUNCIL, ⓦ www.counciltravel.com.

STA Travel ⓣ 1-800/781-4040, ⓦ www.sta-travel.com.

TFI Tours International ⓣ 1-800/745-8000, ⓦ www.lowestairprice.com.

Travac ⓣ 1-800/TRAV-800, ⓦ www.thetravelsite.com.

Travel Avenue ⓣ 1-800/333-3335, ⓦ www.travelavenue.com.

Travel CUTS Canada ⓣ 1-800/667-2887, ⓦ www.travelcuts.com.

Tour operators

Bring It On! Tours ⓣ1-866/883-9070, ⓦwww.bringitontours.com. Ibiza party specialists, with an excellent selection of imaginative hotel- and villa-based clubbing trips; clients get the full treatment, with free club entry and a sunset cruise thrown in.

Central Holidays ⓣ1-800/227-5858, ⓦwww.centralh.com. US agents for Iberia, offering flight deals as well as flight and accommodation packages in three- and four-star Ibiza Town hotels.

European Escapes ⓣ1-888/387-6589, ⓦwww.europeanescapes.com. Villa rentals in rural locations.

Odysseus Travel ⓣ 1-800/257-5344, ⓦwww.odyusa.com. New York-based gay vacations company with choice of packages based in Ibiza Town, Figueretes and Talamanca.

Rainbow Travel ⓣ613/825-4275, ⓦwww.rainbowtravelnetwork.com. Gay tour operator with locations throughout Canada, offering good-value two-week packages in Ibiza.

FROM AUSTRALIA AND NEW ZEALAND

Flying to Ibiza **via London** is the cheapest route, as the city is the main destination for most international flights **from Australia and New Zealand**. You'll have no problem finding an inexpensive charter flight to Ibiza from London between May and October, though if you're travelling to Ibiza in winter it's best to book your (scheduled) connecting flight well in advance. For more on getting to Ibiza from London, see pp.4–5.

The best place to start the search for **tickets** is via travel agents, such as those listed below, or the internet; ⓦwww.travel.com.au and ⓦwww.sydneytravel.com offer discounted fares online. Return **fares** vary according to the season; you'll pay the most during the high season (mid-May to mid-Sept). Regular return economy flights to Ibiza cost around A$1820 in the low season and A$2550 in the high season from eastern Australian cities, and around NZ$2050 and NZ$2700 respectively from Auckland. Garuda, SriLankan Air and JAL usually have the best fares.

Airlines

British Airways Australia ⓣ 02/8904 8800; New Zealand ⓣ 0800/274 847 or 09/357 8950, ⓦ www.britishairways.com.

Garuda Australia ⓣ 02/9334 9970, New Zealand ⓣ 09/366 1862, ⓦ www.garudaindonesia.com.

Japan Airlines (JAL) Australia ⓣ 02/9272 1111, New Zealand ⓣ 09/379 9906, ⓦ www.japanair.com.

KLM Australia ⓣ 1300/303 747, ⓦ www.klm.com/au_en; New Zealand ⓣ 09/309 1782, ⓦ www.klm.com/nz_en.

Qantas Australia ⓣ 13 13 13, ⓦ www.qantas.com.au; New Zealand ⓣ 09/357 8900, ⓦ www.qantas.co.nz.

Sri Lankan Airlines Australia ⓣ 02/9244 2234, New Zealand ⓣ 09/308 3353 ⓦ www.airlanka.com.

United Airlines Australia ⓣ 13 17 77, ⓦ www.unitedairlines.com.au; New Zealand ⓣ 09/379 3800 or 0800/508 648, ⓦ www.unitedairlines.co.nz.

Discount agents

All the agents listed below offer discounted airfares (including RTW tickets) and most can also arrange car rental.

Flight Centre Australia ⓣ 13 31 33 or 02/9235 3522, ⓦ www.flightcentre.com.au; New Zealand ⓣ 0800 243 544 or 09/358 4310, ⓦ www.flightcentre.co.nz.

STA Travel Australia ⓣ1300/733 035, ⓦwww.statravel.com.au; New Zealand ⓣ0508/782 872, ⓦwww.statravel.co.nz.

Student Uni Travel Australia ⓣ 02/9232 8444, New Zealand ⓣ 09/300 8266, ⓦ www.sut.com.au.

Trailfinders Australia ⓣ 02/9247 7666, ⓦ www.trailfinders.com.au.

Unlimited New Zealand ⓣ 09/373 4033.

FROM THE REST OF SPAIN

Getting to Ibiza (and then on to Formentera) by plane or by ferry from mainland Spain or from Mallorca is a fairly simple business. Flying is by far the quickest option: Ibiza is a forty-five-minute flight from Barcelona, or thirty minutes from Valencia.

Fares vary tremendously, depending on the time of year and even the time of day you want to fly. Because availability can be difficult all year round, it's best to book as far ahead as possible. There are also plenty of **ferry** routes to Ibiza from the mainland ports of Barcelona and Dénia, plus fast hydrofoils from Valencia and Alicante in the summer months. Prices on the ferry routes are consistent throughout the year, though there are often special deals available outside the tourist season.

FROM THE MAINLAND

If you want to **fly** to Ibiza, it's best to travel **from Barcelona**, which has more services than any other Spanish city. Iberia fly three times a day between October and April, rising to six times a day between mid-June and mid-September. Expect to pay around €145 for a return ticket throughout the year, though you'll often come across promotional fares for as low as €90 return in the low season. Air Europa (and their subsidiary Spanair) fly twice daily in summer and once daily in winter; fares are very similar.

Though it's a little further from the Balearics, there are also plenty of services to Ibiza **from Madrid**. Air Europa fly twice daily between May and September, and once a day throughout the rest of the year, with economy fares typically around €155 return. Iberia have four daily flights between July and mid-September, and two flights a day during the rest of the year, with economy prices set at around €179 return. Iberia also have two or three daily flights to Ibiza **from Valencia** and a daily flight **from Alicante** all year round; economy tickets from both cities cost around €115 return. Note that off-season promotions on all routes can periodically cut fares to as low as €69 return.

There are regular connections **by sea** between Ibiza and Barcelona, Dénia and Valencia. **From Dénia**, the nearest mainland port to Ibiza, Baleària operate a twice daily hydrofoil to Ibiza Town (€55 per person, 2hr 15min) and a slower ferry to Sant Antoni (€43, 4hr 30min) which also operates on a twice-daily schedule. **From Barcelona**, Trasmediterránea operate four services per week (€47, 9hr); and **from Valencia**, Trasmediterránea operate a daily hydrofoil (June–Sept, €53, 3hr 15min) and a weekly Sunday service for the rest of the year (€37; 6hr). A new daily hydrofoil **from Alicante** to Sant Antoni is also planned to start in June 2003; this route will take three hours.

Airlines in Spain

The airlines listed below all have bilingual websites, which often have details of special offers and last-minute deals, as well as a few English-speaking staff manning the phone lines.

Air Europa ⓣ902 401 501, ⓦwww.air-europa.com.
Iberia ⓣ902 400 500, ⓦwww.iberia.com.
Spanair ⓣ902 131 415, ⓦwww.spanair.es.

FROM MALLORCA

Getting to Ibiza from Mallorca is simple, with frequent air and ferry services, plus a fast hydrofoil connection in the summer months. **By air**, from Palma, Iberia fly seven times daily between May and late September, and five times daily during the rest of the year; an economy ticket costs around €92 return, but fares are sometimes slashed as low as €65 return. Air Europa fly twice daily between May and September, and daily in winter from Palma, with economy tickets costing around €77 return.

There are also excellent connections from Mallorca **by sea**. Baleària operate a twice-daily Palma–Ibiza Town hydrofoil (€30, 2hr 30min) and also a twice-daily Sant Antoni–Palma ferry (€28, 5hr 15min). Trasmediterránea operate a daily Palma–Ibiza Town ferry (€27.50, 5hr) and a daily high-speed hydrofoil between June and mid-September (€3, 2hr 15min).

Ferry companies

Timetables and full details of seat, cabin and vehicle transportation rates are listed on companies' websites, though only Trasmediterránea have an English option. Alternatively, call the company offices direct; there are usually some English-speaking staff on hand. It's advisable to book ahead, especially if you plan to travel in the high season.

Baleària ⓣ902 191 068, ⓦwww.balearia.com.

Trasmediterránea ⓣ902 454 645, ⓦwww.trasmediterranea.es.

Visas and red tape

EU citizens (and those from Norway and Iceland) need only a valid national identity card to enter Spain for up to ninety days. However, as the UK has no identity card system, British citizens must travel with a passport. Citizens of the US, Canada, Australia and New Zealand do not need a visa for stays of up to ninety days. Bear in mind, though, that visa requirements can change, and it's always advisable to check the current situation before you travel.

Spanish embassies and consulates abroad

Australia 15 Arkana St, Yarralumla, ACT 2600 ⓣ02/6273 3555.

Britain 39 Chesham Pl, London SW1 8SB ⓣ020/7235 5555.

Canada 74 Stanley Ave, Ottawa, ON K1M 1P4 ⓣ613/747-2252.

Ireland 17a Merlyn Park, Ballsbridge, Dublin 4 ⓣ01/269 1640.

New Zealand contact the consulate in Australia.

USA 2375 Pennsylvania Ave NW, Washington, DC 20009 ⓣ202/728-2330.

For **longer stays**, EU nationals can apply for a *permiso de residencia* (EU residence permit) once in Spain. A temporary residency permit is valid for up to a year, and you'll need an extension after that (valid for up to five years). Applications

The UK consulate is at Avgda d'Isidor Macabich 45, Ibiza Town ⓣ971 301 818 (Mon–Fri 9am–3pm).

need to be made first with the Policía Nacional on Avgda de la Pau (the E-10 inner Ibiza Town ring road); ⓣ971 305 313. You'll either need to produce proof that you have sufficient funds (officially around €35 per day), or show a contract of employment.

To **work** in Ibiza legally, whether as a holiday rep, English-language teacher or bar worker, you need to obtain the *permiso de residencia*. During the summer months, hundreds of young Europeans (mainly Brits) illegally work the season without a residency permit, thus avoiding tax and legal employment status; accordingly, most are paid very little – typically €30 for a night-shift in a bar or as part of a club's promotional team. Though you may have the time of your life, bear in mind that it's possible (though unlikely) that you could face prosecution if you are caught working illegally. If you're a citizen of the US or Canada, you cannot legally work in Spain without a special application from an employer. However, you can apply at the Policía Nacional office for one ninety-day visa extension; you may be asked to prove you have sufficient funds. After 180 days, all overseas citizens must leave Spain.

Information, maps and websites

The best general **information** about Ibiza and Formentera is available from tourist information offices on the islands, or from the Internet. There's little point contacting the Spanish Tourist Board in advance or visiting their website (Ⓦwww.tourspain.es), as only very general background detail about the Pitiuses is available. The Balearic Islands website (Ⓦwww.visitbalears.com) is a much better source of information, with sections devoted to both Ibiza and Formentera that include features, news and events.

In Ibiza, you'll find **tourist information offices** at the airport, Ibiza Town, Sant Antoni and Santa Eulària, as well as La Savina in Formentera, all of which are detailed within the Guide. Staff usually speak English, are generally very helpful, and provide leaflets on everything from Carthaginian archeological sites to horse riding as well as accommodation lists, detailing self-catering apartments and campsites; however, they won't make bookings for you. Information kiosks are also located on the beaches of Figueretes, Cala Llonga and Talamanca.

There's also a vast amount of written and internet-based information about Ibiza and Formentera, covering everything from contemporary politics to the local football leagues, but focusing mostly on the club scene.

Spanish tourist board offices abroad

Australia 1st Floor, 178 Collins St, Melbourne, VIC ⓣ03/9650 7377, ⓔsales@spanishtourism.com.au.

Britain 22–23 Manchester Sq, London W1M 5AP ⓣ020/7486 8077, ⓦwww.tourspain.co.uk.

Canada 2 Bloor St W, 34th Floor, Toronto, ON M4W 3E2 ⓣ416/961-3131, ⓦwww.tourspain.toronto.on.ca.

Ireland contact the British office.

New Zealand contact the Australia office.

USA 666 Fifth Ave, 35th Floor, New York, NY 10103 ⓣ212/265-8822; San Vincente Plaza Bldg, 8383 Wilshire Blvd, Suite 956, Beverly Hills, CA 90211 ⓣ323/658-7188; 845 North Michigan Ave, Suite 915-E, Chicago, IL 60611 ⓣ312/642-1992; 1221 Brickell Ave, Suite 1850, Miami, FL 33131 ⓣ305/358-1992; ⓦwww.okspain.org.

MAPS

Free city and island **maps** are available in all the tourist information offices, and are generally more accurate than most maps available at home. If you do want to buy a map before you leave, Kompass publish the best (1:50,000) map – it's contoured, includes the main hiking routes and plans of Ibiza Town, Sant Antoni and Santa Eulària. The best map available in Ibiza is by Joan Costa (1:70,000); though if you rent a car or bike, you'll usually be given a reasonable map from your rental company. In Formentera, the maps issued by the tourist board are generally accurate, and should be sufficient for all but the most serious hiker.

However, to really explore Ibiza by foot or bike, you'll need to purchase some Instituto Geográfica Nacional maps. The ten 1:25,000 IGN maps that cover Ibiza include plenty of obscure trails and dirt tracks; they cost €2.30 each, and are available from outdoor specialists Transit, c/d'Arago 45, Ibiza Town (ⓣ971 303 692), as well as most newsagents and bookstores.

WEBSITES

The island's **web** presence is well-established and continues to expand, with a number of local and UK-based sites offering everything from villas to environmental news. Most are Ibiza sites, though a handful focus on Formentera.

Architectural Guide to Ibiza and Formentera
ⓦwww.arquired.es/users/Catany/pitiusas/0_home.html
Informative articles about Pitiusan churches, rural houses and modern architecture.

Diario de Ibiza
ⓦwww.diariodeibiza.es
Online edition of Ibiza's leading daily newspaper, with comprehensive news coverage, but in Spanish only.

Formentera Guide
ⓦwww.guiaformentera.com
Useful Formentera-related site, with good background on the island's culture, history, beaches, flora and fauna.

Formentera Online
ⓦwww.formenteraonline.com
Commercial site with decent information on Formenteran history and tradition.

Global Spirit
ⓦhttp://global-spirit.com/Ibiza
Stylish commercial site with good links to accommodation and property in the island.

Ibiza Friends of the Earth
ⓦwww.amics-terra.org
Information on environmental campaigns, past battles, local green issues and lists of events.

Ibiza Holidays
Ⓦ www.ibizaholidays.com
General island information – beaches, bars and accommodation – plus some news and a good club section.

Ibiza Night
Ⓦ www.ibizanight.com
Ibiza site with extensive historical, cultural and environmental information.

Ibiza Online
Ⓦ www.ibiza-online.com
Reasonably helpful site, with general information and some hotel and villa listings.

Ibiza Spotlight
Ⓦ www.ibiza-spotlight.com
The definitive Ibiza website. Regularly updated, reliable all-round island information, weather and daily news stories, accommodation and property listings, transport detail, plus an entertaining nightlife section and useful message boards.

Ibiza Sun
Ⓦ www.theibizasun.ibiza-show.com
Rough-and-ready journalism from the *Ibiza Sun* newsletter – but it does manage to cover the main stories in reasonable depth.

Live Ibiza
Ⓦ www.liveibiza.com
The best on-line resource devoted to Ibizan culture, this site boasts expert contributors.

Sant Josep
Ⓦ www.sanjose-ibiza.net
Informative site of the southern Ibiza municipality, with good historical background about the region, beach photos and an excellent architectural section.

Internet cafés are listed on p.296.

Health and insurance

Ibiza and Formentera are generally very safe places to visit in terms of health. No jabs are required, and hygiene standards are high, but you should avoid drinking the tap water, which isn't dangerous but tastes revolting. Alcohol and drug abuse aside, the worst thing that's likely to happen to you is an upset stomach.

For minor complaints, go to a **pharmacy** (*farmacia*), indicated by a green cross; you'll find these in all the main resorts and towns. Pharmacists are highly trained, willing to give advice (often in English), and able to dispense many drugs which would be available only on prescription in other countries. A night-rota system ensures that there's always a pharmacy open 24 hours a day in Ibiza and Formentera, ready to supply urgent prescriptions and medical advice; all the local papers print current rotas. In more serious cases, contact one of the English-speaking doctors in the islands recommended by the UK Consulate (☎971 301 818).

For an ambulance (*ambulancia*), dial ☎112.

Ibiza's main **hospital** is Can Misses, located in the western suburbs of Ibiza Town at c/de Corona (☎971 397 000). It's reasonably well equipped for emergencies, but few of the medical staff speak fluent English, so communication difficulties are almost inevitable. There's no hospital in Formentera, but the **health centre** (*centre de salut*) at the km3.1 marker on the La Savina–Sant Francesc road (☎971 322 357) can deal with most medical problems; in really serious cases, patients are taken to Can Misses in Ibiza. You'll also find health centres in Sant Antoni at c/d'Alacant 33 (☎971 345 102), and in Santa Eulària at c/Marià Riquer Wallis 4 (☎971 332 453); both can deal with minor injuries, and have some English-speaking staff.

Despite Ibiza's status as one of Europe most sexually charged holiday destinations, **condoms** (*condones* or *preservativos*) are not that widely available – although all pharmacies stock reliable brands, and some bars have a machine in the male toilets. There's a 24-hour condom machine on c/Antoni Palau in Ibiza Town, just west of the ramp that ascends up the Portal de ses Taules to Dalt Vila.

TRAVEL INSURANCE

Travel insurance is strongly advised if you're not a citizen of an EU state; without it, you'll probably have to pay private hospital rates for any treatment. Spain does have free reciprocal health arrangements with other EU member states; make sure you bring an E111 form (available from post offices) to ensure free treatment. It's worth noting that your E111 does not cover the full cost of prescriptions, dental treatment, or emergency repatriation however.

A travel insurance policy will also cover your baggage and tickets in case of theft, though some home policies do provide some cover whilst abroad. Bank and credit cards often have certain levels of medical or other insurance included,

ROUGH GUIDES TRAVEL INSURANCE

Rough Guides offers its own travel insurance, customized for our readers by a leading UK broker and backed by a Lloyd's underwriter. It's available for anyone, of any nationality and any age, travelling anywhere in the world.

There are two main Rough Guide insurance plans: **Essential**, for basic, no-frills cover; and **Premier** – with more generous and extensive benefits. Alternatively, you can take out **annual multi-trip insurance**, which covers you for any number of trips throughout the year (with a maximum of sixty days for any one trip). Unlike many policies, the Rough Guides schemes are calculated by the day, so if you're travelling for 27 days rather than a month, that's all you pay for. If you intend to be away for the whole year, the Adventurer policy will cover you for 365 days. Each plan can be supplemented with a "Hazardous Activities Premium" if you plan to indulge in sports considered dangerous, such as skiing, scuba-diving or trekking.

For a policy quote, call the Rough Guide Insurance Line on UK freefone ⓣ0800/015 0906; US toll-free ⓣ1-866/220 5588, or, if you're calling from elsewhere, ⓣ+44 1243/621 046. Alternatively, get an online quote or buy online at ⓦwww.roughguidesinsurance.com.

and you may automatically get travel insurance if you use a major credit card to pay for your trip. Travellers from the UK should bear in mind that though travel agents and tour operators are likely to require some kind of insurance when you book a package holiday, UK law prevents them from making you buy their own policy (other than a £1 premium for "scheduled airline failure").

Costs and money

The Balearics are the most affluent region of Spain, with a standard of living above the EU average. Tourist accommodation is around twenty percent more expensive than elsewhere in Spain, while food prices in the supermarkets are also dearer, as most produce has to be imported from the mainland. However, unless you're planning to go clubbing a lot (a seriously expensive business), it's still fairly easy to have an economical holiday in Ibiza and Formentera. Eating and drinking are generally inexpensive, especially in the village bars and big resorts, but as there are plenty of flash bars and pricey restaurants where your funds can take a real hammering, it pays to be choosy if you're on a budget.

The overall **cost** of a trip to Ibiza or Formentera depends on the time of year. While it's possible to find a seven-day self-catering package deal from the UK to Sant Antoni for under £150 in May or October, the same holiday will double in price by late July or August. Similarly, if you're travelling independently, room rates can triple in high season. The hip bars of Ibiza Town and Sant Antoni also crank up drink prices in summer (though elsewhere, bar prices are stable) and car rental costs also increase. Food, restaurant, bus and taxi prices at least remain constant.

If you camp or stay in a simple *hostal* and live frugally, perhaps eating out cheaply once a day, you're looking at a minimum budget of around €38 a day between June and September, including accommodation. In the winter months, budget accommodation prices drop a little, so you might get by on around €30 a day. If you plan to stay in a mid-range hotel, rent a car and eat dinner in a good restaurant, you'll spend upwards of €80 a day. Bear in mind, though, that with entrance fees to the main venues costing €35 and over, combined with high drink prices and taxi fares, it's frighteningly easy to spend substantially more than this if you've come to go clubbing.

THE ECOTAX

All adult visitors to Ibiza and Formentera now have to pay an **ecotax** of between €0.25 and €2 per day (the exact charge depends on the quality of accommodation booked). Children under twelve are exempt. The new tax was introduced by the Balearic Islands government in May 2002 in an attempt to make the region's tourism more sustainable, and provide funding for environmental improvements. The first of these measures will be a clean up of the Ses Feixes and Cala d'en Serra areas, and a new visitor centre for the Ses Salines Natural Park may be funded by ecotax money.

The ecotax was fiercely resisted by most tour operators, the opposition PP party and many hoteliers (who were charged with actually collecting the levy). Many hotel and apartment complex owners dispensed soft drink vouchers to guests as compensation in the 2002 season, and continue to fight the legality of the tax in the courts.

For a table of exact tariffs and more information, check out the website Ⓦ www.ecotaxa.org/index.en.html.

CURRENCY

On January 1, 2002, Spain was one of twelve European Union countries to change over to a single currency, the euro (€). The euro is split into 100 cents. There are seven euro notes in denominations of 500, 200, 100, 50, 20, 10 and 5 euros, each a different colour and size; there are eight different coin denominations, including 2 and 1 euros, then 50, 20, 10, 5, 2 and 1 cents. Euro coins feature a common EU design on one face, but different country-specific designs on the other. No matter what the design, all euro coins and notes can be used in any of the twelve member states (Austria, Belgium, Finland, France, Germany, Greece, Ireland, Italy, Luxembourg, Portugal, Spain and The Netherlands).

BANKS AND EXCHANGE

Banks offer the best rates for changing travellers' cheques and foreign currency – you'll find plenty of branches in all the main towns and resorts and in many villages. The main difficulty is that they have very limited **banking hours** (generally Mon–Sat 9am–2pm), which are not very convenient if you're planning to dance all night and sleep in the day, so it pays to plan ahead a little if you've only brought travellers' cheques. Bureaux de change, found in all the main resorts, often stay open until midnight, but their commission rates are usually higher. Many large hotels will also cash your travellers' cheques, but you'll rarely get a competitive exchange rate.

Travellers' cheques are probably the safest way to carry money abroad, with cheques in sterling, euros, US dollars and most other major currencies accepted in banks and bureaux de change throughout Ibiza and Formentera; you'll need your passport to validate them. All international **credit and debit cards** should function without any problem, and allow you to withdraw money from cashpoint (ATM) machines, which are common throughout the islands – you'll even find them in many small villages. Virtually all restaurants and large stores accept credit cards, but don't expect to pay by plastic in a *tapas* bar or at the corner store.

Getting around

Ibiza has a good public transport system, with buses and boats linking all the main resorts and towns, and there's a very decent bus service in Formentera, considering its tiny population. If you're planning on really exploring the islands, however, you're going to have to rent a car, motorbike or a bicycle, as many of the best stretches of coastline are well off the beaten path.

Hitching is another very popular way to get around the main roads, especially in northern Ibiza. Hitchhikers are not expected to contribute towards drivers' transport costs. Obviously, there are risks involved; avoid hitching alone, and never accept a lift if you feel in any way uncomfortable about the driver.

In Spain, businesses located on main roads use a **kilometre marker** to indicate their location; there are roadside markers at every kilometre along all the main routes in both Ibiza and Formentera. For example, the restaurant *Can Caus* adopts the address Ibiza Town–Santa Gertrudis km 3.5. This means that the restaurant is located 3.5km from the beginning of the road between Ibiza Town and Santa Gertrudis.

BUSES

Buses in Ibiza and Formentera are inexpensive, punctual and will get you around fairly quickly. Services between the main towns run roughly from 7.30am to midnight between June and late September, and 7.30am until 9.30pm in winter. Smaller villages and coastal resorts are less well served, with fewer buses running from around 9am to 7pm all year round. While it's possible to get to every village in Ibiza or Formentera by bus (bar Cala Saona in Formentera), services to isolated hamlets like Santa Agnès are pretty infrequent, so it pays to plan ahead and check the current timetables in advance before you set off, especially on Sundays, when there are fewer buses on all routes, and in winter. Copies of timetables are held at tourist offices and bus terminals, and are printed in local newspapers; you can also visit ⓦwww.ibizabus.com. Services to the more popular beaches and resorts are increased between June and late September.

From **Ibiza Town**, there are services to all the main towns, most villages and resorts, and to Salines beach all year round. **Sant Antoni** and **Santa Eulària** are the other two transport hubs, with frequent services to local beach resorts and good intra-island connections. In **Formentera**, there's one main route across the island, from La Savina to La Mola, supplemented by extra services that shuttle between Es Pujols, Sant Ferran, Sant Francesc and La

Savina. **Fares** are very reasonable on all routes: Ibiza Town–Sant Antoni costs €1.40, while the longest route, Ibiza Town–Portinatx, is €2.10.

Between mid-June and late September the all-night **discobus** service provides hourly shuttles between Ibiza Town and Sant Antoni (passing *Amnesia* and *Privilege*). Additional hourly routes run between Platja d'en Bossa (for *Space*) and Ibiza Town; Sant Antoni and Port des Torrent; Es Canar and Santa Eulària; and Santa Eulària and Ibiza Town. During the rest of the year, the same routes are in operation, but the buses run on Saturday nights only. Tickets cost €1.50 one way; for more information, call ☎971 192 456.

BOATS

Dozens of **boats** buzz up and down the Ibizan coastline between May and late September, providing a delightful – if more expensive – alternative to bus travel. Most services are timed to get tourists to beaches from the main resorts and towns. Boats go from Ibiza Town to Talamanca (€2.50 return), and Platja d'en Bossa (€4.50) from Sant Antoni to points around the Sant Antoni bay (€3.50 return), Cala Bassa (€4.50) and Cala Conta (€5); and from Santa Eulària to northeast beaches, including Cala Pada (€4.80) and Es Canar (€5.80). In Formentera there are boats between La Savina and Espalmador via Platja Illetes (€10) return.

There are regular scheduled daily ferry and hydrofoil connections **between Ibiza Town and Formentera** all year round. Four different operators ply the route; all leave from the same terminal on Avgda. Santa Eulària in Ibiza Town (Map 3, I1) and return from the harbour in La Savina, Formentera. Between June and September there are 25 boats per day (7am–10pm), while the rest of the year there are thirteen daily boats (7.45am–7pm). Tickets cost between €15 and €24 return, depending on the speed of the service (between 30min and 1hr 10min per journey). Consult Ⓦwww.visitbalears.com for more information.

TAXIS

Taxi rates are quite reasonable; all tariffs are fixed, and the minimum charge is €2.50, with an additional €1 charge after midnight, on Sundays and during public holidays. For example, to get to Sant Rafel (for *Amnesia* or *Privilege*) from either Ibiza Town or Sant Antoni, the fare is around €9, while Ibiza Town to Sant Antoni (15km) will cost about €15. The latest fares are posted on the website Ⓦwww.taxi-eivissa.com. Though no taxis are currently equipped with meters, there is a proposal to introduce them in the next year or two.

Taxis for hire display a green light, you can hail them on the street, wait at the one of the designated ranks, or call (see numbers below). You'll have no problems getting a taxi at most times of the year, but demand far exceeds supply on most August nights, when it's not uncommon to wait up to an hour for a ride. Lastly, it's well worth bearing in mind that all Ibizan clubs will pay your taxi fare from anywhere in the island if four of the passengers purchase an entrance ticket to the venue.

Taxi companies

Ibiza Town Ⓣ971 398 483, Ⓣ971 301 794, Ⓣ971 306 602

Sant Antoni Ⓣ971 340 074, Ⓣ971 343 764

Santa Eulària Ⓣ971 330 063

Sant Joan Ⓣ971 800 243

Sant Francesc, Formentera Ⓣ971 322 016

La Savina, Formentera Ⓣ971 322 002

Es Pujols, Formentera Ⓣ971 328 016

CAR AND MOTORBIKE RENTAL

Driving along Ibiza and Formentera's smooth network of roads is pretty straightforward, though to really see the islands you'll have to tackle some terrible dirt tracks from time to time. All the major towns and resorts are well-signposted, but many small coves, especially in northern Ibiza, are not. Take extra care when **driving at night**, as none of the main roads are adequately lit, including the notorious Sant Antoni–Ibiza Town highway, where accidents are all too common. In general, local people are not overtly aggressive drivers, and it's the young British boy-racers you'll have to watch out for.

Renting a car is the best way to explore the islands. Daily rental costs are very reasonable, and most companies will give a discount of ten percent or more if you book a full week. Local companies are usually a little cheaper than the international names: for the cheapest hatchback model, expect to pay around €36 a day in July and August, and around €27 per day the rest of the year. As the number of rental cars is restricted in the Balearics for environmental reasons, it pays to book ahead, particularly in August. All the resorts have a rental company or two, or you can arrange to pick up a car at the airport. You have to be over 21 years old to rent a car in Spain.

Motorbikes and **scooters** are also a very popular means of getting around the islands independently, with rates starting at around €21 for the cheapest motorbike, or €17 a day for a scooter model. In low-lying Formentera, even the least powerful model will be adequate to get two people around, but to explore hilly Ibiza properly you should consider hiring a machine above 100cc. Legally, you must be over eighteen to rent a motorbike over 75cc, and crash helmets are compulsory.

Insurance policies vary from rental company to rental company; it's essential to ensure you have full cover (all the companies listed below include this in their contracts). You should also check if there's an excess waiver amount – obviously, the higher the rate specified in the contract, the more you'll have to pay if you're involved in an accident.

Local car and motorbike rental companies

All the local companies listed below rent out both cars and motorbikes.

Autos Marí c/de la Mar 25, Santa Eulària ⓣ,971 330 236, ⓕ971 332 659.
BK Plaça del Mar 5, Cala Tarida ⓣ971 806 289.
Canals Albert Avgda Dr. Fleming, Sant Antoni ⓣ971 345 571.
Moto Luis Avgda Portmany 5, Sant Antoni ⓣ971 340 521, ⓕ971 340 257, ⓔmotoluis @arrakis.es.
National Ibiza airport ⓣ971 395 393.
Sixt c/Felipe II, Ibiza Town ⓣ971 315 407; Harbourside, La Savina, Formentera ⓣ971 322 559.

International car rental companies

Avis UK ⓣ0870/606 0100, US and Canada ⓣ1-800/331-1084, ⓦwww.avis.com.
Budget UK ⓣ0800/181181, US and Canada ⓣ1-800/527-0700, ⓦwww.budget.com.
Hertz UK ⓣ 0870/844 8844, US and Canada ⓣ1-800/654-3001, ⓦwww.hertz.com.
National UK ⓣ0870/5365 365, US and Canada ⓣ1-800/227-7368, ⓦwww.nationalcar .com.

BICYCLES

With few hills, **Formentera** is perfect bicycle territory, and, as illustrated by the rows of bikes for rent in La Savina, Es Pujols and at the big hotels, **cycling** is an easy and popular way to get around the island. Pick up a *Green Routes* leaflet from the tourist office for details of some good cycle excursions along the island's quieter lanes – most are now very well signposted. **Ibiza** is much more hilly, and its roads more congested, though there are some spectacular routes across the island. Tourist information offices can supply you with leaflets detailing cycling routes, but these tend to be impractical, consisting of vague lines drawn across poor maps, and you're liable to get lost; to really explore by bike, you'll need large-scale IGN maps (see p.20). In both islands, a cheap bike costs around €9 a day, while state-of-the-art mountain bikes start at about €14.

Ecoibiza, c/Abad y Lasierra 35, Ibiza Town (Ⓣ971 302 347; Ⓦwww.ecoibiza.com), organize **mountain bike tours** across the Pitiuses. These include a "Magic Island" tour of southwest Ibiza (€44) that takes in the highest peak and the coast around Es Vedra, and a tour of Formentera (€52). If you're interested in serious mountain bike racing, consult the website Ⓦwww.ibizabtt.com for details of events.

Bicycle rental companies

Autos Ca Mari Harbourside, La Savina, Formentera Ⓣ971 322 921.

Bicicletas/Moto Rent Mitjorn Harbourside, La Savina, Formentera Ⓣ971 322 306.

Tony Rent c/Navarra 11, Ibiza Town Ⓣ971 300 879.

Vespas Torres Sant Jaume 66, Santa Eulària Ⓣ971 330 059.

Communications

Telephone connections between Ibiza and Formentera and the rest of the world are generally efficient, but mail can be very slow, especially in the summer months.

You'll find **telephone** booths in towns and villages all over Ibiza and Formentera; these mainly take cash, but some are exclusively geared up for phonecards, which you can buy at tobacconists. Local calls in the ☎971 Balearic area are very cheap, while national calls are quite expensive, at around €0.75 for three minutes. Make sure you have gathered a pocketful of change before you dial a mobile number, as calls cost around €0.70 a minute. **International calls** can also be made from these booths, at fairly reasonable rates (around €2 for five minutes). However, the most cost-effective way to dial home is by using an international phonecard – there are plenty of options, but the España Mundo card is one of the cheapest. You can purchase phonecards in any *estanco* (tobacconist) shop; look out for the brown and yellow *Tabac* sign.

Most UK **mobile phones** will work in the Balearics, though users of US-bought handsets may have difficulties. Bear in mind that as you have to pay to receive calls from home, you can run up a hefty bill by chatting on the beach. If you are planning a long stay, consider buying a Spanish

DIALLING CODES

To call **Ibiza or Formentera from abroad**, dial 00 plus the relevant country code (00 34 in the UK, Ireland and New Zealand; 011 34 in North America; 0011 64 in Australia), followed by the nine-digit number.

To **call abroad from Ibiza or Formentera**, dial 00 followed by the country code (44 for the UK; 353 for Ireland; 1 for the US and Canada; 61 for Australia; 64 for New Zealand) then the area code minus its zero, and then the number.

mobile phone. Movi Star is the most popular service provider, and you can purchase "pay-as-you-go" handsets from around €60 – the price usually includes some free calls. Alternatively, it's possible to convert your UK mobile to the Spanish network by buying a new SIM chip from a telecom store; these cost around €52, but include €40 of calling credit.

Postal services for international mail are reasonably efficient most of the year, but the system gets clogged in the summer months. Allow a week to ten days for delivery of letters and postcards within the EU, or two weeks for the rest of the world, and up to double that time for parcels. Post offices (*correu*) generally open between 9am and 1.30pm Monday to Saturday, and you can also buy stamps from tobacconists and some souvenir shops.

INTERNET CAFÉS

Internet cafés (listed on p.296) have opened all over Ibiza, and there are also several places where you can surf and send email in Formentera. Most of Ibiza's cafés are concentrated in Ibiza Town (with three on Avgda d'Ignasi Wallis alone) and Sant Antoni. Rates for internet access average €4 an hour. Bear in mind that some internet cafés shut down between October and May.

The Media

It's relatively easy to keep in touch with what's happening in the world from Ibiza. All the main British (and some American) newspapers and magazines are very widely available, and three free English language listings magazines are published in the summer months. You can also hear some decent dance music on local radio, while satellite TV is popular in many bars.

MAINSTREAM PUBLICATIONS

Though Ibiza and Formentera lack an English-language **newspaper**, you'll find all the British broadsheets, tabloids and many periodicals for sale at shops and newsagents in all the major towns and resorts throughout the islands. They usually arrive by 9am the same morning, sometimes a little later in winter.

The most popular Ibizan newspaper is the *Diario de Ibiza*, a Spanish-language daily which covers Ibiza and Formenteran news, plus national and international events. It's essential reading if you're staying for a while, with dozens of short- and long-term house and apartment rentals. You'll also find the latest bus, ferry and plane timetables, plus *El Rastrillo*, a kind of Pitiusan notice board where everything from bar jobs to scooters are advertised.

Mainly geared toward the expat market, the slightly staid monthly *Ibiza Now* magazine concentrates on island news, with brief political summaries, cultural listings and excellent historical content; it's sold in most newsagents. The *Ibiza Sun*, a breezy weekly freesheet, covers the main news stories fairly comprehensively, despite its ranting editorial tone; it's available in many hotels and British bars, and also online (see p.21). The glossy monthly *Ibiza Deluxe* magazine devotes itself to soft focus spreads of Ibiza's ageing moneyed class. Finally, less widely available is the free *La Carta Totamà* magazine, another useful, if rather dry, source of island news and cultural information; it's published in Spanish and English. There are no equivalent publications in Formentera.

CLUBBERS' MAGAZINES

Ibiza has two main **clubbing magazines**, both offshoots of established UK-based titles; they're published between June and September, and are available free from hip bars and boutiques across the island. The monthly *DJ Magazine* is the better publication, despite a slip in standards in recent years, as it does focus upon the wider picture of what's going on in the island rather than the narrow British–Ibizan club scene; you'll also find comprehensive bar, restaurant and club listings included. The other UK-based publication – *Ministry in Ibiza* – is worth picking up for its clubs section, though most of the mag is devoted to the San An teenage pill-popping market, with tales of drug-fuelled misadventures, pictures of bare flesh and gurning geezers.

Finally, the monthly *Dub* (Ⓦwww.dubibiza.com) is well worth a read, with an eclectic selection of articles from a team that knows the island well, plus listings and reviews that cover more than the British scene; you'll find it in Ibiza Town at the *Sunset Café* and *Chill*, and at other bars around the island.

RADIO AND TV

Cadena Cien (89.1FM and online at ⓦwww.clubibizardio.com) is the leading local radio station, with mainstream pop and dance in the day and some excellent night-time DJ shows. Igor Marijuan commands the evening session between 8 and 10pm from Monday to Friday, with guest slots from visiting DJs including Danny Tenaglia and Erick Morillo. On Saturdays and Sundays (10pm–midnight), it's well worth tuning into the excellent Balearia session, a brilliant eclectic selection of music hosted by Mancunian exile Andy Wilson.

Just down the dial, the rival **Dance FM** (91.7FM) concentrates on Euro trance and club favourites, with Ibiza's most popular turntablist, David Moreno hosting the main evening slot between 9 and 11pm. In the high season, both Cadena Cien and Dance FM broadcast live from clubs including *Pin-Up* and *Space*, and there are regular link-ups with the UK's BBC Radio One. A third station, **Ibiza Nueva** (90.6FM) which started broadcasting in November 2002, also concentrates on house and chart music. The Ibiza-based pirate station **Zumo FM** (107.3FM) broadcasts at weekends only; it's run by an English team with talented local collaborators and offers a diverse range of dance music including drum 'n' bass and plenty of soulful house. Shortwave listeners will find the **BBC World Service** and Voice of America both come across crisp and clear at most times of the day in the Balearics.

Television is not a Spanish cultural strong point, with lots of inane game shows and Mexican soap operas. However, dozens of bars in the resorts have all the Sky and BBC channels, with live Premier League and European games broadcast on big screens.

Drugs, safety and the police

Ibiza and Formentera are generally very safe destinations with low crime rates – incidents are very rare indeed, but occasionally bag-snatchers or pickpockets target visitors. Nevertheless, it's wise to be vigilant with your valuables, and avoid leaving anything on display that will attract thieves to your rental car. Plenty of people get into self-inflicted trouble of a different nature, usually involving alcohol and drugs; bear in mind that drink-driving and drug-dealing are dealt with very severely by the local police and courts.

DRUGS

At times, it's easy to forget that **drugs** are illegal at all in Ibiza. Pills and powders are everywhere, and the main lure for many visitors is the notion that the island is the Mediterranean's best-stocked recreational pharmacy. The reality, however, is that **Spanish drug laws** are comparable to the UK, most of mainland Europe and North America: cannabis, amphetamines, ecstasy, cocaine, LSD, ketamine,

GHB and heroin are all illegal. The maximum penalty for trafficking drugs is up to twelve years in prison, and possession of drugs is also illegal – every year, dozens of visitors are arrested for possessing a few pills or a gramme or two of coke. Most are cautioned and released fairly swiftly, but those caught with larger amounts, not considered to be for personal use, face a significant jail term.

If you do decide to indulge, take a few basic **precautions**, and take great care who you buy from; while the chances of being set up by a police informer are slim, the chances of being sold dodgy powder or moody pills from a dealer in a club are much higher. It's also important to bear in mind the dangers of overheating and dehydration after taking ecstasy (MDMA), which affects the body's temperature controls. It's essential to keep drinking sufficient, but not excessive, fluid – around a pint (568ml) of water or fruit juice an hour, or a little more if you're dancing all night in the high-season heat. As a small bottle of water can cost up to €8 in the big clubs, it's also important to make sure you have sufficient fluid funds.

Cocaine – reputed to have replaced salt as the island's primary source of wealth – is omnipresent. Alongside amphetamines (speed), use is also endemic within the bar scene of Ibiza Town and Sant Antoni. Again, if you do decide to take cocaine or amphetamines, ensure that you drink enough non-alcoholic fluids. Though of minimal popularity with clubbers, you may be offered GHB or ketamine; both drugs can be very dangerous if mixed with alcohol, so if you suspect you've taken either, stick to water. The police normally tolerate the possession of small amounts of cannabis, though don't go waving a spliff around in the streets. Again, anyone considered to be a dealer faces serious trouble, and possibly a prison sentence.

There's a massive booze culture in Ibiza's resorts, aided and abetted by bar-crawls organized by tour operators, and

alcohol abuse is the main reason why most people end up in hospital, either through overindulgence or as a result of an accident. Be especially careful when making your way home at the end of a night out, particularly when crossing the main Ibiza Town–Sant Antoni highway near *Privilege* and *Amnesia* – there have been many fatal road accidents on this stretch. It's worth remembering that if you have an accident while drunk or under the influence of illegal drugs, many insurance policies won't pay out, and you could be faced with a large bill.

The emergency telephone number in Ibiza and Formentera is ⓣ112. On getting through, you'll be asked if you want either the police (*policía*), fire brigade (*bomberos*) or ambulance service (*ambulancia*); telephone operators usually speak some English.

Lastly, never drink and drive; quite apart from the safety considerations, the police regularly breath-test drivers in Ibiza and Formentera. The legal alcohol limit is around two alcoholic units for women and three for men. Drivers failing breath tests can expect to pay a fine of €300–600 and face the possibility of a ban.

SAFETY AND THE POLICE

Though **street crime**, such as pickpocketing and mugging, is extremely uncommon in Ibiza and Formentera, it's wise to take some basic precautions. Be careful in the Sa Penya district of Ibiza Town, which has the highest number of bag-snatching incidents, and avoid walking after dark in the alleys above (south of) c/de la Verge, close to the city walls. Similarly, inside Dalt Vila, avoid the poorly lit streets above Plaça de la Vila late at night, as muggings are not unknown. Pickpockets love crowds, so take extra care at Es Canar market and the La Marina night market in Ibiza Town. Thieves also target pavement cafés, snatching banknotes from tables, so keep an eye on your money when paying your bill.

You may not find the **police** to be particularly helpful if you do suffer any trouble. The main problem is likely to be that few speak much English, so you'll probably have to wait around until an English speaker is found. Should you be arrested on any charge, you have the right to contact your nearest consulate (see p.17); though British consulate staff are rarely sympathetic, they do keep a list of English-speaking lawyers. Remember that if you do have something stolen, you'll have to get a police report in order to claim for the loss on your insurance policy.

Sports and outdoor pursuits

You'll find plenty of opportunities for **sports and outdoor pursuits**, from yoga to horseback riding. With a sparkling coastline never more than a short drive away, watersports are especially good. Coastal Ibiza also offers superb scenery for hikers, while Formentera is perfect cycling terrain.

DIVING AND SNORKELLING

Over 70km away from the large cities of the mainland, and virtually free from local heavy industry, the Pitiusan islands can boast some of the cleanest seas in the Mediterranean, the coastlines dotted with blue-flag beaches. With little rainfall runoff, the water is also exceptionally clear for most of the year; visibility of up to 40m is quite common.

SCUBA DIVING

Scuba diving is generally excellent, with warm seas and (generally) gentle currents. Boats tend to head for the tiny offshore islands such as Tagomago and Redona that ring the coasts, where sea life is at its most diverse; however, if you've ever been diving on a coral reef, the Mediterranean may seem disappointingly barren. Schools of barracuda and large groupers are reasonably common, though, and you can expect to see conger and moray eels, plenty of colourful wrasse, plus crabs and octopuses. In addition to the marine life, there's some startling underwater scenery, with three shipwrecks around Illot Llado near Ibiza Town and another in Cala Mastella, plus caves and crevices all around the coastline to investigate.

Sea temperatures are at their lowest in February (around 15°C), and highest in early September (around 25°C).

All scuba-diving schools open between May and October only and tend to charge similar prices. A single boat-dive works out around €40 including all equipment and insurance; you'll save around twenty percent if you bring your own gear. All scuba schools also offer discounts if you book a package of six or ten dives. Night dives incur an extra tariff of between €15 and €33, depending on the site. If you want to **learn to dive**, expect to pay €360–420 for a five-day PADI Open Water course; most dive schools offer advanced open-water, rescue-diver and divemaster training, too, plus other specialist courses. You'll find a BSAC school in Port des Torrent, and there's a decompression chamber in Ibiza Town.

SNORKELLING

Small coves and rocky shorelines offer the most productive **snorkelling** territory: try Cala Mastella, Cala Molí and Cala Codolar in Ibiza, or Caló de Sant Agustí in Formentera. Perhaps the best area for experienced snorkellers and freedivers is the rugged northwest Ibizan coastline, at bays like Es Portitxol and Cala d'Aubarca, where there are very steep drop-offs and deep, clear water. You'll often encounter coastal fish such as ballan, goby, grouper, brown and painted wrasse, as well as passing pelagic sea life such as mackerel or even barracuda. Most resorts have a store where you can buy snorkelling equipment, but as much of it is poor quality, it's well worth renting or buying from a dive school or a specialist fishing store.

OTHER WATERSPORTS

Windsurfing is a popular sport in the Pitiuses – July and August are often the calmest months, so less challenging for the experienced windsurfer, but conditions are ideal for most of the year. Several of the schools listed opposite rent out boards (around €15 per hour) or run training courses (around €21 per hour). There are also several **sailing** schools and clubs in Ibiza and Formentera, and the islands host various competitive events. The most famous of these is the Ruta de Sal regatta (Ⓦwww.larutadesal.com) held in Easter week, a long-established event that retraces the historic salt route between Ibiza, Dénia and Barcelona. For information about sailing, yacht moorings and harbours check the website Ⓦwww.ibizanautico.com. **Deep sea fishing** is another popular sport; contact Pesca Ibiza (see box on opposite), which organizes half- and full-day excursions trawling and bottom fishing.

Operators in most of the main resorts offer **jet-skiing** and **waterskiing** (both around €12 for 15min), a speedy ride on a blow-up **banana** (€8–10 per person per ride), as well as the ubiquitous and very Balearic **pedalos** (around €7 an hour). Sea **kayaking** is also quite popular – expect to pay around €35 for a day's rental, plus a hefty deposit. Finally, H2O Sports in Sant Antoni (see box opposite) charge €38 per person for **parasailing**, which includes an hour's power boat trip – book a day in advance.

Watersports operators and stores

Club de Surf Ibiza Platja d'en Bossa ⓣ971 192 418. Long-established windsurfing school, offering board rental and tuition.

Club Delfin Vela y Windsurf *Hotel Delfin*, Cala Codolar ⓣ971 806 210. Sailing school, plus windsurf tuition and board rental.

Diving Centre San Miguel *Hotel Cartago,* Port de Sant Miquel ⓣ971 334 539, ⓦwww.divingcenter-sanmiguel.com. Scuba school with inexpensive rates (€345 for a dive licence), though not PADI affiliated.

Formentera Diving and Watersports La Savina, Formentera ⓣ971 323 232. One of Formentera's best dive schools; also rents out kayaks, jet-skis and boats.

H2O Sports Opposite *Hotel San Remo*, Sant Antoni harbourfront ⓣ616 538 250. Parasailing, plus waterskiing tuition.

Ibiza Diving Port Esportiu, Santa Eulària ⓣ971 332 949, ⓦwww.ibiza-diving.com. Ibiza's only five-star PADI school, with courses that include Nitrox training.

Pesca Ibiza Edificio Bristol, Avgda 8 d'Agost, Ibiza Town ⓣ971 314 491, ⓦwww.ibizanautica.com/recreation/index.html. Deep sea fishing trips, priced from €105 per person for a half-day trip.

Pesca y Deportes Bonet c/Pere Francés 20, Ibiza Town ⓣ971 312 624. Fishing tackle and snorkelling gear.

Pesca y Deportes Santa Eulalia Molins de Rey 12, Santa Eulària ⓣ971 330 838. Snorkelling, spear-fishing and fishing gear.

Sea Horse Sub Port des Torrent ⓣ971 346 438. The only BSAC-accredited dive school in Ibiza.

Sirena c/Balanzat 21, Sant Antoni ⓣ971 342 966, ⓦwww.ibiza-online.com/DivingSirena. Dive school offering courses and trips to west coast sites.

Subfari Es Portitxol beach, Cala Portinatx ☎971 333 183. Scuba school that offers dives at many of Ibiza's remote north coast sites.

Vellmari Marina Botafoc 101–2, Ibiza Town ☎971 192 884 & Avgda Mediterráneo 90, La Savina Formentera ☎971 322 105, www.vellmari.de. Five-star PADI dive centre that run daily trips into the Ses Salines natural park.

Vela Náutica Avgda Dr Fleming, Sant Antoni ☎971 346 535. Sailing school, with windsurfing equipment, boats and kayaks for rent.

BOAT TRIPS

In all the main resorts, companies offer **pleasure-boat trips** around the coastline. The most popular excursion by far is the day-trip to Formentera, and it's well worth doing for the stunning views of the Pitiusan coastline alone. Trips typically leave around 9.30am and return by 6pm; most visit the island of Espalmador on the way. Prices vary depending on the resort you leave from; expect to pay around €12 per person from Figueretes, and €17 per person from Sant Antoni.

The pick of other Ibiza excursions leave from the Sant Antoni harbour; all are bookable with several companies on the waterfront. The three-hour return trip to Es Vedrà (daily €14) is recommended, passing Atlantis and a series of fine beaches, and including a snorkelling stop in Cala d'Hort. Another good option is the dramatic day-trip up the northwest coastline to Portinatx, passing many isolated coves; boats sail twice weekly, and tickets cost €18 return per person. In Formentera, Cruceros, Harbourside, La Savina (☎971 323 207) organize excellent half- (€50 per person) and full- (€75) day trips on a catamaran around the island; prices include a gourmet lunch.

It's not prohibitively expensive to **charter** a boat. The

English owners of the *Life of Riley* catamaran (☎629 077 356, Ⓦwww.sail-ibiza.com) offer an excellent range of flexible trips, including sunset cruises and day-trips to Formentera, with pick-ups from any Ibiza beach; prices start at €20 per person. Try Ⓦwww.ibizanautico.com for a good selection of boat charter companies, including Tagomago Charters, Port Esportiu, Santa Eularia (☎971 338 101) which have several boats, from simple tub-like craft with an outboard motor (€205 per day) to swanky Sunseekers (€4000 a day); add on €140 for a skipper.

HIKING

Ibiza and Formentera's beautiful coastal paths and inland valleys offer exceptional **hiking**. We've detailed several of the best walks within the Guide, all of which have opportunities for a swim along the way; trainers and shorts are adequate equipment. If you plan on doing a lot of walking, you'll need a detailed map; IGN publish the most useful (see p.20). Though the tourist offices do have some hiking leaflets, the information is pretty hopeless, with appalling maps and vague text. Sunflower Books publish the best specialist walkers' guide to Ibiza and Formentera (see Contexts on p.342).

The only specialist company offering organized treks is Ecoibiza, c/Abad y Lasierra 35, Ibiza Town (☎971 302 347, Ⓦwww.ecoibiza.com), which arranges some excellent "Secret Walks" to remote parts of the island, including some superb hikes around Santa Agnès. Half-day trips cost around €27 per person; full-day excursions are priced from €33–43.

HORSE RIDING, GO-KARTING AND GOLF

In Formentera, Sahona Horses (☎971 323 001), based 500m outside Sant Francesc on the road to the Cap de Barbària, offer some excellent **horse rides** on well-looked-after mounts through woodland, along beaches and across the salt flats. In Ibiza, Easy Riders (☎971 196 511), located 200m along the Sòl d'en Serra from Cala Llonga, is another good option, with fine-looking horses and some thrilling beach and hill rides; or you could try Can Mayans, Santa Gertrudis–Sant Llorenç rd km.3 (☎971 187 388). All charge around €15 for a one-hour lesson, or €48 for a half-day excursion.

There are two **go-kart tracks** in Ibiza; the hilly 300m Santa Eulària circuit, located at km 5.8 on the main Ibiza Town–Sant Eulària road (daily May–Oct 10am–9pm, Nov–April weekends only ☎971 317 744), is the better option, with high-power adult karts, junior karts and baby

YOGA

Ibiza is fast establishing itself as one of the Mediterranean's key **yoga** destinations, with a choice of centres run by acclaimed instructors. The island itself, with its benign climate and stunning scenery, makes an inspirational base, with classes mostly performed in the open air in rural surrounds. All prices quoted below exclude flights and transfers.

Ibiza Yoga

Map 8, I2. Benirràs, Ibiza (UK ☎020 7419 0999, Ⓦwww.ibizayoga.com; May–Oct).

Friendly Ashtanga yoga retreat, situated in a spectacular location a short walk south from one of Ibiza's finest beaches, with seafood restaurants close by for evening meals. Three hours of tuition per day, vegetarian brunch and communal accommodation costs £375 per person per week. A more luxurious villa, with a pool, will also be used from the 2003 season.

Jivana Ashram

Map 9, C6. Near Cala Conta (☎971 342 494; May–Oct). Small

karts. Much flatter and less scenic, the other track is just outside Sant Antoni along the highway to Ibiza Town (daily May–Oct noon–midnight). Kart prices at both tracks start at €9 for seven minutes.

The only **golf** course in the Pitiuses is Club de Golf Ibiza (Ⓣ971 196 152), halfway along the Jesús–Sant Eulària highway at Roca Llisa. It boasts a nine- and an eighteen-hole course, both positioned between patches of pine woodlands under the island's central hills. You don't have be a member to play, but it's an expensive course – green fees are €75, and you'll pay extra for a caddy and for renting a golf buggy, though the price does includes club rental.

Ashtanga yoga retreat run by friendly, experienced German instructors; there's a maximum of eight per class. Accommodation is in comfortable double rooms; there's no electricity, so it's an early-to-bed kind of place. Superb beaches are only a short walk away. The weekly rate, including full board, is €350; a single class costs €19.

Windfire Yoga

Map 8, D4. Can Am, near Sant Miquel (Ⓣ971 187 996, Ⓦwww.windfireyoga.com; May–Oct).
Yoga centre of excellence, run by one of Europe's foremost instructors, Godfrey Devereux, who teaches according to a "Dynamic Yoga" method of Ashtanga. Self-practice options, teacher training and apprenticeships are also available. Accommodation is in teepees, domes and tents, set in the grounds of a hilltop villa with views over the island. Courses cost £300 per week, including accommodation and vegetarian meals.

THE GUIDE

Ibiza Town and around

Elegant and sophisticated, **IBIZA TOWN** (**EIVISSA**) is the cultural and administrative heart of the island. Set around a dazzling natural harbour and enclosed by a backdrop of low hills, it's one of the Mediterranean's most cosmopolitan pocket-sized capitals, full of historic sights, hip boutiques, chic bars and restaurants. In the summer months, the narrow portside lanes of **La Marina** and **Sa Penya** quarters become an alfresco catwalk, as a good selection of the planet's most committed party people, fashion victims and freaks strut the streets in a frenzy of competitive hedonism. By the end of September, however, the pace abates and life becomes more languid: most of the restaurants and bars shut up shop, and Ibiza Town's beleaguered residents wind down and look forward to a well-earned winter siesta, counting their euros and recharging for the next seasonal onslaught.

All this takes place in a setting of breathtaking beauty. Looming above the portside action is historic **Dalt Vila**, a rocky escarpment topped by a walled enclave, squabbled over by all the island's invaders since the days of the

Phoenicians. The fortress-like Catalan cathedral and craggy Moorish castle that bestride the summit are Ibiza's most famous landmarks, clearly visible from all over the south of the island. Below Dalt Vila, Ibiza Town's **harbour** is the island's busiest port, its azure waters filled with a succession of yachts, fishing boats, container ships and ferries. This bustling maritime traffic is actually a new phenomenon, for, as recently as the 1940s, the island's only regular links with the outside world were a sporadic mailboat from Palma and a ferry to the mainland described by British writer Douglas Goldring as a "deplorable, flea-infested old tub". The scene today could hardly be more of a contrast, with sheik-owned yachts gliding in from the Gulf and vast ferries disgorging hundreds of weekending Spaniards eager to join in the revelry.

Occupying the north side of the bay, the **new harbour zone** is an upmarket strip devoted to pleasure and leisure. Here the luxury apartments, yacht marinas, casino and restaurants attract a suitably moneyed clientele, and the ambience is far less raucous than in the old quarters over the water.

West of La Marina, and extending a kilometre or so inland, the **New Town** is far less appealing. Though the area around boulevard-like Vara de Rey is urbane and attractive, the western suburbs quickly descend into a featureless commercial sprawl of concrete apartment blocks and traffic-choked streets. Unless you arrive by sea, this will be your first impression of Ibiza Town, and it's easy to wonder what on earth all the fuss is about.

Points of interest **around Ibiza Town** include the appealing, crescent-shaped sandy bay of **Talamanca**, 2km to the northwest. The village of **Jesús**, to the northeast, is little more than a suburban overspill of the capital, though it does have a couple of decent café-bars and a historic church. Just southwest of the capital lies the resort of **Figueretes**; while it's not the most picturesque beach on the island, it remains popular with holidaying families and also attracts many gay visitors. Finally, 7km northwest of Ibiza Town, the village of **Sant Rafel** is home to the legendary clubs *Amnesia* and *Privilege*, has good restaurants and commands stunning views of the capital from its lofty perch in the central hills.

For reviews of accommodation, restaurants, bars and clubs in Ibiza Town, see pp.214, 232, 248 and 267.

Arrival and information

Ibiza's **international airport** (Map 11, H5; ⓣ971 809 000) is situated 7km southwest of Ibiza Town, close to the Salines salt pans. There's a **tourist office** (May–Sept only Mon–Sat 9am–2pm & 4–9pm, Sun 9am–2pm; ⓣ971 809 118), with helpful staff and a good stock of leaflets, brochures and maps; and you'll also find several **cashpoints** that accept all the main credit and debit cards. **Car rental** companies (see p.33) are located in the arrival lounge, and **taxis** meet incoming flights; though there are usually plenty available, you may have to wait a while in August. There's also an efficient **bus** service between the airport and Ibiza Town (hourly 7.30am–10.30pm; 20min; €1) that operates throughout the year.

Ibiza Town's bus terminal (Map 3, A2) is on Avgda d'Isidor Macabich in the New Town, a ten-minute walk west from the port area; there's a taxi rank on the opposite side of the street, or you can call one of the taxi firms listed on p.31 if you don't want to walk. Services from all over the island arrive and depart from bus stops outside the scruffy waiting room. Arriving by ferry from the mainland or Palma, you'll dock just east of the Estació Marítima building (Map 3, L3) on the main harbourfront, Passeig

Marítim. All Formentera ferries (see p.30) arrive and depart from a separate terminal building (Map 3, I1) on the west side of the harbour.

The efficient **main tourist office** (Map 3, K3) is located opposite the Estació Marítima on Passeig Marítim (June–Sept Mon–Fri 8.30am–2.30pm & 5–7pm, Sat 9.30am–1.30pm; Oct–May Mon–Fri 8.30am–2.30pm; ⓣ971 301 900).

La Marina and Sa Penya

Ibiza Town's pretty, atmospheric harbourside districts, **La Marina** and **Sa Penya** are crammed with hip boutiques, restaurants and bars, all almost exclusively geared to tourists. These twin quarters, often lumped together as "the port", are sandwiched between the harbour waters to the north and the walls of Dalt Vila in the south. Smarter La Marina rubs up against the New Town at Vara de Rey in the west; smaller, sleazier Sa Penya almost topples into the Mediterranean waves to the east.

First settled by the Phoenicians in the seventh century BC, then occupied by the Carthaginians and Romans, La Marina and Sa Penya were left virtually uninhabited for a thousand years after Vandals sacked the town in 425 AD. Rudimentary buildings were constructed in the quarters during this period, but were repeatedly burned down by bands of plundering Vandals, Visigoths, Moors and Turkish pirates. However, by the fifteenth century, despite the continuing threat from pirates, overcrowding inside Dalt Vila forced residents outside the walls, and La Marina and Sa

Penya grew steadily as working-class districts, populated by fishermen, tradesmen and privateers. Life in the harbour-side districts continued to revolve around the sea and docks until the 1960s, when package tourism revolutionized the Ibizan economy. Today's bombastic bar culture has squeezed out most of the local families, who have relocated to the relative tranquillity of the suburbs, renting out their apartments to tourists and foreign workers during the summer season.

The port area's wonderfully crooked warren of streets, alleys and tiny plazas was built organically, with new buildings being added as the population increased. All the houses in the district are whitewashed, and many streets are barely a couple of metres wide, to keep out the glare of the fearsome summer sun. In high season, these almost souk-like alleys are some of the most crowded in all Spain, as a tidal wave of visitors arrives to shop, feast or hit the bars.

ALONG PASSEIG MARÍTIM

The best place to start exploring La Marina is at the southwestern corner of the harbourfront, along **Passeig Marítim**, where a slightly comical-looking **statue** (Map 3, I2) dedicated to the fishermen of Ibiza resembles Dopey of seven-dwarf fame. Heading east along Passeig Marítim, a cluster of upmarket café-bars (particularly *Mar y Sol*, long a favoured location amongst Ibizan high society, affords fine views of the yachts and the docks. Midway along the bay, the modern harbour building/ticket office, the Estació Marítima, juts into the water opposite the tourist office and a large stone obelisk (Map 3, K3) dedicated to the corsairs (see p.311), privateers officially licensed to defend crown lands against pirate attacks. Opposite is a small square, **Plaça d'Antoni Riquer**, named after a legendary corsair. This plaza is one of the best places to view the club parades that characterize La Marina's summer-season nightlife; by midnight, the bar terraces are heaving with drinkers gathered to watch the outrageous procession of drag queens and costumed PR-people promoting events at the big club venues.

Continuing east from the obelisk, Passeig Marítim is lined with another glut of restaurants and bars, plus market stalls in high season. Almost at the end of the Passeig, the tiny square of **Plaça de sa Riba**, backed by tottering old fishermen's houses, is a popular place for outdoor dining, though more for the views than the food. While it's firmly a restaurant quarter these days, many Ibizans still refer to this stretch of the harbour as *Sa Riba* (The Shore) – it's the site of the old docks and shipyards, and boats returning from fishing trips once moored here. At the very end of the Passeig Marítim, a twentieth-century breakwater, Es Muro, extends well into the harbour; you can walk right to the end for an excellent view back over the old town. Steps at the beginning of Es Muro lead up into Sa Penya (see p.62).

ESGLÉSIA DE SANT ELM

Map 3, K3.

Just south of Plaça d'Antoni Riquer, c/Sant Elm leads into a tiny triangular cobbled plaza that holds the **Església de Sant Elm**, open only for mass. First built in the fifteenth century, over the next four hundred years the church often acted as a sanctuary, when besieged harbourside residents sought protection from pirate attacks; their efforts were often in vain, though, as Sant Elm was burned down at least a dozen times. A sturdy, three-storey, functional design with a tiered belltower, the present building was constructed after the last church was destroyed during the Spanish Civil War. The cool interior is home to the shell of a giant clam (which doubles as the church font) and a striking bronze-coloured statue of a beaming open-armed Christ, complete with a 1960s-style Roger Moore hairdo. The other image of interest is the haloed **Verge del Carmen**, carrying a child, which has long been associated with the Ibizan seamen's guild. On July 16 each year, the statue is removed by the fishermen of La Marina and placed in a boat, which then leads a flotilla around the harbour in a ceremony to ask her protection at sea for the year ahead.

PLAÇA DE SA CONSTITUCIÓ

Map 3, J4.

Southwest of Sant Elm, La Marina's main shopping street **c/del Mar**, thick with boutiques and souvenir stalls, leads south to tiny Plaça de sa Font, tight by the city walls and sporting a modest, but now dry, eighteenth-century fountain. From here, head east along c/d'Antoni Palau, nicknamed "pharmacy street" because of its profusion of chemists, to the **Plaça de sa Constitució**, a small peaceful square of elegant whitewashed and ochre-painted old merchants' houses. Here you'll find **Es Mercat Vell** (The Old Market), a curiously squat Neoclassical edifice where fruit and vegetables have been traded since 1873. There's little hustle and bustle in evidence today, and the underemployed traders spend most of their time swatting flies from the rows of fruit or selling the odd apple to tourists. Few locals shop here, which is understandable when you see the prices charged; the haggling has shifted to the New Town, where the main market now resides.

The New Market (Mercat Nou) occupies a large concrete building on c/d'Extremadura in the New Town (Map 3, A3).

Market aside, leisurely Plaça de sa Constitució is still a

great place for a refuelling stop before an excursion into Sa Penya or a steep assault on Dalt Vila through the looming presence of the Portal de ses Taules gateway, which is situated just above the square. Several **cafés** are grouped in the area around the plaza, including the ever-popular *Croissant Show* (see p.249), a legendary and chaotic French-owned patisserie.

SA PENYA

The glamour goes on above the seediness,
like a red carpet over a sewer.

Paul Richardson, Not Part of the Package – A Year in Ibiza

East of Plaça de sa Constitució, the twisted triangle of streets, bordered by c/d'Enmig to the north and hemmed in by the city walls to the south, is **Sa Penya**, the wildest, sleaziest neighbourhood in the Balearics. Until the fifteenth century there were few permanent buildings here, and it was only settled in any concerted way when Ibiza Town began to expand beyond its walls.

A run-down and occasionally even threatening place, Sa Penya is never bland. Cutting through the heart of Sa Penya is *the* gay street in Ibiza, **Carrer de la Verge**, lined with dozens of tiny cave-like bars and a fetish boutique or two, while the dilapidated houses of the streets to the south constitute Ibiza's main gypsy district, home to the most marginalized of Spain's population. Most gypsies settled in Ibiza in the 1960s to work in the construction industry, and have since been subject to the booms and slumps affecting the building trade more than any other section of the community. Sa Penya is beset by social problems – poor housing, high unemployment, very high levels of drug addiction (particularly heroin) and dealing – and few residents have any stake in the tourism sector. Nonetheless, the area does have an unmistakably edgy, underground appeal, an identity derived from the crumbling facades of the dark, warren-like alleys and lanes, and the outrageous streetlife, bars and boutiques, all of which create a vibrant and absorbing scene. If you want to explore Sa Penya on foot, however, it's probably best to stick to the area around c/d'Alfons XII and c/de la Verge, as the area's quieter streets are very poorly lit and can be unsafe at night.

Carrer de la Verge

Map 3, K4–N5.

Despite its inappropriate moniker, **Carrer de la Verge**, or "street of the virgin" (also signposted as c/de la Mare de Déu), is easily the wildest on the island, and one of the essential experiences in Ibiza. If you wander down the street in the daytime, it appears to be a sleepy-looking, whitewashed Mediterranean lane, barely four hundred metres long and hardly worth exploring, as there are no sights to see. By night, however, the street metamorphoses into a dark, urban ravine of S&M and leather bars and risqué boutiques, reverberating to pounding trance techno, trashy drag shows and all-round cacophony.

At its western end, the street begins rather tamely with a strip of straight basement bars and an enticing hole-in-the-wall pizza joint, *Pieda Peks*. On the right, c/des Passadís leads past another cluster of bars including *Noctámbula* (see p.251) and ultimately to c/d'Alfons XII, where many of the club parades finish. Back on c/de la Verge, the atmosphere steadily changes from here onwards: the road becomes narrower, the music and laughter louder and the cave-like boutiques wilder – check out dildos galore at QG, and the wig specialist Atrevete. Most of the bars are gay, and in high season it's barely possible to squeeze between the mass of perfectly honed muscle that fills the street outside. Up in the balconies above the action, drag queens and club dancers preen themselves for the long night ahead.

The gay bars along c/de la Verge are reviewed on p.291–292.

The excesses culminate at the eastern extreme of c/de la Verge, where the street is barely a couple of paces wide, and rows of bars and their customers face each other across the divide during summer-season nights. A frenzy of flirtation, bravado and mischief fills the air as passers-by are assessed, pectorals tensed, and drinks downed like there's no tomorrow. Just before the rocky cliff that signifies the end of the street is *Bar Zuka* (see p.248), one of the island's most fashionable drinking dens. A few paces beyond here, past the flight of steps down to the Passeig Marítim, is **Sa Torre**, a small stone defensive tower with a pointed roof, rebuilt in 1994, from where there are wonderful night-time views of the lights of Formentera and the Botafoc peninsula.

Carrer d'Alfons XII and around

Map 3, K5.

From the western end of the c/de la Verge, it's a short stroll south up c/des Passadís to **Carrer d'Alfons XII** – actually more of a plaza than a street. During daylight hours it's a pleasant but unremarkable corner of Sa Penya, framed by tottering five- and six-storey whitewashed houses on the east side and the city walls just to the south. It's dotted with palm-shaded benches, and bordered by a small octagonal building, the city's old fish market, which is rarely open these days.

At night, however, c/d'Alfons XII is transformed into one of Ibiza's most flamboyant arenas – the final destination for the summer **club parades**. At around 1am, after an hour or so of posturing through the streets of La Marina and Sa Penya, the podium dancers, promoters and drag queens move to the almost amphitheatre-like surrounds of c/d'Alfons XII for a final encore. A surging, sociable throng spills out of some of the most stylish bars on the island to watch the parades, comment on the costumes, blag a guest pass and discuss plans for the night's clubbing.

Dalt Vila

Occupying a craggy peak to the south of the harbour, the ancient settlement of **DALT VILA**, meaning "high town", is the oldest part of Ibiza Town. Colossal Renaissance walls surround this historic enclave, which contains the finest monuments in Ibiza: the **cathedral**, the **castle**, the **town hall** and two good **museums**. Alongside these major attractions are numerous hidden chapels and tunnels, Moorish fortifications and noblemen's mansions, and a warren of steep streets to explore.

Dalt Vila's strategic importance is obvious when you reach the top. Although it's only around 100m above its surroundings, it affords magnificent views over the harbour to the open ocean and Formentera, and inland to the central hills. This summit has been a place of worship for two and a half millennia, as well as the site for a succession of ceremonial structures: Carthaginian and Roman temples, a Moorish-built mosque and the Catalan cathedral that stands here today. These days Dalt Vila is one of the quietest parts of the city, with nightlife limited to the tasteful restaurants of Sa Carrossa and Plaça de Vila and the *Anfora* club (see p.293). In winter, the streets are almost deserted, and even in the high season months you'll find the atmosphere agreeably tranquil and unhurried. Many of the families who lived here for centuries have moved out in recent years, preferring the space of the suburbs. Today, the population is a mix of disparate classes: the clergy (who have lived in the area since the Catalan takeover, pockets of Ibizan high society in their imposing ancestral homes, and wealthy foreigners seduced by the superb views and tranquil atmosphere, all living alongside poor gypsy families who have moved into the houses in the lower half of town.

THE WALLS

Encircling the entire historic quarter of Dalt Vila, Ibiza Town's monumental Renaissance **walls** are the city's most distinctive structure. Completed in 1585 and in near-perfect condition today, the walls – at almost 2km long, 25m high and up to 5m thick – are some of Europe's best-preserved fortifications, and were awarded UNESCO World Heritage status in 1999.

The high ground occupied by Dalt Vila has been fortified for at least 2300 years. The Carthaginians first built walls around the very highest point, close to today's castle, and in the fourth century BC the traveller-historian Timaeus admired the settlement's imposing defences; later, in 217 BC, a Roman attack led by Cornelius Scipio failed to penetrate the **Carthaginian** defences. During the Moorish occupation of the island from the eighth century AD, the city (then called "Yebisah") was extended to the south, and divided into three fortified quarters (the lower, upper and middle towns), each with its own defences. Protected by all three sets of fortifications, the upper quarter, around the cathedral and castle, remained the safest place to live, and was home to the elite. Remnants of these **Moorish** walls survive below the Baluard de Sant Jordi on the Ronda de Calvi, and on c/Sant Josep, where there's a section that divided the middle and lower quarters.

PORTAL DE SES TAULES

Map 4, F2.

The main entrance into Dalt Vila is the appropriately imposing **Portal de ses Taules** (Gate of the Inscriptions), a monumental gateway in the city walls up above the Plaça de sa Constitució. Even the approach is impressive – up a mighty stone ramp, across a drawbridge and over a dried-up moat – all part of the defences necessary to keep out sixteenth-

Battered by centuries of attacks from corsairs, the city walls were crumbling by the sixteenth century. Vast new fortifications, strong enough to withstand the pirates' cannon fire, were planned; the Italian architect Giovanni Battista Calvi produced the designs, and funding came from the Church, the Crown and the sale of salt. Work started in 1554 with the construction of six colossal bastions (*baluards*) for artillery use, and a "ring road", today's **Ronda de Calvi**, atop the broad walls that enabled cannons to be manoeuvred swiftly around the city. By 1575, as the new fortifications were nearing completion, King Felipe II's chief architect, Jacobo Fratín, made a crucial modification: the construction of a seventh bastion, **Baluard de Santa Llúcia**, which enabled the precariously situated neighbourhood of Vila Nova to be included within the walls. An impressive new gateway, **Portal de ses Taules**, was designed to accommodate this alteration, and construction was completed by 1585. Perhaps the greatest testament to the architects' design was the security that followed: Barbary pirates deemed the fortifications too formidable to breach, and the residents of Dalt Vila were never again troubled by marauding buccaneers.

century pirates. A stone *taule* (tablet) mounted above the gate bears the coat of arms of Felipe II and a Latin inscription attesting that the "King of Spain and the East and West Indies" built the fortifications for the benefit of the island. Flanking the *portal* are two white marble statues (a Roman soldier and the goddess Juno), modern copies of second-century figures found nearby by architect Jacobo Fratín when he was constructing the gateway in 1585; the originals can be found in the archeological museum (see p.73).

Immediately after passing through the Portal de ses Taules, you enter the old **Pati d'Armes** (armoury court), a surprisingly graceful, shady arena – the island's very first hippy market was held here in the 1960s beneath its ten sturdy columns, and there's often a busker and a hairy trader or two here today. At the far end of the armoury court, you pass through a second stone gateway, less imposing than the first and constructed as an additional defensive measure. Above its arch are a stone cross and two small coats of arms; the upper belongs to Catalunya and Aragón, who controlled the island in the sixteenth century, while the lower is Ibiza Town's own emblem.

PLAÇA DE VILA AND BALUARD DE SANT JOAN

Map 4, E2.

The inner gateway in the walls leads into **Plaça de Vila**, actually more of a broad, pedestrianized avenue than a town square, its sides graced by elegant old whitewashed mansions, pavement cafés and an assortment of art galleries and boutiques. A fruit and vegetable market was held here until the early twentieth century, but now life in the plaza revolves around enticing the ever-faithful flow of tourists to take a breather on their way to the historic treats above. The restaurants and cafés here reflect this, and though the setting is wonderful, many of the menus offer bland pan-

European food, printed in enough languages to keep an EU translator busy for weeks.

Heading west along the Plaça de Vila, the first path on the right leads up to the **Baluard de Sant Joan**, one of the seven turrets depicted on Ibiza Town's flag. From the manicured gardens on top of the bastion, there are excellent views over the Mercat Vell and La Marina quarter to the harbour, and beyond to Ibiza's central hills.

MUSEU D'ART CONTEMPORANI

Map 4, E2. May–Sept Tues–Fri 10am–1.30pm & 5–8pm, Sat 10am–1.30pm; Oct–April Tues–Fri 10am–1pm & 4–6pm, Sat 10am–1.30pm; €2.60.

From the Baluard de Sant Joan, it's a short stroll along the edge of the walls, past a tiny pyramid-topped watchtower, to the **Museu d'Art Contemporani**, housed in a two-storey rectangular building originally constructed in 1727 as an arsenal, and later used as a barracks and as the stables of the Infantry Guard. Its conversion in 1969 made it one of Spain's very first contemporary art museums, and the collection, though small, is well worth taking in.

Visitors enter into the upper floor of the building, the old arms hall, where temporary exhibitions are staged under its lofty beamed roof. The lower floor (the old ammunition store and former stables) comprises two rooms separated by a metre-thick dividing wall. This is where the pick of the museum's collection is displayed, mostly the work of artists with an Ibizan connection of some kind. The exhibits are frequently shuffled around, but the work of island-born Tur Costa and the challenging abstract art of Ibiza visitors Will Faber, Hans Hinterreiter and Erwin Broner stand out.

PLAÇA DEL SOL AND AROUND

Continuing west from Plaça de Vila, c/Santa Creu passes another row of restaurants, including the fine *Sa Torretta* (see p.234), and narrows as it passes through what was originally part of the lower town of Moorish Yebisah, before leading into **Plaça del Sol** (Map 4, B2). A small, shady square directly above the city walls overlooking the harbour and Ibiza Town, it's an ideal place for a drink or snack. The *Plaza del Sol* restaurant here commands superb views, but you pay slightly over the odds because of this.

West of Plaça del Sol, a flight of steps just before the adjoining bastion of Baluard des Portal Nou leads down into the New Town. It passes through the body of Portal Nou itself and into the Parc Reina Sofía, a small paved arena below the walls that's popular with skateboarders and the site of occasional concerts.

TOWARDS PLAÇA DE LA CATEDRAL

From Plaça del Sol, most people head to the top of Dalt Vila to see the castle and the cathedral. The most direct route is along the Ronda de Calvi, the ancient ring road on the top of the walls that girdle Dalt Vila, which passes Baluard de Sant Jaume and Baluard de Sant Jordi. However, you'll suffer in the summer sun, and a shadier (and more interesting) alternative is to work your way through the heart of the Old Town. From the southwest corner of the square, climb the broad stone staircase of c/Portal Nou. At the top, turn left into c/Sant Josep, its upper side lined by ten-metre high remnants of the original Arab-built fortifications, including a defence tower. At the corner of c/Sant Josep and c/Santa Façç is the unadorned whitewashed facade of the fifteenth-century **Església de l'Hospital** (Map 4, C3), originally a hospital for the poor, but now a low-key cultural centre that serves as a venue for amateur dramatics and occasional art exhibitions.

Adjacent to the steps at the end of c/Sant Josep is the imposing, angular old **Seminari** (Map 4, C3). The Jesuits first used the building as lodgings for their monks between 1669 and 1767, but after they were thrown out of Spain by Carlos III it served as a seminary until the late 1990s, when it was converted into luxury apartments. From the top of the staircase, pretty c/Conquista on the right derives its name from the Catalan takeover of the island in 1235 – some of the heaviest fighting took place on this street. The road also houses the most eccentric hotel in Ibiza, *El Palacio*, a temple to kitsch and chintz that proclaims itself "the hotel of the movie stars". Each rooms has a movie theme (from Charlie Chaplin to Marilyn Monroe), and assorted Teutonic guest wannabes have left their handprints on clay plaques hung on the wall outside, but this is about as close to Hollywood as things get.

At the end of c/Conquista, more steps lead up to the left into c/Sant Ciriac, the first street inside what was once the old Moorish upper town. A few metres along and on the right is a curious little chapel, the **Capella de Sant Ciriac** (Map 4, C5), which is little more than a shrine, set into the wall, protected by a metal grille and embellished with pot plants, candles and incense burners. The chapel is said to be the entrance to a secret tunnel through which the Catalans and Aragonese stormed the upper quarter of the Moorish citadel on August 8, 1235. The arch of a sealed-up passage is clearly visible below the painting of Sant Ciriac on the back wall of the chapel, but local opinion is divided as to the accuracy of the story – the invaders may have used a number of entrances. Whatever the truth, the legend is remembered on August 8 every year with a special mass held here.

Today the upper town is probably quieter than it's ever been, the garrison and market having relocated (along with many of the aristocratic original inhabitants) to the suburbs. Some reminders of the glory days remain, though: **Carrer Major** (Map 4, D5), the continuation of c/Sant Ciriac and the main thoroughfare to the cathedral, boasts numerous grand houses adorned with family coats of arms.

The luxurious *La Torre de Canónigo* apartments on c/Major are reviewed on p.217.

PLAÇA DE LA CATEDRAL

Map 4, E5.

At the eastern end of c/Major, **Plaça de la Catedral** represents the epicentre of Ibizan civilization. Phoenicians were the first to settle this spot, around 600 BC, attracted by the pivotal position above the island's best harbour; by 400 BC, Ibiza Town (then Ibosim) was a crucial city in the Carthaginian empire, with a temple dedicated to the god Eshmun gracing today's plaza. In 283 AD the Romans also built a temple to Mercury here; this was followed during the Moorish period by an Arab mosque, which was later torn down after the Catalans took over in 1235, to make way for the Gothic cathedral that dominates the small plaza today. A cluster of historic buildings also line the north side of the plaza, including the archeological museum and the courthouse; however, it's the sublime **view** of Ibiza Town from the lookout point between these buildings that's the plaza's most arresting aspect, with the sparkling waters of the harbour and forested hills beyond.

Until 1838, when the town hall offices were moved to today's Ajuntament building, Plaça de la Catedral was also the focus of Ibizan political power, being the site of the Universitat (island government) building, to the right of the lookout, which is now occupied by the **archeological**

museum. The late Gothic-style courthouse, and the former seat of the judiciary, the **Reial Curia** building (Map 4, E5), is just to the left of the lookout. Currently being renovated, it's a modest whitewashed building, but the honey-stone coat of arms (belonging to Felipe V) above the double doorway gives the building a certain presence.

Museu Arqueològic d'Eivissa i Formentera

Map 4, E5. April–Sept Tues–Sat 10am–2pm & 5–8pm, Sun 10am–2pm; Oct–March Tues–Sat 10am–1pm & 4–6pm, Sun 10am–2pm; €2.

To the right of the Plaça de la Catedral lookout is one of the two buildings that make up the **Museu Arqueològic d'Eivissa i Formentera**. The other (currently closed) site in the New Town concentrates on the Carthaginian necropolis, the Puig des Molins and other Punic treasures, while the collection here provides an overview of Pitiusan history from prehistoric to Islamic times. It's not wildly exciting, but the logically arranged, well-presented exhibits are worth a browse; you'll need around an hour to have a good look around.

The **museum building** is itself of some interest, with its low, simple stone facade belying a much bigger interior. The middle portion of the structure is mid-fifteenth-century, built in a very functional, unadorned Mudéjar (Spanish Islamic) style, though the old entrance is now bricked up. It housed the **Universitat**, the seat of government for over 300 years until 1717, when Madrid downgraded its power to Ajuntament (town hall) status. On the left, and now serving as the museum's entrance hall, the fourteenth-century **Capella del Salvador** boasts a fine ribbed vault roof and was the seat of the seamen's guild until 1702, when it was moved to the Església de Sant Elm in La Marina (see p.60). On the right, the sixteenth-century **Capella des Joans** is more modest in scale, and now houses the Phoenician exhibits. The final section of the museum, containing the Punic, Roman and Medieval rooms, extends down into the **Baluard de Santa Tecla**, the southeastern bastion which overlooks the harbour.

The museum's first room deals with prehistoric remains and the initial Phoenician colonization. The earliest exhibits, from around 1500 BC, consist mainly of pottery cooking vessels, stone and bone tools and copper axeheads, used by farmers, fishermen and hunters who lived in caves and in high locations, such as the Puig de ses Torrents near Santa Eulària and the Cap de Barbària (see p.196) in Formentera. Dating from the seventh century BC onwards, the **Phoenician** exhibits are more cosmopolitan, reflecting the sophisticated trade routes established by these powerful seafarers: red-glazed ceramic plates and amphorae from mainland Spain, Italian perfume bottles, and alabaster vessels and scarabs from Egypt stand out. Most of the Phoenician pieces were collected from Sa Caleta (see p.177) and the Plaça de la Catedral, the two main Phoenician settlements in the Pitiuses.

However, it was under the Phoenician's relatives, the **Carthaginians**, that Ibiza really flourished. Ibosim, as Ibiza Town was then called, was a key settlement in the Carthaginian (or **Punic**) empire until the mid-second century BC, with several thousand inhabitants, extensive docks from which figs, dates and wool were exported, and potteries that supplied the western Mediterranean with amphorae on an industrial scale. From the first room, steps lead down to the small Punic collection, housed in the tunnel that extends under the Baluard de Santa Tecla from under the old Universitat. Almost all of Ibiza's finest Punic artefacts, however, are in the (currently closed) Puig des Molins museum; here, there's an ordinary-looking stela (an upright decorated stone slab), carved from local limestone, with an image of an unknown robed male figure and a religious inscription dedicated to the fearsome god **Baal**, around whom a cult developed that included offerings of wine, olive oil and the sacrifice of children. Earthenware images of the fertility goddess (and wife of Baal) **Tanit**, who had her own sanctuary at the cave of Es Cuieram near Sant Vicent (see p.113), are also on display alongside plenty of local pottery and coins, and imported curiosities including painted ostrich eggs – a symbol of resurrection for the Carthaginians.

Ibiza was little more than an island backwater within the mighty **Roman** empire and would have had very limited geopolitical significance; hence there are few items in the Roman room of the museum, at the end of the Punic corridor. If the Roman statues look familiar, that's because you'll have passed the replicas mounted on the walls of the Portal de ses Taules (see p.67). There's also an interesting Roman coin or two – Ibiza had had its own mint from the third century BC, and the Romans maintained production within the island during the reigns of Tiberius, Caligula and Claudius. They continued using an image of the Carthaginian god Bes on the reverse side, reflecting the dual cultural nature of the island (there were also separate cemeteries) and the fairly harmonious crossover between Punic and Roman times.

The meagre **Islamic** collection, housed in a small room under the Baluard de Santa Tecla, again reflects the Pitiuses' relatively unimportant status during the Moorish era. Silver and gold coins minted in Córdoba and Morocco, glazed pottery and assorted epigraphic oddities make up the bulk of the artefacts.

The cathedral

Map 4, F5. Daily 10am–1pm; Sunday service 10.30am; free.

Visible from all over the south of the island, Ibiza's most

prominent landmarks are the **cathedral** and adjacent castle that crown Dalt Vila. The former parish church of Santa Maria was granted cathedral status in 1782, after centuries of petitioning by the Ibizan clergy, and is dedicated to Santa Maria de les Neus (Mary of the Snows) – an odd choice, perhaps, considering that Ibiza only gets a light dusting every ten years or so.

Built mostly in the mid-fourteenth century in Catalan Gothic style, the cathedral is a simple, rectangular structure topped by a mighty belltower. Its sombre, uncluttered lines are at their most aesthetically pleasing from a distance, especially at night from across the harbour when the structure is floodlit. Whitewashed throughout, the interior is much less attractive, with somewhat trite Baroque embellishments added between 1712 and 1728 that detract from the hushed, austere atmosphere typical of Catalan Gothic churches. The cathedral's newly-renovated **Diocesan Museum**, due to open early in 2003, will be located in the sacristy and the Chapel of the Blessed Sacrament, and exhibit Catalan art from the thirteenth to the nineteenth centuries, plus assorted ecclesiastical documents, artefacts and relics, including some impressive silver- and gold-plated altar pieces.

THE CASTLE AND AROUND

A rambling strip of buildings constructed in a fractious contest of architectural styles, the **castle** (Map 4, E6) squats atop the very highest ground in Dalt Vila, just southwest of the cathedral. Construction began in the eighth century, although modifications were still being made as late as the eighteenth century. The heavily fortified castle complex housed the governor's residence and contained its own garrison. During the Spanish Civil War, the castle was the setting for one of the darkest chapters in Ibizan history, when mainland Anarchists, briefly in control of the island, massacred over a hundred Ibizan Nationalist prisoners here before fleeing the island. The incident is seen as the basis for decades of local opposition to leftist politics, which was broken only by the election of the leader of the Left-leaning Pacte Progressita coalition as president of the Consell Insular (island government) in June 1999.

Despite its historical significance, the castle complex has been left to decay since the mid-twentieth century. The Town Hall owns the site, and the authorities have squabbled over what to do with the place for the last three decades – various ideas have been mooted, including conversion into a museum or a luxury hotel. The latest plan is to turn the entire complex into a museum of Ibiza, putting all the island's historical treasures and documents under one roof. Some initial renovation work has recently been completed, and there are plans to open two rooms to the public – La Casa de la Ciutat and La Sala de ses Voltes – by early 2003. However, such is the structural instability of most of the castle, it will take many more years for the renovation to be completed.

For the best perspective of the castle's crumbling facade, head south to the **Baluard de Sant Bernat** bastion (Map 4, E7). From the broad stone-flagged apex of the bastion, the decaying profile of the castle complex is laid bare. Just left of the Sa Torreta tower is the sixteenth-century former governor's residence – slab-fronted, dusty pink and with three iron balconies – and rising above this to the left are the towers of the **Almudaina**, the Moorish keep. Smack in the middle of the castle complex is another original rectangular Moorish fortification, the tower of homage; its enigmatic name was probably invented by the nineteenth-century traveller Archduke Luis Salvador. Finally, dropping down in elevation to the left, are the wonky-windowed eighteenth-century infantry barracks.

The southerly views from Sant Bernat are also spectacular, with Formentera clearly visible on the horizon and the sprawling Ibizan resorts of Figueretes and Platja d'en Bossa hugging the coastline just a couple of kilometres away.

VILA NOVA

Retreating back to the Plaça de la Catedral, then onto c/Major, you'll quickly come to a small passageway on the right, some 50m down the street. Known as **Sa Portella** or "Little Gate" (Map 4, D5), this modest little archway is the only remaining Arab entrance to the old city, and today divides the historic upper town from the newer quarter of **VILA NOVA** to the south. Belatedly included in the city walls by Fratín, Vila Nova encompasses the Plaça d'Espanya, the Plaça de Vila and the Baluard de Santa Llúcia.

Through the gateway, the cobbled street ahead, c/Santa Maria (so named because it's the traditional route from La Marina and Vila Nova to the cathedral) passes the legendary **El Corsario** hotel on the left (see p.214), where Picasso is said to have stayed in the 1950s. On the same side of the road is a surviving section of Calvi's walls, rendered ineffectual after Fratín extended the defences south to include the Vila Nova area.

C/Santa Maria ends at **Plaça d'Espanya** (Map 4, G5), a narrow, open-ended cobbled square shaded by palm trees. The imposing arcaded building with the tiled, domed roof that dominates the plaza was originally built as a Dominican monastery in 1587, and also housed a school, providing free education for the poor until the Dominicans were expelled by the Spanish Crown in 1835, and the building was converted to today's **Ajuntament** (town hall).

The tunnel opposite the Ajuntament cuts through the walls to the scrubland of Es Soto beneath the castle.

At the eastern end of the plaza is a recumbent statue of Guillem de Montgrí, a crusading Catalan baron who helped drive the Moors from Ibiza in 1235. It's a short walk from here along the edge of the walls, from where there are fine views of the crooked rock outcrop of the Sa Penya district, and around to the left into c/General Balanzat, home to the **Església de Sant Pere** (Map 4, H4), open only for services (Sat 7pm, Sun noon & 7pm). This whitewashed sixteenth-century church, constructed by Genoese master craftsmen, is one of Ibiza's most handsome, topped by red-tiled domes. It was built as the Dominican monastery's church, and is still referred to the Església Sant Domingo by many Ibizans. Opposite the church, the vast, five-sided **Baluard de Santa Llúcia** (Map 4, H3) is the biggest of all the seven bastions that define the perimeters of Ibiza Town's walls. It was constructed by Fratín thirty years after the other six were built, then connected to Baluard des Portal Nou via an extension of the city walls from Baluard de Sant Joan.

West of the Baluard de Santa Llúcia, pretty **Sa Carrossa** (Map 4, G3–F3) heads back down toward the Portal de ses Taules. A triangular grassy bank, planted with palm trees and flowering scrubs, graces the centre of the street. Amongst the foliage is a miserable-looking statue of **Isidor Macabich**, local historian and author of a formidable four-volume history of the island first published in 1966; despite being known for his sense of humour, Macabich is depicted here as a rather serious figure, with a book at his side. Once asked if he was descended from one of Ibiza's most noble families, he replied: "In Ibiza there are no nobles, we are sons of seamen, of peasants, or of a bitch." Though Sa Carrossa has a slumberous feel during the day, during high-season nights it becomes one of the island's most delightful places to eat out, when a gentle hubbub emanates from the busy restaurant tables lining the south side of the street.

The New Town

Most of the suburban **NEW TOWN** (also known as the *Eixample* or "extension") west of Dalt Vila and La Marina has sprung up over the last thirty years, and holds little of interest. The one appealing area surrounds boulevard-like **Vara de Rey**, bordered with attractive streets brimming with cafés and quirky boutiques. Just east of here is the Carthaginian necropolis of **Puig des Molins**, a hillside littered with tombs, some of which can be explored. The further you get from this central zone, the worse things get, however – the outer suburbs are a depressing world of bland, faceless apartment blocks and broad, traffic-choked avenues. Surprisingly, these dormitory zones are the most lively part of town in the low season, when the unpretentious bars and cafés buzz with business while the hip joints in the port enjoy a long winter slumber.

Taking up the entire northern and western sides of the port, the **new harbour** area is also short on sights, but it does at least provide marvellous views of the old town across the water. The docks and marinas can also be fun to explore and, in any case, you'll have to pass this way to get to the **Botafoc peninsula** and Talamanca beach.

VARA DE REY AND AROUND

An imposing and graceful tree-lined boulevard, **Vara de Rey** (Map 3, H3–G4) is the hub of modern Ibiza, and the logical place to start exploring the area. It's here that you'll find the island's oldest cinema, the Art Deco-style *Cine Serra*, one of the island's most famous café-bars, the *Montesol*, numerous banks and a collection of fashionable boutiques. Vara de Rey can't compete with Barcelona's Ramblas, but the beautiful five-storey, early twentieth-century buildings, many in Spanish colonial style, give the street a certain status and character. Like the Ramblas, the central portion of Vara de Rey is pedestrianized; shaded by palms and poplar trees, it's thick with tourists in high season. Smack in the middle of the avenue is a large stone-and-iron monument dedicated to Ibiza-born **General Joachim Vara de Rey**, who died in the Battle of Caney fought between Spain and the USA over Cuba in 1889.

Just a block to the south, the **Plaça des Parc** (Map 3, H4) is an even more inviting place for a coffee or a snack, night or day, with a myriad of café-bars and restaurants grouped around a square shaded by acacias and palms. There's no traffic at all to contend with here, and the small plaza attracts an intriguing combination of stylish Ibizan denizens and plenty of bohemian characters: ageing New Agers, musicians, artists and hippies. The bars all have plenty of atmosphere, each catering for different punters – the most popular are pre-club favourite *Sunset Café* (see p.251) and classy, comfortable *Madagascar* (see p.250).

PUIG DES MOLINS

Map 3, D6. Museum closed, necropolis open March–Oct Tues–Sat 10am–2pm & 6–8pm, Sun 10am–2pm; Nov–Feb Tues–Sat 9am–3pm, Sun 10am–2pm; free entry.

West of Plaça des Parc on Via Romana, **Puig des Molins** (Hill of the Windmills) was one of the most important Punic burial sites in the Mediterranean, and continued to be used as a city cemetery in Moorish times until at least the tenth century. It was chosen by the Phoenicians in the seventh century BC because their burial requirements specified a site free from poisonous creatures – there are no snakes or scorpions in Ibiza. Noblemen were buried in this necropolis in their thousands, their bodies transported here from all over the empire.

Although the site now has been awarded UNESCO World Heritage status, Puig des Molins today is pretty modest to look at, and appears little more than a barren rocky park, scattered with olive trees and rosemary bushes. However, the hillside is riddled with over three thousand tombs, and excavations over the years have unearthed some splendid terracotta figurines, amphorae and amulets. It's possible to see some of these tombs by following a short trail that winds around the site, passing **Chamber 3** which contains thirteen stone sarcophagi from Punic times, illustrating just how densely packed this hillside is with graves. Most of the finest burial goods have been gathered in the museum building adjacent to the site, though it remains closed, and there are no plans to reopen it again soon. However, it's possible to see a collection of Punic artefacts inside Dalt Vila's **Museu Arqueològic d'Eivissa i Formentera** (see p.73).

NEW HARBOUR

Map 2, E2–G3.

Occupying the western and northern sides of Ibiza Town's bay, the **new harbour** (or Port d'Eivissa) is another modern extension to the city. This area was one half of the capital's vegetable patch, **Ses Feixes** (see box on p.84), until the late 1950s, when the town began to expand to the north. Today, it's a wealthy enclave containing the yacht club, several marinas, the casino and the clubs *El Divino*, *Pacha* and *Angel's el Cel* (see pp.267, 268 & 276).

From the western end of Passeig Marítim (opposite the *Café Mar y Sol*), the harbour promenade of Avgda Santa Eulària heads north past the Formentera ferry terminal building and Club Nàutic, the yacht club. Continuing around the north side of the harbour, you'll pass rows of gleaming yachts in the bay and a line of luxury apartment blocks inland. The Art Deco-style *Ocean Drive* hotel (see p.216), the jogging tracks, exercise stations, palm trees, yachties sporting designer sunglasses and seemingly year-round sunshine hereabouts are reminiscent of Miami and, to a degree, even the vice is here too, in the form of the casino, nightclubs and an upmarket brothel or two.

BOTAFOC PENINSULA

From the *Ocean Drive* hotel, the thin, kilometre-long **Botafoc peninsula** stretches southeast into the harbour, with a road running along its length and a lighthouse defining the final rocky extremity. The three main bodies of land are now connected, the result of infilling in 1885; before this, all three were offshore islands. Over a century later, the environment is set to change again – despite protests from the green lobby – as a huge new dock nears completion, stretching from the lighthouse into the harbour. The new mole, capable of accommodating vast cruise ships, should be finished by the summer of 2003.

There's no reason to linger at the first hill, the residential **Illa Plana** (Map 2, H3–H4), which was used as a plague colony in the fifteenth century. In Carthaginian days, it was the base of a fertility cult centred around the goddess Tanit; dozens of figures dug up here can now be seen in Dalt Vila's archeological museum (see p.73). Beyond here, a wide new highway, built to service the emerging Botafoc dock, clings to the western shore of the harbour around the eastern fringes of Ibiza Town's bay. There are great views of the old town and the ocean from the **Illa Grossa** (Map 2, I6) and **Botafoc** (Map 2, H6) promontories above the road; the latter a much smaller adjunct of Illa Grossa, defined by the sentinel-like **Far de Botafoc** lighthouse at its end. Cava-carrying revellers traditionally congregate here to witness the first sunrise of the New Year. Beyond the

SES FEIXES

Despite its mundane appearance, the large, seemingly barren patch of land west of Talamanca beach is actually a UNESCO World Heritage site. Now choked with giant reeds and scrub bushes, **Ses Feixes** (The Plots) were developed by the Moors over a thousand years ago using innovative agricultural methods. The farmlands were irrigated via an incredibly complex network of *acequias* (dykes), *fiblas* (subterranean water channels) and crop rotation systems thought to be unique to Ibiza, which enabled the land to produce two harvests per year. The principal crops were onions, cabbages, beetroot, melons, and, after the fifteenth century, maize and peppers. The *feixes* remained Ibiza Town's most important farmland until the late 1950s, when the fringes of the fields began to be developed

lighthouse, the new concrete mole juts into the harbour waters, offering photographers an arresting perspective of the fortress-like summit of Dalt Vila from across the waves.

Around Ibiza Town

The suburbs, resorts and beaches that ring the flat land around the capital are not Ibiza's best aspect. However, if you desperately need to cool down, there are plenty of places to swim and chill, and fine coastal **hiking**, with the shoreline north of **Talamanca** beach almost untouched. The area offers little in the way of historical interest, although the village church of **Jesús** is worth investigating.

The suburbs extend to Talamanca and Jesús in the north and **Figueretes** to the south. In the west, Ibiza Town is at and tourism replaced agriculture as the island's main industry. From the edge of the plots, it's still possible to make out the *feixes*, *fiblas* and water gates (*compuertas*) amongst the reeds.

The area is rich in birdlife: grebes, the black-winged stilt, redshanks, egrets, herons and other waders. The Green pressure group GEN and the island government have begun to clean up the two *feixes* (there's another smaller area behind the yacht club on the western side of the harbour) with the aim of creating a natural park. EU money and revenue raised from the Balearic ecotax (see p.26) will pay for the channels to be dredged, water circulation and a new information centre, but as industrial contaminants have been discovered, the work is likely to take years to complete.

its most ugly, with a bewildering tangle of roundabouts, industrial estates and hypermarkets scarring the indeterminate fringes of the capital. Eight kilometres to the west, the village of **Sant Rafel** is worth a quick visit for its ceramic workshops and church, though it's most famous for the **clubs** on its doorstep, the legendary venues of *Amnesia* and *Privilege*.

TALAMANCA

Map 2, H2.

A sweeping sandy bay 2km north of Ibiza Town, **Talamanca** beach rarely gets overcrowded, despite its close proximity to the capital. Development has been fairly restrained here, with hotels mainly confined to the northern and southern fringes, and it's not impossible to imagine the paradisiacal pre-tourism environment. A smattering of bars and some good fish restaurants occupy the central part

A WALK FROM TALAMANCA TO CALA S'ESTANYOL

This easy two-hour-long, four-kilometre hike from Talamanca around the coastal cliffs north of Ibiza Town passes pine forests and the little bay of Cala s'Estanyol, where there's good swimming and a beach restaurant. If you want to shorten the hike, take one of the buses that run hourly to Cap Martinet from Avgda Santa Eulària in Ibiza Town.

Just beyond the crumbling *Paraíso del Mar*, the last hotel on the north side of Talamanca bay, a path follows the shore, passing the swanky *Sa Punta* restaurant, a string of huts housing fishing boats and a scruffy, nameless, summer-only seafood shack renowned for its mussels. The route continues past a rocky outcrop, **Punta de s'Andreus**, which is popular with naturists – although the sharp rocks and strong currents here don't make for particularly pleasant swimming. Beyond here, the path hugs the shoreline as it climbs the cliffs around the *Paradise Club* villa complex. Walk around the cliff side of the complex, and then head inland to avoid the firing range ahead; the path then heads east (right) back to the sea by the main entrance to the *Paradise Club*, where municipal buses terminate. Jutting into the waves ahead is **Cap Martinet**, a thin, saw-toothed rocky promontory that resembles the tail of a stegosaurus.

From Cap Martinet, head north toward the white villa with a slightly ridiculous mock turret, then down through the woods ahead for a couple of minutes to a tiny stony bay, with some shade from pine trees; it's ideal for a swim, a snorkel around the rocks or a picnic lunch. From the bay, walk up the right-hand side of the valley directly behind, following a pretty trail lined with rosemary bushes, and turning right after five minutes down a short dirt track bordered by stone walls. At the end of this trail, you reach the driveway of a cluster of villas; turn left into the drive, and walk for 200m until you reach the villa gateway; turn sharp right here along a dirt lane. Follow the lane for a couple of minutes, then skirt round the second of two sets of black gates and pick your way through a stretch of scrubland towards a gap in the stone wall some 100m ahead. Pass through the hole, and head uphill, taking the middle path that swings to the left; this steep trail climbs quickly though some woods and follows a crevice in the cliffs. After three minutes' walking, the trail levels out and offers sea views, with two jagged rocks visible just offshore; from here, the path descends to an old lime kiln, and after another five minutes or so you reach a sandy-coloured farmhouse. A track swings to the right below the farmhouse, and it's a further five minutes' walk to **Cala s'Estanyol**, a tiny cove with a patch of fine pale sand and sheltered swimming. It's undeveloped apart from a handful of fishermen's huts and the funky *PK s'Estanyol* café-restaurant (May–Oct only).

To return to Talamanca via a different route, retrace your steps to the farmhouse, then walk straight ahead through the farm's gate and take the left-hand dirt road uphill through a pine forest. Ignore two left turns and continue uphill along the winding track, which soon levels out to reveal superb views of Formentera on the horizon. The route is all downhill from here, passing the sandstone walls of a stupendous casament-style house below, until you reach a crossroads adjacent to a cluster of houses. Take the right turn, and a narrow paved road soon starts to descend toward the castle and cathedral of Dalt Vila ahead. It's a further five minutes' walk to the coast below, past the concrete villas of Puig Manya, protected by razor wire and guard dogs. Once you reach the seashore, beside the Sa Punta restaurant, Talamanca is just 200m to the west along the coast path.

of the shoreline, which is popular with European families – the gently shelving beach is ideal for children.

Talamanca's *Bar Flotante* and *Hotel Lux Isla* are reviewed on p.235 and p.215 respectively.

To **get there**, you can walk from Ibiza Town (around 30min) via the new harbour along Passeig de Juan Carlos I or, in the summer, catch one of the half-hourly boats departing from the docks close to the statue of the fisherman in La Marina (April–Oct 9am–1am; €2.50 return; 10min).

JESÚS

Map 1, E4.

Just northeast of Ibiza Town, along the road to Cala Llonga, **JESÚS** is a messy overspill of the capital suspended in suburban no-man's land; just urban enough to boast a happening late-night bar, *Alternativa* (see p.252), but rural enough to ensure that roosters prevent any chance of a lie-in.

Right on the highway, but almost hidden amongst an ugly sprawl of anonymous box-like apartment blocks, is the whitewashed village church, **Nostra Mare de Jesús** (Thurs 10am–noon, plus Sunday Mass), a wonderfully simple Ibizan design that's brilliantly illuminated at night. The church building dates back to 1466 and was originally a convent, but construction work continued under Franciscan friars, who established themselves here in 1498, and wasn't completed until 1549. The church boasts Ibiza's finest altar painting, by Valencians Pere de Cabanes and Rodrigo de Osona. An impressive and expansive work spread over seven main and thirteen smaller panels, with images of Christ, the Virgin Mary and the Apostles, it was deemed of sufficient artistic merit to be spared during the Civil War, when most of the island's ecclesiastical art was destroyed. Opposite the church is a good, no-nonsense café-bar, *Bon Lloc* (see p.253) where there are some interesting old photographs of the church and village on the walls and a very swish terrace café, *Croissantería Jesús* (see p.253), one of the best breakfast spots in Ibiza.

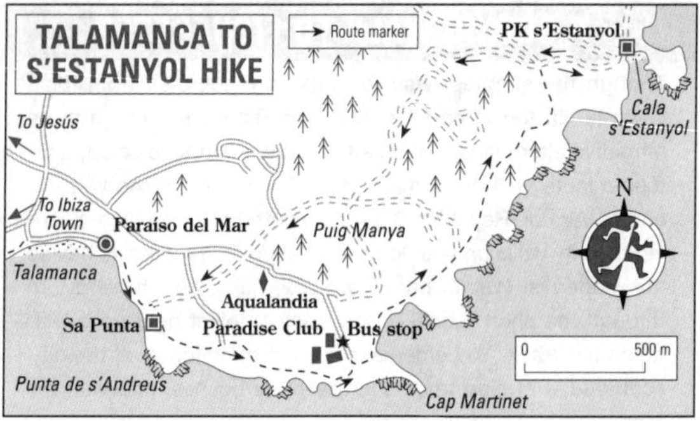

FIGUERETES

Map 2, A5.

The suburb-cum-resort of **FIGUERETES** lies only a fifteen-minute walk southwest of the capital, and is touted as an "up-and-coming" area by estate agents – though, as yet, there are only faint signs of this emergent cosmopolitan identity. However, Figueretes was undoubtedly one of the most happening places in Ibiza during the 1950s, when a bohemian collection of Dutch writers and artists including Jan Gerhard Toonder spent several seasons here; and again in the 1960s, when the area was the focus of the early beatnik scene and the haunt of jazzmen including the bassist Titi and trumpeter Pony Poindexter. However, despite the

A SCENIC WALK TO FIGUERETES

Though the simplest way to **walk** to Figueretes from Ibiza Town is via the fume-filled Avgda d'Espanya, a much more attractive alternative is to take the route around the coast, a fifteen-minute walk from the centre of town. From the western end of Vara de Rey (Map 3, F4), turn left up c/Joan Xico, keeping the city walls on your left. After 200m the road splits beside the modernist *Warhol* bar (see p.252); take the left-hand turn through the short tunnel ahead, then the first right up a pot-holed dirt track. You emerge in a semi-rural corner of the city, scattered with pine trees and rosemary bushes, and with the Mediterranean directly ahead.

Follow the dirt track for 150m or so, and you'll reach the coastal cliffs, where you'll see a phone box. Uncluttered by the sprawl of the modern city, the walls of Dalt Vila to the north look especially impressive from here, while to the south are sublime vistas of Figueretes and Platja d'en Bossa, and over the sea to Es Cavallet and Formentera. Just below the phone box, a spiky tangle of prickly pear cacti and spear-leaved agave plants disguise a precipitous path that snakes down to a tiny sandy **beach**, popular with gay men. Figueretes is just 500m away from the phone box, down the wide dirt track that clings to the cliffs. After a couple of minutes, this track joins up with c/Ramón Muntaner, from where steps lead down to Figueretes' promenade and beach below.

opening of the stylish new Hotel Es Vivé (see p.215) in 2002, there's little evidence today of this funky past in Figueretes; nightlife is limited to a tired collection of expat-run bars and the Blue Rose lap-dancing club, and most of the restaurants are very mediocre. The sandy beach isn't one of the island's finest, either, and is certainly not flattered by the dense concentration of unruly apartment blocks fram-

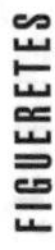

ing the double bay; however, it does at least have some basic seaside appeal, with an attractive palm-lined promenade. Unlike many Ibizan resorts, there's a small resident population here, and in winter when the tourists have gone, elderly Ibizans reclaim the streets to stroll, chat and take the sea air.

Figueretes' main draw is its location – being so close to the capital, it makes a convenient and economic base for serious forays into the dynamic night scene just around the bay. **Gay** visitors have known this for years, and many return annually to the same apartments.

SANT RAFEL

Map 1, D4.

Perched atop the central hills 8km from the capital, **SANT RAFEL** is a largely featureless village just north of the Ibiza Town–Sant Antoni highway that's all but overshadowed by the mighty clubbing temples of *Amnesia* and *Privilege* just to the south. You'll find a moderate collection of stores, cafés and restaurants strung out along its modest high street, Avgda Macabich, which was originally a section of the main road across the island until the current highway between Ibiza Town and Sant Antoni was built. Though Sant Rafel may seem rather lacking in appeal, the village does have several **ceramic workshops** – a couple of which were originally set up by Argentinian leftists fleeing the military junta in the 1970s – leading the Consell Insular to (somewhat ambitiously) declare the village a *zona de interés artesanal*, or artisan zone. Hype notwithstanding, there are a few good potteries in town: Cerámica Es Molí, Can Kinoto and Icardi are all on Avgda Macabich. Local ceramics are usually on show at the annual October 24 fiesta.

Sant Rafel's restaurants are reviewed on p.235; *Amnesia* and *Privilege* are reviewed on pp.265 & 271.

Just 300m east of the high street is the nicest part of the village, centred around the **church**. Built between 1786 and 1797, it's typically Ibizan, with metre-thick whitewashed walls that are visible for miles around, and impressive buttresses. From the churchyard there are stunning views down to Dalt Vila and the sea, as well as glimpses of *Privilege* and *Amnesia*.

The East

From the slender, pebbly beach of Sòl d'en Serra, some 5km north of Ibiza Town, to the rugged cliffs around the hamlet of Sant Vicent in the extreme northeast, Ibiza's east coast represents the sane side of the island's tourism industry, with a shoreline dotted with family-orientated resorts and sheltered coves. Many of the most spectacular sandy beaches, including lovely Cala Llonga and Cala de Sant Vicent, both handsomely backed by towering coastal hills, were developed decades ago into bucket-and-spade holiday resorts, where the nights now reverberate to karaoke and 1980s hits rather than pounding techno-trance – but plenty of wild, pristine places remain. North of the built-up environs of the lively resort of Es Canar, it's just a few kilometres' drive to the tiny, sheltered cove beach of Cala Mastella, and the cliff-backed bay of Cala Boix. A little further north, the kilometre-long sands of Aigües Blanques are the place to bare all in the north of the island.

Santa Eulària des Riu, the region's municipal capital, is a pleasant but slightly mundane town that acts as a focus for the east coast's resorts, with a good restaurant strip and a clutch of appealing bars, cafés and shops. The town has a friendly, family-orientated appeal, with an atmosphere that's markedly different to the teenage histrionics that can plague Sant Antoni or the wild street theatrics of Ibiza Town.

Aside from the historic hilltop **church**, there's little in the way of sightseeing, but the **harbourfront**, with its extensive promenade, is an agreeable place for a wander, and the bars and restaurants in the port area have a fair degree of bustle in the summer months. To the north, the pretty village of **Sant Carles** is worth a visit, with a historic church and a traditional Ibizan farmhouse that's open to the public, a half-decent Saturday hippy market and a good bar or two. Heading towards the extreme northeast tip of the island, around the hamlet of **Sant Vicent**, you'll find some of Ibiza's most spectacular scenery: steep, forested hillsides and sweeping valleys, as well as rugged coves like **Port de ses Caletes**.

Getting around the east is fairly easy. One of Ibiza's main transport hubs, Santa Eulària is connected to the area's chief resorts and villages by regular bus and boat services. However, to get to the more remote beaches, you'll have to procure your own wheels – there are car, scooter and bicycle rental outlets in all the resorts – or take taxis. After midnight, the discobus (see p.30) runs between Es Canar, Santa Eulària and Ibiza Town.

Reviews of accommodation and restaurants in the east start on pp.218 and 235 respectively.

CALA LLONGA AND AROUND

Heading northeast from Ibiza Town to Santa Eulària, you're best off avoiding the heavy traffic on the main C733 highway in favour of the far more scenic minor road that runs to Santa Eulària via the village of Jesús (see p.88) – the turnoff is 1km along the C733, on the right-hand side, next to the pink *El Motel*. Beyond Jesús, this road climbs up the eastern hills, twisting and turning through dense forests of aleppo pine, skirting the lush greens of the **Roca Llisa** golf course (see p.51), and providing sweeping views of the island's interior. Some 8km past Jesús, there's a turnoff on the right for the small family resort of **CALA LLONGA** (Map 5, B9). Set in a spectacular fjord-like inlet below soaring forested cliffs, the 300-metre-wide bay has fine creamy-coloured sand and translucent water. Cala Llonga is purely a holiday enclave, and the place closes down completely for six months after the last visitors have left in late October. Unfortunately, the bay's natural beauty is tainted somewhat by the off-white hotels and apartment blocks insensitively built on the northern cliffs, part of the rampant development in the 1960s.

On the plus side, the gently shelving sands are superb, and the shallow water is usually unruffled by waves. There are full beachside facilities including sunbeds, umbrellas and pedalos, and a **tourist information** kiosk (May–Oct Mon–Sat 10am–2pm). As in many Ibizan resorts, the cuisine is uninspiring and with little variety. The best bet is the *Wild Asparagus*, well-signposted down a track at the rear of the bay.

There are two **bus** services between Cala Llonga and Santa Eulària from May–October (Mon–Fri only).

Sòl d'en Serra

Map 5, A9.

Just 800m south of Cala Llonga, down a bumpy dirt track (you can drive as far as the path that leads down from the cliffs to the beach), **Sòl d'en Serra** is a slender, undeveloped 500-metre-long pebble beach backed by high golden cliffs. The shore is quite exposed here, and the sea can get choppy when there's a strong wind – perfect for an invigorating dip if you're a strong swimmer, but not ideal for small children. The beach never gets busy, even in high season; between October and May, you're almost guaranteed to have it to yourself. Good **meals** and **snacks** are served in the Dutch-owned *Sòl d'en Serra* restaurant overlooking the waves, where there's also a chillout terrace complete with hammocks and sunbeds.

SANTA EULÀRIA DES RIU

Map 5, B7.

In an island of excess, **SANTA EULÀRIA DES RIU**, Ibiza's third largest town, is remarkable for its ordinariness. Pleasant and provincial, the town lies on the eastern shoreline beside the banks of the only **river** in the Balearics, the Riu de Santa Eulària, from which the town takes its suffix, *des riu* (of the river). Apart from an attractive fortified church and modest museum perched on the **Puig de Missa** hilltop just northwest of the town centre, there's little of specific interest. Santa Eulària's shoreline is its best aspect – the two town **beaches** are kept clean and tidy, with gently-sloping sands that are ideal for children, while the recently redeveloped **Port Esportiu** in the harbour bristles with yachts, bars and restaurants.

The grid-like network of streets are filled with functional rather than fashionable stores and bars, most open throughout the year, giving the town a little urban hustle and bustle. While the town centre lacks inspiring architecture, the wide **Passeig de s'Alamera** helps compensate, running from the town hall south to the shore and providing Santa Eulària with an agreeably leafy focal point.

There's a good selection of atmospheric, moderately priced places to **eat** along the main restaurant strip, c/Sant Josep. **Nightlife**, however, is pretty tame; most locals and visitors content themselves with an amble along the palm-lined promenade or a quiet drink in one of the many seafront café-bars.

There are hourly (Mon–Fri 8.30am–8.30pm) **buses** between Santa Eulària and Ibiza Town, and eight services a day on Saturdays and Sundays. Four daily buses (except Sun) connect Santa Eulària and Sant Antoni. Buses also run from Santa Eulària to Sant Carles (three daily, except Sun), Es Canar (five daily except Sun) and Portinatx (two daily, except Sat and Sun).

Some history

Isolated pottery fragments found close to the Santa Eulària River indicate a minor Punic presence here during the first millennium BC, but there's no evidence of a sizeable settlement. The **Romans** constructed a bridge over the river (now the rebuilt Pont Vell), but they left the Santa Eulària bay alone. The region remained a rural backwater for six hundred years, until the **Moors** took control of the island in the tenth century and intensively farmed the Riu Eulària valley, but again, they didn't establish an urban centre. Following the **Catalan** conquest in 1235, a simple chapel was constructed on the Puig de Missa; in 1550 it was burnt down by **pirates**, who remained a constant menace until the early eighteenth century.

Santa Eulària's first streets, c/de Sant Jaume and Passeig s'Alamera, and the **Ajuntament** (town hall) building, were constructed in the late eighteenth century, but the population remained tiny, growing to only a few hundred inhabitants by 1920. The first foreign **travellers** – mainly writers and artists – also began arriving in the early years of the twentieth century, but tourism didn't really become an important factor in the local economy until well after the Spanish Civil War, which split the town politically. New hotels began to be constructed after 1950, and Santa Eulària's economy slowly began to rely on **tourism** rather than its fishing boats. In the 1960s and early 1970s, the relatively unspoiled nature of the place, combined with the

---

Elliot Paul's *Life and Death of a Spanish Town* (see Contexts, p.345) documents Santa Eulària's extreme poverty and social divisions at the time of the Spanish Civil War.

---

presence of the legendary bar, *Sandy's*, attracted a fair number of European jetsetters. Laurence Olivier and John Mills were regular visitors, while Diana Rigg, Terry Thomas and Denholm Elliott even settled and bought houses in the area. However, the glamour faded as the town expanded and geared itself to mass tourism: *Sandy's* has closed, and Santa Eulària today is an appealing family resort rather than a chic destination.

Plaça d'Espanya and Passeig de s'Alamera

Smack in the centre of town, pretty little **Plaça d'Espanya** (**Map 6, F3**), planted with palms trees and lined with benches, is the quiet hub of the Santa Eulària municipality and a good place from which to start exploring the town. The graceful **Ajuntament** (Town Hall) dominates the north side of the plaza. Built in 1795, this sober building exudes provincial restraint, with a stout-arched colonnade flanked by two simple municipal coats-of-arms. In front of the Ajuntament is a small stone monument, erected by the city of Palma in neighbouring Mallorca to honour the local seamen who came to the rescue of the steamboat *Mallorca*, which became trapped on a reef near the island of Redona, just offshore, in 1913.

Just below Plaça d'Espanya, over the busy high street of c/Sant Jaume, **Passeig de s'Alamera** (Map 6, F3–F4) is easily Santa Eulària's most attractive thoroughfare. Laid out at the same time as the Ajuntament, boulevard-like s'Alamera has a shady pedestrianized centre, planted with a healthy collection of well-tended trees and flowering shrubs. In the summer season, dozens of market stalls here add a splash of colour, selling jewellery, sarongs and tie-dye Thai garb.

A tourist information kiosk (May–Oct Mon–Fri 9am–1pm & 4–7pm, Sat 9am–1pm; ⓣ971 330 728) lies at the top of Passeig de s'Alamera.

Along the harbourfront

At the end of Passeig s'Alamera, Santa Eulària's **harbourfront** commands wonderful views of the sparkling, turquoise Mediterranean and the steep wooded hill, Puig d'en Fita, that frames the bay to the south. Below the promenade are the town's two slim, crescent-shaped **beaches**, packed in high season with families enjoying the fine golden sands and safe swimming. The scenery is somewhat spoilt, however, by the obtrusive, concrete apartment blocks ringing the bay, and the unremarkable café-bars that line the promenade.

Heading east along the promenade down the harbourfront, you'll soon arrive at the **Port Esportiu** (Map 6, H4; signposted in Castilian as the "Puerto Deportivo"), an upmarket, yachtie-orientated enclave set around a modern marina. Full of restaurants and bars, it's a popular place for a drink or meal; the location ensures high prices, although the menus tend to be uninspiring.

Continuing east, the harbourfront takes you past rows of gleaming yachts before reaching a rocky promontory some 500m from the beaches, in front of the big modern *Hotel Ses Estaques*, from where there are spectacular **views** back along the Santa Eulària bay. Local legend attests that the small hill beside the huge, modern *Hotel Los Loros*, a couple of minutes further on, was the site of a Medieval chapel that, according to legend, collapsed seconds after the congregation left the building after Mass. There's no evidence to back this up, but the unremarkable site still appears on most maps as **Punta de s'Església Vella** (Point of the Old Church). It's been earmarked as the spot of a new convention centre, with an auditorium and cultural centre – work should begin in 2003.

The travel writer and novelist Norman Lewis lived in a house close to the Punta de s'Església Vella while researching his book *The Tenth Year of the Ship* (see p.345).

Puig de Missa

Map 6, C2.

Behind Plaça d'Espanya, at the back of the Ajuntament, c/Sant Josep is the first leg of the walk up to **Puig de Missa**, the little hill to the west where you'll find the town's sixteenth-century church and ethnological museum; it's an easy ten-minute walk to the top. Pink signs along the route proclaim it a *paisatge pintoresc* (picturesque path), but it's far from scenic initially, passing shops and long, ordinary suburban streets. The route continues to the right into c/Sol, and then left along c/Pintor Barrau, passing the town's main **market** (Map 6, E2; Mon–Sat 8am–6pm). which is situated underground on the corner of c/del Sol and Camí del Missa. It's not a wildly exciting commercial hub, but fine for a quick browse amongst the glistening fish displays and piles of fruit and vegetables.

Museu Etnològic d'Eivissa i Formentera

Map 6, C3. May–Oct 10am–1pm & 5–8pm; Nov–April 10am–1pm & 4–6pm; €2.

Halfway up Puig de Missa, the **Museu Etnològic d'Eivissa i Formentera** has displays based on Pitiusan rural traditions. The main draw here is the **museum building** itself, a classic example of the traditional flat-roofed Ibizan *casament*. You enter via the outdoor terrace (*porxet*) that would have been the centre of family life in the hot summer months. Moving inside, the ticket office is located in the cool, beamed **porxo** (long room), the heart of the household for most of the year, where corn would have been husked, tools sharpened and *festeig* (courting rituals) held. Most of the exhibits here are either carpentry tools or musical instruments, such as oleander wood flutes (*flautas*) and *tambor* drums made from pine and rabbit skin.

All the other rooms lead off from the *porxo*. Up a short staircase, **room 4** houses long black nineteenth-century *gonella* skirts and several flamboyant, billowing dresses from the early twentieth century, made to wear at weddings and fiestas; some are adorned with spectacular *emprendadas* – ceremonial necklaces made from silver, gold and coral. Downstairs, **room 5** is the most unusual feature of the house – a damp natural cave, perfect for wine storage, with a grape press, vat, cask and decanter on display. The **kitchen** (room 6), dominated by a massive hearth and chimney hood, has a modest collection of meat cleavers, mincers, coffee roasters and gourds. All things agricultural have been amassed in **room 7** – ploughs, shovels, yokes, pitchforks and hoes – while the attraction in **room 8** is a huge old olive oil press. Up another flight of stairs from the *porxo*, **room 9** has a nautical flavour, with fishing spears and a framed privateer's licence, the legal certificate granted to Ibizan corsairs (see p.311) by the Crown, authorizing them to attack pirate vessels. Adjoining room 9, **room 10** was originally a tiny bedroom, and a small cot and a bridal chest are displayed today.

Església de Puig de Missa

Map 6, C2. May–Sept daily 9am–9pm.

Puig de Missa's 52-metre summit is dominated by the sculpted lines of Santa Eulària's magnificent fortress-cum-church, **Església de Puig de Missa**, a white rectangular building constructed – after pirates destroyed the original chapel – by the Italian architect Calvi, who was also responsible for the Dalt Vila walls. Dating from 1568, the church has a semicircular tower built into its eastern flank that formed part of Ibiza's coastal defences. Around 1700, two side chapels were added, and also the church's best feature, a magnificent and wonderfully cool porch with eight arches and mighty pillars supporting a precarious-looking beamed roof. The church interior is whitewashed throughout, with little decoration apart from a series of images of a suffering Christ and a huge, typically gaudy, *churrigueresque*-style seventeenth-century altar brought here from Segovia by the Marqués de Lozoya in 1967 – the original interior was torched in the Spanish Civil War. Below the church, just to the south, the **cemetery** is worth a quick look, thick with verdant foliage and spilling down the hill over several different levels. Amongst the predominantly Catholic monuments, one tombstone displays a Star of David, in honour of a member of the tiny Jewish community that has been established in Ibiza since Carthaginian times.

Along the river

Descending from the Puig de Missa via a footpath just before the Ethnological Museum, you soon reach busy c/de Sant Jaume, the old Roman road that connected the capital with the lead mines near Sant Carles (see p.106) – today, it's Santa Eulària's main thoroughfare. Cross to the other side of c/de Sant Jaume and turn right along it towards the **river**; after 100m, take the path that leads down to **Pont Vell** (Map 6, B2), with its three simple seventeenth-century stone arches. These days it's a footbridge – traffic continues along c/de Sant Jaume and crosses the river via one of two modern roadbridges just upstream.

Heading downstream from Pont Vell towards the sea, an attractive path lined with giant reeds and the occasional bench follows the course of the wide riverbed to the town's promenade and southern beach. Just before you reach the river's mouth, a startlingly modern blue suspension bridge (Map 6, A5) connects Santa Eulària with the suburb of **Siesta**, once a rural retreat where the English actress Diana Rigg owned a house, and now a prosperous modern housing estate.

NORTHEAST TO PUNTA ARABÍ

From the seafront promenade in Santa Eulària, an attractive, easy-to-follow **coastal path** follows the indented shoreline northeast to the modern resort of Es Canar. It's a six-kilometre, two-hour walk, with plenty of opportunities for a swim along the way. Walking east along the promenade, in about fifteen minutes you'll reach the rocky promontory of **Punta de s'Església Vella** (Map 5, C7). The path then loops around the bulky, landmark *Hotel Los Soros*, and passes above quiet **Cala Niu Blau**, or "Blue Nest Cove" (Map 5, C7), where there's a 100-metre arc of fine, sunbed-strewn sand and a simple fish restaurant.

Continuing along the coast path, past a cluster of pricey-looking villas, you'll arrive at **Cala Pada** (Map 5, D7) in about twenty minutes; the 200m of fine, pale sand and shallow water here are popular with families, and there are three café-restaurants. It's also a surprisingly well-connected beach, with hourly **boats** to Santa Eulària and Ibiza Town during the summer, when boat operators also offer excursions to Formentera.

Some 500m beyond Cala Pada, the path skirts **s'Argamassa** (Map 5, D7), a compact, fairly upmarket family resort where a scattering of large modern three- and four-star hotels loom over the shoreline. From there the path heads inland, bypassing the wooded promontory of **Punta Arabí**, which juts into the Mediterranean opposite two tiny rocky islets, Redona and Santa Eulària. From here, it's a ten-minute stroll into Es Canar, passing the *Club Arabí* resort, where Ibiza's biggest hippy market (see p.285) is held.

The beaches of Cala Niu Blau and Cala Pada can also be reached via side roads that branch off the main Santa Eulària–Es Canar highway.

ES CANAR

Map 5, D7.

ES CANAR, a compact resort of four- and five-storey hotel blocks, lies 5km across the well-watered plain north-east of Santa Eulària. The inviting Blue Flag beach, with an arc of fine sand, is Es Canar's main attraction, with safe swimming in its sheltered waters. Unfortunately, the accompanying tourist facilities – a strip of British and Irish pubs, souvenir shops and fast-food joints – present a much less pleasant picture, though the special menus and happy hours keep things economical at least.

There are regular buses (May–Oct only, Mon–Sat 7 daily, Sun 3 daily) between Es Canar and Santa Eulària, as well as discobuses in the evenings (see Basics, p.30).

Es Canar is generally a family-orientated place, where children are well catered for and nights revolve around "Miss and Mr Es Canar" competitions and quiz shows. However, it's the weekly **hippy market** (May–Oct Wed only 10am–6pm), held just south of the centre in the grounds of the *Club Arabí* resort, that draws most people to this part of the coast. First held in the early 1970s, it's the biggest in the island these days. On Wednesdays in July and August, Ibiza's worst traffic jams form when convoys of coaches and rental cars besiege Es Canar, and crowds flock to peruse some four hundred stalls. If you join them, bear in mind that you'll be extremely lucky to find anything you haven't seen at home. The whole affair has become very sanitized, and most of the stalls sell the same kind of overpriced tack, from gaudy nylon Bob Marley and Che Guevara banners and junk jewellery to "I love Ibiza" T-shirts. Since the cookshacks were cleared out a few years ago following a health scare, there's nothing very interesting to snack on either.

Cala Nova

Map 5, D6.

A kilometre north of Es Canar around the rocky coastline, the wide sandy bay of **Cala Nova** is one of Ibiza's most exposed beaches, with invigorating, churning waves at most times of year; when there's a northerly wind blowing, it's one of a handful of places in Ibiza where it's possible to **surf**.

There are no surfboards available for rent at Cala Nova, although there's a good selection at the store Kalani (see p.283) in Sant Antoni.

As offshore rocks and the pounding wave action can make swimming tricky, Cala Nova isn't a favourite with families and the sands never get too crowded. There are sunbeds and umbrellas for rent, a small snack bar (May–Oct) and a large, very well-equipped **campsite** (see p.225) at the entrance to the beach. The nearest bus stop is at Es Canar.

SANT CARLES

Map 5, D5.

Of all Ibiza's villages, the pretty, whitewashed hamlet of **SANT CARLES**, 7km northeast of Santa Eulària, is probably the most steeped in hippy history. It first became associated with early bohemian travellers in the 1960s, when vacant farmhouses in the unspoiled surrounding countryside attracted hippy settlers, who quickly made Sant Carles – and specifically the legendary *Anita's* bar – the focus of a lively scene. *Anita's* remains open (see p.254), though these days the scene is less in evidence here than in the *Las Dalias* bar (see p.254), 1km south of the village on the Santa Eulària road, which stages weekly psychedelic trance nights and also hosts a boho Saturday **market** (see p.285). It's worth a browse around the stalls – run by a merry bunch of tie-dye traders, crystal-ball merchants, navel-gazers and chaiwallahs – which proffer *souk*-like stacks of ethnic oddities.

There are also two points of architectural interest. In the heart of Sant Carles, the **church** is a very fine eighteenth-century construction, with a broad, arcaded entrance porch supported by six squat pillars, and a simple white interior with a single nave and a side chapel on the left dedicated to Santa Mare del Roser ("of the Rosary"). In 1936, during the **Spanish Civil War**, the church witnessed a bloody incident which resulted in the death of the village curate and his father. Until recently, the best-known version of events came from Elliot Paul, an American writer based in Santa Eulària during the Spanish Civil War, who reported in his book *Life and Death of a Spanish Town* (see Contexts, p.345) that the Nationalist curate was so at odds with his staunchly Republican parishioners that he was forced to barricade himself inside the church, and even opened fire on the villagers from the belfry before being captured and executed. An alternative view, with more widespread local support, has been put forward by Ibizan historian Rafael Sainz. He asserts that when Republican forces arrived in the village demanding water from the church cistern, the curate refused them entry unless they disarmed. This provoked an argument between the curate (supported by his father, who appeared on the scene with a rifle) and the Nationalist troops. Sainz maintains that neither father nor son fired a shot, but were both quickly overpowered before being executed. Whatever the truth, they were both hung from the carob tree which still stands outside the church.

There are three daily **buses** (Mon–Fri only) between Santa Eulària and Sant Carles.

Es Trui de Can Andreu

Map 5, D5. May–Sept Mon–Fri 3.30–4.30pm, Sat 11.30am–1.30pm & 3.30–4.30pm; open sporadically in winter, call ⓣ971 335 261 to check; €3.50.

On the outskirts of the village, located 250m south of the church along the road to Cala Llenya, the seventeenth-century **Es Trui de Can Andreu** is a fine example of a traditional Ibizan farmhouse, or *casament*. This whitewashed cubist structure displays all the renowned design features of Ibizan house-building style that have been so feted by modernist architects. Tiny windows punctuate the house's exterior in seemingly haphazard places, while all the rooms have a certain organic character, with bowed sabina pine-timbered roofs contrasting superbly with chalk-white, metre-thick walls. The prefix "*es trui*" refers to Can Andreu's colossal olive press, the house's most unusual feature, which

S'ARGENTERA MINES

The s'Argentera hills south of Sant Carles were quarried from Roman times until 1909 and, alongside salt, mining represented the island's only other industry for two millennia. The crumbling brick chimneys of the **s'Argentera mines** still stand 3km south of Sant Carles on the road to Santa Eulària; here, up to two hundred Ibizans were employed on nine different seams, removing over a hundred tons of lead a year as well as small amounts of silver. The mines are not currently open to the public, but there are plans to develop the site into a tourist attraction, with guided tours and a museum.

is kept in the smoke-blackened kitchen. Several other rooms exhibit various Ibizan cultural curios: musical instruments, farming tools including threshers and ploughs, basketry and *espardenyas* sandals. You'll be escorted around the building by a member of the Andreu Torres family, the owners of the house; though they no longer live here, they remain proud of their ancestral home and are keen to point out its unusual features. All visitors are offered a glass of local *hierbas* liquor, and you can also buy Ibizan wine and postcards.

THE NORTHEAST CORNER

East of Sant Carles, Ibiza's rugged **northeastern corner**, between Cala Llenya and Aigües Blanques, is strewn with beautiful sandy beaches, low sandstone cliffs and patches of thick woodland. With only two small, upmarket hotel complexes along the entire shoreline, limited public transport links and no towns in the vicinity, many of the beaches on this exposed coastline are empty for most of the year, and even in the high season things never get too crowded.

The waves can get choppy at the beaches of **Cala Llenya** and **Cala Boix**, while the surf can get really strong at **Figueral** and **Aigües Blanques**, especially in winter. The coves of **Cala Mastella** and **Pou des Lleó**, however, are more sheltered, and for most of the year there's barely a ripple in the pellucid water.

Cala Llenya to Cala Boix

Southeast of Sant Carles, a signposted road weaves 4km downhill through small terraced fields of olive and carob trees, and skirts the La Joya holiday village – one of the island's less intrusive developments – before reaching **Cala Llenya** (Map 5, E6), a two-hundred-metre-wide, bite-shaped sandy bay lying between low sandstone cliffs scattered with white-painted villas. As with many of the beaches on this stretch of the island, the sea can get choppy here and, perhaps because of this, the fine sands never get too crowded – you should have no problem finding a sunbed or umbrella for the day, and there's also a beachside café (May–Oct) for snacks and drinks. Two daily buses run between Cala Llenya and Santa Eulària, via Sant Carles.

Heading north along the coast, the next accessible beach is **Cala Mastella** (Map 5, E5), some 3km from Cala Llenya and reachable via the same road from Santa Carles; the route descends to the shore via an idyllic terraced valley. Barely forty metres wide, Cala Mastella's sandy beach is lovely, set at the back of a deep coastal inlet with pine trees almost touching the sheltered, emerald waters. It's an exceptionally inviting place for a swim, although watch out for sea urchins, some of which are fairly close to the shore. A tiny kiosk (May–Sept) rents out sunbeds and sells drinks, but for fine seafood and grilled fish lunches walk 50m around the north side of the bay to the El Bigotes restaurant (see p.235); you can't see it from the main section of the beach.

North of Cala Mastella, a wonderfully scenic coastal road meanders for 1km or so through pine forest, affording panoramic views over the Mediterranean below, to **Cala Boix** (Map 5, F5). Set below high, crumbling cliffs, Cala Boix is a beautiful sliver of a beach, with coarse sand and pebbles, and the obligatory umbrellas and sunbeds for rent. Three simple restaurants line the headland high above the shore – the Restaurant *La Noria* (see p.236) commands the best views – and there's also the excellent inexpensive Hostal Cala Boix (see p.218) if you need a place to stay. There are no buses to Cala Mastella or Cala Boix.

Pou des Lleó and around

Inland of Cala Boix, a lone country road cuts northwest for 1km or so, past large terraced fields separated by honey-coloured dry-stone walls, until you come to a signposted junction for the diminutive bay of **Pou des Lleó** (Map 5, F5), named "Lion's Well" after a sweet spring close to the shore which is now all but dry. A tiny, pebble-and-sand-strewn horseshoe-shaped inlet, surrounded by low-lying, rust-red cliffs and lined with fishing huts, Pou des Lleó is popular with Ibizan families, who come here for barbecues on summer evenings, but is usually deserted in winter save for a fisherman or two. The only facilities here are a tiny snack bar (May–Oct 11am–sunset) serving delicious grilled fish and cold beers, and the decent *Restaurant Salvadó* (see p.236). Walk around to the left of the bay (north), above the fishing huts, and you'll find two completely deserted coves, both covered with banks of compressed seaweed that form a natural, comfortable mattress for sunbathing.

From the restaurant, it's a further kilometre down a winding road that strikes east towards the coast to a seventeenth-century defence tower, **Torre d'en Valls** (Map 5, F5). Set atop of one of the few outcrops of lava rock in

Ibiza, the tower is in fine condition, but even thougl rungs ascend its wall the door is kept locked. Thei panoramic views over the ocean from here, towards humpbacked island of **Tagomago** (Map 5, G5), 153 ac of privately owned beach and scrubland where Spanish and British royalty occasionally moor their yachts for a day or two. Trips around the island leave from Cala de Sant Vicent (see p.112).

The rural hotel *Can Talais*, high in the hills above Figueral, is reviewed on p.218.

Figueral and Aigües Blanques

After a two-kilometre detour inland from Pou des Lleó, the road loops back to the exposed northeast coast at **FIGUERAL** (Map 5, E4), a small, fairly prosperous, but bland family resort with a clump of hotels, mediocre restaurants and souvenir shops offering postcards and lilos. The narrow, 200-metre stretch of exposed sands is swept clean by churning waves, but swimming conditions can get a little rough, and there are some jagged rocks offshore.

For a day by the sea, though, you're far better off heading for the naturist beach of **Aigües Blanques** (Map 5, E4), or "White Waters", separated from Figueral's slender sands by eroded, storm-battered cliffs. To get there, head inland for 1km, and then turn right (north) and follow the coastal road towards Cala de Sant Vicent; 1km further north and you're at Aigües Blanques, signposted in Castilian as "Agua Blancas". The kilometre-long slice of dark sand here, interspersed with rocky outcrops and crumbling cliffs and buffeted by the ocean, is usually pretty empty, and the beach offers Ibiza's most consistent **surf**, with three-kilometre swells some winters; however, conditions are only ever ideal for a few days a year. Aigües Blanques is also the only official **nudist** beach in the north of the island, and very popular with hippies, who gather at the *chiringuito* at the southern end of the shore – a favoured place to watch the sun rise over the Mediterranean.

Both Figueral and Aigües Blanques are on the Santa Eulària–Cala de Sant Vicent bus route.

Cala de Sant Vicent and around

Map 5, E3.

Ibiza's isolated northeastern tip offers some of the island's most dramatic highland country, dominated by the plunging valley of Sant Vicent, west of the resort of **Cala de Sant Vicent**, the only tourist development in this near-pristine area. Getting there is an attraction in itself: the coastal road north of Aigües Blanques offers one of Ibiza's most magnificent drives, following the corrugated coastline and weaving through thick pine forests, with sparkling waters offshore. Three kilometres after Aigües Blanques you catch a glimpse of Cala de Sant Vicent, its sweeping arc of golden sand enclosed by the 303-metre peak of **Sa Talaia** to the north, and steep cliffs to the south. Unfortunately, property developers have filled Cala de Sant Vicent's shoreline with a row of ugly concrete hotels, but the waters here still offer some of the best swimming in the area. Minimarts, cafés and restaurants sit below the hotels on an otherwise featureless promenade, while behind the prom stands the derelict remains of a concrete house, which served as the hideout of French assassin Raoul Villian after he killed the socialist leader **Jean Jaurès** in 1914 and fled to Ibiza. Villian lived here in near-total seclusion for almost two decades before he was finally tracked down and murdered in 1936.

There are regular buses between Cala de Sant Vicent and Santa Eulària.

Cova des Cuieram

Map 5, D2.

From the shoreline at Cala de Sant Vicent, a good paved road heads inland, slowly climbing westward up the broad, U-shaped valley of Sant Vicent. A kilometre from the bay, there's a small lay-by on the right side of the road, where a sign points the way up a vertiginous path to a cave, **Cova des Cuieram**. A site of worship in Carthaginian times, hundreds of terracotta images of the fertility goddess Tanit were unearthed here when the cave was rediscovered in 1907; some are displayed in the archeological museum in Ibiza Town (see p.73). Consisting of several small chambers, the modest cavern is thought to be in danger of collapse, partly due to the damage inflicted some decades ago by a treasure-seeking lunatic armed with dynamite. Access to the cave is normally prevented by metal railings, although the tourist board plan to run trips in the future (call ⓣ971 301 900 for more information). Open or not, the views from the mouth of the cave (almost 200m above the road) are exceptional enough to warrant the very stiff fifteen- to twenty-minute trek through dense forest.

Sant Vicent

Map 5, C3.

As Ibiza's smallest village, **SANT VICENT**, 3km up the valley from the coast on the road to Sant Joan (see p.117), is easily missed. Consisting of a handful of houses and a fenced basketball court, there are no sights except for the modest, minimalist village **church**, built between 1827 and

1838, with a double-arched porch and an appealing setting in its own tiny plaza, with a solitary palm tree for company. The facade is unembellished except for a small plaque, which confidently proclaims in Castilian Spanish: "house of God and gate to heaven". Around two hundred metres downhill from the church is Sant Vicent's only other feature, an orderly, dark little bar, *Es Café*, which also functions as the valley's post office and shop.

Port de ses Caletes

Map 5, C2.

A tiny pebbly cove, barely 50m across, **Port de ses Caletes** is reachable only via a torturous (but signposted) road from Sant Vicent village that ascends via switchbacks to 250m and then plummets to the sea; it's a bumpy fifteen-minute drive from Sant Vicent. With a ramshackle collection of dilapidated fishing huts as its only buildings, the cove is dwarfed by soaring coastal cliffs, and it's a blissfully peaceful spot, where there's nothing much to do except listen to the waves wash over the smooth stones on the shore or snorkel round the rocky edges of the bay.

JOHN MILLER/ROBERT HARDING

Ibiza Town

IAIN STEWART

Cala de Sant Vicent, Ibiza

ROBERT HARDING

Sant Miquel, Ibiza

IAIN STEWART

Balàfia, Ibiza

IAIN STEWART

Cala d'en Serra, Ibiza

JAMIE BAKER/DEMON LIBRARY

Bora Bora beach bar, Ibiza

IAIN STEWART

Sa Trinxa, Ibiza

The Northwest

From the tiny cove of Cala d'en Serra at the island's northernmost tip to the diminutive village of Santa Agnès in the southwest interior, rugged **northwest Ibiza** is the wildest, most isolated part of the island. An awesome, almost unbroken barrier of towering cliffs and forested peaks, the coastline only relents to allow access to the shore in a few places. Just two bays – **Port de Sant Miquel** and the small family resort of **Portinatx** – have been developed for tourism. Elsewhere, the coastal environment is all but pristine, with formidable cliffs, some over 300m high, offering more possibilities for **hiking** than for beachlife – particularly as sea breezes usually alleviate the heat, even in the height of summer. Though the area is short on sand, the rocky coastline below the cliffs is ideal for **snorkelling**, with thirty-metre-plus visibility and rich marine life, including spiny lobsters, dogfish, moray and conger eels, and peacock wrasse.

The relative inaccessibility of much of the region means that most of the pebble bays and inlets are usually all but deserted, and even in July and August the few sandy beaches never get really crowded. For real isolation, you can hike to the untouched coast around **Cala d'Aubarca** and **Portitxol**; while, if you prefer a few amenities, the stunning beaches of **Cala d'en Serra** and **Cala Xarraca** both have snack bars and sunbeds to rent. Beautiful **Benirràs** is the island's premier hippy beach, where the sun sets to the beat of bongo drums. Inland, the thickly forested terrain is interspersed with small patches of farmland where olives, carob, almonds, wheat and citrus fruits are nourished by the rust-red earth.

The northwest is the most sparsely populated part of Ibiza – of the handful of tiny, isolated settlements, only picturesque **Sant Joan** and sleepy **Sant Miquel** could realistically be described as villages, though all the other hamlets have a whitewashed, fortified church and a bar or two. Many of the villages tend to be associated with a particular produce: **Santa Agnès** is known for its almonds, **Sant Mateu** for its wine, and **Santa Gertrudis** for its apples, apricots, peaches and oranges. Ancient Ibizan rural customs and traditions, some Carthaginian in origin – including dance rituals (see p.287) at remote springs and wells – still survive in the isolated areas. On many hillsides, traditional cuboid Ibizan *casaments* still outnumber modern villas and chalets, while in the village bars the Ibizan dialect of Catalan (see p.334), rather than Castilian Spanish, remains the dominant tongue.

Reviews of accommodation and restaurants in the northwest start on p.219 and p.237 respectively.

There's no **public transport** hub in northwest Ibiza and, while buses do serve virtually every village and resort between May and late September, there are only one or two daily services to the smaller settlements. In winter, schedules are even less frequent, though you can at least get to the main villages (Sant Joan and Sant Miquel). With the exception of one cross-island service that connects Sant Antoni and Port de Sant Miquel via Santa Agnès and Sant Mateu, all services start in either

Ibiza Town (see Chapter 1) or Santa Eulària (see Chapter 2).

To really explore the northwest, you'll need your own transport; **car rental** companies are listed in Basics (see p.33). As many of the best bays are well off the beaten track and at the foot of atrocious dirt tracks, you should also be prepared to do some walking.

SANT JOAN

Map 7, H3.

High in the lofty northern hills of the Serra de la Mala Costa, the pretty village of **SANT JOAN** (San Juan in Castilian) lies on the main highway from Ibiza Town to Portinatx, 22km from the capital. Though only a couple of hundred people live here, the village is capital of the Sant Joan municipality, which comprises most of northern Ibiza, and boasts its own modest little Ajuntament (Town Hall), just above the highway. You'll also find a good, very cheap pension (see p.220), a small supermarket and a bar, and, with regular buses linking the village to Ibiza Town and Portinatx, Sant Joan makes an excellent, tranquil base to explore the attractions of the remote north of the island.

Along with Sant Carles (see p.106), Sant Joan has served as a focal point for northern Ibiza's **hippies** since the 1960s, when a scene developed around the Can Tiruit commune, a legendary hippy hangout. Later it became a primary base for the Bhagwan Rajneesh cult (later renamed the Osho Commune International), where elements of Sufism, Buddhism, Zen and yoga were blended with a good dose of hedonistic sexual libertinism. Rave folk history has it that Bhagwan Rajneesh devotees from California were the first people to bring ecstasy to Ibiza in the late 1970s, when there was the first mass ritual use of the drug on the island.

Evidence of Sant Joan's counter-cultural leanings is

somewhat muted today, though the spirit survives to an extent in the New Age-ish *Eco Centre* café, located in a pretty terraced row in the heart of the village. The region remains popular with a bohemian bunch of artists and writers, however, and the hills around the village are a favoured destination for Ibiza's clandestine psychedelic trance party scene (see p.328).

Dominating the skyline, Sant Joan's eighteenth-century **church**, just off the main highway, boasts typically high, whitewashed walls and an arched side porch. The slim steeple that rises slightly awkwardly from the main body of the building is a twentieth-century addition, which detracts a little from the wonderfully minimalist simplicity of the original design. Inside, there's an unadorned single nave, with a barrel-vaulted roof and a small dome, comprising several segments painted with images of Christ.

There are two daily **buses** between Sant Joan and Ibiza Town.

Sant Joan's bar is reviewed on p.255.

NORTH TO XARRACA BAY

Map 7, H2.

North of Sant Joan, the main highway to Portinatx wriggles down to the coast following a beautiful, fertile valley flanked by olive-terraced hills and orderly almond and citrus groves. The route affords sweeping views of **Xarraca Bay** below, one of Ibiza's most expansive at 2km wide. Dotted with tiny rocky islands, the translucent waters are backed by low cliffs, and there are three small beaches. Four kilometres along the road from Sant Joan, a short signposted turnoff at the km 17 road marker loops past some villas to the quiet beach of **Cala Xarraca**, a thin strip of coarse sand and pebbles no more than 150m long, with a few sunbeds and umbrellas to rent. The solitary bar/restaurant sells full meals and *tapas*, and is a fine spot to watch cormorants and spear-fishermen diving for fish at the end of the day.

A kilometre further along the Portinatx road, **s'Illot des Renclí** is a beautiful 30-metre-wide patch of well-raked sand and very shallow, azure water; just offshore is the tiny islet after which the beach is named. There's a decent fish **restaurant**, also called *s'Illot des Renclí* just above the shore, with tables positioned to give stunning views over the ocean, but no snacks are available. Another kilometre around Xarraca Bay, look out for the signpost to **Cala Xuclar**, a sandy, horseshoe-shaped inlet sprinkled with fishing huts that lies at the mouth of a seasonal river. It's usually very tranquil here, and a few metres to the west there are plenty of rocks ideal for sunbathing, while the waters offer good snorkelling possibilities.

PORTINATX AND AROUND

Map 7, H2.

At the end of the highway, and separated from Xarraca Bay by the sharp contours of Punta de sa Torre, moderately sized, low-rise **PORTINATX** is one of Ibiza's more attractive resorts. It's set around a double bay, with three small sandy beaches, and with well-spaced hotels and apartment blocks built between mature pine trees. Portinatx is a friendly, family-orientated holiday centre rather than an especially happening place – there's a dearth of stylish bars, boutiques or decent restaurants – but it's pleasant enough for a day by the sea, and with several other good beaches nearby it also makes a good base. Somewhat unconvincingly for such an innocuous holiday destination, Portinatx adopted the self-bestowed suffix "*Des Rei*" (royal) after King Alfonso XIII made a fleeting visit in 1929.

The larger of the bays, Port de Portinatx, has two golden patches of sand, **s'Arenal Gross** and **s'Arenal Petite**, where rows of sunbeds are rotated on an hourly basis in high season. The other beach, **Es Portitxol**, at the end of a narrow inlet 500m west of s'Arenal Gross, has well-sheltered water, perfect for swimming and snorkelling; there's also a dive school here (see p.48).

Cala d'en Serra

Map 7, I2.

East of Portinatx, a glorious road with excellent views climbs up the low, sloping hills rising above Ibiza's northern tip, threading through woods and past isolated luxury villas. After 3km, there's a magnificent view of diminutive **Cala d'en Serra**, a remote, exquisite cove framed by green hills; it's reachable via a poor, signposted, and just about driveable, dirt road. The only scar in the scenery is the ugly, half-built concrete shell of an abandoned hotel project just above the beach – though its remains are soon to be demolished as one of the first initiatives paid for by the Balearic ecotax (see p.26). Mercifully, by the sandy shore, this eyesore is all but hidden. The bay's alluring, translucent waters make an idyllic place for a dip, and offer rich snorkelling around the rocky fringes of the inlet; it's a short swim across to a another tiny pebbly cove, which is also accessible over the rocks to the south. Between May and October, a German-run **café**-shack just off the beach serves decent seafood, *bocadillos* and drinks.

You can also reach Cala d'en Serra via a signposted road from Sant Joan, that passes though remote highlands, offering exhilarating views of the indented coast. There are no **buses** to Cala d'en Serra.

BALÀFIA TO SANT LLORENÇ

South of Sant Joan, the north–south highway to Ibiza Town beats a path to two historic inland hamlets that are well worth a quick peek. Six kilometres along the highway, **BALÀFIA** (Map 7, G5), characterized by its castle-like defence towers, is often cited as Ibiza's only surviving Moorish village, though the only thing definitely Arabic about the place is its name. It's certainly one of the most unusual settlements in the Ibiza, though – a cluster of ancient, interlocking whitewashed houses, and ochre-coloured towers where the population once sheltered from pirates. This layout, a common defensive arrangement elsewhere in Europe, never really caught on in Ibiza, where the diffuse population relied instead on coastal watchtowers to warn them of possible danger well before it arrived on their doorstep. Though there are a few "*Privado*" (Private) signs, there's nothing to stop you walking around the hamlet's two alleys to get a closer look at the houses and towers; however, bear in mind that the buildings are people's homes.

The Can Sort organic food market, a fairly modest affair, is held each Saturday in the hills between Sant Joan and Balàfia. To get there from the C733 Ibiza Town–Sant Joan highway, take the turnoff signposted for the "Mercado del Campo" at km 11.9

Sant Llorenç

Map 7, G5.

A kilometre west of Balàfia, down a signposted dirt road off the highway, remote **SANT LLORENÇ** (San Lorenzo in Castilian) is one of Ibiza's least-visited settlements. There's nothing here but a couple of village bars, a handful of houses and a large **church** that seems out of proportion with the rest of the place. A fine eighteenth-century construction, it boasts a broad single-arched entrance porch lined with stone seating, and blindingly white exterior walls. Inside, the nave is divided into five bays and topped with a barrel-vaulted roof, with a single nineteenth-century chapel dedicated to the Virgin Mary.

The wooded hillside above the church has been set aside as the **Can Pere Mosson country park**, a spacious recreation spot with good, waymarked walking trails, barbecue areas and three lookout points offering fine views of the

THE DAY OF THE DRUMS

Since the hazy days of the hippy trail to Marrakesh, Benirràs has been the scene of sporadic **full-moon parties** staged by Ibiza's bohemian population. The assembly declined somewhat in the 1980s, but in 1990, as tension in the Persian Gulf reached fever pitch following Iraq's invasion of Kuwait, the congas and bongos were dusted down, brought to the beach and bashed in a huge rhythm-driven protest for world peace. Since then, the **Day of the Drums**, held to celebrate the August full moon, has become an annual fixture, performed with inimitable crusty gusto. In the last few years, though, the festival has been threatened by the local government, which has spoiled the fun somewhat by laying down strict guidelines: bonfires have been banned, and vehicles restricted to ensure access for the emergency services. The whole future of the event is dependent upon delicate negotiations between the organizers and the authorities. Agreement could not be reached in 2001, when, much to the annoyance of the authorities, hundreds decamped to Cala Jondal (see p.176) and held the party illegally there instead. In 2002, the event was also banned.

hilly heart of the island. The park is popular with Ibizan families at weekends, but deserted the rest of the week.

BENIRRÀS

Map 7, F3.

Three kilometres west of Sant Joan, along the road to Sant Miquel, a signposted right-hand turnoff leads to one of Ibiza's most idyllic beaches, **Benirràs**, a three-hundred-metre-wide sandy cove set against a backdrop of high, densely forested cliffs. Development has been restricted here for decades, and buildings are currently limited to

Future uncertainty notwithstanding, the Day of the Drums is a spectacular occasion, and one of the premier social celebrations for Ibiza's hippy denizens. Dozens of sarong-clad drummers descend to the bay, and a furious rhythm is maintained from before sunset until after sunrise, often developing into a reggae-style sound-clash situation, with two competing teams gathered below the cliffs at the opposite ends of the bay. At such times, Benirràs takes on a magical air, bathed in blue light from the full moon and illuminated by hundreds of candles, while the sweet smell of cardamom-scented *chai* and vegetarian feasts from the cookshacks fills the night air. The celebration has developed into one of Ibiza's unique events, a non-commercial festival that's as much a part of Ibizan culture as the clubs' closing parties and the village fiestas. For a flavour of the occasion, check out the *Waves in the Air* CD on the island-based Ibizarre label, which features many Benirràs percussionists.

three unobtrusive beach **restaurants** (open summer only) and a handful of villas in the hills above. Plans for more houses are currently being vigorously contested by the green lobby.

Legendary in Ibizan **hippy** folklore, and said to have been the site of wild drug-and-sex orgies in the 1960s, Benirràs's distinctly alternative tendencies persist today, and it remains the New Age community's favourite beach. Summer afternoons (particularly Sundays) see the bongo brigade gathering here to bang a drum at sunset or at full-moon time, a tradition that reaches its zenith during the annual August drumfest (see box on p.122). Just offshore, atthe mouth of the bay, lies Cap Bernat – a prominent rock islet that's somewhat revered by mystically minded individuals, who gather here to burn herbs at sunset. It's said to resemble, variously, a woman at prayer, a giant baby, or the Sphinx; however, in the cold light of day, it's difficult to see what all the fuss is about.

SANT MIQUEL

Map 7, F4.

Perched high in the glorious Els Amunts hills, which isolate the northwest coast from the interior, **SANT MIQUEL** is the largest of the villages in this sparsely populated, thickly forested region. The village is not especially picturesque, its main street lined with tiny old cottages that sit somewhat uneasily amongst five-storey apartment blocks; even so, Sant Miquel does retain plenty of unhurried, rural character, and you'll find a good mix of locals and visitors in the bars during the summer.

The settlement dates back to the thirteenth century, when the first walls of the fortified church, **Eglésia de Sant Miquel**, were constructed high on the Puig de Missa hill, a superb defensive position some 4km from the sea, giving the original inhabitants a little extra protection from marauding pirates. Parish status was granted in the early eighteenth century, when a few families were encouraged by Bishop Abad y Lasierra to build houses around the hill-top. It's a short stroll to Puig de Missa from the main street, past a neat little row of terraced cottages and a small plaza, which commands magnificent views over the pine forests and olive groves of the interior. Opposite the plaza is the tiny old post office, which has now been converted into a **bar**, from where you can gaze over the hills with a glass of Rioja. From the plaza, you enter the church via the arches of a walled patio, then pass through a broad porch, which leads into the southern side of the barrel-vaulted nave. The simple altar is to the right, flanked by two large side chapels. The recently restored **frescoes** of the Benirràs chapel, to the right of the altar, are the church's most unusual feature – swirling monochrome vines and flowers that blanket the walls and ceiling, dating back to the late seventeenth century, when construction was finally completed. Below the frescoes is some superb stonework of crosses and octagons.

Ball pagès **(folk dancing) displays are staged in the church patio every Thursday all year round (May–Oct 6.15pm; Nov–April 5.15pm; €3).**

There are five **buses** (Mon–Sat) between Sant Miquel and Ibiza Town; two buses (Tues & Thurs only) between Sant Miquel and Sant Antoni; and two buses (Mon and Wed only) between Sant Miquel and Santa Eulària.

PORT DE SANT MIQUEL AND AROUND

Map 8, H2.

From Sant Miquel, a scenic road meanders 4km north through a fertile river valley to **Port de Sant Miquel**, a spectacular bay that was a tiny fishing harbour and a tobacco smugglers' stronghold until tourism took over in the 1970s. Enclosed by high cliffs that shelter the inlet's dazzlingly blue, shallow waters, and with a fine sandy beach well-suited to children, Port de Sant Miquel's beauty is tainted considerably by the portentous presence of two large and ugly concrete hotel blocks insensitively built into the eastern cliff. Catering almost exclusively to the package tourist trade, Sant Miquel's **bars** and **restaurants** are also disappointing, ranging from the *Happy Friar* English pub to a Wild West-themed saloon bar. The only recognizably Spanish bar/restaurant, the *Marin Dos*, is the best of a bad bunch, with decent *menú del día* – unlike all the others, it's also open all year.

In the summer season, things are pretty lively, with sarong and jewellery vendors wandering along the shore. Pedalos are available for rent; you can also arrange boat trips to neighbouring beaches from a desk on the sand.

Between May and October only there are four **buses** (Mon–Sat) between Port de Sant Miquel and Ibiza Town; two buses (Tues & Thurs only) between Port de Sant Miquel and Sant Antoni; and two buses (Mon and Wed only) between Port de Sant Miquel and Santa Eulària. There are no buses in the winter months.

Cala des Moltons and Torre des Molar

Map 8, G2.

From the western edge of Port de Sant Miquel's beach, a path loops around the shoreline for 200m to a tiny cove, **Cala des Moltons**, where there's a small patch of sand and fine, sheltered swimming. The same, easily followed trail continues past the beach, climbing through rocks and crossing a dirt road, then passing through pine copses. After ten minutes' walk, you'll reach a well-preserved stone defence tower – the eighteenth-century **Torre des Molar**, from where there are good views of the rugged northern coast towards Portinatx.

Cova de Can Marça

Map 8, H2. Daily 11am–1.30pm & 3–5.30pm; €5.

Set in the steep eastern cliffs above Port de Sant Miquel, just past the monstrous hotels, **Cova de Can Marça** is a modest-sized cave system that, though unlikely to get speleologists drooling with excitement, is the biggest in Ibiza. Tobacco and liquor smugglers used its one main chamber and several smaller ones until the mid-twentieth century, after which the cavern was developed as a tourist attraction, with lighting installed and a staircase and pathway constructed. Once you've paid your entrance fee, guides conduct an informative twenty-minute tour (in English) through the dripping chambers.

The cave is about 100,000 years old, and was formed by an underground river that once flowed through the hillside. There are some impressive stalactites and stalagmites, including one specimen that looks like a fat Buddha. An entertaining sound and light show ends the tour, with an artificial waterfall synchronized to cosmic electronic music from Tangerine Dream, who remain big in Ibiza. There's a small café next to the ticket office, where tables afford wonderful views over the turquoise waters below.

From the Cova de Can Marça, a well-signposted, potholed two-kilometre dirt track leads east to Benirràs (see p.123).

Na Xamena and around

Clinging to the vertiginous cliffs west of Port de Sant Miquel, and commanding spectacular vistas over the north shore, tiny **NA XAMENA** (Map 8, F2) consists of nothing more than a small development of holiday villas and the palatial *Hotel Hacienda* (see p.221). Nonetheless, if you're in the area it's worth a detour for the views alone, or for a quick drink in the hotel, popular with supermodels and assorted Euro-showbiz types.

To get to Na Xamena from Port de Sant Miquel, head 800m south toward Sant Miquel village along the main road, and take the signposted paved turnoff on the right. This twists and turns through dense pine forest, passing a turnoff for "Playa Blanca" after 1km – this route leads north toward **Illa des Bosc** (map 8, H2), an islet in the Port Sant Miquel bay. The islet, capped by an exclusive private villa, is connected to Ibiza's northern shore via a tiny sandy **beach**, where there's good swimming. Back on the road to Na Xamena, the tarmac climbs steeply through the pines until you reach some scattered, small whitewashed villas and then the imposing frontage of the *Hacienda*. Adjacent to the hotel, a steep, rough trail descends over rocks, roots and shoots to the foaming, exposed waters below, where you can take an invigorating dip. To reach the trailhead, walk south through the hotel car park, then right down a dirt track after the second holiday cottage, named *Ses Sevines*; it takes around fifteen minutes to walk down to the shore. There's no beach, just boulders and rocks, but there's excellent **snorkelling** in the deep, cobalt waters.

Swinging to the right just before the hotel, a bumpy road heads north to the lofty peninsula of **Punta de sa Creu** (Map 8, F1), where a heliport serves the rich residents of the luxurious houses here. The views from the heliport are some of the most spectacular in all Ibiza, the jutting promontory enveloped by the Mediterranean on three sides, with a brilliant perspective of the golden sands of Benirràs over in the east, and the mighty ochre cliffs around Portitxol and Cap Rubió just to the west.

PORTITXOL AND AROUND

Map 8, D2.

Some 5km northwest of Sant Miquel, the hidden bay of **Portitxol** is one of the most dramatic sights in Ibiza – a fifty-metre-wide, horseshoe-shaped pebbly cove, strewn with giant boulders and dwarfed by a monumental backdrop of cliffs that seem to isolate the beach from the rest of the world. Entirely free of villas and concrete eyesores, the only structures are a ring of tiny stone-and-brushwood huts, owned by fishermen who use the bay as a sanctuary from the rough but rich waters, which plummet to over 90m in depth just a short distance from the beach. In high season, a few adventurous souls work their way to this remote spot for a little secluded snorkelling, but for most of the year Portitxol is completely deserted, a pristine – but also sunbed- and refreshment-free – zone. There's plenty to explore, however: tracks skirt around colossal yellow boulders of earth and rock, and past weird rock formations; the craggy peak that looms 315m above the bay to the west is **Cap Rubió** (Blonde Cape), named for its sandy colour.

Getting to Portitxol is a bit tricky. From Sant Miquel, take the Sant Mateu road to the west, then after about a kilometre and a half, turn off onto a tarmac road to the right, which zigzags up through woods to Isla Blanca, a small, unlovely complex of half-built, whitewashed holiday villas high in the coastal hills. Past here, the road starts to descend to the sea; park up at the small bar-kiosk (summer only), as the road down is in terrible condition from here onwards. From the kiosk, walk for fifteen minutes along the potholed road until you reach an unmarked path, which heads west by a high stone wall just before the second of two hairpin turns. Twenty minutes' more walking along the path, through some stunning cliffside scenery, and you're at the seashore.

Entrepenyas and s'Àguila

Map 8, E2.

There are two equally secluded places to swim within walking distance of Portitxol, both reachable via the same rough road from the kiosk at Isla Blanca. Five minutes' walk past the point where the Portitxol path turns off, the road divides by an abandoned stone hut. Follow the left path for more excellent snorkelling in the deep indigo waters of **Entrepenyas** (Between Cliffs), a small rocky bay strewn with boulders and rocks. The right turn from the hut leads to **s'Àguila** (The Eagle), the more impressive of the two bays, surrounded by grey cliffs etched with rusty orange rocks that plummet into the Mediterranean. There's no beach here, but plenty more giant boulders for sunbathing. Even in August, only a handful of people visit this lonely spot.

SANT MATEU D'AUBARCA AND AROUND

There's little to the tiny village of **SANT MATEU D'AUBARCA** (Map 7, D5), 7km west of Sant Miquel, other than a confusingly aimless collection of lanes, a solitary but friendly store-cum-bar and a typically well-fortified, whitewashed **church**. Completed in 1796, it has a slim, squarish belfry and a fine triple-arched entrance porch, supported by two rows of compact columns, the latter added in 1885. Two tiny chapels, dedicated to the virgins of Montserrat and Rosario, are set at the end of the draughtboard-tiled nave, on the right.

Tourism has barely touched the countryside around Sant Mateu, which remains a rustic landscape, with small fields of brick-red earth separated by low sandstone walls. Much of the land is given over to **vineyards**, and on the first weekend each December, the village hosts an annual festival in honour of the humble but delicious local *vi pagès* (country wine). It's a tremendously sociable event, with around a thousand people gathering from all over the island to drink the new vintage from teapot-shaped glass jugs called *porros*, and feast on *sobrassada* and *butifarra* sausages barbecued over pine- and apricot-wood fires lit on the village football pitch. All the *vi pagès* is free, and the vibrant atmosphere is helped by folk dancing and a live band that usually concentrates on rock cover versions.

At other times of the year you'll have to be content with **visiting a vineyard.** One and a half kilometres west of the village, the **Sa Cova** vineyard (Map 8, A5; ⓣ971 187 046) run by the Bonet family, produces 22,000 bottles a year – two reds, a rosé and a white. They have plans to build an information centre for tourists and start tours, but will give you an unofficial look around and a taste in the meantime. It's best to call ahead to arrange a visit, particularly in the quiet winter months.

Between May and October, on Tuesdays and Thursdays only, three **buses** pass through Sant Mateu on their route between Sant Antoni and Port de Sant Miquel.

CALA D'AUBARCA

Map 8, B4.

Once the main point of sea access for Sant Mateu, the untouched bay of **Cala d'Aubarca**, 4km north of the town, is one of Ibiza's most magnificent. In an island of diminutive cove beaches, its sheer scale is remarkable: a massive tier of cliffs envelop the three-kilometre-wide bay, and a thundering ocean often batters the rocky shore. There's no beach, and it's quite tricky to fathom out a path to the sea; as a result, Cala d'Aubarca remains one of Ibiza's best-kept secrets, completely deserted for most of the year.

Whether it's an internal Ibizan conspiracy to keep the place clandestine, or an oversight by the island's tourism department, there's only one official sign to direct you to Cala d'Aubarca. To **get there** by car or on foot from Sant Mateu, follow the road beside the church that's signposted "Camí d'Aubarca"; after 700m, you reach a junction. Bear left (you'll soon pass a tree on the right with "Aubarca" daubed onto the bark), and follow the road through a large vineyard until you pass a white house with yellow windows on the right. Turn right just after this house, up a dirt road that leads to the wooded cliffs above Cala d'Aubarca. Past the cliffs, the road is in terrible condition, so park up in the woods and walk the final fifteen minutes down to the beach.

When you reach the rugged promontory at the bottom of the dirt road, look out for the **natural stone bridge** carved out of the rock by the waves. With the sand-coloured formations of Cap Rubió to the northeast, and brilliant white patches of chalk at the back of the bay, the multicoloured cliffs are also striking. Several tricky paths, very rough in parts, lead to the sea to the left of the bridge, but for an easier route, backtrack uphill along the dirt trail for 200 metres and you'll meet a clear path that cuts through the woods to the shore, directly below the chalky section of cliffs.

Es Cucons, a remote rural hotel located near Sant Agnès, is reviewed on p.220.

SANTA AGNÈS

Map 7, B5.

Some 7km southwest of Sant Mateu, the tiny hamlet of **SANTA AGNÈS** ("Santa Inés" in Castilian), is made up of a scattering of houses, a couple of streets, the simple *La Palmera* restaurant and the friendly *Can Cosmi* bar (see p.255). There are no specific sights other than the village church, which dates from 1806. It's properly known as

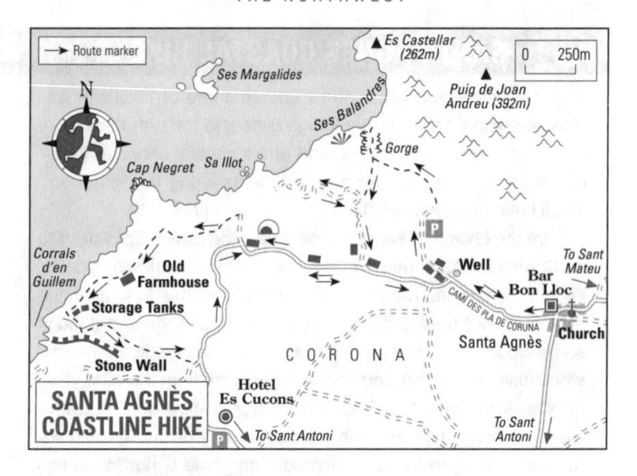

Santa Agnès de Corona (Saint Agnes of the Crown) – a reference to its location in the centre of a two-hundred-metre-high plain, enclosed by low hills on all sides which form a crown-like surround to the settlement. With a patchwork of small, stone-walled fields of ochre earth densely planted with figs, fruit and thousands of *ametlla* (almond) trees, the plain is very beautiful. If you visit in late January or early February, the sea of pink-white almond blossoms is an unforgettable sight, almost as famous in Ibiza as the cherry blossoms in Japan.

Between July and September only there are three buses (Mon–Sat) between Santa Agnès and Ibiza Town; only one bus (Mon–Fri) runs this route during the rest of the year. There's also one bus (Mon–Sat) between Sant Antoni and Santa Agnès (July–Sept only).

SANTA AGNÈS COASTAL HIKE

This circular walk (8km; 2.5hr) explores some of Ibiza's most remote coastal scenery, along high cliffs and through thick forest, past valleys and gorges, and offers several chances for a dip in the sea. There are no refreshments along the route, so you'll have to carry everything you're likely to need.

From the church in Santa Agnès, follow the paved Camí des Pla de Coruna for 600m until you reach an old stone **well** with a pointed roof, where the road bends to the left. At this fork, continue straight ahead up the dirt track, past farm buildings and through some woods. The track cuts through two clearings; keep the drystone wall on your left and, ten minutes' walk from the fork, you'll glimpse the narrow **Ses Balandres gorge**, nicknamed "Heaven's Gate" by Ibizan hippies, with the sea glinting below. The fifteen-minute descent to the water through the gorge is not for vertigo sufferers; the rocky path is quite good at first, but you'll soon have to use a wooden ladder and steps cut into the cliff. Though there's no actual beach at the base of the gorge, it's a great place for a swim or snorkel below the cliffs. If this all seems too much effort, forgo the climb down to the beach and head instead for the lookout (*mirador*) 100m north of the gorge entrance, which affords outstanding views inland to the pine-topped hill of Puig de Joan Andreu, the fortress-like rocky summit of Es Castellar to the right, and the horseshoe-shaped island of **Ses Margalides** below.

Backtracking from the lookout, a rough path, directly opposite the gorge entrance, cuts through a patch of woodland popular with mushroom collectors, who find delicious orange *cepes* each autumn. You'll have to pick your way carefully around fallen trees at times, but after five minutes' walking you'll arrive at a wide dirt road. To the right, it's a steep but easy fifteen-minute hike down to the shore at **Sa Illot**. There's no beach at the bottom, just a strange, almost apocalyptic scene of rusty abandoned cars, smashed stone huts and giant cuboid boulders. Alternatively, ignoring the Sa Illot route, turn left up the same wide dirt road and it's a five-minute stroll back to the Camí des Pla de Coruna.

Turn right along the Camí des Pla de Coruna, and walk for 800m past some villas and farmhouses. The **Corona** plain is beautiful around here, with fields of vines, fruit and almond trees divided by limestone walls. Just after the road dips towards the coast, you get a glimpse of the sea on your right beside the sandstone walls of a villa. Take the rough dirt track off the road here and follow it downhill, ignoring the first path on the left after a few metres. On your right there's a small cave and a hearth that's regularly used by trekkers for campfires. Continue down the dirt track towards the sea and take the next path on your left – it's about 200m from the road. This path continues southwest around the coastal cliffs, dotted with scrub pine and juniper bushes, about 100m above the sea. The trail splits in places, but blue arrows mark the correct way, passing through the rocky headland of **Cap Negret** after another ten minutes' walking. Follow the blue arrows around (not over) a wall, and along the trail, as you make your way through overgrown farm terraces before descending to a lovely clearing in the pines, where there's a long-abandoned farmhouse; the stone structure with a domed roof used to be the house's bread oven. Continuing west, you'll pass through a clump of giant reeds, then reach a series of large, overgrown farm terraces, propped up by substantial stone walls. Walk through the terraces past some old water-storage tanks, and blue arrows direct you inland up the wooded hillside. The steep route is ill-defined at first, but soon joins a dried-up stream bed before continuing up a pine-clad valley. Some fifteen minutes from the coast, the trail levels out and descends gently to the Camí des Pla de Coruna; turn left when you reach this road, and it's a fifteen-minute walk back to Santa Agnès.

SANTA GERTRUDIS DE LA FRUITERA

Map 7, E7.

Smack in the centre of the island, 11km from Ibiza Town and just off the highway to Sant Miquel, lies **SANTA GERTRUDIS DE LA FRUITERA** ("of the fruits"). The village is a diminutive but interesting settlement with an international – and rather bourgeois – character, and offers a glut of bars, restaurants and boutiques out of all proportion to its size. Even in the winter months, tank-like 4WDs and ancient Citröen 2CVs compete for prime parking positions, and a collection of moneyed expats (particularly Germans), farmers, artists and artists-who-farm fill the streetside **café** terraces of *Bar Costa* and *Es Canto*.

Santa Gertrudis's bars and restaurants are reviewed on p.254 and p.238 respectively.

Beside the bars and boutiques, with their Indonesian and Indian clothes and fabrics, trinkets and handicrafts, there's also an excellent **auction house**, the English-owned *Casi Todo* (Ⓣ971 197 023; Ⓦwww.casitodo.com), a few doors down from *Bar Costa*, where everything from gypsy carts and antiques to plastic garden furniture and rusty 1950s motorbikes goes under the hammer once a month. Auction day (check the website for details) is something of a social event, as air kisses are exchanged, property prices discussed and exhibits examined.

Just outside the village, on the road to Sant Mateu, there's yet another rather chichi group of stores, including *Nino d'Agata*, a pricey boutique that specializes in jewellery and sculpture, and the well-stocked *Casa Azul* bookstore. There are also several **cashpoints** (ATMs) in Santa Gertrudis – convenient if you want to embark on a serious spending spree.

The landmark eighteenth-century **Església de Santa Gertrudis**, in the centre of the village, is less austere than most Ibizan churches, with an elevated frontage and small windows picked out with yellow paint. Their interior, though hardly ornate, does have a few sculptural decorations, including some apples and figs on the ceiling (Santa Gertrudis has long been a fruit-growing centre).

If you're in Ibiza in November, try to time your visit to coincide with the village's annual **fiesta** held on the 16th of the month. Aside from the usual Ibizan dancing and folk-rock bands, animals are exhibited, which, due to the village's international character, inevitably take on a global flavour – the prize pigs have included Vietnamese pot-bellied porkers.

Buses between Ibiza Town and Sant Miquel pass Santa Gertrudis (five daily; Mon–Sat only).

Sant Antoni and around

Labelled as the Mediterranean's premier rave resort by the British media, the sex, drugs and dance package unique to **SANT ANTONI** (**SAN ANTONIO**) is as dynamic as you'll find anywhere in Europe. High-rise, concrete-clad and shamelessly brash, San An (as it's usually called) primarily draws crowds of young clubbers bent on engaging in unbridled hedonism, propelled by a cocktail of cheap booze and copious pills and powders. Things can get seriously out of control in the Brit-only enclave of the **West End**, with its unbroken chain of bars, disco-bars and fast-food fryers, but this is really only one side of the story – there are less frenetic sides to the resort, such as the stylish chillout bars of the **Sunset Strip**.

The Sant Antoni municipality has been trying hard to shake off its less-than-wholesome reputation in recent years, introducing restrictions to the notorious holiday-rep-guided bar-crawls and drinking competitions, and belatedly attempting to attract "grey pound" winter visitors. Though the essential character of the resort remains unchanged, the atmosphere has become a little more refined since the excesses of the 1980s, when alcohol-fuelled street brawls were nightly occurrences in the high season. The authorities have also made environmental improvements: further hotel development is now restricted, several streets have been pedestrianized and the **harbour** has been given a face-lift, with a new palm-lined promenade. Cosmetic improvements aside, Sant Antoni's harbour, prized by the Romans, remains the island's finest – a sickle-shaped expanse of sapphire water framed to the south by the crest of 475-metre **Sa Talaiassa** (see p.164), and to the north by the wooded uplands of **Santa Agnès** (see p.132).

Around Sant Antoni, away from the crowded sands at the heart of the resort, you'll find some impressive **cove beaches**; north of town, gorgeous **Cala Gració**, **Cala Gracioneta** and **Cala Salada** are all within a few kilometres of the centre. To the southwest, **Sant Antoni bay** is heavily built-up, a continuous, happy-holiday-geared sprawl that stretches as far as the pretty swimming spot of **Port des Torrent**. A little further west, there's a string of stunning beaches, including **Cala Bassa** and **Cala Conta**, where you can swim in some of the cleanest water in the Mediterranean.

Some history

The cave paintings at the Cova de les Fontanelles, just north of Sant Antoni, thought to be either **prehistoric** or dating from the early **Bronze Age**, are the earliest evidence of human presence in the region, but there's nothing to suggest a significant settlement here at this time. Though local legend attests that **Carthaginian** general Hannibal was born on the island of Conillera, just west of Sant Antoni's bay, it seems that the area was more or less bypassed by his people, as Punic pottery fragments found at the cave chapel of Capella de Santa Agnès are the only proof of their presence here. The **Roman** invaders were certainly impressed by Sant Antoni's natural harbour, naming it *portus magnus* (great port), but they never settled here in numbers either. Their name did stick, however; most rural Ibizans still call the town "Portmany", a corruption of the Latin.

For more on Ibiza's early history, see Contexts, p.301.

For the next two thousand years, Sant Antoni was never anything grander than a small fishing village. The **Catalans** constructed a rudimentary chapel in 1305, as a focal point for the scattered population of no more than fifty families living around the harbour, but the area remained something of a backwater. Successive outbreaks of bubonic plague across the island took their toll, as did sporadic pirate raids. To offer some protection against attackers, in the seventeenth century a defence tower was added to the church built on the site of the Catalan chapel.

In the early twentieth century, travellers from overseas started to arrive, and **tourism** began to impact upon the local economy. The first substantial construction projects began in the late 1950s, and hotels quickly mushroomed around the bay; as in the other mainland Spanish resorts, Franco-directed mass tourism initiatives, characterized by unregulated building and planning controls, unleashed a frenzy of ugly construction. Fishing boats became sightseeing cruisers, and an army of waiters and support staff were recruited from rural Andalucía and Murcia to cater for the northern European visitors who were starting to arrive in droves. By the 1970s, Sant Antoni's high-rise skyline was barely distinguishable from Benidorm or Magaluf, its success built on a cheap package-holiday menu of bacon and eggs, *The Birdie Song*, the sun and *The Sun* – all washed down with jugs of sangria and barrels of San Miguel.

Sant Antoni became a mecca for the Club 18–30 holiday crowd in the 1980s, and the serious problems began.

Drunken rampages by Union Jack-bedecked British louts hit the headlines in Spain and the UK, as policemen and non-British tourists were regularly attacked or beaten up. Tourism declined considerably, and by the early 1990s Sant Antoni had acquired a nefarious reputation, described by one guidebook as a destination characterized by "booze-ups, brawls and hangovers", because "even soccer hooligans need holidays".

The resort's recovery was kickstarted by the British **clubbing revolution**. Though Sant Antoni was a pivotal part of the acid-house scene in the late 1980s, the resort was quite polarized: specialist venues such as the *Milk Bar* reverberated with Balearic Beat classics, while the West End pubs rang to the strains of drunken football chants. However, by 1994, as clubbing became much more mainstream in the UK, the word was out: Ibiza was *the* place to party, with the best club venues, the cream of the DJs and a seemingly liberal attitude on the part of the authorities towards drug use. Propelled by a wave of publicity, young British tourists descended en masse.

Today, non-British visitors are rare in Sant Antoni, and the town is now almost totally geared to the seasonal influx of thousands of UK clubbers. Holidaying families have been all but squeezed out of the picture, deterred by the images of teenage excess beamed back to living rooms by British television programme makers – notably Sky TV. This dependence on clubbing has left San An particularly exposed to the fickle nature of British youth culture and the strength of the pound. By the 2000 season, other Mediterranean resorts, including Ayia Napa and Faliriki had emerged as rival clubbing destinations. These factors, plus the impact of September 11th, combined to make 2002 a poor year for the resort, and several hotels failed to open at all during the season.

Although Sant Antoni could certainly do with some better PR, in many ways the resort has improved considerably in recent years. A swathe of stylish new bars and restaurants have emerged along the Sunset strip and Caló des Moro on the north side of town; while the new beach promenade has cheered up the southern fringes of the resort. Continuing environmental improvements are needed if the resort is to retain its allure, but it's unrealistic to expect a complete change of identity. San An is no St-Tropez, or even Ibiza Town, but remains an inimitably lively resort well-suited to young British holidaymakers – most of whom have the time of their lives here.

For reviews of accommodation see p.221; restaurants p.238; bars p.255 and clubs p.266.

The Town

Sant Antoni's **layout** is simple. The **Egg** (Map 10, H6) is the most useful landmark, at the centre of the roundabout at the eastern end of the harbourfront where the roads for Ibiza Town and Sant Josep converge. Northwest of the Egg is the main body of the town, including the church and the busiest shopping district, the latter concentrated around c/Sant Antoni. South of here, the waterfront promenade (**Passeig de ses Fonts** at its eastern end and **Passeig de la Mar** to the west) skirts the ferry docks, the marina and the bus terminal, while the rocky coast that encloses the west side of town is occupied by the bars of the **Sunset Strip** and **Caló des Moro**. South of the Egg, another promenade curves down past more bars and hotels to the windmill and maritime museum at the **Punta des Molí**.

THE EGG

Smack in the centre of town, in the middle of a grassy roundabout, San An's prominent flat-bottomed, ovoid sculpture, universally known as **The Egg**, was erected by the local government in the early 1990s in honour of the tenuous claim that **Christopher Columbus** was born on the island. Inside the hollow, creamy-white structure is a miniature wooden caravel, modelled on the fifteenth-century vessels in which the explorer sailed.

The shape of the sculpture originates in a story about Columbus himself. When ridiculed for suggesting there was a westerly route to the Indies, Columbus countered by saying he could also make an egg stand upright; challenged, he promptly cracked the base of an egg and placed it on a table.

Arrival and information

Sant Antoni's small open-air **bus terminal** (Map 10, D7) overlooks the harbour at the western end of the Passeig de la Mar. Though it's little more than a glorified bus stop, this is the point where all buses arrive and depart for destinations throughout the island. The **ferry dock** for services to and from mainland Spain is almost opposite the bus terminal, while boat services around the San An bay leave from the eastern end of the Passeig de ses Fonts, near the Egg. If you're arriving by **car**, you're best off leaving your vehicle in the car park just off Avgda Dr Fleming, 100m south of the pyramid-topped *Es Paradis* club.

The efficient **tourist information** kiosk (May–Oct Mon–Fri 9.30am–2.30pm & 3–8.30pm, Sat & Sun 9.30am–1pm; Nov–April Mon–Sat 9.30am–1pm; ⓣ971 314 005) is at the eastern end of the Passeig de ses Fonts, just west of the Egg, and has a good stock of leaflets about the island and municipality. It's easy to find out what's going on in the club scene – the island's main listings magazines (see p.38) covers Sant Antoni fairly comprehensively, and teams of club PR people patrol the streets.

PASSEIG DE SES FONTS

Map 10, G6–F6.

The eastern portion of Sant Antoni's harbourside promenade, broad **Passeig de ses Fonts** benefited from landscaping in the early 1990s, when the luxuriant collection of tropical palms, rubber plants and flowering shrubs was planted. To the west, past the tourist information kiosk, the unsightly string of concrete office and apartment blocks that line the prom are occupied at street level by rows of pavement cafés, where you can eat American fast food or tuck into a full English breakfast while gazing at a Mediterranean harbour. Almost lost in this near-featureless architectural sprawl is the whitewashed **Ajuntament** building, on the corner of c/Bisbe Cardona, identifiable by its municipal flags and modern clock, where town councillors plotted Sant Antoni's transformation from fishing village to full-blown resort.

West of here, Passeig de ses Fonts continues past a series of flashy modern fountains, dramatically illuminated at night, and the docks from which ferries shuttle around the bay. On summer evenings, this area is lined with street sellers and caricaturists, and filled with drinkers heading up c/Santa Agnès to the West End bars (see p.146).

ESGLÉSIA DE SANT ANTONI

Map 10, G5.

From Passeig de ses Fonts, c/Ample leads north to the small plaza that houses the town's large historic church, **Església**

de Sant Antoni, a handsome, whitewashed structure with a twin belfry and a pleasantly shady side porch. What sets the church apart from others in the island is its two-storey, rectangular **defence tower**, on the southeast side of the building; until the early nineteenth century, cannons were mounted at the top of the tower to defend the town from marauding pirates. The building mainly dates from the late seventeenth century, and was constructed over the remains of two simple chapels – the first built in 1305 and the second in 1570, which were badly damaged by pirate attacks.

You approach the church through the twin arches of a cobbled, courtyard-like patio, with the elegant porch and priests' quarters on the left, and an old well to the right. The sombre interior has little decoration, though a little light enters through three small stained-glass windows. A collection of dark oil paintings of Sant Francesc and Sant Antoni line the nave; the altar, coated in gold leaf, replaced a previous Baroque piece destroyed during the Spanish Civil War.

THE WEST END

The Blackpool of Ibiza, cheerfully vulgar, unashamedly unglamorous.

Paul Richardson, Not Part of the Package – *A Year in Ibiza*

The island's most raucous bar zone, Sant Antoni's notorious **West End** is spread over a network of streets centred around **Carrer Santa Agnès** (Map 10, F6–F5), plus the southern end of c/Bartomeu Vicent Ramón and c/de Cristòfol Colom. There's nothing subtle or complicated about this almost entirely British enclave of wall-to-wall disco-bars and English- and Irish-style pubs, interspersed with the odd hole-in-the-wall kebab joint or Chinese restaurant serving fry-up breakfasts. In the summer months, a "Brits abroad" mentality comes to the fore, with the streets transformed into a seething mass of football-shirt-clad, pink-fleshed humanity; understandably, few Ibizans would dream of drinking around here. Once the morning cleaners have the swept up the broken bottles and cleaned up the puke, there's nothing at all to see in the day, and most of the bars are closed.

Attitudes towards the West End tend to be strictly polarized, and after a quick glance at c/Sant Agnès by night you'll be able to tell straight away if it's the kind of place you'll love or hate. If you do decide to hit the bars here, you'll find that, in general, drinks are priced well below Sunset Strip or Ibiza Town averages, and as the disco-bars are usually free to enter it's an inexpensive place to strut your stuff. Though the music is generally party-anthem, happy-holiday house, plenty of decent DJs have cut their teeth and gained a reputation in the better bars, which include the *Simple Art Club* for its House Nation nights, and *Kremlin,* where you'll hear UK garage – both are located on c/Santa Agnès.

PASSEIG DE LA MAR

Map 10, E7.

Back along the harbourfront, the promenade narrows west of c/Santa Agnès, becoming **Passeig de la Mar** once you've passed a statue of a fisherman, complete with nets and catch, who stands on the pavement beside a crop of gaudy Chinese restaurants and several banks. Opposite the statue, it's worth taking a quick look at the **Moll Vell**, the old dock, where you'll often see fishermen mending their nets and fixing reed lobster pots. Further west, you pass the marina and modern Club Nautic (Yacht Club) building, the main bus terminal and a group of bars before you reach the **Moll Nou** (Map 10, C8), the 400-metre-long dock that juts into the harbour, from where huge ferries head for mainland Spain. At the end of the Passeig de la Mar, a flight of steps leads northwards up into c/Alemanya; from here, it's a short walk to the left along c/General Balanzat to the bars of the Sunset Strip.

THE SUNSET STRIP

Map 10, B6.

Stretching for 250m along the rocky shoreline between c/General Balanzat and c/Vara de Rey, Sant Antoni's legendary **Sunset Strip** of chillout bars is one of the most cosmopolitan places to drink in Ibiza. In the day, the setting appears far from ideal – the bars cling to a jagged, low-lying rocky shelf some 50m away from the sea, and it's a tricky scramble over the rocks to take a swim. However, the location starts to make sense towards sunset, when all eyes turn west to watch the sun sinking into the blood-red sea, to a background of ambient soundscapes.

Until 1993, there was only one **chillout bar**, the ground-breaking *Café del Mar* (see p.256), along this entire stretch of coast, and it was very much the preserve of in-the-know clubbers and islanders. By the following year, however, the renowned *Café Mambo* had opened, and by the late 1990s a barrage of publicity led by the massive success of the seminal *Café del Mar* CDs (see p.332) had spread the word, and other bars were quick to get in on the act. Today, there are half a dozen chillout bars here, and the area is very much on the map, with the sunset spectacle an essential part of the "Ibiza experience" for most visitors.

For reviews of bars in Sant Antoni, see p.255.

It's undeniable that the original vibe, created by José Padilla at the *Café del Mar* and nurtured by a small clique of like-minded chillout DJs and producers, has been considerably diluted. Though little can detract from the appeal of spectacular sunsets and evocative chillout music, the hype is incredible in the height of summer, when thousands of visitors congregate, television crews stalk the strip and web cams beam the sunset scene around the globe. The commercialism is unavoidable – all the bars now sell their own T-shirts and CD mixes – but despite these changes, a certain unique atmosphere does survive, especially early and late in the summer season, when things are less high-octane.

The San Antoni authorities are considering building a promenade north from the Passeig de la Mar to Caló des Moro, passing through the Sunset Strip.

CALÓ DES MORO

Map 10, B2.

Some 500m north of the Sunset Strip, the rocky shoreline continues to **Caló des Moro**, a tiny cove with a small patch of sand that's surrounded by a loose scattering of hotel and apartment blocks. The bay makes an inviting place for a dip, with shallow, turquoise water. However, most people choose to patronize the swanky swimming pools of the landmark shoreside bars at the sweeping modernist *Coastline* and neighbouring *Kanya* (see p.257). These hip new establishments have helped Caló des Moro become San An's most happening location in recent years, rivalling the Sunset Strip as *the* premier chillout zone.

To get to Caló des Moro from the Sunset Strip, you'll either have to negotiate the 500-metre-long patch of rocky shoreline that lies between the two, or head to the right along Vara de Rey and then left into Avgda d'Isidor Macabich, turning left again into c/Santa Rosalia, which leads to the bay.

S'ARENAL TO PUNTA DES MOLÍ

From the Egg, a landscaped, palm-lined harbourside promenade runs around the southern fringes of Sant Antoni as far as the Punta des Molí promontory. When it was built, the prom sliced a few metres off an already slimline **s'Arenal beach** (Map 10, H8–H10), which begins just south of the Egg. However, recent municipal efforts to widen the beach by spraying tons of sand towards s'Arenal from an offshore ship seem to have helped redress the erosion. Barely twenty metres wide in places, s'Arenal is nevertheless the closest beach to Sant Antoni, and, despite the harbour waters being less-than-pristine, the entire 500-metre stretch is packed in the summer months. A section of the sea is partitioned off from jetskiers and boats here so that swimmers can enjoy themselves safely, and there are plenty of pedalos for hire. Bordering the sands at the northern end of the beach are three very stylish bar-cafés, *Kiwi*, *Bar M* and *Itaca* (see p.256), all popular places offering good snacks and music.

Just inland from s'Arenal, on the other side of Avgda Dr Fleming, are the town's two vast temples of dance, pyramid-roofed *Es Paradis* and domed *Eden*; nearby is the ugly steel shell of a half-built club, *Idea*, which has been left incomplete for years. South of the clubs, the promenade skirts a row of block-like hotel complexes and a scruffy, seldom-used row of fishing huts before skirting an imposing old **windmill** (Map 10, G12), with a white tower, a conical brushwood-roof and warped wooden sails. The windmill crowns the **Punta des Molí** (Map 10, G12), a quiet, landscaped spot planted with olive trees, lavender and rosemary bushes which juts into Sant Antoni's bay. This promontory is the site of the island's new Museu Marítim, due to open very soon – for more details, contact the tourist office (see p.143). Beside the fenced-off museum enclave, there's a restored well and an old water wheel, as well as panoramic views over the entire Sant Antoni bay.

North of Sant Antoni

There are several decent attractions **north of Sant Antoni**, all reachable via turnoffs from the main road to Sant Agnès. The road soon leaves the town's grim suburbs behind, and climbs steeply towards Ibiza's wooded interior. Though they're within a fifteen-minute walk of Sant Antoni, the cave-chapel **Capella de Santa Agnès** and the twin sandy beaches of **Cala Gració** and **Cala Gracioneta** receive few tourists. Likewise, hardly anyone visits idyllic **Cala Salada**, some 5km away and accessible either by road or the wonderful coastal hike detailed on p.154.

CAPELLA DE SANTA AGNÈS

Map 9, H3. Sat 9am–noon; €1.20.

A chapel set in a cave, the **Capella de Santa Agnès**, down a signposted turnoff 1.5km north of town along the Sant Antoni–Santa Agnès road, has been a place of worship since the third or fourth century AD. Carthaginian pottery fragments found here also suggest that humans visited the site much earlier, but it's not known whether the cave had any religious significance during the Punic era. However, there's little evidence of the chapel's historical importance today: the walls of the tiny, rectangular nave are built into the cave mouth, and there's just about enough room for a dozen worshippers in addition to the low stone altar and statues of Christ and the Virgin Mary.

Capella de Santa Agnès sits beside the car park of a much larger eighteenth-century church, which was never consecrated, and has now been converted into the *Sa Capella* restaurant (see p.239).

CALA GRACIÓ AND CALA GRACIONETA

Map 9, F3.

From Caló des Moro, just north of the Sunset Strip, a path winds around the rocky edge of Sant Antoni bay, beside the leafy grounds of some of the resort's most upmarket hotels; 1km from town, you emerge above a small but gorgeous beach, **Cala Gració**. Gració's elongated patch of fine white sand stretches back 100m from the sea, and the shallow water is wonderfully calm and clear. The beach is popular with British and German families holidaying in the smart hotels and villas close to the bay, but things only get busy at the height of summer. A small snack bar rents out pedalos, sunbeds and umbrellas between May and October.

Set in an old smugglers' cave on the south side of the bay, Cala Gració is also home to the modest **Aquarium Cap Blanc** (daily 10.30am–7pm; €3), which offers a collection of sluggish-looking Mediterranean sea life, including lobster, moray eels, wrasse and octopuses. This natural aquarium was previously used by local fishermen as a storage tank for surplus fish. The whole thing is well organized and popular with children, with wooden walkways above pools containing the sea creatures.

Beside the fishing huts on the north side of Cala Gració, a path clings to the shoreline, leading after 100m to a second hidden bay, Cala Gracioneta. Exceptionally beautiful and peaceful, **Cala Gracioneta**, at barely 30m wide, is even smaller than its neighbour, with a tiny patch of exquisitely fine, pale sand between a low shoreline dotted with pines, and shallow, sheltered waters that heat up almost to bathtub temperatures by late summer. Few people know about this little gem of a beach, and it rarely gets crowded, despite the proximity of the wonderful El Chiringuito restaurant (see p.239), where food is served practically on the sand.

If you don't want to walk, you can also **get to** the beaches by road. From the town centre, take c/Ramon y Calal (Map 10, G5), which becomes the Sant Antoni–Santa Agnès road. Follow the signpost for both the bays, which takes you off the Santa Agnès road and left along c/Johann Sebastian Bach (Map 10, G1), round a roundabout (Map 10, D1), and then northwest along Carretera de Cala Gració for another 1.5km to Cala Gració. To get to Cala Gracioneta by road, you have to do a loop around the coast: follow the same route along Carretera de Cala Gració, but turn right beside the *Hotel Tanit* (Map 9, G3), and then up Carretera de Cap Negret. The road heads northeast for 1km, then west for 2km towards Cap Negret; just before you get to Cap Negret, a signpost on the left directs you south to Cala Gracioneta.

To get to Cala Yoga by road, take the Cala Salada turnoff from the Sant Antoni–Santa Agnès highway (Map 9, H2), continue downhill until you reach a white arched gateway across the road, where the road splits; then bear left downhill towards the sea. You can park above Cala Yoga.

CALA SALADA

Map 9, G1.

Ringed by a protective barrier of steep, pine-clad hills, the small, all-but-undeveloped cove-beach of **Cala Salada** makes an idyllic escape from the crowds of Sant Antoni, just 5km to the south. A deep turquoise colour, the inviting waters here lap against a fine 100m strip of pale sand, and there's a low rocky shelf good for sunbathing. Apart from a line of stick-and-thatch fishermen's huts, a solitary villa and a simple seafood restaurant popular with locals (May–Oct daily; Nov–April Sat & Sun), there's nothing here but the sea and sand. It's reachable via the coastal hike detailed on p.154, or by a serpentine road through the trees, signposted off the Sant Antoni–Santa Agnès road. To the north, about two hundred metres across the bay is an even more peaceful sandy beach, **Cala Saldeta** – you can either swim over or follow a path that winds around the fishing huts.

Cala Salada is one of the best places in the Pitiuses to watch the **sunset**, though you'll have to move around the shore for the optimum view, depending on the season. Winter is possibly the best time of year, when the sun sinks into the ocean between the gateway-like outline of the islands of Conillera and Bosc. Just above the beach, the setting rays paint a villa (appropriately named *Casa Roja*) intense shades of red, crimson and purple.

COVA DE LES FONTANELLES

Map 1, B3.

Half a kilometre inland from Cala Salada, a signposted dirt track strikes off the main road to **Cova de les Fontanelles** ("Cave of the Springs"), named for the spring water that used to bubble up from the cliffs along this part of the coast. Protected by a metal fence (the interior is off-limits

A HIKE TO CALA SALADA

The 5km of coastline between Cala Gració and Cala Salada makes a delightful fifty-minute hike, passing a series of small, rocky coves. The route sticks very close to the shoreline until the last part of the walk, when you have to head inland after Cala Yoga. Starting at **Cala Gració** (Map 9, F3), the trail follows the shoreline, soon reaching **Cala Gracioneta**, then weaves past jagged coastal rocks and through a scrubby landscape of stunted pines and juniper bushes, skirting the smart detached villas of **Cap Negret** (Map 9, F2) and *Hostal La Torre* after about fifteen minutes' walking, where you can get a drink on the terrace. Sticking very close to the shore, the trail continues north, squeezing between villas and the cliffside. Ten minutes after *Hostal La Torre*, the path reaches **Punta de sa Galera** (Map 9, G2), a crooked, sandy-coloured finger of rock that stretches into the sea. Past here, the path winds around two miniature pebbly coves; the second, larger of the two, known as **Cala Yoga** (Map 9, G1), is popular with nudists and hippies. It's completely undeveloped, with bizarre eroded cliffs of stratified rock and a series of shelf-like rock terraces (many

to the public), the cave is a very modest affair, at around ten metres wide, but it harbours the only ancient **petroglyphs** in the Pitiuses. Unfortunately, due to centuries of weathering, the designs can barely be made out, but you can just about detect boats, and the grapes which have given the cave its other name, Cova des Vi (Cave of Wine). Scholars disagree about the age of the rock art, but the images, which have been copied onto display panels, are thought to be either prehistoric or from the early Bronze Age. Les Fontanelles' setting is magical, right beneath the 255-metre hill of Puig Nunó, and overlooking the sea towards the island of Conillera. The best time to visit is **sunset**, when painted with New Age doodles) that are good for sunbathing; the sapphire waters make this a good spot to break your walk with a swim. In summer, an enterprising costume-less hippy sells cool drinks here from an icebox most afternoons; there's even a reiki masseur and reflexologist here, available (in theory) daily from 7pm to 8pm.

From Cala Yoga, it's a further fifteen minutes' walk to Cala Salada. Continue uphill along the poorly surfaced road, leaving the shoreline and ignoring the first turnoff by a villa's large electrical box. Take the next left down a leafy road lined with luxury houses, passing the *Artesia* villa and its 250-metre-long dry-stone walls, and following the road downhill, towards a tennis court on your right. Immediately after the tennis court, a green mesh- and brushwood perimeter fence marks the concrete steps that lead down through a copse to **Cala Salada** (Map 9, G1). You'll emerge just above the beachside *Restaurant Cala Salada* (closed Dec and Jan), from where you can phone for a taxi to take you back to Sant Antoni.

the place is usually deserted except for the occasional hippy and his joint. From the cave, a short path winds 100m down to the waves below, where the rocky shore provides a blissfully isolated spot for a swim.

To **get to** Cova de les Fontanelles, follow the sign from Cala Salada along a signposted dirt track that snakes up the hills. Ignore the first (private) right turn, and after 2km take the second right, where a signpost guides you down another poor dirt track; you'll have to park and walk the last few hundred metres.

Southwest of Sant Antoni

Southwest of the Punta des Molí, a seemingly endless Spanish *costa*-style sprawl of hotels and apartment blocks, mini-markets, souvenir shops, bars and restaurants has spread around **Sant Antoni bay**. Giant shells of half-built hotels loom over the coast road, and the rocky shoreline is broken only by patches of pine woods and a sprinkling of man-made beaches. These small stretches of sand are convenient for a dip if you're staying locally, but if you're after a day by the sea you're much better off continuing west to the far superior **beaches** lying southwest of Sant Antoni; all are reachable by means of a short drive, bus journey or boat trip from the centre of town.

Travelling southwest around the bay, all the beaches and the bay of **Port des Torrent** get very busy with families in the high season. Further west across the dry, littoral plains, things are a bit less hectic at the delightful beach of **Cala Bassa**. However, the very best stretches of sand – the stark expanses of **Cala Compte** and neighbouring **Cala Conta** – are in the far west opposite the arid offshore islands of Conillera and Bosc. Finally, just to the south of Cala Compe, the cove beach of **Cala Codolar** is often overlooked, but has a good sailing and windsurfing school.

SANT ANTONI BAY

Map 9, G5–E5.

Officially, the border that divides the town of Sant Antoni from its "bay" area, which lies in the neighbouring municipality of Sant Josep, starts just east of the Punta des Molí

(see p.149), though the holiday-geared environment remains pretty indistinguishable at first. Gradually, however, as you head around the bay, the area becomes a little less built-up. Plenty of visitors booked on last-minute deals from the UK are allocated accommodation in Sant Antoni bay; though the area is unremittingly touristy, it tends to attract more families than San An itself, so the atmosphere is less raucous.

Almost adjoining the Punta des Molí promontory, **Platja des Pouet** (Map 10, F13) is a slim, unappealing sandy beach blighted by its position right next to the busy coastal road. West of here, c/de Cala de Bou continues around the bay, between apartment and hotel blocks and the attendant commercial sprawl. The road passes two small man-made beaches, **Platja s'Estanyol**, a kilometre from Punta des Molí, and **Platja des Serral**, a further kilometre to the west; both are unattractive and surrounded by large concrete blocks.

The best beach on this stretch, **Platja des Pinet** (Map 9, F5), labelled on some maps as Platja d'en Xinxó, some 3km west of Punta des Molí, is a little more inviting. It's certainly nothing special – a small sandy cove, barely 100m wide, but there's safe swimming in the sheltered waters and three cheap shoreside snack bars. It's possible to waterski or take a ride on an inflatable banana here; there's also a rickety-looking waterslide complex (May–Oct 9am–7pm; two rides E1, ten rides E3.50). Buses between Sant Antoni and port des Torrent pass Platja des Pinet every thirty minutes.

PORT DES TORRENT

Map 9, E5.

The coastal road around Sant Antoni bay comes to an abrupt halt beside the *Seaview Country Club* holiday village, some 5km from the centre of town. A short pathway from the roundabout beside the *Seaview* descends to the pretty, sandy cove of **Port des Torrent**, named after a seasonal stream that originates on Ibiza's highest peak, Sa Talaiassa (see p.164), and empties into the small bay. Nestled at the end of a deep inlet, Port des Torrent's sands are packed with families lounging on sunbeds and splashing about in the calm water during the summer, when a snack bar-restaurant also opens; for the rest of the year, it's empty save for the odd fisherman.

CALA BASSA

Map 9, C5.

A striking horseshoe-shaped bay, ringed by low cliffs and sabina pines, the fine, 250-metre-wide sandy beach of **Cala Bassa** is one of the most popular in the Sant Antoni area, with plenty of sunbeds and umbrellas to rent and three large café-restaurants. From the bay, there's a wonderful view over the sea to the hump-shaped coastal outcrop of Cap Nunó, and the wooded hills of the island's northwest in the distance. The sparkling waters have been awarded Blue Flag status, and there are plenty of watersports on offer, from waterskiing (€20) to banana rides (€7), as well as a roped-off area for swimmers. Cala Bassa does tend to get very busy in high season, when it's well served by regular boats and buses from San An, but peace returns and the beach clears by 7pm, when the last transport departs. To get to Cala Bassa by road from town, take the southbound Sant Antoni–Sant Josep highway; after 5km, take the signposted right-hand turnoff opposite the small village of Sant Agustí – Cala Bassa is 6km to the northwest.

Cala Bassa's peaceful campsite is reviewed on p.225.

CALA CONTA AND AROUND

After a three-kilometre loop around the remote rocky fringes of western Ibiza, the Cala Bassa road ends at the exposed beach of **Cala Conta** (Map 9, B6), which, together with neighbouring Cala Compte, is generally considered one of Ibiza's very best, and has Blue Flag status. Though there are only two small patches of golden sand, it's easy to see why people rave about the place: gin-clear water, superb ocean vistas and spectacular sunsets. There's also a large café-restaurant behind the sands.

Just 100m or so to the north is a second inlet, **Cala Compte** (Map 9, B6), where there are two more tiny sandy bays. Just southwest of the car park, the delightful beach under the coastal cliffs is popular with nudists and has a snack bar. The other beach is more family-orientated, with a good fish restaurant, *s'Illa des Bosc*, named in honour of **Illa des Bosc** (Map 9, B5) directly offshore – though the name means "island of woods", it's now completely deforested, the trees having been felled for charcoal burning over a century ago. Illa des Bosc is reachable via a 400-metre wade and swim across shallow water dotted with three tiny islets; although the crossing is fairly easy when the sea is calm, beware of the currents that can sweep along this section of the coast when things get choppy.

Just north of Illa des Bosc, the much larger island of **Conillera** (Map 9, A3–A4) is visible from most points of Sant Antoni bay, from where its elongated profile resembles a giant beached whale. Many local legends are attached to the island – it's said to have been the birthplace of Hannibal, the Carthaginian general and arch-enemy of Rome, and also the best source of the *beleño blanco* psychoactive herb, collected by pagan practitioners each year and burned during the night of Sant Joan (see p.287).

Topped by a lighthouse, the island is uninhabited today, though scuba divers often visit the waters just offshore.

Two kilometres north of Cala Conta is the beachless, empty bay of **Cala Roja** (Map 9, C5), named after the burned red colour of its low sandstone coastal cliffs. To get there, you'll have to navigate a tangle of bumpy dirt tracks that cut through the parched scrubland. A few lonely fishing huts stand beneath Cala Roja's corrugated shoreline, and it's easy enough to scramble down to the sea for a blissfully peaceful dip; if you have a snorkel, you can swim to some crustacean-rich coastal caves under the bay's protruding coastal rocks. Looming above Cala Roja, the eighteenth-century **Torre d'en Rovira** watchtower crowns the Cap de Torre, a barren, rocky outcrop that affords spectacular views back over Sant Antoni bay and to the islands of Conillera and Illa des Bosc.

CALA CODALAR

Map 9, B7.

Two kilometres inland of Cala Compte, the road takes you past a dirt road signposted for the minuscule cove of **Cala Codalar**, 1km away. It's a pretty little bay, just 40m wide, with fine, pale sand and waters sheltered by the rocky Punta de s'Embacador headland to the north. The beach can get crowded in high season, when it's popular with tourists from the *Club Delfin* hotel just above the bay. There's a simple, nameless snack-shack and a **windsurfing** school (see p.47) here, both open between May and October only.

The South

A dramatic landscape of soaring hills, thick forests and exquisite beaches, **southern Ibiza** is wildly beautiful and largely undeveloped. It's the island's most geographically diverse region, with the highest peak, **Sa Talaiassa**, the shimmering flats of the **Salines salt pans** and drowsy one-horse villages, as well as a craggy coast staked with defence towers. The coastline is lapped by warm pellucid waters and endowed with more than a dozen beautiful **beaches**: from secluded, diminutive Cala Llentrisca, Cala Carbó and Cala Molí, to family-friendly bays like Sa Caleta and Es Cubells, and also the outrageous posing zones of Es Cavallet and Salines.

The area has only three resorts – the quiet bays of Cala Vedella and Cala Tarida in the west, and big, brash Platja d'en Bossa in the extreme east; the rest of the shore is more or less pristine. The most dramatic coastline is around Cala d'Hort in the southwest, an isolated region of soaring mountains and bizarre cliff and rock formations. Here, the mysterious island of **Es Vedrà** and an ancient quarry known as **Atlantis**, a place of pilgrimage for Ibiza's mystic crew, form a kind of "cosmic corner", where fishermen, farmers and hippies have been reporting UFO sightings and weird happenings for decades. Beachlife and unexplained phenomena notwithstanding, southern Ibiza is well worth exploring for the sweeping views and unspoiled landscape alone.

Inland, the rolling, forested countryside is dotted with small attractive villages – serene **Sant Agustí**, affluent **Sant Josep**, and suburban **Sant Jordi**, home to the prettiest church in Ibiza. There are also some very funky **bars** spread across the south, especially at **Cala Jondal**, Salines beach and along the Sant Josep–Ibiza Town highway, plus some great dining options, from simple shoreside *chiringuitos* to elaborate country restaurants.

Getting around the south is easy with your own vehicle, as there's a decent road network and plenty of signposts. Five daily buses run along the main highway between Sant Antoni and Ibiza Town (via Sant Josep), and there are also services to some beaches.

Reviews of accommodation, restaurants and bars in the south start on p.222, p.240 and p.258 respectively.

Sant Josep and around

The attractive municipal capital of southern Ibiza and the hub of the area, **Sant Josep** is surrounded by high, thickly forested hills that include **Sa Talaiassa**, the island's highest peak. To the south of Sant Josep is the sleepy hilltop village of **Sant Agustí**, capped by a fortified church with sweeping views over the southwest coast. Regular **buses** run through the region, passing Sant Agustí and Sant Josep as they trundle along the glorious southern highway between Sant Antoni and Ibiza Town.

SANT JOSEP

Map 11, E2.

Pretty, prosperous and easy-going **SANT JOSEP** has a delightful setting, 200m above sea level in a valley between the island's central hills and, to the south, the green, forested slopes of Sa Talaiassa. Though the village itself is of no great size, with a population of just four hundred, it's the largest settlement in the region; if you're staying in the south, you're likely to visit for its banks, boutiques and restaurants. There's a tidy, trim self-confidence here, best illustrated along the attractive, pint-sized **high street**, where you'll find the arched modern Ajuntament, and just to the west around the exquisite little central plaza, where the Moorish-style tiled benches are shaded by pines. From this plaza you have an excellent view across the main road to the imposing, whitewashed **Església de Sant Josep**, one of the largest churches in the island, dating from 1726. Its most arresting aspect is its superb three-storey facade, with a triple-arched porch that extends out from the main body of the building. The church is only open for Mass, but if you do get to take a look at the capacious, delightfully cool interior, check out the wooden pulpit painted with scenes from the life of Christ, a reproduction of the eighteenth-century piece destroyed when the church's interior was gutted in the Spanish Civil War.

SANT AGUSTÍ

Map 11, E1.

A couple of kilometres north of Sant Josep, a signposted turnoff from the main road to Sant Antoni climbs up to the pretty hilltop village of **SANT AGUSTÍ**, a place so tranquil that all signs of life seem to have been frazzled by the Mediterranean sun. Grouped around the fortified church at the heart of the settlement are a clump of old farmhouses, one of which has been beautifully converted into the *Can Berri Vell* restaurant (see p.240), as well as the village bar, a solitary store and an ancient stone defence tower where the locals once hid from pirates over the centuries. The views across the hilly interior of the island and down to the southwest coast are captivating from the little plaza next to the landmark **Església de Sant Agustí**, which was completed in the early nineteenth century. Designed by the Spanish architect Pedro Criollez, this simple rectangular structure has a stark, whitewashed facade, but lacks the typical frontal porch of most Ibizan churches.

SA TALAIASSA

Map 11, D2.

Towering above Sant Josep is the 475-metre peak of **Sa Talaiassa**, the highest point in the Pitiuses. It's reachable either by an hour-long hike, or a via a well-signposted dirt track that turns off the road to Cala d'Hort and Cala Vedella 2km west of Sant Josep; it's a ten-minute drive to the top from the village centre. Thickly wooded with aleppo and Italian stone pines, the summit offers exceptional views of southern Ibiza from gaps between the trees. You should easily be able to pick out the humpback cliffs of Jondal and Falcó, the Salines salt pans and plateau-like Formentera –

and on very clear days, the mountains of the Dénia peninsula in mainland Spain, some 50km distant. There's a wonderfully peaceful feel here, the silence broken only by the buzz of cicadas and hum of a number of television antennae. In the 1960s, the summit was the scene of legendary full-moon parties staged by the hippy population; misty-eyed veterans still talk about watching the sun set into the ocean beyond the island of Conillera and the moon rising over the Mediterranean in the east. Such gatherings are banned these days, but there's nothing to stop you driving up to take in the sunset or moonrise.

The southwest coast

One kilometre west of Sant Josep, a turnoff from the road to Sant Antoni bristles with brown beach signs directing you to the string of lovely sandy bays that lie along the southwest coast. **Cala Tarida** and **Cala Vedella** have been developed into attractive, small-scale family resorts, while cliff-backed **Cala Molí** and **Cala Carbó** are almost pristine, and are more peaceful places to spend a day by the sea. An isolated, remote region of soaring mountains and bizarre cliff and rock formations, the area also holds special significance for spiritual types, drawn to the weird rock-island of **Es Vedrà**, which lies opposite the fabled beach of **Cala d'Hort**, and the ancient quarry known as **Atlantis**.

CALA TARIDA

Map 11, B1.

A wide arc of golden sand broken by two low rocky outcrops, **CALA TARIDA** is where you'll find one of Ibiza's more appealing resorts, a small, family-orientated collection of low-rise hotels surrounding a pretty bay. In high season, the **beach** gets very busy with German and Spanish holidaymakers, and you'll have to pick your way through rows of umbrellas and sunbeds for a swim. There are plenty of fairly unexciting bars and restaurants to choose from; the best seafood is served at the expensive *Cas Mila*.

Regular **buses** run between Cala Tarida and Ibiza Town via Sant Josep all year round.

CALA MOLÍ

Map 11, B2.

Two kilometres south of Cala Tarida, the serpentine coast road dips down to **Cala Molí**, a fine beach at the foot of a seasonal river bed. Steep cliffs envelop the pebbly cove, which is undeveloped except for a solitary eyesore placed insensitively close to the shoreline, the *Restaurant Cala Molí*, which sells snacks and has a big swimming pool for use of its patrons. However, the sheltered, deep green waters are a much better place for a dip – if you swim across to the cove's southern cliff, you can also explore a small cave. Despite its relatively close proximity to the popular resorts of Tarida and Vedella, Cala Molí never seems to get too busy, probably because it's not served by buses – if you can get there independently, you'll find it's perfect for a chilled-out day by the sea.

CALA VEDELLA

Map 11, B2.

Continuing south from Cala Molí, the precipitous, shady road twists through the coastal pines for 3km, passing pricey-looking holiday homes and the beautifully positioned *Hostal Cala Molí* (see p.222), before emerging above the long, narrow-mouthed inlet that harbours **CALA**

VEDELLA. One of Ibiza's smallest and most attractive resorts, Cala Vedella's profusion of good-quality villas and well-spaced, low-rise hotels are separated into two main developments dotted around the low hills framing the bay. The sheltered, sandy beach is ideal for families, with calm, very shallow water and a collection of snack bars and restaurants backing onto the sands. Between May and late September, Cala Vedella is served by regular **buses** from Sant Antoni and Ibiza Town via Sant Josep.

CALA CARBÓ

Map 11, B4.

A tiny, tranquil cove-bay, **Cala Carbó**, 4km south of Cala Vedella, is a delightfully peaceful place for a day at the beach, and as there are no public transport connections, it never seems to get too packed. The cove gets its name from the Catalan word for coal, which was unloaded here until the 1960s. There's a lovely little sand and pebble beach, backed by low sandstone cliffs, and tempting, calm sea; the mossy, rounded boulders offshore lend the water a deep jade tone. If you have a snorkel, try exploring the southern shore up to the rocky point at the mouth of the cove, where colourful wrasse and large schools of mirror fish are common. Of the two **restaurants** at the back of the bay, *Balenario* serves snacks, drinks and excellent mixed fish platters, while *Can Vincent*, set in a fine *finca*-style building, has a huge terrace ideal for more formal dining.

To **get to Cala Carbó**, take the main road to the south-east from St Josep and follow the signs to Cala d'Hort; Cala Carbó is clearly signposted on the right. If you're up for a pleasant twenty-minute walk, you can also take one of the three daily buses that run from Ibiza Town to Cala Vedella via Sant Josep, and get off at the turnoff for Cala Carbó.

CALA D'HORT

Map 11, B4.

An expansive beach of coarse sand, pebbles and crystal water, **Cala d'Hort**, 4km south of Cala Carbó along a well-signposted road, is afforded special status by Ibiza's hippies. Having one of the most spectacular settings in the Balearics, the beach is backed by the imposing, forested hillsides of the Roques Altes peaks and lies directly opposite the startling, vertiginous rock-island of Es Vedrà, source of countless local legends. With no concrete blocks to spoil the coastline, there's a wonderfully isolated feel here, and the remote location, wedged into Ibiza's south

THE BATTLE OF CALA D'HORT

In 1992, the sparsely populated slopes behind **Cala d'Hort** became the subject of a bitter battle between **environmentalists** and **developers**. The latter planned to build a golf course, a 420-bed hotel and a desalination plant smack in the middle of what is one of the island's most spectacular landscapes – an area of unique biodiversity, home to rare Mediterranean orchids and the highly endangered Eleanor's falcon. Supported by powerful local politicians in the Sant Josep municipality and elements within the then-ruling PP party, the scheme outraged Ibiza's environmentalists, who mounted a protracted campaign, successfully paralysing work for years. Though Cala d'Hort had been declared an ANEI (Area of Special Natural Interest), the developers, Calas de Mediterráneo, continued to lobby. The Sant Josep planners maintained their support for the project, and in late 1998 the green light was given to start work on the golf course.

Most Ibizans were appalled, and the issue ignited a wider campaign against rampant overdevelopment, provoking in west corner well away from all the main resorts and towns, ensures that things never get too busy. Even in high season, you can usually find a quiet spot for your sun lounger and umbrella, and in winter you'll probably have the place to yourself.

There are three good fish **restaurants** by the shore – the best is *El Boldado* (see p.240) on the northern lip of the bay, past a string of fishing huts. If you fancy sticking around in Cala d'Hort, try asking at the *El Carmen* restaurant if there's a room for rent – the owners like to keep it quiet, but there's often some simple accommodation.

Between June and late September only, three daily **buses** on the Ibiza Town–Cala Vedella route (via Sant Josep and

January 1999 the biggest **demonstration** in the island's history, when 12,000 people (one in seven of the population) marched through Ibiza Town in protest at the Cala d'Hort plans. Seasoned political commentators were astounded, and the march is now seen as a seminal event – the day that notoriously apolitical Ibiza woke up. The demonstration ultimately helped lead to the ejection of the PP conservatives in the June 1999 elections, after twenty years in power. In August 1999, after Green Party campaigners chained themselves to bulldozers at Cala d'Hort, the newly elected Left-Green Pacte coalition finally acted decisively, putting a veto on any further development. The **Cala d'Hort National Park** was finally created in February 2002, while the victory of the environmentalists has also had a wider effect, influencing the Balearic government to place a moratorium on the building of new golf courses across the Pitiuses.

Es Cubells) serve Cala d'Hort. The bus stops on the main road above the beach.

ES VEDRÀ

Map 11, A5.

Rising from the sea like the craggy crest of a semi-submerged volcano, the limestone outcrop of **Es Vedrà** is one of the most startling sights in the western Mediterranean. Despite its height (378m), Es Vedra is only visible once you get within a few kilometres of Cala d'Hort – it's hidden by the high surrounding peaks of Llentrisca, Sa Talaiassa and the Roques Altes, which have all been included in a new national park (see box on p.168).

Among the **legends** surrounding Es Vedrà, it's said to be the island of the sirens, the sea-nymphs who tried to lure Odysseus from his ship in Homer's epic, and also the holy island of the Carthaginian love and fertility goddess, Tanit. A reclusive Carmelite priest, Father Palau i Quer, who spent a few weeks on Vedrà in the mid-nineteenth century, reported seeing visions of the Virgin Mary and satanic rituals. Sailors and scuba divers have reported compasses swinging wildly and gauges malfunctioning as they approach the island, and there have been innumerable reports of UFO sightings here. The rock has also featured on the cover of numerous Ibiza compilations and Mike Oldfield's album *Voyager*. It also inspired songs for Oldfield's *Tubular Bells III* and *Tres Lunas*; he lived in a palatial villa high in the hills opposite Vedrà until the late 1990s, but Noel Gallaghernow owns the property.

These days, Es Vedrà is inhabited only by wild goats, a unique sub-species of the Ibizan wall lizard and a small colony of the endangered Eleanor's falcon; you can often see the birds swooping around the island. There are no boat excursions to the isle, but if you're really curious you may be able to get a fisherman to take you over from Cala d'Hort. Boat excursions from Sant Antoni to Cala d'Hort pass close by; for more on these, see p.30.

TORRE DES SAVINAR AND ATLANTIS

Map 11, B5.

Climbing abruptly from the beach at Cala d'Hort, an exhilaratingly scenic road with sweeping views of the Mediterranean heads east between wooded hills towards Es Cubells. Two kilometres on, a right-hand turnoff leads to **Torre des Savinar**, a defence tower built in 1763. The tower has also been known as Torre d'en Pirata since Valencian author Vicente Blasco Ibáñez set part of his buccaneer novel *The Dead Commands* here. The dirt track from the coast road to the tower is in very bad condition, so unless you have a 4WD, it's best to park up after 100m and continue by foot; it's a twenty-minute walk from here to the tower. After ten minutes, you reach the coastal cliffs, where a *mirador* provides an amazing view over the sea to Es Vedrà. This is one of best places in Ibiza to watch the **sunset**, and a small crowd gathers here most evenings. A few metres below this lookout, a path leads down to a small **cave** in the cliff-face – the abode of a hermit, according to local legend.

There are even better views once you get to the two-storey tower itself, set majestically even higher above the Mediterranean. A flight of steps climbs to the upper level, from where there's a jaw-dropping view of Es Vedrà and panoramic vistas across the sea to tabletop-flat Formentera in the southeast, and the undulating form of the island of Conillera to the north. Immediately beneath the tower is Vedrà's sister island of **Vedranell**, which resembles a sleeping dragon with its snout and spiky backbone protruding from the water.

If you look to the east from the tower, you can also see the crooked outline of **Atlantis**, an ancient shoreside quarry that's something of a sacred site for Ibizan hippies and a place that retains a magical feel, with a harsh, eerie beauty. Though lying 200m below, it's easy to make out where the colossal chunks of the sandstone rockface were cut out to be shipped to Ibiza Town to build the capital's magnificent Renaissance walls. If you decide to tackle the steep trail down, bear in mind that many locals are extremely sensitive about the site – treat it with the respect that not all visitors have afforded (some idiot spray-painted the route with "London Posse" in the mid-1990s). Also, remember to bring sunscreen with you, as there's no shade at all for most of the day.

To **get to Atlantis**, it's best to retrace your steps to the cliffside lookout, and then back inland towards the car parking area. Five minutes from the lookout, take the path to the right (east) through scrub bushes; you'll quickly reach the clifftop that marks the trailhead for Atlantis, clearly visible below. The well-trodden path is easy to follow, though very steep, until it flattens out after fifteen minutes beside a natural, pine-shaded campsite. There's a small **cave** in the rocks here, and a beautiful etched image of a **Buddha**, said to have been drawn by a Japanese traveller, that has given this part of the coast its Spanish nickname, "Punta de Buda". A mini-shrine has developed around this image, with an "altar" decorated with trinkets, mirrors, feathers and assorted offerings.

The final descent to Atlantis is quite tricky, as you have to plough your way across towering sand dunes, which are particularly exhausting to negotiate on your return. As you near the shore, the hewn forms of the ancient quarry become clearer, the cut sandstone offset at oblique angles from the bedrock. Between these rock outcrops, shimmering indigo- and emerald-tinged pools of trapped seawater add an ethereal dimension to the scene. There's a great deal to explore, as much of the stone has been carved by hippies with **mystic imagery**. This includes blunt-nosed faces resembling Maya gods, swirling abstract shapes, decades of doodles, engravings and graffiti, and even blocks of stone hanging suspended by wires from the angular rock face. At the extreme edge of the promontory, don't miss the wonderful, partly-painted carving of a Cleopatra-like oriental queen.

The south coast

Ibiza's spectacular **southern coast**, between the headlands of Llentrisca in the west and Cap des Falcó in the east, has more than a dozen small **beaches**, most linked to the main Ibiza Town–Sant Josep highway by minor roads. None has a full-scale resort, and many of the tiny coves have nothing but a seafood restaurant and a few umbrellas to rent. Inland, thick pine forests cover most of the region, and there's just one diminutive village, **Es Cubells**, to tempt you away from the sea.

Public transport is very sporadic throughout the area. **Buses** do pass by **Platja Codolar**, **Sa Caleta** and Es Cubells between May and late September, but you'll need your own transport to get to the other beaches, which are well signposted.

ES CUBELLS AND AROUND

Map 11, D4.

South of Sant Josep, a signposted road weaves around the eastern flank of Sa Talaiassa, past terraces of orange and olive trees, to the southern coast and the tiny cliffside village of **ES CUBELLS**. The settlement owes its place on the map to Father Palau i Quer, a Carmelite priest who visited nearby Es Vedrà in the 1850s. He persuaded the Vatican to fund construction of a chapel here in 1855, on the grounds that the farmers and fishermen of the area lacked a local place of worship. Magnificently positioned above the deep blue Mediterranean, the simple whitewashed sandstone building has now been upgraded to church status. The tiny garden beside it contains a stone plinth dedicated to Father Palau, engraved with an image of Es Vedrà. Although the church and a neighbouring convent building form the nucleus of today's tiny hamlet, Es Cubells still consists of no more than a dozen or so homes, a store and, adjoining the church, *Bar Llumbi*, an inexpensive small bar and restaurant (May–Oct, closed Mon), where you can get decent grilled fish or a *bocadillo*.

Signposted from the church, the minuscule **Cala des Cubells beach** (Map 11, D5) lies 1km from the village, via a couple of hairpin turns. It's one of Ibiza's least-visited spots, consisting of a slender strip of grey, tide-polished stones, with a few sunbeds and umbrellas and a somewhat overpriced restaurant, *Ses Boques*. If you're looking for an isolated place to get an all-over tan, head to the left past a strip of fishing huts, where three tiny, untouched stony beaches lie below grey, crumbling cliffs.

Between May and September, three daily buses pass through Es Cubells on the Ibiza Town–Cala Vedella route.

CALA LLENTRISCA

Map 11, C5.

Southwest of Es Cubells, the road hugs the eastern slopes of the Llentrisca headland, descending for 3km past a sm enclave of luxurious modern villas towards the love unspoilt cove of **Cala Llentrisca**, cut off from the rest of the island by soaring pine-clad slopes. As no buses serve the beach, you'll need your own transport to visit; however, the road progressively deteriorates the closer you get to the cove, and you'll have to park beside the final villa at the end of the road and walk the last five minutes. Bear in mind that there's very little shade, and nothing on the pebbly shoreline except a row of seldom-used fishing huts, with a yacht or two often moored in the translucent bay waters.

ES TORRENT AND AROUND

Map 11, E5.

A small, sandy cove beach at the foot of a dry river bed, **Es Torrent** lies 7km south of Sant Josep. It's not served by public transport; to get there, take the road to Es Cubells, and follow the signposted turnoff that winds down towards the Porroig promontory. Es Torrent's waters are shallow and invitingly turquoise, and offer decent snorkelling around the cliffs at the edge of the bay, or a little further out close to the two tiny offshore rocks, Ses Illetes. Though the beach is lovely, many people come here just for the expensive seafood restaurant, *Es Torrent* (see p.241), very popular with the yachtie crowd.

Two kilometres southeast of Es Torrent, the road passes **Porroig Bay**, a small collection of ramshackle fishing huts set below low, eroded cliffs on the western side of the Porroig peninsula. There's no reason to stop here, but once you've looped around the prosperous peninsula, dotted with luxury villas and a four-star hotel, you can follow a dirt track that continues northeast for 400m to **Cala Xarcó**, a quiet strip of sand that only Ibizans and the odd yachtie seem to have stumbled upon. The coastal sabina pines here offer a little shade; there's also a sunbed or two for rent, and the superb (but very pricey) *Restaurant Es Xarcu*, which specializes in seafood.

If you want to carry on from Xarcó to Cala Jondal, it's a couple of minutes' scramble over the cliff behind the restaurant; you can also drive via a precipitous dirt road from the beach; after 200m, take the first right beside some walled villas.

CALA JONDAL

Map 11, F5.

The broad beach of **Cala Jondal**, lying between the promontories of Porroig and Jondal, lies 9km southeast of Sant Josep via a signposted turnoff from the Ibiza Town–Sant Josep highway. No buses serve Cala Jondal, so you'll have to make your way there independently. A broad, stony seashore at the base of gently sloping terraces planted with fruit trees, Jondal's kilometre-long strip of smooth rounded stones, divided by a dry river bed, doesn't make one of the island's very finest swimming spots, but some of the best beach bars in Ibiza ensure a certain liveliness that sets the place apart from other quiet bays hereabouts.

Relatively few tourists know about Cala Jondal, which attracts mainly an Ibizan and island-based international crowd, and an innovative home-grown dance and chillout scene has developed here since the mid-1990s. Over on the east side of the bay, the legendary *Jockey Club* (see p.259) hosted amazing Sunday club nights for over a decade until licensing problems in the 2002 season forced the venue to close; currently, it's only open for daytime food and drinks, though the owners are trying to regain their dance licence. Next door, the *Yemaná* restaurant (see p.241) is renowned for fresh fish and wonderful cava-based sangria. On the other side of the torrent, *Particular* (see p.259) is one of Ibiza's most stylish chillout bars, where local DJs entertain sunbathers with languid, beatless grooves, while on the far west side of the beach, *Tropicana* serves excellent fresh fruit juices.

SA CALETA AND AROUND

Map 11, F5.

Four kilometres around the coast from Cala Jondal, and reachable by road via the same signposted turnoff from the Sant Josep–Ibiza Town highway, lie the ruins of **Sa Caleta**, the first Phoenician settlement in Ibiza. Established around 650 BC on a low promontory beside a tiny natural harbour, the small site was only occupied for about fifty years, before the Phoenicians moved to the site of what is now Ibiza Town. Today, a high metal fence surrounds the foundations of the village, once home to several hundred people, who lived by fishing, hunting and farming wheat as well as smelting iron for tools and weapons. The ruins are visually unimpressive, but the site is a peaceful place to visit, with expansive views over an azure sea towards Platja Codolar and Cap des Falcó.

To the west of the site, a short path leads to Sa Caleta's **beaches**, three tiny adjoining bays sometimes labelled as "Bol Nou" on maps. The first bay, a hundred-metre strip of coarse golden sand, is the busiest spot, and very popular with Ibizan families on weekends – there are some sunbeds and umbrellas to rent here in summer, excellent swimming and snorkelling, and the good, reasonably priced *Restaurante Sa Caleta*, now open all year. The other two bays, both secluded and pebbly, are to the west of the sandy bay, via a path that winds along the shore below Sa Caleta's low sandstone cliffs – both are popular with nudists.

Six daily **buses** (May–late Sept) pass Sa Caleta, which is on the Ibiza Town–Cala Vedella route.

PLATJA CODOLAR

Map 11, G6.

East of Sa Caleta, a road runs parallel to the ochre-coloured coastal cliffs, heading towards the airport and Sant Jordi. One kilometre along, just as the road heads inland, a sign on the right marked "chiringuito" indicates the start of **Platja Codolar**, a sweeping pebble beach that stretches for over 3km southeast, running close to the airport runway and skirting the fringes of the Salines salt pans. Even at the height of summer, there are rarely more than a dozen or so (mainly nude) swimmers and sunbathers here, and the place would be very peaceful were it not for the regular interruption of jet engines revving up on the runway or screaming overhead. It's also possible to get to the opposite end of Platja Codolar via the main road to Salines beach, turn off at km 3.6 and follow the signposts for the *Cap des Falcó* restaurant.

The far south

Ibiza's most southerly body of land, the promontory that juts into the Mediterranean south of the scruffy settlement of **Sant Jordi**, offers some stunning landscapes. Lining the coastline are three of the island's finest beaches – the resort of **Platja d'en Bossa** and the back-to-back sands of **Salines beach** and **Es Cavallet**; taking up most of the interior are **salt pans**, the island's only source of wealth until mass tourism revolutionized the economy in the 1960s.

Regular **buses** run up and down the main road from Sant Jordi to Salines beach, while the resort of Platja d'en Bossa enjoys excellent connections with Ibiza Town, including the all-night discobus between June and late September.

SANT JORDI

Map 11, I4.

Dismal-looking and traffic-choked, the small settlement of **SANT JORDI** is trapped in a kind of no-man's land between Ibiza Town and the beaches to the south. Almost lost in the featureless suburban sprawl is the main point of interest, the **Església de Sant Jordi**, 200m north of the roundabout around which the town is centred. It's Ibiza's most fortress-like church, with mighty angled walls gashed with embrasures and topped with full battlements – all security measures to keep out pirates; inside, the austerity of the gingham tiled floor and simple wooden benches seem at odds with the gaudy modern altarpiece, installed in 1990.

The only other reason to visit Sant Jordi is for the Saturday **market**, actually more of a car-boot sale, held in the dustbowl of the **hippodrome**, a former horse-and-buggy race track. It's Ibiza's most quirky affair, far less commercialized than the hippy markets, with a good selection of junk jewellery, trashy clothes, secondhand books and furniture. It's open all year and starts around 9am, tailing off by about 3pm; there's no entrance charge.

Hourly **buses** between Ibiza Town and Salines beach pass through Sant Jordi all year round.

PLATJA D'EN BOSSA

Map 11, I4.

A kilometre east of Sant Jordi, and merging into Figueretes (see p.89) to the north, the conventional, *costa*-style resort of **Platja d'en Bossa** is stretched out along the island's longest beach – a ruler-straight, three-kilometre-long strip of wonderfully fine, pale sand. Lining the beach are a gap-toothed row of hotel blocks, many abruptly thrown up in the later Franco years, others still in various stages of construction, while behind lies an unappealing secondary strip of cafés, restaurants, German bierkellers, British pubs, car rental outlets and supermarkets filled with plastic dolphins, lilos and suncreams. Though Platja d'en Bossa is predominantly a family resort, attracting tourists from all over northern Europe, the crop of new **bars** that have sprung up towards the southern end of the resort, close to the club *Space*, now form an embryonic party zone. By far the best-known of these is the beachside club-bar *Bora Bora* (see p.258), where thousands gather to groove in the high-season months.

For reviews of Platja d'en Bossa's bars and club-bars, see p.258.

Despite the concrete and the tourist tack, Platja d'en Bossa is increasingly popular as a base for savvy, older clubbers who have tired of the San An scene and stay here to take advantage of the location – a few kilometres equidistant from Ibiza Town and the sands at Salines. If you follow suit, you'll find that the main drawback is the lack of decent restaurants, most of which serve only fast food or bland "international" fare. However, you can always escape to the restaurants of Ibiza Town, connected to Platja d'en Bossa by half-hourly buses and a regular boat service in high season.

SALINES BEACH

Map 11, I7.

A beautiful kilometre-long strip of powdery pale sand backed by pines and dunes, **Salines beach** is Ibiza's most fashionable place to pose. The sands are interspersed with rocky patches, and beach bars dot the shoreline, which changes from a family-friendly, bucket-and-spade environment close to the *Guaraná* café in the north into the island's premier navel-gazing spot around the über-hip *Sa Trincha* (see p.260) in the south, where clothing is optional. Beyond *Sa Trincha* are a succession of tiny sandy coves, enveloped by unusual rock formations – some were once quarried centuries ago, while more recently, talented sculptors have carved images into the coastal stone, including a Medusa-like figure and a fang-baring dragon wearing a Maya-style headdress. These mini-beaches tend to get grabbed fairly early in the day and jealously guarded as private bays by dedicated – and very territorial – sunbathers. Beyond the coves, the sands give way to a slender rocky promontory, topped at its end by the **Torre de ses Portes** defence tower.

Hourly **buses** run to Ibiza Town from a bus stop just north of Salines beach, close to sorry-looking **La Canal**, a ramshackle wharf where salt is loaded for export.

ES CAVALLET AND AROUND

Map 11, I6.

A kilometre east of the Salines beach car park, via a delightful signposted road around the sparkling salt pans, are the honey-coloured sands of **Es Cavallet**, the second stunning-beach on this part of the coast. Franco's Guardia Civil fought a futile battle against nudism here for years, arresting

BETWEEN THE BEACHES – A HIKE TO ES CAVALLET

South of Platja d'en Bossa, a shady path follows the coastline along the eastern contours of Puig de Baix to the beach at Es Cavallet. It takes a little over an hour to complete the four-kilometre walk, which passes unspoiled rocky coves and meanders through thick forest. The route is easy to follow, and not too strenuous, but there are no refreshments on the way.

The path begins at Platja d'en Bossa's southernmost point (Map 11, I5), next to the *Club Med* windsurfing school, and crosses a narrow, rotten-smelling aqueduct that feeds the nearby salt pans with seawater. It then heads for the conical, sixteenth-century **Torre des Carregador**, which stands above the beach to the south on a rocky outcrop and was built to guard the southern approach to Ibiza Town. There are superb views of the Dalt Vila castle and cathedral in Ibiza Town from its base. Past the tower, the path continues around the diminutive semicircular bay of **Cala de sa Sal Rossa** (Red Salt Beach), and passes a ring of fishermen's huts before climbing up the pine-clad hillside ahead. From here onwards, you're always within fifty metres or so from the sea, climbing up and down undulating slopes thick with thyme and rosemary, and past deserted rocky coves, with La Mola, Formentera's slab-like eastern peninsula, clearly visible for much of the route. Eventually, the path takes you to a paved road that descends to the northern end of **Es Cavallet**, near to the excellent *La Escollera* seafood restaurant (see p.241).

To **get back to Platja d'en Bossa**, take an Ibiza Town-bound bus from nearby Salines beach; the route passes close to the northern end of Bossa. If you've parked close to *Club Med*, get off at the Sant Francesc church and walk 1km to Platja d'en Bossa along a dirt road that skirts the northern section of the salt pans.

hundreds of naked hippies before the kilometre-long stretch of sand was finally designated Ibiza's first naturist beach in 1978. The northern end of Es Cavallet, close to the *Chiringuito* and *La Escollera* (see p.241) restaurants and the car park, attracts a mixed bunch of families and couples, but the southern half of the beach – and the nicest stretch – is almost exclusively **gay**, centred around the superb *Chiringay* bar-café (see p.291). It's a ten-minute stroll over to Salines beach from *Chiringay*, through sand dunes and wind-twisted sabina pines that double as prime cruising territory.

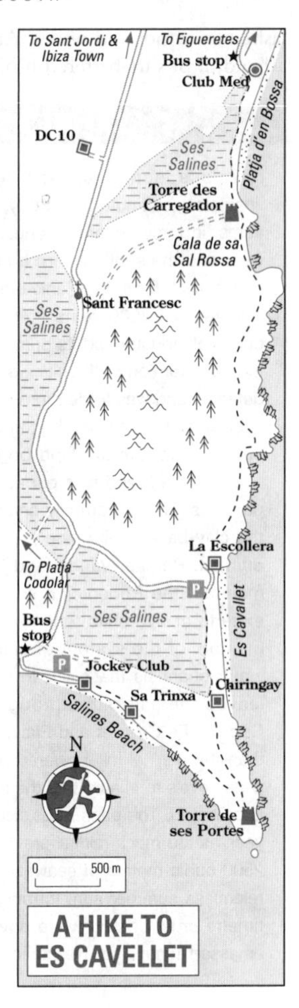

Punta de ses Portes

Map 11, I7.

A fifteen-minute walk south of Es Cavallet's *Chiringay* beach bar, Ibiza's most southerly point, **Punta de ses Portes**, is a lonely, rocky spot, often lashed by winds and waves. Above the swirling currents and a handful of surf-battered fishing huts is another two-storey,

SALINES SALT PANS

Ibiza's spectacular **Ses Salines salt pans** (Ⓦ www.insula.org/saltroute/html/body_ibiza.html) stretch across 1,000 acres, in three separate zones, between Platja Codolar in the west and the southeastern beaches of Platja d'en Bossa and Es Cavallet. From the Punic era until the mid-twentieth century – more than 2000 years – the production of salt was Ibiza's only real industry and its primary source of wealth; salt funded the construction of the city walls and the purchase of arms for defence, and was traded for wheat when harvests failed.

Ibizan salt production began with the **Phoenicians**, who recognized that the flat land bordering the sea in the extreme south of the island was perfectly suited to the creation of salt pans – seawater naturally crystallized here anyway – and that the clay-based soil made a perfect base for large-scale production. Roman, Vandal and Visigoth invaders continued to maintain the Phoenician salt pans, but it was the **Moors**, experts at hydraulic technology, who developed the fundamentals of the system of sluice gates, mini-windmills and water channels that's still in use today. Seawater enters and leaves the salt pans through narrow stone aqueducts at Codolar, Es Cavallet and Platja d'en Bossa, with pumps (rather than the original mill-powered paddles) controlling the flow and water levels to ensure that the maximum quantity of salt residue is collected. The pans must also be flooded at the right time of year, as too much rainfall prevents crystallization. Approximately 2500 cubic metres of seawater is then left to evaporate in the relentless summer sun, forming after three months a ten-centimetre crust of pink-white powder, which is scooped up and amassed in huge salt hills, then exported from La Canal jetty.

sixteenth-century defence tower, **Torre de ses Portes** – almost a twin of the Torre des Carregador at Platja d'en

Until the late nineteenth century, when a steam engine partially replaced the human workforce, labourers carried the entire cargo to the docks by hand in the terrible heat of August and September. These days, tractors, trucks and conveyor belts perform the hard labour, allowing a few dozen employees to do the work previously performed by hundreds. Around 70,000 tonnes of salt are now exported annually; the finest quality is shipped to Norway for salting cod, and the rest to Scotland for salting roads in winter.

As well as producing salt, the pans are also an important habitat for **birds**, being one of the first points of call on the migratory route from Africa. Thanks to a 23-year battle by environmentalists against property developers and politicians, Ibiza's salt pans, alongside those in the important wetlands of Estany des Peix and Estany Pudent in Formentera (see pp.190–191), are now officially protected as a **natural reserve**. You'll see storks, herons and flamingoes stopping to rest and refuel, as well as over 200 species in permanent residence, from osprey and black-necked grebe to Kentish plover. The salt flats are also rich with endemic plant species, such as the pink-flowering molinet, and are regarded as one of the EU's most important wetland habitats. A director and six wardens have been appointed to manage the area and conduct tours, and a visitor centre is due to open at the church in nearby Sant Francesc in 2003. Until then, you're best off viewing the pans at sunset from the Sant Jordi–La Canal road, around the km 3 marker; beware clouds of mosquitoes at dusk and dawn, especially in September.

Bossa – which commands superb views of the chain of tiny islands that reach out to Formentera. One of these, **Illa des Penjats** (Island of the Hanged), was used for executions until the early twentieth century; another, **Illa des Porcs** (Pig Island), was once a pig smugglers' stronghold. Both islands are topped by the lighthouses that guide ships and ferries through the treacherous Es Freus channel between Ibiza and Formentera.

Formentera

Tranquil, easy-going **Formentera** could hardly be more of a contrast to Ibiza, despite being only a thirty-minute ferry ride away. Physically, the island is very flat, consisting of two shelf-like plateaux connected by a narrow central isthmus. It's also very sparsely inhabited, with less than 6,000 people spread thinly over 84 square kilometres of rain-starved, sun-baked land, and there are just three, tiny sleepy villages. This isolation and the languid pace of life attracts a mellow bunch of visitors: cyclists, hippies, birdwatchers, naturists and very dedicated sunseekers.

Formentera's unhurried appeal belies a troubled past. The struggle of eking out a living from the salt pans and the unforgiving soil, combined with outbreaks of the plague and attacks by pirates, led the island to be completely abandoned in the late fourteenth century, and it was only resettled in 1697. All of Formentera's historic buildings – especially the churches – have been fortified to some extent, and the coastline is studded with watchtowers.

Today, for the first time in its history, Formentera's future prosperity seems secure. The economy is totally dependent on summer tourism (almost exclusively Germans and Italians), with visitors flocking in for some of Spain's longest, whitest, cleanest and least-crowded **beaches**. The authorities have followed a relatively sustainable pattern of tourism development, attracting enough tourists to ensure reasonable revenue without feeling the need to cover their best sandy bays with sprawling concrete resorts, and have devised tight environmental controls to prevent future tourism projects.

The sole resort, **Es Pujols**, is a fairly restrained, small-scale affair, with a lively (but far from raucous) summer bar scene and a small club. Formentera's real draw, however, is its magnificent **shoreline** – the clarity and colour of the sea is astonishing, with water turquoise enough to trump any Caribbean holiday brochure. The pick of the beaches are the two back-to-back powdery white sands, **Platja Illetes** and **Platja Llevant**, of the slender Trucador peninsula to the north, and **Platja de Migjorn**, a sweeping six-kilometre sandy crescent that lines much of the island's south coast. Formentera also has a number of less expansive beaches, including the fine pale sands of **Ses Platgetes**, and the sheltered bay of **Cala Saona**, the island's only cove beach.

Inland, the countryside is remarkably beautiful despite the arid climate: a patchwork of golden wheatfields, vines, carob and fig trees, divided by old dry-stone walls. It's best explored by cycling along the "Green Routes" (see p.33), a network of quiet country paths and lanes that connect Formentera's villages. The island's diminutive capital, **Sant Francesc Xavier**, is the most interesting of these, with a striking but spartan church and a number of boutiques and bars. The other settlements of **Sant Ferran** and **El Pilar de la Mola** also have the odd pocket of cultural and historical interest.

Formentera also offers some modest **ancient sites** in the southern Barbària peninsula, as well as the ruined remains of Ca Na Costa near Es Pujols and a Roman fort – but only the foundations of these buildings remain. **Birdwatching** is best at the salt lakes of **Estany Pudent** and **Estany des Peix**, while the wind-lashed extremes of the island – **Cap de Barbària** in the south and **Punta de la Mola** to the east – have a wild, stirring feel, with both headlands crowned by lonely lighthouses and surrounded by stunning coastal scenery.

Getting around

Most visitors choose to get around Formentera independently, and renting a car or bike is easy, with several rental outlets offering bicycles, scooters, motorbikes and cars. Prices are similar from outlet to outlet, but **Isla Blanca** (Ⓣ971 322 559) or **Autos Ca Mari** (Ⓣ971 322 921), both on the harbourside, are reliable options.

Formentera has a pretty reasonable **bus** network, with daily services operating a loop around the main settlements of La Savina, Es Pujols, Sant Ferran and Sant Francesc every two hours or so from 9am until 8pm between May and mid-October; there are three daily services for the rest of the year. Small **boats** also sail up the coast, connecting the main port of La Savina with Platja Illetes beach, and on to Espalmador island just north of Formentera.

For full details of ferries between Ibiza and Formentera see p.30

LA SAVINA

Map 12, C3.

Set in a small natural harbour in the northwest corner of the island, small, orderly **LA SAVINA** is likely to be your first view of Formentera, as all ferries from Ibiza dock here. It has never been a huge settlement, content to busy itself with the export of salt and planks of the sabina pine that give the place its name, and it's a still a sleepy place today, only stirring when the Ibiza ferry steams into port. However, the hubbub doesn't last very long, as most passengers make a beeline for the rows and rows of rental scooters and bicycles, and make a quick getaway to the beach.

Though La Savina is not the most absorbing place in the Pitiuses, the **harbour** is pleasant enough, with a small central marina bristling with yachts from the Spanish mainland and northern Europe. Modern hotel and apartment buildings overlook the marina from the south side of the harbour, housing souvenir shops and cafés at street level that are perfectly placed if you need to while away an hour or so before your ferry departs. All these eating places offer broadly similar menus, but the stylish *Aigüa* (see p.242) has the best food and most comfortable surroundings.

Just behind the harbour, Formentera's only **tourist information** office (Mon–Fri 10am–2pm & 5–7pm; Sat 10am–2pm; ⓣ971 322 057) has a good stock of glossy leaflets about the island's history, environment, hotels, beaches and Green Routes, and the staff are extremely helpful. For **accommodation** information, head next door to the Central de Reservas Formentera office (ⓣ971 323 224, ⓦwww.formenterareservations.com; see p.212), which has an extensive list of apartments and houses for rent.

ESTANY PUDENT AND ESTANY DES PEIX

Heading southeast out of La Savina, the island's main highway passes an ugly sprawl of roadside warehouses that almost obscure Formentera's two **salt lakes**, the island's main wetland habitats. On the left, the appropriately named **Estany Pudent** (Map 12, C3–D**4**), or "Stinking Pond", is the larger of the two, an oval expanse that smells better now that an irrigation channel has been opened to allow seawater in; however, a rotten aroma still hangs in the air most days. Ringed by scrub bush and an unsightly jumble of bungalows, Estany Pudent is not the most aesthetically pleasing place either, but it is popular amongst **birdwatchers**, who come to see common visitors from herons and egrets to black-necked grebes, warblers and even the odd flamingo. Dirt tracks run around the entire lake, and you can get to the shoreline via a right-hand turnoff 500m along the main highway from La Savina, which passes through a small patch of salt pans, as well as other turnoffs from the road between Es Pujols and the Trucador peninsula.

Smaller Estany des Peix (Map 12, C3–C4), to the right of the highway via a turnoff 1km south of La Savina, has a narrow mouth to the sea, and its shallow waters act as an ideal nursery for young fish. The brackish lagoon is no more picturesque than its neighbour, and not as rich birding territory, but there are plenty of terns and ducks and you may encounter the odd wader. Endemic **marine organisms** found in the lake have also been found to have strong cancer-fighting qualities. After four years of successful clinical trials in the USA and several EU countries, an extract from a tunicate found in Estany des Peix will be marketed as Yondelis (ET-743), a treatment for tumours.

PUNTA DE SA PEDRERA AND PUNTA DE SA GAVINA

The route around Estany de Peix from the highway soon deteriorates into a dirt track, heading through scrub bush, spiky succulents and prickly pears towards the remote promontories of the northwest coast. Though there are no sights of any note along the way, the route, marked by brown

Can Marroig signposts, is popular amongst mountain-bikers, and it's nice for a gentle afternoon stroll, particularly if you time your walk to coincide with sunset. Some 500m from the highway, the track swings west around the southern shore of Estany des Peix, passing a string of villas, before continuing another 3km northwest through thorny scrub to **Punta de sa Pedrera** (Map 12, B3), a small, thumb-shaped sandstone outcrop, favoured by Formentera's hippies as an isolated place to watch the sun sink into the sea and take in the expansive views across the Mediterranean to Es Vedrà (see p.170). From Punta de sa Pedrera, blue signs marked "kiosko" lead to the east shore of the promontory 100m below, where the famously testy owner of a dilapidated *chiringuito* sells simple, rather overpriced fried fish and drinks, the only refreshments for miles around.

From Pedrera, rough trails following the low coastal cliffs meander 2km to the southeast through bush and eroded sandstone to **Punta de sa Gavina** (Map 12, B4). Here, a crumbling conical eighteenth-century watchtower, **Torre de sa Gavina**, makes another agreeably quiet spot for sunset watching.

SANT FRANCESC XAVIER

Map 12, C4.

Formentera's tiny capital, **SANT FRANCESC XAVIER**, is a quiet little town 2km southeast of La Savina. The attractive network of pretty, whitewashed streets contains several boutiques and a couple of historic sights; it also serves as Formentera's administrative centre, with the police force, health service and local government all based here. Strangely, though, it's not much of a social centre, and though it does have a fair selection of bars, Sant Francesc's residents have the reputation of being a somewhat sedate bunch. If you've arrived from the mainland or from Ibiza Town, you'll have to get used to very un-Spanish timekeeping – eating before 10pm and drinking up shortly after 11pm – unless you decamp to the late-night pastures of Es Pujols.

The heart of the town is the **Plaça de sa Constitució**, an attractive little square, with a few benches scattered between gnarled olive trunks and sickly-looking palm trees, which is home to Formentera's most notable buildings. Consecrated in 1726, the forbidding, fortified **Església de Sant Francesc Xavier** stands on the north side of the plaza, its stark plastered facade embellished only with a tiny window set high in the wall. Until the mid-nineteenth century cannons were mounted on the building's flat roof as an extra line of defence against pirate attacks, an ever-present threat. Entering the church through the mighty main doors, strengthened with iron panelling, the interior is very sombre and plain, with a single barrel-vaulted nave, five tiny side chapels and a gaudy gold-plated altar. Beside the doorway, the large, alabaster baptismal **font** is its most curious feature, decorated with a crudely executed ox's head and weathered human faces. It's thought to date from Vandal times, but no one is quite sure who originally brought it here.

Adjoining the church to the south is the unpretentious, blue-shuttered old government building, while on the opposite side of the square is its attractive replacement, the **Casa de sa Constitució**. Built from local sandstone, this modern, two-storey centre of island power is draped with the flags of Formentera, the Balearics, Spain and the EC.

Sant Francesc's bars are reviewed on p.260.

A second chapel, the primitive fourteenth-century **Sa Tanca Vell**, 100m south of the plaza down c/Eivissa, is also worth a quick glance. Barely 5m long by 2m high and topped with a simple barrel-vaulted roof, it was originally constructed in 1362 from rough sandstone blocks, and the partly ruined remains were rebuilt in 1697, when Formentera was resettled. Sa Tanca Vell must have been a horrendously claustrophobic place to take Mass or seek refuge from pirates, with just enough space for a congregation of a dozen or so. After the resettlement, it served as the island's only place of worship for thirty years, until the much larger Sant Francesc Xavier was completed. Today, the building is fenced in and not open to the public, but you can get a clear enough view of the exterior through the protective railings.

The only other point of interest in Sant Francesc is the modest **Museu Etnològic** (Mon–Sat 10am–1.30pm; free admission), 100m northwest of the plaza on c/Sant Jaume. It's situated above a little cultural centre, which stages regular free exhibitions by local artists. Housed in two rooms, the museum's collection is not especially interesting unless you have a fascination for highly-polished old farming tools and fishing gear. However, there are a few curious old photographs of the island, including one from the early twentieth century of a very muddy, desolate-looking Sant Francesc. Outside the museum is the tiny toy-town steam train that used to shunt the island's salt to the docks from the salt pans.

CALA SAONA

Map 12, B5.

South of Sant Francesc, an undulating, ruler-straight main road heads through sunburned fields towards Formentera's southern plateau, the Barbària peninsula. Some 2.5km from the capital, a signposted branch road veers west through rust-red fields of carob and fig and small coppices of aleppo pine to the appealing cove of **Cala Saona**, 3km from the junction. The only cove beach in Formentera (and a fairly busy spot in the summer), Cala Saona has temptingly turquoise water, and fine sand that extends 100m back from the coast to the big *Hotel Cala Saona*, the bay's only building.

There's some fine cliffside **walking** south of Cala Saona, along coastal paths that meander past sabina pines and sand dunes and offer plenty of quiet, shady spots for a picnic lunch. The sunset views from this section of the coast are stunning, with dramatic views over the Mediterranean to the sphinx-like contours of Es Vedrà and Vedranell, and to the soaring hills of southern Ibiza.

BARBÀRIA PENINSULA

South of the Cala Saona turnoff, the road gradually begins its ascent of Formentera's southern plateau, the sparsely populated **Barbària peninsula**. The main attraction here is the eerily beautiful, almost lunar landscape itself, capped by a lonely lighthouse and a landmark defence tower. However, along the route there are also a collection of minor archeological sites, all signposted from the road. **Barbària II** (Map 12, C6) is the first and the largest set of remains, though the fenced-off remnants of this 3800-year-old Bronze Age settlement look unimpressive. Originally, the site contained nine simple limestone buildings – bedrooms, workrooms, a kiln and animal quarters – and was occupied for around three hundred years. It's beautifully located amidst small arid fields dotted with carob trees and dense patches of pine, which serve as prime habitats for **birdlife**, including flycatchers and the exotic, zebra-striped hoopoe.

Another 100m or so south, the second set of remains, **Barbària III**, are of a much smaller Bronze Age site.

Excavations have revealed no evidence of human habitation here, and it's likely the ruins were some kind of storehouse or animal pen used by the inhabitants of Barbària II. The final site, **Barbària I**, is right on the fringe of the last barren section of the peninsula, the Cap de Barbària, beyond a patch of pine forest and an ancient stone wall known as Tanca s'Allà Dins. Consisting of a three-metre-wide circular formation of upended stone blocks that may have represented a place of worship, the remains are a little more striking, but practically nothing is known about their significance. Tiny pottery fragments have been unearthed here, but there's no proof the site was ever inhabited.

Cap de Barbària

Map 12, B7.

The most isolated, barren region of the Pitiuses, the **Cap de Barbària**, or "Barbary Cape", is named after the North African pirates who passed this way to plunder Formentera. Looking across the bleak, sun-bleached landscape, dotted with tiny green patches of hardy rosemary and thyme, it's hard to imagine that there was a dense pine wood here until the 1930s, when ruined emigrés returning to a jobless Formentera during the American Depression chopped down the trees to make charcoal.

At the end of the road a white-painted lighthouse, the **Far des Barbària**, cuts a lonely figure on this moon-like plateau, standing tall above the swirling, cobalt-blue waters of the Mediterranean. Gulls, shearwaters and peregrine falcons swoop and hover in the sea breezes, and the occasional blast of warm desert wind serves as a reminder that Algeria is closer than Catalunya. If you pick your way 200m south of the lighthouse, you'll find a cave, **Sa Cova Foradada**, which is worth a quick look. You enter by lowering yourself into a small hole in the roof of the modest single chamber; once you're inside, you can edge your way to the mouth of the cave, almost 100m above the sea, for a stunning view of the Mediterranean.

Northeast of the lighthouse, it's a ten-minute walk over to **Torre des Garroveret**, a well-preserved, two-storey eighteenth-century tower. As Formentera's first line of defence against Barbary pirates, it would have been manned night and day in centuries past, but is no longer open. Formenterans claim that on exceptionally clear days it's possible to see the mountains of North Africa from here, despite the fact that they're 110km away.

SANT FERRAN

Map 12, D4.

Strung out along a busy junction on the main La Savina–La Mola highway, **SANT FERRAN** ("San Fernando" in Castilian), Formentera's second largest town, has an abundance of banks, bars, stores and restaurants. With its two main streets plagued by traffic noise and lined with an unsteady-looking sprawl of apartment blocks, your first impression of Sant Ferran may make you want to head straight out again. However, the most attractive part of town, hidden away a couple of streets northeast of the main highway, is well worth investigating, centred around the pleasantly austere village church, **Església de Sant Ferran**. The church was originally built close to the island's salt pans towards the end of the eighteenth century. However, poor construction methods and the unsuitability of the sandy terrain meant that the structure started to crumble; in 1883 it was taken down, and over the next six years reconstructed stone by stone in today's location. Uniquely in the Pitiuses, its simple sandstone facade, topped with a crude belfry, has not been plastered or white-washed.

Opposite the church is a spacious, paved **plaza**, lined with seats and young palm trees. There's barely a soul to be seen here for most of the year, but during the summer months it becomes a meeting place for young Formenterans and holidaying teenagers, who gather here in the high season's balmy nights to gossip and flirt. The more mature can be found just down the road at the *Fonda Pepe* (see p.260) on c/Mayor, the island's most famous drinking den, or eating at one of the string of restaurants south of the plaza.

ES PUJOLS

Map 12, D4.

Formentera's only designated resort, **ES PUJOLS**, 2km north of Sant Ferran, is an attractive, small-scale affair, popular with young Germans and Italians. It's lively but not overtly boisterous, with a decent quota of bars and a small club. Curving off to the northwest, in front of the clump of hotels and apartment blocks, is the reason why virtually everyone is here: the **beach** – two crescents of fine white sand, separated by a low rocky coastal shelf and dotted with run-down fishing huts, with beautiful shallow, turquoise water that heats up to tropical temperatures by August. It can get very crowded here in high season, when sunbathing Italians on rows of sunbeds pack the sands. There's nothing much to see away from the beach, and most visitors spend the evening wandering along the promenade, selecting a seafront restaurant and browsing the market stalls.

The summer **bar scene** is as lively as you'll get in Formentera, though don't expect cutting-edge tunes – most of the bars play standard-issue Mediterranean holiday-mix tapes. It's not difficult to find the action, mostly centred on c/Espardell just off the promenade and in the streets behind. The hippest spots in town are probably the *Moon Bar* (see p.261), on the road to Sant Ferran, with live DJ mixing and events; while next door is the small club *Flower Power* (see p.279).

CA NA COSTA

Map 12, D3.

A kilometre northwest of Es Pujols, signposted just off the road to the Ses Salines salt pans and overlooking the waters of Estany Pudent, is the fenced-off megalithic tomb of **Ca Na Costa**. The site was first unearthed in 1974, and represents the earliest proof of human habitation in Formentera; as such, it's one of the most important archeological finds in the Pitiuses. It consists of a stone circle of upright limestone slabs, up to 2m high, surrounded by concentric circles of smaller stones. These stand adjacent to a mass grave, where the skeletons of eight men and two women have been found – one of the male specimens, at some 2m tall, is thought to have been a sufferer of gigantism. Archeologists have also unearthed flint tools here not found anywhere else in the Pitiuses, and ceramic fragments indicating that early Formenterans were trading with Mallorca, suggesting a relatively sophisticated early society with established trade routes.

NORTH TO SES SALINES

Map 12, D3.

One kilometre north of Ca Na Costa along the road that skirts the east coast, a signposted turnoff on the right leads to two neighbouring sandy bays, **Platja des Canyers** and **Platja de sa Roqueta** (Map 12, D3), which both offer good swimming in calm shallow water and have kiosks selling refreshments. These twin beaches may not be amongst Formentera's most scenic, but they are popular with families based in the cluster of hotels behind the sands. Continuing north, Formentera's shimmering salt pans, **Ses Salines** (Map 12, D3) swing into view on the right. Though they haven't been in commercial use since 1984, crystallization in the steely-blue pools continues nevertheless, with foam-like clusters of salt clinging to the fringes of the low stone walls that divide the pans. For more on Pitiusan salt production, see the box on pp.184–185.

Together with Estany Pudent and Estany des Peix, the salt pans form an important **wetland** zone, attracting gulls, terns, waders and flamingoes, the latter encouraged (or perhaps confused) by the presence of two dozen pink concrete impostors. The salt pans and surrounding coastal region of northern Formentera, as well as southern Ibiza and Espalmador, are included within a protected "natural park" in which building is prohibited. Plenty of money has been invested in building wooden walkways and roping off the dunes, but until a new visitor centre opens in Ibiza in 2003, the tourist office is the only place to get more information on the reserve's ecosystems.

TRUCADOR PENINSULA

Map 12, C2–D2.

From the salt pans, a slender finger of low-lying land, the idyllic **Trucador peninsula**, extends north towards the island of Espalmador and Ibiza. Virtually the entire length of this flat, sandy promontory is blessed with exquisite **beaches** lapped by shallow waters, but mercifully the developers were never let loose here, and Trucador is now included in the Ses Salines Natural Park.

At the base the peninsula, on the west side of the salt

pans, several paths lead from a small parking area through dense patches of woodland to a slender, sandy beach, **Es Cavall** (Map 12, C3), sometimes called Cala Savina. You'll find two excellent, though slightly pricey, *chiringuitos* – *Big Sur* and *Tiburón* – and wonderful swimming, as well as more shade than you'll find further up the peninsula. Continuing north along a sandy track you pass a huge old windmill, **Molí des Carregador**, that used to pump seawater into the salt pans – it's now been converted into a mediocre seafood restaurant.

Past the windmill, the track continues north through steep sand dunes, passing a signposted right turn that twists around the northern edge of the salt pans to **Platja Llevant** (Map 12, D2), a glorious undeveloped beach that runs along the east coast of the Trucador peninsula. The eye-dazzling stretch of white sand is also where you'll find the large, popular *Tango* beach restaurant.

North of Platja Llevant, the sandy track eventually ends beside a huge car park, packed with hundreds of scooters and bicycles in high season. Just offshore are two small islets, **Pouet** and **Rodona**, that give this slim stretch of beach its name: **Platja Illetes** (Map 12, C2). The sands here are very popular with day-trippers from Ibiza in high season, when you can rent windsurfing equipment from a beachside hut.

You'll have to continue on foot if you want to explore the very narrow final section of the peninsula, barely 30m wide, bordered by blinding white powdery sand that never seem to get too busy. These back-to-back beaches are Formentera's very best, with astonishingly clear, turquoise-tinged water on both sides of the slim, sandy finger of land. A kilometre from the car park, you reach the northerly tip of Formentera, **Es Pas**, or "The Crossing", partially connected to the island of Espalmador by a 300-metre sandbar.

If the sea is not too choppy, you should be able to cross over without soaking your belongings.

Between May and October, regular boats shuttle between La Savina and Espalmador via Illetes beach, (€10 return).

Espalmador

Map 12, C1.

A 1.46-square kilometre expanse of dunes, sandstone rock and fabulous beaches, **Espalmador** has never been much of a settlement. Currently, just one large villa is seasonally occupied, though a small garrison of the Spanish army was stationed here until the early nineteenth century. The one monument, aptly-named **Torre de sa Guardiola** ("Piggy-bank Tower"), on the western flank of the island, is a two-storey eighteenth-century defence tower clearly visible from the decks of Ibiza-bound ferries.

Most people visit the island for the stunning natural harbour of **s'Alga** on Espalador's southern shore, with its dazzling, shallow water and fine arc of white sand. In summer, the sheltered bay bristles with yachts, and is a favoured destination for Ibizan day-trippers. Some visitors take time out to visit the **sulphurous mud pond** a few minutes' walk north of the beach. The pond does get popular with the day-tripping 18–30 crowd, but you'll probably have it to yourself if you visit early or late in the day. The entire crust of the four hectare pool has dried out considerably in recent years because of declining rainfall, but, even in the height of summer, there are three or four small patches of softer mud that you can climb down to for a good writhe around in gooey bliss.

Most Formentera-bound boat-trips from Ibiza stop at Espalmador's s'Alga beach on their way to La Savina.

ALONG THE CENTRAL STRIP: COVA D'EN XERONI

East of Sant Ferran, Formentera's main highway descends towards the **central strip**, an isthmus only a kilometre or so wide in places, with glorious beaches occupying its south coast and a largely rocky shoreline to the north. Just off the highway at the 6km marker, there's a signposted turnoff for **Cova d'en Xeroni** (Map 12, D5; May–October 10am–2pm & 5–8pm; €3.50), a large limestone cave consisting of a single, 40m-wide cavern, that was accidentally discovered in the 1970s when the owner of the land started drilling for a well. His son now conducts regular tours of the chamber's spiky crop of stalactites and stalagmites, though only in German, Italian, Spanish or Catalan. The tour has a certain kitsch appeal, as the owners have lit the cavern with 1970s disco lights, but unless you're interested in gawping at vaguely Demis Roussos and Santa Claus-like formations, it's not really worth the bother.

The main La Savina–La Mola highway does have cycle lanes, but the parallel Camí Vell is a more pleasant, less congested way to get around Formentera's central strip.

Platja de Migjorn

Map 12, D5–E6.

Vying with the Trucador beaches for status as Formentera's finest strip of sand, Platja de Migjorn (midday beach) is a sublime six-kilometre swathe of pale sand washed by gleaming, azure water, extending along the entire south coast of the central strip. Most of it is more or less pristine, with development confined to the extremities – at the western end, Es Ca Marí (Map 12, D5), signposted 3km south of Sant Ferran, is a loose scattering of hotel blocks set back from the sand; while at the eastern end, Mar i Land (see p.206) comprises two large hotels. To get to the best stretch of sand, turn south off the highway around the 8km marker, where a bumpy dirt track passes through wonderfully picturesque fields of wheat and fig trees separated by Formentera's characteristic dry-stone walls. You'll emerge at the sea beside the sand dunes that spread back from the shore, adjacent to *Mogambo* and *Lucky*, two of the best *chiringuitos* in Formentera – both very friendly places serving good, inexpensive food and drink. The legendary *Blue Bar* (see p.260), is also a mere two-hundred-metre walk away through the dunes to the east.

Castell Romà de Can Blai

Map 12, E6.

Around the 10km marker on the highway, a signposted turnoff leads just south to the fenced-in remains of a large Roman fort, **Castell Romà de Can Blai**. The sandstone foundations are all that's left of the square structure, which originally had five towers. The fort guarded the island's east–west highway and the nearby port, Es Caló de Sant Agustí, but little else is known about it.

Es Caló de Sant Agustí and around

Map 12, F6.

Nestled around a rocky niche in the north coast, 2km east of the Castell Romà, the tiny cove of **Es Caló de Sant Agustí** has served as nearby La Mola's fishing port since Roman times. Sitting snug below the cliffs of La Mola, this diminutive harbour of no more than 30m across has never been much grander than it is today, a rocky, semicircular bay ringed by the rails of fishing huts. It's a pretty enough scene, but there's no real reason to stop here other than for Es Caló's two excellent fish restaurants, *Rafalet* (see p.243), where you can dine overlooking the bay, and *Pascual*, a little further inland. The settlement's only other building is the *Hostal Residencia Mar Blau* (see p.224), which makes a superb, tranquil base if you want to linger in the central strip.

The shallow water surrounding Es Caló offers decent **snorkelling**; head for the heavily eroded limestone rocks that ring the bay to the south. However, the meagre scraps of sand don't really constitute a beach; you're better off walking 300m over the rocks (or taking the signposted turnoff from the highway) to the inviting sands at **Ses Platgetes** (Map 12, F5), where you'll also find a good *kiosko* selling snacks and drinks.

LA MOLA

The knuckle-shaped tableland of **La Mola**, the island's eastern tip, is the most scenic part of Formentera, combining dense forest with traditionally farmed countryside. La Mola's limestone promontory looks down on the rest of the island from a high point of 202m, and there are stunning views across the ocean from the steep cliffs that have given La Mola's inhabitants protection on three sides since the area was first settled around 2000 BC.

Getting to La Mola is half the fun. From Es Caló de Sant Agustí, the highway dips before beginning the long climb up, passing a signposted left turn after 500m for **Camí Romà**, or "Roman Way", a beautiful but steep pathway up to La Mola. Part of the original Roman road across Formentera, Camí Romà is popular with hikers, offering a refreshingly shady and traffic-free shortcut up the hill. Back on the highway, at the 13km marker, there's a turnoff on the right for the upmarket enclave of **Mar i Land** (also spelled "Maryland"), where two huge hotel complexes spill down a hillside towards the easternmost section of Platja de Migjorn beach. This section of shoreline, known as **Es Arenals** (Map 12, F6), is usually the most crowded spot on the southern coast. Although there are lifeguards on duty here between May and September, take care if you go for a swim, as the currents can be unpredictable.

The highway continues its steep incline past the Mar i Land turnoff, winding through Formentera's largest forest via a series of hairpin bends that will exhaust all but the fittest cyclists. At the 14km marker, the terrace of *El Mirador* restaurant (see p.242) affords a magical vista over the entire western half of the island, particularly worth taking in at sunset, when the sun sinks into the Mediterranean just beyond the hourglass-like outline of Formentera.

El Pilar de la Mola

Map 12, G6.

The region's solitary village, and something of a social centre for the farmers and hippies who make up most of the area's population, **EL PILAR DE LA MOLA** is a modest, pleasantly unspoiled settlement of around fifty houses, a handful of stores and a few simple bar-cafés strung along the main highway. Most of the time it's a very subdued little place, though there's a flurry of activity on Wednesdays and Sundays in the summer season, when an **art market** (May–late Sept 4–9pm) is held in the village's small central plaza. Much of the jewellery and craftwork is made locally, and tends to be far more imaginative than most of the junk on sale in Ibizan hippy markets; there's usually some live music towards the end of the day as well. On market days, an extra bus runs across the island, leaving at 5pm from La

Savina and passing Sant Francesc, Sant Ferran, and Es Pujols a few minutes later, before arriving in La Mola around 5.30pm; the return service runs along the same route, leaving La Mola at 7pm.

Two hundred metres east of the market plaza is the village church, **Església del Pilar de la Mola**. Built between 1772 and 1784 to a typically Ibizan design, it's the usual minimalist, whitewashed Pitiusan edifice, with a single-arched side porch and a simple belfry.

The only other sights around La Mola are two ancient **windmills** on the eastern outskirts (another pair are signposted just south of the highway), formerly used for grinding wheat. By the 1960s, these windmills had fallen into disuse and became hippy communes – Bob Dylan is said to have lived inside eighteenth-century **Molí Vell** for several months. Though you can't go inside the windmill today, it has been well restored and its warped wooden sails are still capable of turning the grindstone.

Far de la Mola

Map 12, H6.

The **Far de la Mola** lighthouse, set in glorious seclusion at Formentera's eastern tip, lies two kilometres from El Pilar de la Mola, through flat farmland planted with hardy-looking vines. The whitewashed structure, which has a 37-kilometre beam, is something of a local landmark, and was the inspiration for the "lighthouse at the end of the world" in Jules Verne's novel *Journey Around the Solar System*. Verne was obviously taken by the wild isolation of the site, and there's a stone monument to him beside the lighthouse. There's also an excellent café-bar here, *Es Puig* (see p.261), a popular place for islanders to wait for the first sunrise of the New Year over the Mediterranean.

LISTINGS

Accommodation

Most people visiting Ibiza and Formentera have their **accommodation** included as part of a package holiday. However, if you want to make your own arrangements, you'll find a wealth of different options, from superb rural hotels to simple self-catering apartments and campsites. **Prices** are higher here than elsewhere in Spain, especially in late July and August, when demand is so high that 98 per cent of Ibiza and Formentera's accommodation is fully booked. Nightly rates for a standard double room in a top hotel start at €180 at this time of year, and even the cheapest twin rooms will set you back around €34 per night. During the rest of the year, most places slash prices to around half the peak-season rate and, though you should have no problem finding somewhere to stay, there's less of a choice, as many hotels shut down for the winter.

Ibiza Town is by far the most cosmopolitan place to stay, and commands the highest prices; however, rooms in all price bands tend to be small, and it's extremely difficult to find anywhere at all in July and August. Almost all of **Sant Antoni**'s accommodation is block-booked for package holidaymakers, but we've listed a selection of inexpensive, independently-run guest houses. Elsewhere, there are some excellent *finca*-style country hotels scattered through-

PRIVATE RENTALS

During the summer, hundreds of privately owned apartments, houses and villas in Ibiza and Formentera are available to **rent**. Most are unregistered with the tourist board, and are sublet unofficially through advertisements in publications such as the *Diario de Ibiza* and *Ibiza Now*. For flatshares, try the notice boards in cafés and bars – the *Croissant Show* and *Chill* (see p.249) in Ibiza Town and *The Ship* (see p.257) in Sant Antoni are the best places to start a search. **Estate agents** such as those listed below operate on a more official level, with everything from Sa Penya apartments to vast rural *fincas* available on weekly, monthly and annual contracts.

If you can get a group of people together, renting a **villa** can be a very cost-effective solution to the high-season accommodation squeeze. Bear in mind, though, that many places are in remote areas, well away from shops, bars and nightlife, so you'll almost certainly need to rent a car to get around. Some of the **tour operators** listed on p.8 also organize villa and flight packages.

Central de Reservas Formentera ⓣ971 323 224, ⓕ971 323 096, ⓦwww.formenteraresevations.com.

Ecoibiza ⓣ971 302 347, ⓕ971 398 079, ⓦwww.ecoibiza.com.

Ibiza Online ⓣ971 393 400, ⓦwww.ibiza-online.com/accommodation/index.html.

Ibiza Properties ⓣ01883/723861, ⓦwww.ibizaproperties.net.

Ibiza Villas ⓣ01383 820 888, ⓦwww.ibiza-villas.com.

Loco Motives ⓣ & ⓕ971 192 166, ⓦwww.housenation.com/locomotives.htm.

Specifically Ibiza ⓣ971 194 958, ⓦwww.specificallyibiza.com.

out the interior and around the coast, with off-season bargains available. However, if you want to stay right on the beach, it's best to arrange accommodation as part of a package, as most of the resort accommodation is pre-booked by tour operators. In **Formentera**, demand for accommodation considerably outstrips supply in peak season, when you'll have to book ahead. There are no youth hostels in the Pitiuses, but you can **camp** at one of Ibiza's officially designated sites.

HOTELS AND APARTMENTS

Spain's confusing system of **hotel** and **apartment** categorization is best disregarded at the top end of the scale, but if you're searching for somewhere inexpensive to stay, look out for places designated a *casa de huéspedes* (guesthouse) or a *pensión* (pension). In general, price is a more reliable indicator than category, and you usually get what you pay for. At the bottom end of the scale, very few double rooms in the cheapest *pensiones* (costing €30–36 a night in high season) have private bathrooms, but almost all have a washbasin; for around €45, you'll get a bit more space plus an en-suite shower or bath, and for €70–100, you can expect extras such as a television or sometimes air conditioning. At the top end of the scale, above €140 a night, you will get all mod cons, as well as pools, gyms, spas and restaurants on site.

All **tariffs** are officially fixed by the Balearic tourism authorities, and should be clearly displayed in the reception area and on the back of each room door. Normally, there are three different rates: low season (Oct–April); mid-season (May–June & mid-Sept to late Sept) and high season (July to mid-Sept). Some places also impose additional price hikes in mid-August, Easter and New Year. If you're willing to do a bit of bargaining, many proprietors will give you an

ACCOMMODATION PRICES

Accommodation listed in this guide has been graded on a scale of ❶ to ❾. These categories show the cost per night of the **cheapest** double room in July and August, and include the seven per cent IVA tax; where more than one category is shown (eg "rooms ❻, suites ❾") the establishment has a selection of accommodation classes. Winter prices are often slashed to half the high-season rate.

❶ under €35
❷ €35–50
❸ €50–65
❹ €65–80
❺ €80–100
❻ €100–120
❼ €120–150
❽ €150–180
❾ over €180

extra **discount** if things are quiet. Lastly, you should always check if the seven per cent **IVA** (value-added tax) is included in the price quoted.

Unless otherwise stated, all the accommodation listed in this guide is open all year round.

IBIZA TOWN & AROUND

Hostal Bimbi

Map 3, A7. c/Ramón Muntaner 55, Figueretes ⓣ971 305 396, ⓕ971 305 396 May–Oct

Popular with backpackers, this comfortable family-run *hostal* is just a block from Figueretes beach and a 10min walk from the heart of Ibiza Town. Rooms are spotless and tastefully decorated. ❷, with private bathroom ❸

El Corsario

Map 4, F4. c/Poniente 5, Dalt

Vila ⓣ971 301 248, ⓕ971 391 953, ⓦwww.ibiza-hotels.com/corsario
Former pirate's den that's now an atmospheric landmark hotel in the heart of Dalt Vila; Dalí and Picasso allegedly stayed here in the 1950s. The rooms are quite small for the price, but have plenty of character, with beamed roofs and antique furniture; some have dramatic harbour views. Avoid the overpriced in-house restaurant. ❼, suites ❾

Hotel Es Vivé

Map 2, A6. c/Carles Roman Ferrer 8, Figueretes ⓣ971 301 902, ⓕ971 301 738, ⓦwww.hotelesvive.com
Funky new hotel, a Balearic HQ for affluent clubbers and music industry professionals. The building itself is a white-and-turquoise Art Deco landmark. There's a hip bar, a small pool and an excellent, but pricey, restaurant. The rooms are smallish, though all have a/c, and those on the upper floors have sea views. ❼

Hostals Juanito & Las Nievas

Map 3, F3. c/Joan d'Austria 18, New Town ⓣ971 315 822
These two neighbouring, centrally-located *hostals*, popular with young travellers, have clean budget rooms, some en suite. Both share the same management and prices. ❷

Hotel Lux Isla

Map 2, I1. c/Josep Pla 1, Talamanca ⓣ971 313 469, ⓕ971 302 566, ⓦwww.luxisla.com
Small hotel, well-situated 50m from Talamanca's beach and 2km from Ibiza Town. The rooms are bright, modern and comfortable, with attractive furnishings and satellite TV; many have sea views, while a/c is an optional extra. There's also a ground floor bar-café. ❺

Hostal Mar Blau

Map 3, E8. Puig des Molins ⓣ971 301 284 May–Oct
Excellent hilltop location, overlooking Figueretes beach, yet just a 5min walk from the centre of town. The rooms are simply but appealingly

furnished, with terraces or balconies, and small kitchenettes, though they lack full cooking facilities. There's also a bar, dining room and huge rooftop sun terrace. ❹

Hostal La Marina

Map 3, K3. c/Barcelona 7, La Marina Ⓣ971 310 172, Ⓦwww.ibiza-spotlight.com/hostal-lamarina/home_i.htm
Historic portside hotel in the heart of the action. The very stylish, good-value rooms are divided between three neighbouring houses, and there's also another annex in the New Town. Many rooms in the main *La Marina* building overlook the harbour, and have wrought iron beds and mirrors, a/c and satellite TV. There are cheaper, less well-appointed rooms in the *Caracoles* building almost opposite, and also in the *Ebusitana*, a 5min walk away. ❸, *La Marina* ❹

Ocean Drive

Map 2, H3. Marina Botafoc Ⓣ971 318 112, Ⓕ971 312 228, Ⓦwww.oceandrive.de
Just above the Botafoc marina and close to Talamanca beach, *Pacha* and *El Divino*, this is a favourite with DJs and club scenesters. The hotel exudes Miami Art Deco character, with a dramatic floodlit facade visible from across the harbour. Rooms are small but stylish, and all have a/c. Considering there's no pool, summer rates are pricey, but these plummet outside high season. The decent in-house restaurant specializes in Basque cooking. ❾

Hostal Parque

Map 3, G4. Plaça des Parc 4, New Town Ⓣ971 301 358, Ⓕ971 399 095, Ⓔhostalparque@hotmail.com
Superb and very central mid-range hotel. The tastefully decorated, spotless rooms are fairly small, but all have a/c (and heating for winter), and many have wonderful town views. Single rooms are especially good value, and share access to a rooftop sun terrace. Book well ahead. ❹

Hotel Apartamentos El Puerto

Map 3, G1. c/Carles III 24, New Town ⓣ971 313 812, ⓕ971 317 452, ⓦwww.ibiza-spotlight.com/elpuerto
Large motel-style block, with slightly soulless rooms and well-equipped self-catering apartments, some with large sun terraces. There's a swimming pool and a reasonable café on site. Good off-season rates. Rooms ❼, apartments ❽

Apartamentos Roselló

Map 3, F9. c/Juli Cirer i Vela, Es Soto ⓣ & ⓕ971 302 790
Supremely tranquil location with superb Mediterranean views, a 5min walk from Figueretes beach and the Ibiza Town bar action. The comfortable, simply furnished apartments have full cooking facilities, and most have wonderful sun terraces. ❹

Sol y Brisa

Map 3, G3. Avgda Bartomeu Vicente Ramón 15, New Town ⓣ971 310 818
One of the cheapest places in Ibiza Town, a clean and friendly, family-run backpackers' stronghold, close to the port bars and restaurants. The rooms are small and share bathrooms, but are good value. ❷

La Torre del Canónigo

Map 4, D5. c/Major 8, Dalt Vila ⓣ971 303 884, ⓕ971 307 843, ⓦwww.elcanonigo.com
Easter–Dec and New Year
Highly atmospheric apart-hotel occupying part of a fourteenth-century defence tower, in a fine location next to the cathedral in Dalt Vila. Considering the exceptional historic character and quality of the suite-sized rooms, which have either harbour or city views, a/c, kitchen facilities, satellite TV, DVD and hi-fi, the prices are not outrageous. Guests have access to a sauna and steam room and a swimming pool close by. Popular with visiting celebrities, even though it's quite a hike down to the port restaurants. ❾

Casa de Huéspedes Vara de Rey

Map 3, H4. Vara de Rey 7,

New Town ⓣ971 301 376
Excellent central hostel with friendly management and decent notice board. Though not the very cheapest in town, the scrupulously clean rooms (eight singles and three doubles) are simply but artistically furnished with seashell-encrusted mirrors and driftwood wardrobes; all share bathrooms. Streetside rooms are a little noisy in high season. ❷

La Ventana

Map 4, F3. Sa Carrossa 13, Dalt Vila ⓣ971 390 857, ⓕ971 390 145
Atmospheric hotel just inside Dalt Vila's walls. Immaculately furnished with antiques and Asian fabrics, the rooms are small, but have every modern amenity, including a/c and four-poster beds; most have great harbour views. Superb service, an excellent restaurant and rooftop terrace. Book well ahead. ❽

EAST COAST

Hostal Cala Boix

Map 5, E5. Platja Cala Boix ⓣ971 335 224
Situated above stunning Cala Boix beach, the peaceful location and simple, comfortable rooms with fans and sea or mountain views offer excellent value. Breakfast included. ❶

Can Curreu

Map 5, C5. ⓣ & ⓕ971 335 280, ⓦwww.cancurreu.com
Small, peaceful hotel in a converted farmhouse high in the hills 1km west of *Las Dalias* bar (see p.254). Exceptionally comfortable, spacious doubles have private terraces, jacuzzis, satellite TV, hi-fi, a/c and open fires in winter. The beautiful grounds contain citrus groves, a cactus garden and stable (horse riding is €22 an hour). There's also a fine restaurant and pool. ❾

Can Talaias

Map 5, E5. 2km northwest of Cala Boix ⓣ971 335 742,

Ⓕ971 335 032, Ⓔhotelcantalaias@ctv.es
Rural hotel on a remote hilltop, with panoramic views over pine woods to the east coast beaches. The ambience is bohemian – the sylish decor includes objets d'art, Asian fabrics and quirky sculptures. Rooms and suites have a/c and satellite TV; there's even a luxurious Moroccan tent available in summer, and the pool is wonderful. Rooms ❻ suites and tent ❾

Can Pere Marí

Map 5, A8 1km west of Roca Llisa golf course Ⓣ & Ⓕ971 187 134, Ⓦwww.canperemari.com
Tastefully converted nineteenth-century farmhouse, situated in tranquil hilly countryside 6km north of Ibiza Town. The well-furnished rooms all have a/c and stylish bathrooms, and there's a large pool. Breakfast is included, but there's no restaurant. ❼

Ca's Català

Map 6, E2. c/del Sol, Santa Eulària Ⓣ971 331 006, Ⓕ971 339 268, Ⓦwww.cascatala.com May–Oct
Friendly English-run hotel set on a quiet street in the heart of Santa Eulària, close to restaurants, shops and beaches. The en-suite rooms are comfortable but not elaborately furnished, and there's a delightful shady courtyard with small pool and sun terrace. Afternoon tea and cakes are served. No children. ❹

Hostal Rey

Map 6, F2. c/Sant Josep 17, Santa Eulària Ⓣ971 330 210 May–Oct
Pleasant, central and spotless place close to the Ajuntament, where the moderately priced singles and doubles are all en suite. Filling, inexpensive breakfasts are served in the downstairs café. ❸

NORTHWEST

Can Marti

Map 7, H3. 2km south of Sant Joan Ⓣ971 333 500, Ⓦwww.canmarti.com March–Oct

Delightful family-run rural hotel which also operates as an organic farm, set in a remote valley. The accommodation (doubles, a duplex and a cottage) is imaginatively decorated. Rates include bicycle hire; breakfasts are extra. Doubles ❺ Cottage ❼

Can Pla Roig

Map 7, H3. Sant Joan Ⓣ & Ⓕ 971 333 012

Just north of Sant Joan's church, this Ibizan-owned guesthouse is one of the cheapest places in the island. Rooms are simply furnished, with shared or private bathroom, and some have private terraces; there's also a communal kitchen. ❶

Can Pujolet

Map 7, C4. 2.5km northeast of Santa Agnès Ⓣ 971 805 170, Ⓕ 971 805 038, Ⓦ www.ibizarural.com

Luxuriously converted farmhouse in a tranquil location in the hills above Santa Agnès. Rooms are immaculately furnished with antiques, have a/c and satellite TV; suites and a self-contained bungalow are also available, and there's an excellent pool and jacuzzi. No restaurant, but breakfast is included. ❾

Es Cucons

Map 7, B5. 2km southwest of Santa Agnès Ⓣ 971 805 501, Ⓕ 971 805 510, Ⓦ www.escucons.com

Perhaps the finest rural hotel in Ibiza, with a blissfully peaceful setting in the high inland plain of Santa Agnès. Rooms and suites in the superb seventeenth-century converted farmhouse are very comfortable, with sabina-pine beamed ceilings and countryside views; all have a/c and satellite TV, and many have fireplaces. There's also an excellent restaurant, pool and big gardens. ❾

Hostal Cas Mallorquí

Map 7, H1. Portinatx beach Ⓣ 971 320 505, Ⓕ 971 320 594

Attractive beachside hotel in quiet Es Portitxol bay, with nine modern, comfortable rooms; all have sea views,

TV, private bathrooms, a/c and heating. There's a reasonable restaurant downstairs. ❺

Hotel Hacienda

Map 8, F3. Na Xamena
Ⓣ971 334 500, Ⓕ971 334 514, Ⓦwww.hotelhaciendaibiza.com May–Oct
Ibiza's only five-star hotel, set in a spectacular remote location in the rugged northwest cliffs. Rooms are luxurious, and most have terraces with a jacuzzi aligned for sunset-watching, and there are two restaurants, three swimming pools, a gym and a sauna/spa. The only drawback – apart from the price – is that you're far from any action. ❾

SANT ANTONI AND AROUND

Hostal Flores

Map 10, F4. c/de Rossell 26
Ⓣ971 341 129 May–Oct
Mid-range hotel in the centre of town, with fairly large, comfortable rooms, all with private bathrooms, and a popular bar-café downstairs. ❸

Hostal Residencia Roig

Map10, F4. c/Progress 44
Ⓣ971 340 483
Recently renovated central *hostal*, popular with young British visitors. The 37 attractive rooms have pine furnishings, good-quality beds and private bathrooms, and guests can use a pool nearby. ❷

Hostal Residencia Salada

Map 10, F3. c/Soletat 24
Ⓣ971 341 130 Easter–Oct
Spotless little hotel on a quiet street, with very inexpensive singles and doubles, some with private balconies and bathrooms. ❶

Habitaciones Serra

Map 10, F5. c/de Rossell 13
Ⓣ971 341 326 May–Oct
Run by friendly Ibizan family, this simple guesthouse in a quiet location close to Sant Antoni's church has ten basic, tidy and very inexpensive rooms; all share bathrooms. ❶

Pike's

Map 7, B7. 3km east of Sant Antoni ⓣ971 342 222, ⓕ971 342 312, ⓦwww.ibizahotels.com/pikes

Almost legendary, relaxed and idiosyncratic rural hotel, popular with visiting celebrities, DJs and musicians – Wham's "Club Tropicana" video was filmed here. Grouped around a fifteenth-century farmhouse, rooms and suites have Moroccan furnishings, plus all mod cons. There's a top-class restaurant, a swimming pool, sun terraces, a Jacuzzi, gym and floodlit tennis court, and all guests can purchase a VIP all-access club card. ❾

THE SOUTH

Hostel Cala Molí

Map 11, B2. 1km south of Cala Molí ⓣ971 806 002, ⓕ971 806 150, ⓦwww.calamoli.com May–Oct

Friendly hotel, high on the cliffs, with great sunset vistas. Nicely decorated with textile wallhangings, the seven doubles are very good value, and all overlook the sea; there's also a restaurant and small pool. Breakfast is included. ❺

Hotel Jardins de Palerm

Map 11, E2. Sant Josep ⓣ971 800 318, ⓕ971 800 453, ⓦwww.jardinsdepalerm.com

Small luxurious hotel, peacefully situated just above Sant Josep village. The stylish rooms and suites have a/c and cable TV; there's a lush garden, a decent bar and restaurant, and a beautiful pool. ❽

Hostal Mar y Sal

Map 11, H7. Salines beach ⓣ971 396 584, ⓕ971 395 453

Small, basic *hostal* just behind Salines beach. The smallish rooms have private showers; some have balconies and views of the sand dunes; there's also a good bar/restaurant downstairs. The location is pretty isolated, so you may want to rent your own transport, though there are hourly buses to Ibiza Town. ❷

Hostal Pepita Escandell

Map 11, H7. Salines beach

Ⓣ971 396 583 May–Oct
Tiny, very friendly place at the northern end of Salines beach with tidy, basic rooms; some have private bathrooms. There's a communal kitchen and peaceful garden. This *hostal* makes a tranquil seaside base: there are regular bus connections to Ibiza Town from a bus stop close by. ❶

FORMENTERA

Hostal Bahía

Map 12, C3. Passeig de la Marina, La Savina Ⓣ971 322 142, Ⓦwww.hbahia.com.
Medium-sized hotel, situated opposite La Savina's small harbour. All the rooms are bright, airy and spacious, and have a/c and TV; some have private balconies, while others share a large terrace. There's a café-restaurant downstairs. ❻

Pension Bon Sol

Map 12, D4. c/Major 84–90, Sant Ferran Ⓣ971 328 882 April–Oct
Basic, clean and fairly spacious rooms, with shared bathrooms, located above a friendly bar. Just about the cheapest accommodation in Formentera. ❶

Casitas Ca Marí

Map 12, D5. Es Ca Marí, Platja de Migjorn Ⓣ971 328 180 May–Oct
A stone's throw from the western end of Formentera's best beach, these basic, pine-trimmed bungalows all have small terraces and are fully self-catering. ❹

Hostal Centro

Map 12, C4. Plaça de sa Constitució, Sant Francesc Xavier Ⓣ971 322 063
Budget *hostal* across the square from the church, with simply furnished double rooms. The large adjacent restaurant, *Plate*, serves reasonable and inexpensive snacks and meals. ❷

Hostal Residencia Illes Pitiüses

Map 12, D4. Sant Ferran Ⓣ971 328 189, Ⓕ971 328 017, Ⓔhostalillespitiuses@cempresarial.com

Good-value, spacious and comfortable rooms, all with TV, a/c and private bathroom. The German management are knowledgeable and helpful. The only minor drawback is the location on a main road; try and book a room at the rear. ❸

Hostal Residencia Mar Blau

Map 12, F6. Caló de Sant Agustí Ⓣ & Ⓕ 971 327 030 April–Oct

Excellent small hotel, next to the fishing harbour and near Ses Platgetes beach. The bright, attractive rooms offer good value and have panoramic sea views; attractive apartments next door offer similar quality and price. ❹

Hostal Residencia Mayans

Map 12, D4. Es Pujols Ⓣ & Ⓕ 971 328 724 May–Oct

Pleasant *hostal* in a quiet spot 100m away from the main resort area. The modern, pleasantly decorated rooms, either with sea or island views, all have private bathrooms; there's a pool, and the terrace café downstairs serves a popular buffet breakfast. ❸

Hostal La Savina

Map 12, C3. Avgda Mediterránea 22–40, La Savina Ⓣ & Ⓕ 971 322 279, Ⓔ hostallasavina@terra.es May–Oct

Well-run hotel, situated opposite the Estany des Peix on the main road to Sant Francesc. The cheerful modern rooms all have a/c and attractive bathrooms, and most have lake views. There's a small beach just in front of the hotel, a ground floor bar/restaurant and an internet café. Buffet breakfast is included. ❺

Pueblo Balear

Map 12, E6. Platja de Migjorn (For reservations, call the neighbouring *Blue Bar* Ⓣ 971 187 011) May–Oct

The main attraction here is the stunning location, overlooking the island's best beach and very close to a couple of excellent *chiringuitos*. The stylish, self-contained apartments are housed in a superb whitewashed cuboid block. Book well ahead in summer. 

CAMPING

There are four **campsites** in Ibiza: two north of Santa Eulària, close to the resort of Es Canar, and two near Sant Antoni, but none in Formentera. All the sites open between Easter and late October only. They have plenty of shade, a food store and washing facilities; some also have bungalows and cabins to rent. Prices don't vary much between sites; per day, you'll pay a flat fee of €4–6 to pitch a tent, plus an additional €4–6 per person.

Though **camping rough** is illegal in the Pitiuses (the coastal dunes are particularly fragile areas), many people ignore the law and camp in remote areas where they are unlikely to be caught. If you follow suit, make absolutely sure that any fires you light are well contained and are completely extinguished before you leave – thousands of acres of woods are lost to forest fires every year.

CAMPSITES

Camping Cala Bassa

Map 9, C6. ⓣ971 344 599, ⓔccbassa@teleline.es

Beautiful site close to Cala Bassa beach, with full facilities, including a restaurant. Cabins sleeping two to four (€60), caravans sleeping six (€75) and hire tents (€4) are also available. Regular buses and boats run to and from Sant Antoni in the daytime, but you'll need your own transport or a taxi at night.

Camping Cala Nova

Map 5, D6. ⓣ971 331 774

Well-equipped site, 100m from Cala Nova beach and a short walk from Es Canar.

Attractive, self-contained log cabins sleeping either four (€45) or six (€58), plus mobile homes that sleep four (€56) are also available.

Camping Sant Antoni

Map 9, H4. ⓣ617 835 845 (mobile)

Pleasant shady spot just a 5min walk from the Egg, though it can get noisy. One-bedroom bungalows are also available, costing €42 with a bathroom, or €24 without; discounts are available for stays of more than two weeks.

Camping Vacaciones Platja Es Canar

Map 5, D7. ⓣ971 332 117

Popular with families, this site is close to the beach in the resort of Es Canar and has good facilities: a pool, laundry, security boxes and a bar/restaurant. Prices for the cabins (€16–24), caravans (€32–56) and hire tents (€9–16) depend on the season.

Eating

Ibiza offers a huge variety of **places to eat** in all price ranges, from hole-in-the wall takeaways through to cafés, *tapas* bars and restaurants serving everything from sushi and curry to pizza, as well as Ibizan and Spanish dishes. There's much less choice in **Formentera**, however, where there are some decent seafood restaurants and a number of good, informal *chiringuitos*, but little in the way of globally influenced dining. Nevertheless, there are plenty of excellent places to eat on both islands, and the listings below represent the best options across the price scale. Bear in mind, though, that at many places an excellent setting – from a converted chapel or farmhouse to an elegant harbourside terrace – may not be reflected in the quality of the food, particularly at the upper end of the scale.

Cuisine in the Pitiuses is relatively unsophisticated in comparison to other parts of Europe, with many smart-looking restaurants seemingly stuck in a 1970s timewarp – you'll regularly come across period pieces like steak and Roquefort sauce, prawn cocktail, Black Forest gateau and tiramisu. In the **resorts**, most establishments are geared to serving big portions of bland international food to diners they'll probably never see again. However, if you head for village and backstreet bars, you can tuck into the chunks of

SOME COMMON CASTILIAN AND CATALAN FOOD TERMS

	English	Catalan	Castilian
Basics			
	Bread	*Pa*	*Pan*
	Butter	*Mantega*	*Mantequilla*
	Cheese	*Formatge*	*Queso*
	Eggs	*Ous*	*Huevos*
	Oil	*Oli*	*Aceite*
	Pepper	*Pebre*	*Pimienta*
	Salt	*Sal*	*Sal*
	Sugar	*Sucre*	*Azúcar*
	Vinegar	*Vinagre*	*Vinagre*
	Garlic	*All*	*Ajo*
	Rice	*Arròs*	*Arroz*
	Fruit	*Fruita*	*Fruta*
	Vegetables	*Verdures*	*Verduras*
In the restaurant			
	Menu	*Menú*	*Carta*
	Bottle	*Ampolla*	*Botella*
	Glass	*Got*	*Vaso*
	Fork	*Forquilla*	*Tenedor*
	Knife	*Ganivet*	*Cuchillo*
	Spoon	*Cullera*	*Cuchara*
	Table	*Taula*	*Mesa*
	The bill	*El compte*	*La cuenta*

fish, meat or vegetables, cooked in a sauce or served with salad, that make up the **tapas** menu. **Vegetarian** options in formal restaurants are limited, but you'll find that many *tapas* are meat-free, and there's usually fish on the menu. If you don't eat meat or fish, you may have to resort to ordering a couple of starters in restaurants, or eating *bocadillos* or *tostadas* alongside the usual pizzas, pasta and salads.

Breakfast is usually a fairly light affair, often taken in the nearest bar or café. Standards don't vary much, and even in the roughest-looking joints you can expect excellent *café con leche* (milky coffee), *café solo* (a thick espresso-like shot of coffee) or a freshly squeezed orange juice (*zumo de naranja*). The classic accompaniment is a *tostada*: half a baguette, toasted on one side, sprinkled with olive oil and topped with either chopped tomato (*tomate*), ham (*jamón*) or cheese (*queso*). For **lunch**, particularly in the high-season heat, many locals enjoy a *bocadillo* (sandwich) – usually with ham, cheese, egg (*huevo*) or tuna (*atún*); for something more substantial, try the excellent-value *menú del día* (set lunch) deals, which typically include three courses and half a bottle of wine per person.

Dinner is usually taken very late in the summer, between 9pm and 11.30pm; in Ibiza Town and some country eating places, it's common to start ordering after midnight. The rest of the year, most people sit down to eat between 8.30pm and 10pm. Other than in August, it's usually unnecessary to book ahead.

Most restaurants concentrate on grilled meats and fish, usually served with a small portion of seasonal vegetables and potatoes, though there's often a local speciality on offer (see box on p.230). If you just fancy a pizza or bacon and eggs, you won't have to look too far in the resorts, and there's a good selection of Asian restaurants – though the Chinese restaurants are usually pretty dire. Almost every restaurant will give you a basket of bread and thick, rich *all i oli* (garlic mayonnaise) to dip into before you order.

IBIZAN AND FORMENTERAN CUISINE

Traditional **Pitiusan cuisine** is quite distinct from the Spanish-European food you'll encounter in most local restaurants, and you can often find a regional speciality or two on most menus. Many local dishes are very hearty – and a bit heavy in the summer months – such as thick meat stews, fish broths and rice dishes. Perhaps the most famous **meat** dish is *sofrit pagès* (country stew), a carnivore's delight of lamb and chicken (often with rabbit as well), potatoes, garlic, parsley and lashings of lard and oil. As in many parts of rural Spain, pork is the most important source of protein, with the annual *matança* (slaughter) providing the basis for a winter larder of delicious pork-based products. Tasty *tapas* of Ibizan *butifarra* (blood sausage akin to black pudding) and *sobrassada* (spiced sausage) are available in most bars.

Fish (*peix*) and **seafood** (*marisc*) are the other main sources of protein: red mullet (*moll*), sardines (*sardines*), wrasse (*raor*), lobster (*llagosta*), squid (*calamar*), cuttlefish (*sèpia*) and octopus (*polp*) are usually grilled, barbecued or fried, or added to stews. Local fish dishes include *bullit de peix*, a fish broth made with skate, and *guisat de peix*, a stew seasoned with cinnamon and saffron. Dried fish has always been a Formenteran speciality, with skate and tunny commonly used to add flavour to broths or as a salad garnish. Salt cod (*bacallà*) is usually cooked with onions, peppers, garlic, nutmeg and pine nuts to form the rich *bacallà amb salsa* (cod with sauce).

Rice (*arròs*) is another Pitiusan staple, used in many paella-like local dishes such as the fragrant *arròs sec*, with meat, fish, seafood, saffron and lemon, and *arròs amb peix*, with cuttlefish, parsley and peppers. You may also come across *arròs* *amb caragols* (rice cooked with snails), heavily seasoned with thyme, basil and fennel, and *arròs amb col* (rice with cabbage). Among the **vegetarian** options, look out for the traditional **salad** (*ensiam*) of tomato, onion, green pepper and garlic, which is far superior to the bland but more common Spanish *ensalada*, made with iceberg lettuce and tomato topped with sweetcorn and raw onion. To check if a dish is vegetarian, ask if the food is "*sin carne*" (without meat) before ordering – but note that lard and bacon fat is often added to stock and broths. Staple dishes include thick, wholesome *olla fresca* (bean and potato hotpot) and *cuinat* (chard, bean and sweet-pea casserole). Spanish omelette or tortilla, known locally as *truita*, is usually meat-free. In autumn, don't miss the vivid orange *cèpe* and *pebrasso* (milk) mushrooms, especially delicious when fried with garlic butter and served with chopped flat-leaf parsley; you'll find them served in restaurants across both islands.

Local **snacks** include the *coca*, a kind of pastry pizza-pie topped with tomato, onion and roasted peppers, which can also be fruit-based, using apricots or cherries. Dry, flaky spiral **pastries** dusted with icing sugar, *ensaimadas* are very common across the Balearics and are often given as presents. Dry *ensaimada* pieces are also mixed with eggs, milk, cinnamon and lemon rind and baked into a *greixonera* cake. At fiestas, you're sure to come across *bunyols* and *orelletes* (little ears), which are both doughnut-like pastry fritters flavoured with anise. *Flaó* is by far the best Balearic **dessert**, a wonderful crumbly flan made with pastry, eggs, cheese, plenty of sugar and topped with mint.

IBIZA TOWN

El Bistro

Map 4, F3. Sa Carrossa 15, Dalt Vila ☎971 393 203 Easter–Oct daily 1–4pm & 7.30pm–12.30am. Moderate

Classy French-Mediterranean restaurant inside Dalt Vila's walls on Sa Carrossa; food is served on the pavement terrace or in the intimate dining room. Good value, tasty cooking, especially grilled meats – try the pork fillet or lobster salad; wines are well priced, and the service good.

La Brasa

Map 3, H4. c/Pere Sala 3, La Marina ☎971 301 202 Daily noon–4pm & 7.30pm–12.30am. Moderate–expensive

Elegant but relaxed place, with a delightful bougainvillea-filled garden terrace in summer, and a wonderfully atmospheric indoor dining room with a log fire in winter. The Mediterranean meat- and fish-based menu is fairly simple, with seasonal specialities.

Bon Profit

Map 3, H4. Plaça des Parc 5, New Town (no reservations) Mon–Sat 1–3.30pm & 7.30–10.30pm. Budget

Excellent, very cheap canteen-style dining room, with stylish decor, shared

DINING PRICES

Each restaurant listed in this guide has been categorized according to the following grades: budget (under €17), inexpensive (€17–25), moderate (€25–35) and expensive (above €35) per person. These ratings relate to the price for a starter, main course and dessert, and include half a bottle of house wine. *Tapas* prices vary a lot less, typically costing around €1.80–3.50 per portion. Wine is much cheaper than in northern Europe; house wines start at around €5, while a bottle of Rioja is almost always available for under €12.

tables and a bargain-priced menu of Spanish meat, fish and vegetable dishes. Very popular – people queue to eat here in the summer.

Comidas Bar San Juan

Map 3, I4. c/Montgri 8, La Marina (no reservations) Daily 1–3.30pm & 8–11.30pm. Budget

Age-old, family-run place, with two tiny, wood-panelled rooms serving unpretentious Spanish and local dishes – the chicken soup and *embutido* sausages are really tasty. You may be asked to share a table, particularly in high season.

Macao Café

Map 3, N5. Plaça de sa Riba, Sa Penya ⓣ 971 314 707, ⓦ www.macaocafe.com Daily: May–Oct 1–4pm & 7.30pm–1am; Nov–April 7.30–11.30pm. Moderate

Stylish Italian restaurant at the eastern end of the harbour, with an extensive terrace that catches the sea breeze. Great salads, seafood and and grilled meat dishes, and particularly good fresh pasta – try the *spaghetti a la vesuviana*. The decent wine list has some interesting Italian options.

Mayura

Map 3, K5. c/Santa Llúcia 7, Sa Penya ⓣ 971 194 934 May–Sept daily 8pm–1am. Inexpensive

Genuine South Indian food, especially dosas, vegetable and fish curries, prepared with real flair by friendly, extremely helpful owners. Reached via a steep flight of steps from c/d'Alfons XII, it's a little tricky to find, set in a tiny plaza next to the city walls, but the surrounds are evocative.

La Plaza

Map 4, E2. Plaça de Vila 18, Dalt Vila ⓣ 971 307 617 May–Oct daily 1–4pm & 7.30pm–midnight. Moderate–expensive

Elegant Mediterranean restaurant, superbly located just inside the main Dalt Vila gateway, with a fine pavement terrace and tiled interior. There's an excellent selection of meat and fish dishes, and very reasonably-priced pasta.

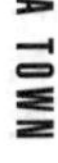

Pasajeros

Map 3, L4. 1st Floor, c/Vicent Soler, La Marina (no phone) May–Sept daily 7.30pm–12.30am. Budget

Tucked away on a tiny side street off c/Barcelona, this cramped, canteen-like diner serves some of the tastiest, best-value food in town: excellent, imaginative salads, filling main courses, plenty of vegetarian options and inexpensive wines. Popular with club workers, so it's a good place to find out what's going on.

El Pirata

Map 3, L4. c/Garijo 10b, La Marina ⓣ971 192 630. May–Sept 8pm–2am. Budget–inexpensive

Authentic, Italian-owned pizza house, in the heart of the port area, where you can eat vast thin-crust pizza on a harbourfront pavement terrace. There's also a hole-in-the-wall takeaway window to the rear, on c/d'Enmig.

Thai'd Up

Map 3, N5. c/de la Verge 78, Sa Penya ⓣ971 191 668, ⓦwww.thaidup.com. May–Sept daily 9pm–midnight. Moderate

Very tasty Thai food, served in a streetside terrace location at the very eastern end of Sa Penya, though there's also a tiny inside dining area. The service is friendly, and the curries, pad thai noodles and spicy soups are fresh and authentic.

Sa Torreta

Map 4, D2. Plaça de Vila, Dalt Vila ⓣ971 300 411 May–Sept daily 1–3.30pm & 7.30pm–1am. Expensive

Superbly positioned inside Dalt Vila's walls, the French-Mediterranean cuisine at *Sa Torreta* is a little more accomplished than the other options along atmospheric Plaça de Vila. The extensive pavement terrace is perfect for summer dining, but for a really memorable setting, book the inside room in one of the original bastions. Good fish, seafood and desserts.

Restaurant Victoria

Map 3, I3. c/Riambau 1, La Marina ⓣ971 310 622 May–Oct 1–3.30pm & 9–11pm,

Nov–April 1–3.30pm & 7.30–10.30pm. Budget
Charming, old-fashioned Spanish *comedor* (canteen), with simple furnishings and a welcoming ambience. It serves very inexpensive but well-prepared Spanish and Ibizan meat and fish dishes, with plenty of robust wines.

AROUND IBIZA TOWN

Bar Flotante

Map 2, H3. Talamanca beach ☎971 190 466. Daily noon–11pm. Budget
Informal, popular café-restaurant, with a large terrace right next to the sea at the southern end of Talamanca beach. The fish and seafood are especially good, with huge portions of sardines, hake and cod served with chips and salad; it's also a great place for a *bocadillo* and a glass of wine.

El Clodenis

Map 1, D4. Plaça de s'Església, Sant Rafel ☎971 198 545 April–Oct daily 12.30–3.30pm & 8pm–1am. Expensive
A good place for a splurge, offering an extensive wine list, exuberant Provençal cooking, and a lovely setting opposite the whitewashed village church. Book ahead for a terrace table in summer; the intimate dining rooms, decorated with Gallic prints, are also richly atmospheric.

Restaurante Soleado

Map 2, B5. Passeig de ses Pitiuses, Figueretes. ☎971 394 811 May–Oct 1–3.30pm & 7.30–midnight. Moderate
The finest restaurant in Figueretes, with a delightful seafront terrace positioned just above the waves, with views of Formentera. The Provençal-based menu includes *ensalada soleado* and dorada fish cooked with pastis-based sauce.

EAST COAST

El Bigotes

Map 5, E5. Cala Mastella May–Oct 12.30–3.30pm. Moderate

Set in a tiny inlet just around the rocks on the north side of a pretty cove, this is one of Ibiza's best-kept secrets. Feast on epic *guixat de peix* (two courses: fish and potato stew, followed by shellfish and rice) and grilled squid at long wooden tables right by the water's edge. There's also a simple dessert and wine list.

Es Caló

Map 5, E3. Cala de Sant Vicent ☎971 320 140 May–Oct daily 12.30–3.30pm & 7pm–midnight. Moderate

At the northern end of the beach, *Es Caló* is the finest restaurant in the area, with comfortable rattan seating and lots of modern art in the large terrace overlooking the bay. Ibizan and Spanish specialities include *buillet de peix*, and there's a nightly barbecue and an extensive wine list.

Restaurant La Noria

Map 5, E5. Cala Boix ☎971 335 397 Daily 12.30–4pm & 8pm–midnight. Moderate

High above Cala Boix beach, with tables below the clifftop pines and superb ocean views. Excellent seafood specialities include paella, *calderata de langosta* (lobster broth) and *guisado de pescado* (fish stew).

Restaurant Salvadó

Map 5, F5. Pou des Lleó ☎971 187 879 Daily 1–3.30pm & 7.30–11.30pm. Inexpensive–moderate

Overlooking an undeveloped fishing bay, *Salvadó* serves some of the freshest fish in the east. The paella and *bullit de peix* are especially good, and the service is friendly.

Taberna Andaluza

Map 6, G2. c/Sant Vicent 51, Santa Eulària ☎971 336 772 May–Oct daily 12.30–3.30pm & 7pm–midnight. Inexpensive

Simple taverna on Santa Eulària's main restaurant strip, with good service and delicious *tapas* – try the baked squid or meatballs – plus wonderful country bread with *all i oli*.

NORTHWEST

Ama Lur

Map 1, D4. Ibiza Town–Sant Miquel road, km 2.3 ⓣ971 314 554 Daily 12–4pm & 8pm–12.30am. Expensive

One of the finest restaurants in the island, about 7km north of Ibiza Town. It serves superb Basque cooking in a formal setting: fish and seafood are the basis of Basque cuisine, so try the exquisite hake, red mullet, swordfish or shellfish.

Bambuddha Grove

Map 7, G7. Ibiza Town–Sant Joan road, km 8.5 ⓣ971 197 510, ⓦwww. bambuddha.com May–Oct daily 8pm–2am; Nov–April Thurs–Sun 7pm–1pm. Expensive

One of the island's most acclaimed places to dine, a superb pyramid-roofed restaurant, built from reeds and bamboo. The inventive Asian-fusion menu includes yellow coconut prawn curry, yaki soba noodles, and Japanese-style bento boxes. Prices have risen in the last year or two, yet *Bambuddha Grove* still offers a great night out, with candlelit tables overlooking lush gardens, and a funky bar area where DJs spin tunes until 4am.

Can Caus

Map 7, E7. Ibiza Town–Santa Gertrudis road, km 3.5 ⓣ971 197 516 July & August daily 1–4pm and 7.30–midnight. Inexpensive

Locals' favourite, specializing in Ibizan cuisine, with bench seating outdoors and a snug interior. Virtually all the ingredients are sourced from Ibiza – the barbecued pork, cross-cut ribs and young goat are particularly recommended.

Can Pau

Map 7, F7. Ibiza Town–Santa Gertrudis road, km 2.9 ⓣ971 197 007 Oct–May, Tues–Sun 1–3.30pm & 8–11.30pm; June–Sept, daily 8pm–midnight. Expensive

Gorgeous converted farmhouse restaurant with a spacious interior and a huge terrace overlooking a lush garden. The Catalan cuisine – with some fairly successful *nouveau* leanings – attracts a moneyed, local clientele.

Es Caliu

Map 7, G7. Ibiza Town–Sant Joan road, km 10.8 ⓣ971 325 075 Sept–June daily 1–4pm & 8pm–midnight; July & Aug 8pm–midnight. Moderate

A carnivore's paradise, this country restaurant serves grilled meat (and nothing else) to an almost exclusively Ibizan clientele. The decor is rustic, with the odd stag's head or stuffed fox on the whitewashed walls, and there's a pleasant terrace for the summer months. Book ahead on Sundays.

Cilantro

Map 7, E7. Santa Gertrudis ⓣ971 197 387 May–Oct daily 1–4pm & 8pm–12.30am. Inexpensive

Delightful garden restaurant, just south of the village church. The evening menu is Asian based, with Vietnamese spring rolls, Malay curries and Thai noodles; at lunchtime, there's more of a Spanish flavour. A good set meal here costs around €10.

Es Pins

Map 7, G6. Ibiza Town–Sant Joan road, km 12 ⓣ971 325 034 1–4pm & 7.30–11.30pm; closed Wed. Inexpensive

Very simple Ibizan restaurant with log-cabin-like decor; the spartan menu has island specialities such as *sofrit pagès* and grilled meats. The three-course set-menu lunches are excellent value.

SANT ANTONI AND AROUND

Can Pujol

Map 9, E5. c/des Caló, Sant Antoni bay ⓣ971 341 407 Thurs–Tues 1–3.30pm & 8pm–midnight. Closed Dec–Ephipany. Moderate–expensive

Excellent seafood restaurant right on the beach, just east of Port des Torrent, with hypnotic sunset views over the Mediterranean. The shack-like surrounds and rickety furniture belie the quality of the cuisine – superb paella, fish and lobster.

Sa Capella

Map 9, H3. Sant Antoni–Santa Agnès road, km 0.5 ⓣ971 340 057 April–Oct 8pm–1am. Expensive

Set in an eighteenth-century chapel just off the Sant Antoni–Santa Agnès road, and patronized by the DJ elite and celebrities. The evocative setting is the real draw here; the salad starters are decent, but the cuisine can't quite match the surrounds.

El Chiringuito

Map 9, F3. Cala Gracioneta ⓣ971 348 338 May–Oct daily 12.30–4pm & 8pm–12.30am. Moderate

Sublime setting right by the water's edge in a sandy cove 2km north of Sant Antoni – it's especially pretty at night, when the restaurant owners float candles in the bay's sheltered waters. The straightforward menu includes swordfish steaks, paella and delicious barbecued meats, and there's a decent wine list.

Kasbah

Map 10, B2. Caló des Moro ⓣ971 348 364, ⓦwww.kasbahibiza.com May–Oct daily 10am–11pm. Moderate

At the far north of the San An bay, with an excellent sunset view, this classy restaurant has an elevated terrace setting, a friendly vibe and a lethal cocktail list. There's a real passion about the cooking in evidence, based upon the finest, freshest ingredients and a desire to experiment. Not surprisingly, *Kasbah* is extremely popular, and you should book ahead. The separate bar area, with leather Chesterfields sofas, is a great place for an evening drink.

Es Rebost de Can Prats

Map 10, F4. c/Cervantes 4, Sant Antoni ⓣ971 346 252 Daily 12.30–3.30pm & 7.30pm–midnight; closed Feb. Moderate

Very traditional family-owned Ibizan restaurant in a late nineteenth-century house, with pleasingly old-fashioned decor and friendly service. Dishes include pork rice, fried octopus, *calamars farcits* (stuffed squid) and local desserts.

Casa Thai

Map 10, I13. Avgda Dr Fleming 34, Sant Antoni ⓣ971 344 038 May–Oct daily 11am–11pm. Budget

Brilliant Thai diner with Bangkok-style, neon-lit outdoor seating next to the fume-filled highway. An authentic selection of curries, stir-fries and noodle dishes are served up at a furious pace. The three-course set menu – three courses plus a drink – is great value.

SOUTH

El Boldado

Map 11, B4. Cala d'Hort ⓣ626 494 537 (mobile) Daily 1–4pm & 7.30–11.30pm. Moderate

In prime position opposite Es Vedrà, this is a stunning location for a meal at sunset. The seafood menu includes the paella-esque *arroz marinera* or *guisado de pescado*, and the staff are friendly. The restaurant is a 5min walk west of the beach, past the fishermen's huts; you can also drive there via a signposted sideroad just northwest of Cala d'Hort.

Can Boludo

Map 11, I2. Camí del Cementeri Nou ⓣ971 391 883 March–Jan daily 9pm–12.30am. Moderate

Funky Argentinean-owned restaurant, set in a converted country house, with a rustic interior and elevated terrace overlooking the island. Prime cuts of Argentinian steak, fish, pasta and special South American desserts. *Can Boludo* is reached via a sideroad marked "Cementeri Nou" that heads north off the Ronda E–20 Ibiza Town outer ring road.

Can Berri Vell

Map 11, E1. Plaça Major, Sant Agustí ⓣ971 344 321 Sept–June Thurs–Sat 12.30–3.30pm & 8pm–midnight; open daily (same hours) July & Aug. Moderate

Atmospheric farmhouse setting, with a warren of rooms and a large dining terrace with views over the village church and the southern hills. The setting is the real draw, although the grilled meats are good.

El Destino

Map 11, E2. c/Atalaya 15, Sant Josep
Ⓣ971 800 341
Mon–Sat 7.30pm–midnight. Inexpensive

Wonderfully peaceful restaurant, just off the village plaza opposite the church, with a small outdoor terrace and a comfortable dining room. Healthy, modestly priced menu with plenty of choice for vegetarians, including decent couscous. Book ahead on summer nights.

La Escollera

Map 11, I6. Es Cavallet beach
Ⓣ971 396 572
May–Oct daily 1pm–midnight; Nov–April 1–5.30pm. Moderate

Superb position at the northern end of Es Cavellet's sandy beach, a huge outdoor terrace – with views of La Mola and Espardell – and a capacious interior. Renowned seafood, such as *zarzuela* (fish and seafood casserole) and paella; meat options include country chicken and rabbit. Popular with Ibizan high society for winter lunches.

Es Torrent

Map 11, E5. Es Torrent beach
Ⓣ971 187 402
May–Oct daily 1–10pm. Moderate–expensive

Deceptively simple-looking place with a wonderful shoreside setting, serving excellent fish, lobster and seafood. As there's no menu, the Ibizan proprietor Xicu guides you through the daily specials – try the *fideuá* seafood noodles.

Yemanjá

Map 11, F5. Cala Jondal
Ⓣ971 187 481
May–Oct daily 1–10pm; Nov–April daily 1–3.30pm & 7.30–10pm. Moderate

Excellent seaside restaurant, the best in Cala Jondal, set close to the cliffs at the eastern end of the beach; grilled fish, good meat dishes, creative salads and cava-based *sangría*.

FORMENTERA

Aigüa

Map 12, C3. La Savina
Ⓣ971 323 322
April–Oct daily 1–4pm & 7pm–midnight. Moderate

Very stylish harbourside bar/restaurant that's a regular venue for chillout events, with comfortable seating and a large terrace overlooking the marina. Spanish and European dishes, interesting salads and a decent *menú del día*. Strangely, the place never seems to get very busy.

El Mirador

Map 12, F6. La Savina–La Mola road km 14
Ⓣ971 327 037
April–Oct daily 1–4pm & 7–11pm. Inexpensive–moderate

Superb views over the island from the terrace and an inexpensive Spanish menu – with good portions of grilled meats and fish dishes – make this one of the most popular restaurants in Formentera. Book ahead in July and August for a table with a sunset view.

La Pequeña Isla

Map 12, G6. El Pilar de la Mola
Ⓣ971 327 068
Daily 1–4 & 8–11.30pm. Budget–inexpensive

Decent, dependable roadside village bar/restaurant, known for its well-prepared Formenteran cooking – roast rabbit, tortilla and plenty of rice-based dishes – served on a covered outside terrace, or in the dining area at the rear.

Es Pla

Map 12, C5. Cala Saona road
Ⓣ971 322 903
May–Sept daily 7–11.30pm. Inexpensive–moderate

The best pizzas in Formentera, straight from a wood-fired oven, plus a wide range of Italian dishes. The setting is wonderfully rustic, with a large dining room and a delightful garden terrace, perfect for summer eating.

Restaurant Rafalet

Map 12, F6. Caló de Sant Agustí
Ⓣ971 327 077
May–Sept daily 1–4pm & 7–11.30pm. Moderate
One of the finest seafood restaurants in the Pitiuses, right on the water's edge, with a comprehensive menu of Spanish and Balearic dishes. Excellent paella and *bollit de peix*, and perfectly grilled squid, sole or prawns.

Rigatoni

Map 12, D4. Es Pujols
Ⓣ971 328 351
May–Oct daily 1–4 & 8–midnight. Moderate
Midway along Es Pujol's beach, with a huge shoreside terrace, this Italian-owned restaurant serves some of the best food in Formentera – particularly the fresh pasta and fish dishes.

Bars and Cafés

Founded on Spanish sociability, and attracting a substantial resident crew of dedicated party people, Ibiza's dynamic high-season **bar scene** is excessive, outrageous and runs around the clock, a summer-long marathon of bacchanalian excess. The action is mostly concentrated in Ibiza Town and Sant Antoni, but there are also idyllic beach bars, club-bars, locals' locals, internet cafés and bohemian hideaways scattered throughout the island. Sleepy **Formentera** is much more restrained, with just a handful of good, no-nonsense village bars, some excellent chillout *chiringuitos* and a small but lively summer scene based in the resort of Es Pujols.

Ibiza Town offers an amazing choice of wildly cosmopolitan drinking dens. Beatnik bars sprang up here in the 1960s after the first wave of travellers descended, but the scene is much more diverse these days. In the La Marina port quarter, many bars offer fine harbourfront views, and a ringside seat for the outrageous club parades that are such a feature of the Ibizan night. Sa Penya, just to the east, has much more of a sleazy, underground feel, full of cavern-like bass bunkers catering to straight, gay and mixed crowds. Dalt Vila is a lot quieter, and there's a classy joint or two on Sa Carrossa, while over in the New Town,

Plaça des Parc and Vara de Rey are perfect for an outdoor beer or a coffee, night and day.

Sant Antoni is very different in character and clientele, but almost as busy in the summer season. The scene is younger, far less urbane and almost exclusively geared to the legions of British clubbers who fill the streets in high season. The hooligan mentality that so characterized the resort in the 1970s and 1980s still survives to a certain extent in the notorious West End, but there's also the **Sunset Strip** and neighbouring **Caló des Moro**, where a dozen or so stylishly designed bars have sprung up around the seafront on the west side of town. The success of these new bars owes much to the *Café del Mar*, the original venue, where the hugely influential DJ José Padilla created the sunset-bar concept, playing ambient soundscapes to the setting sun during his seminal residency in the 1980s and 1990s. In addition, many of the bars around Sant Antoni's revitalized harbourfront now have pools and sunbeds for daytime chilling, as well as terraces for sunset-watching and dancefloors for the pre-club wind-up.

Away from the towns, each village has its own bar-café or two, where good-value *tapas* or more substantial meals are always available. Even the most basic place will have a decent bottle of Rioja or Navarra, and a barrel of *vi pagès* – Santa Gertrudis, in particular, has a number of excellent, atmospheric establishments. Reflecting the area's longstanding association with all things esoteric, **northern Ibiza**'s bars have a distinctly bohemian flavour, especially Sant Carles's *Las Dalias* and *Anita's* in Sant Joan. If you're after more of a clubby flavour, **southern Ibiza** is the place: *km 5* and *Bora Bora* put on live DJ sets and don't charge door fees. Finally, **Formentera** has some of the finest chillout bars in the Pitiuses – perfect for dreamy days by the sea and inspirational ambient music.

There's much less of a distinction between **cafés** and bars here than in most parts of the world. Almost every café in the island serves alcohol, and virtually every bar will serve you a creamy *café con leche*, a *café solo* or one of the hundred or so different varieties of coffee available in Spain.

Unfortunately, the vitality of the bar scene is compromised considerably by the sheer **expense** of it all: drinking in Ibiza can be extremely costly in high season, with prices that send hundreds of fuming backpackers aboard the first ferry out of the island. Harbourside La Marina is an especially easy place to get stung – here, dozens of very ordinary, anonymous-looking bars exist by charging unknowing punters way over the odds for a drink. The terrace bars on c/Barcelona, which employ posses of ponytailed geezer-greeters, are particularly dangerous territory, but in the summer anywhere stylish or well-located in the capital or in Sant Antoni charges around €3 for a small beer and up to €8 for a spirit and mixer. During the low season, though, even the most chic bars slash their prices – but you'll still pay a little more than in mainland Spain. Thankfully, prices are much more reasonable in the smaller resorts and in village bars all year round.

Gay bars are reviewed on p.290.

The drinks may be expensive, but the happening bars of Ibiza Town and San An are the places to ask about club **guest passes** – and also to keep up with gossip and inside island information.

In the last few years, there has been a concerted effort by the authorities to regulate the bar scene. Sound limiters have become mandatory, and bars face steep fines if they crank up the volume. Before 2002, there were a number of superb bars (including *km 5* and *Morgana*) where you could count on dancing without paying an entrance fee.

However, most of these venues have experienced serious difficulties recently, as the all-powerful clubs have pressurized the police to enforce licensing laws stringently, and some of the island's most popular club-bars have been closed for weeks at a time. Obviously, the situation can change quickly, so it's best to ask around for the very latest information.

ALCOHOLIC DRINKS

Wine (*vino* in Castilian, *vi* in Catalan) is generally inexpensive, with a bottle of house plonk rarely costing more than €6, and a decent Rioja or Navarra around €12. Available only in village bars, the local wine, vi pagès, is pretty rough

DRINKS

	English	Catalan	Castilian
Alcohol	Beer	*Cervesa*	*Cerveza*
	Wine	*Vi*	*Vino*
Hot drinks	Coffee	*Café*	*Café*
	Espresso	*Café sol*	*Café solo*
	White coffee	*Café amb llet*	*Café con leche*
	Tea	*Te*	*Té*
Soft drinks	Water	*Aigua*	*Agua*
	Mineral water	*Aigua mineral*	Agua mineral
	(sparkling)	*(amb gas)*	*(con gas)*
	(still)	*(sense gas)*	*(sin gas)*
	Milk	*Llet*	*Leche*
	Juice	*Suc*	*Zumo*

and potent, but very cheap, at around €0.60 a glass. Sparkling wine (cava) is excellent, costing around €15 a bottle; Cordorníu and Freixenet are the most reliable brands. Often deceptively strong is sangría, a wine-and-fruit punch that's delicious when made with cava and a shot of Cointreau. Many restaurants and bars offer customers a chupito (shot) of liquor as a digestif – often a glass of hierbas, a very sweet local spirit flavoured with anise, thyme and other herbs. Spanish cerveza (lager beer) is generally good; the most popular brands are San Miguel, Estrella and Mahon. The most popular mixed drinks include vodka limón (vodka and Fanta lemonade), vodka tónica (vodka tonic) and cuba libre (rum and coke with lime), though you can also get any combination you'd normally drink at home.

All the usual fizzy soft drinks and juices are also available. **Mineral water** (*agua mineral*) is sold in bottles of either sparkling (*con gas*) or still (*sin gas*) – it's inexpensive, and infinitely preferable to tap water.

IBIZA TOWN

Bar Zuka

Map 3, M5. c/de la Verge 75, Sa Penya April–Oct daily 9pm–4am

Seriously stylish bar, with giant antique mirrors, a stately fireplace, imposing modern artwork and a balcony table with harbour views. Less frenetic than many bars in the port zone, it's an excellent place to converse and meet people. The attentive English owners provide good service and information.

Base Bar

Map 3, M4. c/Garijo 15–16, La Marina Ⓦ www.basebaribiza.com May–Oct daily 9pm–3am

Portside HQ for a hedonistic crowd of clubbers, dance-industry faces and well-seasoned rave scenesters, this is the Brits' favourite Ibiza Town watering hole – there's a raucous buzz about the place virtually the entire summer. Run by a veteran party-hard crew, the *Base Bar* has also spawned several CDs.

Sa Botiga

Map 3, F3. Avgda d'Ignaci Wallis 14, New Town Daily noon–midnight

One of Ibiza Town's most elegant bar-cafés, with rattan chairs, monochrome photographs, sandstone walls, a beamed roof and a palm-shaded patio out the back. Delicious *tapas*, a well-priced *menú del día*, draught Guinness and some decent wines.

Can Pou Bar

Map 3, I3. c/Lluís Tur i Palau 19, La Marina Daily noon–2am

With prime position by the harbourside and a quirky, disparate clientele of Ibizan artists, intellectuals and the odd drunk, this is one of the few bars to retain its character all year round. Music is a mere distraction as island politics are discussed and black tobacco puffed in the wood-panelled interior. Tasty *bocadillos* are available.

Chill

Map 3, C5. Via Púnica 49, New Town Ⓦ www.chillibiza.com. Daily 10am–midnight

Friendly internet café, and a popular hangout in its own right, with funky decor, a good notice board and healthy food and drink: Greek and fruit salads, ciabatta sandwiches, brownies as well as huge frothy coffees, herbal teas, fresh juices, shakes, beers, wine and spirits.

Croissant Show

Map 3, J4. Plaça de sa Constitució, La Marina Daily: April–June & Oct 6am–2am; July–Sept open 24hr

Popular café with a superb site under the main gateway to Dalt Vila and a reputation for baking the finest patisseries in town – though service can be defiantly negligent. Steady daytime trade, but the pavement tables are also lively around dawn, when weary clubbers perform a postmortem on the night's action.

Gecko

Map 3, L4. c/Barcelona, La Marina Daily: April–Oct 10am–3.30am; Nov–March 10am–2am

Hip new Anglo–Italian venture, with a funky live DJ mixes, a stylish interior, and a small terrace with seats overlooking the harbour; delicious pasta is available upstairs too. It's a good place to pick up the latest news, as the well-connected owners have been resident in Ibiza for years.

Grial

Map 2, E1. Avgda 8 de d'Agost 11 June–Sept daily 8pm–4am; Oct–May Tues–Sun 9.30pm–4am

Pub-like bar with live, funky DJ grooves that attract a hip, gregarious bunch of island-based regulars. With *Pacha* almost next door, it's a popular pre-club meeting point, and a good place to visit in winter, when the port bars are closed.

Madagascar

Map 3, H4. Plaça des Parc, New Town Daily: May–Sept 9am–2am; Oct–April 9am–midnight

The pick of the cafés on delightful Plaça des Parc, the French-owned *Madagascar* is stylish rather than self-consciously chic, with comfortable rattan furnishings, an outdoor terrace and jazz music. Wonderful juices, shakes and a limited food menu, and the finest mocha-tinged *café con leche* in Ibiza.

Mao Rooms

Map 3, K4. c/Emili Pou 6, La Marina Daily 9pm–3.30am

One of Ibiza's most happening bars, drawing celebs and the fashionista crowd. Owned by the London-based *Chinawhite* club, it hosts a series of well-attended parties, and there are regular sets from visiting DJs. Inside, the decor resembles an oriental opium den, with velvet curtains and luxuriant floor cushions. Decent Thai food is served upstairs.

Montesol

Map 3, H3. Vara de Rey, New Town Daily 8am–midnight

Arguably the epicentre of Ibizan high society, popular with the mature, perma-tanned, Gucci-wearing crowd. Excellent service from immaculately attired waiters, and prices are far from outrageous considering the location and reputation. Either *the* place to be seen, or a tired old joke, depending on your generation.

Nación Tierra

Map 3, K4. c/des Passadís 10, Sa Penya May–Oct daily 9pm–3am

Tiny, groovy bar that draws a sociable, predominantly Spanish crowd, who come for the kicking *caipiriñas* and *mojitos* and the eclectic Latin sounds. The outside tables are ideal for watching the club parades.

Noctámbula

Map 3, K4. c/des Passadís 18, Sa Penya May–Oct daily 9pm–3am

Italian-owned funky bunker with DJs mixing chunky house and garage. The lower-level bar has sculptured aquamarine walls, plenty of nooks and crannies and a party atmosphere, and there's a little chillout zone upstairs.

Rock Bar

Map 3, M4. c/Garijo 14, La Marina May–Oct daily 9pm–3am

Ibizan institution, next to the *Base Bar*, run by some of the best-known faces in the local scene, and drawing a slightly older, more international crowd than its neighbour. The *Rock Bar* has a stylish cream interior, DJ decks and a capacious terrace; the venue is popular with club promoters, so it's a good place to look for a guest club pass.

Sunset Café

Map 3, G4. Plaça des Parc, New Town Daily 9am–2am

Stylish bar-café that attracts an eclectic clientele, including a regular bunch of boho characters from the north of the island. Ideal place for a late breakfast of fresh juice and epic *tostadas* (try *jamón serrano* and tomato). The striking decor combines animal prints, velvet and neo-industrial fixtures; the music evolves from chilled daytime trip-hop and nu-jazz into evening DJ sets.

Teatro Pereira

Map 3, I4. c/Comte Roselló, New Town Daily 9am–5am

Set in what was the foyer of a nineteenth-century theatre, this is Ibiza Town's premier live music venue by night. Jazz bands, mainly playing covers, attract a sociable middle-aged crowd; entrance is free, but drinks are expensive. By day, it's a stylish café, with good creamy coffee, juices and *bocadillos*.

La Tierra

Map 3, K4. Passatge Trinitat 4, off c/Barcelona, La Marina Daily 9pm–3am

Gorgeous little bar, one of the town's most historic drinking dens, steeped in hippy folklore, and the scene of major "happenings" in the 1960s. There's less patchouli oil these days, but the ambience remains vibrant, carried by an eclectic mix of hard-drinking Ibizans and a few clubbers. Musically, things are kept funky, and there are regular live DJ sets.

Warhol

Map 3, F6. c/Ramon Muntaner 145 Daily 9.30pm–3.30am

Über-chic new modernist bar, with cutting edge minimalist design. One of the island's most fashionable places to be seen, *Warhol* draws a loyal Ibizan crowd. The glass walls of the bar area look in on a triangular zen-style garden; DJs spin house and progressive mixes, and there's a good cocktail list.

AROUND IBIZA TOWN

Alternativa

Map 1, E4. Jesús Daily 8pm–5am

Probably the closest thing to an Ibizan pub in the whole island, with four rooms, a pool table and dartboard – but not a football shirt in sight. After midnight, DJs spin house, funk and even Spanish rock to a mixed crowd of clubbers, bikers and island headcases.

Bon Lloc

Map 1, E4. Jesús Daily 7am–midnight

Unpretentious village bar crammed in the early mornings with Ibizan workers downing brandy and *café solo* and puffing Ducados. Later on, it's ideal for *tapas* or an inexpensive set meal – the paella is excellent. Huge historic monochrome photographs adorn the walls, and there's a decent notice board.

Croissanteria Jesús

Map 1, E4. Jesús Wed–Sun 7am–3pm

Efficiently-run breakfast café, with a big pavement terrace and a cheery interior decorated with old Martini signs. Choose between wholemeal toast, flaky butter-rich croissants, muesli, fresh juices, eggs and ham, or opt for the set breakfast menu.

El Motel

Map 1, D4. Ibiza Town–Santa Eulària road, km 1 May–Oct daily 10pm–4am

Bizarre-looking, dirty-pink building in the sub-industrial no-man's land north of Ibiza Town, with a richly deserved reputation as one of the island's premier temples of sin. There's a funky basement bar with a dancefloor and a substantial rooftop chillout terrace overlooking Dalt Vila. Formerly the *Manumission Motel*, the venue hosted legendary parties in the late 1990s; though recently the sleaze has become excessive and the party people have moved on. *El Motel* still hosts the odd good night, but ask around first.

EAST COAST

Alhambra

Map 6, E4. Passeig Marítim, Santa Eulària May–Oct daily 11am–1am; Nov–April Wed–Mon 11am–4pm & 7pm–midnight

Chic Moorish-style café,

complete with domes and minaret, situated in the middle of the harbourside promenade. Delicious Middle Eastern dishes include hummus, kebabs and couscous plus fresh fruit juices, shakes and a full range of alcoholic drinks (including cocktails).

Anita's

Map 5, D5. Sant Carles Daily noon–1am

Highly atmospheric village inn, just north of the church, once *the* gathering point for northern Ibiza's hippies and travellers, and still attracting a mixed bunch of local characters. You can enjoy superb *tapas* in the snug bar or on the vine-shaded patio, or order a full meal in the large dining room.

Café Guaraná

Map 6, G5. Port Esportiu, Santa Eulària Ⓦ www.guarana-ibiza.com May–Oct daily 10pm–6am; Nov–April Sat & Sun 9am–4pm

The funkiest bar in Santa Eulària and the sole venue for pre-club parties in the north of the island, with US garage and house mixes from residents and all the main Ibiza-based DJs.

Las Dalias

Map 5, C5. Santa Eulària–Sant Carles road, km 12 Daily 8am–2.30am

Idiosyncratic bar with a large main room, a good-sized garden terrace and a clientele of farmers and hippies. Hosts the weekly *Namaste* evening on Wednesdays, an Indian-themed night with vegetarian food, live music and a psychedelic trance tent (until 5am), plus assorted rock and jazz events and a quirky Saturday market (see p.106).

NORTHWEST

Bar Costa

Map 7, E7. Santa Gertrudis Daily 8am–1am

Richly atmospheric village bar, with a cavernous interior, monumental hearth and great outdoor terrace. Racks of *jamón serrano* garnish the ceiling, giving a delightful sweet-spicy aroma, the walls are covered in paintings (donated by artists to clear their bar bills). Decent menu and delicious *tostadas*.

Bar Es Canto

Map 7, E7. Santa Gertrudis
Daily 7am–4pm
Balearic bar *par excellence*, attracting a mixed crowd. Jumbo *tostadas* and *bocadillos*, fair prices and a raucous atmosphere, especially early in the morning, when the bar catches the sun.

Cafeteria Es Pi Ver

Map 7, F4. Sant Miquel Daily 7am–midnight
Uncontrived village bar – the 1970s Formica and fake wood decor isn't gunning for listed status approval, but the atmosphere is warm and welcoming. Decent *tapas*, country wine and beers.

Can Cosmi

Map 7, B5. Santa Agnès
Wed–Mon 11.30am–11pm
Famous for serving Ibiza's finest tortillas, *Can Cosmi* is also a great local bar, with a convivial atmosphere, plenty of local characters, very moderate prices and good service. The elevated, ramshackle terrace is ideal for summer drinking, with views of the village church.

Eco Centre

Map 7, H3. Sant Joan
Mon–Sat 11am–9pm
Part ethnic bazaar, part internet café, where northern Ibiza's New Age crew gather to surf, snack, sup and generally wallow in pre-punk nostalgia. There's a lovely back garden, and a notice board covered with information on rebirth groups and spiritual awakenings.

SANT ANTONI

Bar M

Map 10, H8. Avgda Dr Fleming May–Oct daily 9am–3am
Just south of the Egg, this striking purple and silver beach bar, owned by the *Manumission* team, is an essential pre-club venue, with propulsive live mixes from resident DJs, and a packed

outdoor terrace facing the beach. Good food too, from sandwiches to healthy breakfasts.

Café del Mar

Map 10, B5. Sunset Strip
April–Oct daily 5pm–1am
The original sunset bar, the *Café del Mar* initiated the globally influential Ibiza chillout music scene. Resident DJs maintain José Padilla's dreamy sunset soundscapes and raise the tempo with soulful house grooves. Unfortunately, the bar itself is set beneath an unlovely concrete apartment block, and the garish decor is on the trashier side of bubblegum kool. Snacks are available.

Café Mambo

Map 10, B5. Sunset Strip
May–Oct daily 11am–2am
Funky music-geared bar, with a stylish, canopy-shaded, double-deck bar terrace with sun loungers and showers. DJs mix everything from modern bossa nova to electro, switching at sunset to dreamy ambient soundscapes then seamless house grooves. It also hosts many pre-club parties, with big-name guest DJs.

Coastline

Map 10, A3. Caló des Moro
April–Oct daily 10am–2am
This stunning-looking addition to the San An scene has really put the bay of Caló des Moro on the map. Set beneath a sweeping modernist apartment building, there's an extensive sun terrace, three pools, and posh loungers. Often booked for pre-club warm-ups; it's all very flash, but the atmosphere can be a bit flat, and the expensive restaurant is unimpressive.

Itaca

Map 10, H8. Avgda. Dr Fleming May–Oct daily 11am–3am
Pre-club bar, with imposing Neoclassical, temple-like design and in pole position next to s'Arenal beach promenade, overlooking the Sant Antoni bay. Live mixing, guest DJ slots, and an infectious party vibe.

Kanya

Map 10, B2. Caló des Moro
May–Oct daily 10am–4am
Superb orange-and-blue creation, with a pool and sun terrace for blissful daytime chilling, and a restaurant for seaside dining. A class above the West End disco-bars, it's the only venue on this strip with an after-midnight dance licence, and the quality house music draws a funky bunch of Ibizan and British clubbers. Drinks are expensive, but there's no admission charge.

Savannah

Map 10, B6. Sunset Strip
May–Oct daily 10am–2am
Triple-deck bar, towards the southern end of the Sunset Strip, with an elegant hardwood interior, and an extensive terrace with sun loungers and brushwood brollies. DJs play placid daytime chillout tunes and Balearic house mixes after sundown.

The Ship

Map 10, F5. Plaça de s'Era d'en Manyà April–Oct daily 10am–3am
Friendly English-run pub serving British ale; popular with English workers, and a good source of information, with internet access and notice boards full of apartment rentals and jobs.

AROUND SANT ANTONI

Kumharas

Map 9, F5. c/Lugo, Sant Antoni bay April–Oct daily 11am–3am
A non-commercial and radically different take on the standard sunset bar formula, hosting regular chillout events that draw international DJs, musicians and artists. There's a pan-Asian food menu, a "no party anthems" psychedelic-trance and ambient music policy, and plenty of weird and wonderful active art and sculpture. However, the location is uninspiring, surrounded by concrete and far from the town centre.

Underground

Map 1, D4. Ibiza Town–Sant Antoni road, km 7 June–Sept open most evenings midnight–6am

Clubby bar, set in a converted farmhouse high in the central hills, just north of the main cross-island highway. *Underground* attracts a very fashionable bunch of international faces (party promoters here include Jade Jagger). The large dancefloor has a potent sound system, adjacent lounge-around rooms, and a beautiful garden terrace where food is served. Access is a bit tricky: be careful when turning off the main highway, as fatal accidents have occurred on this stretch of road.

THE SOUTH

Ancient People

Map 11, I4. Platja d'en Bossa June–mid-Oct daily 8pm–6am

Funky bar, located beneath the huge Jet Apartments. *Ancient People* successfully promotes a diverse selection of urban beats from drum'n'bass to soulful house and hip hop. Run by a friendly team, the full bar menu includes excellent smoothies.

Bar Can Bernat Vinye

Map 11, E2. Sant Josep Daily 7am–midnight

Scruffy, smoky locals' bar in Sant Josep village, serving inexpensive *tapas* and gutsy *vi pagès.* In summer, tables spill into the delightful plaza outside; the conversation usually centres on the rainfall, pigs and lucrative house rentals.

Bora Bora

Map 11, I4. Platja d'en Bossa May–Sept daily midday–midnight

One of the great success stories in the island, a bombastic beach bar-club set on Platja d'en Bossa's golden sands. Attracting some of Ibiza's finest resident DJs, it peaks some days with several thousand hungry clubbers celebrating one of the island's unique experiences: no door

tax, no moody bouncers, no queues and reasonably-priced drinks.

Jockey Club

Map 11, F5. Cala Jondal April–Sept Mon–Sat 11am–10pm; Sun 11am–6am

Chilled beach restaurant by day, the Jockey Club dancefloor has long been *the* place for island scenesters and Ibiza Town's groove-smitten crew every Sunday night. Unfortunately, due to licensing problems in the 2002 season, its future is uncertain. However, the owners plan to reopen the venue, and it's well worth a detour to dance under the stars to fearsomely funky, tribal club mixes spun by local DJs.

km 5

Map 11, G4. Ibiza Town–Sant Josep road km 5.6 June–Sept daily 9pm–4am Oct–May Wed, Fri & Sat 11pm–4am

Elegant, urbane bar–restaurant set in rustic nowhereland west of Ibiza Town, with a huge garden for relaxed drinking and socializing. The food is great: free-range chicken, steaks and a good vegetarian selection. The venue periodically has problems with its dance licence, but if this has been sorted out, there are few better places in the island than the intimate dancefloor to experience a really Balearic-style night.

Morgana

Map 11, H4. Sant Jordi–airport road km 1 Daily June–Sept 11pm–4am

Striking-looking bar, set in a two storey villa, with a large terrace garden and an internal dancefloor that draws a hedonistic local crowd. Like *km 5* and *Jockey Club*, *Morgana* has recently had problems with its dance licence.

Particular

Map 11, F5. Cala Jondal May–Oct daily 11am–10pm

Very cool beachside bar spread over a large, shady plot, with sunbeds and fine (if a little pricey) food – fresh fish, salads and barbecued meat – plus sumptuous smoothies and blended juices. Fluid, largely beatless chillout sounds from live DJs make this a wonderful place to kick back.

Sa Trinxa

Map 11, I7. Salines beach Ⓦwww.satrinxa.com Daily: April–Oct 11am–10pm; Nov–March 11am–7pm

The definitive Ibizan *chiringuito*, set at the southern end of the hippest beach on the island. Mellow, textural sounds from resident DJ Jonathan Grey, and a neo-Noah's Ark of beautiful Balearic wildlife – clubberati, models, party freaks and Euro slackers – to observe. Serves food, though service can be distracted.

FORMENTERA

Blue Bar

Map 12, E6. Platja de Migjorn Ⓣ971 187 011, Ⓦwww.bluebarformentera.com April–Oct daily noon–4am

The best chillout bar in the Pitiuses, with a blissful location in the centre of Formentera's finest beach and inspirational, beat-free ambient soundscapes. The wooden-decked terrace is idea for sunbathing and stargazing; inside, there's table football and a pool table. Food is served (book a table in advance), but be prepared to wait. To get there, follow the signs from the turnoff at km 8 on the La Savina–La Mola road.

Café Martinal

Map 12, C4. c/Archiduc Salvador 18, Sant Francesc Mon–Sat 8am–3pm

In the heart of the capital, this is by far the most popular breakfast café in Formentera, with healthy set menus that include fresh juices, yoghurt and muesli, plus mini *bocadillos*.

Fonda Pepe

Map 12, D4. Sant Ferran Daily: June–Sept noon–1am; Oct–May noon–midnight

Steeped in hippy history, this legendary drinking den was once *the* happening bar in

Formentera; nostalgia reigns in the bar, with photos and doodles from the 1960s on the walls. It's busy in summer, when the narrow terrace is packed with (mainly German) visitors.

Fonda Plate

Map 12, C4. c/Santa Maria, Sant Francesc Daily: May–Oct 10am–midnight; Nov–April 10am–11pm

Inviting place located just north of the main square in the heart of Sant Francesc. There's a lofty, beamed interior with a fine mahogany bar, and a vine-shaded terrace; plus pinball, pool and bar football. The extensive menu includes tapas, salads, pasta and good juices.

Lucky

Map 12, E6. Platja de Migjorn May–Oct daily 10am–sunset

Excellent Italian run *chiringuito*, smack in the middle of glorious Platja de Migjorn beach, with a short menu of well-prepared salads and fresh pasta, plus fine accompanying downbeat tunes. To get there, take the turnoff for the *Blue Bar* at km 8 on the La Savina–La Mola road, and *Lucky* is signposted once you reach the shore.

Moon Bar

Map 12, D4. Es Pujols–Sant Ferran road May–Oct noon–3am

Stylish bar on the outskirts of Es Pujols, with a huge terrace, modish lighting, and soul, funk and melodic house sounds from island-based and visiting DJs. Serves decent food.

Es Puig

Map 12, H6. Punta de la Mola May–Oct 9am–9pm; Nov–April 9am–6pm

The bar at the end of the world, right next to the Far de la Mola lighthouse, and famous for its legendary *platos de jamón y queso* – huge portions of local and Menorcan cheese, cured ham and salami. It's also *the* place to wait for the first sunrise of the New Year, when the bar stays open all night.

Clubs

Though the hype is monumental, few would contest Ibiza's status as the **clubbing** capital of the world, consistently delivering pure, hedonistic mayhem. Home to some of the planet's most celebrated clubs, plus scores of minor venues, the Ibizan scene is potent enough to break new tunes and influence dancefloors and airwaves from Tokyo to Argentina. Simply nowhere else has the same dependence upon, and commitment to, club culture and dance music – all the greatest house DJs have played here, and all the big players return year after year to move a uniquely enthusiastic crowd. At the peak of the summer season, the atmosphere in the clubs can approach almost devotional intensity, and leading DJs attain almost iconic status.

The **club season** starts in mid-June, with spectacular opening parties, and continues 24 hours a day until the last closing parties in late September. During these months, there's a club or a club-bar open at any time of the day or night – many seasoned campaigners prefer a good night's sleep before an all-day session on the terrace at *Space* or by the beach at *Bora Bora*, rather than a more conventional night on the tiles. By contrast, Formentera is much quieter.

Central to the island economy, clubbing in Ibiza is an

CLUB SURVIVAL

Clubbing in Ibiza is a very expensive affair. **Entrance charges** average around €30, rising to €50 at *Space* and *Pacha*; average entry fees to the smaller venues listed on p.276 are lower, however, at around €15. It pays to seek out **advance tickets** to the large clubs, available in the hip bars of Sant Antoni and Ibiza Town, which typically save you €6 (and include a free drink), or try to blag a guest pass from bar staff. **Drinking** is also very costly, with soft drinks around €6, a bottle of beer around €8, and a spirit with a mixer from €10 to €15. Not surprisingly, most people get livened up somewhere else before they get to a club. Unless you can stomach drinking tap water (which won't poison you, but tastes foul), you'll also have to pay about €6 for bottled water. In the summer heat, with hundreds of thousands of clubbers popping pills and dancing all night (and all day), the dangers of dehydration are obvious: if you take ecstasy, carry enough cash to maintain a steady fluid intake.

The big clubs will pay your taxi fare from anywhere in the island, provided that four people purchase an entrance ticket; you can also get home cheaply via the Discobus service (see p.30).

overtly commercial business. Giant promotional billboards for *Cream* and *Ministry* on the airport road hail your arrival in Europe's club central, and armies of PR people comb the streets and beaches attempting to persuade people that they cannot miss the party. The most flamboyant displays of the island's endemic subculture, however, are the promotional **club parades**: exuberant processions of banner-wielding stilt-walkers, silver spacemen, red devils and horny dwarfs patrolling the bars of Ibiza Town's port area and Sant Antoni's Sunset Strip.

Partly because of the money at stake, few promoters are willing to take risks when booking DJs, so in terms of **music**, the mix can get a little monotonous. Sunny party anthems and pounding hard house cuts are the main sounds, with little experimentation in evidence – tech-house, drum 'n' bass and electroclash remain very peripheral on Ibizan dancefloors. Since the late 1990s, **UK garage** has emerged as an alternative to the dominant four-four house beat, though in Ibiza the two-step garage style is still championed largely by a small number of British rather than island-based DJs. The **chillout** scene, concentrated in bars rather than clubs, is Ibiza's most creative musical genre, fusing nu-jazz, ambient, dub, Latin and Afro beats.

We've organized the club listings by venue rather than by night, as the action can change from month to month. While big promoters such *God's Kitchen* or *Renaissance* usu-

DRUGS

Ibiza was first dubbed "ecstasy island" by *The Sun* newspaper in 1989, and to some extent, the association is justified. Perhaps half the Ibizan economy is dependent upon "techno tourism", and ecstasy is so integral to the clubbing scene that removing it from the equation would take away the reason why many people want to visit Ibiza in the first place.

Nonetheless, ecstasy, cocaine, heroin, speed and acid are all **illegal**, and you could be looking at a jail term if caught with any of these substances. For more on drugs and drug laws in Ibiza, see Basics on p.40. If you are arrested for possession of drugs, inform the British Consulate (☎971 301 818), who have a list of English-speaking lawyers. All other nationalities should contact the relevant embassy in Madrid: US ☎91 587 2200; Canada ☎91 431 4300; Ireland ☎91 576 3500; Australia ☎91 579 0428; New Zealand ☎91 523 0226.

ally set up camp at a specific venue for the season, it's best to consult the **club listings** and DJ lineups in the special Ibiza editions of *Ministry* or *DJ Magazine* (see Basics, p.38) before you set out. Alternatively, check the clubs' own **websites**, or visit ⓦ www.ibizaholidays.com or ⓦ www.clubinibiza.co.uk, which both have a full round-up of the summer club scene.

THE BIG CLUBS

Amnesia

Map 1, D4. Ibiza Town–Sant Antoni road km 5 ⓦ www.amnesia.es May–Sept; 5000 capacity

Musically, *Amnesia* is the most influential club in Ibiza, responsible for igniting the whole British acid house explosion and the resultant global clubbing revolution. On the right night, *Amnesia* can feel more like a live gig than a nightclub, with an audience of thousands facing the DJ stage in the main room, punching the air to trance anthems – all under a dry-ice belching cannon.

The vast warehouse-like main room is almost bereft of decor, save a banner or two bearing the promoter's logo, and its huge dancefloor is ideally suited to trance and hard house. In contrast, the terrace on the opposite side of the club is beautified by lush greenery; there's a dancefloor here, too, but the music concentrates upon less intense US house and Balearic rhythms. Forming an upper level around both sides of the club, the VIP balcony has stylish contemporary furnishings, Asian artefacts and statues.

A lowly farmhouse thirty years ago, *Amnesia* became a hangout for hippies in the 1970s, home to LSD-fuelled parties with music ranging from prog-rock to reggae and funk. After being completely eclipsed by the *Ku*

over the road in the early 1980s, *Amnesia* reinvented itself as Ibiza's first after-hours club, opening at 5am – and successfully enticing the *Ku* crowd with an eclectic mix based on British electronic pop sounds.

In 1985, Alfredo unleashed a haul of dark hi-energy, minimal proto-house tunes and electro Italian club hits, and *Amnesia* quickly became the most fashionable club on the island; its reputation continued to grow over the next few years. However, new noise pollution laws in 1990 led to open-air clubbing being banned, and *Amnesia*'s owners were forced to construct a roof over the club. The demise of alfresco partying, combined with an inappropriate, rather brutal techno-based musical direction meant that *Amnesia* lost its way for a while in the early 1990s. Things improved by the middle of the decade, when the first wave of British clubs, especially Liverpool's *Cream*, together with the club's own *espuma* foam parties, injected fresh passion and new punters. By the 1999 season, with musical director Brasilio poached from arch-rival *Privilege* and installed as the club's head honcho, *Amnesia* secured a dynamic weekly line-up of parties. On Millennium Eve, *Amnesia* was *the* Ibizan club to be in, throwing a free party that was the talk of the island.

The club continued to prosper during the difficult summer of 2002, when numbers were well down in many other venues. Its success was due to a diverse array of promoters and events: *Cocoon* pulling the trance techno crowd, *Cream* serving up fearsome hard house, while *La Troya Asesina* ruled unchallenged as the biggest gay night in Spain.

Eden

Map 10, I6. c/Salvador Espiriu, Sant Antoni Ⓦ www.edenibiza.com May–Oct; 4000 capacity

Eden gives its loyal, young (mainly British) crowd exactly what they want – a raver's delight of pounding house and trance, plenty of club anthems and an orgiastic party atmosphere.

Though it's now Ibiza's most modern venue, *Eden* was considered a bit of a joke for years – a disco throwback where all the leading DJs refused to play. However, serious investment by *Mambo*'s Javier and his crew in 1999 and 2000 resulted in state-of-the-art sound and visual systems, a new industrial-decor refit and multiple new rooms, stages, bars and podiums. BBC Radio One's Dave Pearce and Judge Jules were Saturday and Sunday residents, and, boosted by massive support for *Gatecrasher* and the *Retro* house night, *Eden* had assumed local supremacy by the end of the 2000 season; the club has sustained this success.

Eden's exterior is unmissable at night, bristling with electric-blue-lit domes and minarets. Twin steel serpents flank the lobby, while the interior is minimalist in design, with a huge main room under a domed roof; there's a chillout zone and a spacious back room playing alternative sounds. A Gaudi-esque steel balcony forms the substantial upper-level gallery, housing the VIP zone, VJ booths and more bars. Adjacent is the *Garden of Eden*, a stylish open-air bar-café that doubles as an after-hours morning venue.

El Divino

Map 2, F2. New Harbour
ⓦwww.eldivino-ibiza.com
Easter–Oct and some winter weekends; 1000 capacity

Mustard-coloured, temple-like *El Divino* vies with *Pacha* as the ultimate destination for the seriously solvent, with a stained-glass lobby, opulent restaurant and VIP lounge. Jutting into the Ibiza Town harbour, with water on three sides, it boasts the most enviable location of any club in Ibiza, its arched windows revealing a panoramic view of

the floodlit old town beyond the port.

Built in 1993, the club cannot claim to be especially musically influential (concentrating mainly on vocal house sounds), but it has always attracted a cosmopolitan crowd, with Euro-celebs, Gulf sheikhs, models and mobsters mingling with the mainly Spanish and Italian masses. *El Divino*'s patrons tend to be a bit more restrained than the pilled-up, histrionic Ibiza-virgins elsewhere. The most successful nights in recent years have been Naples-based club *Angles of Love* and Birmingham's *Miss Moneypenny's*, always packing the club with a glam, label-conscious crowd, while MTV have also held weekly parties here.

The best way to arrive at *El Divino* is to catch the club's free boat that shuttles across the harbour from the portside Passeig Marítim every fifteen minutes or so between midnight and 3.30am.

Pacha

Map 2, F1. Avgda 8 de Agost, Ibiza Town ⓦwww.pacha.es Easter–Oct, open weekends in winter; 3000 capacity

When Ibizans are asked to describe the island's favourite club, the *grande dame* of the scene, the answer is usually simply, "*Pacha* is *Pacha*". The one Ibizan club open all year round, *Pacha* is the classiest club on the island, with faultless decor, professional staff, and the best dancers in Ibiza. The decidedly international clientele embraces all ages, from young Ibizans to still-swinging playboys and fifty-year-old salsa fans. Over the years, the most successful partners, including *Made in Italy* and *Ministry of Sound*, have concentrated on uplifting, vocal-rich house rather than slamming techno or trance – music that suits the sophisticated clientele.

Pacha opened in 1973 in a farmhouse on the edge of the capital; the whitewashed exterior of the old *finca*,

framed by floodlit palm trees, still creates a real sense of occasion. Inside, the beautiful main room has a sunken dancefloor and serves international cuisine; you can also dine in a seriously stylish sushi bar. There's a salsa room, *Pachacha*, a Funky Room, *El Cielo*, and a dark Global Room where you'll find more diverse experimental beats. The elegant terrace, spread over several layers, is a wonderfully sociable, open-air affair, with vistas of the city skyline.

On the global stage, *Pacha* is an extremely powerful international dance music force. More than seventy *Pacha* clubs have established a worldwide identity for their chic, Balearic brand of clubbing, yet the *Pacha* headquarters remains firmly in Ibiza.

Es Paradis

Map 10, I7. c/Salvador Espiriu, Sant Antoni Ⓦ www.esparadis.com May–Oct; 3000 capacity

Aesthetically, *Es Paradis* is one of the most stunning clubs in the Mediterranean, a testament to the vision and endeavour of owner and founder Pepe Aguirre. Perfectly proportioned, its square foundation is topped by a beautiful glass pyramid, the venue's retractable roof, which dominates the skyline of Sant Antoni bay. Named in full as *Es Paradis Terranial* (Paradise on Earth), it's the second oldest of the big Ibizan clubs, and celebrated its 25th anniversary in 2000.

Inside *Es Paradis*, the layout is straightforward: an imposing lobby framed by Doric-style columns leads to a blindingly white arena filled with neo-Greco columns, marble flooring and verdant foliage. There are ten bars, a giant tropical fish tank, podium dancers and awesome sound and light systems; encircling the entire building, the upper balcony contains a second room with alternative sounds (it's converted into an art gallery outside peak season). *Es Paradis* started out as a simple outdoor venue, and grew organically until 1990, when its 120-tonne pyramidal roof proved the most innovative and successful solution to the new noise regulations. This set the club up for a consistently successful decade, with water parties (when the whole dancefloor is flooded) and *Clockwork Orange* nights ensuring that the place was consistently packed, drawing a young, almost exclusively British crowd. However, in recent years *Es Paradis* has had to compete with the transformed *Eden* over the road, and the flash Neoclassical-style decor now looks dated. Wisely, the club has teamed up successfully with *Twice as Nice* – the sexy, label-conscious UK Garage scene has proved well-matched with the *Es Paradis* environment.

Pin-Up

Map 11, I4. Platja d'en Bossa
Ⓦwww.pin-upibiza.com
May–Sept; 2200 capacity

Of all the new and revitalized clubs that that have recently emerged in Ibiza, *Pin-Up* has the most potential, and looks set to establish itself as a key venue. The club drew little publicity when it opened in June 2002; however, word spread about a club on the beach, and an eclectic bunch of promoters from Madrid, Barcelona and Paris soon attracted a glamorous, metropolitan gay and mixed clientele.

Pin-up has been built around the shell of the notorious after-hours basement club *Konga*, which attracted mainly a hardcore Ibizan crowd. Since the venue's transformation, *Pin-Up* follows the *Space* formula to the letter; it's primarily a day club, but with a 22-hour licence. The layout also mirrors *Space*, combining a club room and a huge outdoor terrace; the latter is its exceptional feature, right next to the Meditteranean. The terrace contains the main dancefloor and a chillout zone where clubbers can get a coffee or a massage, and relax on stylish sun loungers;

there's plenty of banquette seating under pine trees, and also an upper level VIP area. When the terrace closes around midnight, the old *Konga* basement functions as a nightclub. In complete contrast to its former dark, bunker-like appearance, the decor here is now inviting and contemporary, with white leather seating, electric blue neon lights and abstract visual projections set around a large central dancefloor.

Privilege

Map 1, D4. Ibiza–Sant Antoni road km 6 ⓦwww.privilege-ibiza.com May–Sept; 10,000 capacity

Listed in *The Guinness Book of Records* as the world's largest club, *Privilege* is also home to Ibiza's biggest night, *Manumission*. Formerly called *Ku* (after a Polynesian goddess of love), for ten years it was the most beautiful, extravagant and luxurious club in the island.

Ku originated in mainland Spain's most fashionable resort – San Sebastián in the Basque country – where three local businessmen and a Brazilian built a *discoteca* (also called *Ku*) that became the natural home for the nation's clubbing elite. The founders visited Ibiza in 1978, bought a bar/restaurant called *Club Rafael*, and for the next ten years set about creating the most extravagant, luxurious club in the world.

The sheer scale and splendour of *Ku* was breath-taking. There were myriad bars, numerous dancefloors, phenomenal sound and light systems (the laser shows could be seen in Valencia), a swimming pool and a top-class restaurant, as well as huge terraces planted with pine and palm trees. Cocaine spoons and champagne cocktails were de rigueur, and there was no shortage of celebrities: Freddie Mercury sang Barcelona here with Montserrat Caballé; James Brown performed here; and Grace Jones danced naked in the rain here during a thunderstorm.

After construction of the roof precipitated serious

financial problems, *Ku* suffered badly from under investment, and was usurped by the glamour of *Pacha* and the innovation over the road at *Amnesia*. It wasn't until the creative impetuous and party fever generated by the arrival of *Manumission* in 1994 that the club – renamed *Privilege* the following year – started to turn things around. The 2000 and 2001 seasons were generally successful, with *Manumission* enjoying another solid summer and *Renaissance* filling the venue with an outstanding combination of live acts including Leftfield and Moby plus world-class DJ backup. However, consistency remains a real problem –

MANUMISSION

The predominant club night in Ibiza, *Manumission* (Ⓦ www.manumission.com) has been the biggest Balearic story of the last ten years, and can still be one of Ibiza's great experiences. Held every Monday at the club *Privilege* in Sant Rafel, *Manumussion* (Latin for "freedom from slavery") is always packed; crowds of 8–10,000 are common in high season, predominantly young and British clubbers, but there's also a gay following. The atmosphere tends to be more voyeuristic and theatrical than participatory, with the night built around the show rather than the DJ, a ploy *Manumission* have long used to avoid paying for the industry's most expensive turntablists.

Manumission is, in effect, two brothers, Andy and Mike McKay, and their partners Dawn and Claire. Also employed are dildo-wielding strippers, performing dwarfs, lesbian nurses and fluffy pink bunnies – in a Malcolm McLaren-style publicity drive to shock the British and Ibizan media, and get *Manumission* talked about. Most outrageous of all were live sex shows, starring Mike and Claire, which crowned the club night until the end of the 1998 season – the indignation of the British tabloids while *Manumission* guarantees a near full house once a week, on many days, even in peak season, the vast hanger-like space can be very quiet.

Even so, if you pick the right night, *Privilege* is an unforgettable experience. As you enter, the sheer scale of the venue becomes apparent, with a vast main dancefloor and the DJ plinth positioned above the swimming pool like a pulpit. To the rear, there's a stage for live acts, while two large bar areas – the revamped, pink *Coco Loco* and a double-deck back room – are to the right. Fourteen further bars and a café are scattered around, two VIP zones are on the upper levels,

ensured *Manumission* was the one night on the island that the clubber couldn't miss.

Manumission started out in the mid-1990s as a successful gay event in Manchester's Equinox club. After serious threats from local gangsters, the brothers blew their takings on a holiday in Ibiza, liked what they found, and stayed. Their first foray here was to host a night in Ku's Coco Loco bar at the start of the 1994 season; within a few weeks, they had taken over the main body of the club and were pulling in 6000 punters a night. The formula has remained the same, with stunning parades, floorshows, extravagant costumes, acrobats and stilt-walkers, all supported by a highly-efficient promotional team.

The *Manumission* team have also diversified the brand from the clubbing core over the years, with an unsuccessful *Manumission* movie, and a small-scale holiday operation. Several bar and restaurant ventures have also been attempted, including the fabulously opprobrious *Manumission Motel* – but only *Bar M* in Sant Antoni survives.

and there's even a DJ in the toilets. The vast, metal-framed open-air dome above the café serves as the club's chillout zone.

Space

Map 11, I4. Platja d'en Bossa
ⓦwww.space-ibiza.com
May–Oct; 3000 capacity

A vast cream-coloured structure just off Platja d'en Bossa beach, *Space* is essentially a day venue, kicking off after sunrise when the regular clubs are closing – though the owners have also attempted some night events. This carry-on-clubbing scene attracts a very hardcore crowd, and perhaps the most cosmopolitan mix in Ibiza.

Originally a conference centre, the venue was taken over in 1987 by owner Pepe Roselló, who turned it into a club, and later extended the walls to create its famed terrace. Since the start of the 1990s, Sundays on the *Space* terrace has been one of *the* most fashionable places to be seen, an Ibizan institution that draws an eclectic crowd of Balearic-based clubberati, international party freaks and a big gay contingent. Things climaxed in 1999, when London's now-defunct superclub *home* took over the promotion of the Sunday session. A formidable roster of global DJs helped create the island's most notorious event, beginning at 8am and only closing at dawn on Monday after 22 hours of pure party mayhem. The hype reached fever pitch as the notoriety of the Sunday session grew; this drew ever-increasing numbers, but diluted the Ibizan character of the club somewhat. In fact, the crowding has become so intense that many former regulars now avoid the legendary opening and closing parties completely. The club's management, seemingly unable to get a queue moving or employ a half-friendly bouncer, must also bear responsibility for this.

Space is divided into two parts: a dark, cavernous, bunker-like interior, and a wonderful open-air terrace

IAIN STEWART

Atlantis, Ibiza

IAIN STEWART

Salines salt pans, Ibiza

IAIN STEWART

Café del Mar, Sant Antoni, Ibiza

JAMIE BAKER/DEMON LIBRARY

Manumission at *Privilege*, Ibiza

ROBERT CUNDY/ROBERT HARDING

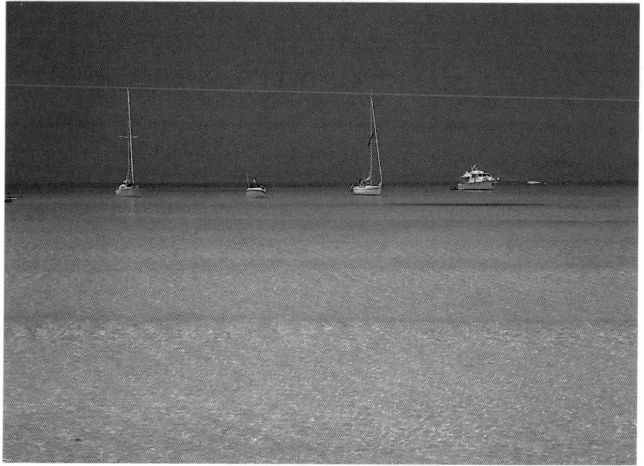

Formentera

TOM TEEGAN/ROBERT HARDING

Es Vedrà, Ibiza

Formentera

IAIN STEWART

Barbària peninsula, Formentera

graced with fine sandstone walls and topped with a brushwood roof. The dark, moody interior is an ideal setting for pounding beats, where minimal lighting helps reduce the sobering impact of the decor (1980s disco tack and holiday-camp-style surrounds).

With substantial rebuilding work necessary over the next few years, which will enclose the terrace with much higher walls, and strict new laws governing noise levels, it will be interesting to see how *Space* reacts. While Sunday guarantees a full house, the competition is now more intense, as emergent rivals *DC10* and *Pin-Up* (see p.270) also now host vibrant day sessions.

SUPERCLUBS OR "DISCO MAFIA"?

The recent downturn in the UK clubbing scene has also had a knock-on effect in Ibiza, with the big Ibiza clubs facing a decline in profits. Many locals now feel the large venues wield too much power and are above the law – all the main clubs routinely flout capacity and licensing regulations. For example, *Amnesia's* June 2002 opening party, which should have closed at 6am, was still raging twelve hours later and eventually wound down at 9pm; while *Privilege*, despite its Guinness-listing as the "world's biggest club" (with a capacity of 10,000), is only licensed for 4000. Many also accuse the self-styled Ibiza superclubs of pressurizing the authorities to close some of the club-bars (such as *Jockey Club*, *km 5* and *AK Morgana*) for weeks at a time on spurious legal grounds. As these smaller venues draw mainly a local crowd, anti-club feeling has grown amongst angry Ibizans, and "Stop Disco Mafia" graffiti now appears around the island.

OTHER CLUBS

Angel's el Cel

Map 2, E1. Passeig Juan Carlos 1, Ibiza Town New Harbour ⓦwww.elcel.net May–Sept; 2,200 capacity

Re-launched in July 2002 after a four year closure, *Angel's el Cel* is a striking and well-situated addition to the Ibiza Town club scene. But though it has the capacity and potential to compete with the big venues, the club has so far suffered from weak promotion and a failure to secure big-name DJs.

Angel's comprises of three rooms: a main room with a sunken dancefloor and modernist decorative touches, a small Funky Room, and the Crystal Zone, which overlooks the Ibiza Town marina. The club also boasts a 12-metre toboggan slide, which transports exhibitionists down to the main dancefloor. Finally, there's an ample outdoor terrace, with lots of foliage and Balinese furniture, plus a bar and comfy chairs, from where there are wonderful views of the harbour's millionaire yachts and Dalt Vila.

DC IO

Map 11, I5. Sant Jordi–Salines rd km 1 June–Sept

One of *the* success stories of the last few years, this daytime club has a raw, unpretentious appeal completely different to the corporate clubs. Forgoing commerce for pure party spirit, *DC 10* has been dubbed "the new *Space*" by a multitude of Ibiza scenesters; at times, the atmosphere here can rival the old acid house days, as a euphoric international crowd of smiling faces dance in the sunshine.

DC 10 is located in a rural corner of Ibiza, a stone's throw from the airport. The terrace, where all the action takes place, is little more than a wall around a paved floor, overlooked by the giant reeds of neighbouring fields, while

the scruffy interior room rarely gets busy. But these humble, rustic surrounds reinforce the appeal of the venue – *DC10* isn't about celebrities in stilettos and roped-off VIP areas, its a place for the Balearic band to get down and really party.

A low key after-hours club scene developed here in the mid-1990s; in 2000, however, *DC10* assumed a more cosmopolitan profile, when the Anglo-Italian *Circo Loco* ensemble started a Monday daytime slot with DJs Fabrizio and Jo Mills. Some amazing sessions followed, including an epic performance by the legendary Danny Tenaglia in 2001. In the 2002 season, the hype reached fever pitch as Norman Cook and assorted superstar DJs clamoured to get behind the DC decks. Sure to be huge in the next few years.

Inox

Map 10, D3. c/Soletat, Sant Antoni May–Sept; 1100 capacity

You'd hardly guess from its modest frontage, but this underground club extends down for two levels below the streets of San An. *Inox* ("steel") opened in 2001, when the owners of *Privilege* gutted the venue and installed new industrial-style decor. The stripped surrounds and zebra print seating look stylish enough, but there remains something not quite Ibizan about the place. During the 2002 season, it adopted an experimental music policy, hosting techno, drum 'n' bass and house nights, and kept drink prices at about half those charged in the big venues, winning favour with young British clubbers and seasonal workers.

Summun

Map 9, G5. c/Cala de Bou, Sant Antoni bay June–Sept; 600 capacity

Over on the west side of Sant Antoni bay, 3km west of the Egg, *Summun* is a well-established venue, hosting a diverse selection of nights, from UK garage MCs to eighties popster crooners. Upstairs there's a bar and a small rear terrace, while the main body of the club is in the basement. *Summun's* bizarre decor would shock a minimalist designer – walls painted with swirling images of pastel angels and gods reclining in alpine scenery, plastercast gourds and fruit hanging from the ceiling, Roman columns and quarry loads of marble. Entrance and bar prices are reasonable by Ibiza standards.

Of the also-rans, **Lucifer** (Map 2, H3) situated in the basement of the *El Corso* hotel near Marina Botafoc has the fundamentals of a wickedly salacious venue in place – a cave-like club room with a potent sound system and a large dancefloor (that used to be overlooked by a devil statue), plus an upper VIP room where swingers and the bondage brigade sometimes gather. Unfortunately, the club has always been very poorly promoted, and despite hosting some decent winter after-hours events, *Lucifer's* future is unclear.

Over in Sant Antoni, in the heart of the town's West End, you'll find an infamous strip of **disco-bars** centred on c/Santa Agnès (Map 10, F5–F6). All the venues – the *Simple Art Club* (probably the most popular), *Koppas*, *Play 2*, *Kremlin*, *Nightlife*, *Gorm's Garage* – open between 10pm and 6am, and draw a very youthful, raucous British crowd. Also in San An, the original dodgy disco, **Extasis** (Map 10, H6), right by the Egg, has little to recommend it. In the south, the tacky **Kiss**, located on Platja d'en Bossa, is prime wet-T-shirt contest territory in summer, and mainly popular with German holidaymakers. It's best avoided, although it has occasionally hosted some credible club nights in winter. Many of Ibiza's best **club-bars** have experienced licensing problems recently, but *km 5*, Cala Jondal's *Jockey Club, Morgana* and *Underground* (see pp.258–259), if open, all have dancefloors and offer a great Balearic-style night out. On a trance tip, the *Namaste* nights at *Las Dalias* (see p.254) are well supported by northern Ibiza's crusty clubbers.

There's very little dance-floor action in tranquil **Formentera**, but Es Pujols (Map 12, D4) has one medium-sized club, *Flower Power* (June–Sept only), offering house and mainstream dance sounds. It's worth noting that in high season, a special boat is chartered by Italian promoters *Made in Italy* to ferry people from Formentera to Ibiza for their *Pacha* nights, leaving around 10pm and returning at 6am; the latest schedule is available at the ferry terminal in La Savina.

Shopping

Ibiza has an eclectic shopping scene; this is a very style-conscious island, where locals and visitors really get dressed up – though there's much less preening and consumer choice in Formentera. Ibiza Town's La Marina quarter is the place to head for all things hip, with dozens of clothing stores and boutiques selling clubbing gear and funky accessories. This area is the heartland of Ibiza's Ad Lib fashion enclave, a globally influential bohemian style, originally characterized by long white flowing fabrics, that evolved in the island during the 1960s. The hippy-chic look continues to define today's Ad Lib style, and the tag is still used to promote the Moda Ad Lib fashion shows, some of the best-attended in Spain.

Ibiza and Formentera's traditional **arts and crafts** – basketry, tapestry and ceramics – are all struggling to survive in the age of mass tourism. Sant Rafel (see p.91) is a good place to find ceramics, while tiny basketry stores full of broad-brimmed Ibizan hats and *espardenyes* (grass sandals) still exist in La Marina amongst the chic boutiques. There are several **galleries** scattered around the island – Ibiza's light conditions and lovely countryside have attracted artists since the early 1900s, and there are hundreds of resident painters and sculptors. In central Ibiza, the Es

Molí gallery in Santa Gertrudis, and the *Bambuddha Grove* restaurant (see p.237), always have some interesting exhibitions by local artists, while in Santa Eulària try Galeria Cascais on the harbourfront below the *Hotel Tres Torres*. In Ibiza Town, Van der Voort in Dalt Vila's Plaça de Vila is the island's most exclusive, and Galería Altamira at Avgda Espanya 29 is also worth a browse. For **antiques**, try L'Occasione at c/de la Verge 47 in Sa Penya, Ibiza Town, or the excellent **auction** house, Casi Todo, in Santa Gertrudis (see p.136).

You'll find auction dates and full gallery and exhibition listings in the monthly magazine *Ibiza Now*, available from most newsagents.

BOOKSHOPS

Casa Azul

Map 3, G4. c/Caieta Soler 9, New Town, Ibiza Town ☎971 392 380

Beautiful bookshop with an excellent range of books on Ibiza, specializing in architecture, design, photographic and cultural titles. The in-store café serves fine teas, coffees and delicious cakes. There's another branch in Santa Gertrudis.

Island Books

Map 6, H4. c/d'Osca 8, Santa Eulària ☎971 331 158

British-owned bookstore, with an extensive range of fiction, travel, Ibizan and Spanish books, with secondhand titles upstairs.

CLOTHING SHOPS

Amaya

Map 10, F5. Plaça de s'Església, Sant Antoni
Large store with inexpensive trendy clothing and party wear accessories.

Ambulance

Map 3, H3. Avgda Bartolmeu Vicent Ramón 5, New Town, Ibiza Town
Funky menswear retailer, with a good stock of street labels (including G Star and Stussy), plus a limited range of beach and club gear.

Boutique Divina

Map 4, D2. c/Santa Creu, Dalt Vila, Ibiza Town ⓣ971 301 157
Ad Lib design par excellence, with racks of flowing white couture for men, women and children. Not cheap.

Can Felix

Map 3, J4. c/Antoni Palau 1, La Marina, Ibiza Town ⓣ971 310 322
A diverse selection of wonderful traditional and modern fans, costume and beaded shawls at moderate prices.

Cuatro

Map 10, G5. c/Ramón i Cayal 4, Sant Antoni
The best bet in San An for select men's gear, including Hustler, Evisu and Maharishi. The service is attentive.

David Ackerman

Map 3, J3. c/de sa Creu 15, La Marina, Ibiza Town ⓣ971 194 745
Very pricey, superbly designed and beautifully crafted ladies shoes, from slingbacks and chunky mules to pony skin sandals.

Diesel

Map 12, C4. c/Santa Maria, Sant Francesc, Formentera ⓣ971 322 116
Large store with all the latest male and female Diesel gear, including sunglasses and accessories.

Envy

Map 3, I4. c/de Montgrí 22, La Marina, Ibiza Town

A friendly, affordable boutique offering groovy, highly individualistic girlie clubwear and accessories.

EGB Man

Map 3, G3. c/Vincent Cuervo 11, New Town, Ibiza Town

Modish menswear boutique, geared towards a gay clientele, with a good range of stylish T-shirts, underwear and well-cut trousers.

Formentera Tattoo

Map 12, D4. c/d'Espardell, Es Pujols, Formentera

Moderately priced surf and skate wear, jewellery, and an in-store tattoo parlour.

Funkin' Irie

Map 3, G4. c/Caieta Soler 7, New Town, Ibiza Town

Zany, English-owned fashionista boutique, with gorgeous street and club wear for men and women; plus a record store well stocked with funky urban vinyl and CDs.

Kalani

Map 10, F4.

34q c/del progrés, Sant Antoni

Surf specialists with boards for hire, plus wet suits, clothing and accessories.

Merhaba Ibiza

Map 2, B4. Avgda Espanya 43, New Town, Ibiza Town ⓣ971 390 569

Warehouse-style store, with racks of very inexpensive girlie boho garb, beaded sandals and beach wear. Per-fect Ibiza gear, though you may get strange looks if you wear this stuff at home.

Sing Sing

Map 3, J3. c/de sa Creu 9, La Marina, Ibiza Town

Affordable Ibiza clubwear for women, with lots of bold prints and ruffled tops – though it helps if you're a size 8.

WAE

Map 3, H4. Plaça des Parc, New Town, Ibiza Town

Great selection of Indian cushion covers, sofa throws and jewellery, plus funky flip-flops and scented candles.

World Company

Map 3, L4. c/de la Verge 16, Sa Penya, Ibiza Town ☎ 971 314 769

Seriously stylish sunglasses, mainly Italian. Prices are inexpensive to moderate, and the service and range are excellent.

HEALTH FOOD STORES

Can Funoy

Map 3, I4. c/Montgrí 6 ☎ 971 310 770

Run by a delightful elderly Ibizan couple, this store sells a good range of quality health food and natural cosmetics.

Ecolandia

Map 10, I11. Avgda Dr Fleming 37, Sant Antoni ☎ 971 803 823

Health food supermarket with an excellent range of fresh organic fruit and vegetables, wine and beer, cereals, milk, Ibiza honey, fresh bread and baby food. The café-restaurant also offers a three-course set lunch menu for €8.

RECORDS AND CDS

With thousands of would-be DJs visiting the island annually, the recommended vinyl and CD specialists below stock an extensive selection of dance music.

DJ Beat

Map 3, K3. Plaça de la Tertulia, Ibiza Town

Megamusic

Map 10, F6. c/Santa Agnès, Sant Antoni

Pacha Records

Map 3, I3. c/Lluís Tur i Palau 20, Ibiza Town

Plastic Fantastic

Map 10, F6. c/Sant Antoni 15, Sant Antoni

MARKETS

If you're after meat, cheese, fresh fruit or vegetables, head for the produce **markets** in Ibiza Town (Map 3, A3), Sant Antoni (Map 10, F3) or Santa Eulària (Map 6, E2). Souvenirs, sarongs, tie-dyed garb and jewellery are the mainstay of the **hippy markets** held in all of the main resorts, though most of the stock is pretty average. There's nothing spontaneous about these hippy markets, either; all are widely promoted, with opening hours and directions available at the tourist offices, and excursions to Es Canar's massive Wednesday market (see p.105) offered by most hotels. The newest of these markets started in 2002, and is held every Tuesday at the Gala Night venue 4km east of Sant Antoni; the Gala Night grounds also have lovely gardens and a pool. The market is served by hourly buses from the terminal in San An.

The best of a bad bunch is the market at *Las Dalias* (see p.106), near Sant Carles, a smaller-scale affair with some quirky stalls selling quality crafts amongst the general tat. For a different flavour, check out the the car-boot-style at the Hippodrome (see p.179) or the **specialized markets**: organic produce at Can Sort (see p.121) and the Mercat d'Art (art market) in Formentera for interesting jewellery and hand-made souvenirs (see p.206).

Festivals

While Ibiza and Formentera cannot claim to host particularly extravagant **festivals**, annual celebrations are an important part of the social calendar and lead to grand family get-togethers. Every single settlement holds an annual *festa* to celebrate the patron saint of the community, and all follow a similar pattern: religious services and cultural celebrations in the church or village square, usually Ibizan *ball pagès* (folk dancing) and often a display from another region of Spain, plus some live music of the soft-rock variety. Bonfires are lit, *torradas* (barbecues) spit and sizzle, traditional snacks like *bunyols* and *orelletes* are prepared, and there's always plenty of alcohol. Some of the bigger events, such as the Sant Bartomeu celebrations in Sant Antoni on August 24 and the *Anar a Maig* in Santa Eulària, involve spectacular firework displays. We've listed the highlights in the festival calendar below; full lists of each village *festa* are available from the tourist board (see p.18).

The customary Pitiusan festival toast is *"Molts anys i bons"* ("many years and good ones").

Throughout the Pitiusan countryside, but particularly in Ibiza, **water-worshipping** ceremonies (*xacotes pageses*) are performed at springs (*fonts*) and wells (*pous*) to give thanks for water in islands perpetually plagued by droughts. Thought to be Carthaginian in origin, the festival-like ceremonies involve much singing, dancing and general celebration. In recent years, the culture department of the Consell Insular has began a restoration programme of Ibiza's historic wells, which are then opened with a fanfare of media publicity with speeches and the like, but traditional events continue unadvertised in isolated spots away from the cameras and reporters. For details of the better-known ceremonies, pick up the special leaflet available at tourist information offices.

FESTIVAL HIGHLIGHTS CALENDAR

February/March

Carnaval Towns and villages in both islands live it up during the week before Lent with marches, fancy-dress parades that poke fun at political figures and classical music concerts.

March/April

Semana Santa (Holy Week) is widely observed, with thousands assembling to watch the Good Friday religious processions through Dalt Vila in Ibiza Town and up to the Puig de Missa in Santa Eulària.

May

Anar a Maig Large *festa* held on the first Sunday in the month in Santa Eulària, with processions of horse-drawn carts, classical music, a flower festival and a big firework display for the finale.

June

Nit de Sant Joan
Midsummer Night (June 23) features huge bonfires and effigy-burning in Sant Joan, Ibiza, and throughout the Pitiuses.

July

Día de Verge de Carmen
The patron saint of seafarers

and fishermen is honoured on July 15 and 16 throughout the islands, with parades and the blessing of boats; celebrations are particularly large-scale in Ibiza Town and La Savina, Formentera.

Festa de Sant Jaume Formentera's patron saint is honoured by celebrations all over the island on July 25.

August

Festa de Sant Ciriac August 8 sees a small ceremony at the Capella Sant Ciriac in Dalt Vila (Map 4, C5) to commemorate the Catalan conquest of Ibiza in 1235, followed by a procession through the town and a mass watermelon fight in Es Soto below the Dalt Vila walls.

Día de Sant Bartomeu Huge harbourside fireworks display in Sant Antoni on August 24, a swimming race across the harbour, a slingshot competition plus the usual concerts and dancing. Also celebrated in Sant Agustí, where there's a football game between bachelors and married men.

December

Wine festival in Sant Mateu, Ibiza, over the first weekend in December.

Christmas (*Nadal*). Candlelit services throughout the Pitiuses on December 25.

New Year (*Cap d'Any*). Big parties in clubs and on Vara de Rey, Ibiza Town, where revellers celebrate the New Year in the traditional manner by eating twelve grapes as the clock strikes midnight.

Gay Ibiza

One of Europe's leading **gay** destinations, Ibiza's scene centres around twenty bars, a club, a network of gay-owned restaurants and a couple of lovely beaches. However, though gay visitors have been made welcome here since the late 1960s, the island remains an essentially **male** destination. There's no real **lesbian** scene as such, but plenty of gay women do choose to holiday in liberal Ibiza Town nonetheless. Check out the excellent **website** Ⓦ www.gay-ibiza.net for up-to-date information, advice, reviews and listings.

For more on Sa Penya, Figueretes and Es Cavallet, see pp.62, 89 and 181 respectively.

With numerous scene-oriented bars, restaurants and boutiques, the **Sa Penya** area of Ibiza Town has become something of a gay village, with the island's only dedicated gay club, *Anfora*, a short hop away inside the Dalt Vila walls. A compact beach resort fifteen minutes' walk southwest of the capital, **Figueretes**, which also attracts plenty of families and straight couples, is the other main centre. Grouped around the seafront are four or five gay bar-cafés, while many of the hotels and apartments in the resort have a predominantly homosexual clientele. Same-sex couples are very unlikely to experience any hostility on Figueretes beach, but many prefer to head 6km south for the glorious sands of nudist Es Cavallet, or to the tiny sandy beach below the *Apartamentos Roselló* between Ibiza Town and Figueretes, where partners can canoodle in peace. Salines beach (see p.181) is also a favourite hangout – the most popular section is to the south of the *Sa Trinxa* bar.

GAY-FRIENDLY ACCOMMODATION

The vast majority of gay visitors choose to stay in Ibiza Town or Figueretes. While you're extremely unlikely to encounter any prejudice in Ibiza, the apartments and hotels listed below are especially gay-friendly.

La Torre del Canónigo
see p.217.

Hostal La Marina
see p.216.

Ocean Drive
see p.216.

Apartamentos Roselló
see p.217.

La Ventana
see p.218.

Hostal Parque
see p.216.

Hostal Mar Blau
see p.215.

Hotel Apartamentos El Puerto
see p.217.

BARS AND CAFÉS

The heart of the gay **bar scene** is the c/de la Verge (see p.63), a wild, 400-metre-long lane that meanders through the Sa Penya area of Ibiza Town. It's lined with over a dozen tiny, atmospheric, cave-like bars, each with its own

pavement terrace. Just to the south, c/d'Alfons XII has another crop of stylish drinking dens, some with great roof terraces, while inside the city walls you'll find a couple of classy places on Sa Carrossa, below the Baluard de Santa Llúcia, itself a popular night-time cruising zone. In Figueretes, the scene is more scattered and less chic, but popular places include the lesbian-run *Monroe's*, *Bar DJs* and *Kitsch* close by on c/Ramón Muntaner, and *Magnus*, which has a big terrace beside the main beachside promenade.

Angelo

Map 3, K5. c/d'Alfons XII 11, Sa Penya, Ibiza Town

May–Sept daily 10pm–3am

Squaring up to *Dôme* on c/d'Alfons XII, and competing with it as the hippest gay bar in the neighbourhood, *Angelo*'s commands pole position for the club parades, but beware the exorbitant bar prices. The interior has recently been extended and smartened up, and now has a/c; there's also a rooftop restaurant.

Capricho

Map 3, L4. c/de la Verge 42, Sa Penya, Ibiza Town

Easter–Nov daily 9pm–3am

One of the busiest bars on gay Ibiza's main drag, with cutting edge tunes, a classy interior, beautiful bar boys and perhaps the most gregarious street terrace in town. It primarily draws a youthful German and British crowd.

Chiringay

Map 11, I7. Es Cavallet beach

April–Oct daily 10am–8pm

Gay Ibizan institution – a superb beachside bar-café, with mellow chilled sounds, a wonderful selection of juices, fruit smoothies and healthy food, as well as a resident masseur. Spread over wooden decks, all the tables have sea views.

Dôme

Map 3, K5. c/d'Alfons XII 5, Sa Penya, Ibiza Town

May–Oct daily 10pm–3am

The most beautiful bar staff, the most expensive drinks, and perhaps the town's best location, in the plaza-like environs of c/d'Alfons XII. As the final destination of most of the club parades, the atmosphere on the terrace outside reaches fever pitch by 1am during the summer, when a funky assemblage of fashionistas, models and drag queens fills the terrace.

Bar JJ

Map 3, M5. c/de la Verge 79, Sa Penya, Ibiza Town
April–mid-Oct daily 9.30pm–3am

Of all the gay bars in Ibiza, *Bar JJ* has probably the best connections to the club scene, and is a good place to score free passes for a night out. The attractive interior has great harbour views, and there's a narrow street terrace. Popular with the French and Spanish crowd.

Monroe's

Map 3, A7. c/Ramón Mutaner 33, Figueretes
May–Oct daily 10am–3am

Run by a larger-than-life British lesbian couple, and featured in the nauseous *Ibiza Uncovered* TV series, this temple of kitsch to Hollywood's celluloid goddess has Marilyn memorabilia on every wall. One of the most popular bars in Figueretes, it draws a mixed gay and family crowd, with regular cabaret shows. All rather tacky and passé, but try telling the regulars that.

La Muralla

Map 4, G4. Sa Carrossa 3, Dalt Vila, Ibiza Town
Easter–Nov daily 10pm–3am

Right next to Dalt Vila's walls, this classy French-owned place is the island's most elegant gay bar, with striking artwork on the sandstone walls and a wonderful mahogany bar. The long, narrow terrace outside is perfect for an amiable evening drink, and the atmosphere rarely gets raucous.

Oríental

Map 3, K5. c/d'Alfons XII 3, Sa Penya, Ibiza Town
Daily 10pm–4am

The chic *Oríental* has quickly become one of the hottest bars on the Ibiza gay scene, with resident DJs providing a pumping soundtrack. Popular with club promoters, it has strong ties with *Amnesia*, which guarantees the terrace is impassable on *La Troya* club nights. Open throughout the winter.

Soap Café

Map 3, K4. c/Manuel Sora 4, La Marina, Ibiza Town

Directly behind the often overcrowded *Croissant Show* (see p.249), *Soap* provides quick and friendly service, a well-stocked bar and the best crêpes on the island. It also has good connections with club promoters, so there are often passes available.

CLUBS

Though *Anfora* is the only gay club in Ibiza, *Pacha*, *Privilege*, *Amnesia*, *Space*, *El Divino*, *Pin-Up* and *Lucifer* all attract a mixed crowd, and all regularly promote gay nights. London's *Trade* used to team up with *Manumission* in *Privilege*, but they've recently jumped ship to host parties in *Amnesia*. There's also a regular *Scandal* night at *Pacha*, but the biggest gay event in Ibiza is the **La Troya Asesina** (see box on p.294) weekly event, held at *Amnesia*. Bear in mind that the Sant Antoni club scene is, by nature, very hetero-sexual.

Anfora

Map 4, E3. c/Sant Carles 7, Dalt Vila, Ibiza Town May–Oct, plus Easter and New Year; 500 capacity

Ibiza's only gay club venue, *Anfora* is nicknamed "Auntie Fora" by many. Set inside a natural cave in the heart of Dalt Vila, it attracts a very international, mixed-age crowd, with ageing drag queens, the leather posse and hip young urban scenesters socializing freely. Musically, the sounds tend to reflect the disparate nature and ages of the regulars, with resident DJs mixing driving house music with camp anthems; in the 2002 season, the new owners also promoted disco fever and military-themed nights. The club's tiny backstreet Dalt Vila doorway is deceptive, as inside there's a large gingham-tiled dancefloor, a central bar and a

LA TROYA ASESINA

The predominant gay night in Ibiza, **La Troya Asesina** (Ⓦ www.latroya-ibiza.com), held weekly on the *Amnesia* terrace, has grown from strength to strength since its inception in the late 1990s. The name is Italian slang for "bad woman". Its success has been built on some inspirational party themes and outstanding theatrics and decor – all masterminded by Brasilio de Oliveira, the legendary artistic director who was the impetus behind *Ku* in the 1980s and early 1990s. *La Troya* is very much an Ibizan creation, with an island-based DJ team headed by DJ Oliver (Ⓦ www.djoliver.com), renowned for his percussive Balearic style driving the mixes.

A night at *La Troya* is Ibiza at its best, with a fabulously hedonistic atmosphere, a beautiful crowd of ripped torso-baring boys, drag queens and Ibiza Town's hetro hipsters. Curiously, *Amnesia's* main room hosts a foam party the same night, which primarily pulls a straight crowd of young Spanish clubbers – though there's never any tension in the air, with many people moving from room to room to sample the contrary scenes. At *La Troya*, the night usually doesn't really get going until 3–4am, and regularly continues until 10am, when a large contingent heads over to *Space* for the after party.

stage (usually used for drag acts). Upstairs, you'll find a sociable bar area, and a darkroom which screens hardcore movies. Entrance (€12–17) is very moderate by Ibizan club standards, and includes a free drink.

Directory

Airlines Iberia is the only airline with an office in Ibiza, at Passeig Vara de Rey 15, Ibiza Town ☎971 300 614 (outside office hours call ☎902 400 500); Air Europa and Go ☎902 401 501; BMIbaby ☎902 100 737; Spanair ☎902 131 415.

Airport information ☎971 809 000.

Electricity The current is 220 volts AC, with the standard European two-pin plug. UK appliances function fine with an adaptor, but North American appliances will also need a transformer.

Emergencies Call ☎112 for police, ambulance or fire brigade.

Internet access There are several cybercafés in the main Ibizan towns, prices are around €4 an hour and connection speeds are usually very fast. In Ibiza Town, try Chill (see p.249), or Surf Net at c/Riambau 4 (Map 3, I3, daily 10am–2am). In Sant Antoni, try Lips.com at c/Sant Antoni 27 (Map 10, D6, Mon–Sat 10am–11pm & Sun 4–11pm), where you can surf while you wait for your laundry, or E Station at Avgda Dr Fleming 1 (daily 10am–midnight). In Formentera, Café Formentera on the main east–west highway in Sant Ferran (Mon–Sat 10.30am–10pm) is well set up and charges €5.30 an hour.

Laundry All resort hotels have laundry facilities. Otherwise, try Wash & Dry, Avgda Espanya 53, Ibiza Town, where you can surf the Web while doing your

washing; or *Lips.com* in Sant Antoni (see above). In Santa Eulària, head for Pernia Izquierdo, c/Isidor Macabich 34; in Formentera, there's Lavamatico del Puerto, just south of the marina in La Savina.

Pharmacies Farmacia Juan Tur Viñas, c/d'Antoni 1, Ibiza Town ⓣ971 310 326; Farmacia Villangomez Mari, c/Ample 12, Sant Antoni ⓣ971 340 891; Farmacia Antich Torres, c/Sant Jaume 50, Santa Eulària ⓣ971 330 097; Farmacia Torres Quetglas, c/Santa Maria, Sant Francesc, Formentera ⓣ971 328 004.

Photography The following photographic shops stock regular, monochrome and slide film; Fotocentro, c/Aragó 70, Ibiza Town; Foto Toni, c/de la Soledat 6, Sant Antoni; Foto San Francisco, Plaça de s'Eglésia, Sant Francesc, Formentera.

Supermarkets Ibiza's biggest and best supermarket is SYP, situated just outside Ibiza Town on the inner ring road, Carreterra Santa Eulària (Mon–Sat 9am–10pm, Sun 10am–8pm. In Formentera there's a smaller branch, on Urbanizacíon Sa Senieta, Sant Francesc (Mon–Sat 9am–8pm).

Time Ibiza and Formentera follow CET (Central European Time), which is 1hr ahead of the UK, 6hr ahead of Eastern Standard Time and 9hr ahead of Pacific Standard Time. Spain also adopts daylight-saving time in winter: clocks go forward in the last week in September and back in the last week of March.

Tipping It's not essential to tip in cafés and bars, but many locals leave some change when they get their bill; in restaurants, ten per cent is sufficient.

Travel agents The following companies can arrange excursions and help with booking flights: Viajes Urbis, Avgda 8 d'Agost, Edificio Bristol, Ibiza Town ⓣ971 314 412, ⓔurbisibz@juniper.es; Viajes Martours, c/Miramar 7, Sant Antoni ⓣ971 340 294, ⓔinfo@viajesmartour.com; Viajes Tagomago, Plaça d'Isidor Macabich 28, Santa Eulària ⓣ971 330 385; Ultramar Express, Avgda Mediterránea 13, La Savina, Formentera ⓣ971 322 136.

CONTEXTS

History

Located almost midway between two continents, the islands of Ibiza and Formentera have been squabbled over by European and North African powers for most of their history. Whilst Catalan and Spanish influence has come to define the recent identity of the islands, Carthaginian and Moorish customs still permeate local cultural traditions, particularly in rural areas. During the modern era, the prosperity and geographical position of the islands – just a short flight from most European cities – has altered things again, and tourism has become the islands' primary industry. Today, Ibiza and Formentera form the most cosmopolitan region in Spain, with a diverse population and a genuinely international outlook.

Prehistory

Until recently, it was thought that the Pitiuses were first inhabited around 1900 BC, just before the Bronze Age. However, in 1994, the carbon dating of sheep and goat bones found at s'Avenc des Pouàs cave near Santa Agnès suggests that Ibiza was first settled much earlier, around 4500 BC, by **Neolithic** people from the Iberian mainland. Little is yet known about them beyond the fact that they were pastoralists who brought their livestock with them, as the only mammals on the island before their arrival were bats. It's assumed that they remained close to the shore, living in natural caves and gradually establishing new settlements around the Pitiuses. The earliest sign of human habitation in **Formentera** is the cluster of important sites in the Barbària peninsula, which date from around 1850 BC, where family groups raised cattle, fished and grew crops. Just to the north, at **Ca Na Costa**, an impressive megalithic burial chamber also dates from the same era, where stone and bone tools, buttons and beads have been unearthed.

Axe heads, arrow tips and other metal utensils first began to be used in both islands at around 1600 BC. As no metal deposits had been discovered locally, the implements would have been imported from elsewhere in the Mediterranean. They were probably produced by the sophisticated Talayotic people, who had by that time established themselves throughout Mallorca and Menorca; and though they never colonized the Pitiuses, they're thought to have exported goods to the south. By the late Bronze Age, around 800 BC, copper, lead and tin tools, and pottery from Mallorca and Menorca, were being traded with the people of Ibiza and Formentera. More settlements had spread across both Pitiusan islands by this time, including hilltop sites at Punta Jondal and Puig Rodó in southern Ibiza, and Sa Cala and La Savina in Formentera.

The Phoenicians

Though the Greeks passed Ibiza and Formentera in the ninth century BC, they never settled in either island. The first colonizers from the east were the **Phoenicians**, skilled seafarers and merchants who originated in the Levant (modern-day Lebanon) and had established ports and trading passages throughout the Mediterranean by 800 BC. They arrived in Ibiza around 650 BC, attracted to the island

It's impossible to draw a line between Ibiza's Phoenician and Carthaginian periods, as the city of Carthage was founded and settled by Phoenicians, and the lack of wars or treaties provide historians with no obvious crossover date. But by the mid-sixth century BC, Carthage had eclipsed the Levantine Phoenician cities of Sidon and Tyre in influence and wealth, assumed dominance over established trade routes, and had become the most powerful settlement in the western Mediterranean. Punic, derived from the Greek word for Phoenician, is usually used to describe the Phoenician–Carthaginian settlements of southern Spain, Corsica, Sardinia and Sicily.

by its strategic position for their main east–west and north–south trade routes between North Africa, the Iberian mainland, Sardinia and western Sicily.

The Phoenicians first settled in **Sa Caleta** (see p.177), above the low cliffs on the south coast of Ibiza, where they established a village of several hundred people, who survived mainly by hunting and fishing. Fifty years later, they abandoned Sa Caleta for the safer hilltop site and sheltered harbour of today's Ibiza Town. They named the new settlement **Ibosim** (Island of Bes), after Bes, a god of dance, usually depicted as a bearded dwarf with a huge phallus. His link with Ibiza is almost certainly derived from his role as a protector against snakes – Ibiza lacks any poisonous reptiles.

The Punic era

During the **Punic era** (550–146 BC), Ibiza became a pivotal part of the Carthaginian empire, although Formentera was never settled. According to the Roman chronicler Diodorus Siculus, the imposing capital of Ibosim boasted a temple to the god Eshmun, a god of healing, atop the peak of today's Dalt Vila, and a "fine port, great walls as well as a considerable number of admirably built houses". The Carthaginians established Ibiza's salt pans (see p.184), and the economy centred around the trading of salt, plus silver and lead mined from s'Argentera in the north of the island. Wheat, olives, figs and fruit were farmed, and pottery was produced on an industrial scale from workshops around Ibosim and exported all over the Mediterranean. Above all, however, Ibiza became rich on the export of a precious purple **dye** extracted from the tiny sea snail *murex brandaris* and used to tint the togas of Roman noblemen.

In addition to its status as trading settlement, Ibiza also came to be regarded as something of a spiritual nerve centre for the Carthaginian empire, a holy place sacred to Tanit, the goddess of love, death and fertility, who was the most revered of all the Punic deities. She was worshipped at various sites throughout Ibiza, but is particularly associated with the **Cova des Cuieram**, and with **Illa Plana** on the Botafoc peninsula. Tanit's association with Ibiza stems from her status as goddess of death – as the island harbours no poisonous animals or reptiles (a main Carthaginian prerequisite for a burial site), it assumed religious significance for the Carthaginians as the most acclaimed burial site in the Mediterranean. They believed that burial in Ibiza would speed their journey to the afterlife, and the wealthy would pay in advance to have their bodies transported to the **Puig des Molins** cemetery (see p.81), which holds over three thousand tombs.

The Romans

The walled city of Ibosim, despite a three-day attack by the Roman general Cneus Cornelius Scipio in 217 BC, remained under Carthaginian control until the final Punic war. After the defeat and destruction of Carthage by Rome in 146 BC, Ibiza made a pact with the victors and obtained confederate status, the greatest degree of autonomy possible under Roman law. For the next two hundred years, Ibiza maintained a dual Roman/Carthaginian identity. Coinage continued to be minted locally, but with Roman emblems on one side and Carthaginian gods Bes or Eshmun on the other, while Punic temples and cemeteries were preserved alongside Roman ones.

This was an extremely prosperous period for most Ibizans. The economy continued to flourish, based on the export of salt, dye, pottery and *garum* (a fish sauce prized by the Romans), and all sectors were boosted by the introduction of slave labour and by new technology that revitalized agriculture. Colossal olive presses and millstones made from volcanic rock were now used, aqueducts were constructed and fish farms established near the modern resort of s'Argamassa, where tuna was salted and dried for export. Hundreds of settlers and slaves moved to near-deserted **Formentera**, where innovative Roman techniques also boosted fishing and agriculture with great success. By 70 AD, the island's population under Roman rule had grown to over three thousand, a figure not reached again until the early 1970s.

This prosperity peaked soon after Roman law was extended to all Hispanic lands in 74 AD, and Ibiza was downgraded to mere municipal status. All traces of Punic identity were gradually erased – Ibosim was renamed **Ebusus**, and the temple to Eshmun was rebuilt and dedicated to Mercury. The economy soon began to suffer as well, as the Romans centralized agricultural production in North Africa under the *latifundia* system, importing vast numbers of slaves to tend their crops. Production of olive oil, *garum*, wine and pottery diminished in Ibiza and Formentera, where there could never be equivalent economies of scale. Swathes of land were abandoned and the population fell; by the end of the fourth century, as the overstretched Roman empire had begun to crumble, Ibiza was little more than a minor trading post, still exporting salt and some lead, but dependent upon extracting taxes from merchant ships for most of her income.

Vandals and Byzantines

More than five hundred years of Roman domination ended when the **Vandals**, a warrior tribe that originated in central Europe, swept through mainland Spain in the early fifth century, conquering the Pitiuses in 455 AD before establishing their main settlement on the site of the former Carthage. Very little is known about Vandal rule in Ibiza, which lasted for just eighty years, but it was clearly a period of great tension, with religious issues causing most of the instability. The Vandals had became Christians during their long migration west, adopting the Arian belief in the concept that Christ and God were two distinct figures rather than elements of the Trinity alongside the Holy Ghost.

Meanwhile, the Catholic **Byzantines** were rapidly expanding from their Constantinople power base and emerging as the main challengers to the Vandals for hegemony in the region. The Byzantines considered the Vandals' Arian creed heretical, and sectarian tensions became acute (though the Romans had been driven out of Ibiza, a Catholic presence remained in the island). Despite a treaty drawn up in 476 AD between the two competing powers, the Vandal king Henrich executed Ophilio, the Catholic bishop of Ibiza, in 483 AD, and there were further martyrs from both faiths across the region.

Tensions continued for another fifty years before the great Byzantine general Belisarius conquered the Vandal power base at Carthage in 533, and the Balearic islands two years later, driving out Arian Christianity for good. Despite gaining control over the Pitiuses, which were of very peripheral interest to them, the Byzantines did not colonize the islands, and it's assumed a primitive form of Christianity, combined with Punic forms of worship, would have continued on Ibiza and Formentera.

The Moors

Almost no records from the eighth and ninth centuries have survived; the islands certainly had very little protection, as they were periodically ravaged by Viking and Norman raiders. The **Moors** first made contact with the Balearics when they pillaged Mallorca in 707 AD; however, they did not gain formal control over the islands until the beginning of the tenth century. For two centuries, Moorish influence amounted to little more than the periodic collection of taxes. This age of great instability was brought to an end in 902, when the Emir of Córdoba conquered the Balearics.

Moorish rule revitalized Ibiza and Formentera, introducing new names (**Yebisah** for Ibiza and Faramantira for Formentera), a new language (Arabic) and a new religion (Islam), though in remote locations a form of Christianity was still practised clandestinely. New and specialized technologies, above all innovative irrigation systems, rejuvenated the agricultural sector, enabling crops like rice and sugar cane to be grown in the arid Pitiusan terrain, and helping to produce two harvests a year in the fields of **Ses Feixes** (see box on p.84) around the harbour of Yebisah Medina, today's Ibiza Town.

For two hundred years, Moorish Ibiza, under tolerant *walis* (governors), was generally prosperous and stable; however, trouble erupted when control of the Balearics passed to the **Almortadha** dynasty of governors in 1085. The Almortadha pursued an aggressive foreign policy, raiding towns in mainland Spain and persecuting Christians in

Catalunya, Pisa and Tuscany from bases in the Balearics, thus provoking a massive invasion of Ibiza in 1114 by tens of thousands of troops from five hundred Pisan and Catalan ships – an action supported by the Pope as a mini-crusade. Though the invading forces massacred most of the island's Muslim population and ended Almortadha control, they didn't take control of the islands, thus opening the door for the next Moorish rulers, the more benign **Almoravids**, and the final dynasty, the **Almohads**.

The Catalan conquest

The key to the **Catalan conquest** of the Pitiuses was the unification of Aragón and Catalunya under Jaume I, which gave the Christian king the political and military strength to expand his kingdom. Mallorca was taken in 1229, Menorca in 1232, and in 1235, Jaume I combined forces with the Crown Prince of Portugal, the Count of Roussillon and Count Guillem of Montgrí to attack Yebisah. The invaders took the citadel on August 8, 1235 after a long siege, possibly entering through an entrance inside the tiny chapel of Sant Ciriac in Dalt Vila (see p.71).

Initially, Catalan rule was very positive for Ibiza (now renamed Eivissa) and Formentera. The islands received a progressive charter of freedom, the **Carta de Franquicias**, which guaranteed freedom of commerce, exemption from military service, an independent judiciary and free legal services for all citizens. Crucially, profits from the sale of salt, the foundation of the islands' economies, were to be retained locally. In 1299, King Jaume II allowed the islands even greater freedom by creating the Universitat, a system of democratic self-government.

These measures, together with the promise of land and a house, were essential to entice reluctant farm workers from the mainland to the islands – not an easy task in the thirteenth century, when the expense and difficulty of transport must have made the Pitiuses seem like the other side of the globe. Under the Catalans, Pitiusan society underwent radical change; Catalan was introduced as the main language, and Catholicism became the official religion. The invaders divided Ibiza into five *quartons* – Eivissa, Sant Jordi, Santa Eulària, Sant Miquel and Sant Antoni – and built a chapel in each region to help establish Christianity in rural areas.

Plague and pirates

The optimism of the late thirteenth century was to prove short-lived, however. **Bubonic plague** in the form of the Black Death first spread to Ibiza from the devastated cities of the mainland in 1348. The already sparse population was reduced to just five hundred people by the beginning of the fifteenth century, while Formentera was left uninhabited.

Plague returned to Ibiza in the fifteenth century, but a more serious outbreak occurred in 1652, when one in six of the by-now 7000-strong population perished. To compound matters, the outbreak occurred during the summer months when salt (the chief source of income) was being gathered; Ibiza was deemed a contaminated port by the salt merchants, and famine inevitably followed.

Pirates were another constant menace. Between the fourteenth and late fifteenth centuries the attacks were sporadic, as Moors seeking slaves pillaged their old colony from bases just a day's sail away in North Africa. The raids multiplied from the start of the sixteenth century, as Turkish buccaneers bombarded the capital with cannon fire, reducing the city's fortified walls to rubble. Complete reconstruction followed (see box on p.66), and after the destruction of Santa Eulària in 1545, the fortifications around the Puig de Missa hill were also upgraded. The first defence tower, Torre de Sal Rossa, was built as part of a network that soon spanned the entire Pitiusan coastline; the towers were constantly manned so that signal fires could warn of enemy ships.

Castilian control

Following the 1702–14 War of Spanish Succession, the victorious **Castilians** assumed control of the Pitiuses and imposed their language (Castilian Spanish) and the name Ibiza. The island suffered for backing the losers in the war: the salt pans were claimed by the new Spanish state, and the Universitat replaced by a Castilian municipal administration with very limited power. The Pitiuses became even more of a backwater, and gradually settled back into provincial stupor. Pirate attacks presented less of a threat in the eighteenth and nineteenth centuries, thanks to the efforts of the **corsairs**; however, although the population grew slowly, life remained desperately poor for most.

The Catholic **Church** was the other dominant power in eighteenth century Spain, and used considerable funds to attempt to restructure Ibizan and Formenteran society around village churches, which they constructed across the islands. Work quickly began on new chapels at Sant Francesc, Formentera in 1724, and in Sant Joan, Sant Josep and Sant Francesc in Ibiza. Later in the century, Abad y Lasierra was appointed as the islands' first Catholic bishop since Vandal times, and Ibiza Town's Santa Maria church was consecrated as a cathedral in 1782. The new bishop quickly authorized the establishment of a dozen new parishes (including Sant Mateu, Santa Agnès and Sant Agustí), but the populace were unwilling to move to these new villages, preferring the independence of the countryside.

Ibiza and Formentera remained very peripheral corners of Spain in the early nineteenth century, with a stagnant

CORSAIRS

Nautical vigilantes authorized by the Catalan (and later Spanish) Crown to attack and plunder enemy ships, Pitiusan corsairs (or privateers) were issued registration certificates as far back as 1356, when the Ibizan-born Pere Bernat defended the Pitiusan coast from Moorish attack. Under the terms of the registration, they were entitled to keep four-fifths of the booty they captured, with the remainder going to the Crown. The **corsairs** only became a force to be reckoned with in the seventeenth century, when, following a long period of devastating pirate assaults, Ibizan corsairs began to regain the initiative, successfully counter-attacking Moorish ships and reclaiming stolen booty (and capturing slaves) from Barbary coast ports. They steadily gained a fearsome reputation in the western Mediterranean as skilled and courageous seamen, and Ibiza's security situation improved, enabling the resettlement of Formentera in 1697.

A corsair would have been one of the main career choices for a young male Ibizan in the late seventeenth to mid-nineteenth centuries. One of the most celebrated was **Antoni Riquer** (1773–1846), born in Ibiza Town's La Marina quarter. Riquer is said to have overpowered over a hundred enemy ships, including a much stronger Gibraltarian craft, the Felicity, in Ibiza Town harbour in 1806, a struggle witnessed by most of the town's population. Evidently, they were impressed enough to name a square, Plaça d'Antoni Riquer, after him; it lies in La Marina on the Passeig Marítim harbourfront (see p.59), opposite a stone monument to the corsairs.

economy and few employment opportunities. Even the option of becoming a corsair was all but ruled out after the French claimed Algeria as a colony in 1830 and began to subdue piracy. Thousands of young men emigrated to

Florida, South America and Cuba, especially from Formentera, which became known as "s'illa des ses dones" (the island of women). The salt pans were sold to a private company (for over a million pesetas, then a colossal sum) by the Spanish state in 1871 in a desperate measure to raise some revenue, and conditions for salt workers worsened under private ownership.

Isolation and civil war

Ibiza only began to recover towards the end of the nineteenth century, when the introduction of regular ferry services to and from the mainland helped ease the island's isolation, and even brought the odd visitor from northern Europe – the first tourists. The initial bohemian travellers in the early 1930s (including the artist and Dadaist photographer Raoul Haussmann) were joined by artists and writers escaping the spread of Fascism across Europe, and represented Ibiza's first proto-hippies.

Though the economic impact of these visitors would have barely touched the island economy, any hopes of an embryonic tourist industry were snuffed out by the **Spanish Civil War** (1936–39). In one of the very darkest chapters of Ibizan history, a previously largely apolitical island became bitterly divided on Nationalist and Republican lines. Atrocities were committed on both sides, but Catalan Anarchists, briefly in control of the island after the expulsion of Franco's Nationalist forces, committed the worst single act, slaughtering over a hundred Nationalist prisoners inside the Dalt Vila castle before fleeing the island. Republicans were hunted down in the ensuing Nationalist backlash; hundreds fled to the hills, and those who were not executed or imprisoned were dispatched to a concentration camp in La Savina, Formentera, where dozens died from malnutrition. The wounds of the Civil

War remain something of a taboo subject in Ibiza, and many local historians still refuse to tackle the matter for fear of stirring up issues that split families over sixty years ago.

Artists and tourists

Ibiza's transformation from isolated backwater in the aftermath of the Civil War into one of the globe's most fashionable tourist destinations has been startlingly swift. By the mid-1950s, two decades after the end of the Civil War, a trickle of bohemian travellers had begun to return to the island. Based at the *Hotel El Corsario* in Ibiza Town (see p.214), a scene developed around the "Grupo Ibiza '59", a collection of artists including Bechtold and Neubauer, and architects including Erwin Boner and Josep Lluís Sert, who worked closely with Le Corbusier.

Sant Antoni was also embarking on the wobbly path from fishing port to resort town during the 1950s, when hotels and Costa-style trappings including the prerequisite bullring that's alien to Catalan culture – sprung up around the town's bay. By the early 1960s, Spain's Franco-directed tourism drive was transforming the whole island, with beach after beach earmarked for development, and the first hotels in Formentera constructed at Es Pujols. By 1965, Ibiza was importing 30,000 tonnes of cement a year, and an army of building workers, waiters and maids from the mainland arrived, swelling the population by 43 per cent during the course of the 1960s.

Beatniks and hippies

Though the roots of the Pitiusan **hippy scene** can be traced back to the first wave of travellers in the early twentieth century, things really took off in the late 1950s, when young beatniks first reached Ibiza. The attraction was simple: a beautiful island just off the overland trail to Morocco, with an established community of artists and Spanish leftists (Ibiza was remote enough from Franco's Madrid power base for dissidents to feel reasonably secure), cheap living costs and a famously tolerant population. At first, the action was concentrated around bars such as *Dominos* in La Marina, and on Figueretes beach, where a small jazz scene developed. Word spread quickly through the travellers' grapevine, and in the mid- to late 1960s, visitor numbers were swollen by American draft-dodgers avoiding the call to fight in Vietnam.

Dubbed *peluts* (hairies) by the locals, Ibiza was quickly adopted as a class A Mediterranean hangout, with Formentera achieving at least a B+ (Bob Dylan lived there for a time, and Pink Floyd recorded the soundtrack to their film *More* on the island). Though Ibiza Town was the main focus of the scene in the early 1960s, Sant Carles, Sant Joan and La Mola later became the main hippy artistic centres, and remain so today. The hippies brought character (and plenty of drugs) to an isolated corner of Europe, putting Ibiza on the map and helping forge its modern identity as a tolerant, hedonistic island. The legendary parties of the 1960s and 1970s initiated the club scene; *Pacha*, *Amnesia* and *Ku* (now *Privilege*) originally had a distinctly hippy identity. Even today, the word "hippy" retains a certain cachet in the Pitiuses long absent in most parts of Europe, and the islands' hippy heritage is now used as a stratagem to entice visitors to the island in the tourist authorities' promotional literature.

Ibiza and Formentera today

Following the return of democracy in 1976 after Franco's death, Ibizan **politics** were dominated by the conservative **Partido Popular** (PP) for over two decades. However in

1999, the left-leaning **Pacte Progressista** coalition, fronted by the charismatic and urbane lawyer Pilar Costa, was elected as leaders of the island government. This epochal result was largely because of the Pacte's opposition to Partido Popular-supported construction and development proposals, including a plan to build a golf course at Cala d'Hort (see p.168). Under the PP, the political agenda had been massively biased towards unbridled tourist development, as blocks-on-the-beach were thrown up around the coastline with little or no regard for environmental considerations. Local people registered their objections to this rampant development with their ballot papers, and since the 1999 victory environmental issues have remained in the forefront of Ibizan politics. Ironically, a flood of new building projects started almost immediately after the election, as desperate developers sought to push through mothballed projects before new building legislation could be set in place, often using licences issued back in the 1980s. Finally, a year after the election – and after a bust-up between Costa and her Green Party environment minister over the speed of change – comprehensive new construction laws outlawed new coastal projects and paralysed several large tourism developments.

The other hot issue is one of **cultural identity**, as the Pitiusan authorities attempt the difficult task of maintaining the islands' Balearic/Catalan heritage. **Language** is a very divisive subject, as the local government steadily adopt a much more stringent attitude to the promotion of Catalan, a controversial topic considering that only 38 per cent of Ibiza's population (a little more in Formentera) speak the local Eivissenc Catalan dialect. This is partly a legacy of the Franco years, when Catalan was banned, but principally because thousands of Castilian speakers migrated here in the boom years of tourism. In the last three decades, a surge of new arrivals (mainly from the EU and South America, but also from North Africa) has resulted in an even more **cosmopolitan** population – according to the 2002 census, nearly twenty per cent of the islands' residents were born outside Spain. Not surprisingly, a recent ruling that all teachers and public servants must speak Catalan has proved controversial, and has resulted in recruitment shortages. Similarly, a directive that Catalan be the main language of education has troubled many parents, whose children already have to struggle with English (and often German) classes.

Tourism remains the linchpin of the Ibizan and Formenteran economies, and it's estimated that over 85 per cent of the working population now earn their living indirectly or directly from the sector. The industry is very seasonal in the Pitiuses, however; even though the official season is May to October, the islands only really fill up for three months, between mid-June and mid-September. Unlike Mallorca, which has established a strong winter season, virtually all Pitiusan resorts shut down completely for the other nine months of the year. Unemployment rates soar in winter, when many locals leave to work in the Canaries or other parts of Europe. Pitiusan tourism is also dangerously dependent on the British market (almost fifty per cent of all visitors are from the UK), and on young clubbers, with little sign of cultural travellers visiting in the numbers that the island government would like.

Despite these shortcomings, the tourism sector still remained buoyant until the 2002 season, which saw a ten per cent drop in arrivals, the first fall for a decade. This slump caused considerable concern in Ibiza (Formentera enjoyed a good season), with everything blamed from the new **ecotax** (see p.26) and the inflationary impact of the euro to September 11th and cheap Turkish holidays. Upon careful analysis, a big disparity between individual municipalities became clear – while hotels in Ibiza Town and rural areas had a decent season, the hotels of Sant Antoni and other resorts suffered badly, being dependent on package holidays. This may represent something of new trend, as the proportion of independent travellers visiting Spain is increasing every year, with people preferring to make their own arrangements. Many of the blockish, 1960s-built concrete hotels in the main Ibizan resorts also look old-fashioned and unattractive.

Ibiza has also undoubtedly gained an **image problem**, acquired from a glut of salacious TV programmes, and, not surprisingly, family bookings have dropped. There's also evidence that the club sector is starting to suffer a backlash against the greed permeating the scene, with teenage clubbers increasingly being tempted to other Mediterranean resorts, where entrance and drinks prices are a fraction of those asked in Ibiza.

Despite these concerns, there remains an irrepressible glamour and allure to the island. With an array of new upmarket rural hotels, improved summer transport connections and a terrific restaurant and bar scene, Ibiza is increasingly drawing more and more wealthy, free-spending visitors – which is exactly what the tourism department and many islanders have craved for decades.

Wildlife and the environment

The Balearics were separated by sea from mainland Spain around five million years ago, when the mountainous barrier between Gibraltar and Morocco that acted as a dam between the Atlantic and the dry Mediterranean area burst. In effect, the islands are continuations of mountains that start on the mainland south of Valencia, and consist mainly of limestone and red sandstone, plus a little basaltic (volcanic) rock.

The name "Pitiuses" is thought to derive from the ancient Greek for pine tree, *pitus*, and **pine forests** still cover large swathes of Ibiza. These consist mostly of Aleppo pine – distinguished by its bright-green spines, silvery twigs and ruddy brown cones – but also of sabina pine near the coast, and some Italian stone pine in the hills. By the coast, there are many varieties of **palm tree**, including one endemic species, *phoenix dactylifera*. Other trees include olive, carob, almond and a rich variety of fruit trees: fig, apricot, citrus, apple, pear, plum, peach and pomegranate.

Formentera is buffeted by the cool, dry *tramóntana* wind from the north, and the hot *xaloc* that blows from the

WILD FLOWERS

One of the delights of the Pitiusan countryside is the astonishing array of **wild flowers**, partly a result of the fact that pesticides and fertilizers are not widely used, and fields are regularly left fallow. The best time of year is spring, when orchids, cornflowers, white rock roses and vast fields of poppies bloom, but even in summer, when the incessant heat stunts most plant growth, there are areas where wild flowers thrive. In the shady torrents you'll see wild oleander and the delicate creamy travellers' joy flower, while sea daffodils and thistles thrive near the coast.

With the first rains in late September, the pale-pink Mediterranean heath flowers open, and herbs and grasses abound. In December, keep an eye out for the brown bee orchid in the woods of southwest Ibiza, and lavender and rosemary flower throughout both islands as early as January.

Sahara, giving the island's limited vegetation a contorted, wind-blown appearance – the trunk of the **sabina** pine is often twisted and bent double by the force of the wind. Nowhere else in the Balearics has the same density of these hardy trees, much valued for construction purposes: the wood is extremely durable and ideal for support beams and window frames because of its highly resinous nature. The fact that the island's main port – La Savina – is named after it is a measure of the tree's importance here. The deciduous **fig** tree, with its large lobed leaves, is another common Formenteran species, its huge branches nearly always propped up by massive scaffold-like supports added by farmers.

Mammals

Other than bats, there were no **mammals** at all in the Pitiuses before the arrival of the first humans around 4600 BC. The first settlers brought sheep and goats with them from the mainland; by 1900 BC, cattle and pigs were being kept in both islands. Though settlers introduced more mammals over the centuries, there's not a great diversity today, partly because of hunting, which remains a popular pastime. The pine marten, for example, is a popular quarry and has been on the brink of extinction for the last few decades.

The largest mammal in the Pitiuses is the rare, cat-like **genet**, possibly introduced by the Carthaginians. Light brown in colour, with a long, bushy, ringed tail, it's an extremely shy nocturnal species, hunting mice and other rodents in the remote forested hills of Els Amunts and the Roques Altes. A much more common sight is the Ibizan hound, **ca eivissenc**, which is also thought to have been introduced from North Africa: images of the same breed are depicted in the tombs of the Middle Kingdom in Egypt (2050–1800 BC). The skinny, rusty brown-and-white hound is a bizarre-looking beast – all ears and limbs – but perfectly adapted to its environment, and is a superb hunter of the islands' plentiful populations of **rabbits** and **hares**. Squirrels, weasels, mice and rats and the North African subspecies of the hedgehog are also found, while Formentera is home to a vary rare subspecies of rodent, called the **garden dormouse** (*eliomys quercinus*).

Reptiles and insects

The dryness of the terrain and the distance from the mainland means there are few **reptiles** and amphibians in the Pitiuses. By far the most commonly found reptile is the

Ibizan wall lizard, which is unique to the islands and has evolved into several distinct subspecies. In Ibiza, the lizard averages 10cm in length and is coloured brown and vivid green, with flecks of blue. The Formenteran variant is slightly larger, and coloured more garishly, an almost electric blue and luminous green. Many of the smaller islands that make up the Pitiuses, including Espalmador, Espardell and Tagomago, also have their own native subspecies, the most spectacular of which is the **Es Vedrà lizard**, an ultramarine colour, with yellow stripes. Despite the dry conditions, the **Iberian frog**, or marsh frog, is reasonably widespread.

The Pitiuses are rich in **insect** life, reflecting the relative lack of pesticides used in the fields. Of the beetles, the staghorn is the largest, but there are also scarab, scarred melolontha and bupredid varieties. Butterflies are plentiful, most exotically the spectacular twin-tailed pacha, which can reach 10cm across, but also the swallowtail, the clouded yellow, Bath white, Lang's short-tailed blue, painted lady and Cleopatra. Dramatic hawk moths such as the death's head, hummingbird and oleander are infrequently seen, while the European mantis is more common. Dragonflies and damselflies are best spotted in marshland areas.

Birds

In contrast to the paucity of mammal species, the Pitiuses are home to a rich variety of **birds**, and the islands are a crucial migratory base for numerous species. Not surprisingly, there's a wealth of **marine birds** on the islands. Of the **gulls**, the most common is the large Mediterranean herring gull, easily identifiable by its yellow beak. On the west coast of Ibiza, it's even possible to see the rarest gull in the world, Audouin's Gull (*larus audouinii*), recognizable by its red beak and olive-green feet. Other winter visitors are the lesser black-backed gull, the black-headed gull, the little gull, and the Mediterranean gull. Seven species of **tern** visit the Pitiuses in autumn and spring, and cormorants and shags are common. Offshore, puffins and razorbills are sometimes seen on isolated rocks, well away from ports and people. Finally, the dull-looking greeny-brown Balearic shearwater, known locally as the **virot**, can still be seen gliding around the capes of Formentera, despite having been hunted until relatively recently.

A wide variety of **marsh birds** reside in southern Ibiza, particularly in the environs of the salt pans and close to Ibiza Town at Ses Feixes. In the rich wetlands, little white egrets, only 50cm or so in height, with thin black bills and yellow feet, are fairly common. Formentera attracts fewer marsh birds, though several species of heron visit both islands, as do bitterns and, less frequently, the white stork, spoonbill, ibis and crane. By far the most exotic wetland bird seen is the European **flamingo**, which, after an absence of a decade or so, is again breeding on the islands, especially in the Ibizan salt pans: over four hundred were counted in the area in October 2002, and over sixty in Formentera.

Other visitors to the salt pans are various species of **waders**, including the black-winged stilt, with its unmistakable red legs. Redshank and greenshank, lapwing, curlews, godwits and five species of plover can also be spotted, plus visiting shoreline and salt-pan waders. Woodcock, snipe and stone curlew favour the freshwater marshes.

Compared with the vultures, red kite and osprey of Mallorca and Menorca, there are few large **birds of prey** on the Pitiuses. Of those that are found, the most spectacular is **Eleanor's falcon**, an elegant predator of migrant birds such as swifts, which resides in Ibiza between April and November. Es Vedrà has the largest colony in the Balearics, but others are frequently seen on the northwest coast near Sant Mateu. The supremely acrobatic, slightly larger **peregrine falcon** is a rare sight now, much-persecuted by pigeon fanciers. Kestrels, marsh harriers and sparrowhawks are more common, plus honey buzzards in Formentera, and the occasional booted eagle in Ibiza. **Owls** include fair numbers of barn owls, spotted even around Ibiza Town, where they prey on sparrows and mice. Other residents are the scops owl and the short-eared owl, the latter unique in that it hunts in daylight – it can occasionally be seen in marshland areas like Ses Feixes.

Of the vast order of **passerines** (perching birds), most of the usual European species are represented. Some of the more unusual ones include the Kentish plover, thekla lark, crossbill, the Sardinian and Marmora's warbler and the blue rock thrush. Some of the most exotic European birds are quite common in the Pitiuses, including the spectacular crested and zebra-winged **hoopoe**, the turquoise-and-yellow **bee-eater**, the kingfisher and the large blue-green **roller**.

Green politics

Until recently, Ibiza's record of **environmental protection** was pretty poor. After decades of rampant development of the island's coastline, Green issues have been forced to the top of the political agenda, and urbanization now rivals tourism for column inches in the local press. The **Green Party** (Els Verds) formed part of the victorious Pacte Progressista alliance that won the 1999 local elections, and despite a very public squabble with the dominant Socialists a year after the historic victory, which saw the Green environment minister Joan Buades leave the coalition, they remain a force to be reckoned with in Ibizan politics.

The issue that ignited Green consciousness in Ibiza was a proposal to develop housing in the near-pristine hills around the **salt pans**, in the extreme southeast of the island. Developers were halted in 1977 by a planning commission, but others returned in 1990 with a proposal to build over six hundred villas. A vigorous and ultimately successful "Salvem Ses Salines" ("Save the Salines") campaign was launched by the Green activists GEN and Friends of the Earth; they managed to secure ANEI (Natural Area of Special Interest) status, and later the Salines achieved international recognition. Today, the region forms part of a Parque Natural (National Park), and is identified as one of Europe's most important wetland habitats by the EU; the Salines are also listed by UNESCO as part of Ibiza's World Heritage Status award.

The battle over **Cala d'Hort** (see box on p.168), a sublime slice of Ibiza coastline, became the focus of the next main Green issue and second big test case between developers and environmentalists. It's fair to say that the proposals to build a golf course marked a turning point in modern Ibizan history, provoking the largest demonstration the island had ever seen and helping oust the Partido Popular conservatives from power. Public pressure and determined campaigning eventually paid off; in February 2002, the coastline around Cala d'Hort was finally given the highest protection under Spanish law – Parque Natural status.

Elected with a mandate to introduce tough new building restrictions, the Pacte took over a year to draw up legislation, which was immediately contested by the powerful construction industry lobby. However, the sweeping **Norma Territorial Cautelar law** introduced in 2000 banned new development within 500m of the coast, cancelling building licences and introducing stricter design and quality requirements for construction. Hoteliers, tour operators, the media and local public opinion were broadly supportive of the new legislation and, though many environmentalists thought it didn't go far enough, the general consensus was that a good start had been made to limit further unsustainable development. Unfortunately, even with this strict new law in place, bitter squabbles between conservative PP dominated town halls and the centre-left island government have erupted over its implementation. In coastal areas, including Port des Torrent and Talamanca, town halls have simply failed to intervene to stop illegal building projects, to the despair of Ibizan Greens, and lengthy court cases have ensued.

Enacted in May 2002, a second key piece of environmental legislation was the Balearic **ecotax** (see p.26), its revenue to be directed towards environmental improvements. The new law was vigorously opposed by most hoteliers, tour operators and the PP – although few tourists complained about the ecotax, detractors blamed the new levy for Ibiza's dip in visitor arrivals during the 2002 season. However, there's no hard evidence to support this, and Formentera enjoyed near-record numbers of arrivals the same year.

The Balearic Beat

Born under the stars in Ibiza, Balearic Beat was Alfredo's baby. Paul Oakenfold and Danny Rampling kidnapped it and raised it indoors in cold, grey London.

Jane Bussmann, Once in a Lifetime

An all-embracing musical style developed by the island's resident DJs in the 1980s, Ibiza's home-grown **Balearic Beat** became a pivotal part of the UK's acid house revolution. It's a positive, optimistic blend, founded in electronica, but fused with afro, Latin and funk charisma, and freed from the incessant four-four thud and two-step beats that dominate UK dancefloors. Though Ibiza's globally renowned clubs may seem the obvious place to get a flavour of the local music scene, a lot of the really creative Balearic action now happens well away from the clubs in the island's secluded beach bars and funky cafés.

The term "Balearic Beat" was first coined in the mid- to late 1980s by visiting English DJs such as Paul Oakenfold and Danny Rampling, to describe the music played by **Alfredo** – a former Argentinian journalist and fugitive from his country's military junta – whose eclectic mixes at

Amnesia fused Chicago house, Italian club-disco, indie and Europop together with a smattering of James Brown and reggae. Many of the big tunes were extended mixes of Woodentops or Cure records considered to be deeply uncool by London's clubberati and music press – but in Ibiza, if it worked then it was used. Fleetwood Mac's *Big Love* and Chris Rea's *Josephine* became Balearic classics, played alongside slamming early house and techno.

Ecstacy – the other vital ingredient precipitating this spirit of open-mindedness – unleashed collective euphoria across Balearic and British dancefloors, seducing the tribe of young Londoners, who brought tales of the scene back to the UK. An early effort by Paul Oakenfold in 1986 to recreate the Ibizan vibe in London had failed – the capital's dancefloors were polarized into soul, rave groove and indie camps at the time, and the Balearic concept of a musical masala proved tricky to translate – but this combination of ecstasy and house music blew the roof off clubland. However, though Balearic classics played an important part in the ensuing UK clubbing revolution, it was the ferocious energy of **acid house** that the UK rave masses really latched on to.

The eclecticism that defined the Balearic Beat is unfortunately rare on the main Ibizan dancefloors today. Alfredo still pursues a diverse, cross-cultural musical direction, even dropping a little UK garage into his devastating sets at *Manumission* and *Space*, and the spirit survives in other isolated corners of Ibizan clubland such as *Pacha*'s Funky Room. In general, however, DJs don't tend to diverge much from house music these days. As many of the biggest club nights are booked by overseas promoters who pay big bucks to import their own DJs, few will take risks or drop the beats-per-minute count. British DJs like John Kelly have successfully championed the **trance** sound, but after the Brits have all left at the end of the season, Ibiza reverts to what works best in the island: positive (sometimes verg-

THE TRANCE SCENE

Illicit by nature, outlawed by the authorities, the **Ibiza trance scene** has organized outdoor parties in the island for over a decade, despite powerful forces stacked against it. Remote rural locations are favoured, with generators and speakers heaved along isolated country trails and coastal paths to settings far from population centres. Ideologically, trance parties represent the antithesis of the Ibizan superclub branding, hype and commerce. Yet it was the spirit and memories of the *Ku* and *Amnesia* clubs (open-air venues in the 1980s) that inspired the original Ibizan trance party organizers to run their own events in 1990. For German-born, Ibiza resident **Sola** – one of the key people in the scene – and her crew, the other main influence was the Goa beach raves of the late 1980s.

The first big Ibiza trance party was held in 1993, at a go-cart track next to the airport; to avoid illegal entry charges, the organizers sold hundreds of clay medallions as party invites. The police were unable to stop the event, but increasing pressure from the authorities, clubs and press forced promoters to seek out remote areas for their events. A game of cat and mouse ensued with the police, as the trance tribe continued to organize four big parties a year. Certain places became legendary, such as the Can Punta hilltop near Sant Joan, a sea cave at Cala Conta and an abandoned bullring near Sant Agustí. One of the most celebrated events took place near the village of **Sant Vicent** in July 1996, at a stunning rural hillside location in the extreme north of the island. Fields became makeshift dancefloors, huge fluro banners and bedouin-style canopies were set up, with tribal, techno and ambient musical zones. The 72-hour party drew 3,000 people, and even *Manumission* were astounded by its scale. The most audacious location, however, was the uninhabited island of **Sa Conillera** in August 1996. Of the 2000 people who gathered on the shore near Cala Conta waiting for boats to the island, only 400 people made it across before the police blocked access to Conillera. The organizers, with equipment confiscated and left with thousands of unsold fizzy drinks, were ruined.

Other parties were broken up by the police, and a war of attrition set in. Party organizers made every effort to promote legal parties, but maintain they were rebuffed at every turn by the discotheque association and police. The clandestine events continued, although in 1997 Ibizan bar owner Miquel Maymó staged a legal event, *Rising Sun*, in a quarry near Sant Antoni. For many, the ultimate event was a three-day party in July 1999 at **Las Puertas del Cielo** ("Gates of Heaven"), a remote location with natural spring water and spectacular sunsets on the northwest coast near Santa Agnès. Speakers and equipment were brought by boat, and dozens of volunteers humped the gear up a cliffside using ropes and pulleys. However, when the same location was chosen in 2001, the police confiscated equipment and used tear gas to break up the party. Then a regular, famous for his perilous cliff-jumping stunts, died after hitting rocks while attempting a huge leap into the sea. The tragedy left the trance tribe in shock; the Ibiza police maintained their extremely tough stance, and no big events were organized for over a year.

Today, the trance scene is fragmented. Out of necessity, **legal venues** have been used much more, with the garden at the *Las Dalias* (see p.254) bar hosting regular events with DJs including the UK outfit *Tribe of Frog*. In 2002, Miquel Maymó also ran a large legal weekly event with a trance dimension, *Kumharas Concept* (Ⓦwww.kumharas.org), in an old zoo grounds in the central hills. The Ibizan trance scene still survives, yet it's hard to imagine organizers getting away with the huge outdoor parties of the past. For many, the scene is slowly fading.

ing on the fluffy) US garage, uplifting house and percussion-rich tracks.

Much broader in terms of sheer musical experimentation, today's **chillout** scene has seen DJs adopting a freestyle approach in the best Balearic tradition. When blended by the don of the genre, José Padilla (who pioneered the chillout concept at the *Café del Mar*), Jonathan Grey or Phil Mison, chillout can include ambient moments, acoustic tunes, British–Asian fusion, Bristolian breakbeats, Jamaican dub, jazzy drum 'n' bass and even a touch of flamenco. In the Balearic sunshine, the only common denominator is that the music must share a positive, engaging feel.

All things considered, the Ibizan scene looks healthy today. Musician-cum-producer Lennart Krarup releases cut after cut of blissful Balearic electronica on his Ibizarre label, while Alfredo continues to champion diverse beats and move feet; José Padilla still comes up with the goods and a battery of other island-based DJ talent (including Andy Wilson, DJ Gee, David Moreno, Reche, Java and Tania Vulkano) provide depth and support.

Discography

The select discography below is unashamedly biased towards the chillout side of the Balearic sound, though there are some rave favourites, and some of the very best hard and deep house mixes. If you're after a really Balearic flavour, you're best off avoiding almost anything labelled "Ibiza" or "sunset" – tags used by record companies to sell cheesy dance hit compilations or duff collections of downbeat tunes. However, we've listed a few notable exceptions.

A Man Called Adam *Duende* (Other). The quintessential Balearic band's second album of sensitive, uplifting songs includes *Estelle*, *Easter Song* and *All My Favourite People*.

Afterlife *Simplicity Two Thousand* (Hed Kandi). Balearic music of real substance from long-term Ibizaphiles, featuring the mellifluous vocals of Rachel Lloyd. The double-CD pack includes a compendium of mixes from Deep and Wide, Spoon Wizard and Chris Coco.

Basement Jaxx and other artists *Atlantic Jaxx* (XL). One of the strongest compilations of the last ten years, with an eruptive samba flavour throughout and moments of pure house magic that include plenty of Ibizan anthems. Basement Jaxx's solo album, *Remedy*, is another Balearic-style masterpiece, blending samba-house with ragga and even ska.

Ian Pooley *Meridian* & *Since Then* (V2). Joyous Latin-soaked dance music, with techno tinges, from the funkiest German on the planet.

Ibizarre *Ambient Ibiza* volumes 1–5 (Ibizarre/WEA). Beautiful, cinematic home-grown sounds created by Lennart Krarup, one of the most influential figures in the local scene, plus Ibizan collaborators.

Jon Sa Trinxa *The Salinas Sessions* & *Beachlife* (Sony). *Salinas* is simply the finest Balearic mix ever compiled – a glorious, exuberant fusion of diverse musical emotions. The genre-free fun continues on *Beachlife*, which can't quite match its predecessor, but still stands head and shoulders above most of the competition. Just don't call it "Ibiza chillout".

Primal Scream *Screamadelica* (Creation). Unequalled indie-dance collaboration, tweaked to perfection by producer Andy Weatherall, which captures the euphoria (and comedown) of the early 1990s, and still sounds startlingly fresh and relevant.

Various *Back to Love* volumes 1 & 2 (Hed Kandi). All the seminal late 1980s rave anthems, plus some rare groove tunes, all beautifully packaged and presented. Volume one includes Joe Smooth's *Promised Land*, Ten City's *That's The Way Love Is* and Ritchie Havens' *Going Back to My Roots*. Volume two serves up more club classics from Rhythim is Rhythim, Lil Louis and Soul II Soul.

Various *Back to Mine* (DMC). Fantastically diverse series, with no fillers or duff tracks. All the imaginative mixes – the best by Nick Warren, Danny Tenaglia, Groove Armada and Faithless – are seamlessly blended, and fizzle with emotion and atmosphere.

Various *Beach House* (Hed Kandi). Quality deep-house selections from one of the UK's most consistent labels, with full-length versions of classic cuts by Blue Six, Bossa Nostra and Sven van Hees.

Various *Bora Bora I* & *II* (React). Propulsive hard house soundtracks of the best beach fiesta in the island, supplied by Ibiza resident DJ Gee.

Various *Café del Mar* volumes 1–4 (React), 5–8 (Manifesto) & 9 (Café del Mar). Definitive chillout series, with the first six compiled by ex-resident José Padilla, and the remainder by Bruno Lepretre. All are worthy purchases, but volume two (with heavy ambient atmospherics from Salt Tank and classy flamenco from Paco de Lucía) and volume six (with Talvin Singh, Nitin Sawhney and Kid Loco) are absolutely essential.

Various *Chillout* volumes 1–3 (Avex). Complied by ex-*Muzik* editor Ben Turner and mixed by former *Café del Mar* resident Phil Mison, these captivating mixed CDs contain a blissful blend of rhythm and melody from the mid-1990s; no fillers, just sublime, emotive electronic music.

Various *Classic Balearic 1* (Mastercuts). Balearic gems from the rave days, from artists including Sueño Latino, Electribe 101, Chris Rea and A Man Called Adam.

Various *Global Underground* (Boxed). This series of double mix CDs are the very finest of their genre. Of the 25 or so pumping hard house and trance mixes from the world's best DJs, the Paul Oakenfold, Sasha, Dave Seaman, Deep Dish and Danny Tenaglia blends are the cream of the crop.

Various *The House that Trax Built* and *Chicago Trax Volume 1* (Trax). Compilations of the seminal Chicago house tunes of

the 1980s Alfredo played at *Amnesia* (including Adonis's *No Way Back* and Phuture's *Can You Feel It?*), as well as Marshall Jefferson's *Move Your Body* and Jamie Principle's *Your Love* and *Baby Wants to Ride*.

Various *Mixmag* series (DMC). Excellent series; highlights are Dimitri from Paris's *Deluxe House of Funk*, which unleashes a lavish blend of funk-house soaked with Latin and jazzy undertones, and Tom Middleton's *A Jedi Night's Out*, an outstanding melange from ambient to filtered tech-funk.

Various *Perceptions of Pacha* (Pacha). Excellent mix, reflecting the soulful deep-house style championed by Terry Farley and Pete Heller, both hugely influential figures since the early days of house music.

Various *Real Ibiza* volumes 1–5 (React). The odd New Age warble notwithstanding, these are solid, good-value compilations in mixed or unmixed format. Volumes two and five are the strongest selections, with key contributions from Ibizarre, Mellow, José Padilla, End of Orgy and Surfers.

Various *Soundcolours* volumes 1–4 (X-Treme). Four wonderful mixes from Phil Mison, seamlessly blending Latin, funk and house tunes in the best Balearic tradition. The first volume includes a Latin house masterpiece by Rey de Copas, while the second has the brilliant Bossa track *Nights over Manaus* by Boozoo Bajau.

Various *Undiscovered Ibiza 1–4* (Undiscovered). Emotional electronic moments selected by *Pacha* resident DJ Pippi, with strong, convincing tracks from Patrice, Oversoul, Afterlife and Plastyc Buddha.

Various *Warehouse Raves* 1 & 2 (Rumour). The first volume includes a collection of formative Balearic music, with 1988 anthem *Let Me Love You for Tonight* by Kariya and Rhythim is Rhythim's timeless *Strings of Life*. Volume two is another strong offering; highlights include Gil Scott Heron's *The Bottle* and the inspirational *Dreams* by Adonte.

Language

Until the early 1960s, when there was a mass influx of Castilian Spanish speakers to the islands, **Eivissenc**, the local dialect of **Catalan**, was the main language of the Pitiuses. Catalan was still spoken after the Civil War, despite the efforts of Franco, who banned the language in the media and schools across Catalan-speaking areas of eastern Spain.

However, although Catalan is still the dominant tongue in rural areas and small villages, **Castilian Spanish** is more common in the towns. Because virtually everyone *can* speak it, Spanish has become the islands' lingua franca. Only 38 per cent of Ibizan residents (a few more in Formentera) now speak Catalan, a situation the Balearic government is trying to reverse by pushing through a programme of Catalanization. Most street signs are now in Catalan, and it's the main medium of education in schools and colleges.

English-speaking visitors to Ibiza are usually able to get by without any Spanish or Catalan, as **English** is widely understood, especially in the resorts. In Formentera, the situation is slightly different: many people can speak a little English, but as most of their visitors are German, the islanders tend to learn that language, and you may have some communication difficulties from time to time. If you want to make an effort, it's probably best to stick to learn-

A FEW CATALAN PHRASES

When pronouncing place names, watch out especially for words with the letter J – it's not "Hondal" but "Jondal", as in English. Note also that X is almost always a "sh" sound – "Xarraca" is pronounced "sharrarca". The word for a hill, "puig", is a tricky one, pronounced "pootch".

Greetings and responses

Hello Hola
Goodbye Adéu
Good morning Bon dia
Good afternoon/night Bona tarda/nit
Yes Si
No No
OK Val
Please Per favor
Thank you Gràcies
See you later Fins després
Sorry Ho sento
Excuse me Perdoni
How are you? Com va?
I (don't) understand (No) ho entec
Not at all/You're welcome De res
Do you speak English Parla Anglés?
I (don't) speak Catalan (No) Parlo Català
My name is... Em dic...
What's your name? Com es diu?
I am English Sóc anglès(a)
Scottish escocès(a)
Australian australià/ana
Canadian canadenc(a)
American americà/ana
Irish irlandès(a)
Welsh gallès(a)

If you want to learn more, try Parla Català (Pia), a good English–Catalan phrasebook, together with either the Collins or Routledge dictionary. For more serious students, the excellent Catalan in Three Months (Stuart Poole, UK), a combined paperback and tape package, is recommended.

BASIC SPANISH WORDS AND PHRASES

Basics

Yes, No, OK Sí, No, Vale
Please, Thank you Por favor, Gracias
Where?, When? ¿Dónde?, ¿Cuando?
What?, How much? ¿Qué?, ¿Cuánto?
Here, Aquí
There Allí, Allá
This, That Esto, Eso
Now Ahora
Then Más tarde
Open, Closed Abierto/a Cerrado/a
With, Without Con, Sin
Good, Bad Bueno/a Malo/a
Big, Small Gran(de) Pequeño/a
Cheap, Expensive Barato/a, Caro/a
Hot, Cold Caliente, Frío/a
More, Less Más, Menos
Today, Tomorrow Hoy, Mañana
Yesterday Ayer

Greetings and responses

Hello, Goodbye Hola, Adiós
Good morning Buenos días
Good afternoon/night Buenas tardes/noches
See you later Hasta luego
Sorry Lo siento/ disculpéme
Excuse me Con permiso/ perdón
How are you? ¿Cómo está (usted)?
I (don't) understand (No) entiendo
Not at all/You're welcome De nada
Do you speak English? ¿Habla (usted) inglés?
I (don't) speak Spanish/Catalan (No) Hablo Español
My name is... Me llamo...
What's your name? ¿Como se llama usted?
I am English Soy inglés(a)
Scottish escocés(a)
Australian australiano/a
Canadian canadiense/a
American americano/a
Irish irlandés(a)
Welsh galés(a)

Hotels and transport

I want Quiero
I'd like Quisiera
Do you know...? ¿Sabe...?
I don't know No sé

There is (is there?) (¿)Hay(?)
Give me... Deme...
Do you have...? ¿Tiene...?
...the time ...la hora
...a room ...una habitación
...with two beds/double bed ...con dos camas/cama matrimonial
...with shower/bath ...con ducha/baño
for one person para una persona
(two people) (dos personas)
for one night (one week) para una noche (una semana)
It's fine, how much is it? Está bien, ¿cuánto es?
It's too expensive Es demasiado caro
Don't you have anything ¿No tiene algo más
cheaper? barato?
Can one...? ¿Se puede...?
camp (near) here? ¿...acampar aqui (cerca)?
It's not very far No es muy lejos
How do I get to...? ¿Por donde se va a...?
Left Izquierda
Right Derecha
Straight on Todo recto
Where is.? ¿Dónde está...?
...the bus station ...la estación de autobuses
...the bus stop ...la parada
...the nearest bank ...el banco más cercano
...the post office ...el correo/la oficina de correos
...the toilet ...el baño/ aseo/servicio
Where does the bus to... leave from? ¿De dónde sale el autobús para...?
I'd like a (return) ticket to... Quisiera un billete (de ida y vuelta) para...
What time does it leave? ¿A qué hora sale ?
(arrive in...)? (llega a...)?
What is there to eat? ¿Qué hay para comer?

Days of the week

Monday lunes
Tuesday martes
Wednesday miércoles
Thursday jueves
Friday viernes
Saturday sábado
Sunday domingo

Continues over...

Numbers	
1 un/uno/una	17 diecisiete
2 dos	18 dieciocho
3 tres	19 diecinueve
4 cuatro	20 veinte
5 cinco	30 treinta
6 seis	40 cuarenta
7 siete	50 cincuenta
8 ocho	60 sesenta
9 nueve	70 setenta
10 diez	80 ochenta
11 once	90 noventa
12 doce	100 cien(to)
13 trece	200 doscientos
14 catorce	500 quinientos
15 quince	1000 mil
16 dieciseis	2000 dos mil

ing Spanish – and maybe try to pick up a few phrases of Catalan. You'll get a good reception if you at least try to communicate in one of these languages.

Getting by in Spanish

Once you get into it, Spanish is one of the easiest languages for English-speakers to learn, with the rules of **pronunciation** pretty straightforward and strictly observed. In Ibiza and Formentera, the lisp-like qualities of mainland Castilian are not at all common – *cerveza* is usually pronounced "servesa", not "thervetha".

Unless there's an accent, words ending in *d*, *l*, *r* and *z* are **stressed** on the last syllable; all others on the second last.

All **vowels** are pure and short; combinations have predictable results.

C is soft before **E** and **I**, hard otherwise.

G works the same way – a guttural **H** sound (like the *ch* in loch) before **E** or **I**, and a hard **G** elsewhere – *gigante* becomes "higante".

H is always silent.

J the same sound as a guttural **G**: *jamón* is pronounced "hamon".

LL sounds like an English **Y**: *tortilla* is pronounced "torteeya".

N as in English unless it has a tilde (accent) over it, when it becomes **NY**: *mañana* sounds like "man-yarna".

V sounds a little more like **B**, *vino* becoming "beano".

X has an **S** sound before consonants, and a normal **X** sound before vowels.

Z is the same as **S**.

Phrasebooks, dictionaries and teaching yourself Spanish

Numerous **Spanish phrasebooks** are available, one of the most user-friendly being the *Rough Guide Spanish Phrasebook*. For teaching yourself the language, the BBC tape series *España Viva* is excellent. Cassells, Collins, Harrap and Langenscheidt all produce useful **dictionaries**; Berlitz publishes separate Spanish and Latin-American Spanish phrasebooks.

Glossary

Ajuntament Town Hall.

Avinguda (Avgda) Avenue.

Baal Main Carthaginian deity, "the rider of the clouds", associated with the cult of child sacrifice.

Baluard Bastion.

Cala Cove.

Camí Road.

Campo Countryside.

Can or **C'an** House.

Capella Chapel.

Carrer (c/) Street.

Carretera Highway.

Casament Ibizan farmhouse.

Castell Castle.

Chiringuito Beach café-bar, which usually serves snacks.

Chupito Shot of liquor.

Churrigueresque Fancifully ornate form of Baroque art, named after its leading exponents, the Spaniard José Churriguera (1650–1723) and his extended family.

Correu Post office.

Cova Cave.

Ebusus Roman name for Ibiza Town.

Eivissa Catalan name for Ibiza, and Ibiza Town.

Eivissenc Catalan dialect spoken in the Pitiuses; it's known as "Ibicenco" in Castilian Spanish.

Església Church.

Far Lighthouse.

Finca Farmhouse.

Font Spring, fountain.

Hierbas Locally produced, sweet herb-soaked liqueur.

Ibosim Carthaginian name for Ibiza Town.

Illa Island.

Kiosko Beach bar or café.

Mercat Market.

Mirador Lookout.

Museu Museum.

Parada Bus stop.

Parc Park.

Passeig Avenue.

Plaça Square.

Pitiuses Southern Balearics: Ibiza, Formentera, Espalmador, Espardell, Tagomago and Conillera are the main islands.

Platja Beach.

Pou Well.

Puig Hill.

Punta Point.

Riu River.

Salines Salt pans.

Serra Mountain.

Torre Tower.

Torrent Seasonal stream, dried-up river bed.

Urbanización Housing estate.

Yebisah Arabic name for Ibiza.

Books

Historically, not a great deal has been written about Ibiza and Formentera in any language. However, in the last decade a steady stream of literature has been published, much of it related to the club scene. An excellent source for books about Spain – new, used and out of print – is Books on Spain, PO Box 207, Twickenham TW2 5BQ, UK, ⓣ020/8898 7789, ⓦwww.books-on-spain.com.

Travel and guides

Hans Losse *Ibiza and Formentera – A Countryside Guide* (Sunflower, UK). Excellent walkers' handbook, with 23 well-organized hikes, complete with accurate maps; plus cycle routes, picnic suggestions and photographs.

Paul Richardson *Not Part of the Package – A Year in Ibiza* (Macmillian, UK o/p). By far the best introduction to the island, this is a compelling, witty look at Ibizan rural traditions and history. The author also examines the impact of mass tourism, hippy heritage, club culture and the gay scene through interviews with some of the island's wildest, most influential and charismatic characters.

History, society and politics

Martin Davies and Philippe Derville *Eivissa–Ibiza: A Hundred Years of Light and Shade* (Ediciones El Faro, Spain). A fascinating, immaculately researched study of twentieth-century Ibizan society and customs, with many rare photographs.

Robert Elms *Spain* (Heinemann UK o/p). This penetrating look at modern Spain from a respected British journalist and broadcaster includes a chapter on Ibiza. Elms interviews an engaging collection of personalities, including the founders of the *Ku* club (now *Privilege*).

Ian Gibson *Fire in the Blood – The New Spain* (Faber, UK). Erudite and highly readable portrait of contemporary Spain, a critical yet passionate look at the country from an Irishman who has been resident in Madrid for over twenty years.

John Hooper *The New Spaniards* (Penguin UK & US). Solid, but slightly dry, introduction to the country from an ex-*Guardian* correspondent. Worth buying just for his description of the hundred-plus ways of ordering a coffee.

Emily Kaufman *A History Buff's Guide to Ibiza* (Tarita, Spain). An incisive, humorous and comprehensive summary of Ibizan history until the Catalan conquest, written by an *Ibiza Now* contributor and island resident.

Music and club culture

Wayne Anthony *Class of 88 – The True Acid House Experience* (Virgin, UK). A rollercoaster tale of the rave years, written by the larger-than-life ex-*Genesis* and *Havin It* promoter.

Sean Bidder *House Music* (Rough Guides UK & US). Definitive guide to the four-four rhythm, presented in mini-encyclopedic format.

Bill Brewster and Frank Broughton *Last Night a DJ*

Saved My Life – The History of the Disc Jockey (Headline, UK/Grove, US). Superb historical study, from the emergence of the DJ as a radio broadcaster in the early twentieth century to today's stadium-filling global superstars. Convincing accounts of the northern soul, disco and dance-hall days and the importance of artists King Tubby, Larry Levan and Frankie Knuckles.

Jane Bussmann *Once in a Lifetime* (Virgin, UK). Hilarious cut'n'paste compilation of art-work, anecdotes and all-round tales of mental-mental mayhem from the rave years, with sub-stantial Ibiza content.

Matthew Collin *Altered State – The Story of Ecstasy Culture and Acid House* (Serpent's Tail, UK). A conclusive account of British club culture and all its mutant derivatives, including hardcore, jungle and the free party scene, with a brief description of the Ibiza clubbing scene of the late 1980s.

Sheryl Garratt *Adventures in Wonderland* (Headline, UK). Candid account of party adven-tures and clubland history from the ex-editor of *The Face*, this is an insider's guide to the British acid house revolution, from its Chicago and Ibizan roots to the Superclub phenomenon.

Ben Turner et al *Ibiza – Inspired Images from the Island of Dance* (Ebury Press UK & US). Lavishly illustrated coffee-table digest of the British–Ibizan clubbing experience, compiled by ex-*Muzik* magazine editor. Most of the writing is straight out of the "Ibiza is magic" school, but there are some provocative contributions from Colin Butts (see p.345) and Dave Fowler.

Wildlife and the environment

Hans Giffhorn *Ibiza – An Undiscovered Paradise of Nature* (RGG, Germany). Limited but fairly well illustrated publication, dealing with the Ibizan environment, landscapes, flora and fauna, with a strong section on the island's wild flowers. The walk descriptions, however, are a bit vague and not terribly useful.

Joan Mayol *Birds of the Balearic Islands* (Editorial Moll Mallorca, Spain). Reasonable, but far from comprehensive, introduction to the region's feathered fauna.

Fiction

Colin Butts *Is Harry on the Boat?* (Orion, UK/Trafalgar Square, US). Set in Sant Antoni, written by a former *2wenties* rep and recently made into a sit-com, this blows the lid on the many faces of the holiday rep world: lewd sexual adventures, money scams and frauds, infighting and general all-round mayhem.

Isobel English *Every Eye* (Persephone, UK). Stylishly written – but profoundly melancholic – tale of a sensitive young English girl who travels from London to Ibiza in the 1950s for her honeymoon.

Norman Lewis *The Tenth Year of the Ship* (Vintage, UK). Superb tale of the devastating impact modernization and speculative investment has on a remote Spanish island after a steam boat link is established. Though the author places the mythical island of Vedra in the Canaries, an Ibizan influence is clearly apparent; indeed, Lewis spent two summers in Santa Eulària researching the novel.

Miscellaneous

Wayne Anthony *Spanish Highs – Sex, Drugs and Excess in Ibiza* (Virgin, UK). Anthony recounts his personal Ibizan highs and lows: massive drug consumption, cocaine psychosis, season-long benders and professional ducking and diving.

Elliot Paul *Life and Death in a Spanish Town* (Greenwood UK & US). Sympathetic portrayal of Santa Eulària's transformation from an Eden-esque fishing village to troubled town plagued by the terror, murder and starvation of the Civil War.

Various *The Cooking of Ibiza and Formentera* (Editorial Mediterrània Eivissa, Spain). Widely available in Ibizan book stores, this book has chapters on the historical influence on the cooking of the Pitiuses, the main ingredients and plenty of recipes.

INDEX

A

B

C

D

E

I

around the world

Alaska ★ Algarve ★ Amsterdam ★ Andalucía ★ Antigua & Barbuda ★ Argentina ★ Auckland Restaurants ★ Australia ★ Austria ★ Bahamas ★ Bali & Lombok ★ Bangkok ★ Barbados ★ Barcelona ★ Beijing ★ Belgium & Luxembourg ★ Belize ★ Berlin ★ Big Island of Hawaii ★ Bolivia ★ Boston ★ Brazil ★ Britain ★ Brittany & Normandy ★ Bruges & Ghent ★ Brussels ★ Budapest ★ Bulgaria ★ California ★ Cambodia ★ Canada ★ Cape Town ★ The Caribbean ★ Central America ★ Chile ★ China ★ Copenhagen ★ Corsica ★ Costa Brava ★ Costa Rica ★ Crete ★ Croatia ★ Cuba ★ Cyprus ★ Czech & Slovak Republics ★ Devon & Cornwall ★ Dodecanese & East Aegean ★ Dominican Republic ★ The Dordogne & the Lot ★ Dublin ★ Ecuador ★ Edinburgh ★ Egypt ★ England ★ Europe ★ First-time Asia ★ First-time Europe ★ Florence ★ Florida ★ France ★ French Hotels & Restaurants ★ Gay & Lesbian Australia ★ Germany ★ Goa ★ Greece ★ Greek Islands ★ Guatemala ★ Hawaii ★ Holland ★ Hong Kong & Macau ★ Honolulu ★ Hungary ★ Ibiza & Formentera ★ Iceland ★ India ★ Indonesia ★ Ionian Islands ★ Ireland ★ Israel & the Palestinian Territories ★ Italy ★ Jamaica ★ Japan ★ Jerusalem ★ Jordan ★ Kenya ★ The Lake District ★ Languedoc & Roussillon ★ Laos ★ Las Vegas ★ Lisbon ★ London ★

RIGA
SINGAPORE
ROUGH GUIDES
TWENTY YEARS

NOTES

* Marina.

* Restaurants.

Lunch:

Caja Jandal -

Cayi vecella -

Dinner:

NOTES

NOTES

NOTES

NOTES

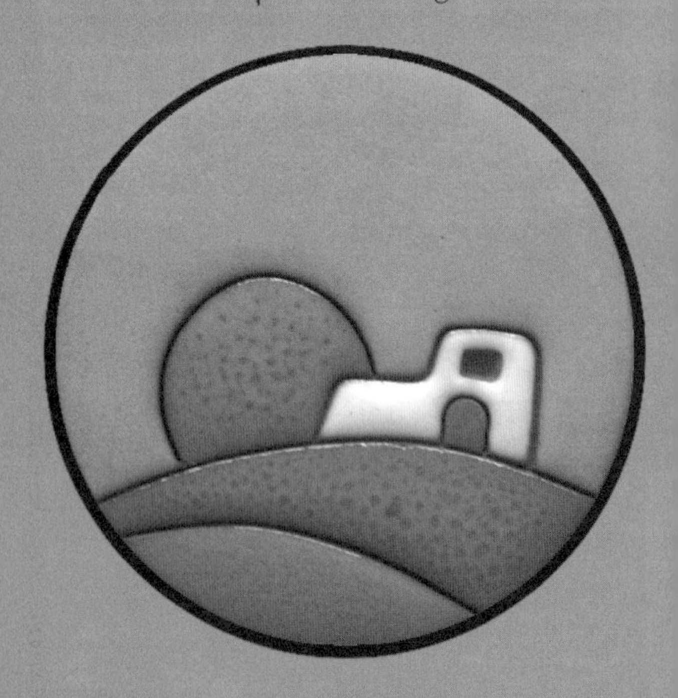

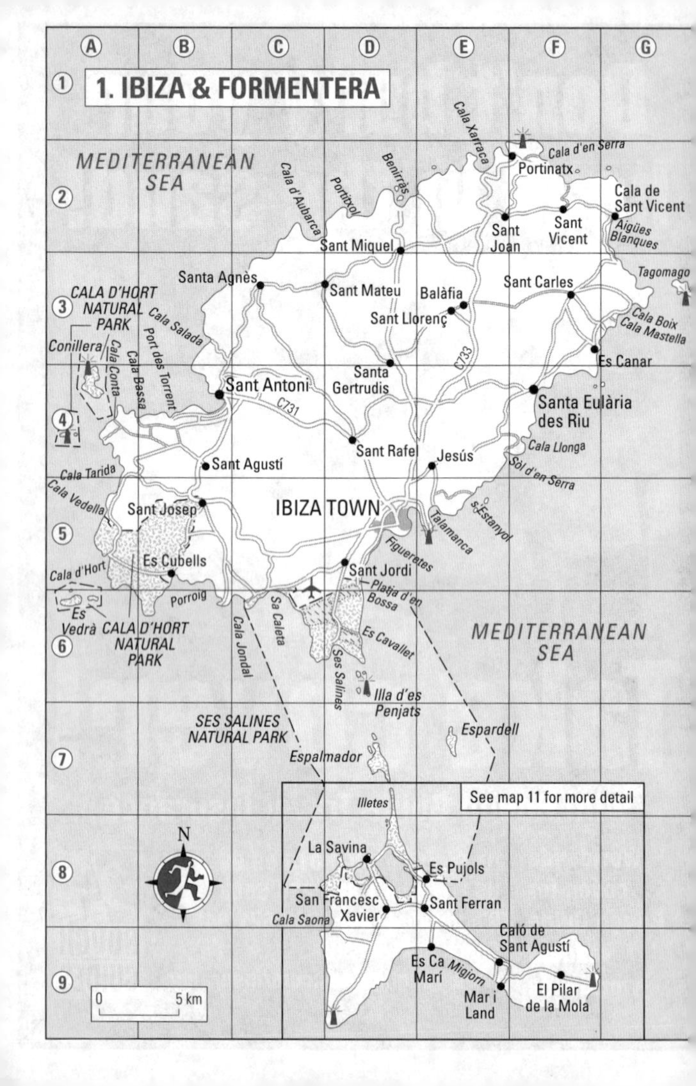
1. IBIZA & FORMENTERA
A
B
C
D
E
F
G
1
2
3
4
5
6
7
8
9
MEDITERRANEAN SEA
Cala Xarraca
Cala d'en Serra
Portinatx
Benirràs
Cala d'Aubarca
Portitxol
Cala de Sant Vicent
Sant Joan
Sant Vicent
Aigües Blanques
Sant Miquel
Santa Agnès
Sant Mateu
Balàfia
Sant Carles
Tagomago
CALA D'HORT NATURAL PARK
Cala Salada
Port des Torrent
Sant Llorenç
Cala Boix
Cala Mastella
Conillera
Cala Conta
Cala Bassa
C733
Es Canar
Sant Antoni
Santa Gertrudis
C731
Santa Eulària des Riu
Sant Rafel
Cala Llonga
Sant Agustí
Jesús
Sòl d'en Serra
Cala Tarida
Cala Vedella
Sant Josep
IBIZA TOWN
s'Estanyol
Talamanca
Figueretes
Es Cubells
Sant Jordi
Cala d'Hort
Porroig
Platja d'en Bossa
Es Vedrà
CALA D'HORT NATURAL PARK
Sa Caleta
Cala Jondal
Es Cavallet
MEDITERRANEAN SEA
Ses Salines
Illa d'es Penjats
SES SALINES NATURAL PARK
Espardell
Espalmador
See map 11 for more detail
Illetes
N
La Savina
Es Pujols
San Francesc Xavier
Sant Ferran
Cala Saona
Caló de Sant Agustí
Es Ca Marí
Migjorn
El Pilar de la Mola
Mar i Land
0
5 km

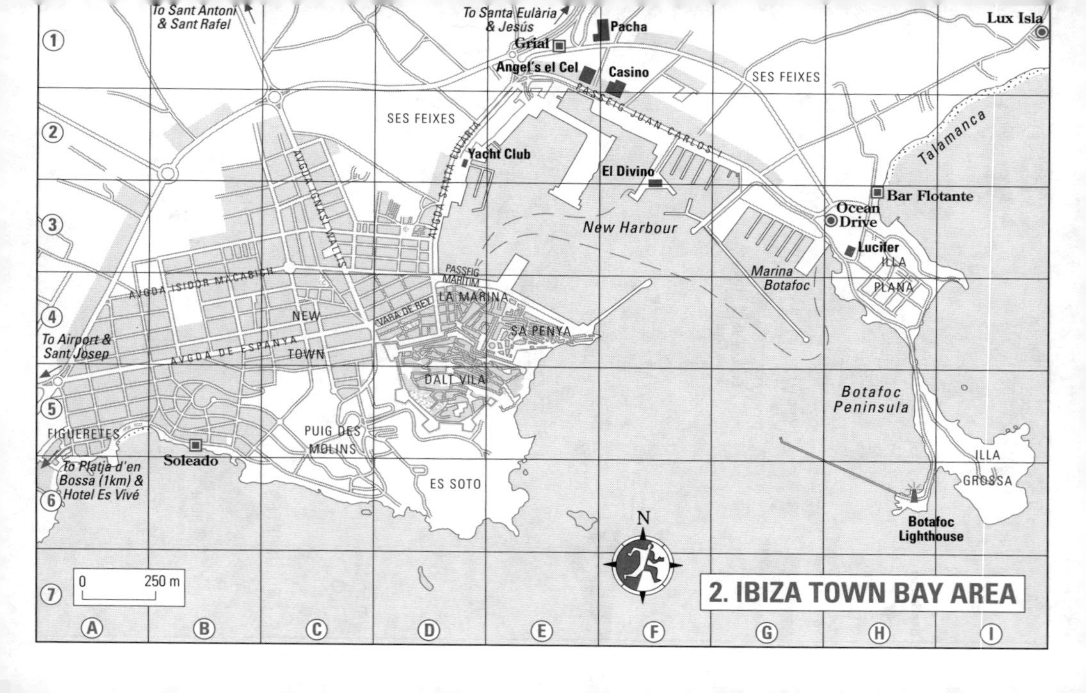
2. IBIZA TOWN BAY AREA
To Sant Antoni & Sant Rafel
To Santa Eulària & Jesús
Pacha
Grial
Angel's el Cel
Casino
Lux Isla
SES FEIXES
SES FEIXES
PASSEIG JUAN CARLOS I
Talamanca
Yacht Club
AVGDA SANTA EULÀRIA
El Divino
Bar Flotante
Ocean Drive
New Harbour
Lucifer
ILLA PLANA
Marina Botafoc
PASSEIG MARITIM
AVGDA IGNASI WALLIS
AVGDA ISIDOR MACABICH
LA MARINA
VARA DE REY
NEW TOWN
SA PENYA
To Airport & Sant Josep
AVGDA DE ESPANYA
DALT VILA
Botafoc Peninsula
FIGUERETES
PUIG DES MOLINS
Soleado
To Platja d'en Bossa (1km) & Hotel Es Vivé
ES SOTO
ILLA GROSSA
Botafoc Lighthouse
N
0
250 m
1
2
3
4
5
6
7
A
B
C
D
E
F
G
H
I

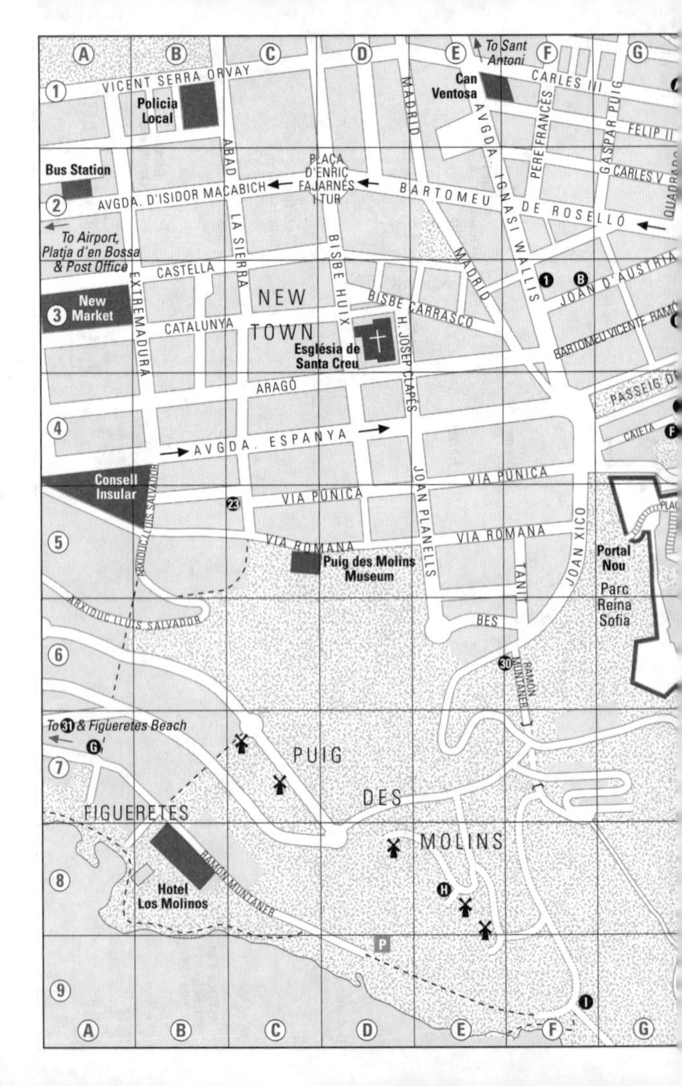

VICENT SERRA ORVAY
Policia Local
Can Ventosa
To Sant Antoni
CARLES III
FELIP II
CARLES V
MADRID
AVGDA. IGNASI WALLIS
PERE FRANCÉS
GASPAR PUIG
Bus Station
AVGDA. D'ISIDOR MACABICH
PLAÇA D'ENRIC FAJARNÉS I TUR
BARTOMEU DE ROSELLÓ
To Airport, Platja d'en Bossa & Post Office
ABAD
LA SIERRA
BISBE HUIX
CASTELLA
EXTREMADURA
New Market
NEW TOWN
BISBE CARRASCO
H. JOSEP CLAPÉS
JOAN D'AUSTRIA
BARTOMEU VICENTE RAMÓN
CATALUNYA
Església de Santa Creu
ARAGÓ
PASSEIG DE
CAIETA
AVGDA. ESPANYA
Consell Insular
ARXIDUC LLUÍS SALVADOR
VIA PÚNICA
JOAN PLANELLS
JOAN XICO
VIA ROMANA
Puig des Molins Museum
Portal Nou
Parc Reina Sofia
TANIT
BES
RAMÓN MUNTANER
To 31 & Figueretes Beach
PUIG DES MOLINS
FIGUERETES
Hotel Los Molinos
RAMÓN MUNTANER

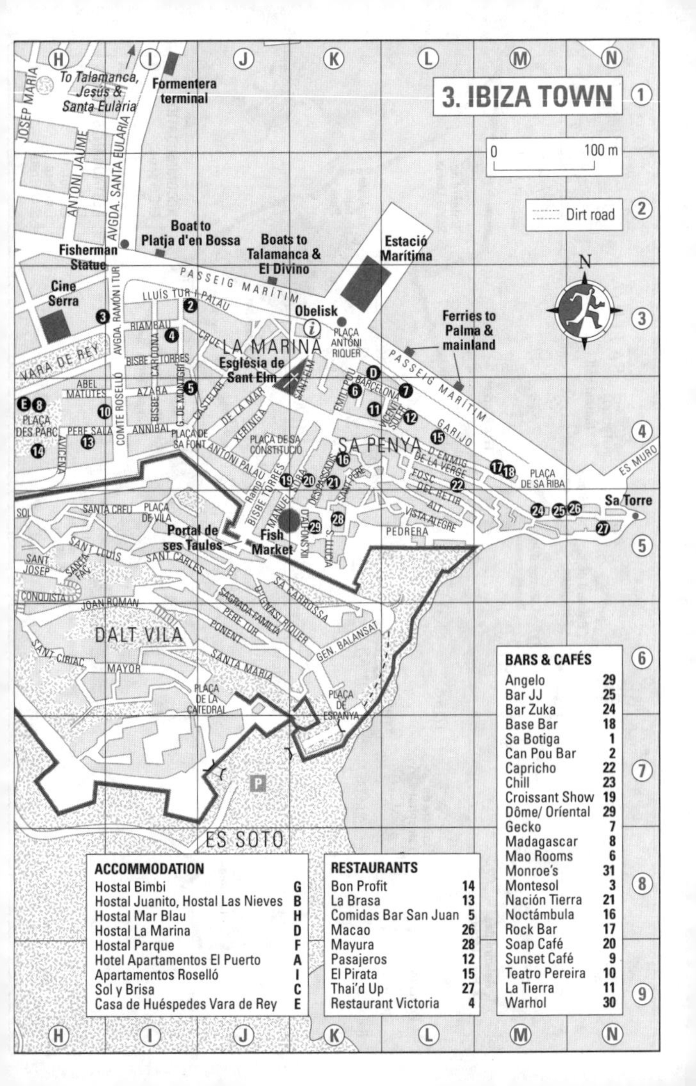

ACCOMMODATION	
Hostal Bimbi	G
Hostal Juanito, Hostal Las Nieves	B
Hostal Mar Blau	H
Hostal La Marina	D
Hostal Parque	F
Hotel Apartamentos El Puerto	A
Apartamentos Roselló	I
Sol y Brisa	C
Casa de Huéspedes Vara de Rey	E

RESTAURANTS	
Bon Profit	14
La Brasa	13
Comidas Bar San Juan	5
Macao	26
Mayura	28
Pasajeros	12
El Pirata	15
Thai'd Up	27
Restaurant Victoria	4

BARS & CAFÉS	
Angelo	29
Bar JJ	25
Bar Zuka	24
Base Bar	18
Sa Botiga	1
Can Pou Bar	2
Capricho	22
Chill	23
Croissant Show	19
Dôme/ Oriental	29
Gecko	7
Madagascar	8
Mao Rooms	6
Monroe's	31
Montesol	3
Nación Tierra	21
Noctámbula	16
Rock Bar	17
Soap Café	20
Sunset Café	9
Teatro Pereira	10
La Tierra	11
Warhol	30

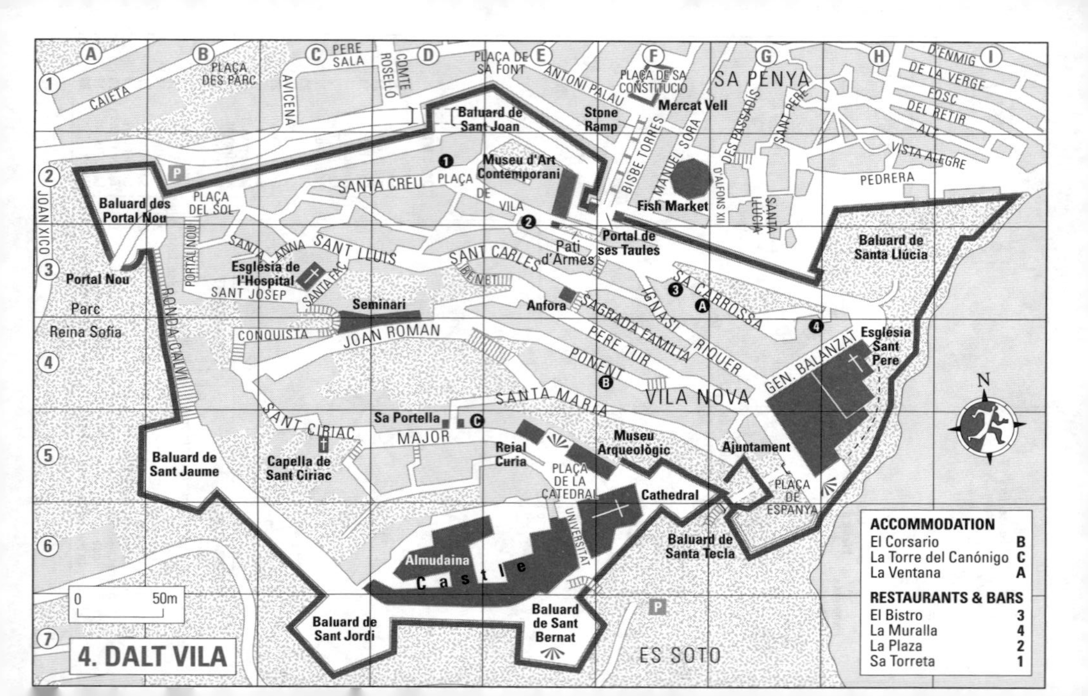
4. DALT VILA
ACCOMMODATION
El Corsario B
La Torre del Canónigo C
La Ventana A
RESTAURANTS & BARS
El Bistro 3
La Muralla 4
La Plaza 2
Sa Torreta 1
SA PENYA
VILA NOVA
ES SOTO
Baluard des Portal Nou
Portal Nou
Parc Reina Sofia
Baluard de Sant Joan
Museu d'Art Contemporani
Stone Ramp
Mercat Vell
Fish Market
Portal de ses Taules
Pati d'Armes
Església de l'Hospital
Seminari
Anfora
Baluard de Santa Llúcia
Església Sant Pere
Ajuntament
Museu Arqueològic
Reial Curia
Sa Portella
Capella de Sant Ciriac
Baluard de Sant Jaume
Cathedral
Almudaina
Castle
Baluard de Santa Tecla
Baluard de Sant Jordi
Baluard de Sant Bernat
Plaça de la Catedral
Plaça de Espanya
Plaça de Vila
Plaça del Sol
Plaça des Parc
Plaça de Sa Font
Plaça de Sa Constitució
Caieta
Avicena
Pere Sala
Comte Roselló
Antoni Palau
Bisbe Torres
Manuel Sora
Des Passadis
D'Alfons XII
Santa Llúcia
Sant Pere
D'Enmig
De la Verge
Fosc
Del Retir
Alt
Vista Alegre
Pedrera
Joan Xico
Ronda Calvi
Portal Nou
Santa Creu
Santa Anna
Sant Lluis
Sant Josep
Santa Fac
Sant Carles
Benet
Conquista
Joan Roman
Sa Carrossa
Ignasi Riquer
Sagrada Familia
Pere Tur
Ponent
Gen. Balanzat
Santa Maria
Sant Ciriac
Major
Universitat
0 50m
N

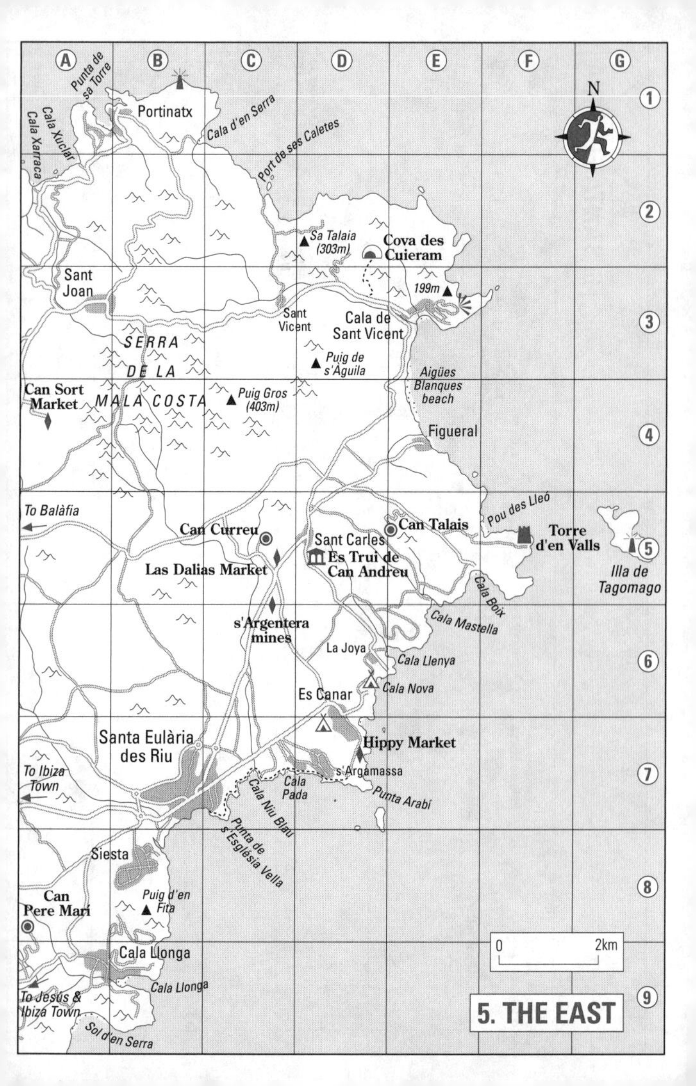

A
B
C
D
E
F
G
1
2
3
4
5
6
7
8
9
N
Punta de sa Torre
Portinatx
Cala d'en Serra
Port de ses Caletes
Cala Xuclar
Cala Xarraca
Sa Talaia (303m)
Cova des Cuieram
199m
Sant Joan
Sant Vicent
Cala de Sant Vicent
SERRA DE LA MALA COSTA
Puig de s'Àguila
Can Sort Market
Puig Gros (403m)
Aigües Blanques beach
Figueral
To Balàfia
Pou des Lleó
Can Curreu
Can Talais
Torre d'en Valls
Sant Carles
Es Trui de Can Andreu
Las Dalias Market
Illa de Tagomago
Cala Boix
Cala Mastella
s'Argentera mines
La Joya
Cala Llenya
Cala Nova
Es Canar
Santa Eulària des Riu
Hippy Market
To Ibiza Town
s'Argamassa
Cala Pada
Punta Arabí
Cala Niu Blau
Punta de s'Església Vella
Siesta
Can Pere Marí
Puig d'en Fita
Cala Llonga
Cala Llonga
0
2km
To Jesús & Ibiza Town
Sol d'en Serra
5. THE EAST

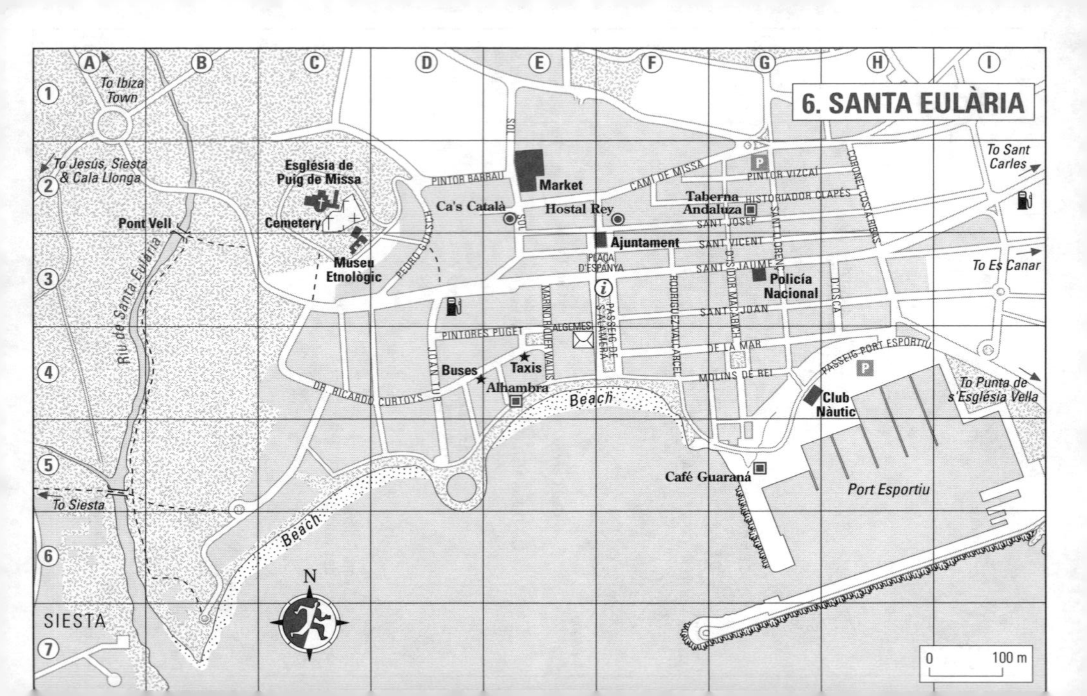
6. SANTA EULÀRIA
To Ibiza Town
To Jesús, Siesta & Cala Llonga
To Sant Carles
To Es Canar
To Punta de s'Església Vella
To Siesta
Església de Puig de Missa
Cemetery
Museu Etnològic
Pont Vell
Riu de Santa Eulària
Ca's Català
Market
Hostal Rey
Ajuntament
Taberna Andaluza
Policía Nacional
Club Nàutic
Café Guaraná
Port Esportiu
Buses
Taxis
Alhambra
Beach
Beach
SIESTA
PINTOR BARRAU
SOL
SOL
CAMÍ DE MISSA
PINTOR VIZCAÍ
HISTORIADOR CLAPÉS
CORONEL COSTA RIBAS
SANT JOSEP
SANT VICENT
SANT JAUME
SANT JOAN
SANT LLORENÇ
D'ISIDOR MACABICH
D'OSCA
DE LA MAR
MOLINS DE REI
RODRIGUEZ VALCARCEL
PLAÇA D'ESPANYA
PASSEIG DE S'ALAMERA
ALGEMESÍ
MARINO RIQUER WALLIS
PINTORES PUGET
JOAN TUR
PEDRO GUASCH
DR. RICARDO CURTOYS
PASSEIG PORT ESPORTIU
N
0
100 m

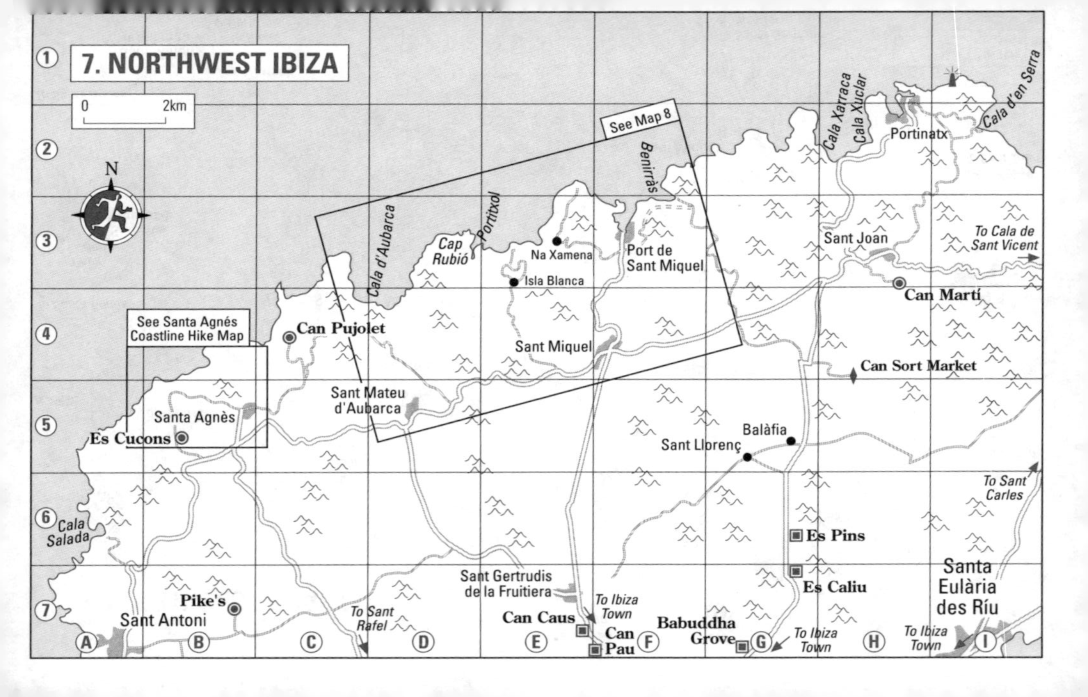
7. NORTHWEST IBIZA
0
2km
N
See Map 8
See Santa Agnés Coastline Hike Map
Cala Xarraca
Cala Xuclar
Portinatx
Cala d'en Serra
Benirràs
Portitxol
Cap Rubió
Cala d'Aubarca
Na Xamena
Isla Blanca
Port de Sant Miquel
Sant Joan
To Cala de Sant Vicent
Can Martí
Can Pujolet
Sant Miquel
Can Sort Market
Sant Mateu d'Aubarca
Santa Agnès
Es Cucons
Balàfia
Sant Llorenç
To Sant Carles
Cala Salada
Es Pins
Sant Gertrudis de la Fruitiera
Es Caliu
Santa Eulària des Ríu
Pike's
Sant Antoni
To Sant Rafel
To Ibiza Town
Can Caus
Can Pau
Babuddha Grove
To Ibiza Town
To Ibiza Town
A
B
C
D
E
F
G
H
I
1
2
3
4
5
6
7

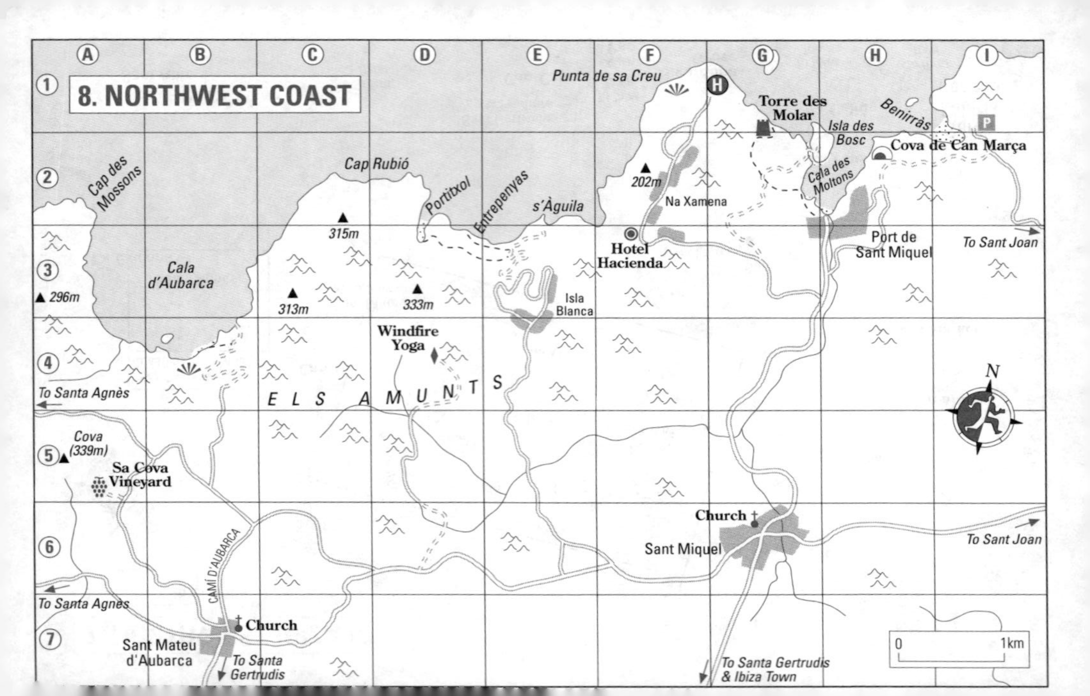
8. NORTHWEST COAST
A
B
C
D
E
F
G
H
I
1
2
3
4
5
6
7
Punta de sa Creu
Torre des Molar
Benirràs
Isla des Bosc
Cova de Can Marça
Cap des Mossons
Cap Rubió
Portitxol
Entrepenyas
s'Àguila
202m
Na Xamena
Cala des Moltons
315m
Hotel Hacienda
Port de Sant Miquel
To Sant Joan
Cala d'Aubarca
296m
313m
333m
Isla Blanca
Windfire Yoga
To Santa Agnès
E L S A M U N T S
N
Cova (339m)
Sa Cova Vineyard
Church
Sant Miquel
To Sant Joan
CAMÍ D'AUBARCA
To Santa Agnès
Church
Sant Mateu d'Aubarca
To Santa Gertrudis
To Santa Gertrudis & Ibiza Town
0
1km

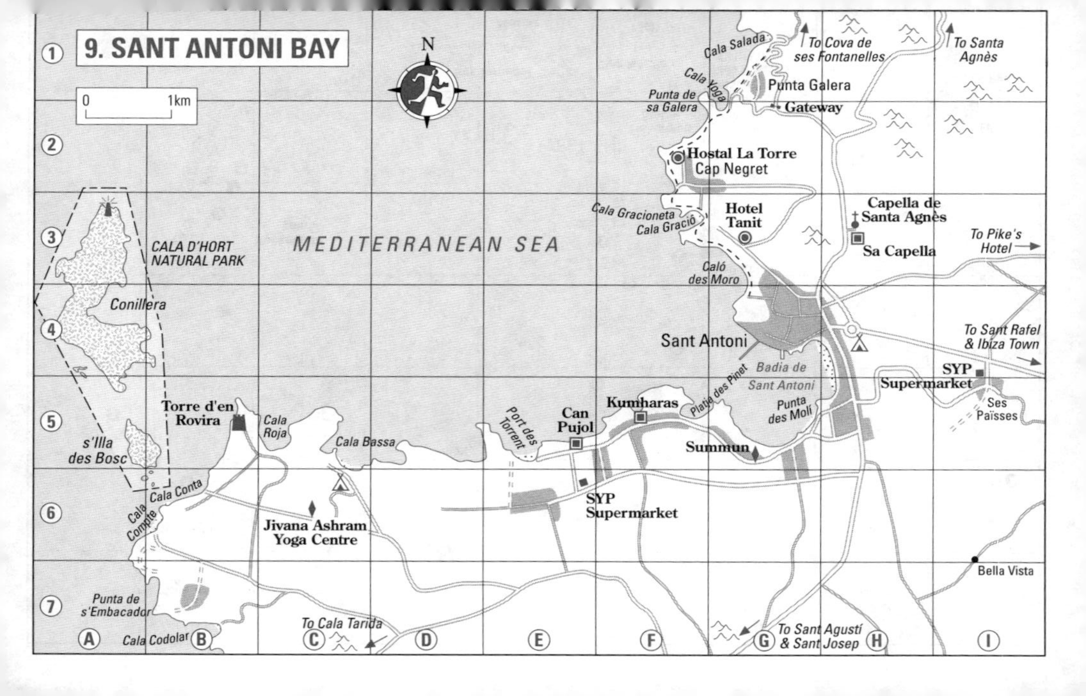
9. SANT ANTONI BAY
0
1km
N
MEDITERRANEAN SEA
CALA D'HORT NATURAL PARK
Conillera
s'Illa des Bosc
Torre d'en Rovira
Cala Roja
Cala Bassa
Cala Conta
Cala Compte
Jivana Ashram Yoga Centre
Punta de s'Embacador
Cala Codolar
To Cala Tarida
Port des Torrent
Can Pujol
SYP Supermarket
Kumharas
Platje des Pinet
Summun
Badia de Sant Antoni
Punta des Molí
Sant Antoni
Caló des Moro
Cala Gracioneta
Cala Gració
Hotel Tanit
Hostal La Torre Cap Negret
Punta de sa Galera
Cala Yoga
Cala Salada
Punta Galera
Gateway
To Cova de ses Fontanelles
To Santa Agnès
Capella de Santa Agnès
Sa Capella
To Pike's Hotel
To Sant Rafel & Ibiza Town
SYP Supermarket
Ses Païsses
Bella Vista
To Sant Agustí & Sant Josep
1
2
3
4
5
6
7
A
B
C
D
E
F
G
H
I

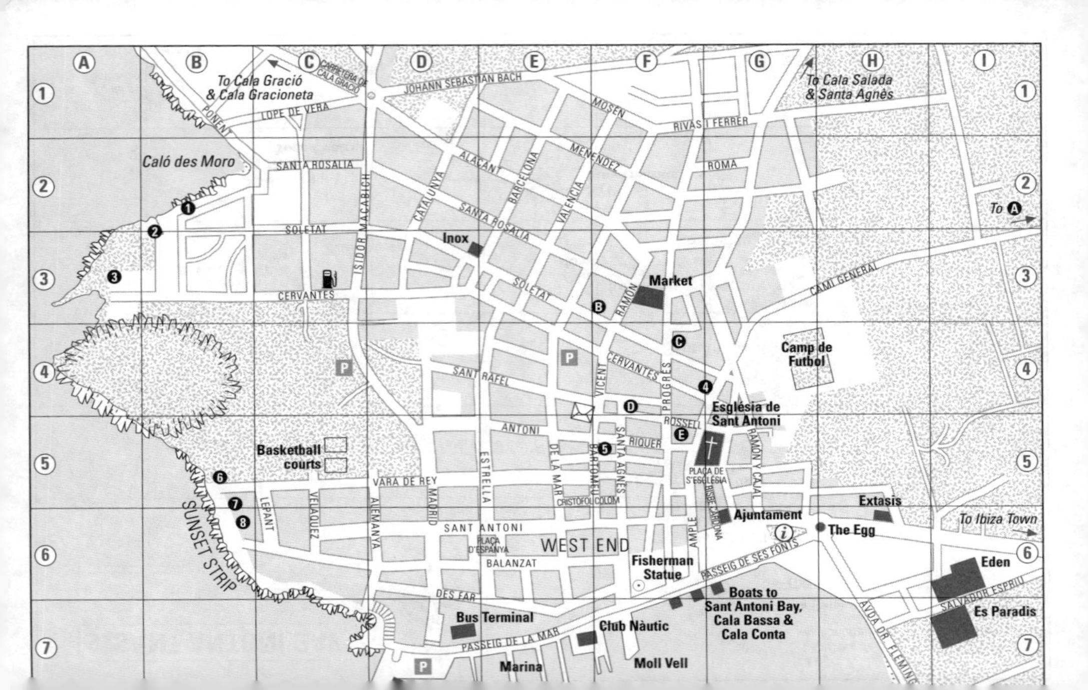
To Cala Gració
& Cala Gracioneta
Caló des Moro
To Cala Salada
& Santa Agnès
To A
To Ibiza Town
Inox
Market
Camp de
Futbol
Església de
Sant Antoni
Basketball
courts
Extasis
Ajuntament
The Egg
WEST END
Fisherman
Statue
Eden
Es Paradis
Boats to
Sant Antoni Bay,
Cala Bassa &
Cala Conta
Bus Terminal
Club Nàutic
Moll Vell
Marina
SUNSET STRIP
JOHANN SEBASTIAN BACH
CARRETERA DE CALA GRACIÓ
LOPE DE VERA
PONENT
MOSEN
RIVAS I FERRER
MENENDEZ
ROMA
ALACANT
BARCELONA
VALENCIA
CATALUNYA
SANTA ROSALIA
SOLETAT
ISIDOR MACABICH
CERVANTES
CAMI GENERAL
RAMÓN
SANT RAFEL
VICENT
PROGRES
ROSSELL
ANTONI
RIQUER
SANTA AGNÈS
BARTOMEU
DE LA MAR
ESTRELLA
RAMÓN Y CAJAL
PLAÇA DE S'ESGLÉSIA
BISBE CARDONA
CRISTÒFOL COLOM
VARA DE REY
MADRID
ALEMANYA
VELAQUEZ
LEPANT
SANT ANTONI
PLAÇA D'ESPANYA
BALANZAT
AMPLE
PASSEIG DE SES FONTS
DES FAR
PASSEIG DE LA MAR
AVDA DR. FLEMING
SALVADOR ESPRIU

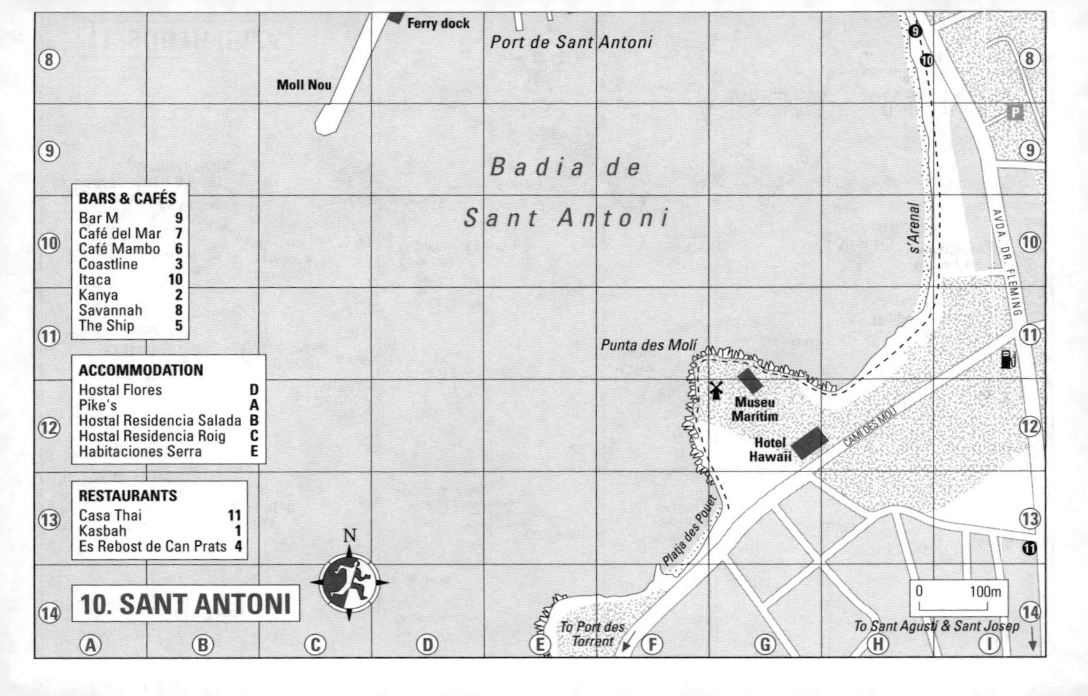
10. SANT ANTONI
BARS & CAFÉS
Bar M 9
Café del Mar 7
Café Mambo 6
Coastline 3
Itaca 10
Kanya 2
Savannah 8
The Ship 5
ACCOMMODATION
Hostal Flores D
Pike's A
Hostal Residencia Salada B
Hostal Residencia Roig C
Habitaciones Serra E
RESTAURANTS
Casa Thai 11
Kasbah 1
Es Rebost de Can Prats 4
Ferry dock
Moll Nou
Port de Sant Antoni
Badia de Sant Antoni
s'Arenal
AVDA. DR. FLEMING
Punta des Molí
Museu Marítim
Hotel Hawaii
CAMI DES MOLI
Platja des Pouet
To Port des Torrent
To Sant Agustí & Sant Josep
0 100m
N

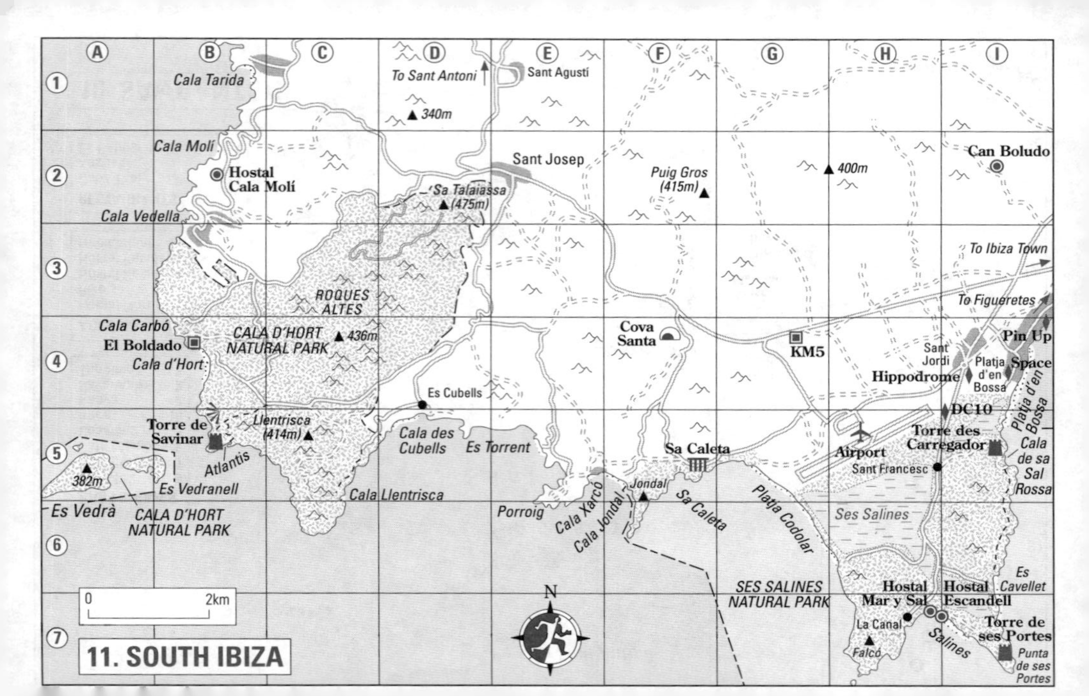
11. SOUTH IBIZA
0
2km
N
Cala Tarida
To Sant Antoni
340m
Sant Agustí
Cala Molí
Hostal Cala Molí
Cala Vedella
Sant Josep
Sa Talaiassa (475m)
Puig Gros (415m)
400m
Can Boludo
To Ibiza Town
To Figueretes
ROQUES ALTES
Cala Carbó
El Boldado
Cala d'Hort
CALA D'HORT NATURAL PARK
436m
Cova Santa
KM5
Pin Up
Sant Jordi
Platja d'en Bossa
Space
Hippodrome
Es Cubells
DC10
Platja d'en Bossa
Torre de Savinar
Llentrisca (414m)
Cala des Cubells
Es Torrent
Sa Caleta
Airport
Torre des Carregador
Cala de sa Sal Rossa
Sant Francesc
382m
Atlantis
Es Vedranell
Cala Llentrisca
Porroig
Cala Xarcó
Cala Jondal
Jondal
Sa Caleta
Platja Codolar
Ses Salines
Es Vedrà
CALA D'HORT NATURAL PARK
SES SALINES NATURAL PARK
Es Cavellet
Hostal Mar y Sal
Hostal Escandell
La Canal
Falcó
Salines
Torre de ses Portes
Punta de ses Portes

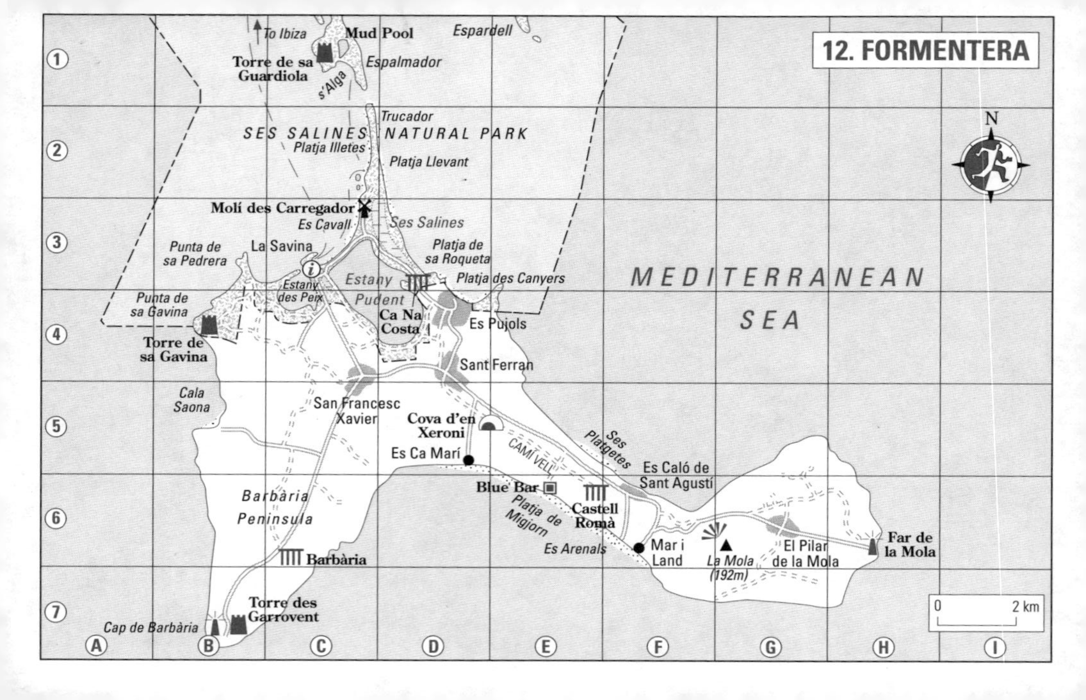
12. FORMENTERA
N
To Ibiza
Mud Pool
Espardell
Torre de sa Guardiola
Espalmador
s'Alga
Trucador
SES SALINES NATURAL PARK
Platja Illetes
Platja Llevant
Molí des Carregador
Es Cavall
Ses Salines
Punta de sa Pedrera
La Savina
Platja de sa Roqueta
Estany
Platja des Canyers
Estany des Peix
Pudent
Punta de sa Gavina
Ca Na Costa
Es Pujols
Torre de sa Gavina
MEDITERRANEAN SEA
Sant Ferran
Cala Saona
San Francesc Xavier
Cova d'en Xeroni
Ses Platgetes
Es Ca Marí
CAMÍ VELL
Es Caló de Sant Agustí
Blue Bar
Castell Romà
Barbària Peninsula
Platja de Migjorn
Es Arenals
Mar i Land
La Mola (192m)
El Pilar de la Mola
Far de la Mola
Barbària
Torre des Garrovent
Cap de Barbària
0
2 km
1
2
3
4
5
6
7
A
B
C
D
E
F
G
H
I